hissed a fat farmer's wife.

Meghan turned to look at her. "I speak the truth, my dear," she said and pulled back her plaid to show the white lock that twisted through her braid all the way to the ground. "I am Meghan NicCuinn, Sorceress o' the Beasts, and I do no' lie! A scarlet thread has been strung on the loom o' our lives and we face danger such as we have no' seen for many years."

There was no doubt the highlanders recognized who Meghan was, for there was a collective sigh and murmur, half fearful, half glad. Many of them looked from her to Bacaiche, and as they noticed the white streak in his black curls and his aquiline nose, so like Meghan's, another, more excited murmur arose.

"Evil times are ahead, have no doubt o' that!" the sorceress cried. "Know, however, that the Witches o' Eileanan are no' gone—they watch out for ye and protect ye still. Do no' fear! We are no' your enemies."

With those words, Meghan turned and led the way into the swirling mist, Iseult limping close behind. Bacaiche wrapped himself in the nyx-hair cloak and became again a hunchback, lurching after her. The mist swallowed their figures and they were gone. . . .

The Pool of Two Moons

Book Two of *The Witches of Eileanan*

KATE FORSYTH

RoC

A ROC BOOK

ROC
Published by New American Library, a division of
Penguin Group (USA) Inc., 375 Hudson Street,
New York, New York 10014, USA
Penguin Group (Canada), 90 Eglinton Avenue East, Suite 700, Toronto,
Ontario M4P 2Y3, Canada (a division of Pearson Penguin Canada Inc.)
Penguin Books Ltd., 80 Strand, London WC2R 0RL, England
Penguin Ireland, 25 St. Stephen's Green, Dublin 2,
Ireland (a division of Penguin Books Ltd.)
Penguin Group (Australia), 250 Camberwell Road, Camberwell, Victoria 3124,
Australia (a division of Pearson Australia Group Pty. Ltd.)
Penguin Books India Pvt. Ltd., 11 Community Centre, Panchsheel Park,
New Delhi - 110 017, India
Penguin Group (NZ), cnr Airborne and Rosedale Roads, Albany,
Auckland 1310, New Zealand (a division of Pearson New Zealand Ltd.)
Penguin Books (South Africa) (Pty.) Ltd., 24 Sturdee Avenue,
Rosebank, Johannesburg 2196, South Africa

Penguin Books Ltd., Registered Offices:
80 Strand, London WC2R 0RL, England

Published by Roc, an imprint of New American Library, a division of Penguin
Group (USA) Inc. Previously published in an Arrow Book edition by Ran-
dom House Australia Pty. Ltd.

First Roc Printing, March 1999
20   19   18   17   16   15   14   13   12   11

for my dearest mother,
Gillian Mackenzie Evans

A witch or a hag is she which being deluded by a league made with the devel through his persuasion, inspiration, and juggling, thinketh she can design what manner of evil things soever, either by thought or imprecation, as to shake the air with lightnings and thunder, to cause hail and tempests, to remove green corn or trees to another place, to be carried of her familiar (which hath taken upon him the deceitful shape of a goat, swine or calf) into some mountain far distant, in a wonderful short space of time.

William West, sixteenth-century English lawyer

THE HUNCHBACK

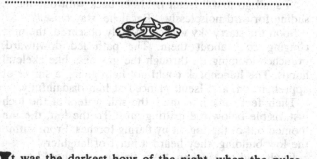

It was the darkest hour of the night, when the pulse runs slowest and the tides of energy are at their ebb, that the three travelers left the woods. They went warily, their heads turning from side to side as they scanned the shadowed landscape. Although it was a clear night and the snowy peaks of the Sithiche Mountains shone faintly in the light of the two moons, the valley below was filled with mist so that their travelers' path sank into a mysterious whiteness.

"Can ye sense anyone ahead, auld mother?" Iseult asked.

"No' on the path, Iseult, though the inn seems quite busy. Let us push on—we can stop and rest soon enough."

"So ye've been saying all week!" Bacaiche snapped, leaning heavily on his rough club. "I'm sick o' stumbling around every night and hiding all day like a frightened hare! When are we going to do something useful?"

The old woman turned and looked up at him. "Come, Bacaiche, ye'll be glad we pushed on when a plate o' hot stew is slapped in front o' ye. Ye've been complaining o' hunger long enough."

"Considering all we've eaten these last few days is shriveled carrot soup!"

"Better to forage on the way than stop for supplies when we have the Red Guards on our trail," Meghan replied grimly, beginning to push ahead.

"I shall go first." Iseult held her back with one hand, sliding forward noiselessly. "Bacaiche, stay close."

Soon the starry sky was completely obscured, the mist clinging cold about them. The path led downward, branches looming up through the grayness like skeletal hands. The hunchback could not help giving a shiver of apprehension, and Iseult glanced at him disdainfully.

Their feet sank into mud, the still waters of the loch just visible below the drifting mist. To the left, the inn loomed out of the fog, lit by flaring torches. From within the low building, they heard a burst of laughter.

Iseult said to Meghan, "Are ye sure we should go in, auld mother?"

"It's damp and foul out here, the ferry will no' arrive for another few hours, and we haven't eaten a proper meal in days," Meghan responded irritably. "Ye can stay out if ye want, but I'm going in!" Pushing open the door, she warned, "Keep the cloak wrapped tightly about ye, Bacaiche."

"I'm no' a fool," he snarled, lurching after her.

The three companions made their way to the fire, stepping over sleeping bodies and bundles of belongings. The fire was the only light except for a lamp on a table where four men were still awake, drinking ale and playing dice for coppers. They looked up, calling, "How are ye yourselves?"

Meghan replied gravely, keeping her cloak wrapped close about her. The innkeeper showed them to a table. "Is it hungry ye are?" he asked. "We have mutton stew if ye'd like it, or vegetable soup?"

"The soup would be most welcome," Meghan replied. He nodded and brought them thick soup in wooden bowls with trenchers of dark bread. "It be a full house ye've got yourself tonight," she said.

He nodded and scratched his beard. "Aye, there's been a witch fed to the *uile-bheist* and so they've been thinking the ferry run will be safe this morning, with the serpent's belly full."

"Indeed!" Meghan exclaimed. "That be lucky for us then."

The innkeeper laughed. "Och, I'll tether some goats at the water's edge. No use tempting the beastie." With that he went back to his game of dice, and the three travelers ate their soup and warmed themselves by the fire.

"Best get some sleep," Meghan said. "There'll be clean straw in the corners."

"Anything will be better than bloody stones, which is all I've slept on in weeks," Bacaiche grumbled. He wrapped the black cloak tighter around him and lurched to his feet. The flickering lamplight played over his hunched back, making him look more sinister than ever. The gamblers glanced at him suspiciously, and he glared back so that they surreptitiously crossed themselves in the age-old gesture against evil.

Soon all was quiet. The only sounds were the crackle of the fire and the occasional snore or sigh of those sleeping. Iseult rested her bow on her knees and stretched her back. Tired as she was after the last few arduous weeks, she had no intention of sleeping. She would stay on guard until they were safely on the other side of the loch. It was her duty and honor to guard the Firemaker Meghan, and despite the quietness of the inn, Iseult knew danger was all around.

For almost three weeks she and her companions had been on the run, harried through the highlands by the Banrigh's soldiers. Iseult had had to grit her teeth to prevent herself from turning and fighting. This game of hide-and-seek seemed cowardly to her, though Meghan had forbidden her to attack them, saying, "We must slip away and leave no trace, for we are no' yet strong enough to start a war."

They were heading now toward the Veiled Forest, the

great, dark forest that covered most of the western shore of the loch. There Meghan hoped to meet with Iseult's twin sister, Isabeau, in the safety of the Celestines' garden, which was concealed deep in the heart of the enchanted forest. At Tulachna Celeste, Meghan said, they would all be safe.

Light was beginning to seep through the shutters when the innkeeper came clattering back down the stairs, tying a scarred leather apron over his kilt and rubbing his curly head. Iseult pretended to sleep, not wanting to draw attention to herself, as he put porridge on to boil and flung open the shutters to the dawn. All around sleepers began to stir, stretching and yawning, and the fire leapt up under the black pot, crackling loudly.

Meghan sat up, looking impossibly old and frail in the cruel dawn light, the donbeag peeping his velvety nose out of her pocket. Iseult helped her up, and Meghan stretched and cracked her back, then gathered her satchel close. "Ye should have slept," the old witch said reprovingly. "I had told ye there was no danger here."

Iseult wondered how she could have known, but shook her head anyway. "I will sleep when I have ye safe, auld mother," she replied.

"Well, prepare yourself for many sleepless nights then, my dear!"

A bell announced the approach of the ferry, and they all went out onto the jetty and watched it cross the dull silver of the water, a broad-bottomed boat pulled along by a weed-draped cable. The crofters bunched together at one end of the wharf, looking askance at Bacaiche's hunched back. He frowned and glared at them malevolently from his peculiar yellow eyes, his black hair tousled and wild, his jaw dark with stubble.

As always the loch was wreathed with fog, but in this cold, fair morning it was a light mist which parted easily before a wayward breeze. As soon as the ferry had nudged against the jetty, the passengers on board were scrambling off and those waiting were jumping on, sacks of grain and bales of hay hastily thrown on and off. No one was waiting around for the loch-serpent to rear his long neck. Through the mist came the nervous bleat of the goats tethered down the shore, and those few animals who were aboard the ferry were tightly muzzled.

The journey across the loch was made with the same nervous haste, the wiry little ferry-master searching the mist with anxious eyes. They were more than halfway across, the walls of Dunceleste looming closer through the mist, when a fat matron suddenly screamed with fright. "The *uile-bheist*!" she cried. Every head whipped around in horror to see where she pointed.

Through the mist came the undulating body of the serpent, rising in great wet loops above the still loch. Its long neck and small head rose high above the prow, and it seemed the loch-serpent would encircle the boat and crush it. Everyone screamed and there was a stampede away from the starboard deck. The loch-serpent gave a great ululating wail, and rubbed its seaweed-colored length against the side. The boat tilted, and Iseult clung tightly to the bench to avoid being flung to the deck. Only Meghan did not scream or fall; she stood straight and still in the prow, looking out into the mist.

The serpent flipped his tail over the prow, doing a complicated rolling maneuver close to the vessel's side so the ferry rocked wildly and almost capsized. Iseult could see how smooth its scaly green-black skin was, and how massive its loops. Casting a wild look at Meghan, Iseult saw the old witch was leaning forward, her gnarled hand stretched out. Briefly a thick loop slid out of the water and rubbed against Meghan's hand, then there was a flick of the great webbed tail and the loch-serpent sank away.

They heard the strange, wild cry twice again, each time farther away. No one else had noticed the moment of contact between Meghan and the loch-serpent, though the ferry-master shook his head and said, "Never ken our *uile-bheist* to come that close and no' take the boat down!"

The shore slid closer. Iseult could see great shoulders of mountains rising from gray-hued woods. Feeling suddenly uneasy, she glanced toward the town. The fog wisped apart for a moment and she saw soldiers waiting by the jetty, their red cloaks lifting in the breeze. "Meghan!" she called softly.

The old woman glanced back at her and nodded, lifting her plaid so it covered the distinctive white lock at her brow. Bacaiche also tensed, and wrapped his cloak more tightly about him. Carefully Iseult loosened the weapons in her belt and flexed her fingers, knowing she was cold and stiff after the night's watch. Meghan looked at her warningly but could say nothing for the ferry was nudging the jetty and the soldiers were already coming forward.

There were thirteen of them, cloaks wrapped close against the mist. As the passengers scrambled from the boat, the captain stepped forward, his plumed helmet tucked under his arm. He was a tall, well-built man with a high-bridged nose and an air of arrogance. He interrogated the crofters, checking their answers against a sheaf of papers he held.

Iseult noticed Meghan had lost her upright posture and was shuffling along like the old woman she was, her back bent almost double. The ferry-master assisted her off the ferry and she clung to his arm, moaning. "It be all right now, ma'am," he said kindly, "the *uile-bheist* be gone now."

The captain looked at the crowd with displeasure. All of the crofters and their wives looked nervous and anxious but were indisputably the very essence of respectability. Then his eyes lit on Bacaiche and a spark kindled there.

"What do we have here?" the captain said jocularly and sauntered over toward them. "A hunchback! Well, we've been told to keep an eye out for cripples and suchlike near Dunceleste. They call the leader o' the rebels the Cripple, do they no'?"

Bacaiche said nothing, just glanced at the man out of

the corner of his yellow eye, then stared at the ground. The captain walked around him, jeering. "Freak! Monster! Escaped from a circus, have we?" As he spoke, he gave Bacaiche a rough shove which sent him reeling back, his cloak wrenched away, its edge still clenched in the captain's fist.

The great black wings confined beneath sprang free as Bacaiche regained his balance. He looked magnificent, his bare shoulders straight and wide as he held the immense span of his wings aloft. Sighs and gasps rang round the crowd.

"Holy Truth!" the captain breathed. "We've got ourselves an *uile-bheist*!"

The soldiers leapt on Bacaiche, dragging him to the ground. He gave a loud screech and tried to fight them off. As he disappeared under a flurry of fists and boots, Iseult blurred into action, throwing her dagger through the throat of the soldier nearest her and spinning on one foot to kick another hard in the stomach. As he doubled over, she elbowed a third in the throat and then kneed him so he dropped like a stone.

She executed a flawless backward somersault, kicking another firmly in the back, sending him sprawling onto the ground. In a flurry of quick, expert movements, she knocked out several more soldiers who rushed her from opposite directions.

The captain shouted, and some of the soldiers holding Bacaiche down left him to attack Iseult. She pulled her dagger out of the throat of the first soldier and plunged it into the back of another feebly struggling to rise, before cart-wheeling out of their range. They spun round to confront her, but she had already pulled her eight-pointed *reil* from her belt and, with a flick of her wrist, sent it spinning toward them.

They ducked, and it flew over their heads to neatly slice the carotid artery of the soldier standing next to the captain. A fountain of blood sprayed the jetty. The captain drew his sword with an oath. Iseult smiled and called the *reil* back to her hand. The captain made a quick swing at

Iseult, who sucked in her stomach so the sword whistled past her midriff with barely an inch to spare. Again and again he thrust, and she smiled as she swayed easily out of reach each time. The captain went scarlet and thrust the sword forward to impale her. Iseult stepped back at the very last moment, then brought her hand down sharply on the back of his neck so he dropped, his helmet rolling across the jetty with a clatter.

Immediately three more soldiers attacked her, but she nicked one behind the knee with her *reil* and punched the other in the side of the head. Hamstrung, the first fell, howling in agony, but the other merely shook his head, dazed, and came at her again.

Iseult dodged his short spear and got in a quick thrust with her *reil*, kicking backward with one foot at the same time, knocking another back to the ground. The third caught her foot, but she punched him sharply under the chin, then stabbed him with the *reil*, held in her hand like a knife.

Another staggered to his feet and swiped at her with his claymore, but Iseult jumped high in the air, bringing her knees up to her chin, then spun in midair, kicking him in the face. She landed in a crouch behind his back and punched him viciously in the kidneys then, as he fell, dragged her small mace from her belt and smashed it into the nose of another as he scrambled round to face her. As he clutched at his face, she grabbed his spear and ran him cleanly through, turning at the same time so the sword being swung at her back sliced off his arm instead. She pushed the dead soldier at her assailant, knocking him off his feet, but another soldier caught her round the legs and dragged her down.

Meghan started forward, but Iseult was fighting so desperately there was no getting close to her. With a series of kicks and blows Iseult overcame the soldier, rolling out of the way as another spear plunged into where she had been just seconds before. Then Iseult was on her feet again. Lightly she bounded away, then unhooked the head of her mace so she could swing it on its leather thong. The soldiers hesitated, and she taunted them. "Scared, are ye? O' a lassie?"

The dazed captain staggered to his feet and swung his claymore toward her. She kicked him in the stomach with both feet, then brought the mace down hard on the side of his head. Again she whirled it around her head, and smashed the skull of Bacaiche's captor. Without waiting to see him fall, she kicked one of the wounded soldiers back to the ground as he tried to reach for his fallen sword, then danced again out of reach.

By now there were only three soldiers left standing and they were reeling with the injuries she had inflicted on them. Iseult was winded, though, and the blood dripping from the wounded made the ground beneath her feet precarious. For some minutes they feinted, but only one came close enough to tear the fabric of her shirt. She beat him back with quick, strong blows, stabbing him through the throat.

Leaning on her sword, she kicked out sideways and caught one in the stomach, but when he fell, he took her down with him. Kicking and punching, she struggled to be free of his weight, but it was too late, the one remaining soldier stood over her and, with a triumphant cry, brought down his sword.

Before the blade could pierce her, he stiffened and gurgled, and the stroke fell awry as he toppled forward, a spear protruding though his stomach. Iseult looked up in amazement to see a stern-faced Meghan release her grip on its handle. "Ye killed him!" Iseult gasped, wiping the blood from her eyes.

"Aye," Meghan replied grimly. "Come, we must get out o' here." She helped Iseult to her feet, and called to her nephew, who was crouched against the fence, holding his stomach and half crying with pain and anger. He staggered to his feet, his enormous black wings trailing behind him. The injured captain tried to rise, scrabbling for his sword, but Iseult lunged forward and killed him with a single thrust of her sword. The crofters scuttled out of her way, as if they expected her to come after

them with her dripping blade, but Iseult was exhausted,
leaning on the sword and panting heavily.

"Come, Iseult," Meghan said again. "We must flee."

The girl pushed her blood-matted curls out of her eyes
and dropped her sword. With slow deliberation she
turned the dead soldier nearest to her down onto his
face, his arms spread. As she arranged his limbs, she
dipped her fingers in the blood of his wounds. Slowly,
with great ceremony, she then touched her fingertips to
her forehead, her eyelids, her ears and her mouth, deliberately tasting his blood.

"Embrace now our mother death as she embrace ye,
and ken the Gods o' White have accepted your blood
in sacrifice," she chanted, then struggled awkwardly to
her feet and moved to the next corpse, removing her *reil*
from his throat and hanging it again from her belt.

Meghan, who had stood silent and still while carnage
and chaos ruled around her, drew herself up straight,
raised her hand and began to intone the rites of the
dead.

"Meghan!" Bacaiche was white, his yellow eyes blazing. Bruises were beginning to discolor his face and
throat. "We do no' have time."

Meghan turned to him. "Iseult is right," she answered.
"We must give due honor to the dead."

So, in the misty morning light, she and Iseult performed the different rites of their countries and religions,
Iseult tasting their blood and turning them to embrace
the earth. Meghan chanting the ancient rites. When they
had finished, Iseult's face was liberally striped with
blood, her lips and teeth black.

The ferry passengers still lay on the ground in positions of supplication, some gripped with fear and horror,
others with wonder intermingled. Iseult picked up the
captain's sword, its hilt intricately cast, its blade black
with blood. "I take this as my spoils o' war!" she announced in a ringing voice. "Take note: I leave the
weapons o' the others, for they fought bravely if
unwisely."

The old witch turned and confronted the crowd. "Ye have seen today the Winged Prionnsa," she said, "Know then that the stories and rumors are true. He does exist, and when Eileanan faces its darkest moment, he will come and save ye all."

One of the crofters said, "Wha' need have we o' a winged man when our Rìgh protects us?"

An expression of deep sorrow crossed Meghan's face. "The Rìgh may no' always be here to protect ye," she answered. "The Red Wanderer has crossed our skies and brings with it omens o' war and destruction. I fear the reports the Fairgean are rising are true, and they say the Rìgh is no' the man he once was . . ."

"Treason!" hissed a fat farmer's wife.

Meghan turned to look at her. "I speak the truth, my dear," she said and pulled back her plaid to show the white lock that twisted through her braid all the way to the ground. "I am Meghan NicCuinn, Sorceress o' the Beasts, and I do no' lie! A scarlet thread has been strung on the loom o' our lives and we face danger such as we have no' seen for many years."

There was no doubt the highlanders recognized who Meghan was for there was a collective sigh and murmur, half fearful, half glad. Many of them looked from her to Bacaiche, and as they noticed the white streak in his black curls and his aquiline nose, so like Meghan's, another, more excited murmur rose.

"Evil times are ahead, have no doubt o' that!" the sorceress cried. "Know, however, that the Witches o' Eileanan are no' gone—they watch out for ye and protect ye still. Do no' fear! We are no' your enemies."

With those words, Meghan turned and led the way into the swirling mist, Iseult limping close behind. Bacaiche wrapped himself in the nyx-hair cloak and again became a hunchback, lurching after. The mist swallowed their figures and they were gone.

THE SPINNING WHEEL TURNS

THE SPRING EQUINOX

SONG OF THE CELESTINES

The Veiled Forest was a dark and forbidding place. Between stands of tall pine were vast moss-oaks hung with great curtains of spidery gray, giving the forest an unearthly feel. Mist drifted everywhere, concealing the great tangle of roots so that Iseult had to pick her way warily. She kept her crossbow nocked and at the ready, for Meghan said many strange creatures inhabited the enchanted forest and Iseult knew she should not have explored so far.

Noticing how long the shadows had grown, she turned and made her way back to the garden of the Celestines. There the setting sun still shone red, and the mist was a mere blue haze beneath the graceful trees. She made her way to the clearing where they had made their camp, and found Meghan pacing in impatience, her brow deeply furrowed.

"About time ye got back!" the wood witch said. "Wash yourself quickly! It's the spring equinox at last, and we must make ready. Tonight the Celestines come to Tulachna Celeste, and happen we shall hear some news o' Isabeau at last."

Iseult obeyed instantly, knowing better than to ignore that tone in Meghan's voice. The sorceress had been

sorely troubled ever since their arrival in the Celestines'
garden, for there had been no sign of Isabeau as hoped.
The garden had been empty of all life but the woodland
creatures and, despite scrying through her crystal ball
every day, Meghan had been unable to discover any
trace of her missing ward.

After the battle on the jetty, the three of them had
hurried as fast as they could into the shadowy gloom of
the Veiled Forest, hearing the alarm bell ringing out
behind them. The old sorceress had been white with
anger. "To think I wanted the Red Guards to believe
we were still on the other side o' the loch! Now the Awl
will have every seeker in Rionnagan converging on the
Veiled Forest! After all these years keeping Bacaiche's
real identity secret, and the elven cat's let out o' the bag
by a wee snippet o' a lass that should've known better!"

"That's no' fair!" Iseult had protested angrily. "It was
no' me who attracted the soldiers' attention! It was no'
me who pulled his filthy cloak off!"

"No, that is true." Meghan's tone was only slightly
softer. "Both ye and Bacaiche are prime fools! Why did
yet no' leave it to me, Iseult?"

Iseult had looked at her in amazement. What could
Meghan have done? Bacaiche would have been beaten
to a pulp if Iseult had not stepped forward, and the lot
of them probably thrown into prison. There they would
have been tortured by the Questioners of the Anti-
Witchcraft League and condemned to die, just like her
twin Isabeau had been. Isabeau had only barely managed to escape her fate, and she had been cruelly hurt
by the Awl first. If Iseult had not fought and killed the
soldiers, their fate would have been as bitter. Yet Bacaiche had said no word of thanks, just limped forward,
his scowl heavier than ever, while Meghan had scolded
her as if she was a child and had acted foolishly instead
of saving all of their lives.

"Well, what is done is done," the wood witch had
said. "I shall just have to see what I can make o' it all.

At least the rumors about the winged prionnsa will be spreading fast after this."

Sulkily Iseult had suffered Meghan's cleansing and purification rites, which the sorceress insisted were necessary before attempting to penetrate the enchanted forest. It had taken them close on a week to make their way through the gaunt, looming trees, but at last they had stumbled out into the smooth lawns and sunlit avenues of the Celestines' garden. In the very heart of the garden was a high hill, perfectly round and symmetrical, with a ring of tall stones crowning its green head.

"Tulachna Celeste," Meghan had said, contentment and wonder in her voice. Iseult was a little surprised. From the way Meghan spoke, she had been expecting the ruins of a grand city, not this hill with its simple ring of rough-hewn stones.

They had climbed the hill in silence and soon had risen above the level of the great trees, almost as high as the hills and mountains behind them. The stones, each twice as tall as Iseult, were topped with other stones, forming archways. The menhirs were all scratched with symbols of suns and stars and moons and running water. Compared to the intricate stone carvings of the tower where Iseult had grown up, they seemed childlike and crude.

Inside there was merely a stretch of meadow, with more tall stones circling a pool of green water in the center. Fringed with clumps of rushes, the water trailed a plume of lush grass and clover to the west where once a stream had bubbled from its depths and run down the slope and into the forest. The joy on Meghan's face had slowly faded as she found no trace of anyone on the hill or in the garden, and gruffly she had bid them make camp and wait. "Perhaps Isabeau will be here soon," she said. "She may no' have been able to find her way easily through the forest."

As they had labored together gathering firewood and foodstuffs that first evening, Iseult had noticed Bacaiche moved more fluidly without the heavy cloak, even abandoning his club. She decided it must be because he was able to use his wings to balance himself, while they were merely a hindrance when pinned beneath the cloak. She began to wonder why Bacaiche had been unable to defend himself at the jetty. He was a tall, strong man with massive shoulders and arms, and a pair of lethally clawed feet. Why had he not used them?

When she had asked him that night, he had looked away, his jaw set. "I thought the People o' the Spine o' the World did no' ask questions."

"I offer ye a question in return, o' course," Iseult answered.

He snapped, "I was turned into a blackbird when I was twelve, if ye remember. I had barely begun to be taught to fight, and although I had to struggle to stay alive while a bird, that is o' no use now."

"I do no' see why no'."

"I was a blackbird for four years, ye fool. I hid among leaves when the shadow o' hawks fell upon me, and flew away when elven cats were on the prowl. What use is that to me now?"

"But have ye no' been spreading rumors o' the coming o' a winged warrior? Are ye no' expecting war? How can ye fight to win the throne if ye canna even defend yourself against a pack o' half-trained soldiers? Ye had to be rescued by a lass and an auld woman . . .."

"Have ye no eyes in your head, Iseult o' the Snows? Life as a claw-footed cripple is no' the path to being a warrior." Bacaiche scrambled to his feet, the flames casting sinister shadows on his face.

"Why no'? Ye could shoot a bow with those shoulders, and ye are strong. Your talons look formidable. I would no' like to fight ye hand-to-hand if ye used those the way a hawk does. And ye could attack from above, which gives ye an advantage."

"How can I attack from above when I canna fly?" Bacaiche flapped his wings derisively so Iseult's red curls were blown away from her face. "Ye think these wings are o' any use to me except to make me a prisoner o'

my own body? I, the Prionnsa Lachlan Owein MacCuinn, son o' Parteta the Brave and direct descendant o'
Aedan Whitelock, am called *uile-bheist* and monster. I
am hunted down like a coney by my own brother's soldiers, forced to live as a fugitive! Ye think I would no'
like to be able to strike back? Ye think I do no' long to
dance with a sword like ye do?"

"I can teach ye," Iseult began.

With a snarl, Bacaiche had jerked away, wrapping the
cloak around him again. "Teach a cripple, Iseult? I
thought ye despised the weak and deformed. I thought
ye believed helpless cripples should be left out for your
blaygird Gods o' White?" Without waiting for an answer, he had lurched off into the darkness, Iseult flushing
with anger and shame. It was true, weak or disfigured
babies were exposed by the Prides, and those crippled
by war or accident pitied and scorned. She was sorry
Bacaiche knew it.

The next morning he had limped off into the forest as
soon as they had finished their porridge. Frowning, Iseult
had washed herself and the dishes in the burn that ran
brown and sun-speckled through the trees. The stone-
crowned head of the high, green hill was framed between
the branches of a massive moss-draped tree. At the sight
of it, serenity swept through her. *What does it matter if
the bad-tempered, hunchbacked fool is angry and will no'
speak with me? He means nothing to me anyway . . .*

Meghan was sitting cross-legged on the ground, pulling
a myriad of strange objects out of the small black pouch
she held in her lap. Her donbeag, Gitâ, scurried back
and forth, carrying what he could to lay in various
mounds on the turf.

"Magic pouch," Meghan explained. "It was woven for
a MacBrann by one o' the oldest and cleverest o' the
nyx. It's a bottomless bag—very useful for moving house
or escaping unexpected attacks. Unfortunately, ye must
take things out in the same order that ye put them in,
and so retrieving anything can be a nuisance."

As the wood witch spoke, Iseult helped the donbeag

sort everything into piles, marveling at some of the extraordinary things Meghan had decided to include. A smith's hammer and chisel were followed by a broken arrow fletched with white feathers, and then by a wedding veil of lace so old Iseult was afraid it might crumble in her hands. There were beautifully woven plaids in blues and greens, red running through like a line of fire, while a dark-brown globe perched unsteadily on top of the tall pile of books.

Iseult picked the sphere up by its ornate stand and spun it. "Where are we?"

Meghan, without pausing in her unpacking, gently floated the globe out of the girl's hands and down onto the grass. "It is no' a globe o' our world," she said reprovingly. "That is one o' only two globes from the Other World, and it is irreplaceable. I keep it in the pouch so that time will no' touch it. Please take great care with my treasures, Iseult. Many o' them I saved from fire and treachery and I would no' like ye to damage them now."

She indicated one of the heavy books, dark with age, with a heavily embossed cover. "That is one o' the great treasures o' the Coven, and I came near death saving it from the Banrìgh. It is *The Book o' Shadows,* and it contains much lore and history, and many great and powerful spells. Now we are safe at Tulachna Celeste, I shall begin teaching ye and Lachlan again."

"More magic?" Iseult asked eagerly.

Meghan nodded, but said, "Ye and Lachlan have much else ye must learn as well. Alchemy and geography and history, among other things. Ye're both ignorant indeed!" At the old witch's words, Iseult sat back on her heels. Her jaw set in a way that Meghan was beginning to know well. "No stubbornness now, Iseult," Meghan warned. "Ye agreed to throw your lot in with me, and indeed I'm glad now that the Spinners brought your thread to cross mine. There is a design in this weaving, that I be sure o'. Ye must be made ready."

Iseult stilled her hands, which had begun to fidget in her lap.

"Besides, why no' take the opportunity to learn what ye can? Knowledge is power, surely ye must ken that. If ye are one day to be Firemaker, as ye wish, ye should want to do the best ye can for your people. I am sure your grandmother does no' wish ye to waste your time here."

Still Iseult was silent, her lashes red crescents against her creamy, freckled face.

"And if I remember rightly, your father first came to the Tower o' Two Moons because he had learnt all that the wise ones o' your land could teach him. He wanted to learn our wisdom and skills, and while he was with us he studied hard."

At that Iseult looked up and said, "Ye are right. To be the Firemaker is to be in *geas* to the Gods o' White. To no' take it on full-heartedly is to no' give all honor to the gods." She paused, and then said in a constricted voice, "I give ye my apologies then, auld mother, and confess both to fear and pride, worst o' deficiencies." Meghan looked a little surprised and went to say something, but Iseult pressed on grimly. "I was afraid ye wished me to learn your wisdom so that ye could win me from the Prides, and turn me to your own path; and I was proud and angry for your nephew has scorned my offer o' coaching when indeed he should ken it was a rare compliment for me to offer at all!"

Meghan's puckered old mouth twitched, but she answered gravely. "Indeed, Iseult, there is no need to apologize—all I wish is for ye to make the most o' your powers. Ye may return to the Spine o' the World any time ye wish, though I would no' like to lose ye at all."

"Then I shall bide a wee and see what pattern the weaver makes o' our lives," Iseult replied just as gravely.

Meghan was pleased at her words, for it showed the girl had at least listened once or twice, but she shut her mouth down grimly and said, "Do no' bother the lad, Iseult, it is no' kind o' ye. Indeed, it was a blaygird enchantment laid on him and he is bitter indeed at the Ensorcellor. He does no' find his life now easy to accept."

Iseult opened her mouth to protest, then flushed and said nothing, remembering the black mood her question the night before had provoked. *Biding with these southerners has made me rude and disdainful,* she thought. *Asking unwanted questions!*

When Bacaiche at last stumped back to the clearing, his curls were lank with sweat, his bare chest and shoulders marked all over with bramble scratches. Meghan beckoned him down to sit by her, her wrinkled face uncharacteristically soft. "Look, Lachlan my lad, I have my father's kilt and plaid for ye. His *sgian dubh* and sporran too. They were tucked away a long time syne. Ye need clothes, ye canna wander around the country in a pair o' Isabeau's auld breeches. Too small by far they are for ye!"

Bacaiche seized the plaids eagerly, his topaz eyes blazing, his black mood forgotten. "Look, the sporran bears the MacCuinn crest—there's a brooch to hold the plaid too." He turned the brooch to examine it, and Iseult saw the device—a leaping stag carrying a crown in its antlers. "I have no' seen the stag rampant syne I was a bairn." His voice thickened. "And the dear auld tartan— my father never wore anything else."

"Nor mine." Meghan caressed the plaid that now hung on her shoulders. With its rich folds pinned together with a great emerald, it was easy to believe she was descended from righrean.

"Who exactly was your father, Meghan?" Bacaiche asked, stroking the dark green velvet of the jacket. "I do no' think I've ever really known what our relationship is. I just remember ye always being there when I was a bairn."

"Aye, I was indeed always there. I was there when your father was a babe-in-arms, and your grandfather and great-grandfather too. Indeed, so many o' your forebears have been dandled on my knee that I have near forgot them all. Great-aunt would be the most accurate description, if we left out about ten greats or so."

So rich with irony was Meghan's voice that both Bacaiche and Iseult were not sure whether to believe her. She smiled and twisted the jewel at her breast. "My father was the Whitelock himself," she said proudly. "I was his eldest daughter, and Mairead the Fair who wielded the Lodestar after him was my younger sister."

"But Aedan Whitelock died four hundred years ago!"

"Nay, three hundred and fifty-nine only. He lived to a grand auld age, my *dai-dein*, though he gave up the throne when he turned seventy, thinking it was time his daughters had their chance. Mairead won the Lodestar and I won the Key o' the Coven in the same year—seven hundred and thirty-four. It's a year I shall never forget."

"But that means ye must be . . ." Bacaiche tried to calculate the years in his mind, but failed.

"Remind me to give ye some lessons in mathematics," Meghan said wryly. "I am four hundred and twenty-seven years auld, though it's hardly polite o' ye to ask. Dearie me, it makes me feel auld to say it, I had almost forgotten how long it has been. Cleaning out the bottomless bag has made me nostalgic . . . Go and put on my father's kilt and sporran, Lachlan, and wear them proudly, for truly he was a great man, perhaps the finest MacCuinn o' them all."

"Ye are calling me Lachlan." His voice was muffled. "Why now? Ye have no' let me be called Lachlan since the enchantment."

Meghan smiled and patted his smooth, brown hand with hers, gnarled and blue-veined. "We are safe here. There is no need to fear listening ears, none can scry on us within the protection o' Tulachna Celeste and none can approach who are no' faery friends. Besides, we declared ye at the jetty. Do ye no' think half o' Rionnagan knows by now that one o' the lost prionnsachan is found? I was no' yet ready to let Maya know that ye were alive and a threat to her power, but the massacre at the jetty forced my hand."

Iseult gritted her teeth and said nothing.

"So perhaps it is time for ye to stop being the Cripple and become a prionnsa again. I shall call ye Lachlan from now on, and so shall Iseult, and when we gather our troops together, they shall call ye the MacCuinn, as they should."

When Lachlan came back from the bushes, he walked with his head high and his wings spread, the kilt swaying above his talons with every stilted stride. "These clothes are no' really in the fashion o' the day, are they?" he said ruefully, though he knew he looked magnificent. He had thrown the plaid over his bare shoulder and pinned it with the stag device, the emerald eye glinting darkly.

"Bring me the shirt and I shall alter it for ye. If ye will let me measure and fit ye, I think I can make ye a shirt with wing-holes as well as armholes."

"Aye," Lachlan replied eagerly and unpinned the plaid, dropping easily into a crouch before Meghan. The firelight flickered over his olive skin, outlining the contours of his chest. Iseult could not help watching for, without his concealing cloak, Lachlan was a beautiful man, all muscle and smooth skin. Even folded, his wings were magnificent, glossy with blue highlights like the wing of a blackbird, while his tousled curls hung over his forehead in a way Iseult found quite disturbing. She reminded herself what a surly, ill-natured man he was, how rude and how ungrateful.

When Lachlan was well shrouded in linen and tied to her by a flashing needle and thread, Meghan said softly, "I ken ye are angry because Iseult spoke to ye about your wings and claws, but indeed it is time ye accepted your state, Lachlan, and tried to make the most o' it."

Surprised, he tried to jerk away. Meghan held him fast, saying calmly, "Lift your arm, laddie." After she had pinned him, she continued, "I ken it has no' been easy for ye and that ye grieve for your brothers still. I miss them myself and hope we will perhaps find one trapped still in the body o' a blackbird . . . Though thirteen years have passed—even under enchantment, I doubt they could have lived so long. I wonder ye managed to survive the four years ye did." She fell silent for a long while.

When Meghan spoke again, her voice was low and stern. "Iseult has offered to teach ye to fight, yet ye are too proud to take up her offer. Much as I abhor violence, she is right, war is coming. If the omens are true, a dark and bloody war it will be. Ye say ye wish to have revenge on Maya for your ensorcelment, and prevent her evil schemes from coming to fruition, yet ye will no' learn the strength and skills ye will need. What kind o' Rìgh will ye be, when ye canna even grasp opportunities when they're offered to ye?"

Even in the dim light of their fire, Iseult could see how red Lachlan had flushed. He gritted his teeth, and said, "Canna ye stay off my back, Meghan! All ye do is nag me and nag me."

"Do ye wish for revenge on Maya the Ensorcellor?"

"Aye, Eà damn the black-hearted witch!"

"Do ye wish to protect the people, as all your forebears have done, ever since our ancestor Cuinn brought them to this land?"

"I suppose so," he scowled.

"Do ye wish to rescue the Lodestar?"

"Aye," Lachlan answered after a moment, his voice unexpectedly gentle. "It's greetin', Meghan, I hear it all the time. I canna bear to have it slowly dying from want o' love and contact."

"Then put aside your pride and accept what Iseult and I are offering ye. Ye have ability, Lachlan, ye just lack discipline and focus. Accept that ye shall never have back your carefree childhood and your strong, unblemished body, and make the most o' what ye have."

He said in a strangled voice, "Ye do no' understand."

"Indeed I do, my lad," and there was more affection and warmth in Meghan's voice than Iseult had ever heard. "My blood boils with anger that Maya can have harmed ye so. But I canna transform ye back, though I've tried all I know. Ye must accept your fate, laddie.

I have thought long and hard on this, and I wonder why else was Iseult brought to us at this time, if not to teach us what she knows o' battle and warfare? I must trust to the weaver to fly the shuttle true, and so must ye, Lachlan the Winged."

Lachlan did not reply. When Meghan had finished altering the shirt, he shrugged it on and submitted to her buttoning the back around his wings, but he said nothing. Scowling, he squatted again by the fire and prodded moodily at the coals with a twig. Iseult risked a glance at him and was disconcerted when he shot her a fierce gaze from under his brows. For a moment their eyes met, then Iseult looked away, embarrassed.

"Ye owe me a question, Iseult o' the Snows," Lachlan jeered softly.

She met his gaze squarely. "That I do."

He lifted an eyebrow in surprise, then turned his gaze back to the coals. "I'll think o' a good one then."

"One should never waste a question," she agreed.

Involuntarily he smiled, though he turned away so quickly that Iseult saw only the crease of his cheek. She smiled to herself, turning her attention back to the spell book.

Every morning after that, Iseult had practiced with her weapons in a clearing in the forest, polishing her moves and stances, keeping her limbs supple and strong. Usually she worked naked, wearing only her boots and weapons belt, but Meghan had suggested she remain in her shirt and breeches in order to protect her fair skin from the sun. Iseult agreed and was glad later when she realized Lachlan was watching her from the shelter of a huge moss-oak. The memory of the time he had watched her bathing still gave her an odd squirming feeling deep in her stomach, and she was glad to keep her linen shirt on, despite the heat.

At first she was tempted to show off some of her more difficult aerial maneuvers. Iseult had been one of the most acrobatic of the Scarred Warriors. Even on foot she was capable of dazzling tumbling and somersaulting runs. Remembering, though, that Lachlan was a pupil, she did what she would do if she were teaching one of her young disciples back in the Haven. She showed how a relatively simple sequence of movements could translate into a powerful defensive move. Over and over she repeated the slow flowing movement of hand and hip, each time extending until at last she rose off the ground in a quick snap of her body, her foot kicking out and up. Without having to look, she was aware of Lachlan's brooding interest, and gradually she began to vary the moves so that he saw how many ways a learned reflex could be used.

By the third day Lachlan was restless, wanting to try the moves out for himself, and only then did Iseult show him what training and discipline could do, throwing herself into a series of cartwheels that ended with a soaring somersault that took her high into the leafy canopy. He came out then, though frowning, his arms crossed over his chest. Since donning the clothes of his ancestor, he had seemed both more righlike and less mysterious. Iseult was conscious of a feeling of anticipation.

"Why do ye always cover your hair?" he had surprised her by asking, tugging at the long tail of her linen cap.

"Is that the question ye wish me to answer?"

"Nay. Though I would like to know . . . . So ye wish to teach me to fight."

"Aye, if ye would like."

"Meghan seems to think it may be o' use. Just try no' to lecture me or put on that superior smirk o' yours."

"So gracious as always, Your Highness."

So while Meghan had paced the clearing and scryed through her crystal ball, Iseult had begun teaching Lachlan how to fight. At first it had been difficult, for he had never worked out whether to stride like a man or hop like a bird. By now, however, he was at least able to defend himself if attacked, and his movements were not so awkward as he limped about the clearing.

Meghan had found the weeks of waiting till the spring equinox difficult and her temper this evening was bitter and hot. As they drank the herbal potion she gave them, the wood witch scolded them angrily, testing them on the rites of the equinox. Both Iseult and Lachlan had learnt them the previous day, but in his resentment at her mood, Lachlan either could not or would not remember them.

"It's about time ye took the rituals o' the Coven seriously, Lachlan! Ye must ken all the chants for all the festivals—they are no' all for show and mystification . . ."

"Why do I need to ken them all? I shall be Rìgh!"

"Ye come from the line o' Cuinn Lionheart himself, and great power is latent in ye. Ye canna wield the Lodestar if the power lies dormant. Ye must learn as much as ye can about your own Skills and Talents afore ye can think o' winning the Lodestar. Ye want to be Rìgh o' all Eileanan? Ye'll need everything ye have o' strength and knowledge and wisdom, and still ye will need more . . ."

"Aye, aye, I ken, ye've told me all this afore," Lachlan muttered.

Meghan clambered to her feet and began gathering together her witch's paraphernalia. "Then why will ye no' heed what I say?" She thrust a load of firewood into Lachlan's arms and piled Iseult's up with wreaths of flowers. Gitâ clinging to her plait, she began to walk through the forest to Tulachna Celeste.

"If it's so important for me to learn the Skills o' witchcraft, why did ye leave me with Enit all those years?" Lachlan suddenly flared, rustling his wings behind him. "She's no Tower witch, just a forest skeelie that sings for her supper."

"Enit may no' be Tower-trained, but she has powerful magic o' her own," Meghan snapped, leaning on her staff to catch her breath. She continued in a troubled voice, "Ye ken why I had to leave ye with Enit. Ye were more than half bird still. Enit can charm any bird, even one as fierce as ye were, more falcon than blackbird, I swear. She could speak with ye in your own language . . ."

"The song o' the blackbird, ye mean," Lachlan scowled. Lifting his head, he sang so sweetly a pang hooked through Iseult's throat and she had to swallow and look away.

"It was dangerous for ye to be with me." Meghan's voice was low and quick. "I was hunted everywhere, with a price on my head and every seeker in the land focusing on me. I hoped the Banrìgh would not find out ye had survived her ensorcelment, and so I had to keep ye well hidden. No one had cause to suspect the jongleurs, and Enit could safely conceal ye and keep ye safe."

"Still, a jongleur's caravan is no' the place to be learning the tricks o' witchcraft," Lachlan responded. "Ye can hardly blame me for no' knowing as much as ye would like, when ye left me to be brought up by gipsies."

"Aye, happen ye are right," Meghan responded with unusual mildness, "but that is no excuse for no' learning now that ye are with me again. Besides, ye ken ye wanted to stay with Enit once ye knew she was working with the rebels. Ye were filled with black rage against the Banrìgh and wanted to be striking against her."

"Aye, because ye would no'!"

"Do no' be a fool," Meghan snapped as she reached the stone-crowned summit. "Ye ken I was working with Enit all the time, I could no' be wandering around in the countryside with a price on my head and a face that every crofter and shepherd knew. Ye just could no' stand to work in shadows, ye had to be out, flaunting yourself and gaining a reputation! Besides, ye ken Enit tried to teach ye some o' the Yedda Skills but ye were as always too impatient, too sulky."

"I could hardly remember to speak, Meghan, if ye remember. It was ages afore I could even summon the One Power again."

"Yet ye were always very strong as a bairn, I still canna understand why ye fear the Power so much now—"

Lachlan opened his mouth to retort, but Meghan held

up an imperative hand, insisting on silence while she made the genuflections necessary before she would cross through the great doorway of stone. When they passed through to the inner circle of stones, the sun was tilted on the far distant peak of the Fang, turning the glacier to rose and lavender. It was sunset, time for the rites to begin.

The spring equinox marked the end of winter and the dead time, and the beginning of the summer months. It was a time when the magical tides turned, a shift in the harmonies of the earth. For the first time since the coming of the cooler weather, daylight lingered as long as the night. Though not as important to the witches' calendar as Beltane or Midsummer's Eve, it was still a key event and was usually celebrated with the burning of fragrant candles, the making of wreaths and the ringing of bells.

Although the three of them were alone in the forest, Meghan intended to celebrate the equinox as fully as if the Coven of Witches were still a power in the land. Once every family would have decorated the house with evergreen branches and chanted the rites, and the bells would have rung out loudly from every village meeting-house. Now that the Coven was outlawed and witchcraft forbidden, only a few would dare celebrate the vernal equinox, and they would do it in secret. Even fewer would endure the hours of fasting and praying that Meghan insisted upon first; and when they spoke the incantations, it would be in low voices and with fearful glances.

Her eyes shut, a wreath of dark leaves on her head, Iseult endured the lonely hours of the Ordeal, thinking of the great snow-capped needles of stone and the white valleys that had always been her home. Iseult missed the Spine of the World. The warmth of these green hills made her slow and soft, and prone to romantic imaginings. Still, she was proud to be following in the footsteps of her hero father, the first of her people to cross the Cursed Peaks and travel in the land of the sorcerers. He had died here, or so she had thought. The dragons had said that he was not dead, only lost, and so Iseult dreamed of finding him and bringing him back in triumph to her grandmother.

The flames were sinking low when suddenly all Iseult's senses came alert. There was an alien presence within the circle of stones. Jerking her tired eyes open, Iseult saw three tall, pale shapes slowly approaching the fire. Silently she fitted an arrow to her little bow, wound it with the hook on her belt and raised it to her shoulder.

Without warning, a gnarled old hand gripped hers, forcing her to lower the crossbow. If Iseult had not recognized Meghan's touch, she would have killed her immediately, but she subdued her instinctive urge to defend herself, and let the bow and arrow slip to the ground.

I said we were safe here, Iseult, when will ye learn to trust me? The witch spoke in her mind. *If ye had fired and killed one o' our hosts, ye would have done great evil, for the Celestines are the gentlest o' creatures, and we shelter here at their kindness. Learn to think afore ye seek to kill, my bairn, for else ye are as evil as those we seek to overthrow.*

Iseult nodded, though she watched the noiseless approach of the mysterious figures with distrust. The Firemaker Meghan may be prepared to extend the hand of friendship to all creatures, but Iseult certainly was not.

The Celestines were tall and slender, with white hair that flowed down their backs. They were dressed in loose robes of pale silk that seemed to shimmer slightly so that a vague nimbus surrounded their forms. In the darkness their faces were indistinct, though occasionally she saw the gleam of their eyes. With the fingers of one hand to their foreheads, they bowed to Meghan. The air was filled with a sonorous humming.

Meghan rose to her feet, bowed, and answered them with the same deep, low croon. It sounded like bees swarming, elven cats purring, leaves rustling, rain blowing.

"It is nigh on midnight," Meghan said softly to her wards. "We shall begin the chanting and dancing soon, and wait for dawn, when the Celestines shall sing the sun to life. Ye may all join in if ye catch the melody; but if ye canna maintain the sound, do no' start. It is a bad omen indeed if the song should falter, and the song o' the Celestine needs stamina and control o' one's breath."

Through the dark came another of the faery creatures, smaller than the others and stooped. When he came closer to the fire to greet Meghan, Iseult saw his face was seamed with wrinkles, his forehead so heavily corrugated that his eyes were hidden in shadow. He and Meghan hummed at each other for some time, the sound surprising Iseult with its flexibility and expressiveness. Although she did not know what they were saying, she heard gladness and welcome, and questions. He placed one multijointed finger between Meghan's eyes, and she bowed her head and let him touch her for a very long time. Then he took her hand in his and let her touch him in the same manner.

So quietly that Iseult did not hear her, another Celestine had come through the outer ring of stones and now stood beside them, humming softly. She and Meghan embraced, and Iseult heard the rising inflection' of an anxious question in Meghan's response.

Iseult had almost fallen asleep when Meghan at last returned to the fire. Lachlan was fidgeting under the gaze of the Celestines, grouped by themselves near the water. He looked up with relief as Meghan ordered them to light their torches, and he nudged Iseult with his claw.

The five white figures stood around the dark pool in the apex of the hill and waited in courteous silence as Meghan led Iseult and Lachlan through the rites of the witches. Iseult was growing used to Meghan's ways, but still she felt awkward and rather silly chanting rhymes and dancing round the fire with those solemn figures watching. Again and again her eye was drawn to them, in both wonder and suspicion. With their long white manes and strong facial structure, the Celestines reminded her of the People of the Spine of the World, and you never turned your back on an unknown Khan'-cohban if you could help it.

It was in the gray hush before dawn when the Celestines at last moved, stepped forward to hold hands around the pool. The burning torches which Iseult, Lachlan and Meghan had carried in their hands were scorched to their base, barely glimmering with flame. The fire had sunk to embers, and Iseult was conscious of the dryness of her eyes and the empty ache of her body after a night without food or sleep.

One by one the Celestines began to croon, some so low the sound was felt as a thrumming in the veins and arteries and organs, rather than heard; others as high and clear as the tinkle of a waterfall. Meghan joined the Celestines around the pool, their slim tall figures towering over hers. Her murmur interlaced with the Celestines, building in blood-troubling rhythms.

The night was beginning to peel away along the horizon when, unexpectedly, a voice of the clearest and most poignant beauty wove through the song. Iseult, crouched by the fire in a daze, looked up and saw that Lachlan had quietly stepped forward to take Meghan's hand and join the ring of singers. His wings were spread, the moonlight marbling the feathers with silver, highlighting the beautiful line of his jaw and neck. Iseult could only gaze at him and listen, filled with helpless longing.

As the stones loomed against the paling sky, birds of all sorts began to sing and carol. Water gurgled as clear, liquid bubbles splashed into life, sending the water in the pool tumbling over the lip of stone and down the side of the hill. Still Lachlan sang, his voice the most beautiful music Iseult had ever heard. The sun rose, embroidering the landscape with color, and the song of the Celestines slowly drifted into silence.

"Och, well done, my laddie!" Meghan cried. "Come and see, Iseult! The summerbourne is running."

In the center of the pool a clear spring now bubbled.

Where the water cascaded down the western slope of the hill, a gaudy train of flowers had sprung up—the tiny crimson stars of waterlilies, golden buttercups, blue forget-me-nots, the white buds of wild strawberries and the heavy pink heads of clover.

The Celestines were humming excitedly, and Meghan turned and embraced her nephew. "It is true, ye have magic in your voice," she cried, and tears were wet on her wrinkled face. "The summerbourne is running, stronger than it has for years! They say it is the best singing o' the dawn since the Faery Decree, for there are so few Celestines left and many are too sick at heart for the singing! Oh, Lachlan, I am so pleased and surprised! Enit said ye refused to use your voice, though she knew it had the power o' enchantment. Ye have Talent indeed—look at the spring, how strongly it flows!"

The youngest of the Celestines, a slim woman dressed in palest yellow, came forward and took Lachlan's hands and gazed intently into his eyes. A surprised expression crossed Lachlan's face, then a look of squirming embarrassment. "That's all right," he said gruffly. "It seemed the thing to do—I could hear the melody building . . ."

After another long, searching look, she moved then to Meghan and the two embraced and wandered off, deep in conversation. One by one, the other Celestines bowed to Lachlan and touched their fingers to the middle of his forehead and then to theirs. He scowled, unsure how to respond, but they merely smiled joyously then followed the course of the summerbourne as it tumbled down the hill. The air was sweet with the heady scent of the flowers, and woodlarks flew overhead, singing furiously. The whole forest seemed alive with gladness, bright leaves quivering, nisses bathing playfully in the overbrimming stream.

Only the oldest of the Celestines remained, running his fingers through the liquid silk of the spring, a buttercup tucked in his beard. His face in the fresh light seemed impossibly lined, as if he had seen much pain and sorrow. His sparse hair and beard were white as that of a *geal'teas,* his eyes pale and glittering. Aware of Iseult's gaze, he looked up and touched his fingers to his corrugated brow. Although he smiled, his face did not lose its tinge of melancholy.

At last Meghan and the Celestine returned from their intent conversation. Meghan's face was bright, her black eyes soft with pleasure. "Come, let us eat o' the flesh o' our mother and drink the water o' her body and let us rejoice, for the seasons have turned and the green months are upon us," she intoned, then her voice thrilled with a deep joy. "And let us rejoice, for Isabeau is alive and on her way to Rhyssmadill! Cloudshadow has seen her, and though Isabeau was sore hurt, she healed her at the turn o' the tides. She gave Isabeau the Saddle o' Ahearn to help her make haste to the blue palace. She says the portion o' the Key which Isabeau carried is safe still. Such a dark load off my mind!"

Meghan turned to Cloudshadow and made the low humming noise in her throat which seemed to be the Celestines' language. The Celestine trilled back, and came and sat by Iseult's side, eagerly breaking the bread and biting into a piece of fruit.

Greetings, Iseult NicFaghan . . .

Iseult looked up and around, but Meghan and Lachlan gave no indication they had heard anything. Then she realized the Celestine was smiling at her and humming gently in her throat. Her eyes were clear and translucent as water.

We of the Celestine do not have the same sort of vocal cords as you humans. We cannot speak your language and it is the rare human who can learn to mimic our sounds. Meghan is the only one I have ever known to have managed it, and it took her centuries. Some of us can speak into your minds, though, if you are receptive. You have the blood inheritance of the Khan'cohbans in your veins. They are cousins of a sort to the Celestines, and so that makes it easier for me to speak to you thus.

"What did ye call me?" Iseult asked.

Iseult NicFaghan. I could just as easily have called ye Khan'derin daKhan'lantha, for both are your names. You are the offspring of the ill-fated union of Faodhagan the Red and Khan'lantha of the Fire-Dragon Pride, many hundreds of years ago. Although your ancestors bred but rarely with Khan'cobhans, you have still inherited some of their qualities—your clear eyesight, your fighting spirit—but I call you by your human name, for that is where your destiny lies.

But I am heir to the Firemaker! Unconsciously Iseult answered without words.

And heir also to the witches' tower. It is time for the descendants of Faodhagan to take their place in human society. A thousand years your family has dwelled apart from their kin. It is time to be united . . . I have met your twin sister, you know. You are much alike, more so than I expected. She has a hard journey ahead of her, but then, I think the cost of your destiny will also be high. You have difficult choices to make, and more depends on your decision than you can be aware of. Do not be afraid, though. Although there is sorrow ahead, there is also great joy.

I do no' understand what ye are talking about.

Always I find it difficult to communicate with humans such as yourself. I have studied your thought and emotion patterns and yet always there is this gap between what I know and what I can say. I am always surprised by how muddled your thinking is, and how vague your emotions.

I do no' think I'm muddled . . .

Amusement rang clearly through the Celestine's mind-voice. *No, of course you do not. Humans never do. I have encountered few races more arrogant, especially when so many are so stupid. Still, the best of you have great minds and hearts, and I try hard not to judge the few by the many.*

Thank you . . .

The Celestine gave a high trill, causing Meghan to look up and smile.

Humans always surprise me. I forget how lightly you

live. It is true your lives are short. I fear the Celestines take everything too seriously, Meghan says we lack a . . . sense of humor, if that is the right term. An odd expression, for how is humor a sense? There are only six senses . . .

My grandmother is always admonishing me for not taking life seriously enough.

Yes, the Khan'cohbans do live heavily. They are conscious always of the weight of death pressing them down.

For the first time in their strange conversation, the Celestine had made a sound. She had said "Khan'cohban" as the People would have said it: a harsh, guttural "Khan," followed by two descending notes—the Gods! Children of. The sound had the same skin-shivering quality as the desolate cry of a raven at dusk.

In the same language Iseult replied, "Life on the Spine of the World is hard."

Indeed it is. We of the forest are fortunate. Or at least, we were. Melancholy now clouded the soft voice in Iseult's mind. *We that you humans call Celestines were once as many as the stars in the sky. We lived in the forests and vales and cared for the land. We had our enemies. Who does not? What you call Satyricorn harried us often, and cursehags and gravenings too. Sometimes the Khan'cohbans came down from the snowy peaks in hordes . . .*

Iseult realized with a start that the complicated bud of wrinkles on the Celestine's forehead had parted and she was being regarded with a third, dark eye. It gleamed with liquid reflections, so bright it struck through her like a sword. Below, her two other eyes were clear and empty.

Involuntarily Iseult started back, and the Celestine regarded her gravely, her long-fingered hands folded in her lap. *The sight of my third eye frightens you? For some reason it always makes humans uneasy, perhaps because they lost theirs so long ago. Yet if I keep it shut, how else am I to see you clearly, or find the means to speak with you?*

Iseult regarded the eye in the middle of the Celestine's forehead. *Ye see me differently through your third eye?*

Indeed. It is hard for me to describe. It is your emotional energies I see, your hidden thoughts . . .

Do we no' have a third eye too? Meghan said something . . .

Yes, but your forehead is smooth, your third eye cannot physically see. It is as much the sixth sense that you use. Your third eye is wrapped in veils, and you must learn to unwrap them. Your sister, of course, her third eye was sealed shut by Meghan, but she suffered a sharp blow to her head and that has shaken Meghan's mark off. She will find the veils unraveling quickly now.

So what do ye see o' me through your third eye?

You are yearning for the winged boy, yet you reprimand yourself for allowing yourself to think about him. He is bad-tempered and arrogant, you tell yourself many times. Be at peace, I tell you, for I feel your destiny and his lie together. The winged boy has enchantment in his voice. This morning saw the strongest running of the summerbourne in years. The summerbourne feeds the forest and the garden and all shall spring into life now and be renewed . . . Do not be angry with me for speaking of what I see. Your emotions are so tangled about this boy I can see very little else.

Lachlan MacCuinn irritates and exasperates me, if that is what ye mean by my emotions being tangled. Other than that I rarely think o' him. Iseult looked down at the fruit in her hand, avoiding the Celestine's three-eyed gaze.

I think I see you more clearly than you see yourself. It is of no use avoiding truth with a Celestine, you cannot lie to us about emotions . . . I must go and walk with my grandfather now, he has missed me much in recent months. Think on what I have said, and be at peace. One cannot always control what one thinks and feels, there is no wrongdoing in discovering one's path lies in a different direction than one has thought.

I am the heir to the Firemaker, Iseult thought defiantly. Cloudshadow rose to her feet, dusted off her pale silk gown, and smiled down at Iseult. *Farewell, Iseult NicFaghan . . .*

Iseult looked up to find Lachlan's topaz eyes fixed on hers, and scowled at him. Immediately he scowled back. *Yearning for that sour-faced lad? I do no' think so!*

DARKSOME LIGHT AND SHINING NIGHT

Dillon the Bold crawled on his stomach towards the ridge, motioning to his lieutenants to keep down, then raised his head to peer over the edge. The path that ran along the fast-paced Muileach River was empty of all life as far as he could see. He waited for a few minutes, listening and watching, then pursed up his lips and whistled, three ascending notes like a bluecap swift. Immediately his second-in-command, Jay the Fiddler, beckoned forward the group of ragged children crouched behind a boulder to the rear. They hurried forward, leading a feeble old man in beggar's robes, whose long, knotted beard was thrust through a belt of rope. He tapped his way across the rough ground with a tall staff, his eyes white and clouded.

"The path is clear ahead, Master, I think it be safe for us to scoot ahead," Dillon said, caressing the black-patched head of his shaggy puppy.

"That be good," Jorge the Seer replied, turning his blind head. "Tonight is the spring equinox and I really think we should hold the rites and do a sighting, though it troubles me to open myself so wide here in the wilderness. If any soldiers be near and see us, they'll know we are following the auld ways and then we'll be in trouble indeed."

"Do no' fear, Master, we shall guard ye and keep ye safe."

"Thank ye, I know ye shall," the old seer replied with no trace of irony in his voice. After the last few weeks traveling in the company of Dillon the Bold and his gang of beggar children, he knew they would care for him with great efficiency.

Jorge had first met the children in the slums of Lucescere, where they had helped him and his young acolyte Tòmas escape the clutches of the Anti-Witchcraft League. The little boy had the miraculous ability to heal by his touch alone, and had drawn the seekers' attention by curing those incarcerated in the Awl's dungeons. Word of the miracle had spread quickly, and riots against the much-despised Awl had broken out. Led by the sturdy, shock-haired Dillon, who was known then by his nickname Scruffy, the beggar children had led the city soldiers in circles while Jorge and Tòmas fled into the mountains. Grateful to Dillon for his help, Jorge had suggested he join their travels but had not expected the beggar boy to accept on behalf of the entire gang.

Jorge had found himself quite unable to tell the ragged, dirty children to return to the slums of Lucescere, however. He had grown up in those alleyways himself. He knew just how harsh a life it was. No matter how arduous traveling through the countryside might be, or how dangerous, the children would be safer with him than living wild off the streets of Lucescere.

After a week in the company of the League of the Healing Hand, as they now called themselves, Jorge had to admit that, rather than the children being under his protection, he was under theirs. Dillon the Bold was the leader of the League, of course, and he had deployed his troops with the ingenuity and expertise of a battle-seasoned general. Although he had lived all his life in the city's slums, several of his gang had been brought up in the country and he had grilled them to find out everything they knew about hunting and tracking in the countryside.

False trails were laid, their tracks covered, roots and berries gathered, camping spots found, snares set for coneys and birds, and patrols ordered to scour the land ahead and behind. Only the eldest girl, Johanna, an anxious-looking waif with long plaits of mousy brown, had begged to be let off the scouting parties, content to forage for food and cook them messy meals instead.

Within days the city of Lucescere had been left far behind, the green foothills steepening into sharp cliffs and ravines filled with forest and the tinkling of waterfalls. Sharp pointed mountains rose on either side, while the river snaked through a deep gorge that forced the small band of travelers to stay on the narrow path. The main problem was that the Red Guards also had to follow the river if they did not want to force a way through the heavily forested ridges that rose on either side. Subsequently the League's journey was a game of hide-and-seek, aided by the long sight of Jorge's raven flying overhead and the old man's prescient witch senses.

The biggest danger was presented by the seekers of the Awl who occasionally accompanied the patrols. Jorge could shield himself with the ease of long practice, but the other members of the gang were more difficult. Tòmas was protected by a pair of enchanted nyx-hair gloves, but the others had no way of hiding their thoughts, and some of them clearly had the potential for working magic. A seeker was trained to search out anyone that had any hint of magical ability, and there was a real danger that one of the children would inadvertently commit some act of magic that would alert a seeker to their presence.

Jorge had already had to forbid Jay the Fiddler from playing his old, battered violin. The thin, olive-skinned boy had played for them one night, and Jorge had been able to see the magic woven into his music as easily as a man with eyes could see the stars in the sky. He had shushed the boy quickly, afraid that what human ears could not have heard from a few hundred yards away, a seeker would be able to sense with ease.

The younger of the two girls, a lissom, mercurial child called Finn, had been quite distressed on Jay's behalf and had tackled Jorge the next morning. "Dinna ye like what Jay was playing last night? Why did ye tell him to stop? He's a flaming witch with the fiddle, I always think! Did ye no' like it?"

"Och, no, it was bonny, Finn, it's just because he is a witch with the fiddle that I stopped him. His music is full o' magic. It's dangerous with so many witch-sniffers around."

Jorge could feel the little girl's bright eyes fixed on him. With a gasp Finn said, "Do ye mean it? Is it really magic? I always said it was!" With a bound she was flying away, no doubt to find Jay and tell him what the seer had said.

Jay came to him later, his voice hoarse with repressed feeling, to say shyly, "Finn said ye think my music has magic in it . . ."

Jorge patted the boy's hand. "Indeed I do, Jay, though I canna tell ye how powerful it is. If the Coven was still in place, I would recommend ye go to Carraig, but the Tower o' the Sea-Singers is now just a pile o' broken stones."

"So there's no hope . . ."

"I dinna say that," Jorge said. "There are still some witches left, my lad, and if all goes well, we will no longer be hunted through the countryside but building the Towers anew. Then all our futures will be different."

Jay the Fiddler was not the only one who seemed bright with potential to the old seer. Finn herself seemed to shine with magical power, and Jorge found himself wondering about her. He asked her about her background, but she was a foundling with little memory of her past. In Lucescere she had been apprenticed to a thief and bounty hunter named Kersey, a brutal man who had beaten her often and set her to stealing for him. The only possession she had which might hold a

clue to her past was a tarnished and battered medallion
which she wore around her neck on a string. She gave
it to Jorge to feel and immediately he felt the tingle of
enchantment. He ran his fingers over it and felt the
raised form of some animal, a dog perhaps, or a horse.
Although he questioned her closely, she had no memory
of how she came by the charm or what it meant; she
only knew it must not pass out of her hands.

"Why did your master no' take it from ye? He must
have known it had magic."

"He was a bloody stupid man," Finn answered. "He
was not a true witch-sniffer, no' like the Grand-Seeker
Glynelda." She gave a little shiver.

"Ye have met the Grand-Seeker Glynelda?" Jorge
asked curiously, knowing that it was impossible that the
head of the Awl should not have sensed the power in
the little girl as he had done.

She nodded, then realizing the old man could not see
her, said in a muffled tone, "Mmm-mmm."

"She knew ye?"

"Mmm-mmm."

"Ye saw her often?"

"No' often. Maybe every couple o' months. Any time
she was in Lucescere she would call for Kersey and he
would take me up to the palace and she would examine me."

"Examine ye how?"

"She'd ask me questions and test me—ask me to find
things for her."

"*Find* things for her?"

Jay interrupted with a laugh. "Our Finn the Grand-
Sniffer! She can find anything that's been lost, Master.
Auld Kersey made a fortune out o' her! People would
come to him and ask him to find all sorts o' things—lost
dogs or jewelry, lovers that had run away! He'd pretend
to go off in a trance, then charge them some ridiculous
amount to find it, while all the time it was Finn who'd
be doing the sniffing. He'd be spending it all on whisky
though, and he were no' a nice man on the drink."

Jorge ran his fingers over the medallion again and wondered at the raised shape. A dog, or a wolf? He wondered if it would be safe to try and reach Meghan, then decided it was too dangerous when there may be seekers in the vicinity. *When we get home, I'll try*, he thought. *Meghan will want to know about a protégée of Glynelda's . . . particularly one with the Talent o' Searching.*

"He was a horrible man," Jay said. "He used to beat Finn if she dinna do what he told her. We were all glad when he died."

Finn had not waited around for the Grand-Seeker Glynelda to bond her to someone else. She had simply gathered her things together and slipped out to join her friends on the street. No one had seemed to miss her. Her only fear was being tracked down by the Grand-Seeker. "But why would she want to?" Jorge asked, which sent Dillon and Jay off into howls of laughter.

"That's what we always say!" Dillon chortled.

Finn said crossly, "Flaming dragon balls! Say what ye like, I ken! The Grand-Seeker had plans for me, she *said* so! She frightened me but I never dared no' do what she told me. I know she was training me up to do terrible things, why else did she have me taught all those things?"

"What things?" the blind old man asked gently.

"Like how to pick locks, or follow someone without them knowing. She even had me taught how to read! Why would she have me read if it was no' to do something bad for her?"

Jorge had almost laughed, though it would have been a bitter laugh. Instead, he managed to say something soothing, as Finn continued rebelliously, "I could no' see why I could no' just hang around with Dillon and Jay—no one cared what they did, why should anyone care what I did?"

Worried about their vulnerability, the old seer had begun to teach the children how to shield their thoughts,

and by the time of the spring equinox, had had some
success. They were all wildly enthusiastic about the idea
of celebrating the turn of the tides. Having found a well-
hidden glade in one of the heavily forested gorges, Jorge
allowed them to have an afternoon's rest, which was
spent cooking a feast of sorts and making thick garlands
of leaves. He was surprised at their excitement and wondered how many chances they would have had to have
fun in Lucescere.

The spring equinox was usually preceded by an Ordeal
that lasted from sunset to midnight, but Jorge thought
it was too much to expect of his young companions, so
he tried to make the children sleep, promising he would
wake them at the turn of the tide. They could not sleep,
though, lying by the fire and whispering and giggling
instead, while Jorge sat as comfortably as his old body
would allow, thinking of Eà and emptying himself to the
cloud-strung night. He knew the moment the tide
turned, he could feel it within him, and so he roused the
sleepy children.

They sat around the fire, wreaths on their heads, a
fiery brand in their hands, as he drew the magic circle
around them with his witch's dagger. He thrust his staff
into the soil at the closing of the circle and began to
chant the rites. Obediently they chanted with him:

> "Darksome night and shining light,
> Open your secrets to our sight,
> Find in us the depths and height,
> Find in us surrender and fight,
> Find in us jet black, snow white,
> Darksome light and shining night."

Silence fell again. Jorge threw a handful of fragrant
leaves and roots on the fire so the flames hissed green
and yellow. He gestured to the children to begin their
dance, their slow step and slide and stamp, as softly he
chanted, "Ever-changing life and death, transform us in
your sight, open your secrets, open the door. In ye we
shall be free o' slavery. In ye we shall be free o' pain.
In ye we shall be free o' darkness without light, and in

ye we shall be free o' light without darkness. For both shadow and radiance are yours, as both life and death are yours. And as all seasons are yours, so shall we dance and feast and have joy, for the tides o' darkness have turned and the green times be upon us, the time for the making o' love and harvest, the time o' nature's transformations, the time to be man and woman, the time to be child and crone, the time o' grace and redemption, the time o' loss and sacrifice, for ye are our mother and our father and our child, ye are the rocks and trees and stars and the deep, deep swell of the sea, ye are the Spinner and Weaver and the Cutter o' the Thread, ye are birth and life and death, ye are shadow and brightness, ye are night and day, dusk and dawn, ye are ever-changing life and death . . ."

The smoke swirled about them, and Jorge began to feel his perception stretching, widening, thin and huge as a wind-stretched cloud. He had not dared open himself to the forces since leaving Lucescere, and he felt a flood of impressions rush through him, dangerously strong.

Sparks fled into the darkness from the leaping flames and he followed them, flying through the night. He saw the river as a tangle of energies, the bright flames of night creatures stalking through the undergrowth, the smaller sparks of the hunted, crouching in the bracken. He saw another camp fire only a few ridges away, and heard the bored ruminations of soldiers and felt the malevolent presence of a seeker. Panic seized his heart—he had not realized anyone was so close!

He tried to turn, to flow back into his body, but the powers had him. Visions flooded through him—red clouds that raced in from the south, rolling with thunder; the glint of swords and chain mail through mist; a tidal wave seething with scales and fins, which rose and swept the plains of Clachan; a white hind running through a tangle of forest, trying to escape a wolf that raced behind, blood-lust red in its eyes.

Meghan is in danger, he thought, then he was whirled

away again. He saw Finn wrapped in darkness; a winged man wielding a bow of fire, shooting flames; a girl that reached out a hand to a mirror, only to have her reflection come alive and grip her wrist. As he fell back towards his frail body, slumped by the side of a dying fire, he saw again the vision which had most troubled him— the eating of the moons, the devouring of light.

Jorge drifted back to consciousness, feeling in his veins the coming of dawn and hearing the pounding of the children's feet as they stumbled around the fire still. He did not know how many hours he had been away. He was tired, so tired he could not lift his hands from his lap nor force his voice to speak. At last he croaked, "Dawn comes, the morning is here and darkness flees." He felt the children collapse as if his words had freed them from the dance, and he felt from them all the same tiredness, the daze of the smoke, the emptiness of the night.

"Let us eat o' the flesh of our mother and drink the water o' her body, and let us rejoice, for the seasons have turned and the green months are upon us," Jorge said, and the children began to laugh and eat the small feast they had so excitedly prepared the night before. The old man knew that for the first time, the bread and water and fruit was more than just food to them; it was the flesh and blood of the earth, filled with power. He knew a tide had turned in them as well.

After they had eaten, Jorge carefully opened the magic circle and doused the fire, then said in a trembling voice, "My bairns, we must find shelter. I need to sleep. Soldiers are close . . . We must hide. Ye must watch over me, my spirit has traveled far tonight and I am tired. Very tired."

He felt their anxiety but could do nothing to help them; he rested his aching head on his hand, trying to control the surging of his heart which beat so loud he thought they all must hear it. Through the pounding he heard Dillon giving orders and the sound of the children's feet as they ran to obey him.

Finn's high voice said, "There's a cave only a few ridges ahead, I be sure o' it . . . Can we support him?"

Then he felt hands under his armpits and he was being supported on all sides by small, loving hands. Letting them lead him, he stumbled along, still clutching the dagger in his hand, the raven croaking with concern as he flew overhead.

Lilanthe lay on the grass, staring up at the dawn-streaked sky. Soon the camp of jongleurs would be stirring and she would have to hide. Now, however, she was free to enjoy the first stirring of the morning. The forests and glades of Aslinn were home to many birds and animals that hopped and scampered about her, quite unafraid. They knew the tree-shifter was as much a creature of the forest as they were.

"Lilanthe!" The sound of the jongleur's voice startled the animals, who scurried away into the underbrush. Dide the Juggler slipped into the glade, carrying a steaming wooden bowl. "It's hot . . ." he tempted.

She tensed, toes curling. Her feet were broad, brown and knotty, and she tried to hide them whenever Dide came near. After a moment he laid the bowl down and backed off a few paces. She only ventured to pick up the bowl when he was a full six feet away, and then she ate frantically, spooning the food into her mouth without pause.

"Ye'll burn your tongue," he said.

She did not answer, only hunching her form closer around the bowl. He lay on his back and began to juggle six golden balls into the air. She watched the balls in fascination as they spun in patterns of ever-increasing complexity. "We'll be splitting from the other carts soon," he said conversationally. "Ye'll be able to come with us then if ye want." She scraped the bowl clean and put it down with a sigh. The golden balls began to chase each other in a high-rising circle. "Would ye like that? Joining our caravan, I mean?"

She did not answer for a long time and he concentrated on juggling. Then she said slowly, "I do no' like your father."

"Neither do I much, sometimes," Dide replied cheerfully. "There's no need to fret yourself, though, it's all bluster. If he likes ye—and I canna see any reason why he should no'—he'll treat ye like a banrìgh." Lilanthe said nothing, twisting the hem of her grubby smock around in her thin, twiggy fingers. "Enit will no' let anything happen to ye. She keeps Da in good order, do no' worry about that."

He got to his feet, rubbing the sparse beard that itched his chin. "Lilanthe, I have to go. Will ye think about traveling more closely with us? These forests are no' really safe, ye ken." Lilanthe smiled at the thought she might not be safe in the forest, but nodded.

As darkness fell that night, the jongleurs boiled up a side of salted pork, broached the barrel of whisky, then sang the evening away. Lilanthe crouched beneath one of the caravans, watching and listening in delight. The music got into her blood and made her want to sing and dance too, especially when Dide played his guitar. Perched on a fallen log, playing like a demon, his music was irresistible. One by one the other jongleurs began to dance, twirling in the firelit darkness until Lilanthe could barely lie still. Even the youngest of the children bobbed up and down on the spot and clapped his plump hands, while his grandmother delighted everyone by dancing a high-spirited jig, bony knees flashing under a flurry of skirts.

Only Dide's grandmother did not join in, crouching in her customary spot by the fire, beads of amber glinting in the firelight. Later she sang, and her voice was so strange and sweet, shivers ran over Lilanthe's body and a knot formed in her throat. She was not surprised to see tears shining on the cheeks of the old woman, for the song had quavered with the intensity of feeling behind it.

After Enit Silverthroat's song, the merry group quietened, the children falling asleep in piles by the fire. The adults stayed up, drinking deeply from the barrel of whiskey and singing ballads. At midnight they began to dance again, but this time their movements were slow and stately and had a ritualistic air to them. Wriggling closer, Lilanthe could hear them chanting softly, and the chorus struck a chord.

". . . open your secrets to our sight, find in us the depths and height, find in us surrender and fight, find in us jet black, snow white, darksome light and shining night," Lilanthe murmured, and found herself thinking of her childhood, in the years before the Faery Decree. Tears stung her eyes, and slowly she turned and slithered backwards into the darkness.

The next morning she was drawn back to the camp by the bustle of packing. Silently she slithered up a tree so she could watch the final farewells of the jongleurs and the last entreaties for the fire-eater's caravan to stay with the others.

"Ye ken the songs just do no' sound right unless ye and Dide and Enit join in," one of the women said, resting on the steps of her cart, a guitar cradled in her arms. "And the acrobatic troupe will sadly miss your wee Nina."

Dide's father shrugged. "Och, well, I've a fancy on me to see the auld ways. Ye ken I be nervous about traveling in Blessèm since that trouble in Dùn Eidean."

"That'll teach ye to cheat at dice!" the woman said, strumming a few notes.

The jongleur gave a sharp crack of laughter. "Obh obh, Eileen! Ye ken I dinna cheat—the dice just seemed to fall my way!" He was tall and very dark, his crimson shirt the same color as his lips, his leather waistcoat grown a little tight across his stomach.

"Och, for sure, Morrell, loaded dice certainly help Lady Luck along! It's up to ye, o' course, but wha' shall ye do in the depths o' the wilds? Eat fire for the amusement o' the birds?"

"I might have a holiday," Morrell answered. "Eà knows I've been working the roads long enough. Besides, I picked Blessèm clean on my last way through, I

doubt ye'll find much left to fill your bellies." She gave
a snort of derision. "No," he continued, "I've a mind to
find some fresh pastures. There mun be some woodcut-
ters and charcoal-burners left somewhere in these forests, and if there's no', well, I still have half a barrel o'
whiskey and a side o' salted pork, what more do I
need?"

"Wha' makes me think ye've some devilry in mind?"
one of the other men said, leaning against the side of
his caravan. "Still, your loss, our gain. I will no' have to
be sharing the takings wi' ye when ye're so drunk ye
canna even light your torches."

"And wha' will your show be without my fire-eating
and Dide's guitar?"

"A lot more reliable!" Eileen chortled at her own
quick wit, then jumped to her feet before Morrell the
Fire-Eater could think of a retort. "No, no, Morrell,
leave me wi' the last word for once! It seems like a guid
way for us to be parting. Happen we'll see your cart at
Dùn Gorm for the summer festivals?"

"Perhaps, perhaps no'. We'll see how well the wood-
cutters pay up and how long my barrel o' whiskey lasts!"

He waved the other caravans farewell as they trundled
off down the wider, smoother road, then called to his
son and daughter to pack up camp. "We've finally got
rid o' them! The road's our own, let's be on our way!"

With one scarred leather boot he kicked dirt over the
coals and stamped them into the ground. Nina came running out of the forest, her mouth stained with berries,
her reddish hair filled with leaves and twigs. "Ye look
like a tree-changer yourself!" her father laughed and
picked her up and swung her around. "Ooof! Ye're getting too big to do that to!"

"I have no' grown at all!" Nina laughed. "Ye're just
getting too fat!"

"Me? Fat? I'm in the prime o' my life!"

"If ye believe that ye have no' looked in a mirror
lately," his mother said in her melodious voice. Snowy
hair combed straight back from her wrinkled brown face,

Enit limped painfully back to her caravan. Lilanthe had not yet met Dide's grandmother, for the old jongleur could not walk easily, crippled with a twisting of her bones that made her fingers look like knobby twigs. She rarely moved more than a few paces from her caravan and guarded its interior jealously.

"Dide!" Morrell cupped his hands around his mouth and bellowed his son's name loudly. "Where in hell's bells are ye?"

"Here, Da! I was just looking for Lilanthe, to tell her the other jongleurs have gone at last . . . She's shielding, though. I canna find her."

Lilanthe crouched lower on the branch. She had been too long alone to give up her freedom lightly. They called for her, then harnessed the mares to the caravans. "Do no' worry, son," Morrell said. "I doubt she'll stop following us after all this time."

"Something may have happened to her. I wish she wouldna shield herself from me."

Lilanthe smiled to herself. It was easy for her to think of trees and sky and wind and sunlight, the thoughts playing on the surface of her mind effectively hiding the thoughts below. It was much harder for humans, who had so little control over their thoughts and so little connection with the world around them. Even Dide, who was surprisingly good at it, was unable to shield as effectively as Lilanthe.

She waited until the horses had plodded almost out of sight, then slipped out of the tree and began to follow them. Morrell's words had caused a brief smart of humiliation, but they were essentially true. Lilanthe had no intention of losing touch with the jongleurs.

It was some hours later that Lilanthe became aware of other minds brushing the edge of her awareness. Cautiously she cast her mind out, and encountered hunger, blood-lust, the hunters' impulse. They were not minds she had ever encountered before, though the thoughts were familiar, akin to the thoughts of a rat-catcher she remembered from her childhood, a man who set packs of rats upon dogs for the amusement of the villagers. Shuddering a little, Lilanthe increased her pace, deciding she should really stay a little closer to the caravans. She wondered if Dide could sense the minds as well, and was answered when he began to call for her, peering anxiously into the glades stretching on either side of the narrow road. She began to hurry forward, casting aside her shield.

Hurry! he thought. *Danger coming!*

Lilanthe ran as fast as she could, but the caravans were swinging out of sight. She felt the pursuit growing closer and swung round to face it, digging her bare feet into the soil. She felt the shiver of changing run over her, felt rather than saw them burst out of the woods and gallop towards her.

There were seven of them, long-haired women with cloven hooves and horns of all different shapes. They wore short kilts of badly cured leather and necklaces of animal and human teeth that bounced against their three pairs of breasts. Down their spines grew a ridge of coarse, wiry hair that ended in a long, tufted tail. Hollering with vicious glee, they waved rough clubs made of wood and stone tied together with cord.

Lilanthe's torso stretched and twisted, her arms lengthening and diverging into slim white branches that dangled towards the ground. Her hair sprouted and grew into long trailers with tiny green flowers clustered along the stem.

They charged her, heads lowered, and she was grateful for her sturdy roots when one hard body after another crashed into her trunk, shaking loose leaves and twigs. Restlessly they leapt around her, butting their horns against her slender trunk, but without the scent of blood to agitate them, they soon galloped after the caravan.

As soon as she dared, Lilanthe reversed the changing process, anxious about the safety of her friends. Knowing there was nothing she could do to protect them, she nonetheless ran as fast as she could in their tracks. She came round a corner to see the caravans backed up against a tree, the horned women cavorting around them. Nina was in the doorway with a frying pan in one hand, just managing to keep them off. Morrell was slashing all about him with his claymore, trying to defend the mares who reared and neighed in terror. Dide was crouched beside Enit's cart, a long dagger in each hand. As the horned women rammed the caravan, he slashed one on the shoulder so blood splattered down her side. The blood only served to excite them, and the caravan rocked dangerously.

Suddenly the woman with seven horns bounded up the steps and rammed Nina, ignoring the frying pan raining blows on her naked shoulders. Nina screamed and fell. Just as Lilanthe thought she must be trampled, Enit began to sing.

The song wrapped Lilanthe's mind in smooth harmonies. She felt her senses benumbed, the frantic beating of her heart stilled. Without realizing it she took a step closer, then another, her body swaying, her eyes half closing. Something close to a purr began in her throat. Humming and swaying, she thought of spring mornings and deep water and starry nights. Closer and closer to the caravan she danced. Part of her mind noted without curiosity the dancing, swaying figures of the horned women. Dide and Morrell were dancing too, and little Nina jiggled about on the step, a blissful smile on her face. The music softened and Lilanthe felt her eyes closing, her breath slowing. One by one the dancing figures sighed and drooped, curling where they lay to sleep.

When Lilanthe woke it was night and she was wrapped in a blanket that smelt of horses. She opened her eyes, wondering why she felt so at peace, so wonderfully rested. Behind her was a stone wall, firelight flickering over it. She lay still, listening to the voices speaking beside her.

"Pretty song teach?" a gruff voice asked.

"It canna be taught, Brun," Enit replied. Her voice was sad. "I had sworn never to use it again. The Yedda are dead and gone, the song-masters lost. What use living in the past? Besides, it be dangerous." Without changing the timber of her voice, Enit then said, "Our tree-changer is awake. How do ye feel, Lilanthe?"

"I am no' a tree-changer," Lilanthe said. "My mother's people are tree-changers, but they will no' accept me either. I call myself a tree-shifter."

"I have never heard o' a tree-shifter afore."

"Neither have I," Lilanthe said. "I think I'm the only one."

"Hmm, I imagine human and tree-changer offspring are rare. I dinna even think it was possible."

"Well, it obviously is," Lilanthe answered and sat up, stretching. "What happened? Who are those horrible women? Where are we?"

"I sang them to sleep," Enit said. "Unfortunately, I sang ye all to sleep too, but the magic is indiscriminate."

"No' sing me," the furry voice said. Lilanthe raised herself on her elbow so she could see who had spoken. It was a cluricaun, a short, hairy creature with a pointed face and large, tufted ears. When he moved, the many small, bright objects hung around his neck clashed and jingled, and Lilanthe remembered that cluricauns were never to be trusted with anything flashy.

"No, that's right, Brun," Enit said. "Why is it ye were no' lulled to sleep? All creatures within sound o' me should have slept."

"Magic songs no' magic to me," Brun said and hopped to his feet so he could stir the pot hanging over the fire blazing in the massive stone fireplace. Above the mantel was a stone shield emblazoned with stars and faint runes of writing, and below it a device of two masks, one weeping, one laughing.

"Cluricauns are immune to magic," Lilanthe said. "Although they have no magic o' their own, they have the ability to sense magic and to resist it."

Enit glanced at her with interest. "Is that so?"

"That is what my mam always taught me."

"Indeed? I thought ye'd been brought up by your father."

"I was. My mam was nearby, though. I often used to climb in her branches, and she would talk to me. She told me many things, about all the forest creatures, and what things were like afore ye humans came." There was bitterness in Lilanthe's voice. "I tried to run to her many times, but she was no' always there, and tree-changers do no' have strong family ties. She did no' understand why I would want to be near her."

"While ye, o' course, wanted your mother like human children do."

"Aye."

"And tree-changers roam at will, do they no'? They have no villages or settlements? Nowhere ye could go?"

"Nay. I've been looking, but when they are in tree-shape they're hard to find. Besides, they would no' want me. My mother always thought I was a very odd-looking creature."

"Bonny lass ye are." Brun smiled at her, showing sharp, pointed teeth.

Lilanthe was amazed to feel blood rushing to her face. Enit smiled and said, "Aye, she's a very bonny lass, if no' quite your average Islander. I'm interested ye woke so early. Look at the others, they still sleep soundly, and I'd bet a full crown that the Satyricorns are still fast asleep."

"Satyricorns? Is that what they were? I've never see one afore."

"Brun has been telling me the forests around here are infested with them. They come from Tìreich originally, I believe."

Enit ladled hot broth into a bowl for Lilanthe and broke her off some bread, her twisted fingers making the task difficult. "Brun says the Satyricorns were released here by soldiers. That makes me wonder whether Maya the Unknown is no' taking advantage o' their natural nastiness to keep these forests clear. Maintaining guards in these forests would be difficult—there are few paths and very few settlements. How much easier to let

Satyricorns roam free, killing anyone who was silly enough to trespass."

"But are they no' *uile-bheistean*? Surely the Banrìgh would execute them?"

"Maya has shown quite clearly she is prepared to make use o' those faery creatures that have qualities she needs."

Lilanthe found she was shaking with anger, her resolve to fight against the Banrìgh strengthened. Why should she be hunted down when the Banrìgh let other *uile-bheistean* live?

Enit nodded. "Indeed, it makes me angry also, my dear. Though I think ye will find most people will turn a blind eye to magic if it serves their purpose, no matter how devoutly they follow the Banrìgh's Truth."

Lilanthe slowly swallowed a mouthful of broth, then asked shyly, "How is it ye were able to cause us all to fall asleep? Surely that was magic?"

"Indeed, it was, it's the song o' enchantment."

"Are ye a witch, then?"

"No' a Tower witch, nay. My mother was a skeelie, my father a traveling minstrel. I grew up deep in the forest and used to sing the birds to my hand and coneys into the cooking pot. I learnt the songs o' enchantment from a Yedda, who tried her best to bring me into the Coven. She said I had magic in my voice and could be a Yedda too if I gave up my freedom. I did no' want to bide, so I got in my wee cart and left, though Lizabet the Sea-Singer was angry that I should say her nay. I have lived as I wished, traveling and singing as I pleased, and now all my children and grandchildren do the same."

"So ye have no' sung the song o' sleep for long syne?"

"Nay, nor any song o' enchantment, though I find to sing at all is to work magic in some way. A spell like I cast today is far too dangerous to do lightly, and besides, I have no heart for it any more."

Lilanthe wiped her bowl clean with the last remnant of bread and only then really looked around her. They were squatting on furs and old blankets piled on wide flagstones so old they were worn deeply in the center. The rafters of the vaulted ceiling were black with age, the walls below decorated with gargoyles. Though Lilanthe had not been within four walls for many years—and had thought it would stifle her to be so again—she felt comfortable and at peace. Through a broken gap in the wall the night flowed dark and warm, and outside she sensed the forest pressing close. The old woman, huddled in shawls, was kind and sang as sweetly as any bird, and Lilanthe had been alone for so long. With a sigh, she nestled back into her blankets, casting a glance over the recumbent forms of the others. Dide was curled on the blankets near her foot, his mouth half open, his olive cheek flushed. He had a tender, vulnerable look about him that gave Lilanthe a strange wrenching in her ribcage. She felt Enit's eyes upon her, and flushed.

"How long will they sleep?" she whispered.

"All night long, I imagine. I hope the Satyricorns will sleep as long. I have no' yet told ye the news. Your friend, Isabeau—Meghan's young apprentice. She's alive! Somehow she managed to escape the witch-sniffers and made her way here, sick with fever. Brun tended her nigh on a full moon, for she was close to death, he says, and then the Celestine hiding here healed her."

The tree-shifter exclaimed in excitement and relief, the cluricaun Brun saying happily, "I knew *she* would make Is'beau better."

"There was a Celestine here?" Lilanthe's eyes gleamed green with excitement.

"Aye, one o' the few Celestines still willing to consort with humans. She is Cloudshadow, a witch-friend who has often helped the rebels in one way or another. She and Meghan o' the Beasts are very close."

"So Isabeau is alive! She really and truly is still alive?"

"Aye, she's alive, though maimed in body and spirit. Brun says Cloudshadow healed her as best she could,

but Isabeau still lost two fingers o' her left hand. She
was tortured, ye see, and given the pilliwinkes."

"What are they?" Lilanthe's voice was faint.

"Thumb and finger screws. They crush your fingers at
the joint . . ."

The tree-shifter gave a shudder. "Poor Isabeau, how
awful! But at least she's alive."

"She was last we heard, but the Satyricorns are on the
prowl, and she had a long way to ride still . . ."

"On her quest."

"Aye—" Enit began, but was interrupted by the cluricaun, who sat up solemnly, rocking forwards and back.

"What force and strength canna get through,
    With a mere touch, I can undo."

When they looked at him blankly, his tail drooped in
disappointment. With one paw he made a gesture, like
unlocking a door. Their expressions did not change, and
he chanted the rhyme again.

Enit said kindly, "I am curious still about the Celestine, Brun. Tell me, what else did Cloudshadow say?"

Brun dropped his paw, bouncing a little in excitement.
"She said Is'beau's head was wrapped in a veil, and that
she had faery blood running in her veins . . ."

"Isabeau's *uile-bheist*!" Lilanthe gasped. "She's a halfbreed like me?"

" 'As much faery as human, if the people o' the Spine
o' the World are included in your classifications,' " Brun
quoted. Then in his normal voice, he said, "And *she* said
that the answer was in the dark stars, and the coming o'
winter is the time."

"The coming o' winter? Dark stars?" Enit whispered,
tangling her gnarled fingers in her amber beads which
glittered with sunshiny fire. "She sounds as enigmatic as
all the Celestines."

Silence dropped over the little party as Enit's eyes
grew dreamy and distracted. Then she stirred and rattled
her beads. "I have told Brun he must come with us. It
is no' safe for him here with the Satyricorns so unsettled.
Even if he can keep them away from the Tower itself,

they will have sent word to the Banrìgh o' activity here-abouts, and soldiers will come, or witch-sniffers." Her voice was contemptuous, and they knew she referred to the seekers of the Awl as much as to the bounty-hunters that plagued the countryside. "There has been too much magic happening for this Tower no' to come under notice."

"Where are we going now? What are we doing?" Lilanthe asked.

"We came to the Tower o' Dreams because we had had news o' someone using the Scrying Pool here and we hoped it was one o' the Dream-Walkers returned. It seems clear, though, that it was the Celestine, and she is gone now. So we'll head into Blessém," the old woman replied.

Immediately the cluricaun stopped his excited capers, his face ludicrously anxious. "Blessém bad," Brun said. "Blessém bad place for cluricauns."

"I shall keep ye safe," Enit promised.

Lilanthe was also shaking her head. "I canna go to Blessém. They will burn me if they find me. I'm an *uile-bheist*, remember. I canna go where there are soldiers."

"I be *uile-bheist* too," Brun said in a puzzled tone of voice.

"They will burn us if they find us. We canna go to Blessém!"

"Be at peace, my bairns," Enit said. "I shall keep ye safe. Do no' look so fearful, lassie. I have smuggled witches and rebels all over the land for near twenty years now! Morrell's caravan has a false bottom where ye can lie if we should come into danger, or ye can lie on the roof, hidden by the carvings. Ye shall be far safer with me, for sure, than here in the forest with the Satyricorns on the hunt and Red Guards on their way. Besides, ye said ye wished to help us. I have a reason for turning back into Blessém."

"What? Why is it so important? Canna we just stay here in the forest?"

"I be afraid no', my dear. Even if I wanted to spend

the rest o' my life outrunning Satyricorns, I wouldna.
Nay, I have had disturbing news from Meghan. She says
a Mesmerd was with the Red Guards that attacked her
secret valley at Candlemas. Also that bairns with Talent
are being stolen from their homes, and she thinks the
Mesmerdean may have something to do with it. I want
to find if this is true, that it is the Mesmerdean and no'
just a rumor. If it is, then I fear Margrit o' Arran mun
be behind it. She is a bad enemy to have indeed, and I
need to be sure she is no' plotting something that will
disrupt our plans."

"What are Mes . . . Mes . . ."

"The Mesmerdean are faery creatures o' the marshes.
They are dangerous indeed, and if the NicFóghnan has
somehow convinced them to aid her in her schemes,
then we may be in trouble indeed. Why the Mesmerdean
would consent to accompany redcloaks, or steal bairns
from their bed, I have no idea. It seems strange indeed.
Why would Margrit NicFóghnan want them to? What
scheme o' hers does it further? These are questions I
wish to find answers for, and so we travel into Blessém,
where most sightings o' the Mesmerdean have occurred.
Happen we may need to go into the marshes themselves
to find the answers. We shall see."

"But they will kill me if they find me . . ."

"Lass, if ye wish to fight against the Ensorcellor, ye
mun face danger and possible death. I canna make that
choice for ye. I will do my utmost to keep ye and Brun
safe, but blaygird times be with us. What is your choice?
Will ye trust me and the Spinners, or will ye try your
luck in the forest?"

The tree-shifter was silent, her hands twisting together
in her lap. "I shall come with ye," she said at last.
"Though I feel sick with fear at the thought."

"That's a brave lassie," Enit said. "Just remember, all
our lives are forfeit if ye are discovered. I have no desire
to end up fodder for the Awl's wicked fires either. We
have many friends scattered through the countryside

who will help us, and jongleurs come and go as they please. So do no' fear, I shall keep ye safe."

The tree-shifter nodded, though her face was white and strained still. Enit patted her hand reassuringly, and said, "We'll get on the road at first light, and we'll plug our ears so I can sing the Satyricorn to sleep again. That would give us a few hours' head start. Brun, why do ye no' pack up what ye will need now so ye are ready to go?"

The little, hairy creature nodded solemnly and began to gather his belongings together. As he crammed a sack full of food and clothing, he softly sang to himself.

"Over the hills and by the burn,
    the road unrolls through forest and fern,
    taking my feet I know no' where,
    happen I'll meet ye at the fair!"

A little prickle of excitement ran over Lilanthe's skin, and she thought to herself that she was being as brave and adventurous as Isabeau herself. After she and the apprentice witch had parted ways, she had felt restless and without direction. Isabeau had made her feel rather ashamed of her aimless wanderings. Now she would be following in Isabeau's footsteps and they could perhaps meet again. She had never felt such a close and natural affinity with anyone as she had with Isabeau the Foundling.

"Why do ye no' sleep some more?" Enit suggested, a black, hunched figure in her shawls and scarves. "It shall be a long day tomorrow."

Obediently Lilanthe lay back on the blanket. Through the gap in the broken wall she could see the stars swarming in a purplish sky. "Dark stars . . ." she pondered. "I wonder what the Celestine meant?"

"At night they come without being fetched, by day they're lost without being stolen," Brun said, pausing in his packing.

"What?" Lilanthe asked.

He pointed out at the night sky. "At night they come

without being fetched, by day they're lost without being stolen," he repeated.

"Och, ye mean the *stars*!" Lilanthe cried, and he danced a little jig, crying, "The stars, the stars!" so that Lilanthe wondered just how much the little creature really understood. She pillowed her head on her arms and heard Brun murmur, "Dark stars and the coming o' winter." For some reason, the words sent a cold thrill over her skin and down her spine, and she wondered if she had made the right decision, joining the jongleurs in their fight against the Ensorcellor. As if sensing her unease, Enit Silverthroat began to sing a gentle lullaby and again the heavy darkness of sleep washed over her.

THE BLACK WOLF

Snow fell out of a leaden sky, swirling in a capricious wind so that the rider rose in his stirrups in a vain attempt to see more clearly. The howl of a wolf drifted out of the forest to his right, and he spurred his flagging horse on mercilessly. The wolves had been hunting him from the moment he crossed the river into Rurach, and the howls were growing ever closer. They came now from the left, so close the mare neighed in terror and plunged on through the snow.

The Seeker Renshaw leant forward, whipping the horse so she broke into a gallop. He could see the wolves now, streaking along behind him. They were great, grey, rangy beasts, eyes yellow with hunger, and they snarled menacingly as they ran. He could see the icy surface of Loch Kintyre to his right and knew Castle Rurach was beyond. He would be lucky to reach its protection, though, the wolves snapping at the terrified horse's hocks. He drew his dagger and plunged it into the breast of one that leapt up to try and haul him from the saddle. The horse broke free of the pack, galloping wildly, and the seeker wiped his blade on his white breeches.

Renshaw heard another howl ahead, and his heart

thudded. He peered through the snowy darkness and saw a wolf sitting on the bridge over the Wulfrum River. Her muzzle was raised to the darkening sky, her black ruff almost invisible in the shadows under the trees. He recognized the beast. She had come close to killing him earlier in the day. He had only just managed to fight her off with boot and dagger and the fleetness of his horse. The mare was tiring now, though, and an early dusk was sinking over the snow-laden fields. The rest of the pack was close on his heels, and he could see other dark forms slinking through the copse of trees.

With a defiant cry he turned the mare's head and forced her off the road and down the bank. The snow was up to his mare's withers, his boots and legs submerged. Then the horse was on the ice, her hooves throwing up splinters of frost as she galloped across the loch's frozen surface. Renshaw heard the clamor of the wolves behind him and, looking over his shoulder, saw they were racing after him. Then the other pack broke from the shelter of the wood and angled across, threatening to cut him off from the shore. He whipped the laboring mare on.

He was only a few yards from the opposite shore, the two packs of wolves converging on him, when there was a great crack as the ice broke. With a scream, the mare was flung forward into the icy blackness. For a moment the seeker was swallowing water, then his head broke free and he grasped the stirrup. The mare was trying desperately to climb out onto the ice, but he dragged her back, using her height to climb out himself. Then he was running, for the castle was looming up ahead, and the wolves had reached the crack in the ice. He fully expected them to feast on his mare, who was still struggling desperately to be free of the icy water. To his horror, they bounded over her head and raced after him, the black she-wolf howling in triumph.

Renshaw ran as he had never run before, hampered by the weight of his drenched clothes, now freezing to stiffness on him. He saw the drawbridge ahead. Thankfully it was lowered, and he pounded up the road, trying to shout. He felt hot breath on his neck and then a great weight took him down, pain searing through him.

Anghus MacRuraich, Prionnsa of Rurach and Siantan, was brooding over a dram of whiskey, the firelight warming his boots, when there was an outbreak of noise and activity below. He raised his chestnut-brown head, but did not move. Soon the castle's chamberlain came, bowing respectfully.

"There is a seeker below, my laird," he said.

Instantly Anghus stiffened. "Here in the castle?"

"Aye, my laird. He was attacked by wolves and barely made it here alive."

Pity, Anghus thought bitterly. He rose to his feet, wrapped his black-woven plaid around him more securely and followed the chamberlain down the long and draughty stairs to the lower hall. There his gillie Donald was waiting, and some of the guards from the drawbridge. All speculating and explaining at once, they led him into the inner bailey, through the bitterly cold courtyards and gardens, the snow-swirled outer bailey, and so to the gatehouse. On one of the guards' beds lay a seeker, blood oozing from a wound to his temple. The back of his crimson tunic was torn, and Anghus could see he had been savagely bitten. He could hear howling and went to the narrow window to look outside. It was fully dark now, but he could see a great pack of wolves churning up the snow on the drawbridge. They were sniffing and growling at the scent of the wounded seeker.

One, a large she-wolf with a black upstanding ruff, was sitting calmly in the very center of the drawbridge, gazing up at the gatehouse with yellow eyes. He could see her clearly in the smoky light of the torches. It seemed as if she looked straight at him.

He knew the wolf. She was the matriarch of the pack that hunted the lands around Castle Rurach. He often saw her when he was riding in the forests. She would step out of the undergrowth and sit where she could watch him, her yellow eyes compelling. The MacRuraich Clan had a long affinity with wolves, their crest a sable wolf rampant, and many in Anghus's family had had wolves as their familiars.

So although the pack around Castle Rurach had grown increasingly bold over the past few years, Anghus allowed no-one to harm them. It seemed his protection had been recognized, for although the wolves had attacked and harassed many a company of soldiers or merchant caravans, anyone wearing the device of the MacRuraich clan was never harmed.

"What shall we do with the seeker, my laird?" the gillie Donald asked. "Shall we throw him back to the wolves? We did no' realize he was a seeker until we'd driven off the wolves and brought him in."

Anghus was severely tempted. He had no great love of the Awl, and neither did any of his people. It would be easy enough to say the seeker had died trying to reach them. He frowned and picked up the sealed scroll the seeker had carried, gripping it tightly. It was marked with the Banrìgh's own scrawl, and he dreaded having to read what was concealed below the seals.

Unfortunately Anghus was reasonably sure the Banrìgh had some method of scrying out those she liked to keep an eye on. Several times she had known things she should not have known. Like the stronghold of rebels that had taken up residence in the Tower of Searchers five years earlier. Anghus had been happy to let the rebels have the burnt-out pile of ruins, as long as they did not hunt out his forests. He could not see what harm they could do there, so far away from anyone.

The Banrìgh had thought differently. She had sent companies of soldiers into Anghus's land and had taken his young daughter hostage in a clever and underhand move, capturing the child as she played by the burn while the women washed the linen. The men had all been absent on a hunting trip and had only heard of the outrage when they returned, six days later.

"She is hostage," the seeker in command had said

coldly, "due to the Prionnsa Anghus MacRuraich's failure to root out rebels and witches as the Rìgh had decreed. If ye do no' lead the Banrìgh's guards to their hiding place, your little girl will be killed."

Anghus's daughter was dear to his heart, and only six years old. As much as Anghus disliked the Red Guards, who had grown cruel and arrogant since the Day of Reckoning, he had agreed to lead them to the Tower. He had been half tempted to try and warn the rebels but had been too afraid of the danger to his daughter to attempt it.

So the rebels had been wiped out, and Anghus had been set to find any who had escaped. He had done so reluctantly but efficiently, wondering who had told the Banrìgh he could find anything once he knew the quarry. For there was no doubt she knew. The wording of the message had been cleverly phrased to show he should not attempt to deceive her by protestations they had escaped him. Only one witch had he let escape, his sister Tabithas's apprentice, and only because he had known Seychella Wind-Whistler for years. As a young woman she had saved both him and his sister from drowning. The three of them had been boating on the loch below Castle Rurach when a fierce storm had blown up unexpectedly. Seychella had controlled the turbulent winds, taking the boat to safety and diverting the storm's path. In memory of that day, he had let Seychella escape, shielding his thoughts when they interrogated him as he had been taught in his years at the Tower.

With a cold and heavy heart, Anghus said, "Nay, tend him, and when he is well enough take him to the castle and put him in the third best bedroom. I will see him when he has recovered his wits."

"Be ye sure, my laird?" Donald said in a low voice. "It be no trouble to dispose o' him. We can do it early this morn, when all are asleep . . ."

Anghus shook his head. "It is too dangerous, my auld friend. Let him live. I shall accept what comes."

When he climbed the stairs to his own quarters, Anghus found his wife Gwyneth waiting for him. Dressed in a warm velvet gown, edged with fur, her fair hair rippled down her back, almost to her knees.

"I heard there is a seeker at the gate," she said in a tense voice. Once beautiful, her face was marked with grief and sorrow now, the luster of her green eyes dimmed. He nodded.

"Have they brought back our bairn?" she asked, twisting her hands together until the knuckles gleamed white. He shook his head, unable to meet her eyes. She slumped in disappointment, turning away.

"I think the seeker has come with further orders for me," he said in a gruff voice. His wife said nothing, just left the room swiftly, her downcast face glistening with tears.

Anghus tossed back a full dram of whiskey and poured himself another, his red-bearded face somber. For a moment he considered defying the Banrìgh. Castle Rurach had never been breached, not even through the long years of civil war that preceded Aedan's Pact and the crowning of the first Rìgh.

The mood of defiance lasted only a moment, however. Sure as he was that Castle Rurach could withstand most forces, he had a healthy respect for the Banrìgh. Had she not thrown down the Towers and all the witches in them? Despite her protestations, the Banrìgh must have some terrible power at her command. How else had she triumphed so totally, that dreadful day so long ago?

Anghus had no great love for the witches or *uile-bheistean,* but neither did he hate them. His own sister had been a witch, and a very powerful one. She had been the youngest Keybearer since Meghan NicCuinn herself. When news came of Tabithas's banishment, he had grieved deeply and railed at the Rìgh who had so suddenly turned against the Coven. But what could he do? He just wished to be left alone with his people, to hunt *geal'teas* through the mountains, to fish the fast-running streams and idle away the bitter winters beside a huge fire, his wife beside him, his children playing at his feet.

He gave a snort of desperate laughter. That was a merry jest! His only daughter had been stolen from him, and his beautiful wife, a NicSian, was slowly fading away with grief. Rurach was a wild, lonely country, not the place for a gentlewoman to overcome such a dreadful loss. There were no parties, no festivals, not even the occasional caravan of jongleurs to distract her from her grief. Although five years had passed, they had had no more children, for his beautiful wife no longer invited him to her bed.

The seeker was well enough to be moved up to the castle the following day. He sent one of Anghus's own men to fetch him, an act that caused the MacRuraich's face to redden in anger. Nonetheless he went, changing first into his kilt and plaid to subtly remind the seeker who he was.

The seeker sat at his ease in one of the carved chairs in Castle Rurach's great hall, a goblet of wine in one hand, his feet in furred slippers stretched to the roaring log fire. His shoulder was heavily bandaged, his arm resting in a sling. He made no attempt to rise to his feet or bow as he should have, instead waving Anghus nonchalantly to a chair. The prionnsa ground his teeth together and sat down.

"Glad indeed I was to wake up and find myself in the castle," the seeker said, failing to address Anghus by his title. "I had heard the wolves were growing troublesome in Rurach but I can hardly believe I was almost killed at your own doorstep. Why have ye no' hunted the wolves down and killed them? See to it."

Anghus was so outraged he could not speak, and that saved him, for it did not occur to the seeker that his commands would not be obeyed. He went on without a pause, "It is almost three weeks syne I left the palace on our blessed Banrigh's orders, and I have run three horses to death to come here . . ."

Anghus's grudging admiration was aroused. *The man must have thigearn blood in him, to travel so far so quickly.* Abruptly his blood chilled. *What urgent business could the Banrìgh have that would drive her messenger to such haste?*

"As ye ken, our gracious Banrìgh is anxious that the recent uprisings o' rebels be squashed fiercely, to reassure the peoples o' Eileanan that peace shall be kept in the countryside. The previous Grand-Seeker failed miserably in this task. In the past few months there have been increased reports of *uile-bheistean* activity, while the cursed Arch-Sorceress has again crawled out o' her hiding place and is wandering the land as she pleases, inciting the peasants to revolt and arousing the dragons' displeasure—"

"I had heard the Banrìgh's guards had attacked and killed a pregnant she-dragon and that was the cause o' the dragons' rising," Anghus replied mildly. He was glad to hear Meghan NicCuinn was still alive, and he smiled inside to think the old witch was still causing trouble wherever she went.

The frown on the seeker's face deepened, and he continued as if Anghus had not spoken. "—the untimely death o' the Grand-Seeker Glynelda was obviously the result o' evil sorceries, thrown as she was by her horse which had been ensorcelled by one o' the Arch-Sorceress's apprentices. The stallion had always been a biddable creature, but after being stolen by the young witch and ensorcelled by her, the Grand-Seeker Glynelda was unable to control him. Consequently the Banrìgh has raised the Seeker Humbert to the position, and he has entrusted me with the task o' stamping out these eruptions o' wickedness in Rionnagan and Clachan."

The Seeker Renshaw paused to preen himself, obviously pleased with his new appointment. He did not notice the frown on the prionnsa's face at the mention of the new Grand-Seeker's name, for Anghus knew Humbert of old. By the time Renshaw glanced up at the prionnsa again, Anghus's face was smooth, expressing only a patient interest. "He has assured me that your country Rurach has been wiped clean, with your noble assistance, and instructed me to request ye to undertake a similar cleansing in Rionnagan," the seeker continued.

Anghus nodded, though he felt sick at heart. It was true that Rurach was remarkably free of rebels and witches, but that was only because the Awl had sustained a ruthless and bloody slaughter over the past five years. The raid on the rebels at the Tower of Searchers had been swift and deadly, and any who may have escaped across the mountains to Siantan or Rionnagan would not return lightly. He had been forced to lead the seekers to where accused witches—mainly frail old women and men—had been hiding, and had had to watch as they were burned at the stake. Even worse, the Red Guards had enacted brutal reprisals against his own people for the aid they had given the rebels and had warned him more would follow if there was any sign of aid given to any enemy of the Crown, be they witch, rebel or faery.

The seeker continued to list the misfortunes which had befallen the Rìgh in Rionnagan. Some of these, like the massacre of soldiers sent against the dragons at Dragonclaw and the subsequent revolt of soldiers in the Sithiche Mountains, Anghus had heard before. He knew of the Cripple, of course, and how he had again and again slipped through the clutches of the seekers. He also knew about the growing discontent of the peasants, due to the constant ravages of the Red Guards, for his own people muttered under the soldiers' yoke as well.

He had not heard the rumors of a winged warrior, though, said to be coming to save the people of Eileanan from disaster, the lost Lodestar blazing in his hand. And he had not heard of the miracle of Lucescere and the uprising of the people against Baron Renton and his soldiers. He found these pieces of news intensely interesting. Perhaps the days of magic really were at hand again. He was surprised by the flash of nostalgia the thought brought him, and he found himself thinking of his sister again, and of the resident warlock who had taught him so much as a child. Both were dead, as were so many others of Talent, and a shadow of anger touched him. He had kept his face impassive, however, and listened carefully to what the seeker was saying.

". . . and so the Rìgh has decreed that the Cripple, as they call him, is the foremost enemy o' the Crown and must be brought to justice. He has instructed me to ask ye to once again lend your services to the Crown and to hunt down this infamous criminal once and for all. Recent information indicates he is in company with the Arch-Sorceress Meghan, cousin of the Rìgh himself. They were last seen near Dunceleste, but disappeared into the evil Veiled Forest and have not been seen since. The Rìgh is anxious that both be captured, and so he instructed me to bring some articles once belonging to the Arch-Sorceress for ye to touch and feel."

Anghus did not need anything to hold. He knew Meghan NicCuinn well from the years before the Day of Reckoning. Meghan had dined at his table and slept under his roof. All Anghus had to do was think of her and focus in on her to know her whereabouts. He did not tell the seeker that, though. He held the age-yellowed silk of the MacCuinn christening robe in his hands and listened to the many stories it told. His face impassive, he shook his head and explained to the seeker that the robe was too old and had been worn by too many to help him as a focus. "I can feel the Rìgh himself," he had said, not wanting the seeker to realize just how clear his clairvoyant skills were. "The Rìgh wore this robe many years after Meghan, and his brothers too. I can sense nothing but a shadow o' Meghan."

The seeker brought out other objects—a knife that Meghan had once worn, and a card with her handwriting on it. After a charade of concentration, Anghus had to admit these were sufficient for him to focus in on the Arch-Sorceress, and Renshaw nodded, satisfied. Before handing everything back to the seeker, Anghus passed his hand one more time over the ancient christening robe, with its long, embroidered skirt.

It was true he felt the Rìgh's life energies more strongly than Meghan's. By concentrating his will, he could tell Jaspar was far to the south, probably at Rhyssmadill, and the Arch-Sorceress Meghan in the highlands of Rionnagan. What puzzled him, though, was that he sensed a third consciousness connected with the christening robe. This was clearer and stronger than either of the other two and seemed located in the north, near Meghan. Although he said nothing to the seeker about it, he puzzled over it for a long time. Who could it be? Meghan and Jaspar were all that were left of a once great and vigorous clan. The Rìgh's three brothers had all disappeared as lads, and the only other NicCuinn, their cousin Mathilde, had died in the fires on the Day of Reckoning. It was a fresh trace; whoever it was had worn the robe after both Meghan and Jaspar. As Anghus nursed his dram of whiskey, he wondered if it was possible that one of the Lost Prionnsachan of Eileanan was still alive.

The seeker's eyes were on his face, but Anghus kept his thoughts well hidden, his face blank. With a niggling sense of unease, he wondered again how it was that his clairvoyant abilities and those of the seekers were acceptable to the Banrìgh, when any sign of magical ability in anyone else led to the torture chamber and an agonizing death. Why was he permitted to live and the Arch-Sorceress Meghan hunted down like a common criminal, an old frail woman who had once been the most powerful witch in the country?

The seeker leant back in his chair and said softly, "And the Banrìgh has instructed me to tell ye that when the Arch-Sorceress and the Cripple are safely in her hands, then ye will be permitted to visit with your daughter and see for yourself how happy she is at Rhyssmadill. The Banrìgh, now that she is to be a mother herself, finds that she has some understanding o' a parent's feelings and does not wish ye to worry for your daughter's happiness."

The words were a knife through Anghus's side—both because of the rush of fervent hope and also because of the chill they gave him. They were a warning, he knew. He wondered for the millionth time why it was he could sense and find anything but his own flesh and blood. His daughter was hidden from him, some sort of spell confusing his sense of direction so that, even though he could tell she was still alive, he had no idea where she was or how she was feeling. He bowed and excused himself, unwilling to let the seeker see how the promise had affected him.

That night Anghus paced up and down his chamber in a fever of indecision. He should have thrown the seeker to the wolves when he had the chance. Then he would not be faced with this unbearable choice. He knew Meghan NicCuinn and wished her only well. How could he hunt her down and turn her over to the Awl to be tortured and burnt at the stake like so many other witches? Yet what choice did he have? The Banrìgh had his daughter, and he could not find her unless he obeyed the Banrìgh's directives. If he wanted to ever see his child again, he had to submit to her wishes, and the sooner he did so, the sooner he would have his lost daughter in his arms again.

The decision made, Anghus felt a weight lift off his shoulders. He let his thoughts begin to dwell on the task ahead and, as always, felt the thrill of the chase begin to grip him. Once Anghus began to Search, he never gave up. Sometimes the chase was short and swift, sometimes long and terribly slow. Either way, he always found his objective. Perhaps, once the Arch-Sorceress Meghan was dead, the Banrìgh would leave him and his family alone . . .

THE THREADS
ARE SPUN

EARLY SPRING

SCHOOLS FOR FLEDGLING WITCHES

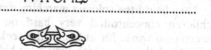

Finn huddled her arm against the old man's back, shocked at the frailty of the bones beneath his rags. They struggled through waist-high bracken, gray-gorse bushes thrusting their thorns everywhere. Clumps of trees offered brief huddles of concealment, but the ridge behind was so steep that they could only retreat a few hundred yards from the path. Jorge was shivering, though the sun had cleared the mountains and was shining warmly on their backs.

"It's horrible to see him look so sick," Jay said.

"Canna ye heal him?" Johanna asked.

They all looked towards Tòmas, who chewed the end of his glove anxiously. "I'd heal his eyes," he answered. "I'm no' allowed to touch him."

Their faces fell, then Dillon said gruffly, "We could no' anyway, there's soldiers nearby and ye ken we have to shield."

The bracken swayed as Parlan emerged white-faced from his scouting trip. "The soldiers are just over the ridge," he whispered.

"Did ye see if there was a cave there?"

"I saw a very narrow crack which could lead to a cave . . ."

"There's bloody well a cave there," Finn said stubbornly.

"Did the soldiers have one o' those witch-sniffers with them?"

Parlan nodded. Dillon chewed his lip, then said, "We'd better lie low, I guess. Everyone keep your heads down. Once they're gone we'll hide in the cave."

They heard the soldiers marching downstream. All the children concentrated very hard on bracken, and it seemed to work, for although the seeker's gaze roamed over the hillside in which they were hiding, the party did not stop and no alarm was sounded. They waited long minutes before supporting the seer's weaving steps down the hill and round the bank of the river to the cave.

It was dark inside. For a moment all was confusion. At last a fire was lit, throwing goblin shadows over the walls. The cave was narrow with a high roof, and it smelt sharply of cat's urine near the entrance. The puppy whined and snuffled around the cave, his tail between his legs.

Suddenly Artair gave a cry and stumbled. "I trod on something," he squeaked. "Look, Scruffy, it be a wee cat . . ."

Straightening up, he showed the body of a kitten nestled in his palm. Fresh blood matted its thick fur. "The puir wee thing," Johanna said. "Look, here's another!"

By the flickering light of the fire they found the bodies of seven cats, five of them mere kittens. All were black as night, with tufted ears. Finn picked one up. It lay cradled in the palm of her hand, its tiny ears folded back against its skull. A fierce tide of pain welled up in her throat, and she bent her head over its body, tears dropping on its blood-soaked fur. "Poor wee kitty," she said.

Suddenly there was an acute pang in her hand and she almost dropped the kitten in surprise. "It's alive!" Finn cried softly and felt a faint scrabble against her palm as the kitten kicked feebly. She had to wedge her thumb against its neck to stop the kitten biting her, even though blood oozed from a long wound on its side.

"Tòmas," she whispered, "what can we do? Ye've got to help it."

Without hesitation he pulled off his glove and touched the kitten's forehead. She stopped her hissing and twisting, her brilliant blue-green eyes slowly shutting. "What's wrong?" Finn cried. "What have ye done?"

"She's sleeping." Tòmas put his glove back on.

Enthralled, the little girl bent over the kitten and saw the wound was knitted together. She looked up, her hazel eyes glowing. "Thank ye, Tòmas!"

"Wha' do ye think ye're doing?" Dillon snapped. "Tòmas, ye dinna! That witch-sniffer's no' far away, Eà damn it!"

"Finn asked me to." Tòmas quickly passed on the blame, and Finn braced herself for Dillon the Bold's sharp reprimand, which she accepted meekly. Asleep, the kitten was as soft as a bundle of *geal'teas* wool, and Finn cuddled her close. At the feel of the little heart fluttering inside the rib cage, Finn's breast again swelled with a feeling close to pain. "What can we feed her?"

Dillon frowned. "Ye are no' thinking o' adopting that animal, are ye? Soldiers do no' have kittens, Lieutenant Finn!"

"But, Scruffy, she'll die unless we look after her," Finn protested. "We canna heal her, then let her die o' starvation."

"Tòmas should never have healed her," Dillon said crossly. "After all I said about the importance o' lying low! If the soldiers come down on us, it'll be your fault, Finn! And stop calling me by the baby name. I be Dillon the Bold!"

"I think they're absolute brutes," Johanna said. "They killed them just for the sport o' it. Those soldiers must have known we could no' have been hiding in this cave if the elven cats were here."

"Why would they have known that?" Dillon's broad, freckled face turned to Johanna with interest.

"Well, elven cats will fight to the death rather than

surrender," Johanna said. "I thought everyone knew that. They're very terry-terry—ye ken."

"Territorial," Finn said absent-mindedly.

"Aye. They're real wild. They canna be tamed, so it's no use ye trying, Finn, ye'll never get it to come to ye. They're only wee, but they can fight!"

"She's only a babe," Finn said defensively, cuddling the furry body closer.

"Makes no difference," Johanna said. "Ye canna tame 'em."

Finn's mouth set stubbornly, and involuntarily she squeezed the elven cat closer. Suddenly her arms were full of writhing, squirming, scratching cat. Sharp fangs sank into her hand and the kitten leapt from her arms and disappeared into the darkness. "Look what ye've done!" she cried and began to search the cave, but there was no sign of the little elven cat. Near tears, Finn let herself be ordered to bed, as her calling woke the others, but it was long before she slept.

In the morning Dillon ordered brambles to be arranged around the cave mouth and patrols were mounted at all times. Finn was disconsolate, though several times the kitten dashed out of the darkness to sink her fangs into someone's ankle. So black was her fur that she could be virtually underfoot and still remain invisible.

Finn filled Jorge's beggar's bowl with water but the kitten would not come close enough to taste it. Johanna, anxious to be of help, promised to help Finn catch some fish. Although they had no hooks or fishing rods, Johanna was surprisingly adept at catching fish with nothing but her bare hands. Tickling trout was a skill her cousin had taught her back in the days when she had lived in the country, and she had caught several fish this way over the past few weeks.

"Do no' worry, wee kit, I'll look after ye," Finn whispered. "Ye mun be so thirsty. Lap up some o' the water and I'll be back with fish as soon as I can." To her surprise, she was answered by a weak, muffled mew, though she could see no sign of the little black cat.

The two girls kilted their skirts up around their knees and braved the freezing rush of the Muileach, wading stealthily to the still waters near the bank. Johanna showed Finn how to slowly bring her fingers up under the body of the trout, fluttering them like the leaves of a water-weed. Johanna caught a fat one almost immediately, but Finn was too noisy and impatient and scared the rest away. They crept downstream to try again, and this time Johanna caught two. "It takes time to catch the trick o' it," she said consolingly as, drenched and dripping, they made their way back to the cave.

After they had all hungrily eaten their supper of fish, Finn crept towards the back of the cave. "Kitty," she called. "Come on, wee one, lap up some water and eat some fish. Ye mun be so hungry and thirsty."

A piteous mew answered her, and she saw the elven cat crouched on a high shelf, its slanted eyes gleaming turquoise in the firelight. Its tufted ears were laid back against its skull and its sharp little fangs gleamed.

"Mmm, fish," Finn whispered. The elven cat's tail lashed from side to side. Moving very slowly, she dipped her fingers in, then held out her fingers for the kitten to smell. Immediately the black cat spat, scratching Finn's hand. Finn was unable to prevent a cry, snatching her hand back to suck the welling droplets of blood. Behind her Dillon and Artair jeered, but she ignored them.

"I be your friend," she said to the kitten reproachfully, trying to project feelings of warmth and security. "I be your friend. I brought fish for ye." Slowly she reached out her fingers again, and again the kitten scratched her.

She sat for a time in silence, subduing her impatience and letting the kitten get used to her presence. The elven cat's natural curiosity asserted itself and, although its ears were still laid back, it crept forward a little, staring at her with bright eyes. Again she dipped her fingers in the fish and held them up for the kitten to see and smell, and this time, although it snarled, it did not strike. She could see its little black nose quivering at the smell of the trout, and so she lifted the bowl and set it close to its paw. This time it thrust its face hungrily into the bowl. Once it was empty, the kitten sat and washed itself while, exhausted, Finn curled up where she sat and slept.

The children were too frightened to venture out of the cave the next morning, having been woken just before dawn by Artair, who reported nervously that a large company of soldiers had just gone crashing past.

Jorge said kindly, "We shall have another quiet day, my bairns, just to make sure we are all fully recovered from the spring rites." He sighed, and Jesyah the raven hopped onto his knee so the blind beggar could scratch his neck. "I am anxious indeed to be home, but a day o' rest shall do none o' us any harm."

Finn spent the long day trying to tame the wild kitten, which had lost its weakness and was full of spite and spunk. Finn's hands were disfigured with innumerable scratches and bites, and even her face and neck were marked. Most of the other children were happy to keep well away and mocked Finn for her foolishness in trying to tame an elven cat.

"They will no' be tamed," Johanna said for the umpteenth time. "Elven cats would rather die than be handled by a human. Give it a rest, Finn."

Instead Finn sat silently as a shadow, staring at the elven cat and trying to emanate love and protection. Every now and again she offered the little cat some more to eat or drink, but mostly she remained still, using every Skill of Silent Communication that Jorge had managed to teach her. The cat occasionally arched its back and hissed, but was demonstrably more accepting of Finn's presence than the day before.

The next evening, after another day of silent communication, the elven cat at last took food from Finn's fingers without trying to scratch her. That night, as Finn slept in her self-exile at the back of the cave, she woke to find the kitten curled against her neck, purring so loudly she thought it must wake the others.

The garden of the Celestines blossomed with all the delicacy of spring. Birds flew with flashes of bright wings, baby donbeags clung to their mothers' backs and, in the clearings, clouds of butterflies danced out their brief, ecstatic lives. Where the summerbourne wound through the green forest, a ribbon of flowers trailed.

As the days grew longer and warmer, Lachlan grew restless, but Meghan merely said, "We shall have to move on soon, so enjoy the serenity while ye can."

"Where shall we go?" Iseult looked up from *The Book of Shadows.*

"Well, the next step is to start gathering our forces. We have rebel camps scattered everywhere, all over Eileanan. Some are tiny, others quite large, as large as a village. We want to start bringing them under our hand and training them up. Lachlan already has his own force, the Blue Guards . . ."

Lachlan's eyes glowed. "They were my father's own bodyguard, but the Banrìgh disbanded them, saying there was no longer any need for them. I ran into one o' their former captains, Duncan Ironfist, who turned rebel with me, and he's been scouting for likely lads and training them up for four years now. He's one o' the few who kens who I really am."

"We need to find somewhere to build a proper base, easy to defend, hard to find, preferably near where the Whitelock and Sithiche Mountains meet," Meghan mused. "That way we can come down from both the west and the north. I wonder . . . I know Jorge has a hideaway near the foot o' the Fang . . . I wonder if that would be suitable? I wish he'd answer my call but he must think it too dangerous to scry. I hope he's safe."

Over the next few days Iseult sparred with Lachlan more fiercely than ever before, trying unsuccessfully to make him use his wings. Even when she knocked his legs out from under him, he kept his wings stubbornly

clamped to his side. Biting her lip thoughtfully, Iseult
began to teach Lachlan a different set of exercises, one
that taught him about the reach and balance of his
own body.

She also decided to make use of the great strength of
his arms and shoulders, and taught him to use her crossbow. She was not surprised to find he had a natural
affinity for the weapon. She returned one day from the
Celestines' fabulous garden with a long branch of ash,
which she whittled into a longbow and strung with one
of Cloudshadow's long, wiry hairs. To her surprise, Lachlan not only learnt to bend the bow but grew quite accurate with the arrows she showed him how to make.

One afternoon she suggested they walk to the nearby
hills so they could watch the birds of prey who nested
in the cliffs. Iseult wanted to show Lachlan how they
used their wings and claws, in the hope he would start
using his.

They wrapped cheese and bread in a napkin and
walked through the Veiled Forest's green avenues. Drifts
of white butterflies danced in the rays of light streaming
through the tree trunks, and a red dappled deer leapt
across their path. Far away a tree swallow warbled its
sweet song to a counterpoint of thrushes and wagtails.
Lachlan began to sing too, his caroling ringing through
the overarching branches, so that birds darted through
the air ahead of them, answering his song with their own.

When at last his blackbird tune died away, Iseult
began to lecture him on strategy and tactics, keeping her
tone as dry as she could. With his dark face alight with
the joy of the song, Lachlan had the power to disturb
her peace, and Iseult wanted no disturbance.

Together they watched a crested falcon hunt down a
coney, its powerful talons snatching the petrified animal
off the ground, Iseult explaining and expounding all the
while. "If ye have no knife or sword to hand, ye can
always disembowel your enemy with your talons," she
instructed, surprised how pale Lachlan turned.

They ate their picnic in the forest and afterwards lay

silent under the trees. Iseult returned from a dream of the snows to find Lachlan's topaz-yellow eyes fixed on her face. He was lying on his side, supporting his curly black head with his hand, his face and shoulders framed by one glossy, black wing. She returned his gaze steadily and saw his lean cheek flush. Iseult's stomach clenched, her blood heating. She forced herself to glance away nonchalantly.

"I would ask ye my question now." Lachlan's voice was low and rough.

She met his intent gaze. "If ye wish," she answered coolly.

"Why did ye leave Tirlethan . . . I mean, were you free to . . . Did ye have no-one to keep ye there?" He stumbled into silence.

She sat upright fluidly, bringing her hands to rest palm upwards on her thighs. "No thought o' leaving the Spine o' the World had crossed my mind afore I met Meghan. I knew, o' course, that one day I would have to leave the Pride and cross the mountains in search o' a mate. Such is the duty o' a Firemaker . . ."

Lachlan glanced at her. Her heart pounding, she continued in a constricted voice, "He must be strong and wise and kind, with blue eyes like those o' all the Firemaker's get and hair with red in it. Only then will the People be sure a true Firemaker will be born to them."

Lachlan turned his face away again, resting his forehead on his arms so she could not see his face. "I knew, therefore, that I must cross the mountains one day. I did no' think this would happen for many years, however, for I have only just reached my sixteenth year. But then Meghan came and said I should travel with her. My grandmother had had dreams of my going, and said I was to find my shadow and my destiny, so it seemed fitting that I should go."

She paused and let her posture relax. She brought her eyes back to Lachlan's face and saw he was scowling, pulling grass to pieces with his brown fingers. He got to his feet and hobbled away, leaning on his club. "A very full and complete answer," was all he said.

Iseult went to bathe her hot cheeks in the clear waters of the burn which tumbled down out of the great granite rocks of the mountains. It was cold, and she rested her wrists in its sparkling iciness, shaken by an unbearable longing for the Spine of the World. She gazed down into the rippling crystal heart, still fascinated by this element of liquidity, so alien to her frozen world. Suddenly she put down her fingers and caught what looked like a tiny snowball. When she pulled her hand out, it held within a strange stone, all pale glimmer like moonshine on snow. She showed Lachlan. He turned a look of dislike and envy upon her, then limped away quickly, slashing at the undergrowth with his club.

She followed him, turning the stone in her hand. It was encrusted here and there with basalt, but everywhere else was milky smooth. After a while she tucked it into her pocket and crept after Lachlan, ambushing him as he moodily stumped along. She did not understand him, and what Iseult did not understand she always wanted to subdue.

Later, when Iseult showed Meghan the stone, the witch turned a piercing look upon it, murmured, "Ah, a moonstone," and tucked it away in the pouch. Both she and Lachlan were quiet all evening, and in the morning Meghan intensified Iseult's lessons to scrying and mind-speaking. To Lachlan's disgust, he was not given the same acceleration, and Meghan would not let him be more than a spectator in their dawn scrying lesson. He complained bitterly, pacing restlessly up and down by the fire, fretting about his fellow rebels.

At last Meghan said gruffly, "Calm down, Lachlan. Ye're like a hen on a hot griddle! I have been in contact with Enit, and she has given the Underground orders to set things in motion. Ye ken she holds all the strings in her fingers—she can manage to tweak them without ye, ye can be sure o' that!"

Most of their time was spent studying, for Meghan

was determined Lachlan should know everything he would need to win the Lodestar and the throne. Apart from geography, politics and history, they learnt astronomy, alchemy, mathematics, and the old and new languages, with any spare moments spent reading one of Meghan's many spell books and scrolls.

Of these, the most interesting was *The Book of Shadows*. So large and heavy that Iseult had difficulty lifting it, its pages were filled with colored maps and drawings, spells, incantations, faery stories, and accounts of battles and crownings, births and burials.

The powers of the ancient book were difficult to penetrate. Its pages seemed to move around, so no matter how carefully Iseult marked a page of interest, when she next picked up the book it would open at a completely different page. Try as she might, Iseult could never return to a page at her own will. It seemed *The Book of Shadows* decided for itself what she should read. Often she wanted to slam it shut in impatience, particularly when it insisted on taking her to embarrassing pages such as love spells or ointments to fade freckles. Lachlan threw it down with a curse every time he read it, causing Meghan to raise her brows, saying, "Dear me, Isabeau worked out how to use the Book when she was a mere toddler."

This made Iseult even more determined to pierce its veil of mystery. Meghan had said one must open the Book with a clear and empty mind, thinking only of what one wished to know. No matter how Iseult emptied her mind, however, she could not seem to control the Book, and she slammed the heavy, embossed covers shut. "Why will it no' answer me?" she cried.

"Ye are asking it the wrong questions," Meghan answered.

"Will ye no' just tell me the answer?" Iseult wheedled.

"Nay," the sorceress replied.

Iseult felt anger tighten the muscles of her neck. "It's no' fair, ye never answer my questions yet ye ask me

them all the time. Asking a question means that ye
owe one!"

"In that case, Meghan owes thousands o' questions,"
Lachlan said laconically.

Meghan frowned. "I am no' here to answer your questions, Iseult. Ye have *The Book o' Shadows*—ye must
learn to use it. *The Book o' Shadows* is a magical book,
it will take ye places sometimes that ye never expected.
Learning is a journey, Iseult, and ye must always travel
it alone."

That night, as they watched the moons rise over the
far-distant forests of Aslinn, Meghan said, "Tell me,
Iseult, do your people have any old tales or fables about
dark stars or constellations?"

"Dark stars . . . I do no' think so."

"Cloudshadow says I must watch the dark constellations, that they hold the secrets."

"What does that mean?"

"If I knew, foolish lass, I would no' be asking ye."

Iseult gazed up at the stars that clustered thickly from
horizon to horizon, forming shapes and patterns that
Meghan gave names to—the Fire-Eater, the Child with
the Urn, the Centaur and His Beard, the Fiery Eagle.

"I do know a story about the moons," she said. "See
Sister Moon's hand-prints clear on Brother Moon's
flank tonight?"

"Hand-prints?" Meghan asked.

Iseult sat upright in one fluid movement, crossing her
legs. In measured cadences, she told how a woman of
the prides, longing to know who her secret lover was,
had pressed her hands into the ashes of the fire and then
looked to see whose skin showed the marks. There, on
her own brother's flank, she saw her smudged hand-
prints. Realizing her lover was her own brother, she
flung herself from the cliff.

"The Gods, accepting her sacrifice, turned her into the
beautiful blue moon that sails our night skies, bringing
us light in the darkness. Her brother, mad with grief and
remorse, flung himself after and was transformed into

the red moon that forever chases his Sister Moon across the sky. They say that once in every five thousand moons, the Gods o' White take pity on Sister Moon and Brother Moon and let them love again, though always under the cover o' darkness."

"That is an interesting story indeed," Meghan replied slowly. "It's no' dissimilar to the tale we tell our children about the cursed love between Gladrielle and Magnysson. They too were turned into moons, but the Celestines tempered the cruelty o' the curse and allowed them to meet again once every four hundred years." Suddenly Meghan's dark, narrow face flushed with excitement. Then she said in a charged voice, "Two moons that reach out to kiss or to bite. O' course! There is to be an eclipse o' the moons!"

"An eclipse? How do ye ken?"

"I remember now. When I was naught but a bairn, my father took Mairead and me through the maze to the Pool o' Two Moons to watch the eclipse. My father was always fascinated by the stars and planets, and I remember him discussing it with Mairead. I was more interested in a dormouse I had found in the garden and carried through the maze in my pocket.

Both Iseult and Lachlan grinned as the wood witch continued. "He bade us watch the moons, and slowly, ever so slowly, they crossed and went black. All the stars sprang out bright, then a great halo of light slowly grew around the merged moons. It was then that my father wrought the Lodestar, in the waters o' the pool that was all lit up with the magic o' the moons and the stars. Look!" She pointed at the two moons, hanging close together above their heads. "See how a dark halo is growing around the moons? See how four rays o' darkness are radiating out from them, as if black beacons were sweeping the stars apart? The dark cross, my father called it. That is what Cloudshadow meant when she said to watch for the dark constellations. She means the spaces between the stars!"

"So what does this mean to us?" Lachlan asked. "Is it a good omen or bad?"

"When Magnysson at last holds Gladrielle in his arms, all will be healed or broken, saved or surrendered . . ." Meghan murmured.

"What does that mean?"

"I will think on it," Meghan replied. "I do ken my head is swarming with ideas. We will see what, if anything, comes o' them. At least we know now the meaning o' Jorge's dreams. An eclipse o' the moons is a time o' great magical significance! There will be power abroad that night!"

"When will it happen?"

"My father wrought the Lodestar on my eighth birthday, at Samhain, the night when the veils between the worlds are at their thinnest. That will be the night. If we can rescue the Lodestar on the night o' the eclipse and bathe it in the enchanted waters, then we can restore its powers. That is what Cloudshadow meant when she said Samhain was the time!"

For two more weeks the League of the Healing Hand hurried through the Whitelock Mountains, managing to avoid the soldiers scouring the hills. Jesyah the raven was invaluable, flying high over the heavily wooded valleys and warning them of any encampments ahead.

The Sithiche and the Whitelock Mountains met just below the great triangular peak called the Fang, but the mountains were so steep, paths through the mountains were rare. One of the few ways to cross from one range to another was a high ridge of bare rock. Called the Goat Bridge because nothing but wild goats would make the crossing, it arched far above the green valleys of Rionnagan.

When Dillon realized that his Master intended them to traverse that narrow bridge, his step faltered. "Mercy me! Ye canna be thinking o' crossing that?"

Jorge looked around. "Ah, ye can see it now, can ye? Good, good. Jesyah, fly for me?" With a hoarse caw, the raven launched himself into the air, scanning the ground with his bright, beady eyes. "Now, Dillon, my lad, lead me forward."

One by one, their exuberance gone, the children followed him, casting scared glances up at the bridge of stone. There was a narrow gap between an outcropping of boulders and the cliff face. Slipping between, they found themselves scrambling up a narrow staircase naturally formed by rock and water. In places they had to climb, digging their fingers into tiny crevices and trying not to look down.

Of them all, Finn found the climb the easiest, having often been forced to break into castles by climbing their outer walls. She darted about like a wild goat herself, the elven cat, whom she called Goblin, bounding along at her heels.

When they at last reached the top, they all flopped onto their bellies on the slanted ridge, their heads hanging over one edge, their feet over another. On either side the ground dived away, nothing between them and the valley floor but dizzying distance. "I'm sacred," Johanna whimpered, clinging to the ridge with both hands.

"I'm scaaaared," Finn mimicked.

"Stop being such a scaredy-cat!" Dillon commanded.

"Soldiers!" Jorge said suddenly. "Get down, bairns, keep your heads low!"

All nine children lay closer to the ridge, their faces pressed against the rough stone, their hearts pounding. Dillon raised one eye above the edge and peered down at the company of soldiers riding through the valley below.

Finding the valley came to what seemed an abrupt dead end, the captain ordered his men to retrace their steps, and the soldiers moved out, not noticing the natural stairway which led to the bridge of stone above. Although they were too far away to hear a word the soldiers said, Dillon noted the lackadaisical attitude of the soldiers and smiled to himself. This was a routine maneuver—the soldiers did not know they were there.

"We'd better be lying still a wee while longer," Dillon said. "Else they'll be seeing us when we cross the ridge."

"How low is the sun?" Jorge asked. "It makes no difference to me, o' course, night and day are the same. Ye may find it difficult to cross after dark, though."

Johanna gave a little cry of distress and hugged her brother closer. Even Finn looked a little concerned, and they all turned and scanned the western horizon. The shadow of the needle-tipped ranges fell dark across the valleys. "Maybe an hour or two left," Dillon calculated.

"Plenty of time," Jorge beamed as the raven flew lazily toward them, his wings black against the bright sky.

Jorge's prediction proved sanguine. By the time the sun had set he had crossed the ridge with ease, but most of the children were still strung out along its narrow length. At last the entire League was safely on the other side, and so exhausted that they camped where they dropped. The dawn breaking over the mountains woke them, and they sat together on the edge of the great expanse of rock, overawed at the vastness of the world spread out before them.

"We can see three countries from here," Johanna said. "Can ye see? That wee silver thread down there is the Wulfrum River, and all that dark forest on the other side is Rurach."

"Rurach," Finn said slowly. She crept closer to the western edge so she could see down to the thickly forested slopes below. Behind them the conical peak of the Fang reared against the brightening sky, its tip wreathed with clouds. "It looks wild," she said softly, "wild and lonely."

"They say the forests o' Rurach still be filled with many strange creatures that are all but gone here in Rionnagan." Johanna gave a little shudder. "It's dangerous indeed, they say."

"It sounds like a place ye'd have adventures in," Finn said softly.

They kept on moving after a scanty breakfast and by noon had descended from the heights into another valley. Each hour they traveled, Jorge grew more excited, his limping step longer and faster. They came at last to a tumbling brook and followed its course up a steep slope, thorny with graygorse and goldensloe. Above them towered great walls of rock, one section much better, as if there had once been a landslide there. The stream bubbled through the rocks behind them, forming a shallow pool where they could wash their hot faces and drink deeply of its cold refreshment. Only then did they look about them and wonder if the Master had not somehow been led astray, for they could see no valley entrance, only massive tumbled boulders.

"This way." Feeling the rock face with his fingers, Jorge walked around the biggest boulder of them all and disappeared.

The children followed quickly, the boulder concealing a narrow, twisting pathway through the cliffs. Once the stream would have gushed freely through the chasm, but the landslide had all but blocked its passageway, and the children had to squeeze through gaps in the fallen rocks to make their way through.

At last they reached the far end, coming out into a broad, long valley surrounded on all sides by a great red cliff like a wave of bloody water turned to stone. At the far end was a small loch, fed by long waterfalls that poured over the edge of the cliffs from the white glacier towering above.

"Jesyah tells me there are many caves in the walls, but the one I have turned into my home is over in this direction." Jorge set off along the corrie's edge, bringing them at last to the far edge of the valley. The loch glimmered a dark green in the overhang of the cliff, the waterfalls frothing into white at their base. Dark openings here and there indicated many small caves. Jorge led the way into one, lighting a witch light at the end of his staff so they could see how cosy it was.

Thick fur rugs covered the floor, and books, scrolls and bottles were crowded on wooden shelves attached precariously to the overarching walls. Dried herbs hung from a badly made rack, and a deep nest of furs and blankets covered the floor. A deeply scarred wooden rod overhead showed where the raven roosted.

"Now out, all o' ye! There is no' enough room in here for all ye lumbering bairns. Ye'll have to find yourselves caves in which to sleep, for this wee crevice is barely large enough for Jesyah and me!"

Excitedly the children raced outside. For the next few hours their cries rang all round the corrie. They discovered caves bigger than any merchant's house, and as ornately decorated, though with pillars and arches of stone rather than cushions and tapestries. They raced through thickets and copses of tress, startling a flock of tree-swallows from their massive nests high in the boughs. They squabbled over the caves, Finn and Johanna at last triumphantly securing the best of them—small but deep, with a spring near the entrance and a smoke-stained crack at the back that showed fires had been lit there in the past.

The boys settled on a cave across the valley from Jorge's. It was much larger than the girls' and had a soft, sandy floor and a high, intricate ceiling. Although there was no natural chimney to lead the smoke from their fire out of the cave, there was a pool of icy-cold water at the very back, and passages that led to other caves, giving them all separate bedrooms if they wished. They began cutting bracken to make mattresses, and Johanna decided to cook them all a feast to celebrate the end of their journeying. The valley was filled with plants and animals, and Dillon was sure he could catch a fish in the loch.

It was near sunset when they sent Connor across the valley floor to fetch Jorge for the feast. When he returned, the little boy was quiet with awe, for the old man striding along behind him was no longer the dirty, shabby beggar they all knew. He had bathed in the loch, and his snowy white hair and beard flowed down over a long, finely woven robe of pale blue. Gilt thread glittered in an intricate border around the hem and collar and sleeves, and a dark-blue plaid was pinned at his breast with a jewelled brooch. He seemed taller, and carried himself proudly, barely leaning on his staff at all.

They greeted him with unusual deference, and seated him by the campfire. He smiled at them gravely, and said, "I have spoken with Meghan at last and she has made a suggestion which pleases me greatly. She wishes me to establish a Theurgia here, the first such school in sixteen years. Ye can all stay here with me and learn whatever I can teach ye."

"I never heard o' a Theurgia afore," Dillon said carefully, not at all sure he liked the sound of it.

"It is a school, bairns. A school for fledgling witches. Do no' feel so dismayed! I can sense your consternation from here. Would ye rather be living hand to mouth in the slums o' Lucescere or here in this safe valley with me and Tòmas?" Obediently the children murmured that they would much rather be here, of course. "All o' the Towers had schools, and bairns would be sent from one to another according to their Talents. If ye had no clear Talent, or if your mentor felt a wider, more general education was necessary, ye would have gone to the Theurgia at the Tower o' Two Moons. It was the biggest o' the schools and the most highly regarded, since acolytes were taught many different Skills there."

As he talked, the warlock ate hungrily, though the children's ardent appetite seemed to have diminished. As Jorge described to them all the things they would learn, they gradually stopped eating altogether, looking at each other in dismay.

Then, as an afterthought, the old warlock said, "Some other news that may interest ye. Meghan asked me to find out from Jesyah as much as I could about the geography o' this valley. When I described to her what he saw, she said she may send us company. It seems she is searching for a place to set up the rebel encampment . . ."

Immediately the boys leapt to their feet, cheering with excitement. "The rebels are coming here? They'll be stationed here, in this valley?" Dillon shouted. "They'd teach us to fight with swords, maybe? And happen the Cripple will come. Is he no' the leader o' all the rebels in the land? Hurrah! Things'll start happening then!" The children danced an impromptu jig around the fire, all thoughts of the Theurgia vanished in their excitement.

It was dark and stifling within the filthy folds of sacking. Sweat stung his eyes, and he twisted against his bonds although he knew there was no escape. He had tested the strength of the ropes for days now, and all he had done was chafe his wrists till they bled. Whoever had caught him had made sure he could not escape.

Douglas MacSeinn was not sure how many days it had since he had been kidnapped from the forests surrounding Rhyssmadill. It seemed like an eternity. He had been riding through the forest when his mare had suddenly reared, neighing in alarm. Something had darted out of the trees directly toward him. He had an impression of fluttering gray, and a strange, dank smell like that of an open grave. Then a great winged ghost was looming over him, its glittering eyes holding his gaze. The world tilted and slowed; the earth rushed past in a blur, then darkness swallowed him.

He had woken much later, bound in ropes and sacking, his head aching, his senses confused. Occasionally the sacking was pulled aside so he could drink water or force down spoonfuls of cold, gluey porridge. Even more rarely, his bonds were untied so he could stumble to a bush to relieve himself. He saw very little at those times, his eyes dazzled, but he heard a deep droning noise. The alien nature of the sound, along with his captors' clawlike grasp, convinced him he had not been kidnapped by humans. *But by what? By whom?*

Douglas shuddered with fear at the idea he was the captive of some demon-spawned *uile-bheist*, and he wracked his brains trying to figure out *why*. Although he was the only living child and heir of the Prionnsa of

Carraig, Linley MacSeinn, their country had been lost to the Fairgean five years earlier. Once one of the richest and proudest of the prionnsachan, the MacSeinns were now refugees from their land, dependent upon the Rìgh for their survival. Kidnapping Douglas in hope of a ransom was futile, for his father, the MacSeinn, simply could not afford to pay.

The rippling sound of water was all about him, and he smelt swamp through the musty odor of the sacking. *Where can I be?* he thought, pushing down the panic rising in his throat.

He was swung into the air and carried forward, the ropes biting deep into his stomach, then dropped without warning onto a very hard, very cold floor. He was unable to help crying out in pain, and he heard a woman's autocratic voice say, "I told ye he was no' to be harmed! Bring him into the throne room!"

Someone dragged him along the floor, and he curled around his ropes, fear freezing his blood. He was tossed in a heap, then the ropes were mercifully cut free. Douglas was able to struggle free of the sacking, gulping great mouthfuls of clean air and rubbing the grime from his caked eyelashes. With an effort he got to his feet and stared at his captors with mingled dismay and horror. They were tall, winged creatures with huge clusters of eyes, out-thrusting proboscis, and three pairs of multi-jointed, clawed arms.

"So, another pupil for our Theurgia," a female voice said. "And a Talented one at that!"

Douglas spun round, staggered and almost fell. With his jaw clenched, he stared defiantly at the woman reclining on a great throne before him. She wore a heather-purple plaid over a black silk gown, with a silver brooch in the shape of a flowering thistle at her breast.

"Who are ye?" Douglas demanded, his voice cracking. "How dare ye bring me here against my will. Ye have no right!"

She laughed, a sweet, silvery sound that brought ice trickling through his veins. "I am the Banprionnsa o'

Arran, and I can do whatever I like, my young cockerel.
Ye are in the Tower o' Mists now, surrounded on all
sides by the Murkmyre Marshes. Ye can no' escape."

"How dare ye kidnap me! My father will be angry
indeed. I am the Prionnsa Douglas MacSeinn, and ye
have no right bringing me here against my will. Take
me home at once!"

"To Carraig, my loud young laird? I have no desire to
lose yet another bright Talent to the wicked, murdering
Fairgean. Nay, nay, ye'll be safer here than in Carraig."

"I want to go back to my father!" Douglas shouted,
his fists clenched.

"Come, Douglas," the banprionnsa smiled, "where are
your manners? Do ye no' realize ye are come to the last
Theurgia in the land? Here ye will be taught to use all
that Talent I sense in ye. Indeed, ye are o' the best and
noblest o' blood and should have a rare potential for
witchcraft and witchcunning. I have the best teachers in
the land, and my library is incomparable. Ye shall be a
great warlock and learn to wield the One Power—"

"No," Douglas cried, "I canna stay here, my father
needs me."

"Ye have made dangerous enemies for one so young,"
Margrit smiled, causing Douglas's heart to sink. With a
chill he remembered his hasty words at the Rìgh's high
table. Was that what the Banprionnsa of Arran meant?
He had criticized the Rìgh's Decree Against Witchcraft
which had led to the death of so many witches, among
them the Sea Witches of Carraig. Many of the sea
witches had had the ability to bewitch the Fairgean with
song, and their death had meant the most potent weapon
against the sea people was lost. He knew his ill-consid-
ered words had caused a minor scandal, for the whispers
had raced around the great hall faster than a bumblebee
could fly. His own father had berated him later, reminding him they were being housed and fed by the
Rìgh and it was rude as well as stupid to castigate him
while living under his roof. Douglas had blushed and

apologized and thought no more about it, but now he began to wonder.

"Ye must take me home, my poor father will be frantic! I do no' want to join your Theurgia. I demand to be taken back to Rhyssmadill!"

The Banprionnsa of Arran threw back her head and laughed, sending icicles creeping down his spine. A young man standing irresolutely against the wall made frantic silencing motions with his hands. Douglas stared at him angrily. He was shabbily dressed, with ink stains on his fingers, so that Douglas thought he must be some sort of scribe. He put his finger to his lips again, gazing at him so pleadingly that Douglas swallowed the indignant words he had been about to shout.

"Ye will learn, my foolish lad, no' to make demands o' Margrit o' Arran," the banprionnsa said kindly. "Khan'tirell! Take the lad away and give him a good whipping for his insolence. Then lock him up with naught but a heel o' bread and a flagon o' water until I see fit to release him."

Douglas tried to escape, of course. Over the next few days he twice evaded the relentless observation of the banprionnsa's servants and was dragged in from the marshes by a Mesmerd, muddy, cold and, although he would never have admitted it, frightened. The first time Margrit showed him three small skeletons hanging from the lintel of the Theurgia's tower. They had been executed by the banprionnsa's chamberlain after staging a rebellion.

"Bright as your Talent is, I shall no' suffer any defiance," she said, smiling kindly. "Do no' try and escape again."

Perhaps it was the smile that had deceived him. Douglas tried again as soon as he was allowed out of solitary confinement. That time Margrit left him for a day and a night in her oubliette, a lightless hole sunk twenty feet below the ground. Before he was lowered into that dark, terrifying closeness, she had nodded to Khan'tirell. The horned man had drawn his dagger and with easy econ-

omy slit the throat of one of the other students, a sturdy
little crofter's daughter. She had been the one with the
least Talent.

"Defy me again and another child shall die," Margrit
said. "Ye see, I sense power in ye, lad, and will no'
lightly let ye slip my fingers."

Douglas was not deceived by the smile that accompanied her words this time. When he was at last drawn up
out of his cramped, dark prison, his face was set as if
carved out of white marble. Both hands were crabbed
all over with black trickles of blood from where he had
dug in his nails. Yet Khan'tirell drew his angular brows
together and said to the banprionnsa, "He is still only a
youth, fifteen o' the long darkness, if that. He either had
help through the night or is a dangerous youth indeed.
Older and stronger men have been broken by the pit."

Margrit grasped Douglas by his thick black hair and
pulled his head back until he was on his knees, back
arched, eyes upturned to hers. She stared deep into his
sea-green eyes and saw pain enough to please her. She
drew her thin brows together, quirked her mouth and
let him go. "He is a MacSeinn," she shrugged. "I would
have expected inner reserves. His apprenticeship has
begun. Feed him, wash him and let him lie in quietness
for a while. When he wakes, remind him the Mesmerdean fly the marshes, the bogfaeries guard the fens, the
golden goddess blooms in glorious death, and my eyes
are everywhere. He shall submit to my will."

Douglas had not endured the night altogether alone.
He had been crouched in shuddering silence when he
had heard the faint sounds of the iron cover being
hauled away. He'd tensed and looked up; someone was
leaning over the dim hole far above.

Do no' be afraid . . . Words had slipped into his mind
as a bulky package was lowered to him on a long piece
of string. He scrabbled at it with urgent fingers and
found the waxy texture of a candle. He kept searching
but to his dismay there was no tinderbox.

Immediately, the candle lit with a blue spark, startling

him so he dropped it. He cursed, and in his mind heard someone say, *Sorry. I forgot ye probably did no' ken how to conjure fire. Hold the candle still, I'll light it again.*

The candle flickered into life again, and by its light Douglas saw a hunk of fine bread, some fish, a fresh bellfruit and, best of all, a bottle of goldensloe wine, all wrapped in a thick but faded plaid. "Who are ye?" he whispered. There was no way the person leaning over the manhole far above could have heard him, but he was answered.

Hush now. We can talk later. I could no' leave ye there in such distress. If anyone comes, do what ye can to hide the plaid, for they'll ken it is mine . . .

Then the manhole slammed shut, leaving Douglas to the precarious flicker of the candle. He sat shakily and drank some wine, then wrapped the plaid about him. Later he was able to eat, and the occasional small sip of wine was like a mouthful of summer light. The candle dwindled quickly, but after it sank away he slept. When he woke to stiffness and fear and pain, the memory of the voice in the darkness was there to give him hope.

His unknown friend had returned later to draw up the bundle. *Do no' defy the banprionnsa,* the mind-voice had whispered. *Speak with courtesy and scheme in silence. It is the only way . . .*

Douglas had many long days to wonder about the identity of his secret friend. Their lessons ran from dawn to dusk, with only a break for a meager lunch at noon. The twenty-seven students of the Theurgia were kept within one tower—four rooms built one on top of the other and connected by rickety wooden ladders that could be drawn up when not in use. Their rooms were cold and damp, the mist rising off the Murkfane seeming to seep into their very bones. The banprionnsa was prone to unexpected visits and exams; their teachers were in turns morose, sarcastic and wrathful, and there was never ever enough food.

Douglas was the eldest of the children, and his courage in outfacing the banprionnsa had made him a hero among them, so he easily ruled them from the very moment he arrived. Closest to him in age was Gilliane Nic-Aislin, who had been stolen with her little sister Ghislaine while traveling to Dùn Eidean to stay at the prionnsa's castle. They were the nieces of the MacThanach of Blessém himself and were able to trace their lineage back to Aislinna the Dreamer, mother to daughter for a thousand years.

There was a boy from Ravenshaw whose grandmother had been a NicBrann; the daughter of a thigearn stolen from Tìreich's shore by pirates; three children from Rionnagan whose apprentice-witch aunt had died in the Burning. Another student came from Aslinn and showed clear signs of faery blood in her angular face and long, multijointed fingers. Yet another had only one eye, centered in features as blunt as if hewn from stone, all scaled with silvery lichen. He had been born of a rape on the Day of Reckoning, his corrigan mother left for dead by the soldiers. Of all the children he was the most sincere in his protestations of gratitude, for the Mesmerdean had saved him from being stoned to death.

Most came from Blessém, the children of lesser lairds and barons, rich merchants and tradesmen. One was the child of a crofter, born of a long line of cunning men and village warlocks. It had been his sister who had died under the chamberlain's knife, and he was frozen still in grief and horror.

Quite a few came from Tìrsoilleir, where witchcraft had been banned for so long it was a wonder Margrit of Arran had been able to find any with Talent. They were wary, sullen children, quick to take offence, and scorning the others for their heathenish ways.

Douglas had only the occasional mind-conversation with his secret friend to sustain him through his homesickness and fear, as well as unexpected relish in the lessons in Craft and Cunning. He learnt faster than even his teachers suspected, urged on by the unknown voice.

It did not take long for Douglas to realize he was not the only one receiving comfort and hope from his mysterious friend. Every few nights someone penetrated the tower while the children slept, hiding small gifts of food and toys. The gifts were always tucked out of sight where none but the children would find them—in the woodpile, under the bundle of rags the girls pretended was a doll, behind the atlas. This was the most popular book in the schoolroom, for not only was it one of the few to have brightly colored pages in it to amuse the smaller ones, but even the eldest children hung over the maps of their countries, dreaming of home. It had seemed clear to Douglas that only someone who watched the children with sympathy would have seen these things, and he was sure it was the same person who had given him the candle and wine.

One night Douglas waited until the tower was still and dark, then he hid in the schoolroom. After more than an hour he was just deciding to go to bed when he heard a faint noise. He crouched low and heard the door open. Someone came silently in. Unsure whether to light his candle or not, Douglas paused, his thoughts hurrying. The quiet footsteps stopped, then the voice said in his mind, *Hush, make no' a sound, she will be listening* . . .

Trying not to even breathe, Douglas crouched obediently still. There were one or two muffled sounds, then a long silence. He was all pins and needles when at last a flame flickered up in the hearth.

It was then that he realized his secret friend was the thin, stooped, stammering young man with the ready blush and uncontrollable Adam's apple that had gestured to him in the throne room. Douglas had often seen him wandering the grounds with a book tucked under his arm and had envied him his freedom.

Douglas opened his mouth to speak but the gangly young man held up a hand, quickly drew a shape about the hearthstone with an ash-smeared finger and beckoned Douglas forward. Stumbling with cramp, the boy obeyed. He sat cross-legged where directed, staying silent as the other scribbled some more in the ashes and sprinkled what looked like salt about.

At last the young man turned about, smiled shyly, rubbed his grubby hand down his shirt and offered it to Douglas, saying, "We can t-t-talk now, the circle is c-c-closed and ashes, salt and earth well-scattered. I am Iain. Be careful n-n-no' to let any part o' your b-b-body pass outside the circle and star, else the s-s-spell will be b-b-b-broken."

They talked half the night that first meeting. The next day, though his jaw cracked with yawning, Douglas listened with even greater concentration to the dried-up warlock teaching them. He had decided his only chance to escape was to listen to Iain, who told him he would need to know much about magic and its applications before he could hope to escape Margrit of Arran.

They had met seven or more times before Douglas thought to notice the heather weave of Iain's shabby kilt, or his distinctive thistle badge. Only then did he realize his dreamy midnight visitor was the Prionnsa Iain MacFóghnan of Arran, heir to the Tower of Mists.

His first reaction was one of shock and suspicion, but as Iain pointed out, if he had wanted to trap Douglas into indiscretion, would he have worn his kilt? Or brought him goldensloe wine?

"In f-f-fact," Iain said, "I want t-t-to escape this place as m-m-much as ye do." He tried to describe to Douglas what it was like to have grown up alone in the middle of the Murkmyre, with no companions but the endless procession of tutors. If it had not been for his books and the mysterious beauty of the marshes, Iain thought he might have tried to kill himself. He had tried to run away several times, but he was closely watched and guarded. Then he told Douglas that his mother had found a bride for him, against his will, and had already poisoned her mind against him.

"She is a N-N-NicHilde," he explained. "My m-m-m-mother has signed an alliance w-w-with the Bright Soldiers o' Tìrsoilleir. In return for allowing them to m-m-march through Arran, we win more land, gain their f-f-forbidden library and a bride for the b-b-b- banprionn-sa's idiot son." There was bitterness in his voice.

"The Bright Soldiers wish to march through Arran? Why?" Douglas's voice was tense. His country had suffered much from the warlike Tìrsoilleirean over the past thousand years.

"I be no' sure—I think they w-w-wish to strike at the MacCuinn, for the Witches' Decree has rid the land o' m-m-m-much o' its strength. My m-m-m-mother says the Tìrsoilleirean have wearied o' marching up and down the streets o' Bride with n-n-n-nothing to strike at. She says b-b-better the MacCuinn than us, for the Bright Soldiers wish to attack someone and we may as well d-d-direct their attention to our ancient enemy, the M-M-MacCuinn, and see what we can gain in the m-m-m-meantime."

Douglas was white as chalk, his vivid sea-green eyes blazing. "We must escape!" he cried. "We have to warn the Rìgh! We canna be allowing the Tìrsoilleirean to attack. They'll burn the crops and murder the people— I have seen what they do when they're on the march. They must be meaning to strike at Dùn Eidean, before marching on Dùn Gorm . . . My father is at Rhyssmadill, and all the clan! We have to warn them!"

Iain had never given much thought to the rest of Eileanan, his country having been independent for a thousand years. He had always heard his mother speak of the Rìgh with contemptuous malevolence, and knew the story of their antagonism as well as he knew his own face. He had thought of the implications of his mother's treaty only in relation to himself, but Douglas's words immediately kindled his concern. He knew at once that Douglas was right. If they could escape and warn the Rìgh of the impending invasion, perhaps much bloodshed and sorrow could be avoided, and the ancient rivalry between MacCuinn and MacFóghnan at last laid to rest.

So an alliance between MacFóghnan and MacSeinn was forged, and the two conspirators began to plan their escape from the marshes and fenlands of Arran. All they needed was an opportunity . . .

BELTANE NIGHT

The week after Fools' Day, Lachlan returned from the forest, his face lit with excitement, and opened his hand to show Meghan a moonstone. "I found it in the burn," he said, suppressed delight in his voice. He shot a look at Iseult, and said, "See, she is no' the only one to find a moonstone!"

"Did ye go looking for it?" Meghan asked sternly, and he quirked his mouth.

"I have," he admitted, "but today I swear I was no' even thinking about it."

"Good," the old witch said and tucked the glimmering white stone away.

She heard from Jorge the very next day. The blind seer and his band of beggar children were safe in his valley hideaway. At Meghan's request, Jorge sent his familiar Jesyah to fly over the corrie and he told her what the raven saw. To Iseult and Lachlan's excitement it seemed sure it was big enough and secret enough to conceal near a thousand men. Talking eagerly about their plans for a rebel encampment, they did not notice the sudden silence from the old sorceress. Then Lachlan said sharply, "Meghan, what's wrong? Ye have had bad news?"

"Aye, Lachlan, in a sense." Meghan's face was paper white, her eyes glittering like shards of black glass.

"What have we to fear?" Iseult said briskly. "Do we need to make defenses?"

"Perhaps . . ." Meghan stroked the velvety brown don-beag as he curled into a ball between her chin and shoulder. "Hush, Gitâ, be still. There is no need to fear." She cleared her throat as her voice cracked, then said grimly, "I am sorry to have to have startled ye. Jorge has had visions of a black wolf on my trail."

"A wolf?" Iseult echoed blankly. "I have killed many wolves, auld mother. There be no need to fear."

"I doubt ye have killed a wolf like this one." Meghan's voice was bleak. "Besides, I should no' let ye. This is a wolf I would be glad to see normally. Come, get back to your studies. There's no need to stand gawking and wringing your hands over a dream. Time shall tell whether it be a true seeing."

She paced the clearing, one hand cradling Gitâ as he burrowed under her chin. "Iseult, where's that broken arrow I pulled out o' my pouch?"

When Iseult had found her the white-fletched arrow, the sorceress sat by the fireplace again, her narrow face pensive. "This arrow is near a thousand years auld," she said slowly. "It was made by Owein o' the Longbow, my ancestor and Lachlan's. I have been watching ye bairns as ye fight and play, and it seems clear to me that Lachlan has the makings o' a very fine archer. In less than a month he already can hit the clout more times than no'."

Iseult looked with pride at her pupil. Indeed he had both the talent and the strength to far outstrip her with the bow and arrow.

"Jorge has had a vision o' Lachlan wielding a bow o' fire and magic. He says Lachlan won many a triumph with this bow. Immediately I thought o' Owein's Bow, which was kept at the Tower o' Two Moons, along with many other objects o' magical significance. When the soldiers attacked the Tower, I locked up the relic room, hiding the door and warding it cannily. Owein's Bow was there. I want to find it and give it to ye, Lachlan. The Bow was made by Owein MacCuinn's own hands and carried by him all his life. His magic should have soaked in deep."

"But ye do no' even ken if the bow escaped the Burning," Lachlan protested.

"Is there any harm in finding out?" Meghan responded irritably.

"But how?" Lachlan drummed his fingers against his book in impatience.

"If ye will let me finish, I will tell ye," Meghan said just as impatiently. "Jorge has gathered around him a motley collection o' beggar children. One seems to have the Talent o' Searching. Jorge says she is amazingly strong, has merely to concentrate her will on what she desires and knows at once what direction it is in."

"But does she no' need to ken what she is Searching for? She has never seen the Bow or felt its psychic emanations, how is she—"

"Lachlan, why do ye argue with me? She can use the arrow, o' course. If she bears her mind upon it, I am sure she'll be able to tell if the Bow still exists. We need to go to Lucescere to retrieve the Lodestar—how much more difficult will it be for the lassie to search the ruins for the Bow first, so ye have it when ye need it most? If Jorge's vision is true, ye shall be invincible with it in your hand."

The idea appealed to Lachlan. His topaz eyes blazed; his swarthy face was alight with excitement. Unable to sit still, he began to stride around the clearing, his glossy wings moving restlessly. Iseult gazed at him in painful tenderness. It was when he was excited like this, his immense vitality bursting its bounds, that Iseult found it hardest to remember that he was forbidden to her.

Meghan had to shush him with a laugh, saying, "Do no' get too excited, my lad, it may have been burnt or lost, or she may no' be able to locate it. It is an idea only, and an idea that shall take some pondering." She turned to Iseult, still gazing up at Lachlan, and cleared her throat to gain her attention. Iseult flushed crimson and bent her head over *The Book of Shadows* once more. There was a suspicion of laughter in Meghan's voice as she said, "I have been watching ye also, Iseult. I have only ever seen one other person somersault as ye do. Is this common among your people?"

"Many o' the Scarred Warriors excel at such defensive maneuvers, but I am considered among the best," Iseult replied with spurious modesty.

"Ye do it very fast and with such power—can ye do it slowly?"

Iseult looked at her in surprise. "I suppose so," she said. She did a leisurely and elegant tumbling run that took her high in the air.

"Beautiful!" Meghan applauded, while Lachlan gave a grunt and scowled at her. He always grew sullen when Iseult demonstrated her ease and grace of movement, the contrast between his own clumsy movements so sharp.

"Could ye jump out o' that branch without hurt?" Meghan asked, pointing to a great twisted branch about ten feet off the ground.

Iseult smiled. "Easy," she said, climbing with effortless agility and bounding off.

"What about that one?"

Iseult frowned and shrugged. "I'll try if ye like."

Lachlan scowled. "She'll hurt herself, ye auld fool," he said disrespectfully.

"I dinna think so," Meghan replied and, sure enough, Iseult managed the twenty-foot drop with no difficulty. Meghan pointed out another, and with a shrug and a grin, Iseult climbed the tree again. From this height she could see over most of the forest. She looked down, and her heart pounded heavily against her ribs.

"Are ye all right?" Lachlan called anxiously. "Do no' do it if ye are afraid, Iseult, the drop'll surely kill ye."

At that Iseult jumped. It was a long way and she fell fast. Her curls blew back from her face, and tears started to her eyes. The woods blurred into a haze of brown and green, then the earth was flying toward her. Terror gripped her, but she prepared her body for landing, loosening her muscles and centering her sense of balance. The world steadied, slowed. She dropped to the ground, and though she stumbled and fell, she did not even bruise herself.

"By Eà's green blood!" Lachlan breathed. His face was white, his body tense. He helped her up and gripped her wrist in his hand. "Ye fool!" he snapped. "What were ye thinking? Ye could have been killed!"

"Meghan would no' have asked me to do it if she did no' think I could," Iseult answered, though now she was on the ground her legs were shaky.

"Indeed I would no', though it was a risk, that I admit. I have seen other witches do such a trick, but was no' sure if Iseult could."

"She might have been killed!"

"Lachlan, my lad, Iseult's mother was Ishbel the Winged. She could float in the air as easily as a bellfruit seed in a breeze. O' course I wondered if Iseult had inherited any o' her Talent. It's clear she has strong powers in air and spirit, and the only other person I've seen to somersault like that was Ishbel."

"Ye think I can fly!" Iseult gasped.

"Perhaps no'," Meghan answered. "No-one needed to teach Ishbel to fly, she did it as naturally as breathing. She used to float above her bed as she slept. I've seen no evidence o' such profound Talent in ye. Still, I wondered. Even if ye canna fly, I can see how the leaping o' high walls would be o' great use indeed."

"Ye are thinking o' the rampart behind the Tower, which protects Lucescere from the forest," Lachlan said.

"Indeed I am. We might set Iseult to practicing jumping while we are here."

Over the next few weeks Iseult found she could jump barriers far greater than her own height and could drop from heights of well over a hundred feet without more than a few bumps. To her amazement she began to be able to control her speed of falling, and by Beltane she could float down as slowly as a feather.

The first of May dawned fresh and clear. Meghan woke them as usual, but as they ate their porridge and drank their tea, she said, smiling, "It be Beltane today. Why do ye no' have a holiday? Ye have both been good, patient bairns and worked hard. No one should work on May Day."

Both Iseult and Lachlan were pleased at the idea, though it soon became clear that Meghan had plans for them. They were to have a May Day feast and invite the Celestines for, as Meghan said, "Ye canna have much o' a feast with only the three o' us!" She needed firewood for the bonfire, plenty of flowers for their wreaths, as well as whatever nuts and fruits they could find. Like Meghan, none of the Celestines ever ate meat, and the amount of vegetables and fruit it took to fill all their stomachs seemed colossal.

Iseult and Lachlan set off into the forest with light hearts. After over an hour of gentle meandering, they came to a path that ran between a stand of moss-oaks, their great silvery trunks writhing upwards in fluid shapes. Iseult followed the trail as it wound up the slope of a hill, thorny bushes pressing all around. At last it led into a small clearing around a tarn. On the tarn's shores was a hut, built of stones and earth. A thin tendril of smoke trickled from the chimney.

"I think we had better go back." Iseult hesitated on the verge of the clearing.

"Because o' a wee hut?" Lachlan jeered, pushing past her. "I dinna think so! Come on, let's go and see who bides here."

"Meghan says . . ."

"Meghan says, Meghan says! Do ye always have to do what Meghan says?"

"Nay, it just makes sense. Meghan said there are many wicked faeries living in the forest, remember?"

"Do no' be afraid, my bonny lass, I'll protect ye!" Lachlan grinned.

"Why, ye couldna protect a duck!" she retorted, following him across the clearing. She looked around carefully, but could see no sign of life. Beside the shack was a carefully cultivated garden, thick with herbs and vegetables, and two beehives were set against the trees. Among the thyme and comfrey stood a small, crooked menhir, with some smaller boulders clustered nearby. A greenberry tree trailed its branches in the tarn, pale lilies floating across its wind-trembled surface.

"I see no one but I feel like we're being watched," Iseult whispered and drew an arrow from her quiver, notching it to her crossbow. Unable to shake off a sense of unease, she moved forward, her bow at the ready. She stepped up to the roughly made door and pushed it open with her hand. Inside she could see a neat little room, with a table to one side, a high-backed chair made from polished branches and three stools. A pot bubbled over the fire.

"There's no one here, but they canna have gone far," she said. "Lachlan, let's go. I do no' think we should be here."

He shrugged his agreement and they stepped away from the cottage, turning back toward the path. Hearing another noise, she twisted round and realized that the boulders had somehow moved.

"Come on, Lachlan, it's no' safe here." She quickened her step, raising her bow so that it was aimed at the tallest of the stones. Immediately her bow burst into flame. She dropped it with a cry. As it hit the ground the flames disappeared and she saw her bow was unharmed. She bent to retrieve it and strong arms suddenly seized her around the waist and dragged her down. Immediately she fought back, but her wrists were caught in an unbreakable hold.

"Lachlan, run!" she screamed, but the winged prionnsa raised his bow and took aim. Immediately his bow turned to a fistful of hissing snakes, which he threw away from him with a curse.

"It's all an illusion!" Iseult cried. "Run! Get Meghan!"

It was too late. Another of the squat, immensely strong creatures had kicked Lachlan's legs from underneath him. "Take them into the hut!" a cracked, querulous voice said. "There may be other human creatures nearby. We dinna want any to see."

Iseult saw the menhir had changed into an old, exceedingly ugly faery. She stood in the herb patch, her clawlike hands clutching a wooden spade. Iseult was heaved to her feet, and she kicked out at her captors. Although she knocked one off his feet, he did not let go and she was dragged to the ground with him. Before she had time to recover, she and Lachlan were dragged into the hut, and the three squat creatures had tied them to the pole in the center of the room.

The old woman sat in the high-backed chair, gray hair straggling all around her warty, wrinkled face. Her long, bumpy nose curved down towards her bulbous chin, a thin seam of a mouth cramped between. Her glittering eyes were merely thin slits under sprouting gray eyebrows.

"A cursehag!" Lachlan groaned. "And hobgoblins too. Just my luck!"

Iseult said nothing, just tested her strength quietly against the ropes as she ran her eyes over every feature of the little room. There was no ceiling, the slats and mud of the steeply peaked roof clearly visible above them. Herbs were hung up to dry in the dim cone, scenting the air. There was a bed built into one wall, neatly made up with homespun blankets.

Around the old woman crouched the three creatures who had wrestled Lachlan and Iseult to the ground. They were short, broad creatures, dark of skin and hair, with bulging eyes and thick fingers like tree roots, bluntly clawed. Iseult tried to remember all she had read of cursehags and hobgoblins.

"Why have ye come here? Wha' do you want?" the querulous old voice asked.

"We were just exploring," Lachlan said. "Ye had better let us go. They will come soon, looking for us."

"They? They? Who is they?"

"Soldiers."

She hissed. "Soldiers! Then we shall kill ye now, before they come." One of the hobgoblins started forward, and Iseult saw he clutched a great sword. Even though it was taller than he was, he had no difficulty in hefting its weight. She recognized it as one of the double-edged claymores the Red Guards carried.

"Nay!" she cried. "We are no' friends o' the soldiers. We mean ye no harm."

"Yet ye come, peeping and prying, snooping and spying, threatening us with your nasty arrows . . ."

"We're very sorry," Iseult said. "We were just exploring a path. We did no' ken this was your place. Forgive us and let us be, and we promise to let ye be too."

"Obh obh, promises, promises, always ye humans make promises. We ken how much your promises mean!"

The hobgoblin with the claymore chuckled evilly and moved the sword menacingly. The old woman checked him almost imperceptibly. Encouraged, Iseult continued softly, "Truly, we mean ye no harm and are sorry indeed to have disturbed ye."

The old woman cackled. "I bet ye are."

"Ye must let us go. More harm will come to ye from keeping us here against our will than by letting us go," Lachlan said. "I am the Prionnsa Lachlan MacCuinn. If ye hurt us, ye shall suffer." The name meant something to her. She looked up, and for a moment her form seemed to blur. Lachlan continued, "Aedan MacCuinn was my forefather. I am his direct descendant. Ye ken they call him the friend o' the faeries. It was Whitelock who drew up the Pact o' Peace and made sure all faeries could live peacefully and without fear."

"Aye, I ken your Aedan MacCuinn. How true were his promises? He said the faeries would never again be bothered and badgered. He said we could all live free."

"His promises were true," Lachlan said eagerly. "I am his descendant and I promise the Pact o' Peace shall be renewed. It was no' the MacCuinns who turned against your kind, it was—"

"Lies, lies! It was the MacCuinn who signed the Faery Decree, the MacCuinn who caused me to be driven from my home! It was the MacCuinn who hunted out poor creatures like my hobgoblins here, and burnt them or drowned them and used them for their amusement. Ye lie!"

"But it is no' his fault, Jaspar is under an enchantment, a foul ensorcelment." It was the first time Iseult had ever heard him speak in his brother's defense.

Her eyes blazed between wrinkled lids. "Lies like all humans, lies and lies."

"My cousin Meghan NicCuinn shall come looking for us! If ye harm us she will be angry!"

"Meghan NicCuinn is dead!" the cursehag snapped. "Now I ken ye are evil liars, like all humans! Meghan o' the Beasts lived before I was ever born, ye think I do no' ken that? If Meghan o' the Beasts was alive, she would never have allowed the MacCuinn to turn against us like that! Ye think to trick me with your lies, but I be canny, I be clever, I ken ye tell no' the truth." She scuttled from the room, beckoning the three hobgoblins with one gnarled hand. "Come, my lovelies, I want ye. We shall kill them and bury their bodies deep, deep in the earth, and none shall ken that they have been here!"

Iseult and Lachlan were left alone. To their dismay, they heard the sound of digging nearby. Their fingers met and gripped.

"I be so sorry, Iseult. Ye were right. We should no' have taken the risk."

Iseult said bitterly, "It's my fault. I should have known better."

"Why is it your fault?" Lachlan said angrily. "Ye always have to take everything on to yourself. I'm the one that wanted to come and have a look."

"I'm the Scarred Warrior."

"I swear, Iseult, if ye say that one more time, I'll strangle ye!"

"As if ye could," she answered scornfully.

He dropped her fingers as if they had stung him. From outside the flimsy walls they heard the sound of metal sharpening. Involuntarily Iseult took hold of his hand again. It was warm and strong in hers, and gripped hers again immediately.

"How long before Meghan will miss us?" she asked.

"Hours yet. She will just think us off exploring still. Ye ken we are always late back." He hesitated then said, "Iseult . . ."

"Aye?"

"Nothing." They stood in silence for a moment, their hands still entwined, then he leant against the ropes, straining toward her. She twisted against her bonds so that she could try and see his face. His mouth grazed her cheek, slipped down. Ignoring the pain in her shoulder sockets, she twisted forward further and their mouths met and clung. Unable to sustain the awkward angle, they had to ease away, their shoulders and arms throbbing. They leaned silently together, her cheek against the feathers of his cramped wing.

"We must escape," he said. "Let me think, let me think."

"I am still wearing my weapons belt," she whispered. "My dagger—if we could work it out of its sheath, we could slice the ropes. Can ye reach?"

He kissed her again, lingeringly. When he finally eased his mouth away, Iseult was trembling. She felt his fingers fumbling at her waist, and she shifted the belt around so he could reach it. "I've found the hilt. How do I . . . ? Oh, I see."

"Do no' drop it!" she whispered. "Careful."

At last with a grunt he drew the knife free and set it against the ropes, sawing desperately. His hands were tied so tightly he could barely move the blade, but gradually the strands parted and they felt the pressure ease. "Getting there," he muttered, grunting again with exertion.

The door opened, letting in a shaft of sunlight. They

both froze, trying to conceal the dagger between them. Iseult, facing the fire, twisted to see around, sensing Lachlan's trepidation. In the doorway stood the hobgoblins, one carrying the claymore, the others a freshly sharpened axe and knife. Iseult strained against her bonds. If only Lachlan had been able to finish cutting the ropes!

The hobgoblins danced around, their broad, flat feet making a slapping noise as they hit the dirt floor. Lachlan pressed back against the pole as the tip of the claymore whistled past his chest. The hobgoblins were chanting in their own guttural language, occasionally shouting a phrase out loud. Glancing frantically around the room for anything that could help them, Iseult thought. *How odd. Meghan always said hobgoblins were peaceful creatures. That is why there are so few o' them left, I thought . . .*

As the old woman appeared in the doorway, Iseult's mind worked furiously. She remembered the illusion of flames and snakes, the boulders in the herb garden, the neatness and cleanliness of the little house. Cursehags were known for their filth and squalor; for their general nastiness of mind and spirit. Would a cursehag refer to the hobgoblins as "poor creatures"? Would her hut be so orderly, her garden so well tended? And as far as Iseult could remember, it was not cursehags that had the power of illusion, but corrigans.

Just as the hobgoblins' chanting grew to a crescendo and the old, bent woman raised her claws to give the order, Iseult cried, "Nay! Please, madam, listen to us! We are your friends! We really are with Meghan o' the Beasts. Lachlan is her great-great-great-nephew, and we are all fighting to overthrow the evil Banrìgh who ensorcelled the Rìgh and made him turn against all the witches and faeries. If ye kill Lachlan, ye will kill Eileanan's best hope! Please listen to us!"

"So ye can tell me more lies?"

"Let us prove ourselves to ye! He really is Lachlan MacCuinn—canna ye see he wears the MacCuinn tartan? And look, his brooch. Lachlan, show her your brooch. I ken ye are no' what ye seem. I ken ye are no' a cursehag. I can see ye think us in league with the soldiers who have been burning and slashing the forest, and who drove ye here in the first place. But we are no', we are no'!"

The old woman abruptly crossed the room and grasped Lachlan's black curls in her hand, dragging his head back. She stared at him intently, noting the white lock of hair, the blue-green tartan. Then with one long, gnarled finger she flicked the brooch that pinned his plaid together, with its device of the stag rampant.

"So," she hissed, "it is a MacCuinn after all." She laughed unpleasantly. "No doubt ye'll raise a fine ransom."

"No' from the Rìgh and Banrìgh," Lachlan said bitterly. "If ye kill me, ye'll be doing exactly what they want. They've been hunting me for years!"

She hesitated, obviously undecided on her course of action.

"If ye free us, we shall take ye to Meghan o' the Beasts, we'll show ye she's still alive," Iseult said persuasively. "I ken she'll be glad indeed to meet a corrigan."

The hideous old woman hissed and drew back.

"I ken ye are no' a cursehag," Iseult said in the same soft, cajoling voice. "Ye be a mistress o' illusion, indeed. Ye tricked us properly! I am a Scarred Warrior. Never before have I been overpowered. But with your cleverness and quickness o' thought, ye caught us fair and square."

"Ye'll gain nothing by killing us, though," Lachlan said sternly. "We are no threat to ye. We fight to restore the grand days o' the MacCuinns, when human and faery lived in peace. Kill me, and the days when ye could move freely around the country and do as ye pleased will never return. Let me live, and I swear when I am Rìgh I shall restore the Pact o' Peace."

The figure of the cursehag suddenly shimmered and changed. In her place stood a beautiful young woman

surrounded by sheets of shining, fair hair. Dressed in a
flowing azure gown, tied close to her breasts with crimson ribbon, she sashayed across the floor to Lachlan,
twining her arms around his neck. "So ye wish to be
rìgh," she said in a lilting voice. "If ye swear I shall be
your banrìgh, I shall let ye go free. See, I am bonny if
I wish. I can be anything ye want. I shall be your banrìgh
and rule with ye."

The corrigan pressed her firm, young body against Lachlan and drew his head down to hers. Iseult heard them kiss.
Pain shot through her, shocking her with its intensity.
She could feel Lachlan pressing back against the pole,
his tightly bound arms quivering. She closed her eyes.

In a rather hoarse voice, Lachlan said, "I canna. I be
sorry, but I canna marry ye or make ye my banrìgh. I
would be lying to ye if I said I could."

"Am I no' bonny enough for ye?" the corrigan
mocked. She kissed him again, hard and passionately.
Iseult could feel her rucking up his kilt so she could
fondle him, and anger sprang through her. She longed
for her hands to be free so she could thrash this pert
beauty and her hobgoblin servants and win them both
free.

Lachlan managed to free his mouth. "It be no use,"
he said, his voice thick and husky. "I canna love ye or
marry ye. I will do anything else I can for ye, but that
I canna do."

"Why no'?" she asked, surprising Iseult with the mildness of her voice.

"My brother was ensorcelled into marriage," Lachlan
said harshly. "He was charmed into an unnatural love,
and so into evil. I shall no' be so bewitched."

In a sudden rage, the corrigan slapped him hard across
the mouth. "Ye understand I shall kill ye? Ye both
shall die!"

Iseult felt Lachlan's fingers grip hers and press the
dagger into them. She began to saw desperately at the
ropes, her hands concealed by Lachlan's wings.

"Ye do no' need to seduce me to gain my help," Lach-

lan said, and his voice was that of a rìgh, full of power
and determination. "I am sworn to help and protect the
people o' Eileanan. If ye let us go, I swear to tell no
one ye are here. Then, when I am rìgh, I shall send ye
your ransom, whatever ye wish for. Gold, jewels . . ."

She stamped her foot. "It is no' gold I wish for," she
hissed. "Why do ye no' succumb to me? Always I have
been able to sway men with my beauty . . . I do no'
understand."

Lachlan said bitterly, "Indeed ye do no' understand.
Beauty is no' the way to win my heart. Maya was bonny
indeed, and her heart was full o' treachery and falseness.
Every beautiful woman I have ever known has betrayed
me. It is true what the Tìrsoilleiran priests say: beauty
hides corruptness, deceit."

For a moment there was silence. Feeling the ropes
unravelling, Iseult risked twisting her head round so she
could see. The hobgoblins were crouched at the corrigan's feet, and she was standing, her downcast face
thoughtful. Then suddenly a shimmer ran over her, and
to Iseult's shock, she saw herself standing where a moment before there had been a fair beauty.

Dressed in grubby breeches and a white shirt, the corrigan now had a head of red-gold curls, bright blue eyes
and a warm skin liberally splattered with freckles. She
heard Lachlan give a little gasp, and then the corrigan
was pressing herself against him again, kissing him and
stroking his muscular arms.

"See, I can be anyone ye want," she murmured with
Iseult's voice. "Ye want this lassie, I shall be this lassie
for ye."

Again Lachlan shook his head, and his wings shifted
restlessly against the ropes. "Ye may look like her," he
said gently, "but ye can never be her."

At that moment, the ropes at last parted and Iseult
almost fell to her knees with the release of the pressure
on her arms. Lachlan staggered forward; then, realizing
they were free, tried to grasp the corrigan. Immediately,
she changed herself to a mouse and scuttled across the

floor. The hobgoblins all sprang forward, seizing Lachlan who was still unsteady on his feet.

Quick as a flash Iseult dived forward and caught the mouse by the tail. The mouse turned to a sand scorpion instantaneously, but Iseult hung on grimly, not afraid that the poisonous tip would strike her. She could feel that she held a knobbly foot, even though Lachlan was screaming at her to let the sand scorpion go. "It'll kill ye if it stings ye," he cried desperately. "*Leannan,* let it go!"

Although the love name stirred her, she did not let go. The sand scorpion turned into a viper, an eagle with a cruelly slashing beak, a slender, snarling shadow-hound. Cut and bruised, Iseult retained her grip as pottery smashed around them, furniture was sent flying, and the very walls of the hut shook as they crashed into them. She knew it was all an illusion and that the corrigan could only escape her if she let go. At last, exhausted, the corrigan regained her natural shape and lay slumped, her foot trapped in Iseult's iron-fisted grip.

She was small and square, her features rough cast as if chopped from stone, her body hunched with age. She had only one eye, surrounded by heavy furrows. Hair as green-gray as moss hung in straggles around her sunken ears, and lichen spread its silvery scales over her drab, leathery skin. Iseult pressed her dagger against her throat.

"Tell the hobgoblins to set Lachlan free," she ordered.

So tired she could barely raise a hand, the corrigan gestured to the hobgoblins. Their faces bewildered, they let him go.

"Lay down your weapons," Iseult said. When they did not obey, she shook the corrigan as if she was a puppet and repeated her order. At another vague gesture, the hobgoblins laid down their weapons. Iseult clambered to her feet, dragging the corrigan upright with her. "Let us take ye to meet Meghan," Iseult said. "She will be glad indeed we found ye. Do no' try any o' your tricks, or I'll kill ye, and then I'll kill the hobgoblins. Do no' think

I speak lightly. It would give me great satisfaction to sink this knife into ye."

The corrigan nodded, her hoary face rigid with fear.

Iseult nodded brusquely at Lachlan. "Lead the way, MacCuinn."

Lachlan looked at her a trifle anxiously, and obeyed. He picked up the bows and notched an arrow to his, aiming at the hobgoblins. "Come along, ye'd better come too," he said gruffly.

They followed the path back through the stand of moss-oaks in somber silence. Iseult's rage was fading quickly, but a certain desolation was creeping over her in its place. She could not forget how the corrigan had kissed and fondled Lachlan, and how it had made her feel. Though she could not have said why, it was Lachlan she was most angry with. He had kissed her only minutes before the corrigan; he had gripped her fingers in his, he had made her weak and foolish.

It took them ages to stumble through to the clearing below Tulachna Celeste, thorns strewing their path, dead branches falling on their heads, vines wrapping around their ankles. The forest did not like Iseult's drawn knife. Even the path led where it had not gone before, and only their woodcraft and sense of direction allowed them to win through.

Meghan was stirring a pot of soup on the fire when they at last blundered into the clearing. She looked up and saw the cowering hobgoblins, the rugged form of the corrigan, Iseult's knife still at her throat.

"What have ye done?" she cried. "Ye poor wee things! Iseult, let her go!"

"No' until I ken she canna trick us any more," Iseult replied grimly. "We were almost worm food, thanks to her."

Meghan came forward in a swirl of gray skirts, holding out her hands. "Och, ye poor thing. Ye're safe now. I shall no' let them hurt ye. Iseult, drop your knife!"

"Fine," Iseult replied and let the corrigan go. With a little moan, she stumbled forward and Meghan helped her to sit by the fire. "Come," she said to the hobgoblins, smiling. "Ye are safe here. Come sit here. I shall keep ye safe."

She led the three squat creatures to the fire and pressed them gently down to sit. Then she turned on Iseult and Lachlan in fury, her dark eyes blazing. "What do ye mean by threatening and hurting these poor creatures? Hobgoblins are the gentlest o' creatures, they'll no' harm a fly . . ."

"Ye should have seen them dancing round us with axes. They dinna look so gentle then!" Iseult retorted. "We barely managed to escape with our lives! As for that . . . that . . . *hag*, she tricked us and threatened us! And tried to seduce Lachlan!"

"I see," Meghan said. Unexpectedly her eyes twinkled. "Well, what were ye doing falling into the clutches o' a corrigan in the first place? I thought I told ye no' to wander off into the Veiled Forest?"

"We were just exploring," Iseult replied shamefacedly, just as Lachlan cried, "It was my fault, Meghan, I made Iseult go into the clearing."

"Indeed? How? I canna see ye forcing Iseult to do anything against her will."

"Indeed he could no'," Iseult responded, remembering how easily she had been persuaded against her better judgement, how eagerly she had returned his kisses in the corrigan's hut. She threw her dagger to the ground, where it stuck upright in the soil, quivering. Then, her face flaming, she marched out of the clearing, towards Tulachna Celeste.

She was walking so quickly her breath began to labor, and she clenched her hands into fists. Behind her she could hear Lachlan calling her, but she shut her ears to the sound. She ran through the circles of stones to the tarn at the hill's apex. There she knelt, washing her face and hands.

Lachlan hobbled through the stones. "Iseult?" he said hesitantly. He came and crouched by her side, and she looked down at her boots, feeling as awkward with him as she ever had.

"I'm sorry," he said at last.

"What for?" she said belligerently.

"I did no' want her to . . . ye ken what," he said haltingly. "I did no' know that was what she was going to do."

"Ye did no' fight very hard." Even to her own ears, her voice sounded petty.

"For Eà's sake, Iseult, I was tied to a pole. What was I meant to do?"

"I do no' ken. Bite her?"

Lachlan swore and lurched upright. She ducked her head, digging at the turf with the toe of her boot. He began several times to say something, then muttered, "What's the use?" and stumped away.

"Gods!" Iseult swore, then flung herself face down on the flowery grass. She lay there for a long time, her thoughts going around and around in circles. At last she sat up and washed her face again, and told herself sternly to stop behaving like a silly lass. She and Lachlan had both thought their death was near. It was natural to have turned to each other. It did not mean that she loved Lachlan, or that he loved her. It just meant they had been afraid of death.

Their destinies lay apart, she reminded herself yet again. He was to be the Rìgh of Eileanan, his life given in service to his people. She was the heir to the Firemaker, her life bound to the Prides. She could not ask him to give up the crown and come with her to the snowy heights, and she would not betray her great-grandmother.

Wondering why her clear and rational thinking only made her feel worse, Iseult got to her feet. It was only then that she realized Meghan was sitting behind her, knitting industriously. "Feeling better?" the old witch asked.

"No' really," Iseult admitted.

"Sann and the hobgoblins are going to stay and share

our May Day feast," Meghan said, folding up her knitting. Iseult scowled. The sorceress smiled and said, "Ye must no' be angry that the corrigan tried to use her powers to win Lachlan over. It is the only power she has. In these dark times we all use what we can to save and protect ourselves. Besides, Lachlan did not succumb, did he? It's a rare man that can withstand a corrigan's allure."

"He kissed her," Iseult cried. "He kissed her for ages!"

Meghan smiled and gave a little shrug. "He is but a man," she answered. "Besides, what do ye expect? The lad's been eating his heart out over ye for weeks, and all ye do is argue with him or fob him off."

"Oh, he has no'!" Iseult refuted this absolutely. "He's the one that argues with me! Or gets all quiet and sulky."

"Indeed, he is no' practiced in the art o' love," Meghan replied. "And I ken he is quick to take offense, and stubborn with it. But then, so are ye, my dear. Two more obstinate bairns I've never known, even worse than my Isabeau, and she was stubborn indeed." Iseult said nothing. Meghan continued, "Give the lad a chance, Iseult. He has been suspicious o' women since Maya first cast her spell on Jaspar, and her ensorcelment o' him only made things worse. Then he has been full o' black rage and despair so long, I fear he has forgotten the more tender emotions . . ."

Iseult made an impatient gesture, immediately stilled. She said nothing as they walked down the slope of the hill. The corrigan was sitting by the fire, stirring Meghan's cauldron. "Better make sure she has no' dropped toadstools into the soup," Iseult said and left Meghan's side abruptly.

By the time Iseult had worked out her temper by gathering a great pile of firewood, she was a little ashamed of herself and sorry she had shown her emotions so clearly. Dragging the massive bundle of firewood behind her, she made her way back to the clearing. Just as she stumped out of the trees, so did Lachlan, on the other side of the shady dell. He was dragging enough firewood to last them a month. Neither was able to help laughing.

"Well, it's a grand bonfire we'll be having ourselves tonight!" Meghan said. "Ye're both good bairns. Come, we'll decorate the clearing and make ourselves a flowery bower for the celebration o' May Day."

Their outburst of involuntary laughter had helped clear the air a little. Both went to wash in the stream, Lachlan stripping to his kilt to better douse his head and arms. Kneeling by his side on the bank, Iseult muttered a gruff apology. She could not look at him with his bare skin all dappled with sunset light. Instead she concentrated on the water veiling her fingers with ripples. He touched her arm. "I'm sorry for making such a mess o' things."

She looked up, straight into his golden eyes. Her heart jumped. She could not look away. Immediately he flushed and glanced away, splashing his face with water. Iseult was unable to speak. After a moment, she leant and placed her mouth on his bare shoulder. She felt all his muscles tense convulsively. His hand gripped her wrist and she looked up into his eyes again. For a moment they stared at each other. There was a clatter of dishes behind them as Meghan moved about the fire. His mouth twisted in a way she knew well, and he moved away.

Iseult washed herself thoughtfully, ducking her head under the water. When she clambered out, groping for her shirt, her fingers closed instead upon silk. She tossed her wet curls out of her eyes and saw Cloudshadow sitting under the tree, holding out a small square of material for her. She took it, and yard after yard of gossamer material billowed out. It was one of the gowns the Celestines wore, woven in one piece from the silk of the weaverworm. Pale as primroses, the gown fitted her perfectly and suited her fiery coloring particularly well. Meghan smiled at the sight of her, and Iseult noticed the flush that darkened Lachlan's cheek, although he turned his face away after one quick, searching glance.

"Do ye remember all I told ye about May Day?" the sorceress asked.

Not sure she remembered anything but Lachlan's gaze, Lachlan's touch, Iseult shook her flower-crowned head.

"It is a very ancient custom, brought over from the Other World by the First Coven," Meghan said. "It's a celebration o' birth, fertility and the blossoming o' all life; a celebration o' Eà as the mother, dressed in her green mantle, bringing life to the field and the womb."

"Why are the Celestines no' singing tonight?" Iseult asked quickly. "We are staying here in the clearing, are we no', rather than going up the hill? Do they no' celebrate May Day?"

"Beltane is a rite o' the Coven," Meghan replied. "The Celestines have their own beliefs, based on the movement o' the sun and stars. They celebrate the equinoxes and solstices, but no' the harvest festivals. They have never cultivated the soil, and so do no' feel a need to goodwish the crops. Beltane, Lammas, Candlemas and Samhain are all change o' season celebrations that have little meaning for the Celestines. They come tonight merely to be with us and share in our feast."

The old witch sent Lachlan off into the forest to find an oak sapling to make the maypole with, then set Iseult to weaving garlands to hang from tree to tree. It had been an exhausting and confusing day and Iseult was content to sit on the ground, plaiting flowers and twigs together. She was unaccountably touched when the bright-eyed donbeag came and curled up on her lap.

Lachlan returned with a slim, tall sapling which they decorated lavishly with ribbons and flowers. The sun had dipped below the trees by now, shadows stretching across the clearing. They knew the Beltane bonfire would be lit at moonrise, and so they hurried to finish hanging the lanterns and strings of flowers, Iseult gently setting the sleeping donbeag down on Meghan's blankets.

The May Day feast was a great success. All the Celestines from the Veiled Forest came, greeting the corrigan with grave pleasure. Sann had brought some of her friends to meet Meghan—the rocky gullies along the ridge had attracted many corrigans. Hobgoblins ran everywhere, shrieking with excitement, their huge flat feet making a slapping sound on the turf. Two cluricauns bounded in from the forest, attracted by the sound of laughter and the smell of food. Nisses darted through the air like waltzing flowers, smaller than Iseult's hand but making more noise than any of the other guests put together.

Meghan insisted that they perform all the Beltane rites, despite their audience of laughing faeries. Lachlan, as the only male present, was made the Green Man, and there was much laughter and teasing as Iseult adorned him with leaves. She was then crowned May Queen, being, as Meghan said, the youngest and prettiest there.

In the flickering firelight, the goldensloe wine warming her blood, Iseult found her eyes continually drawn back to Lachlan's dark, beautiful face. Although there was tension between them, it was not the cold silence of before; rather, an awareness and a questioning. They found it hard to meet each other's eyes, yet were always finding their eyes glancing together. Iseult had to fight a desire to lean toward him, for it seemed he had an aura as intoxicating to her as the wine.

Meghan clapped her hands and bade them all take their places around the maypole. For once Lachlan was the first to obey her, holding out his hand to Iseult. Not without shyness she took it, feeling again how small her fingers felt in his. The cluricauns played their wooden flutes, the hobgoblins pounded little drums, and Lachlan sang a merry country tune that had been danced in Eileanan for centuries.

In the flickering light of the fire, scented smoke swirling up to the stars, Iseult's blood buzzed and sang. Once she would have felt ridiculous dancing around a maypole with a wreath of flowers on her head, but after almost three months in Meghan's company, it felt as natural as breathing.

Once the maypole was wrapped in the green and white and pale gold ribbons, they danced on under the canopy of leaves. Meghan held the hands of a hobgoblin and swung him off his feet, to his great delight. Sann danced with another, then took Lachlan's hands provocatively, dancing as close to him as she could get, her figure blurring into the most beautiful of human shapes. Iseult had no time to be jealous, for Lachlan swung the corrigan away with a smile and grasped Iseult's hands, drawing her into the curve of his arm. He sang as they danced, a wistful, lilting love song, the sound of his voice as always stirring profound emotions in Iseult. She knew he was weaving magic into his song, his black eyes fixed intently on hers. It was a call, a command, a plea, a melancholy longing. She devoured his dark, aquiline features with her eyes, feeling her head swim with fire, aware of no one else. They could have been dancing alone.

At last the dance whirled apart. Lachlan seized her hand, tugging it slightly so that she ducked her head and followed him. As they ran from the clearing, Meghan collapsed by the fire, humming happily with the Celestines and the corrigans, Gitâ curling up on her lap.

As soon as the light of the fire was hidden behind the great bulk of the moss-oaks, Lachlan pulled Iseult to him and kissed her. The warm, breathing darkness of the forest was all around them. His mouth was at her throat, her hands amongst the feathers of his wings. Iseult sank into sensation, amazed at how soft his skin was, how warm and sweet his mouth, tasting of sunshine like goldensloe wine.

They slid to the ground, his wings wrapping her around with silken strokes. Muttering broken words of love, his hand caressed the curve of her knee. His weight pressed her into the ground, his hand sliding up her thigh. Suddenly he leant back, trying to see her face in the shadowy moonlight. Iseult gripped his hand, and he pressed his mouth to her throat. She raised his face and kissed him. His breath caught, and he pressed against her again, mouth hungry.

She woke in the gray dawn, shivering slightly in her nakedness, and saw Lachlan was awake, watching her. He cupped his wing around her, and she shifted closer to his side. At the brush of her naked skin, he bent his head and kissed her, and they made love again, tenderly this time.

Hand in hand they made their way back to the clearing, dressed by now, their bare feet leaving a dark trail in the dew. Meghan was sitting by the fire, wilting flowers scattered everywhere about her. Their footsteps faltered a little, and they smiled self-consciously, unable to meet her eyes.

"So, my bairns," Meghan said, rather sternly. "They say Beltane is a night for loving. I hope it were true passion and no' just my goldensloe wine."

They looked at each other and smiled. Iseult's bare legs were badly scratched from Lachlan's claws, and she examined them ruefully. "I mean it," Meghan said, with both trouble and gladness in her tone. "Ye have changed your destinies this night, do ye understand? Indeed the whole land's destiny. Ye have made a choice that shall transform all our lives."

They glanced at each other, troubled. "And ye wove enchantments through your song, Lachlan. It was wrong o' ye. Ye should never spin such a compulsion."

"I knew too, Meghan," Iseult said softly. "Ye think I could no' have resisted him if I wanted? It was no' a compulsion, more o' a way to . . . communicate. I knew what it was that I was doing."

At that Lachlan gripped her fingers tight. "I did no' mean to ensorcel her," he said abruptly. "I just wanted to . . ." He paused, growing red.

"Aye, ye still do no' know what magic there is in your voice or how to use it," Meghan said. "I wish ye had managed to learn more from Enit. She knows full well the pitfalls o' the songs o' enchantment. Still, at least ye are coming into the use o' it, and cannily, it seems. Och, my bairns! I canna tell ye how glad I am, or how troubled. What a babe ye shall have! Conceived at Beltane, born at Hogmanay with the birth o' the new year! Indeed, a new thread has been strung."

Iseult could only stare at her in dismay.

SPAWN OF MESMERDEAN

T he waters of the Murkmyre lay still, reflecting the cloudy sky, the angular fretwork of rushes and cat-tails, and the graceful shape of a floating swan. The only sound was the rustle of the wind through the rushes.

On the shallow edges of the loch, where a few tree skeletons lifted bare branches to the sky, a long neck-lace of translucent eggs floated amongst the rushes. As the swan spread its crimson-tipped wings and took to the sky, the glistening eggs began to bulge and shudder. Slowly the fragile gelatinous barrier broke, and small, black creatures slithered out into the mud. They had multijointed bodies encased in soft shells, six hooked legs, and their two small antenna were still pliant and slimy with the fluid of their egg cases. Although they paid no attention to each other, each shared a linked consciousness so that their bright clusters of eyes saw not only what was before them, but what each and every one of its egg-brothers saw. Quivering with hunger they crept into the mire, searching for any small insect or fish that they could grasp in their claws and slowly and delicately devour.

Deep in the marshes that stretched on either side of

the loch, a brood of Mesmerdean knew the instant the egg cases broke. Clinging to the branches of massive water-oaks, their silvery wings held stiffly on either side of their body, they rubbed their claws together in satisfaction so a low multitonal humming filled the air. Most were young still, their bodies hard beneath the enveloping gray robes, their eyes iridescent green. Their humming swelled and was joined by a deeper, more resonant tone. From the tangle of trees to the south darted their elder, his long abdomen quivering as he flew in swift, abrupt movements which the eye would find hard to follow. All the Mesmerdean held in their mind's eye the face and shape and smell and emotional aura of Meghan of the Beasts, the witch who had caused their egg-brother's death. Each and every one of the newly hatched Mesmerdean nymphs absorbed into their communal minds that shape and pattern, and with it the desire for revenge. Soon the mourning would be over. Once the nymphets had grown and undertaken their first metamorphosis, the fully grown nymphs would leave the Murkmyre and go in search of she who had tricked and killed their egg-brother. If they should die, their egg-brothers would follow and finish the chase, each successive generation inheriting the hunger for retribution.

Mesmerdean never forgot.

Rubbing their claws together in anticipation, their song of hate caused a flock of snow geese to rise from the trees and circle, trumpeting in alarm. In her tower, built on an island in the center of the Murkmyre, Margrit NicFóghnan looked up from her study of an ancient spell book, and frowned with pleasure.

THE LOOM IS
STRUNG

SUMMER

ISABEAU THE MAIMED

Isabeau lay listlessly against her pillows, staring out of
her narrow window at the wall opposite. She cradled
her left hand close to her breast in a protective gesture. She felt no pain there now, only a dull ache that
came and went and a chill in the fingers that were no
longer there.

The room she lay in was hung with shabby tapestries,
with a thick rug on the floor and a fire burning on the
hearth. It seemed almost sinful to Isabeau, who had lived
all her life in a house built in the trunk of a tree. At
another time she would have revelled in it. Now, however, a deep blackness lay on her spirits, that she could
not shrug off, not at all the command of Latifa the Cook,
nor the teasing and laughter of the flock of maids she
commanded.

All Isabeau could think about was how close she had
come to delivering Meghan's precious talisman into the
Awl's hands. Her guardian had trusted her to carry the talisman from their secret mountain hideaway to the Righ's
palace, yet she had made blunder after blunder. First
she had rescued the surly hunchback from imprisonment
by the Awl, then she had stolen the Grand-Seeker's own
stallion and ridden it into the largest town in the high-

lands—a town where the Grand-Seeker Glynelda ruled. There she had been tortured and condemned to death. Her dreams were haunted by the Grand-Questioner's gaunt face and by the dark, drowning waters of Tuathan Loch where she had been thrown to the loch-serpent. The maimed hand with its missing fingers reproached her, and so she cradled it close to her body and resisted all attempts to bring her into the life of the royal court at Rhyssmadill. The mysterious talisman, hidden in its muffling bag of nyx-hair, had been taken by Latifa, Meghan's contact in the palace, and Isabeau had not seen it or heard of it since, though she felt its absence as a constant ache and desire.

There was a sharp knock on the door. Without waiting for an answer—which was just as well since Isabeau gave none—it opened and a middle-aged woman came bustling in, carrying a bowl wreathed in steam. She was very short and very fat and had a face like a toasted muffin, with two little raisin eyes and a little cherry mouth and a nose that was a mere bump. She came in talking and kept talking the entire time she was there.

"So now, still lying there and staring at the wall and feeling sorry for ourself, are we? Feeling sorry never did anybody any guid, as far as I ken. It's time ye were up and about, for idleness is something I've never been able to bear, and I see no reason to be starting now. Idleness causes talk, especially idleness favored by me, and talk is something we canna be encouraging, for there's far too much o' it already. Seems ye've become a romantic figure to the lamb-brained lassies here, and that I canna be allowing. The only way to stop them wondering about ye is to have ye down there, living and working among them. Besides, I canna be teaching ye anything with ye lying up here like a little misery. So I want ye to eat your broth, then get up and put on the dress I found for ye and come on down to the kitchen. I'll send one of those silly lasses along to show ye the way, so be sure and be ready for her when she comes for I have no' got time to be wasting, like ye seem to."

Isabeau said nothing, turning her face to the wall and cradling her hand closer to her body. As Latifa spoke, she placed the bowl of soup on the side table, took a gray dress from the cupboard, shook it out and laid it over the chair. She cast Isabeau a shrewd glance from her tiny eyes, then continued, seemingly without breath, "Fretting is no' going to do ye any guid, my dear, and much longer in that bed and you'll lose the use o' your legs. No slug-a-beds allowed in my service! So if ye want any more supper, ye'll have to be coming down and getting it. *I* haven't time to be bringing ye trays and neither do any o' my lasses."

The door shut smartly behind her, and Isabeau pressed her cheek deeper into the pillow. *If only they would leave me alone.* She was conscious again of a strange ringing in her head and thought she could hear faint cross-currents of talk. But that was impossible for the stone walls were so thick no sound could penetrate them.

Again the frightening feeling that she was going mad slid through Isabeau's mind. She clenched the fingers of her one good hand, shutting her mind resolutely. That fear had been with her often since she had arrived in Rhyssmadill. Waking from her fever in a state of strange clarity, she had thought she could hear the thoughts of all around her. Feeling as frail as a bellfruit seed, she had lain back on her pillows and stared straight into the deepest recesses of the minds of those who tended her— their secret longings and jealousies, their petty spites and preoccupations.

Later, the sense of clarity wore off and she had thought the feeling merely the effects of fever. It returned, though, in undulations of sound and meaning that washed over her, so that she had trouble concentrating on what others were saying. Sometimes it was like two layers of conversation at once—what the person was saying and what they were thinking.

These brief moments of clarity were usually followed by a crippling migraine in which words, images, ideas and memories, both hers and not hers, tumbled through her mind in whirls of dizzying pain. Then all Isabeau could do was lie and try to remember silence—the silence of the secret valley where she had grown up; the silence of the ruined Tower where she had met the Celestine. At these times she pressed her fingers to her forehead, trying to ease the ache and tumult that seemed centered between her brows.

There was a tap on the door and one of the maids put her head around the edge, her eyes bright with curiosity. A pretty, apple-cheeked blonde called Sukey, she had tied the ribbons of her linen cap under one ear, giving her a jaunty look.

"Obh obh!" she cried. "Wha' do ye be doing still in bed! Is your head aching still? Mistress Latifa can give ye some o' her posset for it, but I wouldna make her come back up here again! Do ye need some help in dressing, with your puir, sore hand? The stable-lads say ye must be a right fool to lose your hand rescuing a silly coney, but me and the lassies think ye be very brave . . ."

Talking as constantly as Latifa and with as little apparent need for breath, the maid pulled back the bedclothes, swung Isabeau's legs out and pulled her into a sitting position. She washed Isabeau's face roughly with a damp cloth and undid the buttons of her nightgown. Isabeau seemed to be as powerless to obey. She looked down at her body as the maid washed her, realizing with a shock just how thin she had become. Her legs were little blue sticks and all her ribs stuck out over a sunken stomach. As clearly as if the maid had spoken, she heard her think, *Puir feeble thing, look at her, no more flesh on her than a string o' auld bones . . .*

Within a few minutes Isabeau was up and dressed in the same outfit as the maid—a gray bodice with a wide skirt over voluminous petticoats, a white pinafore tied over the top. Used as she was to breeches, Isabeau felt like a swaddled babe. Jerking her chin round with one rough, chapped hand, Sukey swiftly tied the white cap on over her shorn head and under her chin. Isabeau put her hand up to her head and felt another pang of grief.

Before she came to Rhyssmadill, her hair had been a mass of fiery ringlets that fell all the way to her feet. However, Latifa had cut it all off in an attempt to bring down her fever. Without the weight and mass of her hair, Isabeau's fever had broken, but she found it hard to forgive the old cook for the loss of her only real beauty. She looked at herself in the mirror and could not see herself in the thin, hunched figure with the pinched face and white cap.

Still talking, Sukey led the way down stone corridors and stairs until they reached the kitchen, which was built in a long low wing away from the main structure of the palace. The massive kitchen took up most of the first floor, surrounded by storerooms, larders, the buttery, the brewery, the curing room, the wine cellar, the cheese room, the herbary where flowers and seeds were hung to dry, and the ice room where jellies and sherbets were made and fresh meat hung. Scullery maids hurried through the corridors, carrying piles of clean linen or steaming pails, and two men staggered past with a great barrel of ale.

Sukey led Isabeau inexorably to the kitchen, which was filled with people tending smoke-blackened ovens, stirring steaming cauldrons on the fires, washing dirty dishes or slicing up vegetables. One was energetically plucking a bhanais bird, the long iridescent tail-feathers stretching across the table.

Isabeau's legs were shaking and she was glad to sink down onto a stool in a corner. She was aware of curious glances from the servants working near her, but all were too busy to pay her much heed, and soon their thoughts returned to the task in hand. Her cheeks stung red at some of their thoughts, but they were no worse than what she had thought herself at the sight of her reflection in the mirror. She leaned her head against the warm stone and closed her eyes.

"Och, guid, ye're up and about." Latifa stopped by

Isabeau's corner. "Come, ye can stir a sauce for me and watch to make sure the spit-dogs run smoothly."

Isabeau had never seen anything like the little dogs which trotted incessantly forward in their wooden wheels, turning the great roasts on their spits. She was unused to dogs, having seen only the rare shaggy sheep-dog in the mountain villages. These two dogs were not much bigger than cats, with flop ears and motley-colored hides. One had a wiry coat, all brindled, with a black patch over one eye, giving him rather a rakish look. The other was mainly white, with silky ears, and short, spotted legs. Latifa passed her a thin, supple cane and told her she was to whip them if they slowed or stopped to scratch or salivated too eagerly at the ever-present smell of meat. Isabeau took it reluctantly and tucked it out of sight as she approached them. Heads hanging, they trotted forward, never varying their pace; their thin flanks were cut and scarred all over.

As Isabeau came near, the little dogs cowered away from her, and she put the switch down. "What are your names, laddies?" she whispered. They cast a glance at her out of dim eyes, and she patted them gently on the head, anger mixing with her pity when they cringed away. Conscious of the other servants watching her, she took up her place on the stool and slowly stirred the creamy sauce in a large, flat pan tucked on the side of the massive fireplace. The heat and the smell of the cooking meat sickened her—it was all she could do not to retch—but Latifa was right, Isabeau had already drawn too much attention to herself with her delirium and her crippled hand. Isabeau was meant to be masque-rading as a simple country lass, sent to the city by her grandmother to take up service. The sooner she started acting the part the better. Still, as she stirred and the dogs ran on, heads hanging, a tear slipped out from under her lashes and trickled down her cheek.

The smell of burning penetrated her dazed senses just seconds before a sharp slap across her ear brought her back to earth with a snap. Tears stinging her eyes, Isabeau jerked upright to see one of the lackeys standing over her. Beside her, the sauce had caught, and one side of the great boar was smoking, the black-patched terrier having taken the opportunity for a vigorous scratch.

"Ye simple-minded fool!" the lackey shouted. He went to strike her again, though Isabeau escaped the blow, tumbling off her stool and to her feet in ungainly haste. The other servants gathered around, exclaiming and commiserating, and one of the maids went running to fetch Latifa. Isabeau slipped away, holding her hand to her cheek, the other clenched to her breast. As she escaped out through the massive arch and into the herb garden, she heard the dogs whimpering as the lackey whipped them.

The long, walled garden was empty of all but a hunched old man tending the beehives lined against the far wall. Isabeau was able to hurry unseen to the shelter of the apple trees espaliered along the wall's length, all budding with new leaves. She crouched on the muddy path behind the hedge of rosemary, her hand to her burning cheek, her head pressed against her knees. They were trembling. After a while, the sun on her back, the contented hum of bees in the flowers, the familiar and comforting smell of earth and crushed herbs, all combined to soothe her. She wiped her wet cheeks on her apron and sat back against the trunk of an apple tree.

"Ye've got your skirt all muddied, lassie. Latifa will no' be liking that at all."

Startled, Isabeau looked up and saw the bow-legged old man leaning on his spade in the herb bed a few squares away. Then she looked down and saw that he was right. Her gray skirt, so fresh and clean only an hour ago, was now bedraggled with mud.

"Ye've got mud on your cheek too, lassie." Involuntarily, tears sprang up in Isabeau's eyes again. "Now, now, lassie, no need to be greetin'. Come and wash your face, and I'll lend ye my clothes brush."

He led her through the garden and out through the arched gateway into a wide paved courtyard. She had

dim memories of coming this way when she had first
arrived at Rhyssmadill, but the fever had had her in its
claws and all she could remember was the endless stone
walkway she had had to traverse to get to the kitchen
from the bridge over the chasm.

From the left came the sounds of the stables and ken-
nels—laughter, shouts, the whinnying of horses, the
sound of a blacksmith hammering steel, the clang of
buckets, the barking of hounds. Just as Isabeau shrank
back, the old man took her hand kindly. They passed
through a narrow doorway into a little suite of rooms,
quiet and dim. He had once been head groom at Lucescere, he explained to Isabeau. He had come to Rhyssmadill with the young Rìgh, and had been given this wee
corner of the stables to himself, so he could potter
around as he pleased.

A small walled enclosure lay beyond. There another
garden flourished, though in old tubs and buckets rather
than beautifully set out in squares and triangles like the
kitchen garden. Although herbs were grown here too,
the tubs mostly held riotous growths of wild flowers.
Isabeau gave a tremulous smile, for here were many of
the flowers she knew, the small, fragrant blossoms of the
meadows and forests.

"This is my secret place," the old man said rather
apologetically. "I miss the highlands, and so have taken
to buying roots and seeds from the pedlars when they
pass. My name is Riordan Bowlegs, while I can see ye
canna be anything but the Red."

"I be named Isabeau," she replied shyly.

In the courtyard was a pump, and he worked it for
her so she could wash her face and hands. She unhooked
the skirt so she could more easily brush off the mud,
sitting on a barrel in her underdress and bodice and
pulling off her cap so her shorn head could feel the sun.
She had tucked her crippled hand under her apron all
the way from the garden; now she carefully concealed it
by her side, hoping Riordan Bowlegs had not noticed.

If he had, he ignored it, bringing her a cup of water to drink. It was warm and tasted of earth.

"There be a natural spring o' water under the rock," the old man explained. "That be another reason why the MacCuinn moved his court here. They pump up the water from the very depths o' the rock. In the royal suite ye have the choice o' seawater or fresh, they say, and ye can even have it warmed for ye, which is too uncanny close to witchcraft for my liking."

"Why would ye want to bathe in seawater?"

"Bloody guid question, lassie, I often ask it myself. They say it be healthful, and an aid to beauty, and indeed ye might believe it, with the Banrìgh so bonny and fresh still. Though if so, our puir MacCuinn should be bathing in it, for he grows thinner and more pinched-looking each day. They say he will no' though, having a healthy misliking for the sea, as a MacCuinn should."

Isabeau sipped her water thoughtfully, filing away this odd fact for future reference as the old man chattered on. "There was an auld castle built here, o' course, before the MacCuinn brought the court down from Lucescere. It was the MacBrann's castle, built in the days when he commanded the harbor. It's too guid a position, here on this great rock, and surrounded on all sides by the firth, for there no' to have been a stronghold here. With its own water supply and escape routes out the sea-caves, 'tis near as strong as Lucescere. Indeed, if it had no' been, I doubt many o' us auld ones would have come with him from the Shining Waters, for Rhyssmadill is far too close to the sea for our liking. I canna see how the folks o' Dùn Gorm can stand it, living down there on the bare shores o' the firth. Ye canna call those puny walls much protection from the Fairgean."

Riordan Bowlegs paused in his slow weeding and pruning to say thoughtfully, "I mean no disrespect, Red, but had ye no' better be hurrying back to the kitchen? I have known Latifa for a long time syne, and she does no' like to be kept waiting."

Isabeau jumped to her feet in a panic, having com-

pletely forgotten her mishap in the kitchen. "Thank ye,"
she gasped, hooking up her skirt. "I'm sorry to have
bothered ye."

"No, bother, lass. Glad to have been o' service. Here,
do no' forget your cap."

Isabeau took her muslin bonnet gratefully and tied it
on again in haste. Riordan said softly, "Some advice,
Red. Latifa does no' like to have lassies under her that
do no' own up to misdoing. Face her square, and she'll
no' be too hard on ye."

Isabeau found this advice sound, and although she endured a tongue-lashing, it was pithy and to the point.
Her punishment was then to be tucked up in bed with
a hot herb posset and some final admonishments, and
allowed to sleep. For the first time in weeks Isabeau
slept soundly and without nightmares, dreaming instead
of a golden-eyed man who wrapped her in the soft darkness of love.

A week after Beltane, Iseult and Lachlan came hand in
hand through the moss-oaks to find Meghan bowed over,
her face hidden in her hands. The discarded crystal ball
lay on the grass, pearly white. Gitâ was standing on his
hind legs, his paws resting on Meghan's hands, chittering
in distress. Iseult's pace quickened. "Auld mother,
what's wrong?"

Meghan's sunken cheeks glistened with tears. "Isabeau . . ."

Iseult's eyes flew up to meet Lachlan's. "What's happened to Isabeau?"

"She's safe, she and the Key . . . all safe." She wiped
her cheeks impatiently. "I'm sorry. I am just so relieved
that Isabeau is safe. She's been sick indeed with the
fever—Latifa was feared she would no' pull through, but
she is young and strong, and the fever has broken." She
took a few deep breaths. "I knew she would succeed.
The Key is safe! We have all three parts now, and all
we need do is join them again. Somehow I must get back
the two parts she holds, but how?"

"Why is this Key so important, auld mother?" Iseult got up the courage to ask the question that had been on her mind a long time.

Meghan looked a little surprised. "Remember I told ye how I had used the Key to hide something I did no' want Maya to get her hands on? That was the Lodestar, a magical sphere that responds only to the hand o' a MacCuinn. I hid it at the Pool o' Two Moons and locked away the maze that surrounds the pool with the Key. I then broke it and gave one-third to Ishbel and one-third to Latifa. I never imagined it would take me sixteen years to find Ishbel again! For all that time the Lodestar has been lying there in cold and darkness, its powers slowly ebbing away. Until we join the Key, we canna rescue it or use its powers to aid us in our struggle."

She sat silently, staring into the ashes. "There is more news, and it is no' good. What the dragons told me about the spell cast on the night o' the comet is true. It *was* a Spell o' Begetting, for Latifa tells me the Banrìgh is with babe . . ."

Lachlan went white. "The cursehag is pregnant? I canna believe it! Sixteen years she's been as barren as a mule! We had banked on there being no heir—I had thought I was the only one. What does this forebode?"

"A new thread has been strung," Meghan replied. "What it means for us, only time will tell."

"She means to be Regent and rule in the babe's name!" he cried. "We have to stop her. A Fairge babe to inherit the throne o' Eilaenan—I will no' allow it!"

"So ye have information I do no'?" Meghan asked sarcastically. "Ye ken the ancestry of Maya the Unknown, when for sixteen years all our inquiries have come to naught?"

Lachlan's cheek darkened, but he continued stubbornly. "If she is no' a Fairge, then I am no' a MacCuinn! Ye have heard her sing, have ye no'? Ye have heard the stories o' how she sneaks out at night to ride down to the blaygird sea? No Islander would swim in the sea for pleasure, or even walk on its shores, in sight o' the waves. She must be a Fairge! She ensorcelled her way into Jaspar's heart using her foul Fairge magic—it is all part o' a plot to overthrow the MacCuinns and win back the coast for the Fairgean . . . ."

"Happen that is true, and Maya is a Fairge. How does she stay so long in her land shape? Ye ken the Fairgean die if away from salt water too long. How can she possibly manage with just the occasional swim? And though her beauty is unusual, and her eyes as pale as any Fairge, she looks as human as any lass I've ever seen. Even in their land shape, the Fairgean do no' look human."

"It is her magic . . . ."

"Perhaps. If so, it is a powerful Talent, to hold an illusion for sixteen years, and under such scrutiny. We ken she is a powerful sorceress, for she transformed ye into a blackbird. And she can charm crowds o' people at a time, and strong witches among them. Yet I have never heard compulsion was a Skill o' the Fairgean, nor the spinning o' illusions. Just because she has thrown down the witches does no' mean she is a Fairge, Lachlan, though I have often wondered if this could be the explanation for her actions. Either way, the babe is a MacCuinn and a soul in its own right, and I do no' want its blood on your hands."

"But—"

"Nay, Lachlan, our plans remain the same. We regain the Lodestar and wait on events. Only when Jaspar has died shall I let ye raise the Lodestar, for no' even for your youthful impatience shall I let the Inheritance o' Aedan be turned by MacCuinn on MacCuinn. Jaspar may have been ensorcelled by a witch from the sea, but he is still the rightful Rìgh and your brother."

"Some brother he's turned out to be!"

"How was he to ken, Lachlan? Have pity on Jaspar, for whatever spell she has laid on him is sapping all his vitality and Enit says he shall no' last the year."

"Now she carries his babe, she has no need o' him," he said bitterly. "She will kill him as she killed Donncan and Feargus! And I am stuck here in this blaygird forest, with my nose in books like a grubby scribe's apprentice, when I should be out there, trying to save him!"

"What could ye do?" Meghan said. "Ye'd burn on the fire as an *uile-bheist*, and our last hopes with ye. No, no, my lad, this is no' the time to lose heart. We have all three parts o' the Key now and are closer than ever to releasing the Lodestar."

"Its song is growing very faint." Lachlan's voice was somber.

"I think Maya means to make sure we canna release it before its song dies out altogether. If Jaspar dies and names the babe heir, then Maya shall rule in truth and that foretells a dark and desperate future for us all. We must get to the Lodestar before the birth o' winter! That means we must join the Key, get into the palace of Lucescere—and remember one wing o' the palace is now the headquarters o' the Awl—rescue the Lodestar and get it into Lachlan's hands."

"Or yours," Meghan's great-nephew said. The wood witch looked grave and said nothing. "Ye can wield the Lodestar too, Meghan," Lachlan said, rather anxiously. "I ken it was ye who really drove off the Fairgean at the Battle o' the Strand."

"Jaspar's hand was on the Lodestar," Meghan said gruffly. "That is what ye must remember."

"Ye told him what to do, though, and lent him your strength."

"Lachlan, I may no' be there to lend ye my strength or my knowledge. Ye must understand that. Ye must unlock its secrets yourself. Why do ye think I have been driving ye and Iseult so hard?"

"What do ye mean? Why would ye no' be with me?"

"We do no' ken the pattern the weaver is weaving, my lad."

"What do ye fear?" Iseult could hear undercurrents in Meghan's quiet voice.

The sorceress looked at her with inscrutable black eyes. "I told ye Jorge has had dreams o' a black wolf hunting . . ."

"But what does that mean?"

Meghan sighed. "Lachlan, can ye answer her question?"

Lachlan said slowly, "A black wolf is the crest o' the MacRuraich clan. They're known for their Searching and Locating Skills."

"Well done, my lad, ye have no' forgotten all ye were taught as a bairn! Aye, I fear the Banrìgh has set the MacRuraich on my trail, and the black wolf is hard indeed to shake off once he has his nose to the spoor . . . I shall have word o' his coming, though, do no' fear."

"He shall no' find ye. I shall keep ye safe, auld mother."

"Thank ye, Iseult," the sorceress replied, with the faintest inflection of irony. "I hope indeed ye shall. But we must take all possibilities into account, always. Anything may happen between now and Samhain. Which brings me to my next point. I wish to give ye your Tests. It is no coincidence ye and Lachlan each found a moonstone, Iseult. That is always a sign ye are ready to pass your apprenticeship test. It is the tradition o' the Coven that the real lessons in witchcraft do no' begin until ye have been accepted as an apprentice. Ye have been angry that I will no' teach ye more o' the skills o' witchcraft and witchcunning but, indeed, such knowledge can be dangerous. Only when ye have passed your Tests can I be sure ye have the discipline needed, and such things are best done in the right time and the right manner.

"Midsummer's Eve is a powerful time indeed, ye canna have a better time to take your Tests. That leaves us only a few weeks to polish up your Skills and have ye ready. This past week ye have both been as distracted as any crofter's lad at your lessons. I ken ye think me a hard taskmaster and wish to spend your days lazing in the sun and making love. Indeed I am glad ye have grown to care for each other and canna deny I had hoped such would happen. But we have no' got the leisure for courting. We have only a short while for ye to learn everything ye may need as rìgh and banrìgh."

"But, auld mother—"

"Hush, Iseult, and let me finish. I think we should stay in the forest as long as we can—at least until Midsummer's Eve so Lachlan can sing the summer solstice with the Celestines and ye can jump the fire together—"

Iseult could keep silent no longer. "But Meghan, ye ken I canna be marrying Lachlan!"

Lachlan looked up swiftly, his swarthy cheek coloring. "What do ye mean?"

"I am in *geas* . . ."

"But ye lay with me—ye said ye loved me!"

"Yes, but . . ."

"Did ye no' mean what ye said?"

"Nay, I did, I just did no' realize . . ."

"But ye came with me into the forest? Did ye no' realize I meant . . . ? Did ye no' know I wanted . . . ?"

"Ye never said anything about *marrying*."

"Ye do no' wish to marry me?" His voice was incredulous.

"But, Lachlan, ye ken I am no' free to do as I wish, that my life has been given in *geas* . . ."

He scrambled to his claws, his eyes blazing yellow with anger. "It was all a lie, then, what we said to each other that night? Ye do no' care for me, is that what ye are trying to tell me?"

Iseult felt anger rise to meet his. "Nay, why will ye no' listen to me? Ye know I am heir to the Firemaker! I canna be betraying my great-grandmother's trust . . ."

"But ye could be Banrìgh o' all Eileanan!" Lachlan gripped her wrist cruelly.

"What is that to me? I know nothing about your righrean and banrìghrean, I just wanted to be with ye . . ."

"But do ye no' see, I want us to be together always! How could ye think it was just for a night or a week? Ye carry my babe—did ye no' realize I meant for us to be married?"

"The Firemaker does no' marry," Iseult said arrogantly, tugging her wrist free.

"Go then! Go back to the snows if that is what ye

want! I do no' need ye!" Lachlan turned and limped
away into the forest, his hands clenched into fists.

"Can your great-grandmother scry?" Meghan asked.
Wondering how the sorceress knew what she was thinking, Iseult shrugged. "I do no' ken," she answered, trying
not to show how upset she was. "The Khan'cobhans can
speak from one mind to another, sometimes over a fair
distance, and my great-grandmother has spoken thus to
me several times."

"Then ye should be able to reach her if ye try,"
Meghan said practically. "Your scrying skills have been
growing in leaps and bounds. She is far away, though,
and there is a range o' mountains between ye which may
muffle your voice. See if you can reach her."

The winged prionnsa did not return to the clearing
that evening. Her throat muscles unaccountably tight,
Iseult tried again and again to reach her great-grandmother but failed every time. At last she rolled herself
in her blankets and slept by the fire, for the first time
since Beltane not slipping off into the forest to be with
Lachlan.

She dreamed she was on the Spine of the World. All
she could see were whirling snowflakes; all she could
hear was the howling of timber wolves. Suddenly she
could hear the crunch of feet on the snow. She brought
fire flickering to life in her palm and held it up so she
could see. The red-gold light flowed over the black-
tipped white mane and snarling fangs of a snow lion,
lifting its muzzle to her breast. Before she could cry out,
the ferocious face tilted up further and it was her great-
grandmother, wrapped in her snow lion cloak.

"Firemaker, I have found you," Iseult breathed in the
language of the Khan'cobhans. "I have been calling and
calling you. Give me your blessing, old mother."

The face beneath the snow lion's snarling mask was
thin, high-boned and very pale. The hair had once been
auburn, but was now so intermingled with gray, only
flashes of fire remained. Slowly the Firemaker raised her
blue-veined hand and made the mark of the Gods of

White on Iseult's brow. "I heard you calling, my great-granddaughter. The restless mountains divide us, though, and I cannot speak with you across their clamor. So I have traveled the dream road to talk with you, feeling that your heart was troubled."

"Firemaker, I have a confession to make," Iseult said.

"Make me your confession and I shall judge," her great-grandmother responded.

Feeling her knees shake, for the punishment of the Firemaker was always just and always severe, Iseult said in a low voice, "I have fallen in love with a man of this land, and lain with him, Firemaker. I am carrying his child."

The Firemaker's eyes gleamed cold and blue in her pale-skinned, autocratic face. "I know this, my great-granddaughter. I dreamed of the child's coming and knew the instant it was conceived."

Iseult waited, but her great-grandmother said no more. She burst out, "What am I to do, Firemaker? I have failed you and failed my obligation as the Firemaker's heir. I have betrayed the Gods o' White." Her voice broke.

"You ask of me a question, Khan'derin. Do you offer me a story in return?"

Iseult's heart sank. She had been too long away from the Spine of the World. Reluctantly she lowered her eyes. "Yes, Firemaker, no matter the question."

The Firemaker sat ramrod straight, her hands upturned on her furs. "I shall answer your question, Khan'derin, and a foolish waste of a question it was too. This is my answer: you must choose the path that you feel and believe to be right for you, then travel that path."

"That is your answer?" Iseult cried. Her grandmother said nothing. Iseult bowed her head, knowing she had been foolish. One did not ask such questions of the Firemaker.

"Now I ask of you a question in return, Khan'derin. Will you answer in fullness and in truth?"

"Yes, Firemaker." Iseult's voice was low. She dreaded her grandmother's questions. They cut to the bone.

"Do you love this blackbird man?"

"Yes, Firemaker," Iseult replied, rather shakily. "I have told myself I must not, and shall not, but I do, I do! I want to have his child, I want to be with him, he shakes me as no one has ever shaken me before . . ." She faltered to a close, knowing her tone was too vehement to please the Firemaker. With an effort she said, "Firemaker, I want to be with him. To imagine my life without him is to see the future as an icy waste. But I must listen to you and hear your judgment. Please help me! I want to do what is right. But know this—I will not leave Lachlan easily. He has his hand around my heart."

The Firemaker took a deep breath. "I have something to tell you, Khan'derin, that perhaps I should have told you before." In the rhythmic chant of storytellers on the Spine of the World, she told again the story of how her twin sister was raised by the Pride of the Fighting Cats to be her rival even though twins were forbidden in the Khan'cohban culture, the youngest born left out in the snow to die. "One day the Old Mother said the daughters of Khan'fella would save the Prides from darkness. The Prides knew then that the child must be allowed to live, though all were afraid."

Iseult had heard this story many times before, but she knew better than to fidget or let her attention wander. Despite her anxiety, she sat still and listened as the Firemaker described her distress, many years later, when her own daughter died in childbirth, along with her baby daughter, leaving her with a mere grandson.

"I begged the gods to tell me why I had been so punished. There was no answer on the merciless wind, and my dreams were filled with omens I did not understand. I was shown the godhead must pass from daughter to daughter, and I railed against the gods that they should pass the Firemaker's powers into the hands of my sister, my enemy.

"At last my grandson left to travel into the land of

the sorcerers. Then came dreams of fire and death and evil sorceries, and I knew my grandson had been lost. Again I cursed the gods of ice and blizzards, and again was sent a dream in return. This is the story of your finding, and one I have told you many times. My heart rejoiced to find you, for I knew you were the child of my grandson. I proclaimed you heir and laughed at the Pride of the Fighting Cats, who had thought Khan'merle, daughter of Khan'dica, grand-daughter of Khan'fella must inherit."

For the first time the Firemaker's story faltered, and she looked away from her grand-daughter. The old woman took a deep breath, then resumed softly. "It was wrong of me to take the dream and twist it to my desire. I knew that the sister of your womb was still living, and that the Gods of White must have some purpose in allowing you both to live. So at the Summer Gathering I broke the silence of generations and spoke to Khan'-merle, Old Mother of the Pride of the Fighting Cats and now named heir to the Firemaker . . ."

"You've disinherited me?" Iseult was aghast.

Her great-grandmother ignored the interruption, though her face stiffened in disapproval. "The Firemaker was a gift of the White Gods to the People of the Spine of the World, in reward for their long exile. She was given to bring warmth and light to the howling night, to protect the people of the Prides from their enemies. The Firemaker is the gift of the Gods of White to *all* the People, and she must serve them in entirety."

Iseult's anger suddenly dissolved in a flood of happiness as she realized what her great-grandmother had said. She was free to follow Lachlan and bear his son as Meghan had predicted. For the moment nothing else mattered, although she knew she was still of the Firemaker's blood, and one day the Gods of White would call her to account.

Her great-grandmother softened her storyteller's stance, dropping her hands to stroke the thick white fur of her cloak. "You shall meet your sister on the first day of winter. It is then the veil between the worlds is thinnest. You have been apart; then is the time to join and be strong. You are like the petals of a rose, joined at the heart. Only together will you be whole. This I have dreamed."

Her fierce blue eyes blurred away, and her sharp-angled face. Iseult was conscious of running, as the snow-whirled darkness overtook her, then she fell through fathoms of darkness. It was with a great sense of dislocation that she woke to see dawn filtering through the leaves of the forest, and Meghan watching her, Gitâ bright-eyed on her shoulder.

"Is all well?" the sorceress asked. Iseult nodded and got to her feet. "Lachlan did no' return? I need to speak with him."

Iseult climbed the steep slope with a buoyant step and found Lachlan crouched against one of the great menhirs. His face was as fierce and wild as she had ever seen it, the eyes red-rimmed, the mouth hard and unforgiving. She knelt by his side, taking his hands in hers. He stared straight ahead, and said nothing.

"My great-grandmother has said I may choose my own path, and I told her I wanted to be with ye. I can marry ye if ye still wish me to."

He looked at her somberly. "Is that what ye wish?"

"Aye, indeed it is. I wish our paths to lie together. Do no' ye?"

He nodded and turned his hand so her fingers were gripped in his. They were trembling. "Are ye sure?" he asked. "I do no' want ye to be sorry later."

"Sorry to be with ye? I'll never be sorry for that."

He leaned his forehead against hers. "Ye must no' say these things lightly," he said. "I need to know, Iseult, I need . . ."

She kissed him, hard on the mouth, and said, "I love ye, Lachlan, I swear it. I want to be with ye, always."

He crossed his arms over her back, so hard she could not breathe or move, his wings wrapping her in darkness. "Ye must promise never to leave me, Iseult," he said, so low she could barely hear him. "Never leave me, never betray me."

"I promise," she said, and knew she had given herself in *geas* again.

Riordan Bowleg's sunny courtyard became a haven for Isabeau through the difficult weeks of early summer. He and the kitchen maid Sukey were the only ones who showed her any sympathy, the other servants impatient with her constant mistakes. She gained some satisfaction from winning over the little dogs, who were as tortured by their proximity to the roasting meat as she was, though for far different reasons. She did not once use the switch, but coaxed them to her with the beef that she surreptitiously fished out of her bowl. She knew the other servants would think her aversion to eating meat odd to say the least. At the worst, it would be seen as being proof of a witch-friend, for many scions of the Coven had abhorred the eating of animal flesh, her guardian Meghan among them. The servants at Rhyssmadill were all ardent witch-haters, and the scullery boys sickened Isabeau with their stories of witch burnings at Dùn Gorm.

She worked hard at appearing a normal country lass, talking only of sheep and crops when asked about her life. Her refusal to use the switch on the spit-dogs did cause some ill-natured teasing, but once the kitchen hands saw how eager the dogs were to please her, the attention died down.

Despite her love for horses, Isabeau avoided the stables. She disliked the impudent stable-lads, and found all the noise and activity too much to bear. Besides, the sight of the horses only reminded her of her friend, the red stallion Lasair, who had brought her from Aslinn to Rhyssmadill faithfully, and near killed himself in the attempt. She had left him running free in the forests of Ravenshaw, but she was conscious of the dangers to him so close to people. The city was filled with discontented sailors, the bored lairds went out hunting nearly every morning, and times were hard with the trade routes closed by the Fairgean.

Mobs of dissatisfied merchants and ship captains filled the great hall during the day, trying to arrange an audience with the Rìgh but being fobbed off by court officials. The winter ice had melted more than a month ago, and the spring tides had retreated, making the conditions perfect for an attempt to sail up the western coast. However, with reports of Fairgean in the seas, the ships were wary of setting out without the promise of protection.

At last the merchants succeeded in catching the Banrìgh and she agreed to send a fleet of heavily armed merchant ships to Rurach and Siantan. They would carry sacks of grain, barrels of ale and whiskey, and great blocks of salt from the Clachan salt basins, as well as finely worked knives and jewelry from the metalsmiths of Dùn Gorm. On their return journey the ships' hulls would be packed with marble, saltpetre and precious metals mined from the Sgàilean Mountains. In the meantime, many of the hungry city folk went foraging in the forest, and Isabeau fretted about both the stallion and the sacred relic the Celestine had lent her, Ahern's Saddle, which she had hidden in the woods.

It was impossible to escape the palace, however, and so Isabeau could only hope they were safe. She did not dare tell Latifa about her fears. Although the old cook looked a lot like one of her own gingerbread men, she ruled the vast staff with inflexible authority. With a large muslin cap tied over her gray curls, and a huge bunch of keys dangling from a hoop at her waist, she seemed to be everywhere at once, eyes darting, nose quivering, fingers testing for dust.

Like all of the palace servants, Latifa expressed a strong devotion to the Banrìgh, though most of them only rarely caught glimpses of her as they bustled here and there around the palace. Among some of the maids, the adoration had grown so intense they harbored velvet scraps from her dresses or slivers of soap from her bath. One morning Isabeau woke in the early dawn and went down to the kitchen early, thinking of wandering in the dim, scented garden for a while. She so often felt stifled and confined within the palace walls. Latifa was in the kitchen, kneeling before one of the great fireplaces.

"Guid, ye have come," she said without preamble. "I wondered if ye would heed my call. I thought we should have a chance to talk. Do no' fear, this hearth is marked with sacred symbols, so is safe from scrying eyes. If ye can, I wish ye to join me down here each morning before the sun is fully risen. Your guardian tells me ye have a Talent with fire and would like to learn more about it. I also need to teach ye about shielding your thoughts for ye are downright noisy, and I will no' have ye endangering me simply because ye do no' ken any control."

"I'm noisy?" Isabeau asked in disbelief. Never had she been so quiet and withdrawn as she had been these last few weeks. How could Latifa think her noisy?

"In your thoughts, ye silly bairn. Ye have no control whatsoever. If ye wish to remain safe here, ye mun never let your mask slip. Ye mun never allow yourself to even think that which ye wouldna want someone to ken. Just because the witches are gone, does no' mean there are no' those that can overhear your thoughts, lassie. I can myself, and ye are shouting yours. Luckily the only ones to have heard them so far are no danger to ye, but I canna let ye go anywhere in the palace until ye learn to control your thoughts."

I do no' understand, Isabeau thought.

The old witch nodded. "Nay, I can see that. It is no' your fault, so do no' look so anxious, lassie. Let me explain. Ye see, Isabeau, Meghan placed a seal upon your third eye, to prevent ye from speaking o' her. She first imposed it on your eighth birthday, for ye brought both her and yourself to the attention of a seeker o' the Awl and caused much trouble. Nay, hush, lass, let me finish. Every day for eight years afterward she reinforced the seal, so ye see, it was very strong. Somehow the seal was knocked loose."

"The Grand-Seeker threw a paperweight at me during

the trial, and it hit me very hard," Isabeau said tentatively, fingering the scar between her brows.

"Aye, that would do it. Such a sudden dislodgment has its price, and I can see ye have been hearing things that ye would rather no' have heard. Also ye've been suffering headaches and dizziness. These are all effects o' the loss o' the veils over your third eye. The Coven believes there are seven veils, usually discarded slowly, over many years. Because o' the way Meghan's seal was knocked away, ye have lost at least the first three veils at one time.

"This is no' the way we would have liked to have it happen. I was planning to remove Meghan's seal slowly and gradually, while teaching ye as much as I could about the use o' the spirit . . ."

"Ye mean M . . . M . . . M . . . She blocked me?" Isabeau was incredulous. Conflicting emotions raced through her—humiliation, anger and hurt, only a little alleviated by a faint relief. It was comforting to know there had been good reasons for her failure at the Trials of Spirit. She had often worried why she did not seem to have any of the preternatural senses that a witch should. That Meghan had deliberately blocked her without telling her infuriated Isabeau, but also made a great many things clear. Why she had not been able to say Meghan's name at any time during her travels, despite ensorcelment, torture or the wish to confide. Why the tree-shifter Lilanthe had not been able to sense her despite an extrasensory perception as precise as Meghan's. The Celestine, Cloudshadow, had said her face was wrapped in a veil not of her making. Now Isabeau understood what she meant.

"It was necessary, Isabeau. Meghan was recognized by the witch-sniffer after that wee contretemps in Caeryla. It got very risky for her to move around in Rionnagan after that. For eight years she had been able to travel through the countryside fairly freely, for noone knew if she were alive or dead, or where she might have fled. Once ye used the Power in view o' a seeker, however, ye drew attention to her and it did no' take long for the descriptions to go out again. Every seeker has dreamed o' capturing Meghan o' the Beasts, last seen in Rionnagan . . ."

"I dinna ken," Isabeau whispered, now feeling guilty, and resentful too.

"She knew that there was a guid chance that she could be captured and she wanted to protect ye. So ye see, it was no' done lightly. Also, I may as well tell ye, Meghan knew ye were very strong and was afraid o' what ye might do with your powers in such dangerous times. So she sealed up your third eye until such a time that ye were auld enough to understand."

Isabeau knew that Latifa was soothing her down, but she felt some of her indignation subside nonetheless. The old cook went on briskly, "Now, we have no' got much time for the lassies will soon be rousing. Show me how ye summon fire."

Isabeau had always had a ready facility with the power of fire, but she had not handled it since her capture and torture. She did so now hesitantly and found that she was only able to summon the merest spark and that soon faded away. Latifa pursed up her lips and said nothing. Isabeau explained stumblingly, but Latifa waved her to silence. "Your sufferings will no' have affected your innate ability," she said kindly. "But drawing on the One Power requires trust in yourself, and I can see yours has been shaken. We shall start at the beginning."

Latifa thrust her podgy hand deep into the blazing heart of the fire and let it lie there, cradling the coals in her hand as if they were onions. "Fire is the strangest o' all the elements, the most dangerous, the most difficult to control," she said. "Like water, it makes a good servant but a cruel master. Ye must always be wary when dealing with fire, for it can twist in your hand like a viper and burn ye. To become a Sorceress o' Fire, ye must be reforged and reforged in the fire like a sword. Purity and strength are what is needed, and to be so tempered, ye need to suffer.

"All said, it is still the kindliest o' all the elements. It warms ye while ye sleep, illuminates your way in darkness, allows ye to cook and eat, to send messages. By the light o' the ceremonial fire we dance and chant, and when we marry it is over the fire we jump. The fire o' the stars shines for us every night, and the fire o' the sun all day. It is in the healing fire o' *mithuan,* and so also the poisoned fire o' nightshade. It is the life spark, and so too the element o' death and ashes. And here is the deepest secret o' fire, for from the ashes comes rebirth. Fire is the element o' transformations."

Latifa's voice slowed to a murmur, and she held out her hand for Isabeau to see. Although it had been resting in the fiery coals all this time, there were no burn marks on her red, chapped hand, nor any sign of strain on the round face.

"The secret o' mastering the element o' fire is in control," she said. "With the other elements precise control is no' always needed, but with fire ye never want to lose your dominance. Your guardian tells me ye have power but little control, and so that is what I shall teach ye first. At the same time ye'll be learning to discipline your own thoughts and to shut out others. It shall take a long time so I warn ye now. Impatience is o' no use to ye with the One Power, and particularly no' with fire. Ye will find it hard, for I can see ye are o' an impetuous and hasty nature. This is one o' the paradoxes o' the One Power—those who have the character and disposition most favorable for a certain element are also the most handicapped in using it. Do ye understand?'

"Ye mean that because I have a fiery nature, I am most strong in the element o' fire, but that I canna learn to use fire properly until I first learn to control my temperament."

"Exactly! I am glad to learn ye are no' such a fool as I first thought. Now, are there any questions ye wish to ask me before the palace starts stirring?"

Isabeau asked shyly, "I was wondering about Maya . . ."

"Never call the Banrìgh by her name like that!" Latifa

admonished. "Who are ye to be speaking o' her like that, a wee snippet o' a lass like ye?"

"But I—"

"Ye mun always remember to mind your tongue, lass," the plump old woman said. "Although no seer can overhear us here, anyone can eavesdrop. Ye mun never forget that a slip o' the tongue could mean your death. What is it ye wish to know about the Banrìgh?"

"She seems to win everyone to her side," Isabeau said thoughtfully. "And she likes to have baths in salt water."

"Obh obh! So ye are no' so dreamy dazed as ye seem. What do ye think it means?"

"I do no' ken," Isabeau said. "The salt-water baths are curious, I have never heard o' anyone bathing in seawater before. I remember Meghan telling me that she has wondered in the past whether the Banrìgh could be a Fairge, and the overthrow o' the Towers due to some crafty plot o' the Fairgean to win back their land. She said the idea was impossible, though, for the Fairgean live in salt water and canna survive long away from the sea. But if the Banrìgh bathed each day in salt water, could that no' explain how she can live on land?"

"Happen it might," Latifa agreed, "though I have bided with the Banrìgh for sixteen years now and I have never seen any sure sign that she was no' human. An impenetrable magic it mun be, to hide her fins and scales so well. Indeed, I canna see how it could be possible, for the Fairgean look nothing like us and have never had the ability to spin illusions, especially no' such a strong one as that mun be! We mun remember that she comes from Carraig where they do no' have the same fear o' the sea as we do. Now run out into the garden and pick me some chives, for I can sense Sukey and Elsie coming down the stairs and I do no' wish them to find us together. Keep your eyes and ears open and tell me anything ye hear o' interest."

Every morning from then on, Isabeau woke early and hurried down to the kitchen, glad to leave her tangled sheets, damp from her restless dreaming. Strangely, to

begin with, all she had to do was watch the fire. Sitting
on a cushion on the floor, she observed as Latifa laid
the fire in different ways and with different woods. She
watched little twigs shrivel to a burning thread, and great
logs smoulder their hearts into hollowness.

Latifa also taught her to shield her mind, so Isabeau
was finally able to shut out the thoughts continually
crowding in on her. Her nights still swarmed with
dreams, both beautiful and terrible, but at least her days
were peaceful and free of pain.

As a cook Latifa was particularly interested in the
senses of taste and smell, though these were lessons that
took place in the bright of day, before the disinterested
gaze of many of the servants. For Latifa's primary
method of teaching Isabeau about the element of fire
was to teach her how to cook. When Isabeau rather
sulkily protested that she could not see what cooking
had to do with magic, Latifa said firmly, "Cooking has
everything to do with magic, ye fool. Cooking is understanding a food's nature and working with its nature and
the elemental powers to turn it into something else.
Wha' else is magic?"

Although Latifa had spent eight years at the Tower
of Two Moons as a child, she was not a fully accredited
witch—she had never been accepted into the Coven as
an apprentice as Isabeau had. Her mother had been the
palace cook, and her mother's mother before her. She
had learnt her kitchen magic at her mother's knee, and
her years at the Theurgia had built on the knowledge
and talents she already had. Unlike Meghan, her skills
were entirely practical.

So Isabeau spent many a long morning following Latifa from pot to pan to oven, from butter churn to ice
room to smoking chamber, as the old cook explained to
her how heat and cold changed the composition of the
food they were preparing. Despite herself Isabeau was
fascinated and learned much about the element of fire
that Meghan had never taught her.

All morning, as Isabeau followed her around the kitchen

wing, the old cook would hold up a laden spoon for Isabeau to smell or taste. The red-haired girl refused to sample anything containing meat, which caused some argument. Despite Latifa reminding her that many of the Coven had never abandoned the eating of animal flesh, Isabeau was filled with horror at the thought. Meghan had taught her to revere all life, and many of the creatures eaten with gusto by the lairds and their servants had been kin to Isabeau's childhood friends. Latifa tried to trick her once or twice but Isabeau's sense of smell sharpened to such an extent that she could detect the flesh of animals even as a supplementary ingredient. Latifa threw up her fat hands and said, "Just do no' let anyone realize is all I ask, ye stubborn lassie, else ye'll have the pot boys gossiping and that I shall no' abide!"

Isabeau was shocked and sickened by many of the customs of the palace kitchen. Cheese-making time came with the summer, and Latifa ordered a lamb to be killed so she could use its digestive juices to curdle the milk. Meghan and Isabeau had always used the juice from the flower of the wild thistle, and it had never occurred to Isabeau that anyone would choose to kill an animal in preference to the long and arduous task of plucking thistle flowers. She had to fight hard to overcome her nausea and could not eat cheese again, even though she knew anyone who noticed would find it strange.

The corpses of murdered boar and deer, delivered each noon by the hunters, were also a trial to Isabeau. She could not understand how Latifa could bear to look at them, let alone cook them and eat them, but the cook oversaw the feeding of up to a thousand people a day. Every day she tasted from countless dishes made from the bodies of slain pigs, sheep, goats, deer, coneys, geese, hens, pigeons, quails, pheasants, sea-stirk and fish.

Isabeau still had not seen the Rìgh or the Banrìgh, nor any of the lairds or courtiers, for none of the servants were permitted to serve in the great dining room. The lairds' own pages served them, the servants only

permitted to bring the trays of food from the kitchen to
the serving table set up along one wall.

Not once did the old cook ask Isabeau to draw upon
the One Power. The girl began to worry in case she had
lost her magical abilities. The last time she had used the
One Power had been to kill the man who had tortured
her. Fervently she told herself that his death had saved
her from great pain and humiliation, even from death.
She had saved the talisman and killed the only person
who knew she had it. It had been a fair death, even a
good one. Still, it seemed something had been broken
in her that would not mend easily and as the days grew
longer and hotter, she wondered if she would ever regain
her powers.

Although the summer dusk was usually long, one evening
it darkened early as the sun sank into storm clouds. Mist
rose from the moist, warm earth, and no birds sang. Iseult
slipped through the dim forest to the glade where Lachlan
practiced his archery. He wore only his kilt, his bare chest
sheened with sweat. As Iseult watched from the shadows,
he drew back the bow with an effort that set all his muscles
gleaming, then let the string go with a twang. The arrow
flew through the air, splitting the arrow already embedded
in the bullseye right down the middle.

"Keen shooting!" Iseult cried.

"Aye, I'm getting good indeed," Lachlan said proudly
and pulled her to him so he could kiss her throat. She
wrapped her arms around his body, kissing his damp
skin. "How are ye feeling, *leannan?*" he asked, and she
made a little moue and tilted her hand from side to side.

"No' very well," she admitted. "Meghan says hurry
back to the clearing. The mist is rising and it makes
her uneasy."

When they returned to the camp, mist was rolling over
the thick roots of the trees in ghostly waves, and Meghan
was tense-faced. "Thank Eà ye are back! I do no' like
this mist, and there's a smell to the air . . . or a

feeling . . . I've been fretting for ye ever since ye left. I think ye should stay close to the fire this night."

By the time they were rolling themselves into their plaids to sleep, the mist curled ghostly fingers over them. Iseult was not surprised at Meghan's unease. The restless eddying of the fog was uncanny; the way it came no further, as if only Meghan's magic was keeping it from pouring over them, drowning them.

It was much later when Iseult woke. The mist was all about her. She lay still and listened. After a moment she slid away from the warmth of Lachlan's body. Shivering a little as dank fingers of fog trailed over her, she scouted around the clearing, dagger in hand. Meghan's bed of mosses and bracken was empty.

Iseult frowned and peered through the trees. She saw the sorceress, her plaid thrown around her shoulders, staring out into the foggy darkness. Meghan sensed her coming and turned, finger to her lips, her face grim.

"What's wrong?"

"Iseult, go and wake Lachlan. Be quick and quiet. Hide in the forest. Head toward Tulachna Celeste when ye can."

"Why?"

"I sense . . . something. A consciousness I am no' familiar with. Dangerous."

Iseult nodded and hurried back. Lachlan had woken of his own accord and was staring out into the mist with compressed lips. Swiftly they dressed and made their way through the maze of twisting roots. Both were keenly conscious of danger.

Meghan was near where Iseult had left her, poker-backed, arms folded over her chest. Even in the gloom they could see how angry she was. "Dinna I tell ye to head for Tulachna Celeste? Why must ye bairns always disobey me?"

"We are no' babes, Meghan!" Lachlan came up to his great-aunt, so small against his bulk yet somehow the more powerful because of it.

"Please, Lachlan, ye must listen to me. There are

strange forces at work here tonight, and I have this dreadful suspicion . . . If what I fear is true, then ye must no' be caught up in it."

"But what—"

"I fear the Mesmerdean have come in search o' me— I remember they are a vengeful race. It crossed my mind when I found that little pile o' marshy-smelling ashes in the tree-house. I had woven a difficult ward indeed on that trapdoor, for I knew they would come in more easily from below once they lit fires. I had other things to worry about, though, and so it slipped my mind. If it is true, and I am no' just a suspicious auld witch, then ye are both better out o' it. Iseult, take my pouch, guard it well, remember the *Book o' Shadows* has all the answers if only ye can learn to master it . . ."

There was a sudden shriek from Gitâ as the donbeag flew to his mistress's shoulder. Iseult swung round and saw a tall, gray figure looming out of the mist. Instinctively she let the arrow fly, but by the time it reached where the creature's glittering clusters of eyes had been, the Mesmerd was gone. It had flitted across the clearing, reaching for Meghan with its claws. Suddenly its gray draperies collapsed as Lachlan drew the claymore and sliced off its head with one swift stroke.

The body of the Mesmerd melted away, leaving such a strong stench of the marshes that Lachlan gagged. "Do no' breathe it in!" Meghan said frantically. "Do no' touch! Come away, quickly!"

Covering her mouth with the end of the plaid, Iseult scanned the fog with her senses as they hurried back through the trees. She felt rather than saw the Mesmerd drifting toward her in a misty cloud. Quick as thought, she pierced its eye with her skewer, and it thrashed in agony, a green ichor welling out of the wound.

She wiped the skewer on the grass, amazed to see its surface mottled with holes as if it had been eaten by acid. The sound of an explosion made her leap to her feet, the skewer held close to her hip. Meghan had bombarded another of the winged faeries with blue witch-fire, and it had erupted into a raging ball of blue-green flame which sent evil-smelling smoke all through the trees.

They stumbled back, coughing and choking at the reek. Gitâ, perched precariously on Meghan's bony shoulder, screeched in warning and the wood witch threw up her hand instinctively. The Mesmerd dropping down from the branches behind her was tumbled away in a wind that came from nowhere. It recovered its balance almost immediately, spreading its translucent wings and darting sideways to attack Lachlan. Iseult threw her *reil* and it whizzed through one of its wings, causing it to shriek in agony, clutching the torn gossamer close to its torso. She plunged her skewer as deep into its chest as she could.

Her gaze was caught by the green shimmer of its iridescent eyes. She felt a strange rushing in her ears, her hands slipping from the skewer's handle to fall limply by her side. Her vision was swirled with green lights; she swayed and fell, hardly aware the dying Mesmerd had caught her in its six arms and was bending its strange face to hers. A sweet tide of painful tenderness swelled through her, and she put up a hand to stroke its glossy shell.

Just as the swampy scent of the Mesmerd's breath flowed over her and her eyes closed, a blissful smile parting her lips, the Mesmerd suddenly stiffened and disintegrated, its draperies floating down to cover the unconscious Iseult.

Lachlan tugged his dagger free, swung Iseult into his arms, her curly red head hanging limply over his arm. Every few strides another Mesmerd darted from the shadows, but Meghan simply enveloped them in fiery blue so that one after the other they exploded into dust. They came at last to the edge of the hill, and Lachlan staggered up the steep slope, Iseult heavy against him. They fell through the gateway and Meghan began to work on Iseult's frighteningly limp body.

"The kiss o' the Mesmerdean is death," she said bleakly as she massaged Iseult's chest vigorously with pungent oils. "I hope I can save her. Why did ye come back for me,

Lachlan? This is exactly what I was afraid o'!" She paused to exhale her own breath into Iseult's mouth, sending her chest rising and falling in artificial rhythms.

Lachlan was white, two heavy lines graven from nose to mouth. "Ye canna mean she's going to die!" he cried. "The Mesmerd barely breathed on her at all!"

"Let us hope that was no' sufficient," Meghan replied. "Do no' stand over me like that, Lachlan. Keep a close watch, for it is only a guess that the Mesmerdean will avoid Tulachna Celeste. They may be creeping up on us now, and the forest is no protection for they can simply fly above the trees."

She put her mouth back down to Iseult's. For long, anxious moments, she breathed into Iseult's mouth, only pausing to pound her chest with her doubled fists. At last her ward coughed and took a breath of her own volition. Soon she was breathing easily, though she did not fully regain consciousness. Meghan massaged her whole body with the strong-smelling oil and poured *mithuan* into her mouth so she coughed and spluttered, moaning in her sleep.

By sunrise Iseult's pulse had steadied and color had returned to her scarred cheeks. Meghan went scouting through the forest and found thirteen little piles of ashes that smelt of the bog. She carefully scraped up every last mote of dust into a pot, which she corked and buried deep. Feeling sick and shaky herself, she then drank several mouthfuls of her precious heart-starting *mithuan*.

"We're in trouble now," she groaned. "If they sent that many in revenge for the one that died in my tree-house, what will they do in reprisal for thirteen?"

"How will they know?" Lachlan replied, stirring the oatmeal in the heavy cauldron hanging over the fire.

"They share a memory," Meghan said. "The only way to rid yourself of a Mesmerdean vendetta is to kill each and every one o' its relatives—egg-brothers, I think they are called. No, if there are any egg-brothers left, they will ken what has happened and they will want me dead. Ye and Iseult too, now." She sighed. "Still, what am I to do if ye never obey me?"

TRIALS OF THE SPIRIT

The week before Midsummer's Eve the palace began to fill with guests, throwing the servants into fevered activity. Isabeau was wide-eyed and over-awed, for she had never realized how much work a banquet of this magnitude involved. All day and half the night Latifa bustled to and fro, ordering chandeliers to be unhooked so the thousands of crystals could be washed, preparing hundreds of sweetmeats, cakes and jellies and plucking dozens of bhanais birds, saving their gorgeous tail feathers to decorate the roasted meat later.

Because of her crippled hand, Isabeau escaped much of the heavier work but Latifa kept her on her feet from dawn to midnight. She was so busy she had no time to wonder about the Banrìgh's mysterious powers or to worry about the apparent loss of her own. Each morning she was up well before dawn to meet Latifa in the kitchen, then she spent all day on the run, ordered here and there by impatient lackeys. If she was lucky, she could stumble to her bedchamber by around midnight. More often she was still awake in the wee small hours, following Latifa as the old cook jingled from one storeroom to another.

She kept her thoughts to herself, finding it easier every

day to lock away her inner self. She put on the character
of a simple country lass, and each day it grew more
comfortable. Meanwhile she listened and watched as
Meghan had told her to, and found much to puzzle her.

The maids' favorite topic was the Banrìgh. They discussed the cut of her sleeves, the way she wore her hair,
and how wonderful it was that she was at last with child.
Their devotion was in such contrast to all Isabeau had
ever heard of Maya the Ensorcellor that it aroused in
her an intense curiosity to see the Banrìgh. Isabeau had
always heard Maya described as evil, manipulative, dangerous and cruel. It was disconcerting to hear instead
how kind, generous and considerate she was.

Two days before Midsummer's Eve, Isabeau asked
Latifa when she would have a chance to see the Banrìgh.
The shyly asked question earned her a sharp slap. "And
who do ye think ye are, to be wanting to rise so high so
fast, and ye just a wee snippet o' a lass from the back
o' yonder! Why, ye must be able to carry a tray without
spilling the gravy before ye'd be allowed to serve anywhere near the Banrìgh, especially now she's with babe,
Truth bless her. So get ye back to your spitting stool
before I box your other ear!"

Her cheek burning, Isabeau stumbled back to her corner. So shocked was she by Latifa's slap that she wept
most of the afternoon, trying to conceal her distress in
her apron. Later that evening, when the kitchen was
empty, the cook gave Isabeau one of her gingerbread
men, hot from the oven.

"Stop your greetin', lassie, your apron is sopping wet
and your eyes look fit to start from your head. Ye should
no' be such a silly lass, asking me such a question in
front o' the whole kitchen! Be patient, I tell ye. Now, I
think ye're in need o' some fresh air and some solitude.
I forget ye're no' used to all this. Take the day off tomorrow. I can say ye've made yourself ill with your sorrow, so eager were ye to see the bonny Banrìgh."

Isabeau's heart leapt at the thought of finally being
able to leave the confining walls of the palace. She had

felt as if the blue-gray walls were closing in on her. Her immediate thought was of Lasair. Would the chestnut stallion still be near the palace? Would she be able to find him?

The next morning she packed up a napkin with some bread and fruit and made her way to the bridge over the ravine, lined with guards. She kept her head down as she crossed, shy of the soldiers, but once she was on the other shore, she leant her elbows on the railing and looked about her with pleasure.

The firth shone in the sunshine, the spires of Rhyssmadill soaring above. The water creamed white on the rocks at the base of the cliff and rushed through the ravine separating the great finger of rock from the mainland. On the opposite shore was the city, all built from the same blue stone as the palace. Hundreds of ships bobbed at their berthing. At the far end of the firth she could see the river-gate which marked the first of the series of locks that controlled the entrance to the harbor. Beyond was a blue shimmer that could only be the sea.

The sight thrilled her to the core. The beautiful, dangerous sea that she had read so much about was only an hour's walk away, pressing up against the seawall the witches had constructed so many years ago. She longed to have a closer sight of it—Meghan said the waters stretched as far as the eye could see and even further.

Today, though, Isabeau intended to trek into the forests of Ravenshaw where she had left Lasair. The Ravenshaw woods pressed up close to the rolling parkland which surrounded the palace, forming a thick barrier along its boundaries. To the north were the rolling hills of Rionnagan, to the east the gatehouse and palace gates, opening into a city square.

Isabeau walked down the long avenue of trees, then cut across the open lawn toward the woods. As soon as the palace walls were safely out of sight, she began casting out her senses. Two boys were fishing on the firth's edge; a gamekeeper was strolling the park, a crossbow slung over his back and two hounds at his heels; and the palace goats were grazing under the trees, minded by two girls in huge white caps. Far overhead a hawk flew, crimson ribbons dangling from its claws. Otherwise there was not a living soul for miles.

Lasair . . . Isabeau called rather tentatively with her mind-voice. There was no response. She reached the edge of the park and slipped through the little gate set in the wall, and into the forest.

It was very quiet in the wood. Isabeau walked slowly but steadily. She had been sick for so long that her strength was much diminished. She did not want to exhaust herself by traveling too far or too quickly. From long habit, she looked out for herbs or flowers and gently pulled up several which she thought Riordan Bowlegs would like for his little garden.

At last she came to where she had hidden the magical saddle and bridle. To her relief they were safe still in the hollow tree, guarded by a magical ward. Wrapped in its blanket, the saddle had remained dry. No mouse or donbeag had tried to make a nest in its stuffing. She gave them both a good rubdown with an oil-soaked rag she had taken from the stable when no one was looking.

It was just before noon, and Isabeau was tired. She sat in the shade of the tree and ate her repast, enjoying the dappled sun on her back. There had been no sign of Lasair and she wondered anxiously if she would ever find him again.

Isabeau was just deciding whether to walk to the seashore when she heard a long drawn-out whinny. Leaping to her feet she called *Lasair, Lasair!* and saw the chestnut galloping toward her through the trees. He came to a snorting halt before her, and she flung her arms around his neck. He pushed his satiny nose into her shoulder and blew affectionately, then rubbed his head against her.

Tears stung her eyes. "I missed ye so much," she told him, and he stamped his foot and whinnied.

Using a fallen log as a mounting-block, Isabeau vaulted onto the chestnut's back and together they galloped through the woods to the gigantic bulwark that kept the ocean away from the land. Perched on its summit, Isabeau had her first good look at the sea.

Between her and the waters was a stretch of bare sand strewn with shells and dried seaweed and ridged with the ancient patterns of tides. Far away the water glittered in the sun, aquamarine and opal near the shore, violet-blue near the horizon. Here and there white-winged birds floated in the salt-scented air. She sat and watched the gentle waves for a long time, knowing why the first humans to Eileanan had called it Muir Finn, the Fair Sea.

The shadows were growing long when the stallion took her back toward Rhyssmadill, leaving her close to the forest's edge so he would not be seen. She wrapped her arms around his neck and rested her head against him for a long time. Then he galloped off into the trees, and she began the long trudge back to the palace. As she wandered through the woods, Isabeau automatically bent and harvested the fruits of the forest, as she had done all her life. Soon her apron was brimming with flowers, leaves and roots, and she had to tie up the edges and carry it like a sack over her back. Berating herself for not acting like a mere country lass, she nonetheless carried the sack through the park, sure Latifa and Riordan Bowlegs would be pleased.

On the opposite shore Dùn Gorm was beginning to prick with lights, and the waters of the Berhtfane shone with sunset colors. Blue and transparent, Gladrielle floated just above the horizon, alone for once as the second moon had not yet risen. Somewhere far above, a hawk gave a hoarse cry, sending a shiver down her arms.

In Riordan's cramped quarters Isabeau washed the horse smell from her hands and face. She untied the apron, and the old groom picked through the flowers and roots with exclamations of delight. Isabeau thought ruefully that she must have been more absent-minded than ever—the apron was over-flowing with groundsel. Although a useful herb, it was a weed that grew in every ditch and field and was usually rooted out by gardeners.

Many a cottager used groundsel tea to relieve a tightness of the bowels, yet too strong an infusion caused great discomfort indeed. She shrugged but wrapped the yellow buds up again nonetheless. The fresh leaves were useful for relieving the pain of mother's milk, and the Banrìgh's maid had been seeking such a remedy only yesterday. Her unconscious mind must have prompted her to gathering it while her conscious thoughts wandered.

The old groom was so pleased with the roots and flowers she had brought back for him to plant that he asked her no questions about where she had been or why she was dusted in horse hairs. Instead they talked about plant lore, and Isabeau promised to bring him new plants every time she was allowed out.

It had been in Isabeau's mind that gathering wild herbs for Latifa would make sure her outing would be repeated. The cook was always bemoaning the difficulty in gaining precious ingredients for her delicacies, what with the trade ships no longer running. Isabeau had been raised by a wood witch, and she knew as much about the properties of plants as any forest skeelie. She had dug up many small herbs and plants that did not grow in the kitchen garden and which she knew Latifa would be pleased with.

The old cook beamed with pleasure when Isabeau presented her with the massive cluster. "Och, ye're a guid lass!" she cried. "How did ye ken I've been in need o' eyebright? No' to mention the antler mushrooms! I'll serve them up to the Banrìgh tonight and see if they tempt her appetite, the puir lass, so picky she has become with the babe turning in her womb."

Isabeau indicated the groundsel with one finger, and Latifa nodded, her black eyes glinting, her jaw set. Then she beamed again, chattering, "Come, ye mun be slavering with hunger. I have a nice pot o' vegetable soup simmering on the fire. I am glad to see the roses have come back to your cheeks. If ye bring me back such a fine bouquet each time ye go out, I swear I'll be sending ye out each day!"

Isabeau slid into an empty chair at the table. Some of the scullery maids nodded, and one of the footboys winked at her. Then she was ignored again as talk turned to the upcoming Midsummer celebrations. Loyal to the Truth as they were, the servants were all very careful not to give the feast any sacred significance, referring to it only as a much anticipated social event. This seemed shocking to Isabeau, who had been taught Midsummer's Eve was one of the most magical of days. Meghan had spun many of her spells and charms on the summer solstice, and it was the most common time for lovers to jump the fire and pledge their troth.

This was one custom that had not changed, she discovered, for there was much teasing and laughter around the table as the servants speculated who would jump the fire together this year. A bonfire had been laid in the great square before the doors of the palace itself, and all the servants would be allowed in the Rìgh's gardens where the feast was to be held. There would be dancing and mummery, with minstrels and jongleurs from all over Eileanan performing. From the embers of the bonfire, torches would be lit and carried in a procession all through the palace, lighting the fires and lanterns within.

The Midsummer Eve festivities would be mimicked down in the city, though there a poor warlock would die in the flames. Isabeau shuddered at the thought and wondered if the city folk would light their lanterns from the ashes of a fire that had consumed a fellow human. She did not understand how they could.

All the servants had to work at some point in the evening, and there was much lobbying for shifts outside the time of the feast and celebrations. Isabeau, as a very lowly scullery maid, had no choice in the matter, of course. She heard from Sukey that she had won one of the worst jobs of all—serving the lower tables during the feast. Not only would she not be able to do more than snatch a mouthful here and there, but she would be serving many of the lairds' squires, who were prone to pinching the maids' bottoms. One small consolation—she would be serving in the lower hall, adjacent to the great hall where the prionnsachan and upper nobility sat. Although she would be in great trouble if she was caught, it was usually possible to peep through the curtain and see the great lairds feasting and carousing. "Ye might even see the Banrìgh," Sukey said with excitement in her voice. "Doreen was telling me ye were greetin' in sorrow for no' having seen her."

The next day Sukey came up behind her and said kindly, "The Banrìgh is playing to the court now, as she does each Midsummer—we're all watching from behind the curtain, if ye'd like to come?"

Isabeau flushed with pleasure, for it was not often that the other serving lasses included her. Sukey led her, half running, through countless stairs and corridors, until at last they reached a gallery overlooking the great hall. Any view to the court below was concealed, however, by a mass of bobbing white caps and gray skirts. Sukey took Isabeau's hand and squeezed through, Isabeau for once not hanging back but taking advantage of her height and slenderness to wriggle past countless whispering, giggling girls, all with sharp elbows and numerous petticoats.

All at once a hush fell over the crowd, the velvet- and lace-clad courtiers milling below, the servants peeping around the curtains and through the carved stone screens of the galleries. Exquisite music spilled into the silence, rising in little running cascades that seemed to reach for, and fail to catch, some unimaginable resolution. Again and again the notes soared upward, and fell down, and prickles ran all over Isabeau's skin. She knelt against the wall and thrust her eye to one of the gaps in the scrolled stonework, but all she could see were the plaid-hung shoulders of the courtiers, a set of wide stone steps, and a man's languid, outflung foot, clad in an ornate slipper.

The music shifted, ran deeper, the beat quickened, and then the hidden musician began to sing. Unexpectedly, her voice was deep, but with such power thrilling through it that Isabeau felt a shiver run over her.

The Banrìgh sang, "My love my honey my honeyed love," rising and rising until the crescendo reached as high as any meadow lark and then at last, so unexpectedly tears sprang in Isabeau's eyes, the pinnacle was reached. "My love my honey my honeyed love, my laird!" Again and again "My laird!" flew to the ceiling so high above. As the last throbbing note died away, the gallery erupted into applause. Isabeau clapped as rapturously as anyone. To her surprise, she was being embraced by all around her, and she hugged them back and joined in the ringing calls from the audience. The footmen and maids no longer hid behind the curtains but hung from the gallery, some weeping, all clapping and stamping their feet.

At last the noise died down, cut in part by a little trill from the Banrìgh's clàrsach. The velvet slipper slowly drew back, and then the Rìgh came languorously forward, wearing a loose green robe over silken hosen. He was slender and dark, with a neatly clipped beard and mustache, and a dreamy, almost vacant expression on his face. He murmured something and held up his hand to bring his wife forward. All Isabeau could see of the Banrìgh were her fine, white fingers, bare of rings, clasped in the hand of the Rìgh.

As the Banrìgh turned to leave, her long velvet train swept over the steps, crimson as roses. Isabeau's heart hammered once, painfully. It was the same color as the skirt of the Grand-Seeker Glynelda. Gripping her cold, sweaty palms together, she sank down to her knees.

"Red, what's wrong?" Sukey asked, bending over her. She was jostled on all sides as the laughing, chattering maids hurried back to their work.

Isabeau shook her head. "Just a wee dizzy," she managed to say, then slowly got to her feet. She leaned against the stone scrollwork to regain her balance, then caught her breath suddenly. Down in the rapidly emptying room, a small woman clothed entirely in black was staring up at her. Isabeau could see how pale her eyes were in the dark, broad face and how intently they were fixed on the gallery. Instinctively she ducked back into the shelter of the curtain.

"That is Sani, the Banrìgh's own servant," Sukey whispered.

Although she was thin and hunched as a swarthyweb spider, the old woman emanated power, as if she were a fully armed warrior. With no lessening of her intense focus, she stood and stared up at the gallery until the flock of serving maids had twittered away. Neither girl dared move until she was long gone, though why, Isabeau did not know.

"She be right blaygird," Sukey whispered. "We all be terrified o' her. I think she be naught but a jealous auld maid, but I still do no' like to go near her." The two girls began to hurry back down the corridor. "She was asking about ye, ye ken," Sukey said idly.

"Asking about me? The Banrìgh's servant?"

"Aye, though why I canna tell. It were when ye first arrived. She asked me and Doreen if there was a red-haired lassie new come to the palace, and if so, where ye came from. We said aye, but that ye were sick unto death."

"Was I really?"

"Aye, we all thought ye'd die for sure, ye were that ill. Anyway, she told us there'd be a penny for us both if we came to her and told her whether ye'd lived or died, and we said aye, that we would, but o' course we did no'. Neither Doreen nor me like to get too close to her, no' even for a penny. Besides, she and Latifa do no' get on so well and we have to live with Latifa's temper, while if we are careful indeed, we do no' have to set eyes on Sani for a sennight or more."

Heels clattering on the stone stairs, the two girls raced back to the kitchen. Isabeau was puzzled and a little frightened by the news the Banrìgh's own servant had been asking about her. She could not see how the little old woman could have had any idea she even existed, let alone know of her connection with Meghan. Isabeau tried to reassure herself that the servant's questions did not mean that she was under suspicion, but she could not help the cold finger of dread that touched her. Isabeau's experiences at the hands of the Awl were still too fresh for her to take any such occurrence lightly.

Once back in the hot, crowded kitchen, Isabeau had no time to worry about Sani as Latifa's orders were flying fast and thick. There was so much to do for the Midsummer's Eve feast that Isabeau had no time or energy to think about anything else at all. That night, even as exhausted as she was by the labor and excitement of the day, Isabeau did not sleep well, her dreams filled with crimson robes and blood.

The day before the summer solstice, Iseult was resting in the shade of a moss-oak when she heard, incredibly, the brazen call of a dragon in the distance. "Asrohc!" she cried, sitting up. "It canna be . . ."

The long bugle came again, sending a shiver of dragon-fear down Iseult's spine so she knew it was no auditory illusion. Then she saw the flash of bright wings and smelled sulphur. "Asrohc!" she cried again and began hurrying through the trees to Tulachna Celeste, sure that was where the dragon would alight, the thorny branches of the forest dangerous to her delicate wings. Sure enough, the golden-green body of the young dragon was circling down from the sky into the circle of stones, her stretched wings almost wide enough to knock down the tall menhirs. On her back were two figures.

Although they were too far away for Iseult to see, she began to run, her sickness of the morning dropping away from her like a discarded cloak. She ran nimbly down the root-mazed avenue, burst from the trees into the open ground of the hill and ran all the way up its steep green slope. Breathless, a stitch in her side, she ran through the stone doorway and into her grandmother's arms.

"Firemaker!" she cried. "Old mother, what are ye doing here?"

The old woman kissed Iseult between the brows, and in the harsh, guttural language of the Khan'cohbans murmured greetings and blessings over her red head.

"I have come to see you wed," she replied. "Did you think I would stay away? My great-granddaughter crosses her leg over the back of the dragon, why should I not also?"

"Iseult, my bonny lass!" a gruff voice cried, and Iseult found herself being hugged hard against the skinny frame of Feld of the Dragons.

"It is so good to see ye, Feld! Asrohc! What are ye doing letting humans cross your back in this way?"

My mother said it was time I stretched my wings, and I had heard thee was to be mated to another of thine kind. Naturally I wished to see him, and see if his heart was big enough and his wings strong enough for a dragon-lord such as yourself . . .

"Meghan told me ye were to be Tested this summer solstice, and needed me here to complete the circle," Feld said, a broad smile across his face, pushing his glasses back onto his nose with one ink-stained finger. "I was to bring Ishbel too, but nothing I could do or say would wake her, and so at last I thought to bring your great-grandmother. She is no' o' the Coven, but a witch nonetheless."

"No witch, but powerful at least," the Firemaker said haltingly in the common dialect. After a thousand years with the Prides, the descendants of Faodhagan had re-membered little of his language, but both she and Iseult had learned from Feld after he had gone to live in the Cursed Valley.

Asrohc announced with a flick of her writhing tail that she was going to hunt something down for her dinner. Iseult warned her with a laugh not to pursue anything in the Veiled Forest if she did not want Meghan and the Celestines after her. "Apparently the Awl has its own flocks in the fields outside Dunceleste. Why do ye no' snack on them?" she suggested. "Be careful, though, ye are still the last o' the she-dragons and do no' want to be losing your life to a poisoned spear!"

Those evil, red witches have broken the Pact of Aedan already, I see no reason why I should not, Asrohc yawned, showing a long, supple tongue as blue as the sky above them. She flexed her translucent-gold wings and launched easily into the air, her shadow darkening the hill before swinging away.

Iseult took Feld's arm in one hand and the Firemaker's in the other and led them down to the clearing, barely able to contain her joy at the sight of two of the people closest to her in the world. If the Firemaker had guarded and directed her winters, Feld had looked over her summers, the two of them teaching Iseult nearly everything she knew.

Iseult felt some trepidation at introducing Lachlan to her fierce, proud great-grandmother. Lachlan flushed and fidgeted under the Firemaker's intense scrutiny, but surprised Iseult by not retreating into his usual surly silence. Instead, he set out to charm the old woman, greeting her with the ritual gesture and salutation of the Khan'cohbans, and treating her with respectful deference. After a while, the Firemaker's stiff back and stern glance softened, and Iseult relaxed in relief.

There was much talk and laughter around the campfire that afternoon. Feld had been much alone over the past eight years, and he mellowed alarmingly under the influence of Meghan's goldensloe wine. They were all shrieking at the sight of him trying to dance a jig when Iseult suddenly looked up and saw a pale, ghostly figure standing under the trees, watching them.

Her immediate reaction should have been a stab of fear. Instead Iseult felt immense happiness well up from deep inside her. She recognized that slender figure surrounded by a nimbus of floating, silvery hair. She had spent eight years of her life tending that fragile form, combing out the great length of hair, coaxing her to swallow water or gruel. It was Ishbel the Winged standing there so gravely. Iseult's mother.

She stood up, saying nothing, staring. Slowly the laughter and teasing died. "Ishbel!" Meghan cried. "Ye've come!"

"Aye, Meghan, I have come," Ishbel answered softly. "I heard your voice in my dreams again and knew ye wished me here. My dreams are often disturbed these days." She sighed and stepped over the tree roots. "Iseult . . ." she said, holding out her hand to her daughter. With color staining her cheeks so her scars stood out strongly, Iseult scrambled to her feet and crossed the clearing to her mother's side. Ishbel's fingers closed over hers. "Ye are with babe, my bairn."

Iseult nodded. Ishbel sighed and tears filled her vivid blue eyes. "To think my baby girls are auld enough to bear their own babes. 'Tis strange . . ."

She sat with them by the fire, Iseult unable to take her eyes off her. Even though she had seen Ishbel the Winged every day during the spring and summer of the past eight years, she had not then known who the sleeping sorceress was.

Ishbel asked for news of Isabeau, and Meghan told her she was safe in Rhyssmadill with Latifa the Cook. Hesitantly, she asked about the Key, and a little of her stiffness left her once she heard Meghan had located all three portions of the Keybearer's badge.

The shadows were growing longer and soon the Ordeal must begin, the night of solitude and fasting all acolytes must endure before being allowed to undertake the tests for entrance into the Coven. Ishbel turned to Iseult and asked shyly, "Will ye walk with me for a while, my daughter?"

Together they moved through lines of light and shadow, both shy and unsure what to say. Iseult said finally, "I often wondered if I was bid to tend ye because ye were my mother."

"I knew always that ye were there."

"Why did ye never wake for me?"

"I wandered in a far place. I did no' ken my way back. I was searching . . ."

"For my father?"

"Aye," Ishbel's eyes filled with tears. "But I have no' been able to find him."

"The queen-dragon told Meghan he was still alive."

She shook her head. "If he were alive, he would have answered me," she said. "Nothing would keep him from answering me."

Iseult bowed her head and clenched her fingers together. She knew dragons did not lie. Ishbel smiled at her sadly, and said, "Your father was a remarkable man, Iseult, I wish ye and Isabeau could have known him."

Iseult nodded her head and told her mother some of the stories the Scarred Warriors of the Fire Dragon Pride told about him on winter nights about the meal-fire. "He was the youngest to ever receive all seven scars," she said. "And he talked with dragons and flew on their backs."

Ishbel told her much about how their love had flowered, saying softly, "Did ye ken ye and Isabeau were conceived on Midsummer's Eve? We thought it an omen o' joy to come at the time. Strange how your path can be twisted so awry . . ."

Her blue eyes overbrimmed with tears again, but she shook away her melancholy, and said affectionately, "Meghan tells me ye have a talent with air."

"Indeed, I seem to. I have always called what I owned to my hand. Then I can jump . . ." She hesitated, then burst out, "Can ye teach me to fly?"

"I do no' ken. I have always been able to do it and have never been able to explain to anyone else how. Perhaps ye may have inherited the Talent, though if so, why do ye no' fly now?"

"Could ye try to explain to me? Or maybe just show me? Meghan says ye can learn many a Skill just by listening and watching."

"Indeed," Ishbel said, floating a few inches above the ground. She swung her legs forward and, slowly and with infinite grace, did a backward somersault. She smiled at Iseult's fascinated and envious gaze and drifted up to sit on one of the massive tree branches far above her daughter's head. She patted the branch affectionately. "Come sit with me, Iseult," she called.

Iseult bent her legs and did a high somersault that brought her within inches of grasping the branch Ishbel sat on.

"Why do ye run and jump?" Ishbel called. "Ye are using muscles and body energy, no' the One Power. Ye are displacing the air, no' the air displacing ye." She slid off the branch and floated down light as thistledown to stand beside her daughter. "Lie on the ground," she commanded. "Close your eyes. Listen to the breeze in the branches. Relax all your muscles, feel yourself light as a feather, light as thistledown, light as a bellfruit seed, lighter . . ."

Her voice blurred into a warm, gentle flow, sweet as honey. After a while Iseult felt as if she were floating. Then Ishbel's voice brought her back.

"Did I float?" Iseult asked eagerly. "I felt as though I did."

Ishbel shook her head. "Ye almost did, my bairn. I felt a change in the air, an energizing. I think perhaps ye could, if ye keep trying. Often we need to accept the possibility o' being able to do something before we can. I feel ye have always concentrated on your body's energies rather than on the world's energies. I will know more after the Tests."

The witches spent the night of their Ordeal on Tulachna Celeste. At the first lessening of darkness, Iseult rose stiffly from her crouch and began her exercises, warming her muscles and quickening her blood. Lachlan joined her silently, naked as she was, then Meghan came from the forest, her gray wiry hair loose around her body. The white streak in it flowed like a river, spreading out like a delta near her feet. Feld was close behind her, embarrassed after so many years spent fully clothed against the cold of the Cursed Valley. He fluffed out his long beard and gazed studiously at the ground.

Ishbel floated down from the sky, startling them all who had looked for her to come along the side of the hill. In the pale dawn, she seemed made of spun ice, so white were her lips and skin and so fair her hair. Only her eyes had any color, and they were blue as ice shadows.

As the witches began to gather, so did the Celestines. Slowly they climbed the hill, their robes ghostly in the wan light. Many more arrived for the singing of the summerbourne than Iseult and Lachlan had ever seen before. *How did they all get here?* Iseult wondered to herself. She had noticed how many of them seemed to materialize between the stone doorway.

Cloudshadow cast her an enigmatic glance out of her crystal-clear eyes. *They traveled the Old Ways, of course. The singing of the summerbourne has made the Old Ways less dangerous than they have been in years, and many of my brethren were eager to hear the winged boy sing and see how strongly the spring runs. Stories of the winged boy have spread far through the hills and forest . . .*

As if knowing the Celestines had all come to hear him, Lachlan sang more beautifully than ever before. These last few months in the forest had seen him overcome his reluctance to use his blackbird voice, and he sang a lilting melody that wove all through the humming and trilling of the Celestines. From deep within the earth the spring of water bubbled again into life and cascaded down the hill. Where the enchanted water wound through the forest, fruits swelled and ripened, berries darkened, and nuts began to bulge in hard green knots within the leaves. Birds flocked down to bathe in the sparkling stream, while nixies cavorted in the shallows, their tinkling laughter sounding like far-off sleigh bells.

The Celestines were all excited by the strength and clarity of the summerbourne, and the air rang with their high-pitched trilling. They all wanted to touch Lachlan's

forehead but Cloudshadow ushered them away into the
garden, knowing the winged prionnsa still had his Tests
to take.

As soon as the faeries had gone, Meghan silently
scratched the shape of a six-pointed star within a circle
into the turf and bade them take their places. Feeling
unaccountably nervous, Iseult obeyed. She knew she
must succeed in the examination if she was to be permitted to join the Coven as an apprentice, and she was
eager to learn all she could of the mysteries of witchcraft
and witchcunning.

Before undertaking the apprenticeship examination,
an acolyte had to again prove themselves in the First
Test of Power, which most would have first undertaken
at the age of eight. Lachlan had passed his First Test
with ease as a child, but since then had suffered enchantment and exile, and no longer possessed the easy confidence he had once enjoyed. Iseult had been given the
First Test by Meghan soon after their meeting, in order
to ascertain the limits of her power so, although she had
been brought up far away from the witches' sphere of
influence, she knew what to expect.

Both she and Lachlan had been extensively coached
all spring and summer for this Second Test of Power,
and they knew their responses by heart. Both were by
nature competitive and warred with each other to do
best. Iseult faltered at the Trials in the element of water,
and Lachlan had difficulty with the Trials of Fire, but at
last they finished, and were told to make their first witch-
ring, as was the custom. Meghan watched critically as
they labored to fashion the moonstones they had found
into a ring. Iseult set the jewel between two single-pet-
alled roses and engraved the silver band with wavering
lines of thorns. It was a device she knew well, her
dragoneye ring set in the same pattern. Lachlan set the
moonstone in a tangle of antlers, with the band engraved
with leaping stags.

It was the usual practice for apprentice witches to ex-
change their first-made ring with their mentor. Since

Meghan was mentor for both Iseult and Lachlan, she had some difficulty in choosing who to swap rings with. Lachlan was her kin, and so had first claim on her. However, the moonstone ring she wore had been made for her by Isabeau only six months earlier, having been exchanged for the ring made by Meghan's previous apprentice, Ishbel. Meghan was very loath to give Isabeau's ring away. Under normal circumstances she would have worn the ring for at least eight years, until her apprentice was admitted fully into the Coven and she was free to take on another acolyte as apprentice.

The presence of Ishbel and Feld complicated matters further. Ishbel was Iseult's mother, but Feld had undertaken much of Iseult's early training. In the end, Meghan decided to let Feld act as Iseult's mentor, for the ring he wore had been made for him by Iseult's father, Khan'tirell. It seemed fitting to the old sorceress that one of the twins should have their mother's ring, the other their father's. Khan'tirell had wrought his ring within the shape of a coiled dragon, a suitable design for a girl who had been raised by the great magical creatures.

This meant Lachlan would receive Ishbel's ring, which Meghan had given to her long ago at her apprenticeship test—it had been wrought by Tabithas the Wolf-Runner and was surely filled with power. Since Meghan NicCunn had been Ishbel's teacher, why should Ishbel not stand as mentor for Lachlan, Meghan's kin? "A potent ring indeed for the lad," she said and kissed Ishbel in thanks.

Once both acolytes were wearing their moonstone proudly on their right hands, the final challenge had to be met—the Trial of Spirit. In this examination Iseult had her revenge on Lachlan for his smugness over her failure at the trial of water. She was easily able to gain emanations from the bogrose brooch that Meghan passed her. She knew it had once belonged to a woman of hot temper and fierce affections, quick with a slap or a kiss.

After she said all this, in halting tones, she was surprised to see Feld wipe his eyes with his long beard and sigh, "Aye, that's my mam, indeed. How clearly ye conjure her for me!"

Lachlan heard no voices from the past, nor saw visions of former owners, nor even gained an impression of emotion from the scarf he was given—all of which would have been acceptable responses. Despite all Meghan's lessons, he could not overcome a reluctance to open his mind. He was both fascinated by, and frightened of, the One Power. Indeed he had seen the worst of it, as Meghan said—his brother ensorcelled and tricked, his brothers transformed and hunted down, himself trapped half bird, half man. Meghan said he had showed exceptional promise when first Tested at eight. He had disappeared when only ten, and was transformed back to human shape when only fifteen. For eight years he had refused to let Meghan or Enit teach him, so embittered with rage that all he wanted to do was fight against the Banrìgh.

The First Trial of Spirit he had passed easily, for he had had to reach out and pluck a thought or image from someone else's mind. The Second Trial of Spirit involved opening himself up to reading the energy vibrations of something else. He had been badly burned by such an experience in the past, having held Maya the Unknown's boot in his hand one day as a child. In what everyone saw as a fury of childish spite and jealousy, he had accused his brother's new wife of being one of the dreaded Fairgean, their country's bitterest enemy. Jaspar had been furious. Only Maya's intervention had saved Lachlan from a whipping. Lachlan would have preferred that to what followed—his beloved brother's cold silences, the distance between them. Only Donncan and Feargus had believed him, and it was only a few weeks later that the Banrìgh had transformed them all into blackbirds and thrown them from her window.

Nothing Meghan said had helped him to overcome his block. The old sorceress had hoped the pressure of the

Tests would drive him on, but he merely shook his head and passed back the scarf, his face shuttered.

Because he had not passed the Second Trial of the Spirit, Lachlan had to pass a Test of an element to compensate, just as Isabeau had had to do earlier in the year. He chose water and easily showed he was able to handle and control the element by spinning it into a whirlpool in the bowl, then changing direction so the whirlpool spun in an anticlockwise direction.

Ishbel smiled at them both gently. "Ye must both now show us how ye use all o' the elemental powers. It is time to make yourself your witch's dagger, to be used in all sacred rites and rituals."

"Take the silver o' the earth's begetting," Feld intoned, "forge it with fire and air, and cool it with water. Fit it into a handle o' sacred hazel that ye have smoothed with your own hands. Speak over it the words o' the Creed and pour your own energies into it. Only then shall ye be admitted into the Coven as an apprentice. Only then shall ye have passed your Test."

Iseult and Lachlan obeyed with alacrity, keen to get the Tests finished so they could rise and stretch. Iseult finished first, accustomed to working with weapons, and said Eà's blessing over her narrow blade with a sigh of relief.

As they walked back down the hill, Ishbel frowned and said to Meghan in an undertone, "Is it no' strange that Iseult is so strong in the spirit when Isabeau was so weak? I would have thought . . ."

Sharp-eared, Iseult looked up in interest and was surprised to see Meghan's lean cheeks color for the first time since she had met her. What was there in the comment to embarrass Meghan? And was it true there was something that Iseult was better at? She was used to finding herself compared to her twin and found lacking. She observed Meghan's flush with interest, but the witch shot her a repressive glance from her bright black eyes and said nothing.

The afternoon was spent in idleness, all the witches

tired after the Ordeal and the Testing. Meghan insisted
Lachlan and Iseult keep apart, so Cloudshadow took the
winged prionnsa away into the gardens with the other
Celestines. Later Iseult heard him singing for them, and
she felt warm tenderness fill her. How much Lachlan
had changed from the surly, suspicious hunchback she
had first known! She wondered if she had changed as
much.

It was late afternoon on Midsummer's Eve when Latifa
came and found Isabeau. She was just about to sit down
at the long table and eat some bread and honey. Somehow she had not managed to swallow a morsel all day.
Her teeth were actually closing onto the bread when
Latifa caught her arm. "Leave that, lassie, ye can eat
later. Come with me. I want ye to clean out the furnace."

Sukey gave Isabeau a grimace of sympathy as the redhead reluctantly got up from the table. All the scullery
maids hated cleaning out the furnace which heated the
water pipes, for it was a long and filthy task normally
reserved for the lowliest of the potboys. Everyone wondered what Isabeau had done to displease Latifa, to be
given such a harsh punishment. Isabeau wondered
herself.

To her surprise Latifa took her in quite a different
direction. They climbed up the narrow back stairs,
higher than the maids' quarters, higher than Isabeau had
ever been before. Through long galleries, narrow corridors and tightly twisting steps Latifa led her, into the
oldest part of the palace. Here the halls were narrow
and of gray stone, not gleaming blue marble.

Her keys clacking at her waist, Latifa paused in the
corridor and held back the folds of an ancient tapestry.
Hidden behind was a door. Latifa fussed through her
loaded keyring and found a long key with an ornate
handle. She unlocked the door and they slipped through,
Isabeau's curiosity growing.

They were in a dark hallway. Latifa summoned a tall
flame from the tip of her finger and gestured Isabeau

forward with her other hand. Isabeau went into the flickering darkness, moving her feet cautiously. Her back to Latifa, she raised her right hand and tried to mimic her. She could summon only a frail flame, though, and so she tucked her hand back under her apron with her crippled one.

They came to a dark spiraling stairwell and began to climb, shadows dancing madly as Latifa huffed and puffed. They climbed into a warm dusk, the staircase winding up into a round tower. At each turn was an immensely tall window facing an ancient door with a dirty and cobwebbed lock. At first the lancet windows showed only gray walls and roofs, unfamiliar to Isabeau even after her weeks exploring the palace. Then the tower grew higher than the building before it and Isabeau could see the dark forests of Ravenshaw. A few more twists and she began to see glimpses of the firth over the palace's peaked roof. Each turn and the view grew grander and wider.

At the apex of the tower was a small room, open to the air through great arched windows, taller than Isabeau herself. The wind poured through the embrasures, tugging at the strings of Isabeau's cap and causing her apron to flutter.

The view made her exclaim in delight, for they could see right across the Berhtfane to the sea. The sun was sinking behind them, the tower casting a long shadow across the palace roof. The water was a blur of violets and blues, the towering islands kindled with sunset. From the other windows the countryside was swathed in a velvety apricot dusk, just beginning to prick here and there with lights. Four tall candlesticks stood at the four corners of the room, at the points of the compass.

"Why have we come all the way up here?" Isabeau asked.

"It's Midsummer's Eve, lassie, surely ye ken that? We o' the Coven try when we can to gather, and this is one o' our meeting places. No window faces it from the palace, and there is none out in the forest to see our lights. At least, so we hope. This palace was built on the site o' a far aulder castle, the home o' the MacBrann clan. The Rìgh's cousin let him have it when he decided to move the court away from Lucescere. Many witches' rites have been held here in the past, and there are reverse spells woven about the tower door to mislead people who may wonder how to get to it. Few even realize it is here, even though ye can see it clearly from the firth.

"I have been hoping and planning to hold the Midsummer rites this year, but with so many people about it is dangerous indeed! Still, Eà is with us, for the Banrìgh is in her bed, bless the babe, and that blaygird evil servant o' hers is down in the town. Some uproar in the docks, and the Rìgh too weak and ill to attend to it. So I canna waste the opportunity. We must take advantage o' the swell in the tides o' power to join the Key. It is our last chance for a month or more, and I would no' dare do it otherwise, no matter how important it is to keep the Key safe."

"What do ye mean by the Key?" Isabeau asked.

Latifa clicked her tongue in annoyance. "In Truth, Isabeau, sometimes I think ye are a halfwit! Did Meghan teach ye nothing? The Key is the sacred symbol o' the Coven, the circle and hexagram. It is carried by the Keybearer, the most powerful witch in the Coven."

"Och, aye, I remember that . . ."

"So I should hope! What did ye think ye were carrying all those months?"

"I was carrying the Key? The Keybearer's Key? No!"

"Did Meghan no' tell ye? In Truth, she has an obsession with secrecy. I keep forgetting. Aye, ye were carrying the Key, or at least part o' it. I have another portion, and Ishbel the Winged had the third. Meghan broke the Key, ye see . . ."

Isabeau was remembering the cryptic words of Jorge the blind seer. He had said she carried "the key to unlock the chains that bind us." Then the Celestine had also spoken about the key. She had said Meghan had locked away the Lodestar with the Key and it could not be freed without it. She had said the power in the Lodestar was dying. *It needs to be touched and held, its power nurtured and used, not to lie in darkness and hollowness,* the Celestine had said. *If it is found and used at Samhain, then indeed all shall be saved or surrendered . . .*

Knowing she had carried a third of the Key suddenly made a great deal of sense to Isabeau. As that one jigsaw piece fell into place, so did many others. *Samhain is the time . . .*

Latifa knelt on the floor of the little tower room and pulled a familiar black bag from her capacious apron pocket. Isabeau gave a little cry of delight and immediately itched to have her fingers on the talisman. Somehow it had grown to be a part of her. Its loss, as much as the loss of her fingers, had made Isabeau feel like only half a person these past few months.

Latifa also pulled out a dagger, a bundle of candles, a bunch of herbs, and a bag of salt. She carefully removed the old candles, dark green and smelling of bay and juniper so Isabeau knew they had been burned for Beltane. She replaced them with tall, white candles that gleamed with sweet-smelling precious oils—rosemary, angelica and gilly-flowers, for healing, consecration, an increase of psychic powers and protection against evil. Isabeau wondered at her choice—normally Midsummer candles were made with lavender and rose for love spells and divination. Latifa knew far more about candlelight spells than Isabeau, however, so she said nothing.

Hearing footsteps on the stairs, Isabeau tensed. Moving quickly for a woman of her bulk, Latifa stepped to the stairwell and peered down. "Toireasa, at last!" she cried. "I was beginning to worry."

The head weaver and seamstress at the palace, Toireasa was a tall, gaunt woman with thick brown hair bundled untidily into a bun at the nape of her neck. Isabeau had met her several times before. She carried a jug of water in one hand. "No need to worry," she said. "It is always hard for me to get away but I always manage it."

Isabeau stood awkwardly, unsure what to say or do.

The seamstress said, "Good evening to ye, Red. Glad to see Latifa's cooking is putting a little meat on your bones."

Before Isabeau could think of anything to say, they heard harsh panting and someone else came slowly up the stairs. Isabeau could only gape at him as he fought to catch his breath after the steep climb. It was Riordan Bowlegs. He smelled of the stables, and there was straw on his jacket. He twinkled at her, doffed his tam o'shanter to Latifa and Toireasa, and laid down his staff on the floor. Isabeau had often seen him leaning on it as he stood ruminating in the kitchen garden, but it had never occurred to her it might be a witch's staff. It was a gnarled hazel branch, polished and oiled to a warm luster and topped with a bulge of wood gleaming with years of handling.

"It is good indeed to see ye, Red, and ye too, Latifa, Toireasa. I had some trouble getting here, the corridors are swarming, and three o' your lackeys took it into their heads to challenge me." He winked at Isabeau and said softly, "Stable-hands are no' permitted in the palace, as ye well ken."

Last to come was a man Isabeau had never seen before. He was dressed in black silk and his black beard was elaborately pointed and curled. His long, white fingers were laden with rings, including a moonstone and an opal. Isabeau wondered that he dared. Jewelled rings were regarded with great suspicion these days. Tucked under one arm was a slender walking stick, embossed all over with intricate silver patterns.

"Isabeau, this is Dughall MacBrann, heir to the Prionnsa o' Ravenshaw and cousin to the Rìgh. My laird, this is Isabeau the Foundling." The slender laird bowed, fingering his curled mustache. Isabeau bobbed her head gauchely.

Latifa laid the fire in a stone dish set right in the very center of the room and gestured for the witches to enter the circle and star. Isabeau was silently directed to sit at one of the northern-facing points, Riordan Bowlegs next to her, with Toireasa to the west and Dughall MacBrann to the east. She sat bolt upright as Latifa drew about them the shape of the circle and pentagram with the point of her dagger.

"Isabeau, make sure ye do no' allow any part o' your body to pass outside the magic circle," the cook warned. Isabeau looked up, wanting to protest that she was not an ignorant acolyte. The still, focused expression of Latifa's face stopped her, and she sat silently.

Latifa sprinkled the circle with water and salt, chanting, "I consecrate and conjure thee, O circle o' magic, ring o' power, symbol o' perfection and constant renewal. Keep us safe from harm, keep us safe from evil, guard us against treachery, keep us safe in your eyes, Eà o' the moons."

She did the same along the criss-crossing lines of the star. "I consecrate and conjure thee, O star o' spirit, pentacle o' power, symbol o' fire and darkness, o' light in the depths o' space. Fill us with your dark fire, your fiery darkness, make o' us your vessels, fill us with light."

Latifa took her place at the apex of the star, lowering herself to the floor with great difficulty. They chanted the Midsummer rites as the sun sank behind the mountains. Isabeau had sung these rhymes since she was a child, and the familiarity soothed her jangling nerves. She could not help feeling afraid. They were performing a forbidden ritual in the very heart of the Rìgh's palace. What if someone heard? What if Sani returned and sensed magic was being performed? What if one of these witches was a spy of the Awl? The dangers seemed so many that Isabeau's heart was pounding in her ears like a drum.

By the time they had finished, it was dusk. The fire illuminated their faces with red; black shadows leaped about the tower room. "It is moonrise," Latifa said softly. "Focus your energies, my friends, guard your spirits. The spell shall begin."

Slowly she pulled the talisman from the bag of nyx hair. At once Isabeau could feel its power beating at her.

It seemed to sing. A slender triangle, the flat surfaces of
its three sides were inscribed with magical symbols. Latifa held it above the fire and let it go. With the scented
smoke trailing around it and through it, the talisman
floated above the flames.

Latifa unhooked the large bunch of keys that hung on
her belt. Isabeau had seen these keys every day since
she had been in Rhyssmadill, for the cook never removed them. On the great hoop hung keys to the storerooms, larders, linen cupboards and cellars. Carefully the
cook detached the keys, of all shapes, sizes and metals,
and laid them together on the floor by her plump knee.
In her hand remained the hoop from which they had
hung. Isabeau found she had difficulty focusing on it.
Latifa made a series of complicated gestures over it,
muttering under her breath. Green fire flared. Suddenly
the power coiling in the magic circle doubled; the song
became a harmony.

Isabeau was now able to look upon the hoop with
clear eyes. She saw it was made of the same dark metal
as her triangle, flat on either side and carved with magical symbols. "It's part o' the Key," she exclaimed.

"Indeed it is," Latifa responded. "Wonderful what a
simple wee charm like a reverse spell can do. I've worn
the Key's circle at my waist for sixteen years and no-
one has been the wiser."

To the east Gladrielle had risen, transparent and blue.
The crimson face of Magnysson was just beginning to
peer above the horizon. Only a few of the island peaks
were still gilded with the last rays of the sun; the rest
swam in shadows. Latifa began chanting under her
breath:

"In the name o' Eà, mother and father o' us all,
I command thee.
By the power o' all gods and goddesses, who are one,
I command thee.
By the power o' the universe, time and space,
I command thee.

Make whole what has been broken;
Make complete what was divided.
By all the power o' land and sea,
By all the might o' the moons and sun—
Make whole what has been broken;
Make complete what was divided.
By all the power o' land and sea,
By all the might o' the moons and sun—
Make whole what has been broken.
Make complete what was divided.
As we wish, as we will, so let it be,
Chant the spell, let it be done!"

As she intoned the words, she suspended the circle in the air above the fire. It floated there, a few inches above the hovering triangle. The tower room filled with moonlight as the last rays of the sun faded. Gladrielle shone silver, mingling with the warmth of Magnysson's light as the larger of the two moons lifted clear of the horizon. As Latifa cried the last few words, the triangle and circle sprang together with an audible click. Isabeau was immediately aware of a difference in the atmosphere; the song of the Key softened into a crooning lullaby.

The five witches watched the talisman float above the embers, a circle crossed with three lines. In the moonlight, the shapes carved on the flat surface were like deep pits. With gesture and muttered word, Latifa replaced the reverse spell, then carefully hung her keys from the rim of the hoop again.

Although Isabeau concentrated all her will, she could not make her attention stay on the keyring. Vaguely she could see the hoop was criss-crossed with metal where before it had been empty, but her eyes slid away before she could really examine it. Latifa smiled at her a little wearily. "It is done," she said. "The Key is no' yet complete, but we have two parts o' it and Meghan the other. We are closer to releasing the Lodestar than we have been in sixteen years."

"Let us hope it is not too much longer," the Prionnsa

o' Ravenshaw said. "The Lodestar has been buried long enough."

They all stretched and murmured, and Latifa opened the magic circle with her dagger and let them all stand and move about. Isabeau was bid to stamp out the fire and clean the room, while one by one the others slipped away. At last only Latifa was left, and she watched critically while Isabeau swept up the ashes with the little pan and brush she had brought, thinking she was to clean the furnace.

"Ye can go and eat now," Latifa said with a smile. "I had to keep ye fasting until after the Midsummer rites, but ye'll need all your strength for the festivities this evening. It shall be a long night."

MIDSUMMER'S EVE

I ain MacFóghnan was roused by a touch on his shoulder. His mother's chamberlain, Khan'tirell, had slipped into his room without making a sound. Iain started and knocked over his inkwell so that a river of dark blue poured over the table.

"K-K-Khan'tirell . . ." he said, mopping up the spilled ink. "How ye st-st-startled me! What is it?"

"Your mother requests the pleasure o' your presence in the throne room," the chamberlain replied in his harshly accented voice. His sharp-angled, fierce face and curling horns belied his smooth manners and expression, as did the three long, parallel scars on either lean cheek that showed white against his skin. Iain was afraid of Khan'tirell, who had been a celebrated warrior among his own people. He knew well the chamberlain regarded him with contempt.

"V-v-very well, tell my m-m-mother I will be along presently," Iain said with a fair attempt at coolness.

"As ye wish, my laird." Khan'tirell left as silently as he had come.

Iain got to his feet immediately and hurried through to his bedroom as he stripped off his ink-stained shirt. He poured water into the thistle-painted bowl from the

jug on the side table and scrubbed his face and hands
vigorously. Slicking back his soft brown hair with urgent
fingers, he scrambled into a fresh shirt. After a moment's
thought, he changed his shabby old kilt for a pair of
black velvet breeches, tied at the knee with purple, a
purple and black doublet, and thistle-embroidered stock-
ings. Best to give his mother nothing to berate him with.
She had been in a foul mood ever since the Mesmerdean
came and told her of the massacre of their egg-brothers
in the Veiled Forest. An entire spawn of Mesmerdean
had died at the hand of Meghan NicCuinn and her companions, and as a result the entire race was withdrawing
into the marshes for the mourning. Only those Mesmerdean in active service to the banprionnsa herself were
to be exempted, and that meant many of Margrit's
schemes had had to be postponed.

Iain ran through the wide corridors to the magnificent
sweeping staircase and hurried down as fast as he could
without losing his step. No-one kept the Banprionnsa of
Arran waiting if they could possibly help it. His footsteps
slowed as he approached the great double doors into the
throne room, and he nervously checked his hair and
clothes before gently pushing the doors open.

His mother was reclining on the purple cushions of
her carved and gilded throne, regarding the rings which
decorated nearly every finger of her hands. On either
side stood long lines of soldiers dressed in long white
surcoats over hauberks and chausses. Their surcoats and
banners were emblazoned with scarlet fitché crosses. At
their head was a Berhtilde. The heaviness of her clothing
could not quite conceal the fact that her left breast had
been cut off.

Iain's step faltered, but he recovered himself immediately. Trying to walk with stately majesty (and all too
conscious he looked a fool), Iain came to the center of
the room and bowed, saying to himself: *Right foot forward, point left leg, bend right leg from the hips, flourish
with left hand . . .*

"My dear, your bow grows more courtly every day,"

his mother purred. "Ye begin to look more like a Mac-Fóghnan. Make your bow to your bride."

Iain stiffened. Straightening, he glanced quickly around the room and saw a slender, fair girl seated on one of the chaise longues against the wall. She was dressed in a humble gray gown, her hair covered in a gray hood. She looked more like a chambermaid at a country house than a banprionnsa. Seated next to her was a hard-faced woman with a distinct beard sprouting from her chin.

Iain bowed as gracefully as he could, keeping his face expressionless. The girl rose rather timidly and curtsied.

"Elfrida Elise NicHilde, I have great pleasure in presenting my son, the Prionnsa Iain Strathclyde MacFóghnan, heir to the Tower o' Mists and all o' Arran. Elfrida is, o' course, daughter o' and only heir to Dieter MacHilde, former Prionnsa o' Tìrsoilleir."

Iain sensed rather than saw the stiffening of the soldiers' stance, the tension in the slight figure of his bride.

"Iain, your bride has traveled far to be with ye. She shall need to rest before the ceremony to be sure to be in her greatest beauty. The wedding shall be tonight, at seven o'clock. Make sure ye are ready."

His heart beating rather fast, Iain bowed his head in acquiescence before sneaking another quick glance at his prospective bride. For months, since his mother had told him she had arranged a marriage with a NicHilde, Iain had had nightmares of a big strapping girl who would out-ride, out-shoot and out-wrestle him. The MacHildes were the descendants of Berhtilde, the greatest fighter their world had ever known, known for her ruthlessness and great strength. This NicHilde was small, with a pointed face and large, fearful gray eyes. Iain felt his nervousness dissolve and he risked giving her a quick smile while his mother was conversing with the bearded lady-in-waiting. To his pleasure she smiled back, her rather plain face lighting with sweetness and charm.

"M-M-May I show ye to your rooms, m-m-my lady?" he asked.

"Ye may," his mother replied, shooting a quick, shrewd look at them both. "Her rooms are your rooms, Iain. I am anxious an heir shall be conceived as soon as possible. I hope they are in presentable order for your new bride?"

Iain blushed, thinking of the tangle of ink-stained clothes, the table piled with books and papers, now all blemished with ink, his unmade bed.

"I gather they are no'," Margrit smiled. She turned to the bearded woman and said conversationally. "They say blood will always tell. My son's father was naught but a minor laird, more interested in hunting and bedding serving maids than affairs o' state. I be afraid Iain has inherited his shortcomings."

This time Iain flushed to the roots of his hair, his fists involuntarily clenching. Margrit smiled and cooed at them sweetly. "Flutter away, my wee doves. Elfrida, my dear, we shall have to find ye something more suitable to wear. Ye look like a serving wench. I shall send my seamstresses to ye. Meanwhile, Iain, try to keep your hands off her. She'll be yours in just a few hours, ye can deflower her then. We want to be sure she is still a maid when the wedding vows are made."

He was conscious of the girl's flush and downcast eyes and wondered why it was his mother was always so coarse when she professed to be so delicately minded. With another small bow, he held out his hand to Elfrida. After a moment of hesitation, she put her fingers in his. They were cold and trembled. He resisted the urge to press them reassuringly, and led her into the hall.

Not a word passed between them all the way to his suite. Iain vacillated between ideas of escape and a desire to reassure her. Only the knowledge his mother would send out the Mesmerdean to hunt him down prevented him from making a run for it then and there. He was red with embarrassment as he ushered her into his untidy sitting room. "I'm s-s-sorry, I d-d-did no' ken ye were coming."

She put back her hood with both hands, revealing pale

gold hair pulled severely into a black snood at the back of her head. Her face was so small and colorless the style did not suit her, making her eyes seem far too large. When he put out his hands to take her hood, she shrank away.

He searched for something to say. "Have n-n-none o' your family come to see ye be m-m-m-m . . ." He struggled for a moment, and at last forced out, "Wed?"

She shook her head. "I have no family," she said in a soft voice. "They all perished in the troubles. My mother died when I was born, my father soon after."

Iain cursed himself for maladroitness. He had been thoroughly taught the history and politics of every country in the Far Islands. He knew the royal family of Tìrsoilleir had been overthrown long ago, the land governed instead by a council elected from the warriors and priests. Despite several successful insurrections by the MacHildes, the council had again and again overthrown the throne and had ruled unchallenged for more than twenty years. The heir to the throne, Dieter MacHilde, had died fifteen or more years ago, trying to break out of the prison in which he had lived all his life. Elfrida must have been only three, for she was eighteen now. She looked younger. He wondered if she had been born and raised in the same prison as her father. He felt pity swell his heart.

Immediately Elfrida looked up, and her soft, pale mouth set tightly. "I have been well treated all my life by the Fealde and the Council. They fed me and schooled me at the expense o' the people, and for that I am grateful. My life has been easy and pampered in comparison with many o' the righteous, and I give thanks and blessing to our holy God that I was permitted to live despite my witch-tainted heritage."

Iain glanced rather wildly from side to side, then said loudly, "Here is something ye m-m-may enjoy, my lady." He quickly wound up a beautiful musical toy and set it to playing a dreamy waltz. Then he took Elfrida's hand in his, and whispered in her ear, "Ye m-must realize ye are in one o' magic's l-l-last strongholds! Do no' let my m-m-m-mother hear ye speak o' being 'tainted.' She will be very angry, and believe m-m-me, ye do no' wish her to be angry with ye."

Elfrida shot a glance at him out of her wide gray eyes and whispered back, "Does she listen to ye in your rooms?"

"She listens everywhere," Iain murmured back.

Elfrida nodded. "I am used to that. I was always spied upon in Bride. Ye must tell me what I am permitted to say and do. Ye need no' fear I shall forget."

Liking his bride more by the minute, Iain led her by the hand to the window embrasure and they sat in the shelter of the sweeping curtains. "Ye m-m-must never disagree with or disobey her," he whispered. "Ye m-m-must never let your face show any emotion she does no' w-w-wish to see. Ye must keep your real thoughts to yourself, and that is hard for she can read your thoughts if ye are n-n-no' careful. She believes ye are strong in magic. Are ye?"

Her face was tense. "I do no' ken. I have never been taught. I . . . know things sometimes . . ."

In Bride suspected witches were burned. Iain knew that and squeezed her hand. She did not squeeze back. "Ye m-m-must learn as fast as ye can. I will help ye when I can."

She nodded, and he bent his head closer to hers. Her skin was marvelously smooth and fine, her scent faint and fresh. He felt his body clench with desire and misgiving, and drew away a little. She looked up at him, gray eyes luminous, and he said diffidently, "How do ye f-f-f-feel about this m-m-m-m-marriage?"

"I am grateful to the Fealde for negotiating such an advantageous marriage for me. I give thanks to our Holy Father for his blessing and forgiveness and pray that I may be found worthy." Again her voice was flat, as if she was repeating something learned by rote.

"Ye do n-n-no' wish . . . ye have no . . . ye are no' frightened? S-s-s-o far away from home?"

"I am glad to be free o' Tìrsoilleir," she hissed unexpectedly. "No matter how awful it is here, it canna be worse than Bride!"

Iain was about to question her more when he became aware of the curtain lifting slightly in a draught. He said loudly, "Look, Elfrida, see how the swans fly? Do they n-n-no' look bonny?"

Elfrida glanced up at him sharply, then twisted in her seat so she was looking out over the misty Murkmyre. Beyond the loch, the marshes were wreathed in gray, but against a clear sky two swans flew, the rose and crimson of their wings flaming in the light of the setting sun. Elfrida gave a genuine exclamation of delight and knelt on the seat so she could watch them disappear over the pearly, scrolled minarets of the Tower of Mists.

Iain held back the curtains and said with only a slight tremor in his voice, "N-n-now I had best be leaving ye, my lady, for ye must be sore tired and w-w-wishing a bath and a rest. Please forgive me the d-disorder o' my rooms; I shall send up a chamberm-m-maid at once."

As he had expected, Khan'tirell had entered his room and was making a show of tidying up some of the scattered clothes. Iain said, "Ah, Khan'tirell, your t-t-timing as always is impeccable. My lady Elfrida is in n-n-need o' assistance. I shall leave her in your good hands."

It gave him immense satisfaction to see the slight flicker of surprise on the Khan'cohban's face. For possibly the first time in his twenty-three years Iain had bested his mother's chamberlain and he had to struggle to keep his face free of expression. Once he had left the chamber, he allowed himself a small smile and then hurried through the grand corridors until he came to the tower where his mother's Theurgia was housed. No guard stood before the ancient, iron-bound door for Margrit was confident her involuntary students would not make another attempt to escape after their last disastrous effort.

Iain easily manipulated the lock open and slipped inside. He locked the door behind him and turned to the

room full of children with his finger to his lip. One never
knew when his mother would be listening.

The room was lined on all sides with books and scrolls
untidily thrust into every shelf. A long table filled most
of the room, much scarred with ink and scratches. On a
sideboard was a loaf of dark bread, much hacked about
by blunt knives, and cold water. Iain wished he had
thought to bring some delicacy from his own plate for
the children. His mother believed half starving her involuntary pupils was as good a way as any to keep them
in subjection.

Most of the smaller children clustered around Iain's
legs hopefully as he drew near the fire, and he had to
shake his head and show his empty pockets before they
let him be. Whispering apologies, he drew up a chair at
the far end of the table where a taller boy was sitting,
desultorily playing cards with three younger lads.

Douglas MacSeinn smiled at him, his seagreen eyes
brilliant, and made a sign with his left hand. Immediately
the other three boys slipped from their place and went
to play a very noisy game by the window. Under the
cover of their laughter, Iain whispered, "She's c-c-
come."

Douglas immediately knew who he meant, and thought,
Time to go . . .

I do no' think so, Iain replied. *I am meant to be preparing for my wedding now. I shall soon be missed. I
think we must wait still.*

But ye canna be marrying the big bosomy blonde!

Iain smiled, and whispered, "She's blonde but no' so
big."

"Ye've met her?"

"Aye. Her n-n-name's Elfrida. There are about sixty
soldiers with her, and apparently another thousand m-
m-making their way through the m-m-mists. It's madness! My m-m-m-mother must have sent bogfaeries to
guide them through, for there is no chance they could
have penetrated the m-m-m-marshes otherwise. I bet she
is making them pay d-d-d-dearly for her assistance."

"A thousand! That's a fair few."

"I think from something Elfrida's w-w-w-woman said that a division o' a similar size is t-t-t-trying to cross the Great Divide, to strike at B-B-B-Blessém from Aslinn."

"Even if they set up ropes and ladders for the soldiers to climb, it'll be slow work crossing the Great Divide," Douglas said confidently. He had tried to climb the three-hundred-foot-high cliff face himself and knew it was no easy task.

"Aye, indeed, but who k-k-k-kens when they began?" Iain pointed out. "It is M-M-M-Midsummer's Eve now. They could have been crossing the Great Divide since the snow m-m-m-melted. That was when my m-m-m-mother signed the alliance, so their plans must have been close to fruition then. Easy enough for them to hide out in Aslinn, for f-f-f-few live in the forests now."

Douglas nodded, his face grim. "Ye're right. We have no idea, really."

"I'll try and find out f-f-f-from Elfrida."

"But she is Tìrsoilleirean! Ye canna be confiding in her!"

"I think I could," Iain said thoughtfully. "But I will no' yet. She has no love for the F-F-Fealde, though, Douglas. Think about it. The Kirk deposed her family and kept her locked up in a p-p-prison all her life. All she wants is to be free o' them."

"I'd wager she wishes to restore the monarchy in Tìrsoilleir," Douglas cried. "She'd be a banprionnsa then."

"M-M-Maybe so. Who kens? I think she'll b-b-be an ally though."

"Ye canna be telling her about our escape plans!"

Iain held his finger up to his lips to warn his friend to keep his voice down. "I will no' t-t-tell her," he whispered reassuringly. "No' yet anyway. After tonight, though, she'll be my w-w-w-wife. I'll have to tell her sometime."

"That soon! Tonight!"

"Aye, my m-m-m-mother does no' believe in wasting

time. Besides, it's Midsummer's Eve—I believe she always p-p-planned for me to jump the f-f-f-fire tonight,
she always holds hard to t-t-traditions."

"Och, Iain, I am so sorry! Ye sure ye do no' want to
make a run for it tonight?"

"No. I think it will be b-b-b-better than I had
imagined."

"Oh, she's a beauty then," Douglas said teasingly.

"No b-b-b-beauty, but a sweet wee lass, and cleverer
than she looks. Both o' us are subject to the will and
ambition o' others, we have that in c-c-c-common at
least."

"Tonight . . ." Douglas mused.

"Aye. I wonder if ye will be allowed to w-w-w-watch.
My m-m-m-mother will make sure there is as much p-
p-pomp and ceremony as possible. I may be merely the
son o' a lesser l-l-l-laird, but a descendent o' Fóghnan
nonetheless." Again there was bitterness in his voice. "I
will ask my m-m-m-mother for permission. It is time to
move to stage two o' our plans."

He asked his mother immediately, pointing out how
wise it would be to give the students some greater freedom and privileges now they understood defiance was
futile. "Did Fóghnan no' say a b-b-blow from an iron
fist followed by a s-s-stroke from a velvet glove was the
best way to break a m-m-m-man's spirit?"

"Fóghnan did no' say it, but it is wise advice nonetheless," his mother said with a grimace. "Ye finally seem
to be learning some sagacity, Iain. I have been pleased
with ye these last few months, ye have been sensible and
done what I have bid ye without any o' these sulks or
tantrums I so despise."

"Thank ye, M-M-M-Mother," Iain responded, his
tongue tangling despite all his efforts. He hesitated, and
said, "It has been in my mind, M-M-M-Mother, that the
students o' the Theurgia may benefit from some t-t-t-
time in the gardens or on the lake. It is midsummer, yet
all are looking rather . . . pale and p-p-peaky. Did ye
no' once tell me that one should d-d-d-develop the body

as well as the mind, that a true witch should be physically strong and p-p-powerful as well as m-m-m-
mentally?"

"Indeed I did, Iain," his mother said warmly. "I have
always deplored the way ye spent all your time with your
head in a book. Ye need strength o' body as well as
strength o' mind to fully realize your potential."

"M-M-My other thought was the children will be
much happier and s-s-s-settled if they grow to love the
m-m-m-marshes as we d-d-do. If they saw how b-b-b-
bonny it is now, with the cygnets just swimming and the
goldenrod and m-m-m-murkwoad blooming."

"True, true," Margrit mused. "I do no' trust them no'
to try and escape, though."

"How can they escape?" Iain shrugged. "They ken
nothing o' the secret paths and byways, and the M-M-
M-Mesmerdean are always aware o' what passes through
their t-t-t-territory . . ."

"And the bogfaeries are under orders to let none pass
that do no' have my authority. Ye are right. If ye or one
o' the warlocks are with them at all times, I see no reason why a few canna get some air and sunshine and
see the beauties o' our fens. I will give directions to
the staff."

"Perhaps as p-p-p-part o' the wedding celebrations?"
Iain suggested. "A w-w-w-wedding picnic?"

His mother shook her head decidedly. "Nay, it is
enough that they are allowed out o' the Theurgia's tower
to see ye wed. Too many concessions too soon will only
lead to liberties being taken. Tell Khan'tirell to keep a
close guard and find them some reasonable clothes. In
fact, tell him to prepare the prettiest o' the girls to be
Elfrida's maids. She has no-one to carry her train and
no attendants other than that hideous woman with the
beard. Has the woman never heard o' plucking? These
Tìrsoilleirean have no idea at all about style. I shall no'
be letting that bearded monstrosity in the wedding party,
ye can be sure o' that!"

"No, M-M-M-Mother," Iain replied meekly, and re-

ceived another glance of approbation from the banprionnsa.

"Ye are pleased with your bride, then, Iain?"

He took a deep breath before answering carefully,
"Indeed, yes, M-M-M-Mother, now I have had time for
reflection. She is o' the very best b-b-b-blood, yet shall
never think herself g-g-greater than Arran, being an out-
cast in her own land. She has Talent, I am sure, but has
had no training and shall be glad for w-w-what we can
give her, and easy to m-m-mould to our will. She was
unhappy in her own land and so is happy to be here,
and no' longing for her home and family all the time. I
think she shall do well."

His mother nodded slowly. "Ye seem to be growing
into a man, my son," she said. "We will see if having a
wife completes the growing process."

Iain bowed his head in acquiescence, trying hard to
conceal his exultation. To gain what he wanted so easily!
Indeed, his attempt at emulating Douglas's poise these
past few months was paying dividends already. Now all
he had to do was suffer the wedding, bed his wife (a
task Iain was beginning to look forward to), and wait
for a chance to break free.

Iseult was woken by her mother kissing her forehead.
Filled with well-being, Iseult stretched in the dappled
sunshine. The clearing was hung with flowers and a wedding feast was spread beneath the huge trees. Meghan
and the Firemaker took her to the pool to be bathed
with Meghan's sweet-scented soaps. She stepped out
onto the grass and the Firemaker took her dripping hair
between her hands and dried it so it sprang into thick,
fiery ringlets that hung down her neck. Cloudshadow
held out her wedding dress for her to step into. Blue as
the summer sky, tendrils of moonflowers in white and
primrose-yellow climbed up from the ground and twisted
along the neckline. She wore no other clothing, her feet
bare, her head crowned with flowers. On one hand

gleamed the moonstone, on the other the dragoneye flashed golden.

From the clearing came the sound of laughter and the pound of the hobgoblins' drums. The cluricauns began to play their pipes, reminding Iseult of the Beltane festivities when she and Lachlan had danced together and loved for the first time. She sipped her wine, feeling its warmth spread through her, and wondered at her serenity. She had never thought to marry, yet here she was, only moments away from her wedding.

Meghan chanted the words of the wedding service as Iseult and Lachlan linked hands by the fire. They made their vows just as the sun was just setting, the clearing awash with golden light. Above the hill of the Celestines, the two moons hung, round as coins.

Three times Iseult and Lachlan ran around the fire, keeping their right hands to the flames, then turned and circled three times again, this time widdershins. Lachlan swung Iseult around and, clutching her wreath, she ran with him around the fire three times again. The hobgoblins drummed in heart-disturbing rhythms, the cluricauns piped away on their wooden flutes, and the Firemaker suddenly gave a long ululation of approval. Everyone laughed and Lachlan pulled Iseult to him, kissed her mouth and prepared to jump the bonfire. At first Lachlan hesitated, but Iseult just whispered to him, "If ye use your wings, ye'll be fine, ye fool!"

He cast her an angry look and ran forward so fast she almost stumbled. When they leaped over the bonfire, he spread both wings and for the first time ever, beat them strongly. Both he and Iseult soared over the flames, which hissed and crackled in the back-breeze, and for once it was Iseult faltering behind.

"Ye flew!" Iseult cried. "Lachlan, did ye feel it? Ye actually flew!"

He gripped her hand so tightly she gasped, and swept her into his arms to kiss her, to the delight of the nisses, who darted about their heads like dragonflies.

Meghan said, "Ye have sworn to be true to each

other, and care for and respect each other, living and
loving with courage and kindness and faith. Ye have
taken strength from the fruits of the earth, ye have
breathed o' the air, drunk deeply o' the water, and dared
the flames. Let now your blood mingle and spill, and
hold handfast, that your troth be given."

Solemn now, Lachlan cut his finger and Iseult's with
the edge of his *sgian dubh,* and they pressed their
wounds together above the fire, their blood trickling into
the flames. Meghan said, "As your blood mingles, so do
your lives and fates. May your path be free o' stones
and thorns!"

The great square at Dùn Gorm was strung with lanterns
and crowded with people. All had come to see the Summer Fair, the festival of the jongleurs. On the road for
most of the year, jongleurs, minstrels and troubadours
came from all over Eileanan and the Far Islands to trade
skills and compete against one another. Many old friends
were briefly reunited at the Summer Fair, and the city
was always filled with travelers who came to watch, listen
and marvel.

Enit Silverthroat's and Morrell Fire-Eater's caravans
had one of the best positions in the square, and the
jongleurs were taking advantage of the large crowd to
show off some of their most dazzling routines. Dide jug-
gled swords in a breathtaking sequence; Morrell swallowed flaming brands and spat out fire like a dragon;
Nina tumbled, cartwheeled and dived through a flaming
hoop, while Enit sang poignant love songs that brought
a prickle to the eyes of many. Now she sat on her caravan steps and gravely exchanged greetings with the jongleurs that passed by. Nobody noticed when a passing
merchant stealthily thrust a large package into her
hands. All eyes were fixed on the great plume of fire
Morrell was exhaling.

Dide caught the flashing swords and bowed with a
flourish. To cheers and whistles, he ran out of the performing circle and ducked back to the caravan. "Sunset,

Coppersmiths Alley," his grandmother said softly as he stepped past her up the caravan steps. He made no indication that he had heard her.

Twenty minutes later he came out of the caravan into the dusky apricot of the summer evening. He had changed out of his sky-blue and crimson into brown breeches. He looked more like a clerk than a jongleur.

"I be going to see if Iven Yellowbeard's cart has come," he called to his grandmother, who nodded vaguely as she stirred the stew over the fire. He plunged off into the crowd, twisting through the maze of caravans. Occasionally he stopped and chatted to a fellow jongleur, scanning the people around him with sharp eyes and his witch senses. Once he was sure none followed him or paid him any attention, he ducked out of the square and into the streets of the city.

By the time the sun was setting he was in the metalsmiths' quarter and strolling down the steps that led to Coppersmiths Alley. Children and small dogs were taking advantage of the warm evening to play in the streets, and a few women were leaning out the windows to gather in their laundry, strung overhead like carnival flags. Dide's heart was beating quickly, but he felt none of the prickle of uneasiness that spelled danger. He paused at the corner and looked about him casually, then stepped down into the dark little alley.

Most of the smithies were shut for the evening, but at the far end a tall door stood open. Dide strode up to the door, hesitated as if trying to make up his mind, then stepped inside.

Once within its gloom, all pretence of casualness dropped from him. He peered through a spyhole cleverly concealed in the wall, while the old man mending a buckle at the bench checked the doors and windows. Satisfied all was clear, some of the tenseness left them and the old man beckoned Dide into the rooms beyond.

They climbed the stairs to the attic, and the old man pulled back a secret panel to reveal a narrow space in the ceiling. With thatch above and plaster and beams below, it was barely large enough for a man to crouch in. Dide would have to crawl down the center beam, which ran the entire row of buildings in this quarter. One misstep and his foot would break through the ceiling into somebody's attic.

He thanked the old man, swung lithely into the ceiling and began to crawl. It was slow and difficult, and Dide had to fight the desire to sneeze as the thatch tickled his nose. He came at last to his destination and felt his knees sag in relief. Carefully he opened the panel and dropped down into the attic.

Dide hurried down four flights of stairs, listening always for any sign of danger, and ducked through the empty house to the wine cellar. He knew where to find the false wine rack, swung it open and slipped through into another large cellar, lit by only one lantern. Within were twelve of his fellow rebels, all dressed in the uniform of the Red Guards. They gathered close around him, clapping him on the back and asking after Nina and Enit. Dide had had many adventures with them all, for most witches were brought to Dùn Gorm for execution and so the rebels were most active in the capital city. Between them they had saved many witches from a horrible death.

Rapidly Dide changed into a red kilt and jerkin. He drew a sword, bundled in a red cloak, out of his bag, buckled the sword about his waist and wrapped the red cloak about him with a swagger. To the laughter of the rebels, he took a few mincing steps about, waving his cloak and saying, "Och, aye, I be a fine soldier indeed! Such a pretty lad in my crimson finery!" Although Dide was anxious about the task ahead, he knew it was up to him to support his men's spirits.

The cellar had a trapdoor in its ceiling which opened into the floor of a storeroom in the Red Guards' barracks. The complex had once housed the Yeomen of the Guard, the bodyguard of the Rìgh. After they had been disbanded, the Banrìgh's Guards had taken it over. None of the Yeomen had thought to pass on the secrets of the military headquarters to their successors. Only the rebels knew of the cellar, thanks to Duncan Ironfist.

Dide clambered up first, carefully shifting the discarded furniture that shielded the trapdoor from view. He kept guard as one by one the rebels followed him into the darkness of the storeroom. Concealing the entrance again, they quietly filed out into a small enclosed courtyard. From beyond the wall came the shouts and thuds of men-at-arms practicing their weapon play.

After checking to make sure no-one was in the yard beyond, the rebels marched out. This was where the danger truly began, for they were in the heart of their enemy's stronghold. The barracks' forces were much depleted, luckily, for many soldiers had gone to reinforce the palace and town guard during the Midsummer festivities.

It was from this point on that Lady Luck would take a hand in the dice game, and Dide was not a gambler like his father. He liked to be sure. The jongleur's jaw was gritted tight as he led his men into the center square where soldiers were sparring and jousting. The thirteen rebels kept an easy motion, stiff-backed and eyes forward, and were not challenged as they rounded the square and exited to the side. Dide breathed more easily and found his hands were damp with perspiration.

They came to the tower where prisoners were kept. A wave of despair and horror swept over Dide, and he resolutely shut his mind to the building's aura. Several of his companions were also sensitive to atmosphere and paled, but their stride did not falter. He was proud of them.

They did not step out into the courtyard before the tower, but waited in the shadows of the corridor, keeping close watch in both directions. The old cook had told them it would take two hours for the contaminated ale to work, and they had timed it closely. Dide could only hope the guards would not decide to wait until they were off duty to celebrate Midsummer.

The door of the tower swung open and a soldier came

stumbling out, clutching his stomach. They retreated before him till he was deep in the shadows, then came
up to him, grasping his arm. "Wha' is it, soldier? Are
ye ill?"

"Eaten . . . something," he retched. "We need . . .
relief guard. The whole lot o' us be taken ill . . . or
poisoned. Must go and get . . . assistance."

Dide hit him lightly on the back of the head with his
sword hilt, and he fell back into one of the rebels' arms.
"Stow him safely," Dide said grimly, "then wait. In ten
minutes or so we shall go in."

When they reported for duty, the guard in the outer
room was greenish and sweating, and he kept his hand
pressed to the back of his mouth. "Thank the Truth ye
are come! That last batch o' ale must have been made
with tainted hops, for I tell ye, man, it is sick as cursed
cats we all are!"

A convulsion ran over him and he ducked for the
inner room, from which they heard the unmistakable
sounds of retching. Dide suppressed a smile. He did not
know how she had done it, but the old cook up at the
palace had come through as promised. No questions
would be asked about the relief guard; the soldiers were
far too relieved to be free to report to the infirmary. All
twelve of them staggered away, handing over the keys
to Dide and warning them to steer clear of the beer.

As soon as they were out of sight, Dide set guards,
beckoning some of his men to follow him as he hurried
up the stairs to the cells above. The jongleur was taking
no chance that someone would come and disturb him.
There was only one prisoner in the tower this year, but
he was important enough for a full battalion of guards.
Dide was anxious to free him and be away.

The prisoner was a warlock called Gwilym the Ugly.
He had once lived at the Tower of Mists, having escaped
there after the Burning, seeking refuge in the only country to still celebrate magic. Ten years later he re-
emerged from the mists and joined the rebels to fight
against the Awl. He never spoke about his time in

Arran, but it was common knowledge among the rebels that it had been the Mesmerdean that had trapped him and brought him to the Red Guards. One did not touch the thistle without pain.

Dide had liked the swarthy young warlock and had found his magic of great use in the past. He had been horrified to hear Gwilym the Ugly had been betrayed and was in prison, waiting to be fed to the Midsummer bonfires. Even if he had not felt drawn to Gwilym, and even if he did not want information about Arran, Dide would still have persuaded Enit to plan his rescue.

The warlock had been cruelly treated. One leg had been crushed in an iron device they called "the boot," which smashed the bone of the foot, ankle and shin. The terrible wound had not been treated, and he was barely conscious. Bruises and cuts marred his face and body, and only one hazel eye snapped open as the door of his cell swung open. He smiled when he saw Dide, wincing as the movement tore a cut at the side of his mouth.

Dide smiled back, wishing fervently that the Awl had not chosen the boot as their torture instrument, for it would make their escape almost impossible.

"Well, ye were never pretty, Gwilym, but truly ye earn your nickname now," he said, working quickly to relieve the warlock's pain. He had known the warlock would have been tortured and so had come prepared. He gave him water to sip and some syrup made from wild poppies and valerian, and bid his men to hold the warlock steady. He then gritted his teeth and used his dagger to sever Gwilym's leg below the knee. Summoning fire, he cauterized the wound and wrapped it well in bandages torn from his shirt.

"Good lad," the warlock said hoarsely. "Help me up, quickly."

"How did they do it?" Dide asked, trying to hide his anguish.

"The Mesmerdean breathed on me but chose to give me a lingering, agonizing death rather than the sweet bliss o' their kiss," Gwilym said wryly. "I can see Margrit o' Arran's fair hand behind it all. I woke when they closed the boot upon me. It was no' a happy wakening."

"Did ye speak?"

Gwilym shook his head. "Nay, I had that satisfaction at least. They have promised me the rack if I do no' tell them my rebel contacts, but it be only a few hours till I am scheduled to burn. They will have to try and screw the information out o' me soon if they are to do it at all."

"We had best get out o' here then," Dide replied.

They had brought Gwilym a soldier's uniform to wear but the kilt showed the dreadful, bloodstained stump and his face was too badly bruised to pass even a casual scrutiny. There was no way they could disguise him as a soldier. They were just discussing what to do when Dide heard his lieutenant's voice, raised in anger.

"Someone is coming." Dide drew back behind the door, gesturing to the other rebels to follow suit. Gwilym sat wearily on the straw pallet, heavy lines of pain graven from his hooked nose to his mouth. He looked down sardonically at his butchered leg before hiding the stump under the rags of the blanket.

The cell door swung open and a red-clad seeker stepped within the cell, a tall, cadaverous man with greasy black hair combed straight off his pale brow. "Ah, ye are awake, witch," he said. "Ready for your next meeting with the Questioner?"

Gwilym said gruffly, "Why do ye bother? Ye tell me I am to be the entertainment for the Midsummer crowds—surely they would prefer to see a whole man burn, no' just parts o' him?"

"Ye think they care? Besides, it will make them think twice about helping the rebels, seeing the great warlock Gwilym the Ugly begging for mercy . . ."

"Och, I will no' beg," Gwilym responded, as Dide's dagger hilt hit the seeker on the back of the head. "But I think ye will."

He raised his hand and pointed it at the slumped figure of the seeker, two fingers extended. Frowning in concentration, he muttered a spell and the seeker's features blurred until they had taken on Gwilym's pox-pitted skin and hooked nose. "Smash his leg, laddies. I think he shall see how it feels to die in agony."

"Ye mean him to burn in your place?" Dide asked, feeling a little sick.

Gwilym nodded, a bleak smile flitting over his harsh features. "It seems befitting, do ye no' think so? He was the one to close the boot."

Dide nodded. The men stripped the seeker of his clothes, throwing the bundle to Gwilym. Grinning savagely, they then jumped on the unconscious seeker's right leg with their heavy boots until blood and bone marrow were seeping from the crushed limb. The pain stirred him in his unconscious state, but they hit him on the head again and he lapsed back into oblivion. Hurriedly they dressed him in the warlock's torn and bloodstained clothes and cleared away any signs that they had been there. This meant Gwilym's severed limb had to be wrapped up and taken away, a task which made them all feel rather queasy.

They locked the seeker in the room, and half carried Gwilym down the stairs and into the guard room where the other rebels were waiting nervously. "How shall we get him to the cellar?" one of the rebels asked anxiously. Dide shook his head. "We canna take him past the practice square like this," he said. "We shall have to try trickery. We can say the seeker was overcome with the same illness as the guards. If that were so, what would we do? Get him a litter, carry him out? Gwilym! That spell ye placed on the seeker—to make him look like ye. Can ye do it to yourself?"

"Ye mean, to make me look like him?" the warlock said warily. "Och, aye. I did no' spend years with the mistress o' illusions herself for naught. I can make myself look like anyone I please. It's called the spell o' glamourie. The illusion does not last long, but it'll be long enough for our purposes."

"Cast the spell then, while we organize ye a litter. We shall carry ye out under their very noses!"

Isabeau returned rather wearily to the kitchen, helped herself to vegetable soup and bread, and sat at the far end of the long table. Servants were milling everywhere, and the kitchen buzzed with talk. Isabeau paid very little attention, eating steadily as she thought about what she had learned that evening. The knowledge that Riordan Bowlegs was a witch was near as astounding to her as the realization that she had carried a third of the Key right to the very door of the Banrìgh.

A flock of serving maids came fluttering in, twittering in excitement. Seeing Isabeau sunk in a dream, they surrounded her with their bell-shaped skirts and high, shrill voices. "Have ye seen them yet, Red?" freckle-faced Edda asked.

"They came on a great boat, with big white sails marked with a red cross."

"They refused to open the river-gates to them at first."

"The hull o' their boat is covered in holes where the Fairgean tried to sink it. They had to plug the holes with oilcloth before they could sail on."

"Fighting Fairgean the whole way!" Elsie cried.

Isabeau said, "What are ye all raving on about now?" She was answered with a babble of voices.

"The Tìrsoilleirean . . ."

". . . came in a boat . . ."

". . . even the women wear armor, and carry swords . . ."

"They want to open trade again . . ."

". . . and fight together against the Fairgean."

". . . Mistress Sani had to go down to the docks, for the harbor authorities wouldna let them in without an authority from the Rìgh, yet the puir man is sunk in a fever and couldna be disturbed!"

". . . there's a priest with them, and ye should smell him! Urgh!" Edda finished triumphantly.

Isabeau was as excited and intrigued as they were. This was the first contact between Tìrsoilleir and the rest of Eileanan in over four hundred years, a truly historic event. She had often wondered about the forbidden land, which she had been able to see from some parts of her valley home. It had looked much like any other land, except for the tall spires of the kirks which rose from every village. Rumor had it that the Tìrsoilleirean had to worship in their kirks as many as three times a day, and anyone who refused was disciplined severely.

Isabeau knew the Tìrsoilleirean had rejected the philosophies of the witches, believing in a stern sun god that punished them mightily for any digression. Unlike the witches, who thought that all gods and goddesses were different names and faces for the one life-spirit, the Tìrsoilleirean believed in one god with one name. They thought their beliefs were the only true faith and that other people must be forced to worship as they did. Many times they had tried to convert their neighbors. When missionaries and traveling preachers failed to win the people to the religion, they tried force.

Meghan had considered them the greatest enemies of Eileanan's way of life, for there was no force as unstoppable as that of fanatics. "It is no' just that they think they are right," she had said. "They are so filled with certitude and religious zeal that they canna or willna allow the possibility o' a different view. To them, there is only one truth, while anyone with wisdom kens that truth is like a multifaceted crystal."

It occurred to Isabeau that the philosophical differences which had once divided Tìrsoilleir and the rest of Eileanan were no longer so rigid. Magic and witchcraft had been outlawed in the Bright Land for hundreds of years. The Day of Reckoning and its fiery legacy must have been viewed with approval in Bride, capital city of Tìrsoilleir. After that the witches' belief in freedom of worship had been replaced by the Banrìgh's vague but strictly enforced Truth, which also believed in only one path. Perhaps the Tìrsoilleirean had come from behind the Great Divide because they hoped to renew their crusade?

The whole court was rife with speculation. The dignitaries remained closeted with the Rìgh who had risen from his sickbed on the news. Soon the whole court knew that the Bright Soldiers had come seeking help against the rising of the Fairgean. The sea people had raided the northern coast of Tìrsoilleir just as they had Carraig and Siantan. Raised as warriors, the Tìrsoilleirean had fought them off for five years, but each spring and autumn the rising tides brought them in ever greater numbers.

Now the tide was rising again with the coming of autumn, the Fairgean were looting and burning coastal towns and villages as far south as Bride itself. The Tìrsoilleirean were suffering terribly from the attacks and had decided to send a fleet of ships around to Dùn Gorm to ask for help and advice while the southern seas still remained free of the fierce, barbarous sea-dwellers.

Isabeau alone seemed to find it strange that the Tìrsoilleirean should decide to seek help now, after centuries of isolation. Although the diplomatic party seemed full of smiles and smooth words, Isabeau wished she could talk it over with Meghan, who would have found their sudden friendliness peculiar too, she knew.

She had little time to wonder, though, for as soon as her soup was eaten, the chamberlain's lackeys were vying with each other to find work for her to do. She tended the spits, gathered herbs for Latifa, helped carry food out to the minstrels and jongleurs, and replaced the half-used candles in the great hall.

Crowds of gaily dressed courtiers and ladies began to throng all through the main part of the palace, and Isabeau was wide-eyed as she trotted to and fro in her white cap and apron. She could not help wishing she was a finely dressed banprionnsa, like the six daughters of the Prionnsa of Blèssém. They wore silk dresses printed all over with roses and lilies, and their golden hair was intricately braided with flowers. None of them noticed Isabeau as she hurried past, too busy laughing and dancing and flirting with their father's squires.

A stir was caused by the entry of the Tìrsoilleirean, who came in under the hanging banners as a closely knit group. In their silver armor and white surcoats, they stood out from the bright silks and velvets of the court, as their stern, wary expressions differed from the idle pleasure on the faces of all about them. Even the pretty banprionnsachan of Blessém stopped their giggling and gossiping to stare at the strangers.

The Tìrsoilleirean were to eat at the high table, a mark of high favor, and much jiggling of the table places had had to be done on very short notice. This meant many of the nobly born squires were squeezed out into the lesser hall where Isabeau was serving. Although a long, high room of grand proportions, the lesser hall was already overcrowded and Isabeau spent much of the evening on the run from one packed table to another. She could not carry the heavy trays with only one hand but she could serve, and so to her dismay she found herself trapped in the lesser room with little excuse to leave.

Isabeau hated having to serve at the tables. The squires were forever pinching her bottom as she poured more wine into their glass. It was Isabeau who would be blamed if she dropped the jug, yet there was little she could do to extract herself from their clumsy embraces without mishap, particularly with the use of only one hand.

As the night wore on, their grabs at her grew more uncoordinated as the wine clouded their senses. She grew more adept at ducking and weaving through them and began to think she would get through the night with only a few boxes to the ear from her superiors. Then a plump squire with food stains all down the front of his jerkin succeeded in capturing her and pulling her down onto his lap. Before she could struggle free, he had ground his hot, sour-breathed mouth against hers. Isabeau, finally losing her temper, bit him. He yelped and

threw her away from him. She fell onto the floor, her
cap tumbling off, her skirts billowing around her.

All the squires howled with laughter. The plump one
lurched to his feet, trying to straighten his crushed and
stained doublet as he peered around for Isabeau.
"Cheeky lass!" he muttered, pressing the back of his
hand to his mouth. "Think she can bite me, eh? I'll
show her!"

Isabeau scrambled to her feet, caught up her muslin
cap and tried to slip away without being seen. The squire
lifted the tablecloth and peered underneath, calling,
"C'mon, lassie, where ye be hiding?" She hid behind the
back of one of the tall menservants and let him shield
her as she tiptoed toward the door.

She had just made it when, to her horror, she saw
Sani standing outside. Although everyone but the serving maids and footmen were dressed in their gaudiest
clothes, the old woman was still clothed in black from
head to foot. She looked like a black beetle amongst a
flock of butterflies.

Behind Isabeau the drunken squire was weaving his
way toward her, his arms held out. She glanced from
him to Sani, feeling trapped. At that very moment the
old woman turned and saw Isabeau, her cap in her hand,
her red curls dishevelled. The pale, fierce eyes focused
instantly, and Isabeau was transfixed. She could not
move or speak, whether from fear or some arcane power
of the old woman, she did not know.

"So, ye are Latifa's grand-niece," Sani said.

Isabeau nodded slowly.

"Recently come from Rionnagan."

She nodded again.

"Ye have cut your hair?"

Isabeau wanted to explain that she had been ill and
feverish, and that her hair had been cut to bring down
her high temperature. She could say nothing, however,
her tongue a plank of wood in her mouth. So she merely
nodded again.

The old woman grinned. "Cat got your tongue?"

"Nay, ma'am," Isabeau managed to say, though her voice sounded high and squeaky. She was conscious of the old woman's eyes—so pale a blue as to be almost colorless—raking over her, and she trembled a little as she stood. Sani's gaze sharpened as she saw the hand bound up in bandages, half hidden by Isabeau's apron. "Injured yourself?" she asked in a silky smooth voice, and Isabeau saw her gaze flick up to the little scar between her brows again.

"Aye, ma'am," she answered politely.

"And how did ye do that? Show me."

Isabeau dug her crippled hand deeper into her skirts. She could think of nothing to say. The story Latifa had told came back to her, and she said breathlessly, "Caught my hand in a coney trap."

"No' very canny o' ye, was it?"

"Nay, ma'am."

In a voice as unctuous as precious oils, the old woman whispered, "Show me your hand, kin o' Latifa the Cook," but before Isabeau had time to react, she felt the plump squire lurch against her back, trapping her arms in his so he could slobber into her neck.

"Gie me a kiss, my bonny lass," he said. "It's Midsummer, time for some loving . . ."

Normally Isabeau would have pushed him away, but with Sani barring her exit and asking her awkward questions, she sagged into his arms so he staggered backward. They lurched against the table, and then to the floor, the squire falling on top of her. She managed to free herself as he lay laughing and wheezing. She crept under the table as a dozen hands hauled the drunk upward. "She's gone again!" he cried. "The tease! Find her, laddies!"

A breathless game of chase-and-hide around the table followed, with Isabeau finally being rescued by one of the serving-men, who reprimanded her severely for flirting with the lairds' attendants. By now thoroughly agitated, Isabeau burst into tears. "It was no' my fault,"

she cried. "He was too strong for me! I've been trying
to get away; I even bit him when he tried to kiss me!"

The serving-man relented. "Ohh ohh! No need to
greet, lassie. Get ye back to the kitchen, and I'll no' tell
Latifa this time."

Dabbing at her eyes with her apron, Isabeau crammed
her muslin cap back over her curls and ran out of the
dining room, going the long way around so she could
avoid Sani still lurking outside the door. She ran down
the wide steps to the entrance hall and into the gardens,
filled with crowds of revellers. Dodging and weaving
through the long lines of dancers, she found at last a
dark corner where she could regain her composure. Her
pulse was galloping and she had to slide down to sit on
the grass, swallowing great gulps of cool night air, before
her blood calmed. *Somehow Sani suspects,* she thought.
How could she ken?

She tried to think but her terror bewildered her, so
that all she could do was grip her fingers together and
try and be calm. *Sukey said Sani was the real leader o'
the Awl. Happen she heard about me from the witch-
sniffer. It must have been big news in the highlands, a
red-haired witch caught and tried. But everyone thought
I died. I was fed to the loch-serpent. No one knew I was
still alive until I got here. No one here knows who I really
am except for Latifa . . .*

The thoughts reassured her, and she repeated them to
herself. She remembered then how the sight of the
Banrìgh's red skirt had shocked her, and how Sani had
looked up at the gallery afterward. Somehow she must
have betrayed herself. Latifa had said her thoughts were
clear as shouts. So perhaps Sani did not really know
anything, had just been alerted by some stray thought
that Isabeau had let slip. So reassuring was this hypothe-
sis that Isabeau got to her feet and straightened her
skirt. Mid-movement she froze.

"So ye've cut your hair," the old woman had said.
And she had first asked Sukey and Doreen about a new
red-haired scullery maid a month or more ago. Isabeau's

limbs began to shake again, and she slid down into a gray heap on the grass. *It was true. Somehow Sani knew . . .*

The prisoner was dragged from his cell close on midnight and paraded around Dùn Gorm's great square in a fool's cap before being tied shrieking to the great pile of timber in the square's center. All the while he begged and pleaded with his captors, shouting that he was no witch but a seeker of the Awl. His guards only laughed. Jongleurs danced all around the square, spinning wheels of fire and spitting out long plumes of flame. Drums pounded, the fifes trilled, and the crowd was filled with excited anticipation. The people of Dùn Gorm had grown used to the death fires of the Awl, and few in the throng felt pity for the screaming man. At last a burning brand was plunged into the kindling and flames roared up the bonfire. As the flames licked up the prisoner's legs, the glamourie dissolved and the agonized features of the burning man were revealed as the Seeker Aidan the Cruel. The seekers lined up before the bonfire recognized their comrade at once, but it was too late to save him. As they shouted for water, his screams were swallowed by bright curtains of flames.

THE VEILED FOREST

Anghus shifted his pack wearily, and said, "No' much further, Donald. I can see the lights o' Dunceleste twinkling yonder. A soft, warm bed would be grand, aye?"

"Aye, m'laird," the gillie replied. "It's sick to death I am o' sleeping on stones. I think I am growing too auld for all this racketing around the country."

Anghus could only agree. They stumbled up the slick cobblestones of the road, the Rhyllster thundering past in swift moving rapids. Ahead rose the walls of the ferry town, and they could hear the clacking of the mill's great waterwheel.

They came through the gates into a courtyard lined with guards' quarters, which led into a wide square, surrounded on all sides by tall, cramped houses with high-pitched roofs. A rowdy crowd, mainly soldiers and merchants, spilled out into the square from an inn, its sign freshly painted with a red dragon breathing flames. Anghus headed that way.

He knew the Arch-Sorceress was only a few days' journey away. She had not moved in all the months that he had been trekking through the mountains. He guessed that she must have some tricky hideaway, for he knew soldiers had been hunting her without respite since word of her first came through in the spring. He knew there was no better way of picking up news than to drink at the same place as the people who had the knowledge you wanted. Besides, Anghus's whiskey flask had been empty for a week, and he was in desperate need of a drink.

The inn was crowded, the two Rurachians having to edge their way past close-packed bodies, many brilliant in scarlet uniforms. Anghus found a seat while Donald shoved his way through to the bar, where four buxom and very pretty girls went a long way toward explaining the inn's popularity.

Perched on the edge of a bench, Anghus listened to the conversation around him. He was to have no trouble in gaining the information he wanted. The talk in the inn was of nothing else but the foul sorceress Meghan and her blaygird companions. At the center of attention was a young piper, no more than seventeen, the only one to have marched into the Veiled Forest and survived. Anghus's eyes widened at his descriptions of the forest. He spoke of shadow-hounds tearing out the throats of soldiers; quicksands that opened under their feet; stones that moved and talked; trees that tangled their feet with roots; paths that shifted, leading the soldiers in circles until they died of hunger and thirst.

Wondering what had become of his whiskey, Anghus turned and saw a band of Red Guards had decided to ease their frustration on his bow-legged gillie. One had snatched his tam o'shanter and was holding it above his head, as another polished the bald crown of his head with a cleaning rag. The gillie's shiny pate was pink with indignation.

Anghus rose to his feet, loosening his sword as one of the soldiers tweaked Donald's long beard. The gillie's face flushed scarlet. "How dare ye!" he roared and head-butted him in the stomach. Knives sprang out, but Anghus stepped into the fray, his sword gleaming. "I would no' make any trouble, lads," he said mildly. "I be the MacRuraich and this is my gillie. Lay one hand on him and I'll consider it an insult to me. An insult to me is an insult to my throne, and ye'll be paying for it with your heads. Do ye understand?"

The leader, a thickset, red-faced man with a swagger, looked Anghus up and down, then said, "Ye do no' look much like a prionnsa to me."

"Appearances can be deceiving." Anghus threw back his faded black plaid so the soldiers could see the wolf device of his brooch. They were uneasy, he could feel it, though the one with a swagger was loath to have his fun taken away.

"Anyone can wear a wolf brooch," he said, twisting Donald's tam o'shanter in his hands. "Does no' mean a thing."

"No one can wear the device o' the MacRuraich clan if they be no' descended from Rùraich the Searcher himself," Anghus said quietly, menace in his voice. "Such irreverence is punishable by death. Ye should be able to recognize my device. Ye are ignorant indeed for a man in the MacCuinn's service."

"I serve the Banrìgh," the man responded.

"Ye serve the Banrìgh?" Anghus repeated incredulously. "Does that mean ye do no' serve the Rìgh? Ye spurn to serve the MacCuinn, descendant o' Cuinn Lionheart himself!"

Suddenly seeing where the conversation was taking him, the soldier rubbed his mustache with his hand. "Nay, nay, I just meant we be the Red Guards, sworn to serve and support the Banrìgh. I never meant . . ." He stopped, laughed nervously, then tossed the crumpled tam o'shanter to Donald, who crammed it over his bald head. "No disrespect intended, m'laird," he said, backing away quickly.

Anghus's declaration of his identity secured them the best rooms in the inn, and he allowed them to bring him hot water to bathe with and take away his mud-stained clothes and boots to wash and brush. He woke in the morning greatly refreshed to find Donald tipping a dash of whiskey into his porridge.

Donald was still incensed from the beard tweaking and muttered away as he served his laird, calling imprecations down on the heads of any who thought a man's beard funny. Only when the tray was empty did he tell Anghus that a seeker was waiting downstairs for him.

The prionnsa groaned. "That's what comes o' declaring myself before a room full o' Red Guards," he sighed. "Bring me my clothes and I'll make ready."

The young seeker waiting in the public room was so thin, the muscles in his cheeks shifted under the tight-drawn skin when he spoke. His long, velvet robe had only two buttons, indicating he was still a lowly servant, only recently recruited to the service. His dark eyes burned with religious fervor, however, and his medallion was brightly polished.

Frowning mightily, the seeker said that the Awl was not pleased Anghus MacRuraich, Prionnsa of Rurach and Siantan, had come to Dunceleste without declaring himself to the Grand-Seeker Humbert and asking his permission to stay in the town first. Anghus interrupted the seeker's grieved tones to purse up his lips and whistle. "Humbert's here, is he? That's cursed bad luck."

All the muscles in the seeker's jaw clenched, so it looked as if he was chewing walnuts. "Is that so? And why would it be bad luck that the *Grand-Seeker* Humbert be in Dunceleste?"

Anghus said, "Now, lad, no need to get haughty. Humbert and I have known each other for a long time. Tell him I'll be along later."

"The Grand-Seeker Humbert requests your presence immediately!"

"Aye, aye, I'm sure that he does. I have a few things to do first, though, so ye just run along and tell him I'll be there shortly."

Anghus did not really have anything to do that could not wait, but it went against his grain to jump at the command of Humbert of the Smithy, who had led the

Awl in Rurach and Siantan over the past seven years, sending many poor old skeelies and cunning men to their death in the flames. Humbert and Anghus had had many confrontations in the past as the laird tried desperately to protect his people. It might, therefore, have been wise to have gone with the seeker, but Anghus just could not do it. He was still the MacRuraich, and he was on the Banrìgh's business. *Let him stew for a while*, Anghus thought unkindly.

The Awl were staying in the best inn in town, a large, steep-gabled establishment with a taste for red velvet and patriotic tapestries. Anghus could not help feeling uncomfortable as he followed the thin young seeker into the public bar. Seekers sat at every table, most poring over the little red volume called *The Book of Truth*, published by the Awl to help disseminate their version of history. Some played chess or trictrac; there were no dice or card games, and very few goblets of wine as one might have expected in such a crowded inn. Many of them raked him over with that disconcerting stare that the Awl taught their seekers. Anghus kept his hand near his sword, and his thoughts closely guarded, as he had been taught as a child.

They went up a grand flight of stairs, and the young seeker knocked nervously on a pair of carved doors and bowed as he ushered Anghus inside. The Grand-Seeker sat behind a massive desk, writing with a fine quill. He was an obese man, his pendulous cheeks pitted with acne scars. His crimson coat strained against the twenty-four small velvet buttons that indicated his rank. He did not look up, the point of his pen scratching in the silence.

Anghus glanced around the luxurious suite, noting the rich silken tapestries and feather-fat cushions. His hazel-green eyes lit at the sight of the whiskey decanter. Without hesitation he splashed a generous measure into a squat, crystal glass and tossed it down. The Grand-Seeker glanced up in irritation. Anghus refilled his glass, sat down in one of the wing chairs and stretched his scruffy boots to the fire.

"Thank ye for honoring us with your presence, Mac-Ruraich," the Grand-Seeker said with heavy irony.

"I am laird o' the MacRuraich clan, and prionnsa o' Rurach and Siantan," Anghus said coolly. "Ye will address me by my title."

"And I am the Grand-Seeker o' the Awl in all Eileanan and the Far Islands, and ye will address me by mine," Humbert answered, his fat cheeks taking on the hue of red plums.

"Certainly O Grand-Seeker o' the Awl in all Eileanan and the Far Islands," Anghus replied equably. "Do ye no' find all that rather tiresome after a while?"

Between half-closed lids he watched the pudgy fingers clench on the quill. He said affably, "A fine drop o' whiskey ye have here, Humbert Grand-Seeker o' all o' Eileanan. Glad I am indeed to be wetting my whistle, for I've been parched ever since I arrived. Seems something has halted the whiskey run, tho' I canna seem to be able to get a straight story on what exactly. A pesky faery-serpent, some say, and others talk o' dragons. Though how can that be? I be sure no dragon would dare peek its snout into Rionnagan with the great Grand-Seeker Humbert in residence in the highlands."

"Wha' are ye doing here?" Humbert asked angrily.

"I be here on the Banrìgh's business, Grand-Seeker," Anghus replied smoothly, inserting just a faint stress of surprise in his tone.

"Show me your authority!" Humbert snapped.

Nonchalantly Anghus handed over the scroll with the royal seal and the Banrìgh's own illegible flourish. "As ye can read there—can ye read, Humbert?—the Banrìgh summoned me to Rionnagan to take in hand Meghan NicCuinn and the leader o' the rebellion, known rather colorfully as the Cripple. Odd ye have no other name for this rebel laird. I was told by your Seeker Renshaw that ye'd seized him several times and each time he managed to slip through your fingers."

Humbert interrupted angrily, but Anghus raised his voice and continued with a smooth overtone of irony,

"I do no' ken exactly why the Banrìgh feels I can be o' service, but there ye are, it seems she thinks I can. Apparently the Awl has had a wee trouble laying these pesky rebels by the heels."

"They are dangerous, ruthless outlaws, condemned to death for treason, murder and evil sorceries," Humbert leant as far forward as his vast paunch would allow him, crushing the quill in his clenched fingers. "The Arch-Sorceress has used her blaygird enchantments to rouse *uile-bheistean* from Dragonclaw to the seas. It is true a dragon flew over the highlands, for I saw it myself, a great golden beast that spat fire at us in contempt! The seas and firths are swelling with Fairgean, wolves are on the prowl . . ."

Anghus started and was sure the little gimlet eyes had not missed it. The Grand-Seeker continued without pause, "The wild beasts o' the field and forest are restless, dogs turn against their masters, even the stars in the heavens have been wrenched awry by their foul sorceries. The dark powers o' these witches are terrible, inciting madness and fear and turning the folk away from the Truth. Again and again have we fought to gain a grip on their throats, and always we are thrown off."

Getting a little tired of Humbert's rhetoric, Anghus yawned, prodded a log with his foot, and finished off his whiskey. "Sorry as I am to hear o' all your travails, the day is getting away and I have business to attend to. Ye asked me what I was doing here, and I have told ye. Listening to ye, I begin to see why it is the Banrìgh wanted me here. The grip o' the black wolf, my friend, is never thrown off. Once I find, I hold. So I shall do as my Banrìgh commanded. I'll find Meghan o' the Beasts and take her to the blue palace myself . . ."

"Och, aye, ye'll just saunter thro' the blaygird Veiled Forest, take her wee hand and lead her awa', I s'pose!" Humbert shouted, his voice losing all traces of refinement. The twenty-four crimson buttons quivered with the strain.

"How I do what I do is none o' your concern!" Anghus retorted. "All ye need to know is that I shall do as the Banrìgh commanded."

"I am the Banrìgh's representative," Humbert said. "Ye report to me . . ."

Anghus laughed. "I do no' think so," he said kindly. "I am still a prionnsa, remember, and laird o' one o' the Eleven Clans. Ye are merely the son o' a blacksmith, even in your fine velvets and gold." He held up a hand as Humbert spluttered with rage. "Aye, aye, I know, ye are the Grand-Seeker o' all the Awl in all o' Eileanan and the Far Islands. I have an excellent memory, Grand-Seeker, and if I remember Jaspar MacCuinn rightly, he would never allow ye precedence over one o' the blood. Ye would be wise to remember it is still the MacCuinn who rules this land, by blood, birthright and the power o' the Lodestar. Maya the Blessed is Banrìgh by right o' marriage only."

"The Lodestar is destroyed . . ."

"Happen that is so, but the MacCuinn still rules, Humbert Smith, and do no' forget it. Now I must be on my way . . ."

"Wait!" Humbert leaped to his feet, snatching the scroll back. Even standing, the Grand-Seeker was a full six inches shorter than the MacRuraich, and he pushed his chair back and stepped out of Anghus's shadow to read the scroll again. Anghus was amused at the way his lips silently moved as he sounded out each word.

Eventually the Grand-Seeker had puzzled out the meaning of the paper, and he stood silently for a moment, his little eyes gleaming. Anghus leaned over and took the paper from between his fingers. "I'll be on my way then," he said.

"Wait," the Grand-Seeker said again, in a milder tone. "Have some more whiskey, my laird." Anghus shrugged and poured himself a half tumbler, then sat on the edge of the desk, one sinewy leg swinging. Masking his irritation, the Grand-Seeker came around the desk to pour himself a glass and drank a mouthful. He swayed back and forth thoughtfully. "So ye believe ye can capture the Arch-Sorceress Meghan and the Cripple."

"I only have a true fixing on Meghan, though I was told the Cripple may be with her," Anghus replied.

"The Cripple is with her, that be for sure, and he be winged, like one o' them angels the Tìrsoilleirean believe in," Humbert said, amazement in his voice.

"But are ye sure he is the leader o' the rebels?"

Humbert frowned and sipped his whiskey. "The former Grand-Seeker, Glynelda, had caught him twice before, once near Lucescere, again heading up through the Pass. It was she who first discovered he was winged. She had been hunting the Cripple and was very sure it was he."

"What proof have ye got? What eyewitnesses to his command o' the rebels, what papers with his signature, what confession?"

"Och, we'll have no trouble getting a confession out o' him!"

Anghus was silent, disliking having to think about the methods used by the Awl for extracting confessions of witchcraft and treason. He had seen Humbert at work and suffered nightmares in consequence. He turned away so the Grand-Seeker would not see how pale he had grown. Humbert saw, of course, and laughed again.

"It is no' enough for me," Anghus said sternly. "I am emboldened to find the Cripple, but I need to hunt surely and canna do so on such flimsy evidence. I need a paper he has signed, or even a scrap o' his clothing . . ."

Humbert glanced up at him sharply, and Anghus thought frantically, *Surely he kens how I search? The Banrìgh must know, and Renshaw certainly did. I should no' have said anything.*

"If the Cripple is with Meghan, then I shall take them both and deliver them to the blessed Banrìgh together. If the leader o' the rebels is no' with her then I shall turn my attention to the Cripple after I return from Rhyssmadill . . ." Anghus continued on smoothly, not showing his inner perturbation.

"Nay, bring the Arch-Sorceress here to me at Dunce-leste, and I shall take her to Rhyssmadill myself," Humbert commanded. Anghus knew the seeker wanted to win all the glory for himself. Although he had been hoping to maneuver the Grand-Seeker into just this position, the prionnsa put up a show of refusal.

"Nay, it makes sense, my laird," Humbert argued persuasively. "If ye need to go on searching for this elusive Cripple, then ye shall save many months in the traveling. Once she is in our hands, we shall soon put a leash on that auld witch. I shall confine her myself with iron shackles and rowan, and weaken her with the Questioning, and she shall no' escape us again!"

Anghus felt no need to tell the Grand-Seeker that his belief witches could be restrained by rowan and iron was a fallacy. He did warn him, however, that the Rìgh might take exception to one of the Awl's Questioners torturing his great-aunt. "Far better let the Banrìgh take the responsibility for that," he said offhandedly and hoped the message had gone home. The idea of his sister's old teacher in the brutal hands of Humbert and his Questioners made Anghus sick to his stomach.

Not wanting to linger in the Grand-Seeker's offensive presence any longer, Anghus submitted to Humbert sending troops with him into the forest. Although he knew they would probably all die or go crazed, he only shrugged and warned the Grand-Seeker that they would have to obey his orders and his alone.

"O' course, o' course," Humbert said, rubbing his hands together and accompanying Anghus to the door. "'Twas a pleasure to see ye again, my laird, and to be working with ye again."

Anghus could only manage a stifled grunt in response.

The gates of the town swung open at dawn the following day. Out marched a cavalcade of men led by a small figure in a kilt and cocked bonnet playing the bagpipes. It was the same piper that Anghus had seen in the inn two nights before. The prionnsa had requested him to accompany the troops, for of all the soldiers sent into the Veiled Forest, he was the only one to have survived mind and soul intact.

To the sound of his bagpipes, ten soldiers in kilts followed in double file, claymores strapped to their backs. Anghus and Donald trotted behind on sturdy cobs, with four cavalrymen all around, pennants fluttering from their spears in the vigorous breeze. Behind them ran the urchins of the town, shouting and jeering.

As the gaunt, moss-draped trees loomed closer, the bagpipes faltered.

Anghus said kindly, "Cease your caterwauling, my lad, I doubt the trees will like it." He swung down from the saddle gracefully, and Donald followed suit. He looked up at the four cavalrymen and said regretfully, "I am afraid we shall have to dismount here. I can see the horses will be o' little use in that nest o' roots. Ye four will need to return to Dunceleste with our mounts and explain to the Grand-Seeker."

"But he said . . ."

"Come, lad, look into the forest. The horses will be nervy and the ground is much broken by the roots o' those trees. I would hate to have to kill one o' the mares because she broke a leg."

"The other three shall return. I shall travel with ye," the leader of the cavalrymen replied, swinging his leg across the saddle and dropping lithely to the ground. He was a tall, black-browed man named Casey Hawkeye, immaculately dressed. A bandolier strapped his claymore to his back, and he carried a long spear.

"If ye come, ye must leave that spear," Anghus said. "And ye must leave your pikes, lads. All other weapons must remain sheathed, unless I give ye the word. If it is indeed true there is a garden o' the Celestines in the woods, the trees will have soaked up their intuitive magic and will ken if ye think o' violence. Keep your thoughts well shielded and your claymores in their strap."

After the others had cantered away, the remaining

fourteen entered the dim, greenish light of the forest in silence. Anghus was immediately aware of shadows that writhed along in their footsteps. Although he never saw anything directly, there was the occasional flicker of movement in the corner of his eye, a sense of being watched, followed, salivated over, brief scuffles of sound. Seeing how the soldiers' heads jerked around at the noise, he said briefly, "Shadow-hounds. No' need to worry. They're merely curious, though if we had meat or were bleeding openly, they'd attack."

They pushed on in silence. It was about an hour later that one of the foot soldiers fell forward with a startled cry. When he scrambled to his feet again, blood welled up from a cut on his forehead. The shadow-hounds swarmed closer, growling and whining, their eyes glimmering green where the light caught their dilated pupils. They scared them away with shouts and waves of the arms, while Anghus bound the cut up tightly.

After several hours of difficult walking, they found it growing chilly, a mist beginning to rise from the earth. The group grew closer together, the soldiers' faces anxious or belligerent, depending on the character of the man. Ashlin the piper was nervy, as was the soldier with the cut forehead. Anghus and Casey were both alert and composed, while it was impossible to tell by Donald's face what he thought, if he thought at all. The brown, craggy features were set into an expression of placid acceptance that seemingly very little could shake—apart from insults to his beard, of course.

Several of the foot soldiers were clearly itching to pull their swords as the mist swirled up around their waists. "Easy, lads," Anghus said. "Let us tie ourselves together, that way we shall no' lose each other."

"How can we ken which way to go?" Ashlin asked. "We canna see our way. Last time we wandered thus for hours, no' knowing which way was east and which way north. Many o' the men just disappeared into the mist, to be heard o' no more."

"That way is north, laddie," Anghus said, pointing off

into the mist. "Ye shall no' get lost if ye stay close to me."

"How can ye ken?" asked Floinn Redbeard, one of the belligerent soldiers.

Anghus knew he must be careful to show no sign of his Talent before these men, for they were seasoned witchhunters, used to accompanying seekers in the field. He stepped up onto one of the thick roots and caressed the moss-oak's trunk. "See how this moss grows here on the trunk?" The soldier nodded suspiciously. "See how the other side of the trunk is bare? This type o' moss grows only on the north-facing trunk. If ye get lost, feel the trunks and head due south. Ye canna fail to find your way free."

"Ye ken a lot about the Veiled Forest for a man who does no' bide here."

"We have many moss-oaks in Siantan," Anghus answered. He tied the rope to Casey's belt. "Are ye called Hawkeye for good reason?" he asked. The tall man nodded. "Good, ye may go first then. Ashlin, stay close to Donald."

One by one they tied the rope to their belts, and then Casey led the way through the curving tree-roots. Although it was mid-afternoon, it seemed dusk, and the gloominess pressed against their spirits.

A wolf stepped out of the shadows, hackles slightly raised, her lips pulled back from her teeth. Immediately a dozen swords sang, but Anghus cried, "Sheathe your claymores! Did I give ye leave to pull weapons?"

He stared at the wolf with incredulous dismay. It was the matriarch of the Rurach forests, her black ruff beginning to silver with age. He could not believe she was here, so far from her natural home. She stared at Anghus with stern, yellow eyes and growled menacingly, the thick hair along her spine stiffening. Donald unstrapped his bow. Anghus motioned him back. "She shall no' hurt us," he said, though he had no idea how he could be so sure.

He untied the rope from his belt and stepped out of

his companions' sight and hearing. The wolf kept her fierce eyes fixed on his face, growling still. Anghus said in a low voice, "What is wrong, black wolf? I had thought we were friends o' a sort. Is there danger ahead?" She would not budge, growling still. He took a careful step forward, and then another, and she snarled. "I shall have to let them kill ye if ye do no' let us past," Anghus warned. "I do no' wish to do that."

She moved restlessly, whining a little. He took another step, and she growled but did not leap. A few more steps and his hand would be on her head. He took them slowly, holding his breath, and his fingers just touched her thick ruff. For a moment her yellow eyes met his, then she turned and slunk away.

He made his way back to the chain of soldiers, staring haughtily at their angry, incredulous faces. A few of them stirred uneasily, but he faced them down and, with only a few mutters, they fell into line. Everyone knew the MacRuraichs had an odd affinity with wolves.

As the afternoon sunk into an early night, the shadow-hounds slunk closer and closer, their black, undulating bodies rippling along on either side. They made camp in a small clearing, though the wood was so damp Donald's efforts to light a fire failed. The gillie was rather affronted when Casey Hawkeye took over, but the cavalryman soon had a bonfire burning. The flames glowed upward into the fretted canopy, carving deep shadows into the tree trunks. In the flickering light the trees seemed to sway as if shifting from foot to foot. All through the forest, black forms writhed, green eyes bright as candles.

Anghus organized a roster for the night watch, and they ate in near silence, then rolled themselves in blankets. They were woken in the early hours of the morning by Ashlin's frantic calls. The soldier on guard had been killed by shadow-hounds, his throat torn out. It was the soldier who had cut his forehead. He had been taken silently from the shadows, but the scuffle that had broken out over his body had woken Ashlin, sleeping uneasily. The boy was white and queasy as he stood with his dagger drawn over the soldier's dismembered body. He had managed to drive the shadow-hounds away with a flaming torch pulled from the fire. The huge, black creatures still swarmed silently around the edges of the clearing however, blood-lust bright in their eyes. No one slept again that night.

As soon as the darkness had lifted enough for them to see the moss-oaks looming through the mist, they continued on their way. The soldiers were unhappy and tense, but followed Anghus's orders quickly enough. He insisted on tying them all together again and warned them to keep their swords sheathed. Several hours later a soldier blundered into the nest of a swarthyweb spider and was bitten. His death throes were awful to watch. They hid his body under leaves and branches, knowing the shadow-hounds would dig him up even if they buried him, and continued in silence.

Soon after dusk closed over them, a swarm of shadow-hounds leaped from the undergrowth. They came in a great snarling wave, writhing about each other's bodies like a nest of snakes. Three soldiers lost their lives in seconds, throats torn out by the great hounds' wicked teeth. The others scrambled together, back to back, their great claymores whistling. Although black bodies were soon heaped up on either side, another soldier went down, then another.

Anghus's face was grim; he knew better than anyone how difficult it was to slow a swarm of shadow-hounds. One alone was hard to kill; together their strength and savagery were virtually unstoppable. He thrust his dagger into the breast of one, the green fire in its eyes flickering out, only to find another sinking its fangs into his arm. Pain zigzagged through him, but he managed to slash at it with his dagger. The shadow-hound hung on grimly and he sank to one knee.

Suddenly a dark streak flashed through the trees, falling on the swarm of shadow-hounds from the rear. It was the wolf. She sunk her fangs into the neck of the shadow-hound and dragged him off Anghus. Snarling and yelping, they rolled together on the ground, then the wolf rose, her fangs dripping with greenish-black plasma. Side by side the wolf and Anghus fought, till at last the swarm wavered and broke. In seconds the misty clearing was empty of all but five panting, cursing men, and the wolf, who lifted her muzzle and howled in triumph. On the ground lay seven of their number, and three times as many shadow-hounds.

They walked no further that day. By the time the bodies had been disposed of, their wounds strapped up, and a dram of whiskey thankfully swallowed by all, it was fully dark. In the distance shadow-hounds howled, while the forest pressed close, more menacing than ever. The wolf had disappeared into the shifting undergrowth again, but Anghus knew she was nearby.

"We are going about this the wrong way," Anghus said. "It is no use fighting the forest; we shall never win through. I want ye all to go back."

Casey Hawkeye shook his head. "We canna be doing that, my laird," he answered respectfully. "We were sent to help and protect ye and canna be turning back because the way is difficult. We knew it would be dangerous before we came."

"But I will do better without ye," Anghus said impatiently.

"How can ye? This forest is evil; ye need us to keep ye safe, my laird."

Anghus could not explain to him why he was safer without them. He merely repeated impatiently that he wanted them all to turn back.

"We have our orders, my laird."

"Aye, and I'm the one giving them to ye. I want ye to turn back."

"We are under orders from the Grand-Seeker himself," Casey replied. "Nothing ye can say will convince us to go against him. Our death in this forest will be far kinder than what the Grand-Seeker would do to us if we disobeyed him."

Anghus ground his teeth in frustration, but knew there was little he could do. Instead he sat in moody silence, taking swigs from his flask and wondering where the wolf had got to. He could hardly believe she had followed them all the way into the Veiled Forest. Her appearance filled Anghus with confusion. His heart had leaped at the sight of her, but he was conscious all the time that there was some vital clue he was missing, a nagging sense of recognition that puzzled him sorely.

It was a long, nerve-wracking night. Casey Hawkeye again built a massive bonfire, and set flaming torches all around the clearing, but the darkness beyond winked with eyes great and small. Three times the shadowhounds descended upon them, only thrust off with fierce fighting and the brief reappearance of the wolf. In the morning they saw the dirt about the clearing was thick with tracks, including the clawed prints of hobgoblins.

With flame and axe and sword, they slashed and burned their way through the tangle of bramble and briar, the forest black and forbidding all around them. Donald was at one shoulder, Casey at the other, Floinn protecting the vulnerable young piper behind. Anghus knew he was close; so close he could smell Meghan in his nostrils and taste her in his throat. The forest fought them each step of the way, but the thrill of the chase was racing through every vein and artery. His excitement infected the others, and together they struggled forward, allowing nothing to slow them or separate them. They did not stop when darkness fell, but pushed on, smoky torches gripped tight in every hand.

At last they fell through the last wall of thorns, and before them stretched open grass, velvet in the moonlight, with shapes of trees and bushes flowing above. The air was sweet-scented; a light breeze ruffled their sweat-damp hair and cooled their scratched faces. The mist had disappeared so stars crowded overhead.

"The garden o' the Celestines," Anghus sighed. "Sheathe your weapons, lads. They'll do us no good here."

Reluctantly they obeyed, and Anghus sniffed the night, scenting his prey. She was close, very close. He set off through the garden, his boots crushing fragrant flowers beneath. The others followed him, silent in awe and anticipation. Ahead loomed a high hill, rising out of the trees. The tall stones that crowned it shone white in the moonlight.

"She will be there," Anghus muttered. He raised his voice slightly, and said, "Ye must no' come any further. Stay by the stream and do no' pull your weapons. Ye are now in the garden o' the Celestines and ye are no' welcome here. One act o' violence or disrespect now and all could be lost. Nay, Donald, ye must stay too. I will no' need ye."

"But my laird . . ." Donald protested.

Anghus shook his head. "Stay, auld friend, and guard my back."

Alone, the Prionnsa of Rurach moved silently through the great trees. He was conscious of being watched, but made no aggressive move, and the hidden watchers did not show themselves. He came through a clearing to the base of the hill and left his sword and dagger concealed beneath a bush. A stream came tumbling down the side of the hill, and he washed himself carefully in it, revelling in its crystal freshness. Only then did he begin the climb.

Meghan NicCuinn was sitting against one of the great stones, looking out across the forest to the loch, which gleamed brightly in the moonlight. She looked up at his footsteps, and smiled. "Greetings, Anghus MacRuraich. I have been expecting ye. It has been a long time indeed syne we last saw each other."

"Nigh on twenty years, my lady," he answered and bowed to her.

"That long? Och, o' course, it was before Tabithas became Keybearer."

"Aye," he replied, melancholy in his voice. "Ye ken I have come to take ye to the Awl?"

"O' course I ken. Why else do ye think I am here

waiting for ye? There is time, though. Bide a wee, Anghus, and we shall talk. The past twenty years have no' been kind to ye, I can tell."

"Nay, cruel years indeed they have been."

"Ye miss your sister, that I can see. Ye have no' yet found her? That surprises me."

"I canna fix my heart upon her. She is hidden from me by strange and troubling shadows."

"But ye are the MacRuraich, Anghus, canna ye see through these shadows?"

He shook his head and slowly sat down beside her on the grass. Her stern face was illuminated by the moonlight, her eyes deepest in darkness. "Why?"

"I do no' know."

"I too have trouble finding her," Meghan said. "She is close now, though. I have had speech with her."

"With Tabithas? Tabithas is here! Where?" In an instant he was on his feet.

"Sit, Anghus, she shall show herself soon enough if she so wishes. Ye are no' seeing very clearly, are ye?"

"Nay," he answered, a break in his voice.

"I heard about the witch-hunts in Rurach and Siantan these past few years. It does no' seem like ye, Anghus, to have subjected your people to such harsh and heartless dealings."

"It is no' me that is to blame!" Anghus cried. "The Awl has its heel hard on our throats. The new Grand-Seeker is a brutal and cunning man who takes pleasure in breaking people to his will . . ."

"So he has broken yours?"

Anghus spat in disgust. "Nay, let a miserable, spotty-faced peasant lad like Humbert o' the Smithy break the will o' the MacRuraich? I do no' think so!"

"So what has happened to ye, Anghus? Do ye no longer rule your clan?"

"They have my daughter," he said quietly, his head down, shoulders slumped. "They stole her from me five years ago."

"Och, I see," Meghan replied softly. "It was then the

witch-hunts in Rurach grew so savage. They threaten her life if ye do no' do what they wish."

"Aye."

"There have been many who died by the fire in Rurach, some with power, very many with only a little. Why were they so harsh?"

"Humbert o' the Smithy was leader o' the Awl there and determined to make his mark and win favor in the Banrìgh's eyes. He sought to punish me as well, I feel, for he was born in Siantan. Many there still hate and resent the MacRuraich clan for ruling their country, even though it was won peaceably by marriage. He and the Banrìgh stole my bairn and set me to hunt down the rebels who had been hiding out in the Tower o' Searchers, as if I were some filthy paid assassin to do their blaygird work. But they had my daughter, and my people were suffering the backlash o' their displeasure. I dared do nothing else."

"Ye did no' hunt down Seychella Wind-Whistler, she who had been apprenticed to your sister."

He glanced up at her in surprise and chagrin. "Nay, I did no'. I lied to them, and said that all were dead. How did ye ken?"

"She came to me in my secret hiding place to help me with a job I had on hand then. I heard all the news from her, though worried I had been for a long time about the state o' affairs in Rurach and Siantan. She is dead now. A Mesmerd kissed her life away."

"A Mesmerd! One o' those blaygird faeries from the marsh? But how? Why? Were ye in Arran?" His voice expressed intense disbelief, for he knew Meghan would never have risked hiding in the misty fenlands of Arran where the MacFóghnans ruled.

She did not tell him where she had been the last sixteen years, instead saying wryly, "The Mesmerd was in league with a troop o' Red Guards and a seeker. Strange bedfellows I ken, but then I find the MacRuraich and the Banrìgh strange bedfellows as well."

Anghus flushed, and bit his lip. "I am sorry indeed to

hear Seychella is dead," he said gruffly. "She saved my life one time, and broke bread under my roof."

"As have I."

He said nothing.

Meghan laid her hands on his arm. All the muscles were tense and knotted. She said softly, "It is a cruel compulsion, to take your daughter and hold her life and safety over your head. I knew o' your coming and I waited for ye. I ken there is no escaping the black wolf once he has begun to hunt. I shall come with ye peaceably, as ye knew that I would. I have one question for ye first."

"What is it?" His voice was strangled in his throat.

"Why have ye no' hunted down your daughter as ye have hunted me? The Talent is strong in ye. Indeed, if ye were no' heir to the throne o' Rurach, we would have asked ye to take your apprenticeship and join the Coven. Ye should have been able to Search her out easily, a child o' your blood and bone."

"Ye think I have no' tried!" Anghus roared, temper breaking free. "I have Searched the whole land from shore to shore for her. I ken she is still alive, but somehow they have hidden her from me. My own daughter, hidden to my eyes!"

Meghan was silent, her eyes fixed on his face. With a broken groan, he told her the whole story. How his Talent had tricked and misled him again and again, making him feel Tabithas was near when all the time she was far away; making him throbbingly aware of his daughter without allowing him to fix her position.

"How do ye ken Tabithas was far away?"

"She was no' near me," he answered. "So many times I was as aware o' her as if she was in the next room, but never, never, was she there."

"Did your daughter have the Talent?"

He nodded brusquely.

"Did she wear your device?"

He nodded again.

She said thoughtfully, "It occurs to me a reverse spell

could have been placed upon the crest. A simple trick, easy enough for anyone with a small amount of skill and training, but highly effective in a case such as yours. Each time ye fix upon her, the medallion would repel ye in the opposite direction. She could no' find ye either, for the reverse spell would work against her own Talent as well. All ye would need to do to find her is go against your natural impulse. Fix on her, then go where your Talent tells ye no' to go."

His eyes were blazing with hope and excitement. "Could it be that simple?" he cried. "All these years, and I was kept away by an elementary reverse spell!"

"Happen that is the reason. It is only a guess, Anghus, but the only one that I can think o'. Try it if ye will. In the meantime, ye should perhaps know the blind warlock Jorge has been gathering together bairns o' Talent to begin a new Theurgia. Among a bevy o' beggar children he made friends with was a young lass with strong Searching powers. She wears around her neck a battered medallion that feels like a dog or a horse. Do ye perhaps think . . . ?"

Her question was not answered, for Anghus was on his feet, already pacing restlessly. "Could it be my Fionnghal?" he asked. "The Grand-Seeker Glynelda always said she was at Rhyssmadill with the Banrìgh, but I have searched every corridor and storeroom o' the palace and every street and courtyard o' Dùn Gorm and no' a trace o' her did I find."

"If she be your daughter or no' I canna tell," Meghan replied. "Such a strong Talent as she shows is rare . . . and I remember now Jorge told me she had been raised under Glynelda's hand. This lass was never at the palace, though. She was apprenticed to a thief and bounty-hunter in the Awl's pay, in Lucescere."

Anghus frowned and his hand moved unconsciously to his side, where the hilt of his sword normally hung. "I hope then that she is no' my daughter," he muttered. "A cruel apprenticeship indeed for my young lass."

"Any young lass," Meghan said.

The prionnsa nodded. "True indeed," he answered.
For a few moments more he paced to and fro on the
moonlit grass, then he turned to the witch and said, "Do
ye think it is the same with Tabithas? Will I find her if
I Search against the pull?"

"Nay," Meghan said. "Ye canna find Tabithas for ye
were looking for her in the wrong form. Ye were expecting her to be the same as ye have always known
her. She is different, though, far different. Her mind and
soul are no longer what ye knew. Anghus, Maya has a
very strange and terrible power, one I have never heard
o' before except in Other World faery stories. She can
transform people into any creature she likes. Tabithas
was turned into a wolf. She has lived in the forests
around Castle Rurach a long time syne. She is near.
Indeed, she waits in the forest."

Anghus was flabbergasted. He could only stare at her
as if she had spoken in a different language. In the growing light, Meghan could see his wide-open mouth. "Tabithas. My sister. Ye say she has been turned into a wolf?"

"Aye, so it seems. She came here last night. We
talked. She has no language left but that o' the beast.
Sixteen years she has been trapped in the body o' a wolf,
unable to reach anyone. She says she tried to speak with
ye many times, but your mind was closed. Slammed shut.
After a while she gave up. She ran with the wild wolves
o' the forest and won their allegiance. They have been
biting and nipping at the Banrìgh's heels all this time,
though since the rising o' the comet they have struck
in force. Tabithas remembers the calendar o' the Coven;
she knows the year o' the comet is always momentous
indeed."

"Tabithas. A wolf."

"Aye, I fear so. It is ironic, is it no'? Maya seems to
have a touch o' wit in her enchantments. I wonder how
many brave witches are now toads or rats?"

Anghus shuddered. From his pocket he pulled an ornate flask, which he uncorked and bent to his mouth

rapidly. He swallowed a mouthful, and then another, and put the flask down dazedly.

"The wolf that followed me here," he said. Meghan nodded. "That wolf with the silver-tipped ruff. She is Tabithas." Meghan nodded again. "I canna believe it."

"I'm sorry, Anghus, my lad, but indeed it is true. She tried to stop ye, but when ye would no' stop she came with ye. I convinced her last night to let me speak with ye and try and find the reason for your hunt."

"It does no' change anything," Anghus said suddenly. "No' any o' it, ye telling me about the reverse spell on Fionnghal or that the Banrìgh turned my sister into a wolf. I ken your witch-tricks; I know how ye witches can twist words until a man can no longer tell what is right or true . . ."

"And do ye feel what the Banrìgh does is right or true?" Meghan said in a terrible voice. "Are ye happy in her service, MacRuraich, descendant o' witches?"

He twisted away, his face set hard. "That has nothing to do with it, Meghan. I have sworn to this task; I dare no' risk my daughter on your word alone."

"Ye ken I do no' lie," she said sternly.

"How do I ken that? What is the Witches' Creed now? Ye swore no' to kill but have no' soldiers been killed by ye and your companions, many o' them?"

She bowed her old head. "That be true. Know I do no' kill lightly, nor lie easily. Yet both I have done in this struggle, for indeed it is a fight to the death. But I shall neither lie to ye nor harm ye, for I have broken bread and eaten salt with ye, and ye are the beloved brother o' my friend, who I loved and who loves ye still."

"I do no' wish to do this, Meghan," Anghus said desperately. "But I have given my word and canna break it."

"I know," she said simply. "I am ready to go with ye."

"What o' your companions? Where are they?"

"I am alone," she answered.

He paced a moment more, then turned and nodded. "So

be it. I am sorry, Meghan. Beware that scum, Humbert. He is a cruel man, and he longs to break you. I am ordered to deliver ye into his hands."

"Ye do no' take me to the Banrìgh yourself?"

"Nay, he countermanded her orders. He wants ye for himself."

"Was that your doing, Anghus?"

"I put the idea into his head," Anghus admitted. "I do no' ken if it was wise."

Meghan nodded. "I thank ye for it, Anghus," she said with renewed vigor. "I would have submitted to ye, fellow child o' the First Coven and friend. I see no need to submit to the Banrìgh's menial. Come, let us go. It is near dawn."

They were just walking into the dawn-scented forest when a small brown creature soared out from the trees and landed on Meghan's shoulder. It was a donbeag, the sails of skin between his paws unfurled. He chittered excitedly and rubbed his velvety head under her chin.

"Gitâ!" the old witch exclaimed. "Why have ye returned?" She stopped and stared into the forest. "Nay!" she cried. "Go back!"

As Anghus spun on his heel, he saw two young people leaping out from behind the shelter of the moss-oaks. There was a young hunchback, wrapped in a heavy cloak and holding a longbow, an arrow cocked and pointing directly at him. The other was a slim figure in a white tam o'shanter and breeches, holding a dagger threateningly.

"Let Meghan go," the hunchback cried, and limped forward a few steps.

"I thought ye said ye were alone," the prionnsa said to Meghan accusingly.

"I thought I was," she answered in chagrin.

"My orders were to capture both the Arch-Sorceress and the leader o' the rebels, named enigmatically the Cripple. Is this he?"

"Nay," Meghan answered. "He is a mere lad. Ye think he has the wit or wiles to lead the rebellion?"

"Let her go, I say!" the young man called again and lifted the bow so the barbed head of the arrow pointed directly at Anghus's heart.

"Bacaiche, put down the bow!" Meghan cried.

Incredulity sprang onto their faces. "But auld mother!" the other called, and Anghus could tell by her voice that she was a lass, although her hair was cropped short and she wore boys' clothes.

"I told ye both to go. Why have ye disobeyed my orders yet again?"

"Ye think we would go so easily?" the girl cried. "We knew ye were in danger. Ye thought we would just leave and let ye be captured?"

"Iseult, do ye no' understand? Ye must care for your babe now; if Bacaiche is killed or captured, the child is our only hope. Ye ken what needs to be done. Why have ye disobeyed my orders?"

"We shall no' let ye be captured by the Awl!" The hunchback hobbled forward a few more steps, his face twisted with hate, the bow raised threateningly. Anghus felt sweat spring up all over his body, and kept his eyes fixed on the arrow.

"Nay! Ye shall let the MacRuraich take me. Have I no' made myself clear?"

"Nay," the girl responded in her oddly accented voice. "I canna let ye sacrifice yourself, Meghan. We need ye. Ye are the Auld Mother, the Firemaker. We must protect ye."

Meghan laughed a little bitterly. "Iseult, I do no' need ye to protect me," she answered gently. "I am more than four hundred years auld and have been looking after myself all that time. Ye endanger me now. I want ye and Bacaiche to go, quickly and quietly. Do ye understand?"

They were puzzled and indecisive. The man with the longbow let the arrow droop until it pointed to the ground, so Anghus heaved a silent sigh of relief. Then the girl suddenly leaped forward with the speed and grace of a striking snake, and he found himself with the wicked-looking dagger against his throat. "We are going to go now, with Meghan. I shall no' kill ye if ye let her go without trouble."

"Iseult, ye do no' understand," Meghan said quietly. "We could go now, but Anghus will just follow us. No matter where I go, he will follow."

"But we will hide . . .."

"He will find us."

"But . . .."

"Iseult, the only way to stop a MacRuraich on the hunt is to kill him. He has sworn to track me down, and if it takes him a decade, he will do it."

Her arm shortened, and he felt the blade piercing his skin. "Then I will kill him," the girl said matter-of-factly.

"Nay, do ye no' understand I would rather give myself into the Awl's hand than have ye harm him? If I had wanted to escape, ye think I would no' have done so? He is the MacRuraich. A whole land—in fact, two lands—need him and depend on him. He is the last o' his line, and it is a great line, the bloodline o' Rùraich the Searcher who first found this land for us and marked it on the star map. I have broken bread and eaten salt with him, and I shall no' allow ye to hurt or kill him. So put down your sword, Iseult, or it is angry indeed I shall be."

The dagger dropped. Anghus put his hand to his throat and felt blood. The girl said in a bewildered voice, "But we want to rescue ye, Meghan . . ."

"If there is any rescuing to be done, I shall do it myself. Now, go, Iseult, take Bacaiche and bring him to safety. All my hopes are riding on ye." She disentangled the donbeag from her plait and, despite his attempts to creep back into her arms, handed him over to the girl. "Keep Gità safe for me, Iseult, and guard the pouch well. Head for the rebel encampment as I told ye. Do no' worry about me. I shall see ye again when the time is right. Now I must go and face the Awl. If I am killed, it is your job to find Isabeau and join the three parts. Nothing must prevent ye from finding the Inheritance!"

Iseult nodded, and she and the hunchback stepped back in the trees.

"Wait," Anghus said, and to his surprise his voice croaked. He looked down into Meghan's narrow, wrinkled face and said firmly, "I was given your christening robe to hold, Meghan NicCuinn."

She understood immediately. She glanced at the young man, still wrapped from throat to toes in the great black cloak. "I see," she said. "Well, then ye ken there is another MacCuinn still living. Take off your cloak, Lachlan."

The young man drew back in protest. Meghan nodded at him. "Anghus knows who ye are, Lachlan, ye canna hide such things from the eyes o' a MacRuraich."

Reluctantly he undid the ties of his cloak and let it drop to the ground. Freed from its concealing folds, he was revealed as a strongly built man, dressed in the Mac-Cuinn tartan. His muscular legs ended in talons like a bird of prey. From his shoulders sprang two glossy black wings. Slowly he stretched them out and flexed them. Anghus's breath caught.

"He is Lachlan Owein MacCuinn, youngest son o' Parteta the Brave. Maya transformed him into a black-bird when he was just a bairn. As ye can see, we have no' found the magic to repel her evil enchantments." Meghan's voice was hard and cold as the first crust of ice on a pond.

"I am sworn to bring him in," Anghus said bleakly.

"Nay, ye are no'," Meghan replied firmly. "Ye said yourself ye were told to capture the Cripple, leader o' the rebellion. Lachlan is no' the Cripple."

"But . . ." Lachlan exclaimed.

"He is a mere lad," Meghan said contemptuously. "True, he has spent the last few years tickling the nose o' the Ensorcellor, but ye think he has the cunning, the cleverness, to plan and command all those spectacular escapes, all over the country? He was only seven when Maya ensorcelled the Rìgh and brought the Towers down. Do ye seriously think he was auld enough or

clear-sighted enough to begin organizing an underground resistance then? For that was when the rebellion
began, in the aftermath o' the Day o' Betrayal. Many o'
the Cripple's most daring exploits occurred when Lachlan was still trapped in the body o' a blackbird. I freed
him when he was just fifteen, and he is now only twenty-
three years auld, and no' very wise. Ye canna seriously
think he is the Cripple, do ye?"

Lachlan made a strangled noise in his throat and
started forward, but the girl held him back with a hand
on his arm.

"I am sworn to hunt down the Cripple. If this is no'
he, who is?"

"A traveling jongleur named Enit Silverthroat," Meghan
said promptly.

"Meghan, no! How can ye?" Shock broke Lachlan's
expressive voice.

"Enit is now is Blessém," Meghan continued. "She is
the real leader o' the rebels, the one they call the Cripple. It is true many think Lachlan is the Cripple, and we
have no' ever let anyone know the truth. But it is Enit
who planned and commanded each and every movement
o' the rebels in the past sixteen years. She is the one
ye seek."

"Meghan, stop! How can ye betray her so?" Lachlan
was sobbing with anger and frustration.

"Trust me, my lad," she said, very low.

Anghus nodded his head. "Very well. I shall deliver
ye to the Grand-Seeker as sworn, and then I go in search
o' Enit Silverthroat."

THE HIGH-PRIESTESS OF JOR

Sani looked up and down the corridor before softly closing the door and locking it. Only when she was satisfied no one was listening did she cross the room to the tallboy where the Mirror of Leyla was hidden.

Reverently she drew the silver hand-mirror out of the drawer and laid it on the table. It was a very old looking-glass, a sacred relic of the Fairgean royal family, and a powerful aid to far-seeing. With it, Sani could keep an eye on her spies and her enemies, communicate with her king and those seekers trained in the skill of scrying, and eavesdrop on private conversations.

Sani was strictly forbidden to touch the mirror without direct orders from Maya. The king of the Fairgean was far too jealous of his own power to give such a powerful icon into the hands of a high-priestess of Jor. Even after sixteen years, Sani still resented his decision. She was an initiate into the deeper mysteries, able to call upon the powers of Jor as her own—the mirror should have been hers, not trusted to the hands of a halfbreed.

His interdiction had never stopped her from using the mirror as she pleased, of course. The old priestess knew, even if the king did not, that Maya was not to be trusted.

Sani firmly believed in keeping the reins of power in her own hands, even if that meant using the magical mirror in stealth.

In recent months it had grown increasingly difficult to find the privacy. Maya spent most of her days lolling in the pool in her suite of rooms. She dreaded having to go into the great hall where she was mobbed by impatient merchants wanting news of the trade flotilla. Her stomach was in constant disquiet, so she could not face the wild boar the lairds hunted down in her honor. All in all, she was as vague and distracted as Sani had ever known her.

It was only by the sea that the Banrìgh found release. Normally Sani disapproved of Maya spending time by the water, for the Banrìgh could afford no suspicions attached to her. This morning, though, the wily old priestess had opened the casement window so the salt-scented breeze blew through the whole room. "Look how the firth sparkles," she had said. Maya had drifted across to the window, the invigorating wind blowing her hair straight back from her brow. "Ye need some fresh air," Sani had cooed. "Look how pale ye grow."

"I need to swim," Maya said faintly.

"I can tell anyone who asks that ye are sleeping . . ." the old servant said and watched Maya's face color with pleasure. So Maya had made her slow way down to the stables, ordered her horse to be saddled, and ridden down to the beach, where the sea breezes caressed her face and cooled her blood. It was dangerous, of course. Too many people could notice when she returned with damp hair and sandy clothes. It was a risk that had to be taken, though. Sani needed to use the mirror.

She sat at the table, making a complicated gesture over its silvery surface and concentrating on Latifa the Cook's grand-niece, the red-haired scullery maid. Sani was not always able to focus in on the girl, but this time the mirror worked. She saw the girl sitting on a stool, feeding scraps of meat to the mangy dogs that turned the spit. Sani pursed up her lips in disappointment. Always she hoped to catch the lass out in some act of witchcraft or wrongdoing. But she always seemed innocent enough, working as hard as any of the other maids. She watched a while longer, then waved her hand over the mirror to banish the image.

The priestess had first seen the redhead in the week after May Day. The girl had been sick and weak, collapsing into a fever immediately after giving Latifa the Cook something concealed in a bag made of nyx hair. Sani knew well that such bags were designed to muffle the force of objects of magical power. Despite all her efforts, however, she had been unable to discover what it was the girl had carried. Sani did not like not knowing. It made her uneasy.

Sani was convinced the girl was the same redhead as the one who had caused so much trouble up in Rionnagan. First she had helped the winged *uile-bheist* to escape. This was a major blow, for it seemed certain he was the mysterious Cripple who had captured the hearts and minds of the common folk. Even worse, the secret fear that he may be one of the Lost Prionnsachan was now a certainty. There could be no other explanation for a winged man with the voice of a blackbird and the white lock of hair that marked all the MacCuinn clan.

The red-haired witch had supposedly been tried and executed, but within a month came news that she was alive and in company with the Arch-Sorceress and the winged *uile-bheist*. It seemed she was a warrior-maid as well as a powerful witch, for she slaughtered an entire troop of Red Guards at Tuathan Loch. The trio had disappeared into the mysterious depths of the Veiled Forest, and all attempts to flush them out had failed. It was not long afterwards that Sani saw her in the mirror, in Latifa's chamber. Although it seemed incredible the girl could have crossed the entire length of the country in such a short time, Sani knew already that she was a very dangerous witch with powerful forces at her command. Perhaps it was true Meghan had charmed the dragons and they now served her. Or perhaps the girl could fly as they said Ishbel the Winged had done. Certainly she had somersaulted through the air as nimbly, by all accounts.

Sani's initial response had been to have the girl killed immediately. A pillow over her face in the night, some hemlock in her tea, a stumble on the stairs—such things were easy to arrange. Caution held her hand, however. Alive, she could be tricked or tortured into revealing the Arch-Sorceress's plans. Once dead, the girl could tell no secrets.

It was not Sani's way to take hasty action. Her plans had been decades in the making, and decades more in the doing. She worked in shadows and in silence, planting a seed here, a suggestion there, then waiting with long and cunning patience to reap the rewards. Why, she had been nurturing Maya's powers for thirty-five endless years; she could afford to let the red-haired witch live a little longer.

So for two months Sani kept her own counsel, and in all that time she saw nothing to confirm her suspicions. It was true that she too was affected by the heat, even more than Maya. Priestesses of Jor were used to physical deprivation, however, and so Sani suffered in silence. She did not have the option of riding on the seashore or spending all day in a pool of cool salt water. She slept in the pool, of course, for without long immersion in seawater she grew sick and dehydrated. During the day, though, she must wear heavy clothes to hide the gills at her throat. She did not have Maya's ability to trick the eye, for the Fairgean could not spin illusions. That was a Talent Maya had inherited from her human mother and Sani relied on her spells of glamourie to hide her own Fairgean features. For this reason she could never leave Maya's side for long, since the glamourie soon wore off and needed to be renewed frequently.

Sani had begun to wonder if she was mistaken about Latifa's grand-niece. Red-gold hair was uncommon, but not so rare that Sani could be sure this girl was Meghan's apprentice. She could be just what she appeared to be, a rather simple country lass that just happened to have hair the color of newly minted pennies. True, there was the mysterious bag of nyx hair, but could there not be a natural explanation for that? Many relics of the Towers turned up in odd places, and it was possible that the lass had had no idea the bag had magical properties. It could have contained a gift from Latifa's sister, tucked into the bag for ease of carrying . . .

Then on the night before Midsummer's Eve, after the Banrìgh had sung for the court, Sani had heard such a cacophony of emotion from the girl that her suspicions had again been aroused. Such an agony of terror, and all at the sight of crimson-colored velvet. She searched out the girl and, seeing her crippled hand, at once knew two things that she had not known before. Firstly, she was now certain this redhead was the same as the one who had killed the Grand-Questioner. She remembered what she had forgotten before—the witch at Caeryla had suffered the pilliwinkes, a cruel torture which crushed the hand.

The second realization was that she could not be the girl traveling in Meghan's company. This thin, pallid lass with the crippled hand had certainly not killed an entire troop of Red Guards. Therefore there must be two red-heads. The trick was knowing whether Latifa's grand-niece had been captured and tortured by mistake, or whether both red-headed girls were connected with Meghan.

Sani ground her teeth in frustration and tried without success to make the mirror focus in on her enemy. That old witch was a sea-urchin spike in her foot that should have been drawn years ago. Everything had gone wrong since that first sighting of Meghan in the spring, and Sani dreaded the anger of her king.

She had only one hope left. It was several months since they had sent a seeker to Rurach with orders for its prionnsa, Anghus MacRuraich. He must be on the hunt by now, and if anyone could track down the slip-pery Arch-Sorceress, he could. Her fingers twitched at the idea of having Meghan in her hands. Meghan and that disgusting freak, the winged *uile-bheist*. More than anything Sani wanted to know how Meghan had managed to transform him back from a blackbird. He should have been trapped in the body of a bird forever.

Sani knew all too well how damaging the young Mac-Cuinn's testimony could be. No one knew of Maya's powers. No one knew the shape-changing ability she had inherited from her Fairgean father had been transmuted into the capacity to transform anyone into any shape she chose. Only Sani knew, and a few of the priestesses of Jor, and the king himself, Maya's terrible father. If the winged *uile-bheist's* story became common knowledge, it could destroy all that Sani had worked for.

It was more than thirty years since the high-priestess had recognized the latent powers in the young halfbreed daughter of the king. Maya's mother had been a Yedda, a sea witch trained to use her voice to ensorcel the Fairgean. A beautiful woman, black haired and blue eyed, she had been stolen from the Tower of Sea-Singers in one of the Fairgean's fierce raids. The king had seen her and wanted her. The blow aimed to kill had instead only knocked her unconscious. When she woke, he tore out her tongue so she could not sing, and used her for his pleasure. Maya had been conceived almost immediately, and so the king had let the Yedda live. A male Fairge was admired for his potency, and many of the king's offspring had been killed in the wars against the humans. He would not kill the human woman while she carried his child.

Nine months later Maya was born. Disgusted that she was a girl, the king lost all interest in her or her mother. In Fairgean politics, daughters were worth much less than a well-trained sea-serpent or a cave that offered shelter from the icy winds. It was not uncommon for a female Fairge to be given to another male at the toss of a stirk-knuckle. The priestesses were the only females the men would listen to, and few would dare raise a hand against them. Most Fairgean women therefore longed to be chosen for Jor, but few had the abilities required.

Sani had not realized Maya had the power to change people's shape until much later. It was her ability to make people do what she wanted that had first attracted the high-priestess's attention. The witches called it compulsion—to override someone's will with the strength of your own. The priestesses of Jor called it *leda*, which meant simply "mind-force."

At that time the Fairgean were living on a few bare rocks in the northern sea. Only the most powerful of the men were allowed on the rocks; everyone else lived on rafts made from driftwood and dried seaweed. Many Fairgean children drowned before they had learnt how to use their fins, for competition for food and raft space was fierce. Many were not adverse to pushing some other woman's babe into the sea to make more room for her own. The Yedda had no voice and no status. Both she and the babe should have died fairly soon. Yet somehow the babe never went hungry and never had to fight for somewhere to sleep. As she grew, her powers became more obvious. She even ensorcelled food out of the men, and that was peculiar enough to capture Sani's interest.

So she took Maya away from her mother and the over-crowded, flimsy rafts, and back to the tiny island given over to the sisterhood. The next day the Yedda no longer clung with desperate tenacity to the raft. She simply let go. Noone cared enough to stop her from sinking away below the water. A Fairgean could stay underwater for up to fifteen minutes before being forced to surface for air. They were designed to live in water so cold, great mountains of ice sometimes floated past. Humans were not. The king's whore would have died quickly.

On the dark, cold island of the Sisterhood of Jor, Maya grew to adulthood. She was trained to instant obedience to both her father and the priestesses and indoctrinated with stories of the Fairgeans' greatness. She was taught to have one desire only—to win glory in her father's eyes and revenge her people against the evil humans who had stolen their land and their seas. Sani had been glad to see she had inherited her mother's human beauty, for that would make the winning of the Rìgh's heart that much easier. She had also inherited her human mother's talent with music, and Sani guarded that secret carefully for if the king knew, he would tear out Maya's tongue in fear she might use it to ensorcel him.

Sani undertook most of Maya's training herself, which she was grateful for as she came to realize the strength and range of Maya's abilities. Not only was her *leda* unusually strong and subtle, particularly when she played her clàrsach or sang, but she had the ability to draw strength from others without them realizing. Most people had only the strength of their own will and intelligence to draw upon, but Maya borrowed magical power from all around her. This meant her strength was without limits.

Of course, those she borrowed strength from gradually failed. If Maya continued long enough, they sickened and died. Her husband Jaspar had lived longer than any other human, and Maya had borrowed so constantly from him that she would be hard put to manage when his life at last flickered out. Of course, once they had realized Maya was not going to conceive easily, they had stopped draining him quite so heavily, finding alternative sources of power instead. They could not risk Jaspar dying before they had a clear claim to the throne. None of them had realized it would take Maya sixteen years to conceive and that an ancient and powerful spell would be needed to achieve procreation.

The power to transform had only revealed itself when Maya was almost a grown woman. Sani's plans had taken definite shape then, and she had approached the king with her idea. He hated it, of course, for it meant relying on a woman's wits, not a man's brute strength. But his final attempt to win back the coastlands had failed catastrophically at the Battle of the Strand. The

Fairgean forces had been so broken that it would be many years before they again had the strength to attack. Reluctantly he had given his permission.

Sixteen years the plan had been unfolding, and nearly all their strategies were complete. Come winter, the babe would be born. The Rìgh would be allowed to slip into death, a mere husk of the ardent youth he had been. The Banrìgh would permit the people to make her Regent, and would rule in the babe's name. Then at last the humans' power would be broken, and the Fairgean would once again rule the waves.

Sani was wrapping the mirror in its tattered silk when she saw the silvery surface begin to swirl with clouds. Someone was trying to contact her. Hoping desperately that it was not the Fairgean king, Sani gazed into its depths.

Slowly the swirling clouds settled into the chubby, choleric face of the Grand-Seeker Humbert. He was sweating with mingled unease and excitement, for of all the seekers he was most sincere in his hatred of all things witch-tainted. He strongly disliked using the same skills that the Awl burnt witches for and would have much preferred to send messengers. Sani had no patience with his discomfort, however, and told him he either had to use the scrying bowl she gave him or she would find another Grand-Seeker. Ambition won over authenticity, and Humbert obediently contacted Sani once a week. It was not his usual time, however, and it was clear he was laboring under some intense excitement.

"We have the Arch-Sorceress!" he blurted out as soon as the courtesies were done with. "The MacRuraich came in with her no' half an hour ago! I do no' ken how he managed to capture her, but she's chained up with iron and rowan in the town square this very minute!"

Sani hissed in satisfaction. "I want her here!" she said in her sibilant voice. "How quickly can ye bring her to me?"

"By river is the fastest way, o' course," Humbert replied. "I will arrange for her to be brought down by barge."

"If she escapes again, I'll rip out your heart and eat it!" she warned. She saw Humbert blanch, and smiled.

"She shall no' escape, I swear it!" he cried.

"She had better no'," Sani replied, sweet as poisoned sugar, and banished the Grand-Seeker's ashen face from the mirror. As she wrapped the magic looking-glass up and put it away, her pale eyes were shining strangely. Once the Arch-Sorceress Meghan NicCuinn was dead, nothing would stand in her way.

THE CAPTIVE

Meghan was led through the streets of Dunceleste
with her wrists in iron shackles. She walked
with her head high and her black eyes scanning
the crowd with interest. Her gray plait was pinned at
her nape, and a huge emerald clasped together the folds
of her finely woven plaid. Despite the chain, the jeering
crowd, and soldiers riding all around her, she looked
more a banprionnsa than a condemned outlaw.

Every now and again a stone or egg or rotten fruit
was thrown at her, but always the missile reversed its
flight mid-air and flung itself back in the face of the
thrower. The more forceful their heave, the harder the
corresponding blow. The witch did not even look, or
move a finger, or show any sign that she had noticed
what was happening.

She reached the main square and saw there a crudely
built platform with a large wooden cage hung from a
gallows. She smiled in genuine amusement, and the soldiers nearest to her felt their uneasiness increase.

"Get ye in," they ordered gruffly, moving to grasp her
arms, but a strange dizziness came over them. As they
paused to recover their balance she stepped forward and
climbed the stairs unassisted. She was small but had to

bow her head to enter the cage, which rocked wildly at
her weight. Showing surprising nimbleness for one of her
age, she sat down cross-legged in the very center, lifting
her plaid clear of the straw and manure which littered
the floor.

"Charming," she said. "Quarters fit for a banprionnsa.
I gather from this that Humbert o' the Smithy fancies a
public discussion. I had heard he was no' very wise and
now I ken it is true. Tell him I am looking forward
to speaking with him. In the meantime, I would like
some water."

"No water for the prisoner," the sergeant ordered.

"Och, it is no' for me."

He ignored her, and she pulled her large bag toward
her and undid its buckle. First she pulled out her knitting, causing one of the soldiers to smile involuntarily.
Then, to their bemusement, she withdrew a bundle of
gardening tools. She took out her little rake and spade
and began raking the floor of the cage, pushing the dirt
to the four edges. Fastidiously she swept underneath her,
dusting off her skirt and wiping her fingers on a cloth.

As she labored, a flock of pigeons flew down, circling
the cage and settling along the top of the gallows. A fat
gray cat with orange eyes gracefully bounded up the
steps and slipped in between the bars to curl up on her
lap, purring loudly, paws kneading. Dogs threaded
through the crowd, tails wagging, and a great carthorse
ignored the cries and whip-blows of his driver to drag
the huge dray right up to the platform, nudging the cage
with its roman nose. She patted it through the bars, and
it nudged again, setting the cage swinging and the cat
miaowing in protest.

Tucking her tools away neatly, Meghan pulled out a
little canvas pouch and poured a selection of seeds into
her palm. The crowd pressed close to the platform, anxious to see what she was doing. The soldiers had to keep
them back with crossed spears. Meghan smiled at them,
carefully planting the seeds around the inside of the
cage. She took out a pinch which she blew into the air.

Tiny parasoled seeds drifted out. She did so four times, at the points of the compass, then looked down at the sergeant and said, "As ye see, I need some water."

"No water for the prisoner." The sergeant's neck turned red.

Meghan shrugged, saying, "What the Red Guards forbid, Eà provides."

To the surprise of the crowd, it began to rain, a light, blowing shower. It had been threatening for the past hour or so, but it seemed eerie that it should begin just at that moment. They wrapped their plaids tighter about them, and pulled on their tam o'shanters, wondering what would happen next. As quickly as it came, the scatter of rain passed over and the sun came out, the cobblestones steaming.

A soft sigh rose from the crowd, and the sergeant jerked his red coat nervously. Small green tendrils were winding their way up the bars and soft leaves were spreading over the beds of straw and manure. Soon flowers were budding, and Meghan's cage became a sweet-scented bower.

The sergeant attempted to break off the flowering branches, then noticed daisies flourishing in the cracks beneath his feet. Despite all his attempts to grind them to death, they soon made the cobblestones a cheerful patchwork of stone and golden flowers. Meghan took a silver goblet from her bag, poured herself a glass of goldensloe wine and reclined back on the soft bag. The cat in her lap purred loudly, paws kneading constantly, eyes mere slits of topaz.

The Grand-Seeker Humbert paused on the steps of the inn in chagrin. The whole square was decked with flowers, and the filthy witch-hag rested at her ease while the crowd murmured and smiled, the hostile voices now drowned by cries of wonderment. Worse, her shackles of iron and cage of rowan wood had had no effect at all upon her foul sorceries. He pulled his crimson robes tighter about him and walked down into the square.

Twelve seekers followed him, an arrowhead of red that stilled the crowd and stiffened the spines of the soldiers.

He raised his pudgy hands and exulted, "We have ye now, sorceress!"

"Have ye, Humbert?"

He struck out at the cage with his fist, and the cat spat at him, arching her back. Meghan stroked her plush gray fur and smiled gently at the Grand-Seeker. Her black eyes were fixed on his face with tolerant interest.

"For sixteen years ye have evaded the grasp o' the Awl, but now I, Humbert, fifth Grand-Seeker o' the Awl, have captured ye!"

"Actually it was the MacRuraich," Meghan answered. "I really do no' think ye had anything to do with it at all."

"Shut your mouth, witch! Ye dare speak thus to the Grand-Seeker!"

"Is he new to the position that he needs to remind himself who he is?"

Humbert grasped a pike from a soldier and attempted to stab Meghan through the bars, but the pike was long and very heavy and somehow the cage swung about so the pike was tangled. Humbert was almost dragged off his feet, and a few people in the crowd laughed. He dropped it, putting a finger in his collar as if the high-necked robe was too tight.

"Meghan NicCuinn, ye are charged with high treason, sorcery, murder, conspiracy against the throne, and foul heresies. It is alleged ye plot to overthrow our rightful Rìgh and Banrìgh and are in league with the wicked rebels terrorizing the countryside. Under the laws o' the Truth, if found guilty, ye shall be condemned to die by the fire."

Meghan said nothing. She stroked the gray cat and sipped from her wine. Humbert's fat cheeks reddened. "Ye shall be taken and put to the Question this evening," he said hoarsely. "We shall wring a confession from ye—and the names o' your evil conspirators."

"Have ye forgotten I am the Rìgh's kin, Humbert?"

Meghan said. "After the Burning I was offered full amnesty if I went to the Rìgh and submitted myself to his will. That has never been repealed."

"Ye have been named as an enemy o' the Crown and charged with sorcery and treason . . ."

"My great-nephew is the ultimate arbitrator o' justice in this land, Grand-Seeker," Meghan said with the faintest sneer in her voice. "It is for him to decide my guilt and to administer appropriate retribution."

Humbert's face was purple, his bulbous nose threaded with engorged capillaries. Sweat sprung up on his face, and he again fingered his collar as if it were too tight for him. "The Anti-Witchcraft League was set up by the Banrìgh herself and does no' report to the Rìgh."

"Nonetheless, the Banrìgh does no' rule—she is Banrìgh by marriage only and subject to her laird and husband, Jaspar MacCuinn, who is Rìgh by blood and birthright."

"The Awl was set up with the blessing o' the Rìgh." Humbert pressed his hand to his heart.

"Aye, indeed, but I doubt he gave permission for his role as judge and judicator to be superseded."

"It is the right o' the Awl to question whomever they believe to be a witch, to establish guilt and—"

"But ye ken I am a witch," Meghan said reasonably. "I do no' deny that charge. I see no reason for ye to torture me to establish something everyone kens." And she waved her hand in the air so blue witch-fire trailed in an arc. The crowd drew back with a hiss, and the Grand-Seeker pointed at her and cried, "See, the foul witch works her sorcery!"

"What do ye think I have been doing since I first walked in through the gates o' Dunceleste?" Meghan spoke in the tone of voice normally kept for a not very bright child. "Do ye think the blossoming o' the square was mere coincidence?" She smiled and waved her hand again. Flowers began to rain down on the square, and children ran about laughing, trying to catch them. A few landed on Humbert's head and shoulders, and he

brushed them away irritably, not noticing a daisy had
lodged perkily in his stiff curls, just behind his ear. A
ripple of laughter ran over the crowd, and one of his
seekers stepped forward and whispered to him. The
Grand-Seeker's round face flushed purple with rage, and
he swiped at the daisy with his plump fingers. Somehow
he kept missing it, his fingers merely pushing it into a
more rakish angle. The laughter intensified. His second-
in-command neatly plucked it out and threw it away,
and Humbert tried to regain his dignity.

"Take her away!" he roared.

Meghan sipped her wine, then said softly, "I warn ye,
Humbert, I shall no' allow ye or your evil-hearted min-
ions to lay a finger on me. Ye think ye could have caught
me if I had no' allowed myself to be taken into custody?
Attempt to question me and I shall be forced to forego
your kind hospitality."

"Ye canna escape the hand o' the Awl!" Humbert
hissed in response.

Meghan smiled. "O' course I can," she replied kindly.
"I have done so before, I shall do so again. I am only
here because it suits my purpose. Remember I escaped
the clutches o' Maya herself on the Day o' Betrayal. She
and her blaygird servant thought they had me, and yet
when they closed their fingers, I was gone. Ye think ye
are more powerful than Maya the Ensorcellor?"

"Speak o' the blessed Banrìgh with some respect!"
Humbert roared.

"I give respect where respect is due." Meghan made
sure her voice carried to the far edges of the crowd.

He spluttered, grasping his collar with both hands as
if it was strangling him.

Meghan said sternly, "And remember, there is more
than one way for me to escape. Believe me when I say
I would rather die than submit to your torture. A sorceress understands the way her body works. I am auld, very
auld; it would be easy enough to still my own heart
before ye could lay a hand on me. With me would die

all my secrets, and your beloved Banrìgh would no' be
at all pleased with ye should that happen."

The Grand-Seeker struggled to speak, his face so engorged with blood it seemed his eyes would bulge from
their sockets. Meghan leant forward, fixing Humbert
with the full force of her sharp, black eyes. "Oh, yes, it
is true a sorceress can stop the beating o' a heart," she
said conversationally. "Once ye understand the mechan-
ics o' the body, it is an easy enough trick. A heart such
as yours would be as easy to still as closing my hand."
Holding up her thin, blue-veined hand, Meghan clenched
it into a fist, and Humbert gave a sharp cry and staggered. He tore at his collar, and his jacket sprang open
as the buttons burst. Breathing harshly, his hand pressed
to his breast, he stared at the sorceress, mesmerized.

Meghan sat back, her hand returning to the fur of the
purring cat. "O' course, such things were forbidden by
the Coven, who swore never to use the One Power to
hurt, only to heal and help. The Coven is gone now,
though, and I suppose the creed we once swore to no
longer stands. Still, I think it would be best for ye all
around if ye send me to the Rìgh and Banrìgh for questioning, do ye no'?"

"Send ye to the Rìgh and Banrìgh for questioning,"
he repeated.

"Aye, send me to the Rìgh and Banrìgh. Soon would
be best."

"Soon," he repeated.

"Good man," she said approvingly and took another
sip of her wine.

Humbert looked about, bewilderment on his face. The
seekers were gazing at him in dismay, the soldiers were
barely able to hide their contempt, and many in the
crowd were openly laughing. He bit his lip and ordered
the soldiers to lock Meghan up for the night and prepare
to sail south in the morning. Then, with his collar still
unbuttoned, he turned and retreated into the inn.
Meghan smiled, picked a flower and threw it to a little

girl staring up at her, who caught it with a delighted laugh.

The soldiers began to strip away the flowers and vines, strumming the cage with their spears but not daring to come any closer. The crowd still surged and murmured, even though it was raining again and dusk was closing in over the town. The rattle-watch walked the square, rattling stones in his can and calling, "Sun is near to set, it be wild and wet, time to light your lamp, get out o' the damp."

Meghan knitted placidly, the cat still sleeping on her lap. A young boy hovered white and anxious at the edge of the crowd. Meghan looked at him and smiled gently. "She is your friend, this cat?"

He nodded, jumpy as a young colt. She stroked the plush gray fur and tickled her under the chin. "Your friend wants ye to go home with him now, orange-eyes. Thank ye for your company and support."

The cat yawned and stretched her fat paws, rubbing her back against Meghan's knee before strolling over to the edge of the cage. Lithely she leapt down and the boy picked her up with a shy glance at Meghan, before running back to his mother. Meghan smiled and said to him, *Ye should see if orange-eyes will deign to speak with ye. Cats rarely take the trouble with humans, but if ye try, she might.* At his startled jerk and glance, she knew the boy had heard her.

The soldiers opened the cage, ordering her to cease her evil sorceries and submit to being taken to safe quarters for the night. Meghan folded up her knitting and tucked it away in her bag. She fussed over the bag's interior for a while, despite their orders to cease. The sergeant leaned forward to grasp her arm, his other hand swinging back to strike her across the face. Suddenly he snatched his hand back with an oath. A wasp had darted from the folds of her clothes and stung him on his hand. He gripped his wrist in pain, staring with horror at the red swelling.

"Do ye have any feverfew syrup? That be the best for

wasp bites," Meghan said helpfully. "Or lavender oil. Keep it in cold water to keep the swelling down."

The sergeant swung toward her as if wanting to try and strike her again, but checked his movement, shouting instead, "Take her to the mill—we shall lock her in there for the night with the rats and the grain-snakes."

Meghan laughed. "Rats are more my friend than ye are, soldier. Such company is no hardship for me. But I warn ye—rats know more secret ways in and out of this sewer-riddled town than any of your raw recruits. If ye wish to keep me another night, I would devise a better keeping-place than that."

The sergeant chewed his mustache in indecision, then cried, "We'll lock ye in the inn's wine-cellar then!"

Meghan examined her nails. One of the guards said diffidently, "Be there no' rats in cellars too?"

The sergeant was taken aback, then angry, but he controlled his temper, saying, "Somewhere away from beasts. And plants. Somewhere with no easy way out, where we can guard all the exits."

"May I suggest the best room in the inn?" Meghan said. "It has been a long time syne I slept in a comfortable bed. I can promise ye'll no' have to worry about me leaving unexpectedly. Indeed, ye'll have trouble shifting me in the morn!"

The sergeant's eyes darted about, but all his soldiers' faces were impassive. He spat on the bluish lump on his hand, and said, "Take her to the inn! And someone get me some feverfew syrup!"

Meghan woke in the early dawn, disturbed by the unaccustomed sounds of the town waking. Out in the meadows the goatkeep was blowing his horn to call the goats out to pasture. The bakery was alive with the thump of dough on wood, and the clatter of bread ovens in the coal. The rattle-watch was making his rounds, declaring "a gray dawn, chill and forlorn."

She smiled and looked about her. If not the best room in the inn, it was still very comfortable. A hard and narrow bed, but then, anything softer and Meghan could not have slept, her old bones used to tree roots and stones. They had given her only a thin blanket, but she had had her plaid and three mice had come to keep her company. They had left her without food or water, but she had packed a great deal of food for she knew the Awl was unlikely to feed her well, and she had simply hung the jug out the window before she went to sleep. It should be brimming over now, for it had rained all night. She had been happy to eat a solitary meal and had enjoyed a few glasses of goldensloe wine with her flat bread and cold potato omelette.

The ashes in the fire blazed into life, and she huddled her plaid closer about her as she sat up in the bed. The mice squeaked protestingly and burrowed deeper into the blanket. She tweaked one pink tail and put her narrow, bare foot out of the bed. The boards were cold as ice, and she pulled it back in. No need to freeze herself—or to hide her magic, now she was in the Awl's very headquarters. With a grim smile, Meghan lay back on the pillows and prepared her breakfast.

The window casements opened, the jug hanging outside lifted itself in and flew across the room, the window banging shut against the cold wind. The jug splashed water into the bowl on the wash table before setting itself down beside it. The wash bowl then swung through the air and hung mid-air above the fire. A bag of oats extracted itself from the half-open pack, flew across to the fire and poured a measure into the bubbling water. A whirl of salt spun out of another pouch as the water and oats stirred briskly together. Soon a smooth porridge was puckering and popping away, and then the bowl waltzed with a spoon over to the bed. Meghan tasted the porridge gingerly. "Och, a wee bit hot!" she exclaimed and blew on it.

She left the bowl for her captors to wash, bathing straight from the jug and braiding her hair tightly. How she missed Gitâ, who had always helped her plait the great length of her hair. By the time she was dressed, the soldiers were kicking open the door and she was able to receive them, straight-backed and neat.

The cage, swept free of dirt, had been thrown onto the back of a wagon. They hustled her out, and with difficulty she climbed on board and settled herself in the cage again. "Humbert no' here to say goodbye?"

They shouted, "Quiet!," pressing close about the cage so all she could see were their red cloaks. She took out her knitting, paying them no attention, as serene as if she was safe in a cottage somewhere. Every now and again one would grow too bold and attempt to strike her. Each time the wagon lurched or a foot slipped, and the fist fell awry. Each time the menacer would injure himself instead. Soon most of the soldiers were bruised and cut, glowering with superstitious fear and frustration.

As the cart rumbled toward the town gates, the streets again thickened with onlookers. The mood was distinctly different from the previous procession through the town. Many still threw overripe fruit and stones, but again the missiles rebounded on the thrower, no matter how cunning the toss. At first the soldiers ducked instinctively, but they soon found no harm came to them if they did not attempt to harm Meghan. To the guards' consternation, some in the crowd threw flowers—always melting away so quickly none could tell whose hand had thrown them. Each of the secret supporters found their good wishes returned threefold. Some found coins in the street, or a sick child miraculously healed on their return. Others won a longed-for contract or a lucrative job.

The cart rumbled through the heavy gates and down the steep, winding road that lead from Dunceleste to the loch below. Loch Strathgordon was the second in the string of lochan called the Jewels of Rionnagan, its banks built high with jetties, warehouses and inns. Because of the rapids that flowed between it and Tuathan Loch, the lower loch was the disembarking point for passengers from the south and the place where goods were loaded and unloaded.

The cage was swung from the back of the cart straight onto the barge, the Red Guards taking no chances. A sharp eye was kept out for any attack by rebels attempting to free the sorceress, but nothing happened as the bargemen poled the low, flat boat away from the jetty. The boat was caught by the current and drawn down the loch toward the river. The water gleamed gray and silver, a brisk wind ruffling its surface. Dark green forest pressed close on the western shore, with the mountains towering above. On the eastern shore, green meadows and orchards rolled down to a wide valley, speckled with the steep roofs of villages. Meghan remarked to no one in particular, "It is many years since I last took a pleasure cruise on the Rhyllster. It is bonny, is it no'?"

The river journey from Loch Strathgordon to Lucescere Loch took more than a week, and all attempts to starve or intimidate the witch failed. She ate better than the soldiers, her pack filled to the brimming with the wild produce of the Veiled Forest. She heated all her food with her finger, a trick that made her think of Isabeau, who had always been too impatient to wait for the kettle to boil. She knitted or read during the day and wrapped herself in her plaid to sleep each night, not showing any signs of discomfort. Her cage was a playpen for mice and rats, causing many a soldier to shudder. The only time she was allowed out of the cage was to relieve herself over the side of the boat. They had at first insisted she perform such tasks in her cage, under the eye of all the soldiers, but Meghan had magically deposited her wastes in the Grand-Seeker's breakfast bowl until he relented. How she had managed such a trick exercised all their minds, for the guards had kept a close watch on her without seeing anything untoward.

They rode the rapids from Loch Braemer to Lucescere Loch with nothing happening to alarm them. The Grand-Seeker had been sure that any attempt to rescue the sorceress would occur during this part of the journey, for the Rhyllster's course ran through thick forests and deep gorges before tumbling down into the great stretch of loch below the Shining Waters.

They reached the Lucescere Loch just before sunset, and the bargemen dropped anchor well away from the tumult of froth where the waterfall plunged into the loch. Wreathed in rainbows where the sun glinted through the high-flying spray, the Shining Falls fell almost two hundred feet down a steep cliff face. The domes and towers of Lucescere seemed to float on the curve of the wave above.

Meghan sat in her cage, staring up thoughtfully at the city, now silhouetted against a color-streaked sky. She tickled the nose of a huge black rat with a straw until it sneezed, batting at its whiskers with its paws. "It may be time to leave the sinking ship," she murmured with a twisted smile. She drew her crystal ball out of her bag and stared into its milky depths. The soldiers about the cage shifted uneasily but dared make no objection. She sat lost in its depths until the sky overhead was prickling with stars; then she tucked it away with a sigh.

It was near midnight when the guard in the bow of the boat heard the sound of leathern wings swooping near. He shook off his odd sleepiness, got to his feet and stared up at the sky. A faint noise from the stern made him turn. He saw Meghan step out of her cage, the padlock somehow open, the chain falling away. "Oy!" he cried. "Wha' do ye think ye're doing?"

He saw with horror that the dozen soldiers who guarded the cage were all slumped on the deck, asleep. The Arch-Sorceress turned at his words, then looked up. He heard flapping right above him and glanced up instinctively. Slender serrated wings were silhouetted against the roundness of the moons. He saw wild, flying hair, the flash of gleaming eyes, then a bare foot caught him on the back of the neck and slammed him to the floor. Dazed, he raised himself high enough to see the black-winged creature catch Meghan in its arms and lift her away. Although he shot arrow after arrow into the night sky, it was too late. The Arch-Sorceress was gone.

THE WEAVER'S SHUTTLE FLIES

Autumn

THE WINGED PRIONNSA

The raven flew down to a branch of a pine tree and cocked his glossy head. He gave a harsh caw, and Iseult raised an eyebrow at Lachlan. "He said it's no' too much further," Lachlan replied, hunching against the rain.

The great bulk of the Fang shouldered out of the mountains ahead, its peak wreathed in dark storm clouds. It had taken them several weeks to cross the country from the Veiled Forest, for they had kept to the hidden paths, not daring to go into any of the mountain villages. They came to a burn tumbling down a steep slope, and followed its course through great thickets of thorn bushes. Goldensloe plums, beginning to wither on the branch, hung on either side, while a red cliff towered above, great boulders littering the slope. Jesyah flew down to the top of one giant rock, gave a caw of amusement and disappeared from view.

Iseult and Lachlan followed cautiously, finding a narrow, winding passageway through the rock. The donbeag, perched on Iseult's shoulder, chittered in curiosity. Guards hiding among the rocks above challenged them, but Lachlan was known to them, and so they were allowed to continue.

Soon they could hear hammering and shouting and the crack of sword on sword. A horse neighed, sounding incongruous in the narrow passageway. Lachlan pressed ahead, leading the way into a huge corrie surrounded on all sides by high walls of stone pitted with caves. Tents covered the meadow, and everywhere armed men were working and practicing their weapon play. At one end was a loch, fed by thin waterfalls that poured down from the lip of the glacier far above. Iseult lifted her eyes to the symmetrical peak of the Fang, briefly visible through a rift in the storm.

"The Skull o' the World," she whispered.

She had no time to do more than give the mountain, sacred to the people of the Spine of the World, a lingering glance. As soon as they stepped out from the shelter of the passageway they were again challenged by guards. Lachlan, his golden-topaz eyes brilliant with excitement, called out to them. Cries of greeting echoed around the corrie, and a huge man in a blue jerkin and a faded kilt came striding out of the crowd to grasp Lachlan's hands.

"Duncan!" Lachlan cried. "It is good indeed to see ye!"

Duncan's face was square, deeply tanned, and disfigured by a knotted scar that ran from his ear into his bushy black beard. His nose had been broken so many times it was hard to tell what shape it once would have been. He was thickset as an old oak tree, the muscles of his arms bulging. Iseult thought she would not like to engage in single combat with him.

He pulled Lachlan into a bear hug from which he emerged ruffled and short of breath. "Ironfist, when will ye give up trying to crack my ribs?" he wheezed, holding his side. Duncan grinned widely, showing black gaps where teeth were missing, as Lachlan was hailed from all sides. "Look, there's Jorge!" Lachlan cried. "Let's go speak with him."

He gestured toward an old man standing at the far end of the loch. A snowy-white beard flowed over his chest, reaching past his waist. He was dressed in a pale blue robe, and the raven was perched on his shoulder.

As they skirted the loch, Jorge lifted his shaggy head, and Iseult saw with horrified pity that he was blind. At that very moment, he startled her by smiling in welcome and calling, "Bacaiche! My dearest lad! I am so glad to see ye!"

"Ye may call me Lachlan now," the prionnsa replied majestically.

"Ye've declared yourself?"

"Virtually."

"Och, I am so glad. It is time for ye to proclaim who ye are. Indeed, I think ye should have done so earlier but Meghan was too afraid o' the possible consequences." Then, with a smile in his voice, he said, "And who is the lassie?"

"My wife," Lachlan replied proudly. "Iseult Nic-Faghan, I would like ye to meet Jorge the Seer, who did much to help me when I first found myself again in the body o' a man."

"Obh obh! Your wife! With babe too, I can see. Congratulations to ye both, though surprised I am indeed to hear it. NicFaghan? That is no' a name I ken, and I know all the clans, even the lesser ones. Though, mind ye, it has echoes . . ."

"Iseult is descended from Faodhagan the Red," Lachlan replied.

"From Faodhagan! But surely that family died out a thousand years ago?" Jorge paused, then exclaimed, "O' course, it is Isabeau ye remind me o'! Ye are twins? Faodhagan was one o' a set o' twins, that I do remember."

"They look exactly alike," Lachlan said. "I had forgotten ye had met Iseult's sister."

"Indeed I did, I was one o' the witches at her Testing. May I touch ye, Iseult? I canna get a clear picture o' ye if I do no'."

Reluctantly Iseult let the old man clench her head in his gnarled fingers. Khan'cobhans did not like to be touched by strangers. His filmy white eyes repelled her but she swallowed her distaste and stood still until he at last let go. The whirling sensation his touch brought passed away, and she saw he was smiling.

"Meghan must have been pleased to ken there were two Isabeaus," he said.

"I am Iseult, and by all accounts quite different from my sister."

"Obh obh, no offense intended, lassie. I just meant it was rare to find two young witches o' such power and potential. I can see for myself that ye are quite different from Isabeau."

"But ye are blind, what do ye mean ye can see?"

Lachlan gave a stifled protest, but Jorge said, "I do no' see with the eyes o' the body, my dear."

He led them to sit on a fallen log, asking, "But how can this be, the discovery o' a new clan? I had thought there was some terrible tragedy with the Red Sorcerers. She murdered him and killed all who tried to stay her hand, did she no'?"

Iseult slid down to the ground, crossed her legs and upturned her hands in her lap. Lachlan rolled his eyes. She ignored him, telling Jorge the tale of Sorcha the Murderess and how the line of the Firemakers had begun. He listened with great interest, nodding his shaggy white head and saying afterward, "NicFaghan. Aye, it fits. Daughter o' Faodhagan."

Laughter rang all around the clearing as children raced through the trees. Iseult slid her hand to her stomach, just beginning to swell the fabric of her shirt. The seer smiled and said, "Ye carry twins, did ye ken?"

Iseult's dreamy smile turned to a horrified stare. "Twins! I had hoped . . . ."

"Aye, twins, born o' the MacCuinn and NicFaghan lines. Happy news indeed! But why are ye so distressed, my child? Twins are forbidden? By whom? Och, I see. Do no' fret yourself, my dear, twins are no' forbidden in Eileanan, particularly no' twins born o' a sorceress!" Then he sighed, and said, "Actually, they are just now, but soon, my dear, soon! The Coven will be reborn, and your twin witches will be welcome indeed!"

"But I am still in *geas* to the Gods o' White," Iseult murmured, arms crossed tightly over her lap. Neither Jorge nor Lachlan understood.

There was a feast that night to welcome back the hunchback, with music and singing and many tales told of the rebels' escapades. Duncan performed a surprisingly dainty jig over crossed claymores, his kilt swirling. One of the beggar lads played the fiddle till toes tapped and fingers rapped, and burly soldiers danced arm-in-arm about the bonfire. Lachlan sang them rousing war songs till the soldiers cheered and banged their claymores against their shields, then he crooned tender love songs till there was not a dry eye in the crowd. Even Iseult's eyes were damp, her heart swelling with love for her husband. It was when he sang that Lachlan moved her most, his blackbird voice so piercingly sweet and flexible that it seemed to express all the things he could not say to her.

After Lachlan's song had died away, Duncan Ironfist strode to the center of the crowd and held up one huge hand. "Laddies, tonight is special indeed, for our auld friend Bacaiche the Hunchback is among us again. Many o' ye here have fought with him over the past eight years and know well his courage and daring."

Cheers rang out among the rebels, and Lachlan smiled and dipped his head, the cloak of nyx hair wrapped close about his throat. Duncan smiled around at them, his ham-sized hands on his hips. He waited for the uproar to die down then continued, "Now I ken ye laddies are all loyal to the Coven and wish for the guid auld days to return. Since the MacCuinn married the wicked Unknown, the state o' affairs in Eileanan has gone from bad to worse. The Red Guards strut around the countryside, taking what they want from croft and cottage, dishonoring our women, killing our lads, burning anyone who stands up to them. People are starving in the countryside, the rivers are filling again with the wicked Fairgean, and the blaygird Banrìgh rules the courts and the army."

There were hisses and cries from the crowd. Duncan again paused for maximum effect, taking a swig from the whiskey flask in his hand. "Rumors in the countryside tell o' a prophecy—they say a winged man will come to save the land, bearing the lost Lodestar in his hand. He shall come with dragons at his shoulder and all the powers o' sorcery at his command. He shall be Rìgh and save us from death and disaster!"

Lachlan stepped forward, unfastening the clasp of his magical cloak. "I give ye Lachlan Owein MacCuinn, fourth son o' Parteta the Brave!" Duncan shouted, then he knelt, his great claymore held like a cross before him.

To an amazed silence the nyx-hair cloak slid to the ground and Lachlan spread out his great, night-black wings. He was wearing the MacCuinn kilt and plaid, the stag brooch at his breast, the *sgian dubh* thrust into his leather gaiters. He looked every inch a prionnsa.

Even Iseult, who had seen the transformation from hunchback to winged prionnsa many times now, could not contain a gasp of admiration. There were sighs of astonishment from the crowd, then the night was ripped apart by shouts of excitement and recognition. "He is winged!"

"The prophecy is true!"

"A MacCuinn—one o' the Lost Prionnsachan!"

"We are saved!"

"We canna lose now!"

"Hurray for Lachlan the Winged!"

Cheers rang out again and again, and a thousand men knelt before him, their swords held out in supplication. Lachlan bowed his head gravely. He told the story of his enchantment, his years trapped in the body of a blackbird, his transformation back into the body of a winged and clawed man. He told how he had sworn revenge on the Banrìgh for her evil sorceries and had joined the rebels and fought with them in every land across Eileanan. He told them how he had been caught by the Banrìgh's Guards, and how he had escaped, naked as a newborn babe, with nothing but the cloak of illusions to protect him. He told them his great-aunt Meghan o' the Beasts still lived but had given herself into the hands of the Awl so that he might remain free. This news was greeted with groans of dismay.

Lachlan held out his hand for Iseult and told the soldiers she was born of the line of Faodhagan the Red, was a witch and a warrior in her own right and was carrying twin babes, heirs to the throne. Iseult stepped into the circle of light, the rebel soldiers cheering until her cheeks crimsoned with embarrassment.

"It is time for us to strike at the very heart o' Maya the Unknown's power!" Lachlan cried. "We shall ride for Lucescere, to win the city for our own and to retrieve the Lodestar! With the Inheritance o' Aedan again in my hand, there shall be no stopping us! On with the rebellion!"

The clanging of claymores on shields, the stamping of feet, the clapping and cheering rang around the corrie until Iseult had to cover her ears with her hands. "Long live Lachlan MacCuinn! Long live the winged prionnsa!" the rebels shouted. "Eà bless Lachlan MacCuinn!"

Finn woke early and bounced out of her bed of bracken, tumbling the sleeping elven cat to the cave floor. "Wake up, Jo!" she cried, but the other girl only murmured in protest. Finn ran out into the fresh morning, her bare toes curling in protest as she stepped onto the dew-laden grass. The sun gilded the leaves of the trees, the loch shone blue, and overhead the mountain peaks glittered with snow. The broad sweep of the glacier was so dazzling in the sun that Finn had to shield her eyes with her hand to stare up at the Fang, its steep sides symmetrical as any cone. The Fang was not often clear of cloud, and for some reason it strummed a familiar chord in her when she saw it like this, white-capped and sharp-pointed.

The rebel camp was already stirring, thin trails of smoke rising from the breakfast fires, and soldiers feeding the horses picketed against the cliff. Finn danced through the meadow toward the camp, hoping to see more of the new arrivals in the light of the morning.

Finn had been thrilled to the core by the wondrous and romantic events of the evening. She and the rest of the League had had front row seats, mainly due to Jay's expertise with the fiddle. Lachlan MacCuinn's magical cloak had dropped at their very feet, and the shadow of his wings had fallen across their faces. They were all now committed heart and soul to Lachlan MacCuinn's cause.

Finn easily wheedled breakfast for herself and the little cat from the under-cook, who tousled her matted chestnut-brown curls and called her "a wee rascal." With Goblin perched on her shoulder, she made her way through the tents and bedrolls till she came near where Lachlan the Winged and his party had spent the night. She easily evaded the guards set to protect his campfire, and crouched where she could watch the flap of the tent without being seen. By the time she had eaten her bread and bacon, the banprionnsa had come out and was stretching in the sunshine. She was dressed like a lad in breeches and a loose shirt, with her red curls tied back in a bunch at the back of her neck. As Finn gazed in admiration, the blue eyes swung around and stared into the shadows where the little girl was hiding. Once she discerned the size and shape of the hidden watcher, her frown smoothed away.

"Come out, lass, I shall no' hurt ye," she said. "What's your name?"

Skipping delightedly into the sunshine, Finn told Iseult her name and all about the League and Tòmas, their mascot, who could heal by the laying on of hands. She told her about the past four months in the corrie, and how they had formed their own battalion, despite the jeers and laughter of the soldiers.

The League of the Healing Hand had more than tripled since the rebels came, for there were many children among the camp-followers. Dillon had ordered Johanna to sew them a banner, which Connor carried tied to a stick. Featuring an oddly shaped golden hand on a blue background, the children were very proud of it.

Each day the League practiced maneuvers under the anxious eye of their general, Dillon the Bold. They had had few weapons to begin with but had begged, borrowed and stolen from all over the camp until all thirty-two of the League had sharp daggers to thrust through their belts. The elder boys had persuaded the soldiers to begin training them in the use of short swords and crossbows, and Finn was very cross that the soldiers refused to teach her.

"They say a lassie canna learn to shoot!" Finn said aggrievedly.

"Och, they be fools!" Iseult cried. "I shall teach ye myself, and we'll show those soldiers how well a girl can shoot!"

This pleased Finn very much indeed, and she begged for a lesson there and then. Iseult shook her head and said she first had to attend a war council.

"They are letting ye go to the war council?" Finn was wide-eyed, having learned to her cost how little the soldiers thought of women in war.

"O' course I am! I'd like to see them try and keep me out."

Finn heaved a blissful sigh and asked if she could come too. Iseult shook her head. "Nay, Finn, I'm afraid that may be stretching the generals' forbearance too far. There is something I would like ye to do for me, though." She rummaged around in a small pouch at her waist, drawing out a broken arrow, dark and brittle with age. "Jorge has told us that he thinks ye have a talent for finding things."

Finn shrugged. "People are always asking me to find something for them."

"Ye sound as if ye wish they would no'."

Finn crimsoned and looked at the ground, her hands

twisting the hem of her ragged dress into a knot. "They always want me to find bad things," she muttered.

"Well, I want ye to find something for Lachlan, something very important, that may help us win," Iseult said gravely.

Finn looked up, her hazel-green eyes shining. "I would love to find something for ye and the winged one!" she cried. "What?"

Iseult explained about Owein's Bow and how it had been hidden in the witches' tower at Lucescere. Finn's face fell. "I'd rather eat toasted toads than go back to Lucescere. I was apprentice to a witch-sniffer—the Grand-Seeker Glynelda herself bonded me. I ran away, and I'll be beaten badly if they catch me."

"Glynelda is dead," Iseult reassured her. "There's a new one, from Siantan—he bides at Dunceleste, no' Lucescere. Ye would be safe."

Finn shook her head. "They all know me, all the seekers in Lucescere. They ken I helped Jorge and Tòmas escape . . ."

Iseult's blue eyes were thoughtful. "Mmm, that could be a problem," she responded. "Though our plan is no' to go into the city ourselves, for we canna risk Lachlan falling into the hands o' the Awl. We think to breach the rampart from the mountains."

"How?"

Iseult smiled ruefully. "That is one o' our problems. I was going to try and jump it . . ."

"But it's two hundred feet high!"

"Aye, I ken. I do no' think I can do it now, the children weigh heavy on me and I have been sick . . . Hopefully we shall come up with a solution in the war council."

"Goblin and I could climb it for ye," Finn offered.

Iseult looked at her in surprise. "It is meant to be unclimbable," she objected. "It is smooth as ice and curves outward. No-one has ever climbed it."

"Goblin is an elven cat," Finn said. "She climbs these

cliffs and the rampart canna be higher or smoother than them."

Iseult looked at the cliff that enclosed the corrie like a frozen wave. It was near three hundred feet high in places. "Your cat climbs that?"

"Aye, as easy as walking a path. Ye should see her! Her claws are very sharp."

"But ye have no claws . . ."

"No, but ye see, the witch-sniffer I was trained by was really a thief, and one o' the best. He could steal a jewel from the Rìgh's own crown if he wanted to. I climbed into many a house or castle for him and find most walls have crevices or ivy or something I can cling to."

"They say this rampart has nothing. No' even a crack."

"All walls have cracks. But if ye like, I could tie a thread to Goblin and a rope to the thread . . ."

"Aye, but surely your kitten canna be tying the rope up securely?"

"No, but she could go around a projection and then jump down again so the rope can be pulled up."

"Ye'd have to train her first though, and that we do no' have time for . . ."

"Och, I'll just tell her what to do, that's no problem!"

"Ye can talk to the cat?"

Finn nodded. Iseult looked at her with interest. It seemed this little girl had great powers indeed to have found herself a familiar when so young.

"How can ye be sure the projection is secure? We dinna want the rope to be coming undone when ye are climbing it."

"Och, Goblin will no' want me to fall. She'll make sure the string is secure."

Iseult looked at the little girl with admiration. "A grand idea indeed. Happen I should take ye with me to the war council!"

Finn straightened in pride. "Really?"

Iseult smiled briefly. "No, sorry, Finn, war councils are no' really the place for lassies, no matter how canny.

I'd like to see ye climb the cliff, though, and see if we canna devise a way to ensure ye can breach the rampart. It would be dangerous though. Red Guards patrol the auld tower, and ye heard Lachlan tell how he was caught there."

"I could disguise myself!" Finn cried in excitement. "I be just a lassie, the soldiers will no' ken I am rebel if I disguise myself."

Iseult said, "Maybe. We'll see." She stretched and added, "I must wake my sleepyhead husband if we are ever to get our plans finalized. Run along now, Finn, and we will talk later."

With the tiny black cat a silent shadow at her heels, Finn went running through the camp, shouting with excitement. She had met the banprionnsa and was to help them breach Lucescere! Just wait till she told Scruffy!

The war council took many hours, even though Lachlan and Iseult had gone over the plan with Meghan a hundred times, polishing it and looking for flaws. Partly the delays were caused by arguments between the different divisions of the rebel army, but most of it was due to the generals refusing to listen to a word Iseult said. Women were never trained for warfare in Eileanan, and women who knew how to fight were regarded as unnatural as a lamb with two heads. The only country in which women warriors were common was Tìrsoilleir, and the Berhtildes were generally regarded with horror due to their love of sacrifice and self-mutilation.

The fact that Iseult still had both her breasts reassured them slightly, but she had to defeat several of the rebel leaders before they would believe she really could fight. Cathmor the Nimble was the most agile of them all when it came to hand-to-hand combat, yet Iseult disarmed him with a few fierce, swift movements. Then Duncan Ironfist stepped up with a jeer and a jest, and she somersaulted right over his head so he spun around, lost his balance and was knocked flat with a powerful blow of her foot. She downed three more in such rapid succession that the soldiers looked at her with awe and lined up to try their mettle against her.

She had gone to such lengths to prove herself that it was afternoon before she was able to rather wearily outline the plan of attack. With Meghan's map of Rionnagan pinned to the side of the tent, Iseult demonstrated her points with her skewer, answering all the generals' objections with a patience most unnatural to her.

After sundown the cooks brought in stew and bread. As Iseult ate, she was pleased to hear the excitement in the soldiers' voices as they argued over the plan. By midnight they were all agreed and it was only the smaller details that still needed to be worked out. By two in the morning every leader knew exactly what he and his men were meant to do, and Iseult and Lachlan were being saluted with tankards of ale.

Like all successful military campaigns, it was a simple plan. Lachlan, Iseult and Duncan were to travel with a select group of soldiers down through the Whitelock Mountains to the forest behind Lucescere. From there they would infiltrate the city, relying on the beggar children to rouse the guild of thieves and make contact with rebel leaders already hiding out in the slums. The soldiers were to be called the Blue Guards, as Lachlan's father's bodyguard had been.

Jorge was to scry to one of the warlocks in the rebel camp in the Whitelock Mountains. There were close on five hundred rebels scattered throughout the south, and they would be secretly gathered on the far side of the Ban-Bharrach River. The remaining soldiery in the corrie would march through Rionnagan to infiltrate Lucescere from the north, led by Cathmor the Nimble. Thus the attack would come from three directions at once, with the gates to the city being opened by their allies within.

"Wha' about the Lodestar?" the soldiers all cried. "Once ye have the Lodestar in your hand, nothing will be able to withstand us!"

Lachlan had known this question would come, but had

no intention of telling the soldiers that he and Iseult first
had to recover the other two parts of the Key and join
them into one before they could even hope to recover
the lost orb. He said only that the Lodestar was hidden
within Lucescere and could only be recovered with great
difficulty. He also told them that the song of the Lodestar was dying, and the closer winter came the less likely
they would be able to rescue the Lodestar in time.
"Meghan o' the Beasts says it will die if it is no' found
and touched," he said bleakly, "so we canna be relying
on the Lodestar's powers."

As he and Iseult finally trudged to their tent, it was
this last problem that occupied both their minds.
"Meghan said she would make contact with Isabeau and
make sure she brought the other part o' the Key to
Lucescere," Iseult said softly as she undressed. "Yet how
are we to be sure Meghan got the message to her?"

"We canna," Lachlan replied in somber tones. "We
canna be sure o' anything."

Isabeau lay in the yellow grass, chewing on a straw,
while Lasair cropped contentedly behind her. The sun
on her arms was warm, but the wind off the sea was
keen. She rolled over, looked up at the cloud-hazed sky
and sighed. If it were not for her rides through the forest, she would have found her life in the palace this last
month very difficult. Sani seemed always to be watching
her, and Latifa was short-tempered and anxious.

Both Latifa and Isabeau had been very disturbed at
the news of Meghan's capture. The idea that her beloved
guardian was in the hands of the terrible Awl had distressed Isabeau greatly. If the Grand Questioner had
tortured her so cruelly, what would they do to the Arch-
Sorceress Meghan NicCuinn?

Meghan's true identity was as much a cause of Isabeau's shock as the news of her capture. She had never
known her as anything but Meghan of the Beasts. It had
made her feel rather strange to know her guardian was
a banprionnsa, descendant of Cuinn Lionheart himself.

In her heart she cursed the sorceress for her secrecy and lack of trust. Would she not have done things differently if she had known?

The old cook had been afraid not only for Meghan's safety but also for her own. She had been intimately connected with the rebellion for sixteen years and was one of Meghan's most useful spies. If under torture Meghan revealed the names of the witches and rebels she knew, Latifa was sure to be denounced.

A week later, however, word had come that the Arch-Sorceress had escaped. Gossip whispered of evil sorceries and strange beasts; all anyone knew for sure was that the Grand-Seeker Humbert had hung himself in his fine quarters on hearing the news. His successor, Grand-Seeker Renshaw, had his men beating the forests and hills around Lucescere, but there was no sign of Meghan.

Isabeau had had to hide her excitement, pretending to be as frightened as the rest of the palace servants. She kept her head down and worked diligently, waiting for Meghan to contact her. Loneliness was seeping into her bones, despite the crowds that surrounded her every day. She wished she could have found a friend at the palace. All her life she had dreamed of a companion who felt as she did, a friend and confidante she could tell her secret heart to.

Isabeau scrambled to her feet and wandered along the seawall, looking out at the clear ripples of water creeping over the sand below. A few hundred yards along was a break in the bulwark where one could climb down to the sand dunes below. Although only two iron posts had rusted through, it was enough for Isabeau to squeeze her slim body through.

Isabeau swung easily down the ladder, though it was so long her arms were aching by the time the beach was finally beneath her feet. She sat, unlaced her boots and wiggled her toes in the sand. Shells and dried wisps of seaweed decorated the dunes, and she gathered some as she walked the long distance to the water's edge. A reef ran out into the sea, forming a small lagoon where the water was crystal clear and flickering with shoals of fish that gleamed with fluorescent lights. In seconds Isabeau was paddling in the foam. She kilted her skirts up through her belt so her legs were bare to the knee. *No one else would come so near the seashore so there's no chance of anyone seeing,* she thought defiantly.

Isabeau had been brought up so far from the coast that many of the stories she had heard about the sea's danger had had a fairy tale quality, not quite believable. She had no fear of water, having been taught to swim by otters as a very young child. Many of her contemporaries at the palace were too afraid to even duck their heads under the pump in case a Fairge's webbed hand should reach out and strangle them. Isabeau was rather contemptuous of such fears, though not so derisive that she would dare go deeper than her knees.

This lonely stretch of coastline was one of the few places on Eileanan where there were calm waters and a natural harbor. Across the river's mouth was a series of massive gates, joined by a sequence of canals. Within their shelter, the navy and merchant ships rested in the Berhtfane, safe from storm and invasion.

The locks had been built by the witches in the time of Aedan Whitelock, after the end of the Second Fairgean Wars. Meghan said they were an engineering triumph, allowing ships to be raised and lowered at will, but keeping the Fairgean out. The MacBrann of the time had designed them and overseen their building, and for four hundred-odd years they had not failed.

On the opposite side of the firth began the Strand, a long expanse of sand that curved around into the salt marshes of Arran. The Strand extended the entire length of Clachan, undulating with dunes where sand lions hunted and sea-stirks roared and fought each spring.

Before humans came, the Fairgean had ridden the spring tides each year to bear their young on the soft dunes of the Strand. The male Fairgean had hunted the sea-stirks for their rich meat and thick coats; the females had taught their babes to swim in the calm waters, and harvested the seagrapes to store for the winter.

It was at the Strand that most of the battles against the Fairgean had taken place. It was here Parteta the Brave had died, three years before Isabeau was born. There the young Jaspar had raised the Lodestar against the Fairgean and driven them back into the seas. *Never to be seen again,* the tale had always ended.

The thought of the Fairgean made Isabeau's stomach twist, for the sea-dwelling faeries had been seen again in the waters to the north. A cloud crossed the sun, turning the water to steel-gray. She turned and hurried back the way she had come. Her footsteps were already blotted out by the rising tide, and her wet legs were cold.

It took a long time to climb the rusty ladder again. Isabeau looked up to see how much further she had to climb, and froze. Someone was watching her. They leaned over the bulwark, the sun behind them so all Isabeau could see was the dark shape of their head and shoulders. Her blood began to drum in her ears. She could not decide what to do. With the tide on the turn, it might be difficult to find another breach in the bulwark, designed specifically to keep people out. She really had no choice. Her legs heavy as lead, she began to climb again.

The watcher said in a deep feminine voice, "Ye're brave, walking the seashore. Are ye no' afraid o' the Fairgean?"

Isabeau replied carefully, "To tell ye the truth, I'm a wee disappointed."

"Oh? Why? Ye did no' see any Fairgean? Ye were wanting to?"

"I have never seen the sea before. It's so calm. I have always heard it is dangerous, and filled with strange, marvelous beasts. I must admit I was hoping to see *something*—a sea-serpent perhaps, or a flying fish. But I only saw birds."

"It was unusually calm today; it's been such a still, warm day. It's still summer, so the tides are low."

The woman had one of the most compelling faces Isabeau had ever seen. Her face was square, the line of her jaw strong, her skin a clear olive. Her silky hair was cut straight across her brow and again near her ears, curving in two black, glossy wings against her wide cheekbones. Every time she moved her head, blue lights darted over its inky surface. Her eyes shone a silvery-blue between thick, dark lashes. A dark plaid was wrapped loosely around her.

"Do no' let the sea deceive ye," the woman said. "Even in summer, the sea is dangerous. That is when the sea-adders teem, and the young sea-stirk bulls begin to test their strength. Besides, the sea and the sands are always treacherous. There are poisonous fish that look like rocks, and doom-eels, and sand scorpions—their venom will kill ye in seconds, so ye must always keep a wary eye out."

"I'll no' be going down there again!" Isabeau wriggled through the railings.

The stranger continued teasingly, "I had no' got to the reefs and whirlpools and swordfish and sea-serpents . . ."

"Enough, enough!" Isabeau dusted off her feet and put her boots back on. "What a fool I am! After all the lectures, still I go paddling the first chance I get!"

The stranger gave a low, infectious chuckle. "Ye can still go paddling, as long as ye ken what ye are doing."

"Which I do no'! Ye seem to, though. Were ye born near here, to be knowing so much about doom-eels and sand scorpions?"

"Nay. I would stay away from the sea if I were ye," she said, her voice suddenly changed. It had grown cooler, more reserved, as if she, like Isabeau, had remembered she should be more cautious. "It be dangerous, and besides, people do no' like it. I gather ye are a stranger here, but ye should know the Clachans are superstitious indeed about the sea. Ye should no' walk through Dùn Gorm with sand on your skirt." She stopped and held out her hand. "I must be going. Remember what I said—stay away from the sea. Goodbye."

Isabeau grasped her hand and thanked her. In the shadows under the trees, she could hardly see the other's face. She saw a flash of teeth as the other smiled, and then she was gone. Only then did Isabeau call Lasair.

Even though they galloped all the way back to the palace, Isabeau was still late. She hurried around to the stables, knowing she had to clean herself up before showing her face in the kitchens. If the servants saw her water-bedraggled dress, they would be suspicious indeed.

Riordan Bowlegs was smoking a long clay pipe and cleaning a harness. He took one look at her and grew very distressed. "Ye've been to the sea," he accused. "Look at ye! Red, ye canna be paddling and playing about in the sea. Do ye no' understand? Look at your dress!"

She tried to make light of it, but he seized her chin so she had to look him in the eye. "Red, no one but witches and faeries dare look upon the sea. Ye do no' want the Awl asking questions about ye! Stay away from the sea!"

She nodded, saying, "I understand." Riordan's agitation was valid, she knew. She certainly did not want to draw the Awl's attention to her again. Nonetheless she was conscious of deep disappointment. Her stroll along the seashore had fascinated her, for there was something about such a huge mass of water, shifting and murmuring, that enchanted the eye and the mind. She had also been strongly attracted to the dark-haired woman. All the way home she had wondered if she would ever see her again. It seemed unlikely, and Isabeau was sorry for that.

Late that night Isabeau was sweeping out the dairy room, trying to stifle the yawns that cracked her jaw, when she heard an urgent squeaking. She glanced up and saw a huge black rat perched on the top of the butter churn. It ran back and forth, its long tail twitching restlessly. *Must come,* it said to her in its high-pitched squeak. *Big mother rat want.*

Careful, little one, she said, covering a yawn with her hand. *They have a cat here who would eat you in one gulp!*

The rodent squeaked in dismay and ran round the rim of the great barrel. *Must come,* it said again, standing on its hind legs, its beady eyes bright with fear.

Not now, she squeaked back, thinking it wished to show her its nest of babies. *Must sleep.* And she put away her broom and trudged up the many stairs toward her room, rubbing her heavy eyes and wishing she had not walked so far that day. The rat followed her some of the way, but bolted at the sight of the kitchen cat sitting on the landing, washing its striped golden head with one paw. His flight led him into the granary, where a careless maid had left the lid off one of the grain bins. All thoughts of his message were lost in the delight of a feast of uncracked wheat.

OUT OF THE MISTS

he closer to Arran the jongleurs traveled, the wilder and more infertile the landscape became. To the east the land sloped down into stagnant salt marshes, here and there broken by shallow salt-water lochs and firths. At the horizon was the gray shimmer of the sea. Lilanthe stared at it as she walked, having never before seen any water greater than a forest pool. It dipped in and out of sight as the road meandered through the wild grasses.

It had been a busy few months. They had traveled the length and breadth of Blessém, even dipping down to Dùn Gorm for the Midsummer festivities. Since the Red Guards had their headquarters in the blue city, Lilanthe and Brun had spent two weeks at a rebel safe house in Blessém. The old lady who owned the safe house had a beautiful garden where Lilanthe had been able to sink her roots in peace.

When Enit returned to pick the faeries up, another caravan was traveling with them—a friend they had met at the Summer Fair who was as shy of crowds as Lilanthe and Brun. To the tree-shifter's dismay, Dide spent a great deal of time with the stranger—a dark, short man with a hooked nose, a sardonic smile and a wooden leg.

Despite herself, Lilanthe was jealous and withdrew into a cold silence. After two weeks away from her, she had been hoping for some indication that the young jongleur had missed her, but he seemed hardly to notice they were together again.

The jongleurs had gathered a great deal of interesting information during their travels in Blessém. The children's disappearance was being blamed on strange winged creatures that hypnotized their parents into immobility. The same gray ghosts had been seen just before the headquarters of the Ancient Guild of Fireworks Magicians had exploded with an amazing display of skyrockets, shooting stars and flaming wheels. The guildmaster's body had not been found among those in the charred ruins of the factory, and one of the town drunks swore he had seen him being carried away by the ghosts, along with many bulging sacks and barrels. Since the same winged creature had saved an *uile-bheist* from an angry mob some months ago, they were thought to be in league with the rebels.

Dide had frowned, whispering in his grandmother's ear, "Surely we have no such creatures working with us?" Enit had shaken her head, her eyes hooded, and Gwilym had snorted with bitter humor. "A gray ghost that appears silently out o' mist and enraptures its prey? Mesmerdean for sure! That means the Thistle's fair fingers are dabbling in this pie. I daresay she wanted the *uile-bheist* for her Theurgia—it must have had some magical power that she wants to harness for her own use."

Enit had decided to head toward Arran itself, to visit a friend of Gwilym's who might be able to help them understand the reasons behind Margrit of Arran's bizarre activities. With the rebels' plans in such delicate balance, Enit Silverthroat wanted no surprises.

By sunset they had reached the edge of the marsh, which rustled mysteriously with rushes, sedges, bulrushes, and cattails. Blue-legged herons flew overhead, croaking their hoarse song. A thick blanket of mist hung over the road ahead, bare tree branches writhing free.

Morrell put Nina up on the seat beside her grand-mother. He walked at the mare's head, one hand resting on the hilt of his dagger. Mist floated toward them, the sky behind darkening to a strange green color. Their shadows before them were long and flat. Though the sun still struck at their backs, storm clouds were ominous on all sides. They all looked at the mist trailing over the road, then up at Enit. She smiled at them encouragingly, and said, "Fear no', I have no intention o' tackling the marshes at night. Let's make camp, and we'll push on in the morning."

Gratefully they set up camp, the horses cropping dis-tastefully at the thin grass. When Lilanthe sunk her roots into the soil, she found it sour and unsatisfying, quite unlike the rich loam of Blessém.

The next morning the caravans were wreathed in mist. All of them felt uneasy, remembering the tales they had heard of Arran. Gossip said it was a brave man who dared travel into the Murkmyre without permission. Many tales were told of men who went in and never came out, or stumbled out years later with mad eyes and stuttering tongue, unable to describe the horrors or marvels he had seen.

Gwilym the Ugly was the only man they knew who had ever seen the Tower of Mists but he was reluctant to talk about his time there and had grown moodier as the fenlands approached. He had not agreed to return to Arran easily, but Enit's spies had told him that Mar-grit of Arran was traveling to Rhyssmadill for the Lam-mas Congress. Only then did he succumb to their arguments, but it was clear he did not relish the prospect of entering the marshes again.

Over their porridge they argued about the best course of action. Enit had to stay with her caravan, unable to walk more than a few steps without pain; Nina also should stay. "To keep Granddam company," Dide said hastily when the little girl pouted her lip. He thought

Lilanthe should also stay, though he agreed with Enit that the cluricaun could prove useful, being impervious to magic and the marshes of Arran steeped in it.

Lilanthe said in a stifled voice that she wanted to go. Gwilym said harshly that she was a fool. "I have no wish to step one foot—or even a wooden stump—over the border o' Arran. No' even if Margrit NicFóghnan is away. If ye had any sense, lass, ye would no' either." Lilanthe said nothing. He laughed sardonically. "I, curse the Spinners, have to go, being the only one to ken the paths through the marsh."

"Someone needs to stay behind and help guard the caravans," Dide argued.

Morrell snorted. "As if a tree-shifter is any more use than an auld woman an' a bairn. One o' us should stay, ye ken that, lad." Dide hesitated, not keen to give up the chance to see Arran, and Morrell guffawed. "I have no desire to tickle the banprionnsa's nose, Dide, ye can go. I shall stay and catch up on some well-deserved rest."

"Very well," Dide replied and began to prepare himself for the trip into the marshes. He did not dress with his customary gaudiness, wearing instead a gray tunic over breeches and hose of a soft brown. Gwilym thrust two daggers through his belt and a *sgian dubh* into his boot. He held over his lap a tall staff he had spent the last few weeks carving and polishing.

With a set expression on her face, Lilanthe also prepared herself, packing food, a warm plaid and a dagger. After a moment's hesitation, Dide dug out one of his golden balls and gave it to Lilanthe. "In case something goes wrong," he said. "Call through the sphere. I will find ye."

She nodded and smiled, feeling an odd stiffness in her cheeks. With a subdued Brun trotting at their heels, they bid the others a quiet goodbye and followed Gwilym down the track.

On either side the mist swirled over mud and rushes, smelling of decay. Noises were muffled in the fog, and they all turned their heads, straining to hear. Soon they came to a fork, and Gwilym silently headed to the left. For the next three hours they tramped through the fens, trees looming out of the haze.

At last they stopped to rest, eating the food they had packed, washed down with well-watered greengage wine. They saw a swamp-rat, large as a cat, swimming through a patch of water. It bared its notched fangs at them, and Lilanthe shrank back with a cry she could not suppress.

Soon after the track petered away and they had to pick their way through squelching mud and floating islands of grass and soil. Gwilym led the way, prodding the ground before him with his staff, finding it difficult to keep his wooden peg from slipping in the mud.

After an hour of such slow walking, the smell of peat smoke mingled with the stench of the bogs. Gwilym quickened his pace, leading the way to a hut built into a low mound. If he had not pointed it out, Dide and Lilanthe would have walked straight past it for the hut's roof was thatched with peat and grew as thickly with sedge and mosses as the bank behind it. The door was only four feet high and made of weathered driftwood the same gray as the marshes. Gwilym rapped upon it, and a gruff voice called out, "Aiieee?"

Quirking his mouth into a smile, Gwilym nodded at his companions and pushed the door open. They all bent their backs and entered, only the cluricaun short enough to stand freely in the dark, smoky room within.

It was a tiny room, furnished roughly with benches and a table made from driftwood and decorated with frail marsh-flowers. A small creature was stirring a pot over the peat fire. She turned as they came in and bared her fangs in a smile. She had purplish-black skin rippled with dark fur, and wore a brown dress with a shawl wrapped around her sloping shoulders. She had only four fingers and four toes, and large, black eyes of great luster.

She was a bogfaery and her name was Aya. She spoke very little of the common dialect, but her wizened face

and the sounds she made were amazingly expressive.
Aya had been nanny to the banprionnsa's son and heir
most of her life. At last she had got so old the many
stairs were too much for her, and Iain MacFóghnan had
arranged for her to return to the bogs, as she so fervently wished.

She threw up her dark, wrinkled paws and moaned
when Gwilym said he had need of information from her.
Each time Gwilym tried to speak, she covered her ear-
holes with her paws, rocking back and forth. "Bad man
ban no' like," she moaned. "Bad man go, bad man no'
say goodbye, no' even to my little man, ban very mad,
my man sad."

He grasped her paws and pulled them down, saying
harshly, "Aya, I am sorry indeed I had to go the way I
did, without any farewells, but what else could I do? Iain
knew I had to go."

"Ee-an want go bad."

Gwilym turned away, his wooden stump dragging on
the floor. "The Mesmerdean would no' have let her only
son pass unchallenged." He made an impatient gesture,
and turned back. "Aya, tell me what has been happening
since I left?"

"Bright men."

"Bright men?"

"Sun shine on arms, legs." She struggled to express
herself, waving her paws over her limbs, then pointing
to the silver daggers at Dide's waist. "Bright. Shine. In
sun. Clank."

"Silver men?" She nodded vigorously, and they stared
at each other blankly. Brun repeated softly, "Bright
men, silver men, bright in the sun they shine."

The bogfairy nodded enthusiastically, and Gwilym
asked, "I'm sorry, Aya, I do no' understand. What else
can ye tell me?"

"My man, little man, married man."

"Iain?"

"Ee-an."

"What has that cursehag been doing to him?" Gwilym

dug at the mud floor with his stump. They stared at him, and he clenched his hands and said, "It's no use, I have to speak to Iain. He's the only one who will know anything o' any use."

"But . . . are ye no' talking about the prionnsa? The Thistle's son?"

Gwilym nodded and sat down with a jerk on one of the sedge-strewn beds cut into the bank. "Iain hates the cursehag as much as I do," he replied heavily. "We have to get a message to him somehow. It will be dangerous indeed. I'd bet a half-crown that Margrit has no' taken her blaygird Khan'cohban with her—he'll be lurking around somewhere, no' to mention the Mesmerdean and bogfaeries and wisps, all o' which report all they see. Ugly, ye fool, what are ye doing here?"

"Ugly is here because he knows it is the best and truest thing to do," Dide said firmly. "Ugly is here because he is at heart a good man, if a trifle jaundiced. Ugly is here because he wants to help his friend the juggler."

"Ugly's here because he is a fool," Gwilym replied, smiling into his beard.

"I go my man, I go ask my man," Aya said, her anxious, seagrape-black face upturned to theirs.

"Aye, take a message to Iain," he agreed. "We shall have to try and meet with him, if at all possible. The Mesmerdean elders may all be with Margrit—though it is turning cooler and soon they will be growing their winter husk and looking for mud in which to lie . . . Iain will ken. Somehow we must arrange a safe meeting."

Iain bent down and hugged his old nanny with delight. "More bog-cookies, Aya! For my pretty wife? Come and give them to her yourself, she was hoping ye would come and visit soon." He did not miss the imploring glance the bogfaery cast him from her huge, black eyes or the tentative point of her knobbly finger. Tucked beneath the cookies was a note, and with a quickening of his pulse Iain thought he recognized the scrawl.

Ten minutes later he was heading toward the Theurgia's Tower, trying hard to hide his excitement. He could feel his eyes shining and his cheeks burning, but he relaxed his shoulders as much as he could, feeling the Khan'cohban's eyes on him.

"Truly the Spinners are w-w-with us!" Iain whispered as soon as the clatter of the other children getting their tea rose around them. "I have a m-m-message from a friend—he wants to m-m-meet with us and t-t-talk. Douglas, this is our chance! It canna be coincidence that Gwilym the Ugly should return to Arran at just this t-t-time. He always said we would one day escape from here—he must have returned for me! And M-M-Mother away and the M-M-Mesmerdean sulking because o' the massacre o' their egg-brothers—it's the Spinners watching over us, for sure."

Douglas's eyes were gleaming bright. "At last! I felt I would run stark staring mad if I could no' warn Papa somehow about the invasion. I could no' stand it any more! Knowing they were threatening to strike into Eileanan and no one but us knowing anything! We have to get out and warn them!"

"This m-m-may be our only chance. It is time to put our plan into action!"

That night, as Khan'tirell served him his evening meal, Iain said casually to his wife, "Elf, ye are l-l-looking a wee pale. How are ye feeling yourself?"

"I am feeling a wee pale too, I must admit."

"Ye are spending too much t-t-time within, why do ye no' go and sit in the garden tomorrow? Ye need some sunshine and fresh air, and ye ken M-M-Mother wishes ye to keep well for the babe."

"O' course, Iain. It is just that it is so hot in the garden."

"I should t-t-take ye rowing on the loch," Iain cried. "It is always cool on the loch—we could take a p-p-picnic."

"Could we?" Elfrida cried, clapping her hands.

"Khan'tirell, would ye order a p-p-punt for to-morrow?"

"Very well, my laird. Where do ye plan to row?"

"Perhaps we'll go n-n-north to the forest. My lady will like to see the g-g-golden g-g-goddess blooming."

"Oh, yes!" Elfrida said.

"I think perhaps too dangerous for . . ."

"Nonsense!" she cried. "Am I no' NicHilde?"

"Yes, my lady," he bowed, eyeing her slim form spec-ulatively. Iain wished she had not reminded him that she came from a long line of warrior-witches, but she drooped a little and toyed with her food, sighing, "Be-sides, it is no' as if I wish to go too close, what with the babe and all. I would like to see them though, I have heard they are bonny indeed."

"The cygnets will all b-b-be swimming, ye will like them, Elf."

"Oh, how lovely! Iain, why do we no' take the chil-dren with us? They will love the cygnets too, and we can make a feast day o' it!"

They could feel Khan'tirell weighing up the idea. El-frida said cooingly, "I find I love the sound o' children's laughter about me at this time."

Iain flashed her a warning glance but the horned man made up his mind and nodded. "Very well, my laird, I will order boats for ye all and bogfaeries to row and two Mesmerdean to scout the way for ye."

"Oh, do we have to have those awful blaygird crea-tures!" Elfrida gave a not entirely artificial shudder.

Iain said casually, "Surely, Kh-Kh-Khan'tirell, that is no' necessary? I do no' need M-M-Mesmerdean to scout the path to the glade o' the golden g-g-goddess. I have been m-m-many times, and it is a simple matter o' scull-ing up the river."

Khan'tirell said nothing, just snapped his fingers at the servants to pour more wine, and they knew he had not changed his mind.

The next morning they set off in the pearly hour after dawn. One of the six long punts was loaded with ham-

pers and blankets. Elfrida sat propped in silken cushions
in the prow of another, with Iain facing her, and the
other children were crammed in the other punts, a warlock in every stern. Little Jock, the crofter's boy, was
crammed in with the wicker baskets and the bogfaeries.

Khan'tirell himself jumped lithely into Iain's punt and
the prionnsa's spirits sank. He had hoped the Scarred
Warrior would not feel it necessary to accompany them,
and had even chanted a goodwish upon it as he dropped
off to sleep. It had not worked, and now their escape
would be much more difficult.

By eight o' clock the mist had burned away and a
bright summer sky stretched overhead. Sunlight danced
on the water of the loch behind them, but under the
overarching water-oaks it was cool. The bogfaeries poled
slowly, so the passengers had plenty of time to exclaim
over the wildlife. Fluffy pink cygnets played in the shallows, the swans drifting nearby. An iridescent green
snake coiled on a low branch; birds rose crying from the
rushes, while the black, wrinkled paws of bogfaeries bent
aside the bulrushes to peer at them. Occasionally one
called to the bogfaeries poling the punts and were answered in the same high, wailing, "Aiieee!"

By noon they had rounded a corner to see a low hill
crowned with tall trees rising to their left, while before
them stretched the glittering waters of the Murkfane. A
rich, exotic scent was beginning to drift through the air.
Elfrida lifted her face, sniffing luxuriously. Iain leaned
forward to touch her knee: "Try no' to breathe in the
smell, Elf—it is the lure o' the g-g-golden g-g-goddess
and will cause ye to become d-d-drowsy."

Khan'tirell directed the bogfaeries to pole the boats
in close to the shore. As they scrambled onto solid
ground Iain pulled aside the hanging branches of a willow, and all the children cried aloud in astonishment.
Before them a flower rested on the ground, taller than
their heads, lily-shaped and yellow as summer sunshine.
Its outward curling petals surrounded long stamens
bending under the weight of thick pollen. Purple-red

spots scattered the lower petal, like a path leading to the crimson bed of the pistil. Deep within was a round globule of golden honey. The air was heavy with the delicious smell.

The great, green stem, covered in sharp bristles, writhed out from the same source as a hundred more. Each stem, as thick as a man's body, carried one of the drooping yellow flowers, while huge green leaves thrust up overhead.

"They're beautiful!" Elfrida cried.

"And d-d-deadly," Iain replied grimly. "She's carnivorous—her b-b-beauty and scent is designed to lure the unwary in. She is most dangerous in the late afternoon— the potency o' her perfume increases t-t-toward sunset, as she likes to d-d-digest overnight."

Elfrida recoiled. "It eats meat? Would it eat us?"

"If she could," Iain responded. "My ancestors used to f-f-feed anyone who disagreed with them to the g-g-golden goddess."

He picked up a handful of pebbles from the ground. "Watch!" he called. "The g-g-golden goddess will sn-sn-snap shut if she feels more than two or three t-t-touches in quick succession—like something walking down her spotted path."

Iain threw some of the pebbles down the throat of the flower, and instantly the petals furled shut. The other flowers about it stirred and rustled, their stems twisting toward them as if scenting them. "They can feel our warmth," Iain said and directed them all back a few paces. He bent his head and stammered softly to Elfrida, "The mead we drank on our w-w-wedding night was m-m-made with the honey o' the g-g-golden g-g-goddess— they say it is a p-p-powerful love potion."

Elfrida lifted her gray eyes to his and blushed. She remembered well the passion she had felt after drinking the honeyed wine. Iain smiled at her and squeezed her hand. "The honey is much prized," he said again in a louder voice. "Along with m-m-m-murkwoad and rys seeds, it is one o' Arran's premier exports. It is very dangerous to c-c-collect, however. We have m-m-many bogfaeries trained to pluck the honey globule, and every year we lose q-q-quite a few."

He took a long stride forward and the flower shifted slightly, opening her petals to better display her crimson heart, studded with the gleaming ball of honey. Carefully Iain placed one foot on one of the rich red spots and leaned forward, his head and shoulders disappearing from view. Elfrida gave a little cry, but just as the petals closed Iain stepped out again. He opened one hand to show the students the globule of honey he held within. "Ye only g-g-get one chance," he explained, "one touch and the petals will c-c-close. Timing is important." Slipping his other hand into his pocket, he then carefully poured the thick honey into a jar and snapped the lid tight. "We will d-d-drink it together l-l-later, my love," he said to Elfrida, who colored again and laughed.

The bogfaeries poled the boats along the willow-hung shore of the loch till they came to the low water-meadow that spread along the western shore. There the boats were tied up, the bogfaeries scurrying to unpack the picnic. They climbed a gentle slope, the ground firmer with each step, and came to a grove of tall trees.

To the north they could see the beginning of the forests, backing to the purple smear of the Great Divide. It was only half a day's journey beyond to the border with Aslinn and Blessém. Iain felt his pulse quicken with excitement, and he glanced at Douglas, who grinned in return.

They sat on blankets and cushions laid out by the bogfaeries and ate the sumptuous feast they served. To Iain's anxiety, Khan'tirell refused any wine, which they had laced with a sleeping potion, prowling the hilltop with tireless grace instead.

The bogfaeries were bringing out fruits and sweetmeats when Douglas suddenly bounded to his feet. "I'd like to propose a toast! Ladies, gentlemen, charge your glasses." The bogfaeries hurried around with the bottles of wine. Douglas waited until every glass was brimming, then called, "A toast to the babe! Heir to the Tower o' Mists and all o' Arran!"

Everyone cheered and drank deeply. Iain said pleasantly, "Ye do no' d-d-drink to our babe, K-K-Khan'-tirell?"

A pale, bright eye flashed his way, then the Khan'cohban came forward, his angular face wary. He accepted the glass a smiling Elfrida handed him and drank a mouthful. His mouth twisted a little and he bent to place the glass down. Douglas shouted, "And a toast to the proud parents, may they be as happy in forty years as they are now!" Again Khan'tirell drank, and was turning away when Douglas cried, with a devilish glint in his seagreen eyes, "And o' course, a toast to our gracious benefactress, Margrit NicFóghnan o' Arran!"

Everyone cheered and drained their glasses, and Khan'tirell was forced to follow suit. The clearing resounded with chatter and laughter as he bent and put down his empty glass, then moved away again. Elfrida and Iain looked at each other with consternation. There had been enough poppy juice and valerian in that wine to drop a stag, yet he seemed unaffected. Already one of the warlocks was snoozing on his cushions, and the others were yawning behind their hands. Yet as Khan'-tirell prowled amongst the trees, his gait was as graceful as ever. Iain shrugged. He had prepared for that eventuality.

The children played a game of chase and hide, Douglas, Gilliane, Iain and Elfrida lay on the cushions and talked, while one by one the warlocks began to snore. "What about the Mesmerdean?" Elfrida whispered anxiously. "How will we overcome them?"

"The M-M-Mesmerdean ken what it is we do; remember they can read our emotional energies as c-c-clearly as we can read words on a page."

Elfrida's color ebbed away. "They know?" Her voice came out in a squeak.

Iain nodded. "O' course. I k-k-knew that was the first test. If they w-w-wished to stop us, they would have communicated their unease to K-K-Khan'tirell. I w-w-watched them as I spoke; they were interested but made no m-m-move."

"Why?" Gilliane was intrigued. "Surely they serve your mother?"

"Mesmerdean serve no species but themselves," Iain replied reprovingly. "Ye m-m-must understand that—they have never been our servants. They choose to ally themselves with m-m-my family because we love the marshes as they do. There is no d-d-danger a MacFóghnan will ever drain the f-f-fenlands."

"But they do what your mother tells them."

Iain laughed. "Sometimes. At the m-m-moment they have withdrawn their support because they are all in m-m-mourning. A week or two before Midsummer's Eve a whole string o' egg-brothers were k-kkilled by my mother's enemy, the Arch-Sorceress. No' only the elders o' that s-s-string but all o' the elders are l-l-l-lamenting. It will be several m-m-months before they offer help again."

Iain cast a quick glance at the Khan'cohban and was glad to see he was shaking his horns in a perplexed manner. His gait had slowed, and every now and again he stumbled. Still, the shadows were lengthening and they had arranged to meet their friends at sunset. He would have to take steps to make sure Khan'tirell was not on their trail. He stood up, stretched and made his way toward the Scarred Warrior.

"My laird, it is growing late, I think we should begin making our way back to the Tower," the Khan'cohban said in his guttural voice.

Iain slipped his hand into his pocket and withdrew the pollen-dusted stamen of the golden goddess flower. He had broken it off while harvesting the honey and had hidden it in his pocket. He lifted the stamen and blew on it so a cloud of golden dust enveloped the horned Khan'cohban. He coughed and choked, then swayed on his feet. For a moment he struggled to maintain consciousness, then he fell where he had stood.

"Quickly! It's time!" Iain called, and his companions scrambled to their feet and began quickly sorting through the leftover food and shaking out the blankets. Only the eldest of the children had known of the plan, for the younger children would never have been able to keep it secret. While Douglas hurried to prepare the boats, Gilliane quickly drew the others to them and told them what they intended.

A few of the children were frightened or confused. The Tìrsoilleirean students were belligerent and shouted that the others were fools. "My lady will only hunt ye all down again," they cried.

"But the Tower o' Mists is the only Theurgia in the land," another cried. "Here is the only place where ye can learn magic."

The corrigan boy was frightened. "*Uile-bheistean* are murdered in Eileanan!" he cried. "If I go with ye, how will I ken ye will no' betray me to the Red Guards!" The tree-shifter shrank against him, her wide green eyes scared.

"We will do all we c-c-can to keep ye safe," Iain said. "My friend fights with the rebels—they do no' consider the faeries *uile-bheistean*. They w-w-work to free Eileanan o' the Faery and Witches' Decrees."

Arguments broke out, and Iain said in exasperation, "We do no' have t-t-time for this. Ye either return to the Tower o' Mists with the warlocks or ye come with us now. What will ye do?"

In the end all the children chose to accompany Iain and Elfrida. They filled their pockets with the leftovers from the picnic, armed themselves with sharp eating knives and bundled together blankets. Kind-hearted Elfrida covered the warlocks and the chamberlain with the spare blankets so they would not get cold sleeping out, and they left them some food, though not much.

They all piled into three of the boats, and Iain smashed the bottoms of the remainder. Now they were actually making their breakout, he was tense and white.

None knew better the consequences if their escape attempt should fail.

The bogfaeries had been watching with wide, anxious eyes, and Iain bent to them and gave them strict orders not to wake the warlocks or try and contact the Tower. They had been trained to obey him without question and so although they were frightened and unsure, they bobbed their seagrape-dark heads in acquiescence.

The boats sailed smoothly away from the shore, their wake rippling the still waters apart. The children exclaimed with amazement and Elfrida looked at Iain with a touch of fear. "I did no' ken ye could do that," she said.

He laughed. "Propeling a boat without oars or pole is the first lesson I ever learned! Truly, it is easy."

"Will ye teach me?"

"I'll surely try," he answered. "I do no' ken if ye have a Talent with air and water, which is what ye need."

The sky overhead was bright with sunset color, rose and violet and apricot-yellow. A light breeze had risen, ruffling the water so the reflected colors blurred together under the prows of the punts. They came to the mouth of the river and slowed, Iain anxiously scanning the shore. He gave a shout of excitement as a stocky man in gray stepped out from the shelter of a weeping willow, his hand raised in greeting.

The boats swerved to the bank, and the man and his companions all scrambled on board. The boats swung out into the river again, heading smoothly against the current.

"Gwilym, ye auld rogue! It is truly ye! Ugly as ever, I see."

"Uglier," the man smiled grimly, indicating his wooden leg.

"Ye've lost a leg! What happened?"

As Gwilym explained how he had escaped being burned on the Midsummer fires, the others eyed each other, making tentative introductions. Lilanthe was amazed to see a girl in the other boat who had a tangled

mane of leafy hair and an angular face like hers. She
stared at her and met her eyes, green as a spring leaf.
Tree-changer? she thought tentatively, and was delighted
to hear back, *I dinna call myself that, I be only half a
tree-changer!*

Me too! I call myself a tree-shifter . . .

Tree-shifter?

My mother was a tree-changer, my father human.

Other way around for me.

*Really? Your father was a tree-changer? Ye are still a
half-breed, just the same as me.*

I thought I was the only one . . .

Me too!

They smiled at each other across the expanse of water,
and Lilanthe felt happiness well through her. So long
she had been alone, a *uile-bheist* unlike any other *uile-
bheistean.* Now she knew there was another tree-shifter
and suddenly she did not feel quite so alone.

For another half an hour the boats sailed smoothly up
the river, the forest on the banks growing thicker and
more varied with every passing mile. It was almost dark
when they heard a long, drawn-out cry behind them.

"What was that?" Douglas exclaimed.

Iain tensed and looked up at the sky behind them.
The sound came again and they saw a flight of swans
soaring far to the east, their crimson-tipped wings catching the last of the sun. Behind them the swans pulled a
shapely sleigh that seemed to carve a path over the
clouds.

The prionnsa swore and banged his hand on the side
of the boat. "Kh-Khan'tirell must have woken, Eà damn
him! He has called out my m-m-mother's swans. We will
have to abandon the boats!"

"Why?"

"They can see us too clearly on the river—ye can see
he has ordered them to bring M-M-Mother's sleigh so
he can fly in search o' us. It will no' be long before they
catch us up." He swore again and said hopelessly, "I

should have known the sleeping p-p-potion would no' knock him out for long!"

"The swans pull along a sleigh?" Elfrida asked, feeling rather sorry she had never had a chance to try it out. A sleigh pulled through the air by swans sounded most beautiful and romantic.

Iain nodded. "We will p-p-push on until we reach firmer ground," he said, more to himself than anyone else. "It is only four hours' walk from there, and Kh-Kh-Khan'tirell will no' ken where we took to the ground."

The boats speeded up until a curve of wave streamed behind each boat. The children squealed and hung on as they raced up the river. Behind them came the call of the swans again, and Iain said, "They have picked him up. He's on our trail now! His eyesight is exceptional, even in the dark. We must abandon the boats now."

With a swerve and a splash, the boats headed to the shore. Under the shelter of overhanging branches they all clambered ashore, careful to choose a solid spot to put their feet. Iain then sent the boats scooting upriver again.

"We canna fight Khan'tirell," he explained to Dide. "He's a Scarred Warrior and trained in all forms o' warfare. With the swans, he'll be able to catch up with us very quickly. Our only hope is to stay concealed in the marshes and try and reach the border on foot." He sighed. "I had hoped we would no' have to face the marshes. It would have been so much easier to simply sail up the river and into Aslinn!"

With the coming of night the mist rose, swallowing up the path and wrapping chilly arms about them. Iain and Elfrida went first with the smallest of the children trailing behind. Dide and Gwilym followed up the rear, keeping a close eye out for any sign of the Khan'cohban. The others were strung out between, Lilanthe walking beside Corissa, the other tree-shifter, talking eagerly. The cluricaun stayed close to Lilanthe's side, for once free of jokes and gymnastics.

It was slow and difficult walking. Although Iain and Gwilym had lit witch-lights at the end of rushes and passed them all along the procession, the mist swirled all around them, hiding them from each other's eyes. The children were tired and inclined to be fretful, and Iain was carrying a sleepy-eyed Jock on his back. Again and again one of them slipped from the path and had to be hauled out of the mud. Worst of all, they could sense eyes all around them in the marsh. Occasionally they saw the ghostly shape of a Mesmerd keeping pace with them, hovering above the treacherous surface of the bogs.

"Do n-n-no' be afraid," Iain whispered. "Hear how they hum? They are just c-c-curious—they will no' harm us if we do no' try and harm them."

Several times they saw a few pallid lights flickering to the side. Sometimes the light hovered so near they seemed part of their procession; other times they glimmered out in the marsh, drawing them away from the path. "Keep your eyes on me!" Iain cried. "It is easy to wander off the path; keep close."

The little cluricaun seized Lilanthe's hand and said earnestly:

"Seize her and she shall flee,
only shadows in your hand.
Follow her and she will lead ye
to bottomless bogs and quicksand.
Ignore her, and she shall see
your foot secure on steadfast land."

"What did he say?" Corissa asked, and Lilanthe said, "It's a riddle. He asks them all the time. What is it, Brun?"

The cluricaun repeated the riddle, and Iain looked up, amazed. "He means a wisp. That riddle is an auld, auld one—he's talking about a will o' the wisp."

"Wisp," Brun said, trotting beside Lilanthe. "Will o' the wisp . . ."

"That's right," Iain said, surprise still in his voice. "That is a riddle I thought only those o' Arran would know. Those t-t-trickster lights are will o' wisps and they will indeed lead ye astray if ye f-f-follow them. Be careful they do no' deceive ye."

The will o' the wisps danced alongside for close on another hour, but at last the path grew wider and firmer, and the trees looming up out of the mist were those of the forest, not of the marsh. "We are almost at the border," Iain said, unable to keep the relief out of his tired voice. "If everything has gone according to plan, Gwilym's friends should be waiting for us." He turned and looked down the long, straggling line of exhausted children but could not see the one-legged warlock anywhere. He pushed on, but turned often to scan the drifting mist, hoping it would reveal the stocky figure of his friend. The swamp fell behind them, trees rising black all around them. Firelight flickered ahead, and they hurried forward. Filthy, their clothes torn to rags, they stumbled through the dark shapes of caravans and fell to their knees before the fire.

An old woman leaned forward, piles of amber beads on her chest glinting with fire. "Welcome! Ye must all be exhausted! Glad we are to see ye indeed!"

A little girl was dancing about in excitement, greeting the other children and offering them hot soup and bread. Mid-skip she stopped and said, "Where's Dide?"

With grateful cries the children had dropped to the ground, rubbing their aching legs and huddling into the rugs against the predawn chill. Elfrida was walking amongst them, helping serve food and whispering reassurances. She paused and looked up at the little girl's words.

"Aye, where is he?" a swarthy man asked, his thick earring glinting.

"And Gwilym? Where's the ugly man?" Nina asked, bursting into tears.

Lilanthe and Brun, suddenly realizing Dide was not

with them, turned to scan the night. Iain stood up, his face going white. "Where's Douglas?"

Elfrida shrugged unhappily. "I thought he was just behind us."

"Ye mean they have no' come out? They're lost in the marsh?" Lilanthe's voice rose in sudden fear.

"I hope no'," Iain replied grimly. "If they have w-w-wandered from the path, I have no' got m-m-much chance o' being able to find them."

"Perhaps they will find the way . . ." Elfrida said comfortingly.

Iain shook his head. "The marshes have many dangers," he said. "Even Gwilym does no' know them all. If we do no' find them soon, we never will."

Dide had stopped to wait for Gwilym the Ugly, who had again slipped in the mud and fallen. He knew better than to offer his hand, waiting till the warlock had struggled to his feet before moving to his side. "Tasting the mud again, Ugly?"

"Mmm, I'm so glad to be back I simply have to kiss Arran's sweet soil at every opportunity," Gwilym responded sardonically. He brushed off his mud-smeared tunic with his hand. "I look like a mudsprite," he said ruefully.

"What's a mudsprite?"

"One o' the more delightful faeries o' the bog," Gwilym answered. "Mudsprites lie just below the surface of the mud and pull unwary passers-by in."

"Charming."

"Indeed, like so many things o' Arran. It is a charming place indeed."

"Ye think so?" Douglas's voice preceded him out of the darkness. "Personally I think it a horrible place, I'll be happy if I never have to come here again."

"Happen we should get out o' it before we start worrying about returning," Gwilym replied, not bothering to explain he was being sarcastic.

They looked around and realized the procession had

already moved out of sight. "Let's hurry," Douglas said, shivering a little.

They could see the faint, dancing blur of Iain's witchlights and set off in pursuit, Gwilym holding his staff high so the light at the apex spread before them.

"I canna hear the others," Douglas said. "Should we call, tell them to wait?"

"It's risky enough showing the lights," Gwilym said. "If the Khan'cohban hears shouting, he'll be on our track in a flash."

They pressed on into the misty darkness, hurrying now. Gwilym slipped again and fell with a curse, and Douglas tried to help him up, only to have his hand thrust away fiercely. "I can manage, thank ye," Gwilym said roughly. "No need to wait for me, I'll catch up."

Douglas opened his mouth to protest, caught an admonishing glance from Dide, and shut it again. He led the way instead, testing the path ahead with a stick. Once he gave a scream and pointed shakily at two huge eyes staring at him out of the darkness. Gwilym brought the witch-light flickering up, and they saw a huge frog sitting placidly on a log. It was squat and broad, as high as Dide's waist, with bulbous eyes that gleamed orange.

"That thing does no' eat humans, does it?" Douglas's voice shook.

Gwilym shook his head. "Nay, insects and Mesmerdean only."

"It eats Mesmerdean?"

"The creatures' only natural predator," the warlock answered.

"Glad to ken something gets those nasty creatures," Douglas murmured. "Let's hurry, I can feel them watching us."

"It will no' be Mesmerdean watching so near the frogs."

"Well, something is watching us and I do no' like it!"

They left the frog behind, its deep belling tone ringing through the forest, and hurried in the direction of the wavering line of lights. Gwilym was frowning, his harsh-featured face set in grim lines. Once he called, "Iain!" but there was no response.

"I thought ye said no' to call?" Douglas objected.

"I think we should try and catch them up quickly." Gwilym's voice was bleaker than ever. "I have a very bad feeling."

"Hey, the path seems to have disappeared," Douglas said suddenly. "I canna feel any firm ground on either side."

Gwilym pushed up next to him, raising his staff so they could see further. On all sides mud puckered and gurgled. They were standing on a floating hillock which teetered under their weight. "But the lights . . ." Dide said, pointing. Ahead floated a few pallid balls of light, flickering slightly, enticing them on.

Gwilym groaned. "Wisps! We've been led astray by bloody wisps!" He struck his forehead with the heel of his hand. "Fool!" he grated. "Gwilym the Fool."

They turned and were gingerly making their way from hillock to hillock toward the trees, in search of firmer land, when Douglas suddenly gave a shriek and toppled into the swamp. He was sucked under quickly, only his desperate white face visible above the mud. Quick as thought Gwilym flung himself down and reached out his staff to the boy. Douglas caught hold of it, but they had a hard struggle to draw him free of the quicksand.

At last he was hauled out, plastered with evil-smelling mud. "Something pulled me in," he cried. "I felt a hand on my ankle."

"Mudsprites!" Gwilym groaned. "Just what we need."

They huddled together on the hillock. "What do we do now?" Dide cried. He saw a pale hand creep out of the mud and swiped at it viciously with his staff. It withdrew quickly, and there was a plop of mud nearby.

"Hope we did no' wander too far from the path and that the others realize we are missing soon and come to search for us," Gwilym said. "Otherwise, try and survive the night."

Douglas swallowed. "Ye say that as if ye do no' think it is likely."

"That's because I do no' think it likely," the warlock responded. "We are in the middle o' mudsprite field, we have a Khan'cohban hunting us, and all the snakes in this blaygird bog are poisonous. I got out o' this marsh alive once; I do no' think I can rely on my luck a second time."

Douglas was very white under the mud and rotten leaves sticking to his face. "If we just retrace our steps . . ."

"We can try," Gwilym said in a weary tone.

They saw another line of dancing lights to their far left. "Do ye think . . . ?" Douglas cried hopefully.

"It'll be wisps again," Gwilym said and sat down on a half-submerged log. "Better get used to them, lad, else ye'll be following them deeper into the marsh."

Dide gradually became aware of a prickle at the back of his mind. He shook it away, but it returned in greater force. Suddenly he plunged his hand into his pack and drew out a golden ball. It shone dimly in the darkness. He stared into it incredulously. "Lilanthe?" he whispered.

Dide. Are ye there?

Lilanthe?

Aye. We are searching for ye. Do ye ken where ye are?

Dide gave a sardonic laugh. *Somewhere in the marshes . . .*

Iain wants to ken if ye can see landmarks. He says ye may die if we do no' reach ye. There are many dangerous things in the bog, he says we must find ye soon, that his magic had been keeping many o' the creatures away . . .

There is too much mist, I canna see anything.

I can sense ye . . . I will lead Iain to ye.

No, Lilanthe, it's too dangerous . . .

But the tree-shifter had broken off the contact, and Dide was left staring into the ball. He looked up and told them what she had said. Gwilym said heavily, "She will no' be able to find us, the marsh gases confuse the mind and everything looks the same."

"She has strong mind-powers," Dide said slowly. "If anyone can find us, it is Lilanthe."

The three of them rested a while, beating off the mud-sprites with their sticks and sharing some food. A bright green snake slid by, watching them with narrow, black eyes, and all around them giant frogs sang. "At least we are safe from the Mesmerdean while the frogs sing," Gwilym said dourly.

"How come? I thought we were safe from them anyway."

"*Iain* was safe from them," Gwilym replied. "The Mesmerdean know who I am. They have caught me once before to please Margrit—one may decide to do so again."

"Well, ye are cheerful company," Douglas said, whacking at a pair of bulbous eyes floating toward him through the mud. "Remind me never to spend a night with ye in a swamp again."

"Believe me, if we come through this night alive I shall never go anywhere near a swamp again," Gwilym said. "May Eà be my witness."

Dide . . .

Lilanthe? Where are ye?

I can feel ye close now. Can ye light a flare o' some sort?

Dide obliged, sending a tall blue flame shooting up into the night.

"If that does no' bring the Khan'cohban down on us, nothing will," Gwilym sighed.

They heard a cry across the field, and then a chain of white-blue lights came bobbing toward them.

Careful, it's bog and quicksand, Dide projected anxiously.

Iain is cutting down some sort o' tree with big leaves, Lilanthe responded. *He and Brun are throwing them into the bog, making a path. Can ye see us?*

Aye, I think so. If they are your lights and no' more o' those wicked wisps.

I can see your light. Hang on, we'll be there soon.

Dide relayed the message to the others and was glad to see Douglas's tense face relax a little. The mist was beginning to pale, and the mudsprites made a concerted rush at their hillock as if anxious to drown them before the sun rose. They had ten minutes of hard fighting, throwing off the mudsprites with boot, stick, stump and fist, before Iain reached them over his impromptu bridge. He dismissed the faeries with a flick of his hand and a contemptuous word, and they sank back below the mud with a splash and a gurgle.

"Led astray by wisps!" Iain said, a smile cracking his tired, muddy face. "Gwilym, I be surprised at ye, intrepid marsh explorer that ye are."

The warlock smiled in return and allowed them to help him cross the sinking bridge of glossy leaves, too tired to insist he needed no help.

Lilanthe and Brun were waiting anxiously on the shore, both covered in mud and leaves from head to toe. Lilanthe had never looked more like an *uile-bheist* but Dide walked straight out of the bog and into her arms, hugging her fiercely. He found he had tears in his eyes. "Clever lass!" he cried. "I never even thought o' the ball! I gave it to ye in case ye got lost, no' I!"

Lilanthe could not speak, content to have Dide's arms hard around her and his face wet on her neck. She hugged him back, her own eyes prickling with relief, while birds sang around them in the dawn.

If the Khan'cohban had seen their distress flare, he was too far away to reach them in time. Iain was able to lead them out of the marshes and into Aslinn without further incident. They were greeted with cries of relief. It had taken Iain and Lilanthe much longer to rescue their three companions and retrace their steps than expected, and it was now fully light. They were all too exhausted to walk any further and collapsed onto the blankets to rest.

"Ye canna sleep now, we have to warn the Rìgh!" Douglas cried. "We have to tell him the Bright Soldiers are coming."

"The Bright Soldiers?" Dide echoed sharply. "Ye mean the Tìrsoilleirean?"

"Aye, they signed a t-t-treaty with my m-m-mother. They plan to invade Eileanan." Quickly Iain told them about the Bright Soldiers' schemes.

Gwilym and Dide glanced at each other. "Aya meant their armor shining in the sun," the jongleur murmured. "And no doubt heard them called the Bright Soldiers, as they always are."

"And that explains the reports o' strangers and lights in the marsh," Gwilym replied. "Though what did they want with the firework magicians?"

"We have to head for Rhyssmadill! My father is there and the Rìgh—they'll be taken by surprise!" Douglas warned.

"When did M-M-Mother say they intended to attack? After the Lammas Congress? We'll never make it, n-n-no' even if we had flying horses to ride on," Iain said. "We could head for Dùn Eidean though, G-G-Gilliane and Ghislaine's grandmother is the d-d-dowager banprionnsa and the city will listen to her."

"What about Rhyssmadill?" Douglas cried.

Gilliane said diffidently, "I could try and send a dream message to my mother. She and my father went with my aunt and uncle to Rhyssmadill."

"Ye can send dream messages?" Dide's voice was excited.

"My mother is a NicAislin," she replied, shrugging. "I travel strange places in my dreams and so does Ghislaine. I have never been taught how but the banprionnsa was sure we could learn to be Dream-Walkers—that is why she stole us."

"So we will head for Dùn Eidean to warn the Mac-

Thanach's m-m-mother, and Gilliane will try and warn Rhyssmadill . . ." Iain began.

"I do no' want to go back into Blessém," Lilanthe cried. "These last few months have been a nightmare, I dinna want to go through that again."

Gwilym was also shaking his head, as were the two half-faeries from the Theurgia. "They tried to stone me to death in Blairgowrie," the corrigan boy said, his one eye obdurate as stone. "Do no' tell me ye can keep me safe in Blessém! Everyone kens they hate *uile-bheistean*."

"I am going back to the forests," the tree-shifter Corissa said.

"But do ye no' wish to help us?" Douglas asked, incredulous. "All o' Eileanan is under threat!"

She shrugged. "Wha' is that to me? I care no' who rules as long as I can run free as I please. Humans have done naught but ill to me."

"How can ye say that?" Douglas was incensed. "If it was no' for us, ye'd still be in that blaygird tower!"

"If it was no' for humans, I'd no' be in the tower in the first place," Corissa pointed out, calmly devouring a second bowlful of vegetable stew.

"Do no' judge all humans by the few ye have known," Enit said gently. "But o' course, ye are free to go as ye please. May I make some suggestions?"

Everyone nodded. The old woman said, "We have to get word to the cities quickly, and I canna see that a pack o' children on foot are the way to do it. If it is true the Bright Soldiers plan to attack Dùn Eidean and Dùn Gorm, the whole countryside will go up in flames. Ye will all be killed. Nay, I have a much better plan."

"What? What will ye do?" they cried.

Enit's eyes twinkled. "I shall scry to my friend Muire in Dùn Eidean. She is maid to the dowager banprionnsa herself. She will have the news in a minute, rather than weeks. I shall also send news to the rebels in Dùn Gorm and elsewhere, telling them to prepare for the attack, and contact Meghan NicCuinn who will relay it to a spy

o' hers in Rhyssmadill. I hear her spy has had the ear
o' the Rìgh since he was a lad." She laughed at their
expressions. "I have friends everywhere, my bairns. I
have traveled this land in my caravan since I was a
mere lass."

"W-W-What about us?" Iain asked, rather crestfallen.
Their imaginations had been running wild with the idea
of saving the whole land and being heroes.

"Why do ye no' join the rebellion? I shall take ye into
Rionnagan. The rebel camp is gathering there—and an
auld friend o' mine has already gathered there many
children o' Talent for a Theurgia."

Immediately there was an outcry, and Enit laughed.
"Be at peace, my bairns, Jorge the Seer is the gentlest
o' men and his Theurgia will be quite unlike that o'
Margrit o' Arran's! Besides, it need only be for a short
time. Perhaps the land will be saved and ye can travel
where ye wish."

Enit filled her silver bowl with water and set it by the
fire, staring into it for a long while. At last she looked
up, her wrinkled face weary. "I have spoken with Muire
and she is hastening to tell the dowager now. She swears
she can convince her to take action and warn the city
in time."

The children cheered in excitement, and Douglas and
Iain shared a weary grin. Enit said more slowly, "I canna
reach Meghan. We scry the same day each week, always
at dawn but she has no' answered me these last few
weeks . . . I feel uneasy. Dide, perhaps ye could try and
reach Bacaiche?"

The old jongleur called birds from the forest to her
hand and attached coded messages to their legs, speaking to them earnestly in their language before throwing
them up into the sky. Meanwhile Dide stared into the
bowl, his face darkening. At last he looked up and said
bleakly, "Enit, I have spoken with my master. Meghan
has been taken. And she has set the MacRuraich on
our trail."

The old woman played with her beads, her eyes

hooded. At last she looked up, and said, "Indeed, I was afraid that is what might have happened. Meghan told me the black wolf was on her trail. Well, we had best be moving. The last place we were seen is Blessém, let us put as much ground between us and the blessed land as we can."

THE WOLF HUNTS

The howl of a wolf reverberated around the valley, and the glum-faced soldiers riding along the narrow path hunched deeper into their cloaks. Anghus MacRuraich was unable to control his start of pleasure. He looked around eagerly and saw the shape of a wolf silhouetted against the crimson glow of the rising moon. The wolf howled again, muzzle raised to the sky, and Anghus had to stifle the desire to shout his sister's name. He saw Floinn Redbeard make the age-old gesture against evil, and wondered again how he could rid himself of his unwelcome escort.

He had spent the week after Meghan's capture in the hot, submerging embrace of alcohol. He only stopped drinking when the black fumes finally overcame him. When he woke again, it was to reach for the silver flask. He was sick at heart, angry and, for the first time in his life, bewildered. What was he to do? The revelations Meghan had made about his sister and daughter had turned everything topsy turvy. Tabithas a wolf? His little daughter Fionnghal an apprentice thief and beggar? His own Talent twisted back on itself by a simple reverse spell? He longed for his wife. If only Gwyneth were with him, to wrap him in her pale silken hair, her pale silken body, to soothe his brow with her cool mouth, to tell him she loved him. It had been so long since she had said she loved him.

It had been his faithful gillie who had jerked him out of his fug of misery. On the fifth morning he had stood by the prionnsa's bed until at last Anghus had rolled over and peered at him from eyes that felt like they had been scorched in with pokers.

"Obh obh, so ye've decided to wake," Donald had said, adding belatedly, "my laird." He passed his master a glass of water, which Anghus pushed away, demanding whiskey instead. "Ye've drunk your flask dry again, my laird," Donald answered meekly.

"Then get me some more!"

"Soon enough, my laird. I have some food for ye first, and some tea."

"I do no' want tea, Eà damn ye!"

Donald did not answer, plates clinking as he set up the table for Anghus. He brought his master cold water and a towel and, after a glowering moment, Anghus washed his face and head, groaning and complaining. He lurched from the bed to the table where he picked at his food irritably, too proud to ask again for his whiskey but not wanting anything else.

His gillie stood before him, his tam o'shanter twisting in his hands so his bald scalp shone in the lamplight. "Wha' are your plans, my laird?"

Anghus laughed, an ugly sound. "To send ye in search o' the water o' life, my man."

"As ye wish, my laird. I mean, after that."

"Is there anything after that?"

"That is for ye to say, my laird. I just wish to ken when we plan to leave this place, my laird."

"Now, never, what does it matter?"

Donald did not reply, his big hands gripping his tam o'shanter. Then very deliberately, he pulled it on, picked up his plaid and prepared to leave. Suddenly Anghus called, "Nay, man, bide a wee." He paused, obviously struggling for words, then said abruptly, "I'm sorry, Donald, a bad laird I am to ye indeed."

Donald's face softened almost imperceptibly. "Ye are troubled, my laird."

"Aye." Anghus regarded his hands, then said huskily, "I do no' ken which way to turn, Donald. The path before me is unclear."

Knowing what a difficult admission that was for a MacRuraich to make, Donald took off his tam o'shanter again. The shiny dome of his head was pink. He listened in silence as Anghus told him what Meghan had said. "I have promised to search for the Cripple as the Banrìgh instructed. I have given my word on it. Yet I know I have been told only lies about my Fionnghal. Meghan may have given me the clues to searching her out. Everything, all o' me, yearns to track her down."

"Then why do ye no'?"

"To do so would be rebellion, Donald, can ye no' see that? I have a royal order, signed by the Banrìgh's own hand. I have given my word, and a MacRuraich's word is his bond. If I break my word, am I any better than them? Besides, I canna take such a risk. I have to look to my people, and they have suffered enough at the hands o' those blasted Red Guards."

"Aye, and angry they are indeed, my laird, and hiding their weapons in the thatch as they used to in the auld days. Ye ken ye are their laird, and they will follow ye no matter wha' road ye take."

Anghus looked sharply at the gillie's wrinkled, apple-cheeked face, but it was open and guileless as ever. He replied slowly, "The MacRuraichs have always been faithful to the MacCuinns."

"My laird, I do no' understand how searching for your daughter is a declaration o' rebellion," Donald said, with a slight stress on the third last word. Anghus stared at him. The gillie went on slowly, "Besides, is it no' just the Banrìgh's squiggle on that piece o' paper? Ye have sworn no oath o' loyalty to the Rìgh's wife, only to him."

Anghus nodded. "That is true."

"And do they no' think the winged lad is the Cripple, and did they no' tell ye to hunt him down? If ye follow him to this rebel camp, where ye think your daughter may be, are ye no' just following their orders? It is only Meghan o' the Beasts who told ye he was no' the Cripple."

Anghus's hazel-green eyes glowed brightly. "Indeed, indeed, that is so," he said. "And who are the Awl to be questioning my movements anyway? It is no' as if I were some shoddy witch-sniffer, having to report my every movement."

He got up and asked irritably for his boots. "Surely ye've had them cleaned by now!"

Donald crammed his tam o'shanter back on and said he would go and retrieve them from the bootboy. Anghus, rummaging through his pack for a clean shirt, said, "And do no' forget my whiskey, Donald, else I'll pluck your beard for ye!"

Anghus had not been able to avoid having an escort thrust upon him, though he had persuaded Humbert that a seeker would be more likely to hinder him than help. So he and Donald had ridden out from Dunceleste with six soldiers, among them the three who had lived through their journey to the heart of the Veiled Forest.

They were on the trail of the winged prionnsa, and a torturous trail it was too, leading through valley and dale, back down into the forest and over some difficult rocky terrain. If he had not been following an extrasensory trail as well as a physical one, Anghus would never have been able to track him.

Although he gave no hint of his intentions, the men knew enough about tracking to know he was following someone. As Anghus seemed to know the path regardless of physical signs such as footprints, broken branches, or dead coals hidden by earth, the men began to look at him askance. Floinn Redbeard in particular was suspicious. Staring at Anghus with his watery blue eyes, he asked one day where it was the prionnsa was leading them. "There be nothing in these mountains but woolly bears and coneys, m'laird. I thought ye were meant to be on the trail o' that blaygird Cripple, but it seems to me we're just chasing our tails."

Anghus said calmly, "Then do no' trouble yourself, Floinn, I am no' lost. A MacRuraich is never lost."

As he repeated these words, which had become over the centuries something like a mantra, it occurred to him how ironic they were at this point in history. One could argue that all MacRuraichs living were lost—Tabithas, Fionnghal and himself, all lost and changed beyond recognition. The thought made him weary. It cost him an effort to spur his horse on, and he could not mask his expression from either Donald or Casey Hawkeye. He was conscious of the latter's intent blue eyes on his face, and wondered what he was thinking.

Anghus knew he had to rid himself of the soldiers before he got too near the rebel camp, but he was loath to commit to any action that would narrow his options. So violence was out of the question. He had to wait for an opportunity to trick them instead. It came during the course of the second week, when they were so deep in the mountains that the soldiers would have difficulty in finding their way out without assistance. Anghus did not want word getting back to Humbert too quickly. He did not want to harm the soldiers either, particularly the young piper with his ungainly wrists and doglike eyes, or the keen-eyed Casey. So when he saw the weather beginning to worsen he rode down toward the forests.

They were trekking along a ridge in single file when the storm that had been threatening all day broke over their heads with a crash of thunder. "It's dangerous out here in the open," Anghus shouted. "Let's look for shelter as quickly as we can."

With the downpour obscuring their eyes, the soldiers all plunged into the forest after Anghus. The prionnsa, hiding in the thick underbrush, heard them crashing through the bushes. He whistled like a tree-swallow, and soon Donald wriggled silently up beside him, leading his horse. He had already muffled the riding tack and had his hand over the mare's nose to stop her from whickering.

Both Anghus and Donald were seasoned hunters and foresters, and they had no difficulty in losing the soldiers in the tangled undergrowth. They slipped silently back to the outskirts of the forest and resumed their journey.

Some time during the night they heard something in the woods behind them and concealed themselves warily in the undergrowth. It was Tabithas, tracking them nose to ground. It was the first time Anghus had come close to the wolf since Meghan's revelations and he was surprised at the wave of emotion which overwhelmed him. He found himself on the ground, his arms full of whining, wriggling wolf, tears mingling with the rain on his cheeks.

"Tabithas, Tabithas, is it really ye?" he asked, and she yapped and thrust her head under his chin for him to scratch.

He stared into her yellow eyes, searching for some resemblance to his sister, but there was no sign that the wolf had ever been a woman, let alone a powerful sorceress. Grief and anger filled him, and he leaned his head against her thick ruff. She whined and licked his cheek, her tail wagging furiously, and he swallowed the knot in his throat. "I canna believe it is really ye," he said hoarsely, and she leaned her bulk against him, looking up at him with such a clear expression of understanding and sympathy on her lupine face that he suddenly no longer doubted this silver-ruffed wolf was indeed his sister Tabithas.

By sunrise they were far away from the forest where they had left their companions, tired, hungry and thoroughly chilled. Both were wet through to the skin, and their clothes clung to them clammily. "Should we stop, my laird?" Donald asked. "The sides o' my stomach are fair clemming together."

Anghus shook his head. He had an uneasy feeling, and the wolf seemed to share his anxiety, for she looked back often, her lip lifting in a snarl. "Nay, those Red

Guards are trained trackers and we've left more o' a trail than I would have liked. Let us push on while we can."

They ate as they rode, Anghus swallowing a few mouthfuls of whiskey to warm his blood. He felt strangely vulnerable, as if a few layers of skin had been flayed away. He had kept his heart and mind locked up for so long, but now all his careful defences seemed to be dissolving. "Soon I shall find her, my Fionnghal," he said to himself. The wolf barked and looked up at him as she ran alongside the horses, unnerving them with her wolf smell.

By noon Anghus was sure they were being followed. Every hair on his neck was bristling, his spine felt stiff and tense, and the wolf stared back down the trail with raised hackles and a low growl. He decided he had best see who it was before taking decisive action, so he and Donald concealed themselves in an outcrop of boulders. After about ten minutes they saw Casey Hawkeye come trotting out of the woods. Behind him rode Ashlin the Piper, his wayward knees and elbows showing he had not yet mastered the art of riding. Casey pulled his horse to a halt and dismounted gracefully, kneeling to examine the ground. Anghus and Donald had wrapped their horses' hooves in cloth to try and conceal the prints their hooves made in the soft mud, but an experienced and keen-eyed scout would still be able to identify the blurred marks left behind. Casey Hawkeye was evidently such a scout.

"Lose 'em or lump 'em?" Donald asked.

Anghus played with his crisp beard, then came to a decision. "Talk to them, I think. I like both Casey and the lad, and do no' wish to hurt them. We've used just about every trick we ken to shake them and they obviously do no' wish to be shaken. I would like to know why."

He rose, stretched and made his way down to the path. By the time Casey and Ashlin rode around the corner, they were sitting at their ease on boulders by the wayside, smoking their pipes. Casey reined in and

observed them with expressionless blue eyes. Ashlin was
not so reticent. His eyes lit up, a broad smile broke over
his freckled face, and he clumsily urged the horse into
a trot.

"So ye've decided to catch us up," Anghus said pleasantly, knocking out his pipe. "We wondered what happened to ye. Have a seat, we were just thinking about
some lunch."

Casey regarded him thoughtfully, then dismounted
and strolled over to them, leading his horse. Ashlin was
talking excitedly. He obviously thought that Anghus and
Donald had become separated by accident in the storm,
and he was delighted to meet with them again. Casey
had no such misconception; Anghus could tell by his
caged expression that he knew perfectly well that Anghus had lost them on purpose.

"And what happened to your delightful associates?"
Anghus asked as they prepared a makeshift repast.

Casey answered carefully, "They seem to have got
themselves lost."

"Such a shame we do no' have time to wait for them,"
Anghus replied.

"For some reason they seem to think ye continued to
head south into the woods," Casey said. "I heard them
cry out they had found tracks . . ."

Anghus's eyes gleamed green. He wondered if the soldier had had anything to do with that. Casey Hawkeye
was a dark horse indeed.

"Wha' a pity. I was just beginning to feel an affection
for Floinn Redbeard," Donald said.

They saw Casey's hard mouth quirk at the corner, and
knew the cavalryman had found the red-haired giant as
objectionable as they had. Anghus began to wonder if
he should take Casey into his confidence. He had found
the cavalryman a good companion in times of trouble,
cool of head, strong of arm and keen of eye. Surely it
was too much of a risk, though. Nothing Casey had said
had shown he was anything but loyal to the Banrìgh.
Anghus was still hoping to keep his intentions a secret—

he was not ready to declare Rurach and Siantan at war with the Rìgh, which is what any overt act of rebellion would mean.

The cavalryman accepted the food Donald handed him. "I wonder what it is ye hunt, my laird," he said, very politely.

"Hunt?"

"I have no' been able to help noticing the black wolf's nose is to a trail."

"Indeed?"

"Aye. I have heard that the black wolf never gives up the hunt once his—or her—nose is to the trail."

Anghus laughed. He decided he liked Casey Hawkeye. "Unless a more attractive scent crosses his path," he said. "Any wolf will abandon a trail gone stale and auld when one more to his—or her—liking comes along."

Casey smiled and got out a long clay pipe, thoughtfully cramming in tobacco. Ashlin the Piper was listening closely, not sure he understood what was being said. Casey lit the pipe with his thumb and puffed away peacefully.

Donald and Anghus exchanged a glance, eyebrows raised. "Ah, ye're a smoking man," the gillie said agreeably and brought out his own worn leather pouch. "But how is it ye can afford smokeweed on a cavalryman's pay?"

"My uncle Donovan is harbormaster at Dùn Gorm. The traders from the Bright Land were kind enough to gift him with a cord or two as they come through the rivergates. I had a parcel waiting for me at Dunceleste when we rode in from the Veiled Forest."

"Are ye a whiskey man too?" Anghus asked, bringing out his silver flask.

"And me a highlander," Casey said sadly. "That ye could be asking such a question."

Anghus poured them all a dram, Ashlin's noticeably smaller. "To the future, then, my friends!"

Iseult woke early the morning after their war conference, troubled by how much of their plan still relied on luck and happenstance. Gitâ was curled on a cushion and chittered to her as she dressed. She stroked him, knowing how much the little donbeag must miss Meghan.

As soon as she stepped outside she became aware of being watched, and smiled. "Where are ye hiding this time, Finn?" she called.

A chestnut-brown head popped up from behind a stack of barrels, a tiny black head with tufted ears appearing beside it. "I be here, Iseult," Finn called back, crawling out on her hands and knees.

"Do ye want to come to the loch with me?"

"Aye!" Finn jumped about in excitement, her legs below the short, ragged dress very skinny and very dirty.

"Do ye no' have any other clothes? Ye must be cold in that auld rag."

"Well, aye, I am almost always cold, but I've worn nothing else for years," Finn replied in surprise. "It used to be big for me—now I'm busting out all over."

"Do ye no' have any shoes?" Iseult asked, looking at her filthy bare feet, cut all over from thorns and sharp stones.

Finn's expression of surprise deepened. "Where would I be getting shoes?"

"Winter is coming, we shall have to see what we can do for ye," Iseult said, leading the way through the noisy camp.

Finn laughed. "It snows in Lucescere in winter; the puddles all freeze over and the wind through the auld city cuts like a dagger. I am used to it now."

"Nonetheless, there must be a cobbler here, and probably someone who can sew too. I shall make sure all ye children are warm before winter comes!"

Iseult stripped off to immerse herself in the loch, and after a while Finn joined her in the icy waters, splashing and squealing. Iseult made her wash the matted dirt out of her brown tangles and scrub her filthy feet with a bristled brush. The sound of her squeals brought the other children out of their caves, and soon the loch was bobbing with small heads, the air ringing with their shouts.

Afterward Iseult made Finn show her how the elven cat climbed, and she watched with amazement as the kitten scrambled swiftly and easily straight up the out-curving cliff. Her sharp claws seemed to dig into the very rock face, and Finn said longingly, "See, if I had claws like that I could climb as easily!"

An idea presented itself to Iseult like a gift from Eà, and she made her way back to the camp thoughtfully, Finn dancing and chattering along beside her. After they had eaten, Finn devouring half of Iseult's breakfast, they sought out Duncan, and Iseult explained her idea to him.

"Could we no' make shoes that are clawed like a cat's? Our wee Finn here says she can climb most walls but needs something to help her if there are no cracks or crevices. It seems she must be the one to breach the rampart behind the Tower o' Two Moons, but it is well known for being as smooth as glass. If we could attach spikes to her feet, would that no' help?"

"Well, we have a cobbler, o' course, but I dinna ken if he could make anything like that," Duncan said dubi-ously. He took Iseult and an excited Finn along to meet him, nonetheless, and after much exclamation the cob-bler said he would try. He also promised to make sturdy boots for all the children if he could find the time, though he said the soldiers' feet must come first. Iseult also found the soldiers' tailor and asked him to make the children some warmer clothes before they left. He simply altered some old clothes to fit them, and soon all of the League of the Healing Hand were dressed in woolen breeches, cross-gartered under the knee, with long-sleeved tunics and jerkins on top.

The next weeks were spent preparing for the journey and working with the soldiers. Iseult found the rebels were mostly poorly trained, many of them mere crofters' sons or runaway apprentices. She and Duncan worked closely together and found a rapport beginning to grow between them. Although the big-shouldered man had hidden his feelings well, he had been both doubtful and suspicious of his laird's new wife. After a week observing her efforts, some of his doubt left him and he began to respond to her more readily.

Iseult also joined the daily hunting parties and impressed the soldiers greatly with her hunting prowess. *Meghan is no' here now,* she told herself. *Better to win the men to our cause than confuse them by Meghan's peculiar notions.* Nonetheless, she found she could not eat much of the meat, preferring the roasted roots and vegetables.

As summer swung toward autumn, their preparations intensified. Lachlan and his party had to leave first, for they had a long and difficult trek ahead of them through the Whitelock Mountains. It was necessary for them to cross the Muileach River in order to come down behind Lucescere, and so that meant they had to climb deep into the mountains to cross the river near its source. There was no other way of fording the fast-running river.

Finn was determined to disguise herself before going anywhere near Lucescere, despite all Iseult's reassurances. She decided to dye her hair blonde, and keep her distinctive elfin features well smeared with mud. None of them knew how to dye brown hair blonde, but Iseult simply drew *The Book of Shadows* out of the pouch and asked it. The pages riffled over by themselves, to the children's amazement, falling open at last on a recipe that promised to bleach hair with a paste made from the ash of barberry branches. Finn's head was wrapped in this putrid mixture for most of a day, and when at last the ashes were washed free, her chestnut-brown hair was a pale blonde.

That afternoon the cobbler came to Iseult with a collection of small but sturdy boots. He and the blacksmith had also designed and made a frame with twelve sharp, curved spikes for Finn to strap over her boots, with cruel-looking clawed gloves for her hands. The blacksmith had also made sharp skewers that could be hammered into any crack to give Finn a handhold.

Not allowing anyone to watch, Finn took them away to the end of the corrie. For the next four days she climbed trees and rock walls, practiced techniques with ropes and pulleys, and at last said she was ready to show Iseult and Lachlan.

In high excitement, the League swarmed around the little girl as she solemnly strapped on her claws and prepared to climb the cliff. Slowly but surely she clambered up the steep, smooth slope, making sure the hooks were dug deep into the stone before attempting to trust her weight to it. She slipped several times, but each time was able to cling on, though Iseult's heart was in her mouth.

When Finn eventually reached the top of the three-hundred-foot cliff, cheers and whistles ran out all around the corrie. "She's just like an elven cat herself," Jay muttered to Dillon. "That's what we'll call her from now on—Finn the Cat."

Two days later Anghus and his men rode into a valley at the very foot of the Fang. Anghus's Talent told him the winged man was straight ahead but there was nothing but a towering red cliff. He tried to sense Fionnghal but each time his perceptions grew confused and jumbled to the point of nausea, and so at last he desisted.

Early the next morning a cavalcade of soldiers came marching out of the very rock itself. Anghus and Casey glanced at each other in surprise, for they had seen no crack or fissure in the wall. Then Anghus cried out softly, for at the head of the cavalcade marched the hunchback, wrapped again in the black cloak.

By his side was the tall woman, a white tam o'shanter pulled low over her red-gold curls, and a blind old man with a raven on his shoulder. Behind them marched a troupe of children, led by a small boy who proudly carried a crude flag—a yellow hand on a blue background.

Anghus scanned the troupe of children anxiously, looking for the chestnut-brown hair of his daughter. The only girls among them were fair, one with a bunch of curls pale as flax. As his eyes passed over her, dizziness washed over him. He could not see, blackness whirling before his eyes. He took a step, meaning to call out to the MacCuinn lad, but his head was spinning, he could not tell which way was up or down. He stumbled and fell, rolling down the rocky hill.

Bruised, his hand and temple bleeding, he lay still. Faces dipped about him. He heard the MacCuinn lad shouting orders, then he was being carried. He was aware of a vast emptiness, sorrow, disappointment. Tabithas was whining at his side, tugging at his sleeve, trying to make him get up. His internal compass was spinning—he did not know where he was, he did not know what he did here. All he knew was that he was lost.

THE LAMMAS CONGRESS

A week before Lammas Day, the witch-banprionnsa
of Arran, Margrit NicFóghnan, rode into Rhyssmadill. She came with a long train of servants and
dependents, and a wagon loaded with gifts for the Rìgh.
The kitchen hummed with gossip—everyone wondered
what brought her to Rhyssmadill, and why the Awl had
allowed a sorceress into the palace.

Isabeau sneaked away to catch a glimpse of her. She
was a tall woman, dressed grandly in black velvet with
gold brocade and lace. Her face was only delicately
lined, but it was cold and disdainful. At her breast she
wore the crest of the MacFóghnans, the flowering thistle.
So rare was it for a MacFóghnan to visit a MacCuinn
that the Rìgh got up to receive her.

He had been very ill, spending the days in his great,
canopied bed. Latifa was concerned about him and made
many a hot broth or posset to try and tempt his appetite
and build up his strength. Isabeau was usually with her,
for Latifa's herb lore was not as wide and deep as Isabeau's. She was shocked by the Rìgh's sunken cheeks,
the grayness of his skin, the irregularity of his heartbeat.
He was only a few years past thirty, but he looked like

an old man. She shook her head and met Latifa's eyes gravely, for he had the look of death about him.

The servants had been kept busy preparing for Lammas Day, an important festival in Eileanan. Not only was it the celebration of the first harvest, but the day when crofters and farmers paid their rents and taxes to the lairds, the lairds paid the prionnsachan, and the prionnsachan paid the Rìgh.

The great hall at Rhyssmadill was thrown open for gifts of grain, rams, silks, precious stones and minerals, finely worked metals and bags jingling with coins. The prionnsachan came from all over Eileanan, some having spent a month in the traveling, for Lammas Day was traditionally a time to speak with the Rìgh and discuss problems and negotiate loans. With the land in turmoil from the raids of the Fairgean and the rebels, the Lammas Congress was expected to be tumultuous.

Gwyneth NicSian came, representing her husband Anghus MacRuraich of Rurach and her own homeland of Siantan, now joined as the Double Throne. She was a very beautiful woman, with a long, pale plait. She brought a wagon load of rare timbers, sacks of charcoal, and luxuriant snow-lion furs.

The Prionnsa of Carraig, Linley MacSeinn, returned after an unsuccessful attempt to cross the mountains into Carraig. He was coiled up tight as a spring with anger and grief, for his son and heir had disappeared from the court in early spring, and all his attempts to raise the men and arms to win back his country had failed. Once the MacSeinns had been a rich clan, trading in furs, fish, base metals and Fairgean scales, but its wealth had been lost with the invasion of Carraig. A proud man, the prionnsa obviously found his position difficult, and there was much speculation in the kitchen about what he would have to say at the Congress.

From Tìreich came the MacAhern clan, who had traveled through Ravenshaw to get to Rhyssmadill. The prionnsa, Kenneth MacAhern, caused an absolute sensation by riding in on one of the famous flying horses. It was a deep-chested, honey-colored animal, with rainbow-tinted wings and a pair of spreading antlers. The MacAhern rode without saddle or bridle, as all thigearns did. One did not tame a flying horse with such constraints.

Piquant as the arrival of the horse clan was, it did not excite near as much interest as the diplomatic party from Tirsoilleir continued to do. The white surcoats of the Bright Soldiers were to be seen everywhere in the palace and city. Some carried a long, oddly shaped weapon over their shoulders called a harquebus, which the potboys said shot out fireworks with a loud bang. Isabeau could not see any reason for a weapon that shot fireworks, and the idea made her uneasy. Her sleep was filled with nightmares, many which took the shape of silver and white soldiers.

Her bad dreams had increased in frequency and intensity until Isabeau was reluctant to close her eyes at night. She dreamed she was trying to escape through mist, running desperately away from something, someone, only to have her feet caught by mud, her body by thorns. She had dreams of war, filled with blood and flame. She had dreams of love, both beautiful and strange. Sometimes the face that bent to kiss hers was dark and passionate; other times it was alien, with great glittering eyes.

A few days before the harvest festival, her guardian appeared in a dream. Isabeau was filled with pleasure as sharp as pain at the sight of Meghan's narrow, wrinkled face and glittering black eyes. She was shrouded in shadows hovering like dark wings about her. *Isabeau . . . She* called as if from a long way away. *Isabeau, ye must come. Ye must come* . . .

Where?

To Lucescere. To the auld palace. Ye must come with the Key . . .

Meghan, where are ye?

Come to Lucescere. Ye must bring me the Key. Isabeau, I need ye. Come to Lucescere . . .

When Isabeau woke, she crept down into the kitchen where Latifa was stoking up the fires. The keyring at the cook's belt jingled, and Isabeau looked longingly at it. Her months carrying one-third of the Key had left her with a yearning she found hard to shake off at times. Keeping her voice low, she told the old cook what Meghan had said.

Latifa frowned, and clutched her keyring. "It be far too dangerous for ye to set out for Lucescere by yourself," she said. "Particularly on the suggestion o' a mere dream. Very few have the ability to walk the dream road and ye are still only a fledgling witch—I have never seen any evidence ye have that Talent! If Meghan wanted me to give the Key into your hand, she would have told me so. Yet she does no' answer me when I scry to her, and we have heard nothing o' her since she disappeared. I canna be letting the Key out o' my hand just because ye've had a nightmare."

"But Meghan said—"

The cook's voice softened. "It be natural that ye dream o' her, worrying about her as ye mun be. And ye are a nervy thing, I can see ye have no' been sleeping. Dreams are chancy things, my lassie, often naught but fragments o' the sleeping mind."

"But why would I dream o' Lucescere, it means nothing to me . . ."

She shrugged. "Lucescere is a fabled city, spun about with rainbows and auld tales. I think it is natural for ye to dream o' it." Though she spoke kindly, there was an edge to her voice, and she caressed the keyring with possessive fingers.

"But—"

"It was just a dream, lassie. Let it rest."

Meghan began to haunt Isabeau's dreams, as frequent as the beautiful, golden-eyed man or the alien creature who brought her such bliss, as frequent as the dreams of flame and blood. In desperation Isabeau drank chamomile tea before she went to bed, but even in her deepest sleep the dreams still came.

During the day, the guests were amused by jongleurs and troubadours, while the gardens were turned into a sort of fair, with stalls handing out sherbets, jellies and cups of ice-cold bellfruit wine. Small groups of men talked quietly in corners, occasionally erupting into sword fights or wrestling matches. The women flirted and gossiped and whispered behind their fans.

Isabeau was filled with curiosity and excitement. This was closer to her expectations of life in the Rìgh's palace—a court filled with prionnsachan and banprionnsachan in gorgeous clothes, swirling with intrigue. She longed to eavesdrop on the Lammas Congress, and wondered if there was any way she could conceal herself in the conference room. She might pick up invaluable news for Meghan and the rebellion and restore herself in the eyes of her guardian. For Isabeau had been unable to throw off a sense of failure, despite the successful joining of two parts of the Key. She had been so cocksure when she had parted ways with Meghan, but it had only been with the help of the Celestine that she had completed her quest at all. Now Isabeau's strength and health were slowly returning, she wished to be involved in the rebellion once more.

The morning of the Lammas Congress, as she and Latifa were making fat yellow candles for their Lammas sabbat, she expressed her wish rather wistfully to the old cook.

"So ye wish to hear what the prionnsachan say? Well, ye have worked hard and are no' so bad at shielding your thoughts now. I shall let ye listen in when I do, but ye must keep your mind carefully guarded."

"So ye were planning to watch the Lammas Congress?"

Latifa smiled at her, her little raisin eyes disappearing into folds of skin. "Indeed I was. Ye'd think I'd let slip such an opportunity? O' course I have to listen. It is very dangerous, though, Isabeau. I shall only let ye watch with me if ye stay quiet as a mouse."

Isabeau nodded excitedly.

"And I do no' mean your body, for we shall be well away from the conference room. I mean your mind, my lassie. The Banrìgh's blaygird servant shall be listening and watching too, and we do no' want to draw her attention. So ye must curl up your impatient, questing thoughts and keep them locked up tight as ye can."

Isabeau nodded again, and knew she could do it. These last few months had taught Isabeau much about screening her thoughts. She could even hide herself from Latifa now, which made the cook rather grumpy.

They watched the conference from the safety and privacy of Latifa's room. The fat old cook lit candles all around them, ones made with murkwoad, hawthorn and rose, to aid divination and clairvoyance. Isabeau thought it was very interesting how Latifa added precious essences to her candles to aid her own Skills, and she stored away the recipe for future use.

Latifa bid Isabeau stare into the heart of the fire. With the sweet smoke clouding her senses, she became absorbed in the patterns of fiery light and darkness. The room behind her faded. She experienced a sensation of lightness, giddiness, as if she was floating. She let herself drift. It was as though Latifa had touched her on the top of her skull but there was no physical connection. She felt herself drawn up into the air, as though Latifa were pulling her by her hair. She could see nothing but flames, but it was as if she was turning, twisted into Latifa's fabric like a strand of wool is twisted into a thread. There was a sensation of spreading. She was light and fragile as dust motes floating in sunshine. Then she saw shapes in the embers of the fire and heard words.

Gwyneth NicSian was describing the reign of terror the Fairgean had implemented all along the coast of Siatan and Rurach. Many of the fisherfolk and sea-hunters had been massacred, coastal villages from Morrigan Bay to the Wulfrum had been raided, river trade had halted as boats were sunk and capsized from below, and the mountain villages were flooded with refugees. They did not have enough grain for the merchant ships from Rhyssmadill had never arrived.

"Also," the banprionnsa continued in a careful voice,

"the continued absence o' my husband, the MacRuraich, makes finding solutions to our problems difficult."

"The Prionnsa is away on the Rìgh's business and canna be recalled," Sani said in her sibilant voice. Isabeau wondered why the Rìgh did not speak for himself. She tried to see the Banrìgh's servant, but in the fire-pictures she was merely a black, hunched shape.

The MacAhern said his people had simply withdrawn from the Tìreichan coast, taking their caravans into the hinterland. They missed being able to exercise their horses on the sand dunes, however, and supplementing their diet with fish and crustaceans. The Tìreichan were also keen and canny traders and regretted the closing of the trade fairs. In the five years since the Fairgean had begun raiding, the summer fairs had gradually been abandoned and this greatly hurt the wealth of the Mac-Ahern's people.

The MacSeinn tried hard to keep his deep sense of betrayal out of his voice but it rang through every word. His land had been invaded. His people had been brutally massacred. He, the laird of the MacSeinn clan and direct descendant of Seinneadair the Singer, was a refugee, dependent on the kindness of others. His eldest son had been killed in the invasion. His daughter had died in the scramble to escape. His last living child had been stolen from the Rìgh's own court.

"If we had struck hard at the Fairgean and driven them from Carraig when first they invaded, perhaps the whole country would no' now be suffering," he said earnestly. "They have built themselves a base in my land and have used it to strike at others. We should have nipped them in the bud five years ago! It is no' too late."

The MacThanach had not suffered much human loss at all, Blessém being protected from the sea by Aedan's Wall. He had plenty to say nonetheless. Many of the missing children had come from his territories. Two of them were his own kin, and descendants of Aislinna the Dream-Walker herself. "Something has to be done to find out who is stealing all the children," he shouted.

He complained about the dangerous creatures in-festing Aslinn, so the trappers, charcoal-burners, forest-ers and miners were afraid to go about their business. The MacThanach needed base metals to make plough-shares, charcoal for his whiskey vats and timber for the building of new crofts. "Why do your Red Guards no' clear the forests o' the blaygird horned faeries, instead o' causing trouble in the provinces with their drinking and whoring? My grain is rotting on the docks, and yet Siantan is rioting for lack o' bread. We must get the trade routes open again!"

This caused an uproar, for the fleet of heavily armed ships that had been sent north at Midsummer had simply disappeared. No word had come from them since they sailed out of the firth into the Muir Finn. Dughall Mac-Brann of Ravenshaw said they had been sighted by his father's people off the coast, but the lookout at the mouth of the Wulfrum had scanned the sea without suc-cess for the past month.

"I have heard reports o' pirates in the seas again," Dughall said. "Apparently they're hiding in the Fair Isles. Could they have attacked the fleet?"

"It must be the Fairgean," the Admiral of the Rìgh's navy said. "My sailors ken how to throw off an attack by those blaygird pirates. Only the Fairgean could have sunk an entire fleet, with their sea-serpents and whales."

He was attacked from all sides with criticism, and when he responded his bluff voice was defensive. "Ye must realise, my lairds, no work has been done on the navy's fleet for nigh on fifteen years. His Highness the Rìgh said the Fairgean were defeated, and he needed the money for other things. We've maintained only a skeleton fleet, and many o' those ships are old and ill-kept. Most o' our men were conscripted to serve in the Red Guards, and so our forces are much depleted. Can we no' call them back to the navy to help us get our ships in order?"

"We need the Red Guards to hunt down the rebels,"

Sani responded. "In fact, the Rìgh has signed an order for each clan to assist us with two hundred more men."

There were sighs and groans all around the room. Sani said suavely, "I ken ye all wish to knock the rebellion on the head, for those wicked outlaws have been raiding all over the country."

"But what about the Fairgean?" the MacSeinn cried. "They are far more dangerous than a handful o' rebellious youngsters!"

"I think the Rìgh is in a better position to decide what is the greatest threat to this country," came Sani's hiss.

Dughall asked about the Lodestar. "There are rumors," he said in his cool, mocking voice, "that the Lodestar was no' destroyed by the witches on the Day o' Reckoning, but was hidden somewhere in the ruins o' the Tower o' Two Moons. Surely our blessed Rìgh would know if the Lodestar was still intact? It is our greatest weapon against the Fairgean, perhaps our only weapon now."

The soft, feeble voice of the Rìgh spoke for the first time. "I do no' know, Dughall," he said with weary affection. "I have long heard the song o' the Lodestar and thought it must be whole still, and undamaged. But the song has faltered, and I know now it was only my memories tormenting me. The Lodestar was destroyed by Meghan o' the Beasts, something I thought she would never have been able to do. But she is a ruthless, coldhearted witch, and her powers were obviously enough to overcome the powers o' the Inheritance o' Aedan. So there is no hope. We canna rely on the Lodestar to help us fight off the Fairgean."

The meeting dissolved into acrimonious argument. Linley MacSeinn said bitterly, and with no attempt to lower his voice, that the murder of the witches had done nothing but throw the rest of them to the Fairgean. Alasdair MacThanach warned him he was speaking treason. The MacSeinn said, "I do no' care. It is the truth. For a thousand years the witches defended us against the terrible sea people and now they are gone, we have no

defense but to abandon the coast. We canna survive
without the freedom to sail the seas!"

Around and around the arguments went, and tempers
began to rise. The Rìgh spoke rarely, and when he did,
it seemed as if he had been hardly listening at all. Maya
was not present, but her servant Sani spoke as confidently as if she were the Banrìgh herself, and certainly
no one challenged her or spoke to her with disrespect.

Indeed, by the end of the Congress, she was the most
vocal of all, speaking on behalf of the Rìgh as well as
his wife. It seemed to Isabeau that she was subtly encouraging the tension and indecision, rather than looking
for solutions, but no one else seemed to notice the way
she goaded the MacSeinn and mocked the Admiral, or
if they did, no one dared say anything. She even derided
the Rìgh's cousin Dughall when he urged they divert
funds to the navy, build up the fleet and defend the
coast. With a few smooth words, she made him seem
nothing but a pleasure-loving fop who had wasted away
his inheritance on gaming and fripperies.

Then Margrit of Arran and the leader of the diplomatic party from Tìrsoilleir were both admitted. The
NicFóghnan came with protestations of friendship, offering to help Eileanan with men and supplies in its fight
against the Fairgean. Jaspar thanked her and accepted
her help rather warily.

Baron Neville of St. Clair made a long and flowery
speech about their common ancestors and their need to
join together in this time of trouble. He described how
the Fairgean had attacked their northern coast in the
past few years. The Fealde had tried to make a treaty
of peace with the Fairgean, but their messengers had
returned with their hands and tongues cut off.

He touched delicately on the Rìgh's own losses, then,
with many flourishes, asked for permission to bring in a
flotilla of merchant ships to trade with Dùn Gorm. He
talked about their need for grain, wine, salt and glass.

At that point the MacThanach's constant objections
began to die. The prionnsa of Blessém was very suspi-

cious of the Bright Soldiers and had been vocal against them. As soon as Baron Neville began talking about trade, however, his interjections dried up, though he did mutter in the Rìgh's ear something about his cousin having had nightmares. "Happen we'd best be careful," he murmured.

He obviously did not want the other prionnsachan to hear him, though Latifa and Isabeau heard him clearly due to the cook's sound-enhancing powers. The sharp-eared Sani also heard him and hissed, "Ye would endanger an important trade agreement because your foolish cousin had a few *dreams?*"

"She's a NicAislin," the prionnsa muttered meaningfully, but the Rìgh either did not hear or did not care, for he said nothing. The MacThanach sat back in his chair with a shrug. Isabeau wondered if the prionnsa's cousin had had the same nightmares that she had— towers in mist, flowers of flame, silver soldiers shouting, "Die! Die!," blood in fountains.

When Baron Neville at last came to an end, the Rìgh sighed and said, "Thank ye, my laird. This is, o' course, something we shall all need to ponder on. Perhaps ye will wait for us in the lobby while we hear what our prionnsachan have to say."

Rather unwillingly the Baron Neville and his followers left the room, and those left behind all argued in circles, Sani's hiss gradually silencing any that stood against the Tìrsoilleirean. When the Lammas Congress at last broke up, differences between the prionnsachan and the Rìgh were deeper than ever. The only clear action decided on was allowing the fleet of ships from the Bright Land to come through the sea-gates into the Berhtfane. Isabeau wondered why she was the only one to find the Bright Soldiers' protestations of friendship false. Even Latifa was excited by the idea of the trade fair, wondering if they would bring any scorchspice with them.

"I've no' been able to make scorchspice stew in decades!" Latifa said as she harried Isabeau back down to the kitchen, "If that do no' quicken Jaspar's appetite, nothing will!"

The Lammas festivities lasted for a week, culminating in the Common Ridings, when all the townspeople poured out to ride the marches, beating the boundary stones with willow switches to fix them in the communal memory. This was a riotous parade accompanied by much laughter and drinking, and it ended with a feast in Dùn Gorm's great square. The Rìgh was usually lightly beaten with the willow switch at the end of the Common Ridings to remind him he was a servant of the people, but this year he was too ill to leave the palace.

Isabeau had thought she would be too busy to get away but, two days after Lammas, Latifa realized she had run out of stonecrop, used in the Rìgh's medicine. No one knew how to find wild herbs like Isabeau, and so she was sent out to find some in the forest. She did not tell Latifa that she knew exactly where to find the rare plant, wanting as she did to have a few hours to spend with Lasair. She rode first to the clearing where the plant grew among the stones of a ruined cottage and carefully tucked it within her pocket. Then she and Lasair cantered on through the forest, enjoying the warmth of the day.

She tried to stay away from the sea, but Lasair turned that way naturally and she thought, a little guiltily, that it would do no harm to have a look. Soon she was breathing in the fresh saltiness of the sea breeze, then she could hear the tumult of waves on the rocks. She rode up to the headland where the sea rushed up through a hole in the cliffs, fountaining into the sky and making an eerie noise. Lasair found the sound unsettling, and so she let him graze as he liked. She lay on the edge of the cliff, looking down at the sea below. She was just about to head for home when she heard a soft footstep behind her.

"I see ye did no' take my advice and keep clear o' the sea," a husky voice said.

"Nay," Isabeau said. "though I have no' been down on the sands again."

"Too frightened o' sand scorpions?" the black-haired woman asked. Isabeau nodded, and the woman said with a flare of her nostrils, "Och, the sand scorpions only come out at dawn and dusk, there be no need to fear them now."

"Does that mean we can go down?"

The woman frowned, then shrugged and said, "Why no'?" She balked at climbing down the ladder, however, saying, "Nay, I ken a much better place for getting down to the sands. Come and I'll show ye."

Isabeau was torn. She was eager to pursue her acquaintance with the black-haired woman, but did not want to reveal Lasair, who was cropping grass in the next clearing. If she told Lasair to leave her, though, she had no way of getting home.

Only a few seconds' thought decided her; she sent a mind-message to the stallion, then followed the woman along the edge of the cliff and toward the river. That way, the woman explained, they could avoid the dangerous rocks and cliffs of the Ravenshaw coast, instead wandering the sand dunes of the Strand.

First they had to cross the river, but the woman led her to one of the massive gates that blocked the river. It took them only a few minutes to cross the narrow walkway that ran over the great iron girders. Isabeau stared into the locks, fascinated by the sharp drop between the level of the Berhtfane and that of the firth on the other side.

"What is your name?" the stranger asked.

"Isabeau," she replied shyly. "Though mainly they call me the Red."

"I can see why!"

"What's your name then?"

There was a slight hesitation, then the other replied, "Morag."

Morag was a mysterious person indeed. She kept a plaid wrapped close about her body and did not remove her boots to walk on the sand, nor kilt up her skirt through her belt, as Isabeau did. She told Isabeau nothing about herself, withdrawing whenever Isabeau tried to probe for more information. She gave enigmatic answers to such questions as where was she born or where did she live, and sometimes would not answer at all. Isabeau did not like to press for more information, being reluctant to discuss such matters herself. Isabeau gave no hint of her own secret life, even though she strongly suspected Morag to be a witch.

For there was nothing Morag did not know about the seashore. She drew a diagram in the sand to explain the moons' pull on the tides. She showed how one could tell how high the tide rose. Isabeau's eyes widened to see seaweed caught on the rocks of the bulwark fifty feet above her head. She picked seagrapes for her and taught her how to tell when they were ready to eat. They prodded a doom-eel with a stick and watched how he lashed out with his fluorescent-tipped tail. Morag even dug up a sand scorpion's nest to show her the tiny, deadly creature, who turned his tail over his head to shield its beady eyes from the sun.

With her plaid fallen away from her body, Isabeau noticed for the first time that Morag was with child. The way her friend unconsciously cradled her stomach reminded Isabeau of a pregnant woman she had once seen in a highland village. That woman had been far closer to her birthing day and so the mound hiding the baby had been considerably larger. Nonetheless, the posture, the fist in the small of the back to ease the ache there, even the dreamy, dazed expression that sometimes crossed Morag's face, reminded Isabeau irresistibly of the highlander.

"Morag!" Isabeau cried. "Ye're having a baby! I had no' realized."

"Aye," her friend replied, her hands unconsciously stroking the bulge of her stomach. "It is no' due for a few months yet."

"Your husband must be pleased!" Isabeau exclaimed,

hoping to elicit some more information about her mysterious friend. Morag only nodded, smiled and changed the subject, however.

It was a long walk back to the palace from the beach. Isabeau was weary and footsore by the time she trudged across the bridge, though her eyes sparkled bluer than the sea itself with excitement. In that one afternoon she had learned more about the sea than in all Meghan's years of training.

Isabeau was scolded thoroughly for her tardiness in returning with the stonecrop herb and was told she would not be allowed to leave the palace grounds again if she was to take such liberties. She sighed and returned to her spitting-stool to dream of the sea. One day perhaps she would see a sea-serpent or blue whale, or even a Fairge. Morag had described to her how the mysterious sea people swam through the waves with their young clinging to their long hair, singing and whistling and diving for pearls. She thought it must be a wondrous sight.

Isabeau had arranged to meet her new friend a week later, so on the appointed day she sneaked out of the kitchen without telling anyone where she was going. Hopefully Latifa would think she was running an errand for one of the other servants and, with the palace still so crowded, would be so busy she might not miss Isabeau at all.

Isabeau had another reason for her trip into the forest. She had been fascinated by the horse lairds from Tìreich and troubled by the fact she still had the magical saddle and bridle. Cloudshadow had told her the riding tack belonged to the MacAhern clan and that its loss troubled them greatly. So Isabeau had decided to give it back to them.

As always Isabeau rode Lasair, who had an uncanny sense of when she wanted him. She had only to walk to the edge of the palace park and the stallion would be there, prancing with delight to see her. That morning she directed him to the hollow tree where she had hidden the saddle and bridle, and spent some time polishing its worn leather. She then saddled Lasair, who submitted to the magical bit and buckle as he would never have to any other form of constraint.

Isabeau urged Lasair to a canter down the long forest meadows, her tousled curls as red as his mane. Horse and rider moved in perfect rhythm, fused into one. Never had Isabeau felt the magic of Ahearn's Saddle so powerfully; it was as if they galloped on sparks, as if they would launch away from the ground and climb those streaming rays of sunlight high into the clouded heart of the sun.

At last Isabeau reined Lasair in and leaned forward to bury her face in his mane, stroking his damp neck. She regretted her decision now. The saddle had brought her and Lasair from Aslinn to Rhyssmadill in record time and given them the strength to keep moving long after their natural reserves had run dry. Now they were both strong again, the riding tack made the stallion fleeter than a bird and she as expert a rider as any thigearn.

Their swift passage had taken them near the highway that wound out of the western gate and into the forest. It was the main route from Rhyssmadill to the western lands, and was the way the horse lairds must pass on their journey home.

Isabeau removed the saddle and urged the stallion back into the forest, then sat on a waystone and waited. She heard them first, a low drumming that caused the ground to vibrate, leaves beginning to scatter. Then she smelled them, horse and sweat and dust, and then a cloud of fine powder billowed at the turn of the road. She got up, wiping hands damp with nervousness on her skirt. A cavalcade of horses and riders came round the corner, flags and pennants fluttering, metal bits and rings sparkling. At their head pranced a tall, antlered beast, rainbow-winged, with a dull golden hide feathered with color around its powerful hocks.

Isabeau tucked her crippled hand behind her and gave the most graceful curtsy she could manage. Kenneth

MacAhern raised his hand and the parade came to a stamping, jingling halt. The antlered creature shook its delicate head and pranced, neighing in disdain. So fascinated was she by its color-stroked wings that she could hardly pull her eyes away, but she looked up at the MacAhern and said, "Please, my laird, I have something which I believe belongs to ye."

He looked at her with shrewd hazel eyes, and she was conscious of at least six arrows aimed directly at her. Her color rose, but she met his eyes steadfastly and gestured to the saddle and bridle perched on the wayside. He glanced at it, then his gaze grew intent. With one easy, graceful motion he dismounted and the flying horse reared, spreading its wings. He strode past her and examined the saddle closely, then lifted it in his arms and came to her side. "How did ye come by this? How did ye ken it was ours?"

"It was given to me. I was told it belonged to ye, and its loss troubled ye."

"Who gave it to ye?"

Isabeau spoke with difficulty. "A friend. She had found it in an auld barn."

"Ye ken what it is?"

She nodded.

"Ye have a horse. Why do ye no' keep it for yourself?"

Wondering how he knew about Lasair, she said softly, "I want to. When I ride with the saddle, I feel I ken what it is to fly. But Lasair is a free horse—I have promised him never to use whip or spur, saddle or bridle . . ."

A smile crinkled his brown cheek, and the riders behind laughed and murmured. "Ye have a heart unto a Tìreichan. We too think our horses free," the MacAhern said to Isabeau. "I thank ye for the return o' the saddle. It is one o' the great relics o' our land and it has been missing for many generations. What is your name?"

"Isabeau."

"No family name?" She shook her head, and he

frowned, staring at her consideringly. "That is strange. Ye have the look o' the blood about ye."

"I'm a foundling," she told him.

He looked her over slowly and keenly, stroking his beard. "Do ye wish to travel with us? Is that why ye brought back the saddle?"

She shook her head. "I am apprenticed, I canna leave," she replied, though she cast a longing look at the glossy, muscular horses beginning to shift restlessly.

"Yet ye have the heart o' a thigearn. Your horse runs along the edge o' the forest, anxious for ye—and ye hide him from our view. Ahearn's Saddle makes ye feel that ye can fly. If ye wish to leave with us, we shall take ye."

"Thank ye but I canna leave. I have a task here," she tried to explain.

"So what can I offer ye in return for the saddle?"

Surprise crossed her face. "Nothing. I want nothing. I just wished . . . The saddle is no' mine. It helped me and supported me when I needed strength, but I need it no longer. It seemed fateful that ye were here, and I know no' when I would have the chance again. So I brought it. It's yours."

"Well, I thank ye again, Isabeau the Foundling." The MacAhern's long, brown fingers unfastened the brooch at his breast, and he gave it to her, pressing it into her calloused palm. "If ye change your mind, or if ye need my help, come to Tìreich. Give this to any o' my people and they will bring me to ye."

She glanced down at it, seeing the design of a rearing horse and flushed. "Is this no' your family crest? Should ye be giving it to me?"

He laughed. "It is only a trinket, lassie. I do no' wear the heirloom to ride through foreign lands. That is kept safe in Tìreich, I assure ye. Nay, I am glad to give it in return o' the saddle, which is a princely gift indeed."

Isabeau was about to protest again, but he bent and said to her softly, "We o' the horse clan do not believe in gifts without reciprocation. That means a debt is owed and we do no' like to be indebted."

She closed her fingers over the brooch and nodded. "Then thank ye, my laird," she said clearly, and he smiled and leapt onto the back of the flying horse.

"Then I look forward to meeting ye again, Isabeau the Foundling. I am sure the Spinners will bring the threads o' our lives together again."

It was the first time Isabeau had heard reference to the Spinners in months, and her eyes stung with tears. She nodded and stood back, and the flying horse sprang forward, its rainbow-colored wings outstretched, framing the tall man on its back. With a shout the other riders followed, streaming past Isabeau in a blur of chestnut, bay and black. Dust coated her but she stood watching until the entire cavalcade had passed.

She called Lasair to her and he came galloping out of the trees, his ears pricked with interest. He stared down the road, and she stroked his glossy neck. "Would ye have liked to have gone with them, Lasair?"

He neighed and shook his mane and pawed the ground, and she said, "Ye would no' have run quite so free in Tìreich, I think."

Hiding the brooch in her nyx-hair pouch, Isabeau swung onto Lasair's back and they trotted into the forest, a squall of rain rattling the leaves above. For some reason Isabeau felt lighter, freer. She was glad she had given back the saddle, and thought it was what Meghan would have wanted her to do.

Once she reached the coast, Isabeau dismounted and let the stallion graze as he wanted. She leant against the bulwark and looked at the sea. The sky above the far-distant islands was a clear apple-green. Long rays of sun slanted through the clouds, lighting the beach with warmth. It was cold and windy on the headland. Isabeau began to pace up and down, anxious to get down to the beach. At last, deciding Morag could not come, she scrambled down the ladder and wandered through the dunes. It felt good to be out in the fresh, damp air. Seagulls rose with the wind, screeching with joy. Isabeau lifted her head and screeched back at them, *Yes, wind strong, seagull flies, yes . . .*

Far away, silhouetted against the pale green sky, was a flock of white sails like giant seagull wings. Isabeau watched them in fascination, wondering what it must be like so far out to sea. The ships must be sailing in from the Fair Isles, and she wondered if perhaps it was the missing fleet returning to Eileanan. She laughed at her hopeful imagining—more likely it was the fishing flotilla, returning with nets filled with herring. Though she had never seen fishing boats with so many fat-bellied sails.

Pink clouds, lit beneath to molten gold, banded the sky from horizon to horizon. Their fiery ardor cooled. Isabeau saw the first shimmer of light from the rising of the moons glide across the rough, gray seas. Suddenly a freezing cold wave wet her to the waist, and she realized she had wandered far along the shore.

Isabeau glanced about her in sudden fear. She realized the tide had turned. Large, foam-flecked waves were galloping toward her. The sun had sunk behind the forest, and the shadow of the bulwark stretched over the sand, dusk turning the dunes to violet and gray. Already waves were splashing the massive wall further around the bend. If she was not quick, the way back to the ladder would be cut off.

Isabeau hurried back across the sands. Waves ate at her footprints. The tide was coming in with frightening speed. The sand that had been so warm twenty minutes ago was now scalloped with foam. She began to run.

Water was swirling above her knees when she at last reached the ladder. She had to struggle to climb it with the weight of her dripping skirts. With her feet still bare, the barnacles on the rungs cut her feet cruelly. The boots slung round her neck hampered her every move. Waves sucked at her and for a moment both her feet were swept off the ladder. She clung on and managed to pull herself higher.

Shaking with fatigue and cold, she could only climb slowly. It seemed as if the water was reaching for her with clawed hands, so fiercely did it tug her down. She was beginning to fail when a deep, feminine voice called to her from above. "Quickly, lassie, else ye'll be dinner for a sea-serpent. Reach for my hand."

With a fresh burst of energy, Isabeau clambered up the slippery steps and managed to grasp Morag's wrist. Strong fingers closed around hers and hauled her up the last few feet.

Isabeau clung to the iron poles and looked back down at the sea, now heaving gray and threatening against the stone bulwark. "It rises so far," she gasped.

"O' course it does, that is why the wall was built so tall. Quick, wriggle through. Ye look weary indeed, and I do no' want ye falling back into the sea."

Isabeau's legs were trembling so much she could hardly manage it, but slowly she made her way along the outside of the bulwark.

"Why did ye go down to the shore?" Morag's voice was stern and a little frightened. "Did ye no' remember the autumn equinox is only a few weeks away? And it's been stormy, the tides are running higher than they have since the spring!"

Isabeau nodded, angry with herself for forgetting. She turned and looked out to sea again. She could not believe how quickly the tide had turned. She gave a gasp. "Look!"

In the great swell thundering into shore were a number of sleek, black heads. They rode the waves as easily as any sea-stirk, diving and leaping out of the water as if enjoying the savage surge of the current. They were too far away to see anything of their features, but Isabeau had no doubt they were Fairgean. Morag looked where she pointed and a strange expression settled over her face.

"Come!" she cried. "We must be away from here!"

"Surely we are safe?" Isabeau asked. "They canna breach the wall . . ."

"If ye can climb the ladder and squeeze through the fence, what makes ye think the Fairgean canna?" Morag replied gravely. All color had gone from her cheeks, and she had crossed her arms over her breast as if afraid.

Fear flooded through Isabeau, and she took a few steps back from the bulwark. With a fast-beating heart, she stared at the Fairgean still cavorting in the waves off the beach. Her dream of seeing the sea people had come true, but Isabeau could only be afraid.

Morag said, "I must be getting back. Be careful, Red. Do no' go down to the beach with Fairgean in the waters—they will drag ye in and drown ye without hesitation." She heaved herself into her side-saddle, standing on a log so as to be able to put her foot into the stirrup.

Isabeau did not even wait for her horse's hooves to fade away before calling out with her mind for Lasair. He sensed her alarm and came at a gallop, and she swung on to his back without waiting for him to stop. He cantered all the way to the edge of the forest, only her riding skill keeping her on his back as branches whipped out of the dusk and massive tree trunks loomed close on either side. At last, scratched and bruised, Isabeau slid from his back and leaned her forehead against his damp neck. She thought frantically, *Be careful, Lasair.*

To her great surprise and joy, she heard faintly: *And ye . . .*

FIREWORKS

Donovan Slewfoot leaned on the railing, watching the pearly dawn tide swell toward him. Behind him the city was quiet and shuttered, but over the peaked islands the sun was easing out of a white mist. He slumped further along, staring with despondency at the rust circling the great bolts. The gates needed a good overhaul, but the Rìgh would not authorize the expenditure. The bulwark was in even worse condition, and seeing the great stones crumbling stabbed Donovan with anxiety. There were Fairgean in the seas, and the Rìgh could not see the wall should be repaired? Indeed, there was something strange about the MacCuinn's apathy. For all their faults, the MacCuinns had never been indifferent to the welfare of the people.

Out of the mist loomed the graceful shapes of a fleet of six great ships. The sails drooped from their masts, but the ships sailed in smoothly, carried by the force of the tide. Donovan Slewfoot frowned and packed his clay pipe thoughtfully, cramming the tobacco deep into the bowl with his spatulate thumb. The tobacco used to be given to him by traders from the Fair Isles when they sailed in with their cargo—a gift to speed the process of cargo checking and raising the ships through the locks.

The Fair Isles were the only place in all of the Far Islands where the plant would grow, for it liked a temperate climate. Tobacco and snuff were consequently rare and normally reserved for those with deep pockets. Donovan Slewfoot considered it one of the privileges of his position as harbormaster.

He lit the pipe, moodily watching the ships sail into the firth. They knew, these Tìrsoilleirean ships, that the best time to enter the Berhtfane was on the incoming tides. They seemed to know the times of the tides near as well as he did. And this tobacco he smoked, they had known to slip him a cord of it as they came through his gates. How had they known, and where did they get the tobacco? It surely did not grow on Tìrsoilleir's cool plains. He wondered about this as he wondered about many things that had happened these past years. But Donovan took his orders from the Rìgh, and the MacCuinns had said, "Let those white-sailed ships in."

One by one Donovan Slewfoot let the ships through the gates and into the locks. The tide lifted them and carried them, one by one, into the peaceful waters of the Berhtfane. Each one of the six gave him a cord of tobacco, with a nod or a stiff smile. Each one seemed innocent enough, the decks clear of anyone but brown-armed sailors and a few soldiers. But the hair on Donovan Slewfoot's neck lifted, and he put the tobacco away with a twist of his lip, and a feeling he should perhaps tell someone his thoughts. But who?

That night Dughall MacBrann was restless and unable to sleep. He was much troubled by the latest letter from his father, who lived in happy seclusion on the family's estates on the far side of Ravenshaw. The MacBrann was elderly now, and so absorbed in his many eccentric inventions and contraptions that he was rarely aware of what went on around him. His letters usually rambled on without much coherence, but this last letter was even more muddled than ever. In between describing his latest flying machine, exultation over a new litter of pups from his favorite hound, and complaints about his son's prolonged absence, Dughall's father had mentioned a visit by a horde of Bright Soldiers. Three paragraphs later, he had mentioned they had come wanting use of Ravenshaw's many hidden ports and bays, and two pages later, he said they had offered a ludicrous amount of money for the privilege. It had not occurred to the Mac-Brann to tell his long-suffering son what reply he had made, though a cryptic postscript that said, "sent them off with a flea in their ear" could have referred to either the Bright Soldiers or the puppies.

Dughall MacBrann could not have explained why his father's letter gave him such a profound sense of unease. It was not the scattered half thoughts, unfinished anecdotes and peculiar expressions which disturbed him so, for that was the usual epistolary style of the Prionnsa of Ravenshaw. It was not the knowledge that the Tìrsoil-leirean had asked his father for permission to use the bays, although that was food for thought indeed. It was not his telling of the sighting of strange ships in the seas, nor the stories of Fairgean in the rivers. It was a prickling down his spine that Dughall knew well. He felt danger hovering. It was this that had kept him tossing and turning in his bed, and this which caused him to quit his bed some hours before dawn.

He sat up, pulled on his long velvet bedgown and his fur-lined slippers, and made his way to the door. The palace was dark and hushed. He hesitated for a long moment, then made his way up the grand staircase to the Rìgh's quarters on the top floor. The bleary-eyed guards nodded to him and let him past, knowing Dughall MacBrann was the Rìgh's closest friend.

Dughall knew the other prionnsachan scorned him for remaining on good terms with Jaspar, for Dughall's mother, Mathilde NicCuinn, had been killed by the Red Guards on the Day of Reckoning. The shock of her death had caused his father—always an eccentric—to slip into amiable madness. Many of the lairds despised Dughall for his weakness in so meekly accepting his

mother's murder, although many had also lost relatives
in the Burning. "Young Dughall thinks to restore the
MacBrann clan's fortune," they whispered, "by being
the Rìgh's lickspittle . . ."

Dughall ignored the whispers. Indeed, what else could
he do? Since Dughall had discovered Jaspar in an agony
of guilt after the Day of Reckoning, the cousins had
been closer than ever. Jaspar had always been his best
friend as well as his cousin, and Dughall knew the power
of the enchantment laid upon him. He had decided long
ago to stand by Jaspar, and though the decision cost
him dear, he had never wavered from the course he had
set himself.

Jaspar slept, one arm flung over his head, his dark
curls damp with sweat. Dughall wrapped his robe more
tightly about him and sat in the chair by the bed. The
fire was sinking into embers, and it was growing cold as
the night swung toward day. He watched his cousin's
face, illuminated only by the flicker of the dying fire,
and castigated himself for being a fool. There was no
danger. Jaspar slept. The palace was quiet. He should
be in bed, sleeping the dreams of a man who had no
greater worry in life than how to pay his latest gam-
bling debts.

Dughall felt ice slide down his spine again, and he
clenched his fingers. It was no fancy, this presentiment
of danger. Dughall had felt it many times before, and
always that chill finger had preceded pain and loss and
sorrow. He propped his head in his hands, and prepared
to watch the last few hours of the night away.

The Bright Soldiers had spent the afternoon exploring
the fabled blue city of Dùn Gorm. Bride, the capital of
Tìrsoilleir, was large and grand, but not near as beautiful
as this dreamy and ornate city built from blue-gray marble. As they walked the streets, never faltering from
their rigid formation, they had passed other Bright Soldiers and touched their fists to their hearts, murmuring,
"Deus Vult."

That night, as the inns in the city filled with dissatisfied merchants, rowdy squires and riotous sailors, the Bright Soldiers had knelt in their cabins and said their prayers. When they had finished—some time later—they had lain down in their bunks with their swords by their side, and slept.

In the dark before dawn, when even the most determined reveller had finally stumbled into sleep, they rose, washed their bodies in cold water, dressed in their chain mail and prayed again. "Deus Vult!" they whispered. "Deus Vult!"

There were now fifteen Tìrsoilleir ships at rest in the Berhtfane. Six were galleons, with four masts and yards of furled sail. Six were three-masted caravels, faster and more maneuverable but dwarfed by their ponderous cousins. The rest were merchants' carracks, with two square sails and a mizzen.

From each ship small boats were lowered, some filled with soldiers that rowed with muffled oars to shore. The others were piled high with straw and manned by one man only, bare-chested and bare of foot. The straw-filled dinghies drifted across the harbor, flowering into flame. As sparks began to drift into the rigging and flame crept up the anchor ropes, the men dived under the water and cut the Eileanan ships' rudder ropes so they could not be steered.

Great tongues of flame began to billow from one merchant ship, and there were cries of confusion. Showers of sparks flew into the night like fireflies. Within twenty minutes most of the Eileanan ships were funeral pyres, the screams of those on board filling the night. The city was awake now, lights springing up all along the harbor wall, and somewhere an alarm bell was ringing. The men on board pulled back tarpaulins to reveal great breech-loading cannons on the ships' deck. Signals were sent to the other ships to do the same, and the caravels began to maneuver closer to shore. The cannons had only a short range and they wished to do as much damage as possible to Dùn Gorm.

The admiral of the Tìrsoilleirean navy was waiting for daylight before firing the cannons. They were difficult enough to load and aim without attempting to do so under the cover of darkness. He was also waiting for the signal from the shore that would tell him his soldiers had disabled the Red Guards' military headquarters and taken over the harbormaster's tower. Outside waited another fleet of Tìrsoilleirean ships, heavy with soldiers, and the gates needed to be opened to allow them into the Berhtfane.

At last it was light enough for him to see the streets were filled with fighting. He frowned. Obviously the soldiers had failed in their surprise attack. He was surprised to see many of the men resisting the Bright Soldiers were not dressed in the red uniforms of the Banrìgh's Guards, and he wondered who they were, to fight so fiercely. He raised his hand, then dropped it sharply.

From every ship the cannons boomed, pelting the city with solid bronze balls. He coughed, enveloped in clouds of foul-smelling smoke, and wiped his streaming eyes. When the black smoke cleared, he was pleased to see the city had suffered a great deal of damage.

Again and again he ordered the cannon to fire, not only on the city fortifications but also on Rhyssmadill itself. It was a difficult target for the ships, towering so high above their masts on its great finger of stone, but anything the Admiral could do to ensure the palace fell quickly was worth the attempt.

The fire had sunk to ashes, the darkness and silence in the chamber complete, when Dughall lifted his head. The urge to pick Jaspar's wasted figure up in his arms and carry him away was almost overwhelming. Suddenly the fear that Jaspar had died in his sleep surged through him, and he felt around on the pillow until he found his cousin's frail wrist. A pulse still scurried there. It quickened at the touch of his fingers, and a feeble voice said, "Who's there?"

"It is I, Dughall." He felt the wrist slacken in relief.

"Ye come to watch me sleep, Dugh?" The Rìgh's voice was sleepily affectionate. "Ye are afraid I shall die in the night?"

"I am afraid," Dughall answered hesitantly. "I fear for your safety, Jaspar, though ask me no' why."

"My death is close," Jaspar whispered. "I can feel it."

"Obh obh! The cracked cup lasts longest, ye ken that!"

"They said, when I was but a bairn, that I had Talent," Jaspar mused in the darkness. "Give me this, Dughall—if any Talent be left in me, it is to ken the coming o' my own death."

Dughall was shaken. "I hope no', Jaspar, for these be times when we need a strong Rìgh."

"I want to return to Lucescere. I miss the Jewels o' Rionnagan gleaming in the light, I miss the Shining Waters, I miss the gardens and running through the maze. Do ye remember how we used to play chase-and-hide in the maze? They say it disappeared the day the Tower burned." Jaspar sighed. "Sometimes I still think I can hear the Lodestar calling . . . My babe will need to be bonded to it, it canna be the first MacCuinn in four hundred years no' to touch the Lodestar . . ." His voice came in spurts as his energy failed him.

The sense of danger was now so close Dughall felt it at his shoulder, breathing a polar wind down his spine. "Jaspar," he said urgently. "Something is wrong! I can feel it."

"It is almost dawn. I would like to see the dawn again before I die."

"I could help ye to the window," Dughall said eagerly.

"I canna walk. My legs shake, and my heart pounds like a drum."

Dughall bent and gathered his cousin's form to his breast, frightened at how light he was. Jaspar had never been tall, like most of the MacCuinns, but he weighed no more than a child now.

"Take me to the west window," Jaspar begged. "I want to see the dawn on the Whitelock Mountains. I do no' want to see the sea." He gave a superstitious shudder, and pressed his arm closer about Dughall's neck.

Dughall carried him across the suite and set him down so he could draw back the curtain and open the long windows. Jaspar leant against him, shivering in the cold. With an exclamation, Dughall stripped off his bedgown and wrapped it around the Rìgh's emaciated form. He helped his cousin over the doorsill, and they stepped out on to the small balcony.

In his luxurious suite of rooms in the royal wing of the palace, Baron Neville of St. Clair leaned on his window sill and watched the first bright blossoming of flame with austere pleasure. "Deus vult!" he cried, and rubbed his hand lovingly over the sword-hilt.

The guild-master of the Ancient Guild of Firework Magicians had been useful indeed. With a little persuasion, he had surrendered the secrets of making gunpowder, and now the Bright Soldiers were assured of victory.

The recipe for gunpowder had been carefully guarded by the Ancient Guild for over a thousand years. The guild sold their magical substance to the prionnsachan at a very high price for blasting, quarrying and metal smelting. The secrets of making the explosive powder had been brought from the Other World, but the white crystalline substance used to make it was rare here—found only in the northern countries of Siantan, Carraig and Tìrsoilleir.

For many years saltpetre had been among those countries' most lucrative exports, for all Eileanan loved fireworks and all the prionnsachan needed explosives for their industries. The Ancient Guild of Firework Magicians had been one of the wealthiest of all the guilds, and the most secretive about their activities.

The fireworks powder had always been used in weaponry, but both muskets and cannons were slow to load and fire, prone to exploding at the wrong moment, and completely useless in damp weather. With saltpetre so rare, its use had primarily been reserved for industrial reasons, particularly in the past four hundred years. Since Aedan MacCuinn set himself up as Rìgh, there had been none of the civil war which had divided Eileanan for so long, and so the use of such high-powered weaponry had fallen out of use.

Tìrsoilleir had been no exception. Although its many limestone caves were rich in saltpetre, there had been no civil war in the Bright Land since the last attempt of the MacHilde family to regain their throne. The dour soldier society did not approve of fireworks, and so the Ancient Guild of Firework Magicians had only a small factory in Bride. After the Fealde, God bless her soul, decided to rid the world of the heretical, witch-loving Eileanans, they had tried to buy the secret from the guild, but they had all preferred to die rather than give up the recipe.

This had presented only a temporary hitch to their plans, fortunately. There had been enough stocks of the gritty gray powder at the Bride factory to allow the legions to be trained in the use of the harquebus, and to allow the military engineers to design a more efficient cannon that could be bolted to the ships' decks. By the time their gunpowder was running out, they had signed a treaty with the Banprionnsa of Arran. She had no gunpowder herself, nor saw any need for it with her foul sorceries, but she commanded the Mesmerdean, who could infiltrate any stronghold. The marsh demons had led a company of Bright Soldiers into the heart of Dùn Eidean itself and had helped carry away sacks of gunpowder, as well as the slack body of the guild-master. With the Mesmerdean's hypnotic talents, they had easily beguiled him into giving up the recipe, and killed him afterward, along with anyone else who knew the secret in Blessém.

It had been a clever plan, this surprise attack on the Rìgh, and had been carefully coordinated. The treaties with Margrit of Arran and the pirates of the Fair Isles had allowed them to attack Dùn Eidean and Dùn Gorm simultaneously. The diplomatic party had flattered the

Rìgh's conceit and paved the way for the fleet of merchant ships at a time when all of southern Eileanan was hungry for trade. The galleons, welcomed in the Berhtfane with open arms, had concealed soldiers and siege machines. The stealing of the gunpowder recipe gave the Bright Soldiers the weapons with which to fight off the superior force of the Rìgh.

It had been a stroke of genius to strike in the aftermath of the Lammas festivities. The barracks were all nursing hangovers, and Rhyssmadill was stuffed with the riches of the land which the prionnsachan had paid in tithes. Already the Fealde was planning a cloth-of-gold tapestry to drape the altar of Bride's cathedral and a jeweled cross to hang above it.

The rich lands of southern Eileanan would be theirs! The corn and barley fields, the saltpans, the abundant forests, the mountains rich in ore and jewels, the life-giving river, the huge harbor and gentle shores would all be theirs. Baron Neville's austere lips almost smiled. "Deus vult!" he murmured.

His lieutenant, Benedict the Holy, stood by his side, the only sign of satisfaction on his impassive countenance the faint gleam of his eyes. "Time, do ye think, my laird?"

"Aye, time indeed," Baron Neville replied and picked up his helmet, fitting it over his cropped gray hair with finicky care before striding from the room.

The upper floors of the palace were very quiet. A few lanterns glowed in the corridors, but otherwise all was dark. Baron Neville loosened his dagger in its sheath. If he felt any compunction about the task he was about to perform, no sign of it showed on his ascetic features. His grim mouth was folded firmly, and his fingers were steady. The twelve other Tìrsoilleirean who had been quartered in Rhyssmadill itself would now be creeping toward the drawbridge, prepared to do what they could to speed the fall of the palace. Even if they were unable to damage the mechanism to open and close the bridge, they could kill or wound many of the guards on duty and perhaps wedge open the portcullis to the inner bailey.

Their white cloaks streaming behind them, Baron Neville and Benedict the Holy climbed the grand staircase to the highest floor, where the Rìgh and Banrìgh's personal quarters were. The guards at the top of the stairs jumped to attention, their spears crossing smartly. If they thought it odd to find the leader of the Tìrsoilleirean diplomatic party creeping through the palace in the wee small hours, they had no chance to express their puzzlement. Both died quickly and silently, their bodies hidden behind the tapestries that hung over the stairwell.

The guards outside the Rìgh's door died as quickly, though their bodies were left to lie where they had fallen. The baron's fingers trembled with excitement as he eased open the door of the Rìgh's suite of rooms. It was dark inside. The fire was dead, the only light sliding through a crack in one of the curtains. He tiptoed across the rug, the knife in his hand slippery with sweat, Benedict at his back. The baron had never before been in the Rìgh's own quarters and so had to guess where the bed was. His fingers encountered the soft plushness of the velvet coverlet, and he followed it higher until he felt the swell of a pillow beneath his fingers. His heart hammering, the baron and his lieutenant raised high their daggers. With loud cries of "Deus vult!," they thrust their knives deep into the yielding softness of the bed. Again and again they stabbed, shouting, "See how witch-lovers die, MacCuinn?"

To the west, the outline of the mountains was just beginning to lift from the darkness. The moons were setting, round as wheels of cheese and near as orange. Even Gladrielle was bright hued, while the shadows on Magnysson's rump were heavy, like the marks left after the slap of a hand.

Dughall was filled with ice inside and out. He smelled burning, and from the corner of his eye saw the ugly stain of smoke against the paling sky. Together they watched the mountains spring to life before them, and breathed in the smoke-tainted air. Danger was cold steel against the nape of his neck. From the Rìgh's bedroom, they heard exultant voices crying: "Deus vult! Die, witch-lover!"

Immediately all Dughall's misgivings crystallized and he knew exactly what he had feared. Jaspar turned his head, his body rigid. "Bright Soldiers."

"Aye," Dughall whispered. He drew Jaspar back into the shelter of the wall, dread coiled like a snake in his belly. They were unarmed, dressed only in thin night-gowns and slippers. For the Bright Soldiers to have penetrated the Rìgh's own suite meant the guards must be dead. Any moment the Tìrsoilleirean would realize the Rìgh's bed was empty, and they would search the suite.

"They will murder Maya!"

"Quietly, my Rìgh, else they will find and murder us," Dughall replied, casting his mind about for someone who could help them. He sent an urgent mind-message to Latifa, hoping she was awake, hoping she would heed the call. He knew the old cook worshipped the ground on which the Rìgh trod and had the force of character to overcome any objections the guards might have to obeying her orders.

From the harbor came the sound of explosions. The wind turned acrid, smoke billowing past the spire. It was brown against the pale sky. Within the room there was the sound of shouting. The Bright Soldiers had evidently discovered the Rìgh was missing from his bed. Dughall pressed back against the wall, one hand clamped on the Rìgh's thin arm. The curtains swished aside and a man stepped out, a dagger held at the ready.

In one clean, swift action, Dughall stepped forward and kicked the soldier hard in the small of his back. The man stumbled forward and half fell over the stone balustrade. For a moment he teetered, shouting with alarm, the knife falling from his grasp. Dughall did not wait, but caught the man about the legs and tipped him over. With a scream he fell, his white-clad body tumbling over and over. It took him only a few seconds to fall hundreds of feet to the steep-angled roof below. He landed with a sickening thud.

His witch senses screaming beware, Dughall whirled around in time to see another man rushing toward him through the billowing curtains. He too wore chain mail beneath his white surcoat, the scarlet fitché cross like a stain of blood on his torso. Dughall had time only to lurch sideways as the dagger in the soldier's hand whistled past him. It struck the stone wall, missing his stomach by inches, but before Dughall had time to do more than regain his balance, the dagger struck again. It penetrated deep into his side, bringing with it a cold so intense Dughall could do nothing more than cry aloud and fall to his knees. The dagger stabbed again and Dughall threw up what power he could to deflect the blade. The soldier hissed through his teeth as the dagger was wrenched awry in his hand and kicked Dughall brutally in his wound, crying, "Sorcery!"

For a moment Dughall could muster no will, no desire, to strike back. He forced his eyelids to open and saw the burly figure sail over his head. His eyes were wide open, staring with terror, his mouth shrieking. Dughall clutched his bleeding wound with both his hands and looked up at Jaspar. The Rìgh's hand was stretched out, the fingers splayed. Horror and triumph were mingled together on his face. He said shakily, "Seems I have more Talent left than I thought I did."

A long line of Tìrsoilleirean marched up the highway, the rising sun glinting on their silver mailshirts and the winding line of their pikes. As they marched, the Bright Soldiers surveyed the rich countryside with covetous eyes. They did not notice that the fields were empty of workers, despite it being harvest time and the sun already risen. Neither did they notice the absence of the fine flocks for which Blessém was famous. Not one white fleecy sheep or one milk-heavy goat was to be seen anywhere in the meadows, although the goat-keep should have called the goats to pasture hours ago. Unheeding they marched on, filled with the glow of righteousness. They were professional soldiers, not farmers. Most had lived all their life in the military barracks in Bride, and they had a profound contempt for the farmers who provided their food and materials.

The Berhtilde raised her hand, and the long line of soldiers stopped in perfect time. She rose in her stirrups and stared down the valley. On a low hillside to the west the walls and spires of Dùn Eidean rose above the placid waters of a small loch. The soldiers fingered their swords and harquebuses and prepared themselves for the battle to come. They had already sent on their messengers to beguile the city and confidently expected to find it open and waiting for them. They knew the prionnsa and his family were still traveling back from the Lammas Congress, so there was no one in the city to take command.

The Berhtilde frowned. Although the city was too far away to see more than its shape, she did not share the confidence of her soldiers. It had occurred to her that more people should be out and about. Blessém was closely populated, the villages lying no more than a day's walk away from each other. Yet they had seen no one since they had struck camp and marched for Dùn Eidean. She shrugged and gave the order to march on.

By the time they reached the shores of the loch, the soldiers were as grim-faced as she was. Not only were the gates of the city shut tight, but outside a large force of men were drawn up in squares and columns. Many were dressed in the uniform of the city soldiery, but there were also five hundred men and women armed with pitchforks, axes and rusty swords. There was implacable determination on their faces. With a curse, the Berhtilde realized all their advantages of surprise, numbers and position were lost. The Blessém folk had the walls at their backs and advantage of height, and there were nearly as many of them as there were of the Bright Soldiers. Nonetheless, none had the advantage of their war training nor any gunpowder. With a gesture, she ordered her soldiers into position. The Fealde of Bride had said Dùn Eidean must be taken, and so taken it would be.

Donovan Slewfoot had woken well before the dawn, as he always did. He had eaten his porridge with a dash of whiskey, as he always did, and had gone out to smell the wind. He was still greatly troubled, but his first pipe of the day helped soothe him, and he leaned on the railing, enjoying the ripple of stars in the water.

The first flowering of flame had caused him to straighten, clenching his pipe in his big fist. As one ship after another began to burn, he hurried back into his gate-tower and began to sound the alarm. He rang the bell until his arms ached, and then hurried out to see what he could.

Red light from the burning city shone on the sails of a fleet of ships sailing toward him out of the dawn, while a band of Bright Soldiers hurried toward the watch-tower, grim determination on their faces and long swords in their hands.

He knew at once what they intended. If the Bright Soldiers gained control of the river-gates, their remaining soldiers could be brought safely within the bulwark and all of southern Eileanan would lie open to their forces. If he could somehow manage to jam the gates, then those dozen galleons would be forced to turn and tack against the tide to avoid being shipwrecked on the shore. At best they would sail straight into the gates and be destroyed anyway. Donovan Slewfoot had been harbormaster of the Berhtfane for thirty years. He had worked on the canals since catching a foot in the gates' machinery as a mere lad. He knew the gates better than he knew the craggy lines of his own face. He knew exactly what to do to sabotage them.

Working quickly, he lay on his back and inched under the massive chains, an iron spanner in his hand. Carefully he wedged the spanner into a gap that would prevent the chains from shifting, at least for a while.

The pounding on the massive door at the base of the tower stopped, and for a moment there was silence. *Given up already?* Donovan Slewfoot thought with a wry smile. Then there was an almighty bang that made him clap his hands over his ears, and the tower filled with evil-smelling smoke. The harbormaster was taken aback. *Wha' sorcery is this? Surely the Bright Soldiers are as witchcraft-fearing as the rest o' Tìrsoilleir . . .*

The sound of feet pounding up the stairs caused his heart to slam. Limping as fast as he could, Donovan Slewfoot went out onto the walkway and locked the door behind him. As he hurried across the top of the gates, he heard the soldiers whipping the great horses into motion. Slowly the wheel turned, and the gates began to swing apart. Donovan still had some distance to cover before crossing the crack where the two arms of the gate met. With a sinking feeling he hastened his gait, trying to reach it before the gates swung too far apart.

Just then the gate shuddered to a halt and he was thrown to his knees. The crack between the gates was only a foot apart but it was a long jump for an old man with a crippled foot. Donovan Slewfoot wedged his stick under his arm, prayed to Eà and jumped. Thanks to his quick reflex in catching hold of the rail, he made it.

Behind him the Bright Soldiers were signaling to the ships bombarding the city with fire. As he hurried along the walkway, he saw a caravel turn and head toward him, unfurling its mizzen sail to catch the dawn breeze. Then he saw the dark mouths of the cannons, and it dawned on him what they meant to do. *The fools!* he thought as he loped forward, desperate to reach the opposite shore. *Do they no' understand the Berhtfane will flood?*

There was a massive boom. Smoke billowed out of the cannons. Ten bronze balls crunched into the first of the gates. As they shuddered under the force of the cannonballs, water spurted through the spiderweb of cracks, quickly turning into thundering water-jets. Just as the gate smashed under the force, Donovan Slewfoot threw himself onto the eastern shore. Though water poured over his body, dragging him sideways, his powerful hands clenched the railing and held him firm.

When at last the flood subsided, Donovan stood on the wall and looked to see the results of the Bright Soldiers' action. It was far better than he could ever have hoped for. Not only had the fleet of galleons hoping to enter the gates been swept away by the force of the escaping water, but chaos reigned among those ships left in the habor. The Rhyllster had not flowed freely to the sea in over four hundred years, and the level of the Berhtfane had sunk alarmingly. Many of the burning ships had sunk, littering the harbor with obstacles the Tìrsoilleirean ships found difficult to avoid in the relentless outward sweep of the river. Some had been smashed upon the wrecks, others had run aground on the rocky shore. Many of the caravels and carracks had survived, being more maneuverable than the top-heavy galleons, but their decks were in confusion. It would take some time for the Tìrsoilleirean ships to regroup, and with the river-gates gone, the harbor was no longer the safe haven it had been. The ship commanders would now have to contend with the tides, the river and the Fairgean.

Unfortunately, most of the Bright Soldiers were safe on shore and the fighting in the town was fierce, smoke pouring from the burning buildings. Donovan Slewfoot gripped his club and began to limp toward the city. He still had a few fighting years left in him, praise Eà!

Isabeau had been woken by the first explosion. She sat up in bed, rubbing the sleep from her eyes, trying to catch the last remnants of nightmare. Again the ships' cannons sounded, and she scrambled to the floor, sure now the sound of attack was no dream. Her narrow window looked out onto the stables and offered no view of the firth, so Isabeau wrapped her plaid around her nightgown and ran out into the corridor. The halls were filled with other servants, in nightgowns and nightcaps, all milling about uselessly. Isabeau hurried through to the upper floor where there was a window which overlooked the harbor. There she found a crowd watching the lurid play of the city in flame.

Isabeau stared out at the harbor, alight with burning ships. Her sharp eyes saw the dim shapes of the Tirsoilleirean caravels slipping about the harbor leaving behind trails of flame and destruction. She saw the vicious fighting spilling into every street and square in the city, and the galleons at the wharf unloading great wooden platforms which she knew would be transformed into siege machines for the taking of Rhyssmadill. It seemed her dreams had been prophetic.

Isabeau slipped back to her room and dressed hurriedly. She swiftly packed a few belongings in her satchel and caught up her plaid from the chair, then she hurried back through the crowded corridors, casting out her senses in search of Latifa.

To her surprise she felt Latifa high in the palace. For a moment she hesitated, but instinct told her she should stay close to her mentor. Latifa had the Key, and Isabeau knew she could not let it be trapped by a long siege when Meghan needed it in Lucescere. At the worst, she would have to take it from Latifa by force or trickery, but Isabeau was sure the cook would see the seriousness of the situation as clearly as she did herself.

Confusion reigned in the high-ceilinged halls. Servants were running everywhere, still dressed in their nightclothes. Sprawled across the floor of the front hall were the bodies of three Bright Soldiers. Although she had seen death before, there was something about the pools of blood glistening on the marble that sickened Isabeau.

A band of guards ran down the stairs, their swords drawn. From the inner bailey came the sound of fighting. Isabeau hurried up the stairs. Someone grasped her and shouted in her face, ordering her to fetch water to help quell a screaming, weeping woman. Isabeau shook herself free and hurried on, all her senses attuned to the proximity of danger.

She reached the palace heights. There were no guards at the head of the steps, and she saw blood on the pale blue marble. Her heart pounded in her chest. Keeping close to the wall, she slipped down the corridor. Two bodies were slumped before the Rìgh's own quarters, their throats cut horribly. Blood was splashed on the walls and puddled on the floor. Isabeau heard Latifa's voice and hurried forward, her stomach churning.

The Rìgh was sitting up in his bed, a furred gown thrown round his bony shoulders. Lying against him was Dughall MacBrann, his white nightgown drenched with blood. His face was pasty, his breathing quick and shallow.

Latifa was on her knees by the bed, tearing his night-gown open. She was still in her nightclothes and would have looked absurd at any other time, her great bulk unhindered by corsets, her gray hair screwed up into papers. She turned her head as Isabeau ran in.

"Guid lassie! Did ye bring your herbs?"

Isabeau shook her head, trying to control her ragged breathing.

"Never mind, we can use the Rìgh's medicines for now. Come help me, the laird has been stabbed. An attempt was made on the Rìgh's life, but he is safe now, thank Eà!" In her perturbation, Latifa did not realize she had used a witches' oath and Isabeau cast a scared glance at the Rìgh's face. He was pale but composed, and gave no reaction to the cook's words. He held Dughall firmly against his shoulder.

It was an ugly wound. After they had cleaned it thoroughly, Isabeau carefully stitched the ragged lips of skin together and dabbed it with a herbal potion to quicken the healing.

Isabeau was just knotting the makeshift bandage together when feet hammered up the stone stairway. They all tensed and looked to the door. Latifa got to her feet and stood tight-fisted before the bed as if ready to guard the Rìgh with her own body. It was a brigade of palace guards, swords drawn.

"We are under siege, Your Highness!" the leader cried. "The Tìrsoilleirean have attacked the city! Dùn Gorm is lost, and the soldiers are at the palace gates!"

The Rìgh began to issue quick orders, his eyes feverishly bright.

"We must get ye to safety before they break through the gates!" Dughall cried. The Rìgh began to make objections, but his cousin cried frantically, "Think o' your unborn babe, Jaspar, think o' Maya! Ye canna stay with the Bright Soldiers at your very gates."

"Rhyssmadill will no' fall," Jaspar said, surprised. "Rhyssmadill has never fallen."

"The river-gates have been destroyed, Your Highness," the soldier said desperately. "All o' Clachan and Blessém lie open before the Tìrsoilleirean army, and Dùn Eidean's beacon has been lit—we can see its glare from the highest tower. We should retreat and regroup, prepare to defend the highlands."

"Lucescere!" Dughall cried. "We must get ye and the Banrìgh to Lucescere! Ye will be safe there."

"Lucescere," Jaspar repeated dreamily. "Very well, we shall go to Lucescere. Latifa! We must make ready. Start packing up—take only what is needful for the journey to Lucescere. Guards! Call the chancellor! Rhyssmadill must no' fall!"

The green meadows around Dùn Eidean were churned into mud, stained with blood and littered with the bodies of the slain. Many wore the silver mail of the Bright Soldiers; most wore the brown homespuns of crofters.

On the city ramparts an old woman stood, wrapped well in velvet and furs against the wind. Tears ran down the wrinkles of her face. She shook her fist at the battle that raged around the base of the ancient walls.

Suddenly there was a massive explosion that shook the city walls. Black smoke mushroomed above the walls, and the Dowager Banprionnsa coughed and covered her mouth with her hands. When the smoke drifted clear, she realized with horror that a hole had been blown in the outer wall. The Bright Soldiers were cheering; and the defenders broke and ran, scrambling to get back as the invaders charged in a silver-glinting wave.

"Damn ye!" she shouted, but her words were caught by the wind and tossed away. She watched helplessly as the enemy prepared to fire again, and an idea came to her. She had been born in Siantan, home of the mighty weather witches. As a girl she had spent eight years at the Tower of Storm, as had all the children of the great lairds. Although witchcraft and witchcunning were not taught until a child had been accepted into the Coven as an apprentice, she had learned many a trick from the older students, including how to keep rain away from picnic days.

The Dowager Banprionnsa did not know what evil sorceries the Bright Soldiers used to so destroy the ancient wall of Dùn Eidean, but clearly the element of fire was involved. She shut her eyes, clenched her fists, and chanted under her breath:

"Come hither, spirits of the west, bringing rain,
Come hither, spirits of the east, bringing wind,
Come hither, spirits of the west, bringing rain,
Come hither, spirits of the east, bringing wind,"

until she felt a fine mist of rain dampen her face. She opened her eyes and saw a gray deluge sweeping across the loch toward her. Far below, the Bright Soldiers manning the cannons were desperately trying to cover their fuses but the rain was soaking into everything. She saw them curse and throw down their flint boxes in anger, and smiled wearily. For the first time in decades she gave thanks to Eà, standing on the city walls with the rain pelting her gray head. The cannons did not fire again.

The palace was thrown into turmoil as the retreat was ordered. Latifa the Cook sent servants scurrying into every storeroom and larder as she packed provisions for the journey. Out in the courtyard, horses neighed, rearing in terror at the smell of smoke and fear. The servants of the prionnsachan still in residence scurried to pack their fine velvets, while screams of hysteria rose from every fine suite of rooms. The palace seanalair was shouting orders, while grim-faced soldiers ran to arm the walls.

The carriages of the aristocrats were the first to leave, guarded heavily. As they rumbled over the bridge, the guards on the outer walls shouted in dismay. The gates into the city had fallen, and fighting was spilling into the park. The coachmen whipped up their horses and the gilded carriages swayed wildly as they raced down the road toward the back gate.

Isabeau was frantically helping the other servants pile the wagons with barrels, baskets and parcels. She could hear the sound of fighting very close, and the screams of pain and hatred sent adrenalin pumping through her veins. "Quickly, Isabeau!" Latifa cried. "The enemy are upon us—we must flee! They will close the gates and raise the drawbridge any moment now!"

Another fully laden wagon thundered out of the courtyard, piled high with bags of gold, precious plate and jewels, the tiny form of the Chancellor of the Exchequer perched amongst the trunks and sacks like a bird. There was only one wagon left, the great bulk of Latifa already perched on the seat with the driver. Isabeau threw her satchel up, then suddenly remembered the little spit-dogs still tied to the spit-wheels in the kitchen. She raced into the kitchen, untied them in haste and ran back, a dog under each arm. She managed to scramble onto the wagon just as it wheeled around, the driver whipping the horses frantically. She would never have managed it if it had not been for Sukey, who reached down and seized the dogs so Isabeau could vault onto the laden back. Sukey's tight grip saved her from tumbling off as the wagon thundered out of the palace gates and across the narrow bridge. Behind them the gates slammed shut and the drawbridge shuddered upward.

"Ye fool!" Sukey said, her round cheeks for once without any color at all. "Must ye be always risking yourself for a dumb animal!"

Isabeau could only hug the spit-dogs to her, breathless. As the wagon swung onto the road, fighting surged up against it. One division of Bright Soldiers had managed to strike through the defending soldiers and was trying desperately to stop the Rìgh's retreat. She saw soldiers, their faces distorted with the lust of battle, press close to the side of the wagon, and she shrank back with a cry. Their silver mailshirts flashed in the sunshine, their claymores and maces clotted with blood and flesh. Ahead a line of white-clad soldiers lifted harquebuses, resting them on wooden stakes driven into the ground. They exploded with a loud bang and a cloud of foul-smelling smoke, and many of the Red Guards fell. Again the harquebusiers fired, and the driver of Isabeau's wagon tumbled off his seat, a red flower blossoming between his eyes. The horses plunged madly, and Latifa seized the reins and urged the terrified horses into a gallop. They surged over the line of harquebusiers before they had had time to reload, knocking them beneath the iron wheels of the wagon. As the Bright Soldiers screamed, Isabeau covered her face with her hands.

The wagon thundered on, the Red Guards forcing the Bright Soldiers back. Isabeau looked back at Rhyssmadill. Its delicate spires were half obscured by thick billows of black smoke as the city beyond burned. Desperately she wondered if Lasair would know to flee, or if he would wait for her along the fringes of the park. She sent a frantic mind-message, but there was no response.

They reached the backwoods gate, the soldiers securing it behind them to slow any pursuit by the Bright Soldiers. The forest pressed in, so that branches scraped the side of the wagon, the wheels rattling with broken twigs. One of the outriders trotted up close and held up a hand to Isabeau. With a glad cry she recognized Rior-

dan Bowlegs and called to him. "Guid to see ye, Red,"
he called back. "Do no' be feared now, will ye? Riordan
Bowlegs will look after ye!"

Isabeau sat back, feeling much happier. A stir of excitement quickened her blood. For weeks she had been
worrying about the Key and how to get it to Lucescere.
Yet here she and Latifa were, traveling to the old palace
in the Rìgh's own party. Indeed, the Spinners had taken
a hand in the weaving.

ing to another, and books. "No, ye've woken, my laird,
ye're no' rightly. And I ken ye've been eating yourself
ill like I'd be daith o' strapped to yon bed. Are ye
had ached "Watha" as the whisper being her to
cry vanished...man now...

ON THE ROAD

Why...yet where are...
I" mused Lady Cul...be said. "Donald,
...to are in the tent, he that could, and did
exclaiming, "Come tha! Damna! so's so...
For there are close...his danger... something...
his run...

by the Cnoc'dh lo a the "I decause for...our
tribe, hearts. Anghu had smiled... there's any
danger...

I'll take to his bow ye know where to find as my

The wolf ran swiftly, her nose to the ground, her
long, lean body bounding over rocks and bushes.
Far below the Muileach River thundered through
its gorge, and the faces of the men riding close behind
were wet with its high-flung spray.

Anghus was white-faced and tense-shouldered, his
face still raw and bruised from his tumble down the hill.
He had woken more than a day after the departure of
the winged prionnsa, feeling as if he had drunk a dram
too many. His head aching, his throat parched, he had
opened his eyes blearily as the wolf had nudged him
with her nose. Disorientated, he had stared up at the
canvas overhead. "Where am I?"

"We be at the rebels' encampment," Donald had said
soothingly, holding a cup of water to his lips. "Lie still,
my laird, ye've taken a nasty knock."

Anghus had swallowed water obediently, trying to
make his brain work. The roof of the tent was wavering,
coming toward him, receding. He closed his eyes, set his
hands flat to the ground, trying to regain his equilibrium.

When he opened them again, a stranger was standing
against the tent flap, a tall, lithe man with daggers bris-

tling in his belt and boots. "So, ye've woken, my laird," he said very politely. "And how are ye feeling yourself?"

"Like I fell beneath a stampede o' *geal'teas*," Anghus had replied. "What happened? What am I doing here?"

"A very guid question, my laird," the man answered suavely. "A question I'd be liking an answer to myself."

"Who are ye? Where am I?"

"I, my laird, am Cathmor the Nimble, son o' Desmond Cobbler. Ye are in the heart o' the rebel camp, and I'd be warning ye, my laird, no' to make any hasty moves for there are close on five hundred men surrounding this tent . . ."

"By the Centaur, do ye think I feel up to making any hasty moves!" Anghus had snapped. "Where's my daughter?"

"I'd like to ken how ye knew where to find us, my laird?" There had been a silky undercurrent of menace in the rebel's voice.

"I followed the MacCuinn lad," Anghus had replied, shading his eyes with his hand. "Where is he? I saw him riding out . . . Where's my daughter?" The quality of the silence made Anghus uncover his eyes, and he saw Cathmor had unsheathed his dagger, frowning fiercely. "For Eà's sake, man, I'm no enemy o' yours or o' the MacCuinn."

"Are ye no' in Maya the Ensorcellor's service? Did ye no' capture Meghan NicCuinn and give her into the hands o' the Awl?"

"Well, yes, but she understood . . . Put the dagger away, lad, ye're unnerving me. I see I shall have to tell ye the whole story, and then ye'll understand." Briefly and hastily Anghus had explained the events that had led him to the rebel encampment. "So ye see, I just want to find my daughter. Meghan said she thought she was here."

Cathmor had stared at him calculatingly. "She's no' here, my laird. There was a young lassie named Finn, but she rode out with the prionnsa."

"Where have they gone?"

"That I shall no' tell ye, my laird. The prionnsa recognized ye, put ye into my care and told me to keep ye safe." There was a slight stress on the last words.

"Have a heart, lad. I swear to ye I care no' what ye are planning."

"So ye say, my laird. Indeed, it does no' matter for soon we shall be gone. We shall keep ye here until ye can do us no harm, then ye shall be free to go. For some reason, His Highness did no' want me to silence you permanently." Cathmor had caressed his dagger, adding, "Do no' think I shall no' kill ye if ye try anything, though, my laird. We have all fought too long to risk our plans now."

Nothing Anghus said had changed the rebel's mind. To his frustration, the prionnsa and his gillie were confined to the one small tent, Casey Hawkeye and the young piper to another. Tabithas paced the floor restlessly, whining, but each time they even looked outside they were menaced with claymores.

The next day they had heard the unmistakable noises of a large body of men packing up and moving out. Their guards kept them incarcerated for another day and night, then drugged their food so all four men and the wolf fell into a heavy sleep. When they had woken, the corrie had been empty.

At Anghus's command, Tabithas had put her nose to the ground and led them on the trail of Fionnghal's party. Through the valleys and gorges the wolf tracked her, the men riding close behind, until they came to the raging torrent of the Muileach River. They had been following the jagged course of the river's gorge for several days now, but had not been able to catch up with the winged prionnsa's party. Although Anghus was light-headed and sick still, he spurred his horse on relentlessly, certain now that the beggar-girl they called Finn was his missing daughter.

They rounded a great boulder and came to an instinctive halt, staring ahead with fascinated eyes. Before them loomed a towering cliff, its craggy surface slick and black

with the spray flung back from the river, which burst out
of the cliff face several hundred feet above their heads.
Boiling and frothing with the power of its escape, the
waterfall poured down the cliff face in a white torrent,
plunging into the gorge below.

Tabithas ran back and forth at the edge of the cliff,
whining, gazing up at Anghus with troubled eyes.

"How can Fionnghal have just vanished into thin air?
Find her, Tabithas!" The wolf whined again, running
back and forth, her nose to the ground. Then she looked
up at the prionnsa, wagged her tail briefly, then ran and
jumped off the edge of the cliff. She fell down, her dark
body twisting, and hit the water with a splash. "No!"
Anghus screamed, as she disappeared under the foaming
torrent. "Tabithas, no!" But it was too late. The wolf
had gone.

Isabeau sat by the fire, stirring the great cauldron of
soup. Overhead, branches made a puzzle of the gray sky;
on either side moss-covered boulders kept a multitude
of slender, golden-leaved trees back. All along the road
soldiers were setting up tents, hobbling horses, gathering
firewood and scouting the paths that ran into the forest.

The Rìgh's ornately carved traveling carriage listed at
a peculiar angle on the road ahead of her. It had lost a
wheel that afternoon and the soldiers were still trying to
repair the broken axle. All the other carriages trailed
along the road behind the MacCuinn's, unable to move
forward until the cartwright was finished. The soldiers
were gruff and tight-lipped—trying to guard the Rìgh
and Banrìgh in such circumstances was not what they
wished for at all.

The three weeks since they had fled the palace had
been slow and frustrating. Potholes had made the journey a bone-jarring nightmare, while skirmishes with bandits had kept them all on their guard.

Isabeau was in a very bad mood indeed. Setting up
camp meant rest for the occupants of the lairds' luxurious carriages, but a great deal of work for the servants.

Every bone in Isabeau's body ached, her limbs were thoroughly chilled, and she was sick of being ordered around. Her crippled hand did not save her from having to lug heavy buckets of water, drag loads of kindling, or run errands for laird, lackey, soldier and groom. Since Isabeau had not allowed anyone to tend the scars, her hand ached from the unaccustomed exertion, and some of the ugly scars had split, so her bandages were stained with blood as well as dirt.

It was the evening of the autumn equinox. If Isabeau had been at home, she would have been celebrating the rites with Meghan, but here no one seemed to care that day and night were again equal, the forces of male and female, light and darkness, good and evil, for a short time in perfect balance.

There were still a few hours till sunset. On an impulse, Isabeau threw down the wooden spoon and caught up her plaid, slipping away into the forest. What did it matter if none of the other witches concealed about the Rìgh's party dared celebrate the equinox? She had been raised by Meghan of the Beasts and knew better than to let Eà's seasonal changes go past without celebration.

It was the first time she had managed to get away from the camp since they had left the palace. If Latifa had been nearby, she would have had no chance of escaping, but the old cook had gone to vent her temper on the servants setting up a tent for the Rìgh and Banrìgh to sleep in.

The MacCuinn's health had worsened since their journey began, and Latifa was irritable and anxious. None of Isabeau's potions seemed to help, and the red-haired girl was not hopeful of the Rìgh's recovery. Her only reward for her efforts had been a box on the ear that had made her head ring, and a warning from Latifa that she would hold Isabeau accountable if the Rìgh died on the journey. Isabeau had muttered that surely that was a matter for Gearradh, she who cuts the thread, which had only earned her a blow to the other side of her head.

Isabeau's ears were still red and tender, and her feelings toward Latifa rancorous. She climbed the hill in an excess of energy, driven on by her resentment, and only paused when her breath grew sharp in her side.

They were high in the mountains now, the road following the rapids of the Ban-Bharrach River as it tumbled toward Lucescere. The needle-tipped peaks of the Whitelock range towered above them, the higher slopes shining with ice. Among the somber evergreens, the brilliant autumn foliage of maple and beech brought sweeps of color. Small waterfalls dashed down the rocky hills, feeding the Ban-Bharrach. Isabeau had to cross one, jumping from boulder to boulder.

She lay on her stomach among the greygorse, watching the camp below, and was pleased to see Latifa's fat form standing by the fire, spoon in one hand, her mouth open as she bellowed Isabeau's name. Isabeau chuckled, wriggled away, and began climbing again. She was determined to at least chant the equinox rites, and she wanted to be well away from the camp before doing so. She reached the crest of the next hill and began to trot down into the valley on the far side. She could hear the tinkle of a waterfall and veered that way.

She was almost at the base of the slope when she heard voices. If the conversation had been in a language Isabeau recognized she would simply have gone in a different direction, but the oddness of the voices made her pause to listen. They rose and fell in melodic rhythms, with a whistling inflection that was unlike anything Isabeau had ever heard before. She knew the languages of most animals and faeries of the land, yet this high-pitched, echoing sound baffled her. Carefully she pulled back a branch and looked down into the valley.

Two figures were sitting on a log just below her. Between them they held something which glimmered and flashed. It was a hand-mirror. Staring into its silvery face, the two people crooned and warbled in that strange language, and to Isabeau's astonishment, the mirror answered in a deep bass tone. As powerful and resonant as the ocean, the voice spoke for a very long time. After it had finished, the smaller of the two figures leaned forward to answer, and Isabeau realized with a sharply dropping heart that it was Sani.

Very slowly Isabeau let the branch drop back into place and began to inch away. She had no desire to let Sani know she was being observed. Luckily the old woman was too absorbed in the mirror to hear the rasp of leaves beneath Isabeau's boots. She was able to regain the safety of the forest without being heard, and hurried away, her heart pounding. She had no doubt that Sani had been communicating through the mirror as Meghan did with her crystal ball. What language had she spoken, though, and to whom? And who had the other hooded figure been? Isabeau had no doubt it was the Banrìgh herself, and she was fairly certain they must have been speaking the language of the Fairgean. It was the only faery dialect Isabeau did not know.

At first she thought to hurry back to the camp and tell Latifa what she had seen. Isabeau's ears still stung, though, and she had no desire to face the old cook's wrath just yet. She decided to find a lonely hilltop and watch the sun set and the moons rise as she had planned to do. Plenty of time to tell Latifa—particularly when there was little she could do, here in the wilderness.

Isabeau reached the hill's crest, which gave her a clear view over the forest. The sun had dipped behind the mountains and the shadows of trees stretched long across the hillside. The sharp peaks were black, the sky golden, the forest singing with the snow-scented breeze, the moons translucent and scarred. Peace flooded her, healing her. Raising her arms to the cloud-streaked sky, she intoned the incantation to Eà, as she had done every solstice and equinox of her life.

Afterward she set off back down the hill, much calmer after the renewal of her contact with the natural forces of life. It was dark under the trees, but Isabeau had uncanny eyesight, seeing nearly as clearly at night as she did during the day. She scrambled through the birches, the little twigs snapping in her face, and began to hurry back toward the road.

The noise of a large body crashing through the undergrowth stopped her in her tracks. She pressed her back against the bole of a mossy-trunked hemlock and listened intently. In the light of the two moons filtering down between the tree branches, she saw a tall horse cantering toward her. She recognized its finely drawn head and proud carriage immediately.

"Lasair!" she cried and ran forward to meet the stallion. He pawed the ground and tossed his head, and she threw both arms around his neck, pressing her face against his silky coat. "I have been worried indeed about ye," she scolded. He gave a hurrumph of disdain and pushed his nose against her. She stroked it lovingly, and he snorted, dancing a little.

The sight of the stallion cheered Isabeau immensely. She had been fretting about him ever since their flight from the palace, worried in case the Bright Soldiers found him, or the Fairgean swimming in from the sea.

She was just telling the stallion to be sure to stay out of sight when she heard hooves trotting along the road behind her. She patted his nose, ignoring his jittery prance, the roll of his eye. Very faintly she heard a word in her mind. *Danger . . .*

Go, Lasair! Be careful . . .

He shook his head violently, pawing the ground, but she pushed him away and slipped through the forest toward the road. Crouched in the shadow of a huge fallen tree, Isabeau could see the track clearly, even though the moonlight fell through a criss-cross of tree branches. A black mare, nervous of head and ears, was picking its delicate way through the stones of the road.

Isabeau stiffened in surprise. She knew that mare. But what was her seaside friend doing here, in the lonely forests of the Whitelock Mountains, three weeks' away from the sea? On an impulse, she stepped out into the road. The mare shied, and the white hands on the bridle gathered up the reins quickly. Before she could spur the horse on, Isabeau cried, "Morag? It's me, Red. Wait!"

For a moment she thought Morag would urge the mare on so she gave a soft whicker of reassurance to the mare, who quietened, and said gaily, "It is Morag, is it no'? I would recognize your bonny mare anywhere. What are ye doing here?"

Morag put back the hood of her cloak. "Red? What are ye doing here?"

"I asked first!" Isabeau said.

Morag hesitated, then said, "I travel into Rionnagan. I have been cooped up in a stuffy traveling carriage all day and was stiff and restless. I thought I would ride poor Fleet-o'-Feet for she's been on a lead-rope for days."

"Are ye camped nearby then? What a coincidence!"

"Aye, we've had a slight accident, a broken axle . . . ." Morag paused, and Isabeau's eyes widened in astonishment. Surely it was too much of a coincidence to expect two separate broken axles in such close proximity? But how could Morag be traveling in the same party as herself? Isabeau knew most of the servants by name, and all of them by sight. It was true she rarely saw any of the aristocrats, who traveled well ahead of Isabeau's coach and had their own servants and meal-fires. Still, there were only a dozen in entirety and she had seen most of them as they strolled along the road on sunny afternoons, stretching their legs. She had never noticed Morag among them.

A hawk screamed, right overhead. Isabeau stepped back instinctively, and the mare shied. Suddenly there was a shrill neigh. Lasair dashed out of the woods, his eyes rolling white. He reared over Morag's mare, hooves flashing. Deep in her mind, Isabeau heard his distressed call: *Beware! Evil! Hurt you . . .*

Morag dragged her horse's head backward, trying to get away from Lasair's flailing hooves. The stallion reared again, screaming with rage. Isabeau tried to catch his mane, but he defied her, dancing away.

No, Lasair! Friend!

No friend! Enemy! Enemy! Evil . . .

One of the stallion's hooves caught the mare on the shoulder. She reared and Morag was tossed from the saddle, landing heavily on the ground. She gave a cry of pain and bent over, her face drawn. Lasair reared over her head, neighing wildly.

Isabeau ran to the stallion's head. "What have ye done, ye stupid horse?" she screamed and tried to catch hold of his mane.

Evil. Enemy. The stallion danced back, not allowing her near.

"This is my friend! What have ye done to her?" Isabeau half sobbed. She bent over Morag, who was groaning. A hawk screamed again and again, and dived at Lasair's head. He reared and struck out at it with his hooves, but it evaded him and flew shrieking into his face, extended claws trailing colored ribbons.

With a neigh Lasair tossed his head and cantered away into the forest. *My enemy . . . beware . . .*

"My . . . babe," Morag panted. "My . . . babe!"

To Isabeau's horror, she saw a spreading stain on Morag's riding skirt. "My . . . babe," she gasped.

Isabeau was gripped with a paralyzing indecision. She clutched Morag's hand. "Can ye walk?" she asked, but the white pain on Morag's face answered her. She was rocking back and forth, and the stain on her skirt spread and spread.

"Latifa . . ." Isabeau scrambled to her feet. She knew the old cook was an experienced midwife. "I canna leave ye here, it's dark already and the wind is cold. I'll take ye back to the camp, I ken someone who can help ye." Morag only groaned.

Panic coursing through her, Isabeau went to catch Morag's horse. Although Lasair's commotion had unnerved the mare, Isabeau calmed her enough to lead her to where Morag was crouching, her lip gripped between her teeth.

Getting Morag onto the horse's back exhausted Isabeau, who was already worn out after her climb. She was finally able to heave the pregnant woman's bulk into the saddle, with the help of the fallen log, and she began to lead the horse back through the forest.

The moons had risen into a bank of storm clouds, and it was darker than ever under the trees. Any stumble by the mare caused Morag to groan. Several times the pregnant woman was almost unseated as the mare shied at a shadow. Each time she managed to cling on. Isabeau peered through the darkness and saw the guards several paces before they saw her. Nonetheless, her heart hammered when they brought their swords up, crying "Halt!"

"I must find Latifa," Isabeau cried. "Woman . . . injured. Having a babe!"

A flaming torch was thrust into her face, and the guard exclaimed in recognition, "Red, it's ye!"

The flaring light played over the mare's nervous hocks, and he cried incredulously, "Fleet-o'-Feet!" and hastily raised the torch high. In distress, he called, "Guards! Quickly! It is the Banrìgh!"

Immediately there was an uproar. Isabeau gripped the reins, bewildered and so tired she hardly comprehended what he meant. Guards were running in all directions, shouting. Lights sprang up. Two of the guards tenderly removed Morag from the saddle. She fainted into their arms at the movement.

"Get Latifa!" Isabeau cried, trying to get near her friend. They held her back with hard but kindly hands. "Ye do no' understand. She fell from a horse! She's having a babe! It will die!" Isabeau sobbed.

The guard snapped orders, and soldiers went running in all directions. Isabeau was unsure why her plea for help had been answered with such enthusiasm, but she was grateful. She sank back on her heels in the middle of the road, unable to take her eyes off that awful, dark stain spreading over Morag's lap.

Suddenly Latifa was there, her round, brown, face creased with anxiety. Torches were flaming all about them. "Oh, my Eà!" Latifa cried, heedless of who was listening. "It *is* the Banrìgh!" She gestured imperiously to the soldiers. "Out o' my way, ye fools!" She took one look at Morag's face and posture and tore the crimson cloak off the soldier's back.

"Give me your cloak, ye great blithering idiot!" she cried, using it to shelter the groaning woman from the soldiers' eyes. "Your Highness," she said gently, "I need ye to sit up. Come now, that be right."

Morag was unable to respond, her breath coming in hoarse pants.

"We canna let her be having the babe here on the road, in the view o' all. Run get me a tent, and build me a fire, as quick as ye can. Isabeau, get your herbs and think what is best to calm the babe for the birth."

Isabeau sat stock-still, her mouth agape. She could not believe that Morag was the Banrìgh, the woman she had been brought up to think of as her enemy. She could not believe it. She kept thinking there must be some mistake, but surely Latifa would not make such a mistake?

Latifa helped Maya sit up, pressing her fingers on her grossly distended stomach. Maya screamed and beat at Latifa's hands with her own. "Gently, my dear, gently," Latifa chided. She said to Isabeau, "The royal babe is no' due for a month! This is dreadful, indeed. Wha' happened?"

Isabeau, trembling with fear and anxiety, tried to tell her. Already in shock at the suddenness of Lasair's attack, she was frightened and dismayed by the realization that her friend Morag was the Banrìgh, the most powerful woman in the land. Everything had happened so fast. She stole little looks at the Banrìgh's white, sweat-glistened face, as she lit the fire—now so used to flint that she never even thought of lighting it with her mind. This was her greatest enemy, the woman she had sworn to topple. The shift in perception was too much for her to deal with.

Latifa had unbuttoned the Banrìgh's dress and was

peering at the swelling bruise on her side. "Bring the candle closer, Isabeau," she murmured. "She's bleeding still. We'll have trouble saving the babe . . ."

Maya heard her and began to scream out. "No, no, ye must save my babe!" she cried. "Ye must save my babe!" Somewhere overhead a hawk screamed.

"Calm yourself, my dear," Latifa said placidly. "I shall do all I can. Ye must be calm, for the babe is distressed enough. Tell me, are ye having contractions?"

Maya nodded, her eyes dark with fear and pain. Latifa laid first her hands then her ear against the Banrìgh's belly. "Now, Your Highness, ye mun do exactly wha' I tell ye."

"No, I canna, no' yet," Maya moaned. "It's too early, it's no' time yet."

"It may be too early for ye, Your Highness, but this babe is ready to be born."

As Latifa eased her into the birthing position, the Banrìgh shook her head and resisted, saying, "No, no, this is wrong—I need . . . water." Isabeau tried to give her water to drink, but she only sobbed and pushed it away and asked for Sani. The old woman could not be found, however, and Maya cried again for water, only to shake her head weakly when Isabeau brought the beaker to her mouth.

It was a long and difficult birth. Isabeau had never seen a child being born before, and Maya's agony horrified her. She knew a great deal about what herbs to use in childbirth, however, for that was one of the primary skills of any skeelie.

For some time they were afraid both mother and child would be lost. They could not stem the bleeding, despite the infusions, and Maya's breathing was shallow and erratic, her pulse skipping under Isabeau's fingers. Latifa had to turn the babe in the womb and draw it out almost unassisted by the mother.

She was a small, red, wrinkled thing, covered with yellow scum. The old cook cut the cord and tied it expertly. Outside the hawk was still screaming.

Isabeau immersed the baby in a basin of warm water, washing away the birth fluids. The little girl's fingers and toes were distinctly webbed, and her skin had an odd, iridescent shimmer. On her neck, just below her ears, were three, flat translucent slits, almost invisible on the pale skin. Isabeau showed Latifa, who frowned and said softly, "Odd. They say babes in Carraig are sometimes born with webbed fingers like a frog's, but I've never seen marks like that before."

Maya struggled to see the baby, but could not find the strength to sit up. Latifa rapidly wrapped her in linen and gave her to her mother. "Ye have a bonny daughter," Latifa said briskly, her face not showing her perturbation.

Bitter disappointment distorted Maya's face. "A daughter! Nay! It canna be."

"Indeed she is, only a wee one still and weak, but she'll grow."

Maya pushed the child away. Tears were flowing down her face. "No!" she cried. "I must have a son. I have to have a son. A daughter is no use!"

"How can ye be saying such a thing about your wee lassie?" Latifa said comfortingly. "I be sure daughters are at least as useful as sons . . . ."

Maya shook her head and began to sob. "A daughter is no use," she repeated. "I must have a son!" She pushed the swaddled babe away so fiercely the wailing little girl almost fell to the ground. Latifa said nothing more, just handed the baby to Isabeau and set herself to soothing Maya.

Isabeau sat wearily on the ground, rocking the infant in her arms. The baby punched out with tiny fists, her face red and crumpled. A tide of tenderness welled up in Isabeau, and she touched the soft palm with one finger. Immediately the baby's fist closed upon it. She looked up and saw Maya's eyes fixed on her and the baby. They were dark with fear and dismay, and some other emotion Isabeau found hard to identify. She thought it was hatred.

THE THREAD IS CUT

CUT

WINTER

LUCESCERE PALACE

Isabeau sat by the fire, rocking the wailing baby in her arms. "Shush, Bronwen, shush, my lassie," she crooned. Latifa knelt on the hearth, stoking up the fire. Her small black eyes were red-rimmed, her round, brown face creased with crying. The Rìgh had almost died in the early hours of the night, and only Isabeau's herb lore had kept him alive. She knew the recipe for Meghan's *mithuan,* a potion that contained foxglove, hawthorn berries and lily of the valley, which could stimulate any heart, no matter how weak.

Since their arrival at Lucescere Palace, Isabeau had rarely left the royal suite. Care of little Bronwen had fallen almost entirely on her shoulders, for Maya was weak and disinterested. The Banrìgh had not recovered after her severe hemorrhaging, and lay still in bed, blue shadows under her eyes. Ever since she had been carried up from the carriage, she had lain there, her face turned away.

The royal suite was composed of seven long, high-ceilinged rooms, all connected by carved and gilded doors. The Rìgh and Banrìgh's bedrooms each opened into a dressing room and sitting room, with the center room converted for the moment into the royal nursery.

This is where Isabeau now slept, in a cot not much larger than Bronwen's and far less ornate.

From this cloud-blue room Isabeau moved between the Banrìgh's suite and the Rìgh's, coaxing them to eat, to drink her teas and to look at their beautiful daughter. Realizing that Isabeau's knowledge of healing was greater than hers, Latifa had handed over much of the nursing of the royal couple to the girl while she tried to get the palace kitchens back into order. Ostensibly the cook was still in charge, but she was so upset by the Rìgh's rapid decline and so nervous at the prospect of the future, that she was not her usual efficient self. Often as she and Isabeau moved softly about the suite in the hush of the night, the old cook wept a little and wrung her hands. She had helped Jaspar into the world, she confessed to Isabeau, and had never thought he would die before she did.

The responsibility weighed heavily on Isabeau, who was constantly wishing for Meghan's knowledge and wisdom to help her. Of all her charges, Isabeau was happiest about the baby, for Bronwen was growing quickly and seemed already to recognize her step and voice. The Banrìgh was exhausted and weak from loss of blood, but nourishing food and plenty of bed rest should soon have her back to her usual self. It was the Rìgh Isabeau was truly concerned about. His heart was beating erratically, and his breathing was shallow. One could not use the *mithuan* too often, for foxglove was poisonous and could do more harm than good if used too frequently. She had given him a syrup made from wild poppies to help him sleep instead, but was listening carefully for any change in his breathing.

"Happen the babe wants her mumma," Latifa said, heaving her great bulk to her feet. "She's been greetin' for half an hour or more, should ye no' take her to the Banrìgh?"

"The Banrìgh is sleeping," Isabeau replied, "and I do no' want to wake her—her sleep has been disturbed indeed these past weeks. I canna think what is troubling her, she does no' seem to want to even look at her daughter, let alone cuddle her or suckle her."

"A new mother often suffers an oppression o' the spirit," Latifa said knowingly. "Once her strength has been built back up, she'll love the wee bairn, do no' worry about that."

"She's barely looked at the babe," Isabeau said, rocking Bronwen back and forth in her cradle. Indeed, she did not like to say so, but it seemed to her that Maya felt nothing but revulsion and resentment toward her little girl. Jaspar had been absolutely delighted with his daughter, and he was far weaker than Maya.

Latifa bustled out, leaving Isabeau and the baby alone. It was a windy, stormy night, and the rain howled around the eaves of the old palace, rattling a loose shutter somewhere. Isabeau gave a superstitious shiver and wrapped her shawl closer about her neck. Two nights ago a hawk had thrown itself against the window of the Banrìgh's room, smashing the glass. It had been stunned by the impact, lying on the floor amidst shards of glass. The Banrìgh had screamed and cried to Isabeau to get it out. Isabeau had knelt and picked up the bundle of feathers, and it had slashed her arm with its cruelly curved beak, despite her whispered reassurances.

Isabeau could speak the language of hawks and was shocked to be so mistreated. She had thrown the bird out the window and fastened the shutters tight, calling to the guards to find a glazier. Blood from her cut had splattered the floor, red across the broken glass. It had seemed like an omen.

Many things were troubling Isabeau. The odd language she had overheard Sani and the Banrìgh use in the forest the night of the baby's birth, and Sani's disappearance that night. The bags of sea-salt that Maya tipped into the hipbath before bathing, and the way she insisted on locking the doors, despite their fears for her safety. When at last she let them in, the floor would be awash with water.

Latifa could no longer mock Isabeau's suspicions. It

seemed certain that the Banrìgh must have Fairge blood, and her baby daughter too. "But how?" Latifa whispered, her round face distressed. "How could she hide her true nature from me for so long? My poor Jaspar, it'll break his heart if he knew. Ye mun no' tell him, Red, he loves his baby so. Promise me ye shall no' tell him."

"We must tell Meghan!" Isabeau cried. "Surely she should know."

"Ye think I have no' tried to reach her? She does no' answer my calls. I think she mun be dead!" Latifa rocked back and forth, her old face screwed up like a child's. "Wha' am I to do, wha' am I to do?" she whispered.

It was over two months since Meghan had escaped the Red Guards and in that time there had been no word of her whereabouts. Isabeau felt as if she had been abandoned or forgotten, and she wished that Latifa had a clearer idea of what Meghan's plans had been. The birth of winter was now only a week away, and Isabeau felt an increasing anxiety. What was she meant to do? All she knew was that Meghan had said she would be in contact, yet there had been no word from the sorceress.

Rocking the sleeping child in its cradle, Isabeau fell into a tired reverie. It was very quiet. Isabeau had built the fire up high, for it was cold. Staring into the flames, she thought of her carefree childhood, riding wild horses, swimming with otters and climbing trees with donbeags and squirrels. On many a stormy night like this she and Meghan would be snug in their tree-house, drinking tea as the old witch told her stories of the Three Spinners, or the Celestines. At the thought of the old wood witch, tears swelled up in her throat. *Meghan, where are ye?* she thought.

Isabeau . . .

Isabeau started upright, her foot slipping from the cradle so Bronwen protested in her sleep, tiny fists nudging at her fast-shut eyes. *Meghan . . .*

I am here.

Where? Where are ye?

I am no' far. How are ye yourself?

I have missed ye so much. So much has happened . . .

Latifa told me about your hand. I be sorry, Isabeau, so sorry.

Isabeau felt tears sting her eyes. She looked down at her useless hand, bound up and hidden under her apron.

Isabeau, there is an auld saying—I do no' ken if it will mean anything to ye but I remember Jorge repeating it to me after he was blinded. They say only the lame can love, only the maimed can mourn . . .

Isabeau said nothing. She scrubbed her cheeks with her sleeve and thought bitterly to herself, *Maimed I am indeed.*

Of course Meghan heard her thought, and her answer came, quick and stern. *All o' us are maimed in some way, Isabeau. Life does no' leave us unmarked. Ye have lost two fingers. What o' all those witches who lost their lives? I am sorry indeed that ye have been hurt, but I am glad it was no' worse.*

Where have ye been, Meghan? I have wanted ye so badly . . . Despite herself, Isabeau could not keep her sense of betrayal from tainting her mind-voice.

My thoughts have been with ye, Isabeau. I have no' dared scry to ye, it is too dangerous. Tell me, what news?

The Banrìgh has had her baby.

I heard. What happened? It is six weeks too soon, surely, even more.

Lasair kicked her horse and she was thrown . . .

Who?

Lasair, my horse. I mean, my friend the horse. The red stallion . . .

The horse that galloped the Old Way. Cloudshadow told me. He kicked Maya?

Her thoughts tumbling over themselves, Isabeau struggled to tell Meghan what had happened.

Well done, Isabeau, very well done. One o' my greatest dreads was the birth o' that child come Samhain. She may have had powers at her command that we would much rather she did no'. In one way, it is a shame the babe did no' die . . . I feel your reaction—did ye work to save the child? Well, she is a NicCuinn, no matter her mother, so in that sense I am glad. What o' Jaspar?

He is fading fast, Meghan, it will only be a few more days, if that.

Ye must keep him alive a little longer! Meghan's mind-voice was roughened with grief and urgency.

I canna, Meghan. He would have died weeks ago if it were no' for the potions I have wrought for him.

I knew ye would have the skills to help him, it was one reason why I sent ye to Rhyssmadill when I could no' be going myself. Are ye sure ye canna help him live just a few days longer?

I have kept his heart beating long after it should have stopped, and he has no will to live. Ye have heard about the attack o' the Bright Soldiers?

Aye, I have. I had dreams o' its coming.

So did I . . .

Indeed? That is interesting. I wonder if ye have the gift o' prophecy . . . Isabeau felt a thrill of pride. Meghan continued, *It is unlikely though. I have no such Skill, and I dreamed o' its coming. I think that must mean someone was sending dream-messages.*

Did ye send one to me?

O' course I did, foolish lass, more than one. I am glad to see ye heeded them.

Innate honesty made Isabeau admit, *Latifa would no' believe me. I did no' ken what I would have done if we had no' had to flee the Bright Soldiers.*

Ye must keep the Rìgh alive until after Samhain, Isabeau. We canna rescue the Inheritance until then.

Ye mean the Lodestar?

Quiet, foolish lass, even if ye have protected your circle there may be others listening who can penetrate such flimsy wards as yours must be. The Banrìgh seems to have a Scrying Pool o' some sort, so she can overhear—

Protected?

There was a long silence, then Meghan said urgently,

*Have ye found me by accident, Isabeau? Has Latifa no'
been teaching ye to scry? Ye have sprinkled the circle
with water and ashes . . .*

No . . .

There was no answer. Isabeau fell to her knees before
the fire, calling *Meghan, Meghan . . .*

Faint came to the answer, *I shall send someone to ye.
Quiet now, lassie, it be too dangerous!*

The next morning Isabeau woke scarcely refreshed at
all. She had tossed and turned half the night, troubled
by uneasy dreams. It had stopped raining, the sun struggling out from behind the clouds. She washed and fed
and dressed Bronwen without her usual enjoyment, and
took the baby in to see her mother.

Maya had no desire to see her daughter and waved at
Isabeau to take her away. She inclined her head and
turned to take Bronwen out again. The Banrìgh said,
"How are ye yourself, Red? Ye look a trifle pale."

"Fine, thank ye, Your Highness," Isabeau responded,
still awkward around the woman who had been her secret friend and was now revealed as her secret enemy.

"Ye seem to be here at all hours o' the day and night.
Why do ye no' have some time for yourself? Leave the
babe with the wet nurse." The Banrìgh's voice was so
kind that Isabeau blushed and smiled in spontaneous
gratitude, and she had to remind herself who Maya was
as she changed her shoes and caught up her plaid.

In the neglected garden, leaves choked the fountains
and were piled in drifts around the roots of the trees.
Hedges ran wild, and the beds were riotous tangles of
roses, columbines and nettles.

It was in her mind to look for the maze concealed at
the heart of the garden. Latifa had told her how Meghan
had hidden the Lodestar at the Pool of Two Moons,
locking away the labyrinth with the Key. Although Isabeau had no inkling of Meghan's plans, she knew they
had to do with the Lodestar and the maze.

After three quarters of an hour, she was tired and
frustrated. She sat under a spreading oak tree and stared

up at the sky through the gray branches. It occurred to her she was going about this the wrong way. Meghan had said to her many times, "A problem is like a tangle o' thread but what seems complicated can always be made more simple. Find the end of the thread and pull the tangle undone."

So Isabeau sat and puzzled it out. After only a moment she smiled and got to her feet with renewed vigor. Kilting her skirts up through her belt, she cursed the impracticality of women's clothes. Soon she was high in the branches and had a view over the length and breadth of the garden. At the far end she saw the blackened timbers and stones of the ruined witches' tower, only one spire remaining to pierce the blue-hazed sky. At the other end were the golden domes of the palace. All around was the tangle of bare branches rising above evergreen hedges and shrubs.

Isabeau smiled in triumph, for through the tree boughs she could see a small golden dome in the deepest part of the garden, much smaller than the domes of the palace but as burnished bright. She swung down to the ground, finding her body stiff after her months at Rhyssmadill, then headed toward the dome.

She came to a high hedge with black clusters of berries buried deep in its red leaves. It was too high and dense to see through, so she walked to the corner, the hedge stretching along as far as the eye could see. By craning her neck she could just see the golden dome beyond. So she followed the hedge along, rustling the leaves with her feet and enjoying the crisp smell of the air.

Soon she came to a parterre garden with a scrolled stone bench on either side. Lavender hedges grew in knots around rose bushes, tangled and heavy with rosehips. It was enclosed within the hedge, with an archway at one end that led back into the garden. At the other end she could see where the hedge had been trained into another archway, but there was no way through.

Isabeau stood on the bench and tried to see over the hedge. This time the golden dome was in a completely different place—she had been walking away from it, not toward it. Puzzled, she followed the hedge to its end, turned east and proceeded along a high stone wall. She came to a promenade lined with tall cypresses. It led her curving away from the dome, yet when she proceeded the other way the dome sank away behind the trees. When she next caught a glimpse, it was behind her again. Isabeau began to smile. She turned her back on the dome and walked away from it and, sure enough, soon the dome was to the west and she had wandered again into the knot garden.

Now grubby and hot, Isabeau decided to abandon the maze and head toward the ruined tower. She had heard so much about the Tower of Two Moons from Meghan that it was almost a pilgrimage for her. Ten minutes of swift walking brought her onto the wide lawn before the ruin. She stood looking at the charred rafters, the smoke-stained walls, the broken colonnades. Enough of the existing structure remained to tell of its original beauty, and she found she was weeping.

She wiped her cheeks with her hands and cast a quick glance about her. The massive rampart which reared on either side was closely guarded, and she had to wait until the sentries had passed out of sight before exploring further.

She did not want to see any more of the scorched and broken buildings, so she went straight to the one remaining tower. She walked slowly from one hall to another, marveling at the carvings and mosaics. It reminded her of the Tower of Dreams, although before its destruction it would have been much bigger and grander than the small witches' tower in the forests of Aslinn.

She climbed the grand staircase until she was on the top floor, and went out onto a delicately carved balcony with slim columns holding up pointed arches. Staying well within the shelter of the pillars, Isabeau stared down over the garden. As she had expected, there was a clear view of the labyrinth. Grown from yew trees and

hedges, the intricate whorls of the maze circled a stretch
of green water. Around the pool were tall stone arches
and a paved area, with shallow curving steps. At the
western end of the pool was a beautiful round building,
held up with flying buttresses and roofed in brass-green.

She memorized each turn of the maze until she could
conjure its shape on the dark of her eyelids, then hurried
back down the stairs. She had been gone longer than
she had expected, and she wanted no one to wonder
what she had been doing.

It was quiet in the palace. Latifa nodded to the guards
outside the Rìgh's door, her arms weighted down with
a tray, and they opened the gilt-painted panel. She went
inside the dim, firelit room, surprisingly noiseless for her
great bulk, and put the tray down on one of the tables.
The Rìgh slept, watched over by Isabeau who nodded
wearily to the old cook from her chair by the fire. In
her lap she held the sleeping baby, stroking the soft,
dark down that covered her head.

"He sleeps at least," Isabeau whispered. "I have given
him some more poppy syrup, but I worry for him, Latifa,
his heart is erratic and his breathing uneven."

The cook nodded, her brown face crinkled with concern. "Stay with him, Red. It is late, I ken, but I do no'
think he should be left alone."

Isabeau nodded, and Latifa went through the nursery
to the Banrìgh's rooms. All was quiet, and the cook wondered again what had happened to her old enemy Sani,
who had disappeared the night Bronwen was born. Despite several days of searching, there had been no sign
of her anywhere in the hills around the camp, and when
they had told Maya, the Banrìgh had half closed her
eyes and said simply, "Sani must have decided she was
needed elsewhere."

The cook unpacked the tray, refilled the Banrìgh's
water jug and stoked up the fire, panting a little as she
bent over the coals. *I be getting too fat for all this,* she
thought, and suddenly glanced over her shoulder.

In the shadows of the great bed she could see the Banrìgh was watching her. Her silvery-blue eyes gleamed a little in the flickering light. She smiled as soon as Latifa turned, and said huskily, "Ye are so good to us, Latifa, where would we be without ye to support us and look after us?"

Latifa flushed. "Thank ye, Your Highness."

"Ye're always so loyal," the Banrìgh said, her voice huskier than ever. "Ye love the Rìgh as I do. I am so worried about him, Latifa. These final betrayals have broken his spirit, I fear." She moved her head restlessly so her silky dark hair fanned out on the pillow. "If only I had no' failed him so badly . . ." Her voice broke.

"Wha' do ye mean?"

Maya lifted a hand in a desultory gesture. "I failed to give him an heir."

"But ye have a bonny little girl—she is only a wee thing, I ken, being born so early, but she is strong and healthy . . ."

"But she canna rule," Maya replied.

"O' course she can," Latifa cried. "She is only young, I ken, but we've had a Rìgh that was only a child when he inherited . . ."

"But she's a lass!" Maya cried, temper flashing out.

"That does no' matter, my lady, wha' made ye think it would?"

Maya's face was a study of conflicting emotions. Even in the flickering light, Latifa could see bewilderment, hope, guilt, and something else—almost like triumph. "Ye mean girls can inherit the throne?"

"O' course. We've had many a banrìgh rule, how can ye no' ken that? Why, Aedan's daughter Mairead the Fair was the first banrìgh, she ruled after him. And there was Martha the Hot Tempered, and Eleanore the Noble—her daughter Mathilde inherited, although Eleanor had four sons. We have no' had a woman inherit for six or more generations now, but that is because the MacCuinns are always overblessed with sons—that must be why ye did no' realize."

"No one ever talked to me about the line o' inheritance because I was barren so long, I suppose," Maya said, and Latifa squeezed her hand in sympathy. The Banrìgh said slowly, "So there are cases where a daughter inherited the throne even if there were sons born, other male heirs to the throne?" She spoke as if the idea was completely bizarre and alien to her.

Latifa smiled. "O' course."

The Banrìgh sat up. "But she is so young, how can she rule?"

Intent only on comforting the Banrìgh, Latifa said, "But the Rìgh will name ye Regent, until Bronwen is auld enough to rule on her own behalf. That is the usual custom." The pale cheek curved. Maya sat up straighter, shaking back her glossy hair.

"O' course the heir has always needed to be favored by the Lodestar," Latifa continued. "The Lodestar responds to the inner character o' he who holds it. We had civil war once when the youngest son was named as heir by the Lodestar and the eldest son challenged him for the throne. He was a cold, ambitious man, no' concerned with the welfare o' the people the way the Rìgh or Banrìgh should be—"

Maya interrupted her. "So if Bronwen had the Lodestar, there would be no doubt o' her right to rule? But if someone else took it, they could challenge her?"

A wary expression crossed Latifa's face. "The Lodestar is lost."

"But if the Lodestar was no' lost . . ."

"The Lodestar is lost," Latifa said. "Besides, there is no one else to challenge for it . . ."

As her words trailed away, Maya said softly, "What about the Arch-Sorceress Meghan, is she no' a NicCuinn? If Bronwen can rule, can no' she? And what about Jaspar's cousin, Dughall? He is the son o' a NicCuinn, can he no' wield the Lodestar?"

"MacCuinns have always bonded with the Lodestar at birth," Latifa replied uneasily. "Dughall MacBrann could have been given the Lodestar to hold, but he was no', since he was raised in the MacBrann clan."

"But he could have been?"

"Och, aye, indeed he could have, having MacCuinn blood. I do no' ken whether he could bond with the Inheritance now or no'—it has never been done except as a babe."

Maya was silent for a while, her fingers restless amongst her blankets. "How auld are babes when they are first bonded?" she asked, just as Latifa began to leave the room.

The old cook looked back over her shoulder. "A month or so."

Maya said softly, "My babe, Latifa. Does she sleep? May I hold her?"

It was the first time she had asked to see the baby, and Latifa's heart bounded with joy. "O' course, my lady," she replied and went through to the Rìgh's suite with a light step.

"The Banrìgh wants her babe," she said jubilantly to Isabeau, who immediately frowned and held the sleeping child closer to her.

"She sleeps."

"It will no' harm her to be held by her mother for a while, Red. Let me take her through."

Isabeau rose to her feet, adjusting the babe so she slept within the crook of her arm. "Nay, she'll wake if we hand her around too much. I will take her."

Latifa followed her back into the Banrìgh's suite, cooing over the sleeping child. "See how thick her lashes are? Jaspar's were just like them when he was a babe. She is dark as any MacCuinn too, though o' course there is no white lock . . ."

Maya was sitting up, looking more vital than Isabeau had yet seen her. She held out her arms for the baby and, feeling oddly reluctant, Isabeau handed her over. Bronwen woke and began to wail, rubbing at her screwed-up eyes with both tiny, crumpled fists. Isabeau stepped forward to take her back and soothe her, but

Maya frowned and gestured her away. Rocking slightly, she began to sing a lullaby.

Her voice was low and husky, thrilling with tenderness. Almost at once the baby quietened, staring up at her mother's face with unfocused blue eyes. Then she smiled, a dreamy baby's smile that caused a lump to come into Isabeau's throat. Chuckling a little, Bronwen reached up for her mother's curve of night-black hair. Maya shook her head so her hair tickled the baby's face and Bronwen laughed.

Glancing at Latifa's face, Isabeau saw the cook was entranced by the sweetness of the song. Tears glistened in her little black eyes, rolling down her fat cheeks. She clasped her hands at her breast and gave a little sigh as the lilting lullaby came to a close. "Come," she whispered as Maya tenderly began to sing another tune. "Let us leave the Banrìgh wi' her babe. I think all will be well now."

his precious world. In horrified silence the owl watched
as the old fable was enacted in phosphors the rocks still
.....ed away in the foam, lay weak as he was, lashed to
..... safer .....
unto .....
the .....

THE TOWER OF TWO MOONS

..... jumping through hoops, each face .... had been
tangled with simper fish. ..... walked up to six men-
men on stairchers, and the forefathers filed, with wild
little bunch walking weakly beside, and various un-
naturally funny. The others were so understated, howling are and the sapphire of dust soul unholy friend.
..... admiration by .....
Out-day they ..... and rest on processing joining
them there were .... moment conversings were away, hung-
gry and had been blown to steel babies and young cells
.....
.....
.....
been opened in six contents. Lucius .....
.....
.....
older they would have been as line .....

The moons drifted amongst clouds, their light falling
haphazardly upon the forest. Ahead looked a lofty,
crenellated rampart, black against the sky. Finn
was tense with excitement. Her stomach fluttered, and
she twisted the hem of her tunic into knots. At her heels
scampered the elven cat, so dark and small she was
totally invisible in the night. In the satchel on Finn's
back were her climbing gloves and boots, and she was
dressed from head to toe in black. Her bleached hair
was covered by a dark tam-o'-shanter and her neck was
muffled with a thick black scarf that she could draw up
to conceal her face.

It had taken them more than a month to travel from
the Fang to the western wall of Lucescere, slowed by
the difficult terrain and stormy weather. It had been a
painstaking and difficult process crossing the Muileach,
for the river thundered out of the very mountain itself,
carving a deep, sheer-sided gorge through the rock. Finn
had had to climb across the cliff face, driving in stakes
and tying ropes to them to form a precarious bridge the
soldiers could cling to.

Jay had almost fallen, saved only by the safety rope
the soldiers had tied to his waist. Tragically he dropped

his precious violin. In horrified silence they all watched as the old fiddle was smashed to pieces on the rocks and swirled away in the foam. Jay wept as he was hauled to safety, but no one badgered him, feeling tears tight in their own throats. Jay's fiddle-playing had enchanted them all.

The journey through the Whitehart Forest had been fraught with danger. No human had walked its dark avenues for sixteen years, and the forest was thick with wild boar, timber wolves, woolly bears, and various unfriendly faeries. The wolves were especially active, howling around the campfire at night and slinking through the undergrowth by day.

One day they disturbed a nest of gravenings, giving them their worst moment. Gravenings were always hungry and had been known to steal babies and young children if they could not find lambs, chickens or coneys to steal. They certainly could have lifted six-year-old Connor in their claws and carried him away if they had been allowed to reach him. The Blue Guards soon beat them off, though, and they screeched away, their filthy hair trailing behind them.

They encountered no soldiers in the Whitehart Forest, for the woods between Lucescere and the mountains were never patroled. Once there had been a gate that opened in the huge rampart, but this gate could only be unlocked by those of the MacCuinn clan, and so had not been opened in sixteen years. Lachlan thought the Red Guards might not even know it existed.

It was Finn's task to climb the wall and open the gate for the rebel force camped in the forest outside. Lachlan had given her the MacCuinn crest, which was the only way to open the gate. Although the walls around the ruined witches' tower were only lightly guarded, it was still a difficult and dangerous task for an eleven-year-old. Iseult had to remind herself she was only five years older and would have been as impatient with their concerns when she was Finn's age. Resolutely she thrust her fears away, whispering to Finn, "Are ye ready, lassie?"

Finn nodded, gripping her hands together in nervous anticipation. She was confident she could climb the wall, having practiced using her clawed gloves and boot frames every day since leaving the corrie. It was the possibility of being captured by the Red Guards and taken for questioning by the Awl that so perturbed her. Finn had been free of the Awl for a year now and had no desire to fall back into their hands.

She picked up the warm, furry body of her kitten and snuggled her close to her chin, finding comfort in the faint purr that thrummed the tiny body. *It is a long way, Goblin, are ye sure you can make it?*

The kitten's purr deepened in response, the soft paws kneading the skin of Finn's neck. The little girl carefully tied the string around the elven cat's neck and checked it was securely fastened to a long piece of cord, which was in turn tied to a slender but strong rope. She gave the kitten one final head rub, then put Goblin down. With a barely audible miaow, the kitten leapt for the wall and began to climb, her claws digging into the ancient blocks of stone. Within moments she was invisible, even when one of the moons drifted out from behind the clouds, criss-crossing the ground with squares of silver.

The rope jerked sideways, and they all followed it, knowing the kitten was searching for something to thread the cord through. There would be iron racks for weapons that the slender little cat could easily climb through. They all had to trust that she would choose one out of the direct line of sight of the patrols.

The trailing rope came to a halt, and they waited nervously, watching the battlements for any sign of guards. Suddenly the rope flew upwards, making a slight swishing sound as it whipped through the dead leaves of the forest floor. In the forest behind them they heard wolves howling, and they moved restively, hands on their weapons.

"What's happening?" Dillon whispered, but Finn did not know and was too wound up to answer. After a long, anxious wait, she felt a warm, furry body winding around her ankles and with a sob of relief picked up the elven cat, who rubbed her head under Finn's chin. "She's done it!" she whispered. "Quick, pull the cord and tie the rope!"

"Let us hope it is well hidden," Iseult said grimly as the soldiers hastily fastened the rope to a spike hammered into the base of the wall, threading it through a special hook on Finn's belt, giving her a taut belay to cling to as she climbed. She had insisted such precautions were unnecessary but Iseult was taking no chances on the little girl falling.

Finn began to climb. It was more difficult than she had imagined. The rampart was angled slightly outwards so she was climbing at a steep angle, and the massive stone blocks were so cleverly fitted that there were no cracks between them. Here and there mosses had loosened the mortar so Finn was able to hammer in a spike to rest her foot or hand upon. Mostly though she had to rely on her clawed hands and feet digging deep into the glossy surface of the rock. The elven cat bounded along beside her, occasionally giving a tiny mew of encouragement.

Finn slipped only once, her hooked hands not gaining enough purchase on the rock. If it had not been for the rope clipped through her belt, she would have tumbled a hundred and fifty feet to the ground below. Instead she swung wildly, trying without success to catch the stone again with her steel claws.

At last the little girl was able to hook one glove into the stone, and then a foot. Finn completed her climb with her heart hammering so loud her ears rang. She clambered over the battlements and sat on the floor, her head bowed. As she tucked her spiked gloves and boot frames back in her satchel, the elven cat waited on the flagstones, tail curled over her paws.

The rampart ran the entire length and breadth of the city, a broad walkway along the top for the guards to patrol. Every two dozen feet was a watch-tower, which concealed a staircase leading down to the ground. Finn

slipped quietly along to the nearest tower, listening carefully before easing the door open.

She descended the dark stairs, the elven cat slipping
before her, and came out in a colonnade, slender stone
pillars holding up an arched stone ceiling. Beyond was
a lawn, and she could see tall hedges and trees.

Lachlan had vividly described the layout of the gardens and tower to her, and so Finn knew exactly where
to go. The gate had been designed as an escape route
and so was cleverly concealed in the carvings that decorated the western wall. When Lachlan was a boy, the gate
had been used frequently for picnics and horse-rides in
the forest. Nonetheless, knowledge of the gate's whereabouts had been confined to the family and a few trusted
servants, and so Meghan had been sure the Red Guards
would not know of its existence.

Silent as the elven cat at her heels, Finn flitted through
the delicately arched cloisters until she came to their
end. Before her were shallow stone steps with a wide
curving balustrade, decorated with urns thick with this-
tles and weeds. Beyond was a broad garden, surrounded
on three sides by the towering rampart.

Seven watch-towers lined the western wall, all joined
by the walkway. Finn knew this was the most dangerous
part of her expedition, as she would have no warning of
when the patrols were passing. She waited until both
moons had been obscured by clouds, then ran down the
stairs, across the wide courtyard and into the garden.
From tree to bush to statue to hedge she ducked and
weaved, trying to time her movements with the swift
pace of the clouds.

The entire length of the great western wall had been
carved with tall arches, inscribed with intricate knots and
ribbons of stone. At the apex of each arch was a carving
of a stag's head with a crown between its outspreading
antlers.

Within every third archway a simple urn was set,
which once would have cascaded with flowers. The others held small carvings, about the size of a fist. Finn

knew these were the crests of the thirteen witches of the First Coven, alternating with the emblem of this Tower—two crescent moons and a star. The one she wanted was the seventh from the corner. She told Goblin to stay hidden in the shadows, took Lachlan's brooch out of her pocket, then ran swiftly down the wall.

She saw the distinctive stag shape at once and reached as high as she could, just managing to insert the crest into the carving. It fitted perfectly, and she pushed it in with a click. Immediately, the wall of the archway swung free under her hand, a crack of darkness widening.

The gate opened silently and easily, swinging outwards into the dark forest. She slipped through and gave the League's secret signal, the three note whistle of the bluecap swift. Feeling anxiety knotting her entrails, Finn waited, casting nervous looks back over her shoulder into the garden.

She whistled again and, to her relief, was answered this time. Out of the darkness came her companions, the puppy Jed bounding ahead, muzzled to keep him quiet. "Quick," she whispered. "The patrols have been twenty minutes apart, and one is due any second!"

Lachlan pushed to the front, sinister in his closely wrapped black cloak. Even in the darkness she could see the exultation on his face. "At last," he whispered. "I be home at last."

As the soldiers silently followed him, he took back the crest from Finn and pinned it to his breast, under the folds of the cloak. "Pull the door to but do no' let it click shut," he whispered. "We may need to withdraw in a hurry."

"Remember, there must be no sign that we've been here," Iseult hissed. "If ye must kill, do so silently and dispose o' the body where it canna be found."

"Aye, my lady," the soldiers whispered, and then scattered along the wall, their claymores drawn. One by one they made their way through the gardens, grateful for the rising wind which hid their running footsteps in the scatter of dead leaves and brought clouds to cover the sky. Several times they had to freeze as patrols marched along the walkway above or around the inside of the rampart.

They came to a broken archway, stained with smoke. Peering through, Finn saw a wide green garth, cypress trees planted all along its length. In the middle was a dry fountain, broken statues caught in strange contortions in its center. Beyond was a massive building, much of it in ruins. As Finn stared, the moons broke free of the bank of storm clouds and spilled down on the blackened skeleton of a high vaulted roof. At the far end one spire still stood, its graceful height set with tall, pointed windows. The cloisters ran all round its length and great flying buttresses sprang out into the overgrown garth.

Finn gave a superstitious shudder and clutched the medallion she wore around her neck. She had heard stories about the ruined witches' tower all her life and, seeing it black and ravaged in the moonlight, found it easy to believe it was haunted by ghosts and banshees. Hundreds of witches had died here on the Day of Reckoning, spitted on the Red Guards' spears or burnt to death in the bonfires. She clutched the kitten closer to her and hurried after Iseult and the others, hoping they would not have to hide out in the tower for long. Although Finn had little fear of anything living, ghosts terrified her.

They reached the base of the tower and slowly eased open the huge oak door. Within was darkness, and one by one they slipped inside, feeling their way forward. The sound of the door closing behind them made Johanna squeak, and Finn clutch her kitten closer.

"Light a candle, *leannan*," Lachlan whispered, and after a few anonymous shuffles and bumps, candlelight flickered up. "Hopefully, if the guards see anything, they'll think it banshees and will be too frightened to come and see," he said, throwing back his cloak so he looked again like a winged prionnsa.

Iseult held the candle high, shielding the flame with her hand, and slowly made her way forward, looking about her with interest. They were in a great hall with a grand staircase at one end and many doors and corridors leading off into other rooms. The hall was paneled with ornately carved oak, the floor paved with worn flag-stones. Gargoyles grinned at her from the top of massive stone pillars, curving into arches overhead.

They found a room with a fireplace and carefully hung black material over the windows so they could light a fire and more candles without fear of discovery. They knew that the guards would not come near the tower unless their suspicions were fully aroused, and so as long as they kept quiet and allowed no light to spill through, they should be safe. The smell of the smoke was a poten-tial danger, but all were cold, tired, and hungry, so Lach-lan thought it was worth the risk.

The soldiers worked swiftly and surely to set up a makeshift camp and prepare a meal. First they made up a bed for Iseult, who had found the journey through the mountains tiring. She was six months into her pregnancy now, and finding it difficult to maintain her strength and vitality. She subsided onto the blankets thankfully, trying to ease the ache in her back. One of the rebels gave her a cup of hot broth and a flap of unleavened bread, and she broke her fast gratefully.

"Let us sleep now," Lachlan said. "It's very late and we are going to need all our strength the next few days. Byrne, Shane, take the first watch. Wake me if there is anything untoward at all, whatever it is."

The two soldiers he had named nodded, though they looked about them uneasily. Shadows were dancing all over the carved walls and it was clear they did not relish keeping watch in this ancient, ghost-ridden building.

Lachlan smiled at them. "Do no' fear. If there are ghosts here, they will no' harm us. I am a MacCuinn and this is my home. Ye will be safe."

The palace grounds were wrapped in darkness, the guards blowing into their hands to keep warm, when the secret gate in the rampart slowly creaked open. One by one, the dark, lithe forms of wolves poured in through the aperture, running swiftly to the shelter of the trees. They ran so low to the ground, on such silent padded feet, that none of the guards patrolling the rampart noticed a thing. The gate swung shut behind them.

In the morning the tower did not seem quite so spooky. All but Lachlan had slept well, it being their first night indoors for months. Lachlan had not retired when the others did. The Lodestar was very close, and he could hear its plaintive murmur always in his ears. It was so faint he was tense with fear it might die out before he had a chance to save it, and so he sat brooding by the window till Iseult came and drew him back to their blankets. Even then he did not sleep well, tossing and murmuring its name.

Even his restlessness could not disturb Iseult, who was tired out after the rough journey and finding the weight of the growing twins increasingly draining. Listening to the rain patter against the mullioned windows made her feel oddly at home, and she had slept deeply and dreamlessly.

They explored after breakfast, Lachlan leading the way and telling Iseult stories about the tower—from tales of the ancient past when the tower was first built by Owein Longbow, to anecdotes about his carefree childhood when he and his brothers had run free through the gardens and palace, teasing the witches and playing hide and seek in the tower's many buildings. As always, thoughts of his brothers made him melancholy, and Iseult drew close to him, hoping her warmth would help him throw off his dark mood.

Somewhere above them was Owein's Bow. Finn could feel it, compelling her onwards. She had spent much time fondling the broken arrow over the past few months and could feel the strengthening tug of recognition that showed the bow was nearby. Lachlan was eager to get his ancestor's bow into his hands and so they hurriedly climbed flight after flight of the great staircase.

Meghan had carefully described the layout of the tower to Iseult and told her how she had concealed the treasures behind a hanging tapestry in the upper levels. Finn charged ahead, not needing any directions, the tugging at her consciousness drawing her ever higher.

"Can ye feel it, Finn?" Iseult asked anxiously. "Do ye ken where it is? Meghan said the relics room was on the top floor and she hid the door behind a tapestry, but every bloody wall is covered with tapestries! I do no' want to have to lift every single one!"

Finn nodded, her hazel-green eyes dancing. "Easy-peasy," she said and led the way down the hall and around the corner. A huge cloth depicting a white hind being hunted through a forest hung down from the ceiling eighteen feet above.

"Are ye sure this is the right one?" Iseult asked.

"Aye, canna ye feel it? The bow is beyond."

Iseult stood before it, going over in her mind the procedure Meghan had taught her. She knew this was the most dangerous part of her task, for the sorceress had warded the door cleverly and completely. Taking a deep breath she hooked back the tapestry and, with careful gestures and chanted words, removed the wards one by one. Luckily her memory had been well trained, and she was capable of memorizing even such a complicated sequence as this.

Her heart hammering, she gently took a long key out of her pouch, inserted it into the cobwebbed lock and turned it with a screech of rust. No witch-fire scorched her flesh so, heaving a sigh of relief, Iseult pushed the door open.

Within was a small, dark room, piled high with strange objects. The little cat Goblin pranced in, tail held high, whiskers twitching. *Smell mouse,* she said.

No mouse-hunting! Finn replied sternly. *Looking for a longbow . . .*

Goblin had no idea what a longbow was, but thrust her little black nose into all the corners obligingly. Candlelight danced madly over the walls as Iseult lit the candles with her finger. The children all crowded in, but with a stern expression Lachlan told them there was not enough room and they would have to wait outside. He reluctantly allowed the three ringleaders—Dillon, Jay and Finn—to follow him and Iseult inside. "Only if ye are quiet and careful, though, bairns—this room is full o' auld and precious stuff and I do no' want ye breaking anything!"

Carefully they began to pull things out. Finn's eyes gleamed at the sight of a velvet and gold jewelry box packed with necklaces, bracelets and rings. Jay found a silver goblet with a strange crystal in its slender stem, and Dillon a brooch and arm-ring made of gold and sapphires, and a pouch of ancient coins, so tarnished it was impossible to see what land they came from.

Finn picked up a curved hunting horn embossed with dark metal and saw it was etched with the shape of a wolf, just like her medallion. She thrust it through her belt, just as Lachlan and Iseult found the bow at the back of the room, half hidden behind a huge gilt harp.

It was near as tall as the winged prionnsa, beautifully shaped and carved, with a quiver full of white-fletched arrows next to it. Lachlan carefully disentangled the bow from the harp and lifted it out, his topaz-yellow eyes brilliant in his dark face. He tested it and the bowstring snapped with a twang.

"To be expected after so long stuffed in a damp room," Iseult said. "We shall have to restring it." Lachlan's black head and her red one bent over the longbow, husband and wife absorbed in examining the carvings along its length.

By the flickering light of the candle Finn saw a violin case resting on the table. Carefully she unfastened the ornate silver clasps and opened the case. Within was the most beautiful fiddle she had ever seen, nestled in blue velvet and shining golden-brown. It had many more strings than Jay's fiddle, raised over an elaborately carved wooden bridge. Its graceful neck was long and slender and carved at the end into the shape of a beauti-

ful woman, her eyes blindfolded. Finn had never seen a
fiddle like it. She stroked the lovely wooden face with
one finger and called softly, "Jay!"

The tall, thin boy put down the chalice he was examining and came to her side. "Look what I found for ye,
Jay," she whispered, and had her reward in the light that
sprang up in his eyes.

"A viola," he cried. To Finn's surprise and pleasure,
he hugged her with one thin, stiff arm before reverently
lifting the viola out of the case and cradling it in his
arms. "She's beautiful," he whispered and lifted it to his
chin. His fingers trembling slightly, he ran the bow over
the strings and a pure, sweet sound rang out.

Lachlan and Iseult whirled around, fingers to their
lips, but Jay had already lowered the bow and was reverently examining the strings. "Sorry," he whispered. "No-
one could hear from here anyway, we be so high up."

"We canna be taking any risks," Iseult reproved. "It
is daylight now and the guards will no' be so afraid o'
the tower that they would no' investigate the sound o'
music."

"Och, they'll think it a ghost," Finn said cheerfully.
The gladness on Jay's face as he stroked the gleaming
viola had caused a corresponding happiness to well up
inside her. Her friend had been sad and quiet ever since
the loss of his violin, and she had missed his rare smile.

Lachlan, the bow in his hands, the quiver full of
arrows over his shoulder, said irritably, "Finn, all we
need is one soldier who does no' believe in ghosts for
us to have a troop marching through the ruins looking
for the mysterious violin player."

"Viola," Jay corrected him, receiving an angry glance
in return. Lachlan did not like to be corrected.

"Put it back, Jay, and all the rest o' the stuff too.
Dillon, put that bag o' coins down! Ye'll no' be able to
use them anyway, they be far too auld."

"That's no' fair!" Finn cried, disappointed at the way
the light died out of Jay's eyes as he reluctantly put the

viola back in its case. "Ye get to have the bow, why canna we have what we want?"

"The bow belonged to my ancestor," Lachlan snapped.

"So? That do no' mean it belongs to ye, necessarily. We've come all this way and broken into the palace grounds for ye, and ye will no' even let Jay have an auld fiddle to replace the one he lost." Finn's voice was rising. Iseult laid her hand on Lachlan's tense arm, and he remembered how much he needed the League of Healing Hand in the coming few days.

"Very well then, ye can all have one thing and one thing only. As payment for all your help." Despite his words, Lachlan's voice was reluctant so the children wasted no time in swarming into the room and pawing over its contents. Lachlan made an exasperated sound but gave no complaint, running his fingers over the carved bow instead.

Finn already had the hunting horn tucked in her belt, so she got out of the others' way, sitting with Jay on a dusty table and laughing as the other children got dirtier and dirtier by the minute. Johanna could not decide between an exceedingly ugly tiara, a jeweled bracelet or a ring, but in the end settled on the bracelet, knowing how dangerous it was to wear rings and how difficult for a beggar girl to find anywhere to wear a tiara.

Her brother Connor took a musical box that played a haunting melody when its painted lid was lifted. Dillon chose a tarnished sword. Although long, it was light and made a hissing sound as he feinted at his shadow. Anntoin was so enchanted with Dillon's choice that he rummaged through the room until he too found a sword, heavier and less graceful than Dillon's, but nonetheless a sword. Artair was mollified with a jeweled dagger, since there were no other swords in the room, and Parlan surprised everyone by choosing the silver cup with the crystal in its stem. "Pretty," was all he said.

They ran down the stairs to describe their treasures to Jorge. Only Finn did not follow. Goblin had disappeared into the dusty clutter, and Finn was hunting for her on her hands and knees. She heard a soft miaow and crawled under the table, calling, *Goblin, where are ye?*

While Anntoin had been searching for his sword, he had opened a large chest against the wall and black material was now spilling out of it. The elven kitten was curled up in its warm folds, invisible against its blackness. Only the wink of her gleaming eyes revealed her to Finn. When the little girl picked her up, her fingers brushed against the cloth and she felt an odd tingling. It was a sensation she had felt before. Her medallion gave it to her, as had the hunting horn and viola she found earlier. With the elven cat curled on her lap, she drew the material out of the chest and examined it as well as she could in the dim light.

It was a cloak, very finely woven, with raised patterns interlaced along the hems. She stood up and wrapped it around her. It fitted her perfectly, the material raising the hairs on her arms as it brushed against her. For a moment her whole body tingled, then she grew used to the sensation, twirling about so the material swirled about her. It was very warm and felt fine as silk against her skin.

Although there was a great deal of material, it folded up into such a small bundle that Finn was able to slip it into her pocket. She felt a momentary pang of guilt, Lachlan having said they could only have one thing each and Finn now had two. *I was the one who climbed the wall,* she thought and went bounding down the stairs after her friends. Despite her quick rationalization, she kept the cloak hidden away and did not tell anyone what she had done.

They spent the day exploring the rest of the building, playing with their new things and learning trictrac from Lachlan, who had found a board and dice abandoned in one of the rooms, as if some witches had been in the midst of a game when the Red Guards had struck.

Finn, Jay, Dillon, Artair and Anntoin grew increasingly tense as the afternoon wore on. That night they again had to risk discovery by the Red Guards and make their way out of the palace grounds and into the city. None of them had heard any news or made contact with their comrades since leaving the corrie. Neither Lachlan, Iseult nor Jorge could risk going into the city. The blind seer had caused too much trouble the last time he was in Lucescere. Tòmas could not go for the same reason, even if anyone had been prepared to risk him, though he wistfully expressed a desire to see his friend Ceit Anna, the nyx who lived in a cave behind the waterfall.

So Dillon had volunteered himself and his lieutenants for the task, arguing that none knew the city as they did, who had lived on its streets all their lives. They knew where to go and whom to ask, which the Blue Guards did not, and could make contact with the rebels hidden in the city without arousing suspicion.

Lachlan knew a secret way out of the palace grounds into the city, for he and his brother Donncan had often sneaked into Lucescere when they were meant to be at their lessons. More than twelve years had passed since Lachlan and his brothers had been transformed into blackbirds, though, so the prionnsa had no idea whether the drainpipe would still be there. It was an alarmingly tenuous possibility, and if it should prove unviable, the children would have to search for an alternative. The palace was heavily guarded, and any ragged child found prowling around would be instantly thrown into the dungeons. Although Tòmas said confidently that he would call Ceit Anna to rescue them again, Dillon preferred to stay out of the Red Guards' grasp.

Until Lachlan knew what was happening in the rest of the country, he could not relax. So delicate was the balance between success and failure that one misfortune was all it would take to overthrow their plans. He wanted to know what news there was of Meghan, and whether she had escaped the Awl. He wanted to know where his brother Jaspar was and how he was faring. He wanted confirmation that the rebels were ready to strike if needed, and that they had infiltrated the city successfully.

In particular, the League of the Healing Hand were to seek news of Isabeau, for without her they could not join the dismembered Key, and without the Key, Lachlan could not get to the Lodestar hidden away in the maze. Meghan had assured him Isabeau would somehow get the two parts of the Key to Lucescere, but with the sorceress in the hands of the Awl, her confidence did not reassure him.

SAMHAIN EVE

ightning flashed, illuminating the ruined buildings uncannily. One by one the boys ran from the doorway, always choosing the darkness that came after the flash so that the dazzled eyes of the guards would be less likely to see them. The puppy Jed ran at Dillon's heels as always, his ears flapping.

Finn stayed till last. Despite all the reassurances that Glynelda was dead, she still feared falling into the hands of the Awl. Trying to overcome her attack of nerves, she crouched in the shadow of the great doorway. Goblin put one paw out, miaowed pitifully and drew it back again. Finn scowled. Like the elven cat, she hated getting wet.

After a moment she took out the cloak she had found that afternoon and wrapped it about her, pulling the hood over her head. She tucked the elven cat into one pocket, stepped out into the rain and flitted silently across the garth.

She crept up behind the boys, who had gathered in the shelter of a great yew tree. "Where's that blasted Finn?" Dillon peered back toward the tower. "She's always doing her own thing, she should stay close and no' get into trouble."

"Why?" Finn replied cheekily, and the others all jumped and looked about them in bewilderment. Realizing the cloak was blending into the gloom so they could not see her, she put back the hood and stuck out her tongue at Dillon.

"Shut up, Finn," he said rancorously. "This is no time to be fooling around. Let's get out o' here as fast as we can."

The palace at the end of the garden was blazing with lights. Two guards marched along the flagstones, but their faces were lowered against the rain and they did not even glance in the children's direction.

Staring with bright-eyed curiosity up at the palace, they made their swift and silent way around the side, freezing whenever sheets of lightning irradiated the sky. Luckily the gardens surrounded the palace on all four sides and so there was plenty of shelter from hostile eyes.

A long avenue stretched from the front of the palace to the gates into the city, lined by bare-branched trees. On either side was an expansive lawn, offering little cover. Lanterns blazed in the great courtyard before the palace doors, casting their radiance far across the lawn, while the city was bright with lights as well.

"Something must be up," Dillon muttered. "There be soldiers everywhere!"

They looked at each other and shrugged. It took a long time to cross the garden, and by the time they reached the corner their hearts were all hammering. They found the drain at last, half buried in leaves and hidden behind the hanging branches of an evergreen bush. Jay slithered through first, Finn following as soon as he gave the signal, stripping off her cloak and folding it away first. She did not want it ruined by mud. Anntoin almost got stuck halfway through, but with Dillon pushing and the others pulling, they at last hauled him through. Artair scrambled through and Dillon came out hard on his heels, and they grinned at each other in delight. They were safe inside the city.

Despite the rain, the streets were filled with people. It was the eve of Samhain, and the city was carousing. Lanterns hung everywhere, and the crowds were dressed in brilliant colors, defying the night of death.

In sharp contrast to the gaiety of the city folk was the blank misery of the beggars clustered in the corners. A few were begging for food or money or a place to stay, but most were just sitting on bundles, their hands lying helplessly.

Peering out from the dark side-alley, Dillon and Anntoin exchanged glances. Lucescere had always been known for its beggars, but never had they seen so many, particularly in the fine streets near the palace. Many were dressed in the neat, plain clothes of artisans or crofters; they carried children, shepherds' crooks, bags of tools and, incongruously, silver teapots and ladles.

The children slipped into the busy thoroughfare one by one. They had split into three groups, Anntoin and Artair as always pairing off, Dillon declaring himself best able to scout alone, and Jay and Finn shrugging and standing together as directed. They had only a few hours to gather what information they could, for they had to be back before midnight. Midnight and the day of the dead.

Iseult looked up from *The Book of Shadows*, which she was trying to read by the capricious light of the fire. "What's wrong, Gitâ?"

The donbeag was running back and forth in front of the door, chittering in distress. He looked up at Iseult and made a high, sharp sound, as if in pain. She got up. "Are ye hurt? What's wrong?"

He stood up on his hind legs, resting his front paws on the door. "Do ye want to go out? Is there danger?"

She opened the door carefully, her *reil* in her hand, ready to throw. The guard sitting opposite jerked up his head and, seeing Iseult, scrambled to his feet. "I be sorry, my lady, I was just . . ."

"No need to apologize," Iseult said, following Gitâ as

he scampered along the hall. The donbeag led her to the narrow side door, put his paws up on the wood and looked up at her, squeaking again. Very carefully she eased it open, expecting to see guards approaching. To her horror, Gitâ immediately bolted out into the stormy night. Within seconds his small body had disappeared from view. Although she called him, with both her mind and her voice, he did not return.

Dillon moved easily through the maze of alleys, the black-faced puppy bounding at his heels. They both sniffed the air luxuriously, enjoying the familiar city stench. Never would Dillon have thought he could miss Lucescere so much. After seven months in the mountains it was a relief to be elbowing his way through tight-packed bodies, lifting a few purses just to keep his hand in. Dillon had been born in Lucescere. Until he left to travel with Jorge and Tòmas, he had lived all of his twelve years in these cramped, filthy streets. It was good to be home.

Soon the spray from the waterfalls was mingling with the rain so all the walls glistened with water. Barefoot, he was conscious of the chill striking up through his feet. *Ye've got soft*, he chided himself and quickened his pace, rubbing his arms.

He sidled down a narrow alley, careful not to meet the eyes of any of the people squatting along the walls. They were dirty, scarred, pockmarked and squint-eyed, bristling with daggers and almost as ragged as Dillon. This was the poorest quarter of the city, the home of thieves, cutthroats and curse-mongers. Here you could arrange a kidnapping or a murder for a handful of pennies. Even after all his years living on the streets, Dillon found this part of his journey a test to his courage.

Occasionally he saw the flare of torches as revellers ran down one of the wider streets, singing and chanting against the demons of the night. In this evil-smelling passageway there was no light and no singing. He evaded the grasp of a thin man with a crimson eyepatch,

who called him "my pretty," and he had to jump aside
to avoid a knife fight, catching Jed up in his arms so the
puppy would not be rolled on. As he hurried down the
alley, he heard a cry go up from the watching crowd,
and then saw the trickle of water running between his
feet turn red.

His heart pounding, he ducked through an archway,
making his way through a maze of filthy courtyards and
twisting steps until he was below the lip of the waterfall.
On one side the water thundered down, white and
churning over sharp, black rocks. Rickety shanties were
built into the side of the cliffs, coated with slime. Dillon
climbed the stairs of one and knocked on the door.

A young man answered, dressed only in an old kilt,
his black hair ruffled. He was yawning. "Wha' do ye
want," he snapped, before his bleary eyes recognized the
beggar boy standing on the step, a shaggy white pup in
his arms. "Scruffy!" he cried and hauled him over the
lintel, casting sharp glances up and down the alley.
"Wha' be ye doin' here? Up to no guid at all, if I ken ye!
This is no' the time to be wandering Murderers' Alley by
yourself, no' at all!"

"Why?" Dillon asked.

The man looked at him sharply, rubbed his head vigorously with both hands, and said, "None o' your business that I can tell."

"How be ye yourself?" Dillon asked, perching on a
rickety table while his old friend Culley pulled on a
woollen shirt and splashed whiskey into a glass, first wiping it out with the tails of his shirt.

"So-so," Culley answered. "I spent more time in the
bloody baron's blaygird dungeons, thanks to ye, charged
with treason and inciting rebellion, o' all things. I was
lucky to keep my head, and many o' my mates were no'
so lucky. Ye left a fine tangle behind ye, Scruffy, when
ye went off wi' that lad wi' the healing hands."

"Indeed? We heard there'd been fighting . . ."

"Och, aye! It were grand. The streets ran red with

their blood, but at last they beat us back and we had trouble avoiding the widow-maker, that I can assure ye."

"How did ye?"

Culley laughed, and tapped his nose. "So wha' is it ye are wanting wi' me, lad? I ken ye have no' appeared on my doorstep after half a year gone just to hear how my health is. Wha' do ye want?"

"Do I have to want anything, Culley?" Dillon said, hurt.

"I be no fool, Scruffy."

He laughed. "I need to see His Highness, King o' the Thieves."

Culley raised one brow. "Ye be a plucky lad, that I have to say for ye."

"It be very important, Culley."

"It always is wi' ye, Scruffy. Wha' be your business?"

Dillon eyed him consideringly, then said abruptly, "All right, I'll tell ye but ye must promise me no' to flap your gums unless I give ye leave, or ye'll have me to answer for."

"Obh obh! Threats now, is it? All right, all right, keep your kilt on! I willna tell a soul unless ye say so."

Dillon told him nearly everything—the only thing he did not tell was where Lachlan MacCuinn and the Blue Guards were hiding. That was one secret that was best kept, he thought. Culley whistled once or twice in surprise, but otherwise waited until Dillon was silent again. Then he said slowly, "It all ties together. There's been some auld biddy whispering in His Highness's ear this past month, saying the same sort o' stuff, all about Samhain and the winged lad who's going to save us all. We've been told to spread the tale, for there are many here who have no' heard it, being refugees from the countryside."

"Why? How come so many people in the city?" Dillon asked. "We've had no news in a month or more."

Culley guffawed. "Well, make yourself comfortable, my lad. How long have ye got?"

By the time he was finished, Dillon was white. Bright Soldiers controlling Dùn Gorm, Fairgean in the river and lochan, the Rìgh forced to flee to Lucescere—no wonder the palace had been so closely guarded, so brightly lit! What would Lachlan say when he discovered his brother was at the other end of the garden?

Culley tossed down the last of his whiskey, and said, "Well, His Highness will be most interested to hear all your news. He's had to move a lot lately, for the Awl have been searching the houses and dragging away anyone they suspect o' being a guild member. We've had a hard six months here indeed."

He took Dillon back through the city, heading into the prosperous merchants' quarter. The streets were wide and swept clean of refuse, and lanterns swung every few paces, their light blurred by the constantly falling rain. Revellers sang and danced through the streets.

"I did no' expect to see the Samhain festival," Dillon panted.

"The Awl had banned it but then the Rìgh said the people needed something to keep their spirits up, and that he would rather leave this life ringed with fire and song than in bleakness and fear."

Dillon's heart slammed. "The Rìgh is dying?"

"How can ye no' ken? We have been holding our breaths every day this week, and they say it is only the skills o' his healer that keep him lingering on."

"We have had no news."

"They say the shock o' the attack, and the jolting o' their retreat through the mountains . . . and the Banrìgh giving birth on the road, all—"

Again Dillon exclaimed, stopping in their swift walking to stare at Culley. The rebel took his arm and led him on, saying, "I canna tell ye all the news in the street! Keep quiet and I'll take ye to the safe house."

They came to an ornate gate and slipped through, giving a password to the guards standing in the shadows, then they walked up a short drive, edged by thick shrubbery and lined with the delicate shapes of winter-bare trees. Ahead was a grand house, the roof steep above the tangled network of twigs, many windows lit with golden light. Dillon tugged at the tattered hem of his shirt and called Jed to heel with a quiver in his voice. Big houses made him nervous.

They were let into the house by a man with a smooth, silent way of moving which made Dillon even more uncomfortable. A serving maid took them up to a long sitting room overlooking the garden. Rain lashed the windows, and Dillon was very glad to stand before the fire, steaming and shaking out his shirt. He looked about him warily, noting the gilt-framed pictures, the cushions and brass jugs, the thick carpet, the velvet chaise longue and fat-seated chairs.

There were many people in the room, most of whom ignored Dillon. He recognized the King of the Thieves, an old man with a wispy beard and intelligent dark eyes with a gleam of mischief lurking deep within. Near him was his daughter, a thin woman with a wild mass of dark hair. She wore a cutlass thrust through her belt, and Dillon knew she would have a dagger somewhere under her skirts.

Among the rough clothes and loud voices were several men who wore ornately trimmed velvet doublets and embroidered hose. One of these, a man with a pointed gray beard, was evidently the master here for he directed the serving maid to bring more ale and some food. By his side sat an old woman, dressed neatly in gray. She had very bright black eyes that seemed to pierce right through Dillon, and gray hair streaked with white. She said nothing but listened carefully to everything that was said, and watched everyone's expressions and body language closely.

The King of Thieves was shaking with laughter. "If it is no' my auld friend Dillon the Bold!" he said. "Somehow I thought we had no' seen the last o' ye, laddie! Come sit wi' me and tell me all your news!"

Reluctantly Dillon left the warmth of the fire and came to sit on a stool by the old man's feet. Carefully he told him what he had told Culley, aware that the old woman was listening to every word. Also listening intently was a tall man with a red beard and chestnut curls. Although he lay back in his chair with his scuffed boots on the table, swirling whiskey in a glass, his eyes were very alert.

The old woman spoke only once, asking after the health of Jorge, Lachlan and Iseult. Staring, wondering who she was to call them by their names, Dillon told her all was well. Her wrinkled face relaxed a little.

Taking a deep breath, Dillon asked, as politely as he knew how, if the Guild of Thieves was still supportive of the rebels and if they were willing to give their aid, should it be needed over the next week.

The old man laughed till he wept and had to swallow a dram of whiskey before he could get his breath back. Wheezing, he mopped his cheeks with his beard and said, "Eà love ye, lad, ye are here now in the headquarters o' the rebels themselves. O' course we're wi' ye! We've been chewing our nails to the quick, wondering if this winged lad was going to show his face as we'd been told. The city is bursting wi' men—the MacCuinn said none can be turned away and so rebel and refugee came in together, and who can tell who is what?"

Dillon asked for, and received, many details of numbers and position, and they discussed how the rebels were to be informed that the time to rise had come.

The old woman leant forward. "Tell Lachlan he must ring the tower bell. It can be heard all over the city. All he needs do is ring the bell and the city will rise."

Dillon nodded, finding it hard not to fidget under her gaze. She had a thin, autocratic face with a high-bridged nose that reminded him of someone. As he was trying to puzzle out who, the maid returned with a tray of food, and he was given a bowl of soup to eat and some fine white bread unlike anything he had eaten before. As he wolfed it down, the old woman sat and told him a great deal of news that Culley had not thought to mention. As he listened, Dillon's eyes grew rounder and rounder. Lachlan was not going to like any of this at all!

There was suddenly a whirring sound and then chimes
rang out. Dillon looked about in surprise, realizing the
sound came from an ornately carved box on the wall.
"It is eleven o'clock, laddie," the old woman said.
"Should ye no' be returning to your friends? It is Samhain, ye know."

Dillon scrambled to his feet. "I did no' hear the rat-
tlewatch," he said with a strong note of curiosity in his
voice.

"Nay, but dinna ye hear the clock?"

Dillon had never even heard of a clock, and she
amused him by opening it up so he could watch the little
wheels spinning and clacking inside. She pressed her
hand on his shoulder. "Have courage, laddie, all will
be well."

Dillon was jogging back through the rainy darkness
when he stopped abruptly. He had just remembered who
the old woman reminded him of, with her high-bridged
nose and the white streak through her hair—it was Lachlan himself.

"Where did ye get the smokeweed from?" Jay asked
curiously.

Finn cast him a wicked glance out of her bright hazel
eyes. Puffing luxuriously she said around the stem of the
pipe, "Nicked it, o' course. I've been dying for a smoke!
That's one benefit o' returning to civilization. There's an
inn—let's go get some ale."

The inn had been decorated with turnip lanterns, hol-
lowed out and carved with fearsome faces through which
the light of candles shone. It was packed with people
escaping the rain, and it stunk of wet, unwashed hair
and beer. A troupe of minstrels was playing, and Jay's
face brightened. He hailed the guitarist and was greeted
with friendly warmth. "If it is no' the Fiddler himself!
We missed ye at the midsummer fair. Come grab a
bow."

Finn slid into a booth and let the wriggling cat out of
her jerkin. With an upraised finger she ordered some

beer and sat back with a happy sigh. It had been a long time since she had heard Jay play. He picked up the violin and drew the bow over its strings with a flourish.

While Jay worked his magic, Finn puffed at her pipe and listened to the conversation of two men behind her, their tongues growing looser as the ale in their tankards grew lower. They were both eel-fishers who had fled with the rest of their village when the first Fairgean had been sighted in the Rhyllster. Unlike most of the refugees, they had been lucky enough to find work, cleaning out the palace fishpond and restocking it. The eel-fishers thought they were blessed indeed to have so improved their lot in life.

As Jay brought another swinging tune to an end, there was a scattered round of applause and a few coins were flung his way. Jay frowned and gathered them together. "No' a guid crowd tonight," he said to Finn as he slipped into the bench seat beside her.

"Nay, the mood is no' pretty," she agreed. The eel-fishers behind her were the only ones who seemed to be in a cheerful mood. Everyone else was bemoaning the weather, the state of the nation and the bleakness of the future. In her dark corner, Finn had heard many tragic tales.

She was straining her ears to hear the slurred words behind her when there was a disturbance by the door. She looked up, and immediately her blood turned to iced water. Crowding through the door were six Red Guards, their faces hard and suspicious, their spears at the ready. With them was a seeker, gaunt and hollow-cheeked, with many small buttons running from chin to waist. Finn recognized him. It was the Seeker Renshaw, who had been Glynelda's right hand man. An involuntary moan of fear escaped her lips. Jay turned to her, surprised, and she made a stiff-fingered gesture toward the door.

"The seeker knows me," she whispered. "I have to get out o' here."

Jay was a little puzzled. He and the other boys often

thought Finn overplayed her supposed consequence to the Awl to make herself seem more important. But there was no denying her cheeks were ashen and her fingers trembled now.

"Sit tight," he whispered. "Your hair is white now, he probably will no' recognize ye."

Finn nodded. Under the cover of the table she slid the elven cat down to the ground. *Go, Goblin, hide.* She felt the kitten's head nudging against her bare ankle, and then she slipped away, invisible in the shadows.

All the customers in the inn were looking decidedly nervous, many leaning back into the shadows. The innkeeper was dragged out from the kitchen, his face as white as the flour coating his hands. "I be a loyal subject o' the Rìgh," he protested. "Ye canna believe I'd have anything to do wi' those blaygird rebels!"

The seeker folded his hands together and stared at him with the skin-peeling gaze of the Awl. The innkeeper cowered against the wall. Finn's hands were sweating, even though her body seemed coated in ice.

"Jay," she whispered, "if they nab me, ye do no' ken me. Understand? Pretend to be drunk or stupid, anything. Just do no' let them take ye as well."

"They will no' take ye, idiot," Jay whispered back, but she stared at him with huge, piteous eyes until he promised.

With a cry of triumph, two Red Guards came back with armfuls of swords they had found hidden in the herring barrels. The innkeeper fell to his knees, pleading his innocence.

Finn shrank back in her corner and tried to pretend she was in a drunken stupor, her eyes shut, her mouth hanging open. If she had not been so frightened she would have allowed a thin dribble of saliva to fall, but her mouth was dry and her pulse racing so fast she could not bring her usual thoroughness to the deception.

The customers were searched and questioned, all denying they knew anything about the rebellion. The seeker stood still, scanning the crowd with heavy-lidded eyes. He watched as Jay was dragged to his feet. The boy clutched the violin, muttering he was "naught but a puir fiddler, playing for my supper."

"Who be this, then?" the soldier demanded, seizing Finn by her shirt and dragging her forward along the bench seat. "Just a beggar lass," Jay responded, while Finn slumped forward, letting her fair locks fall over her face.

"A wee bit young to be in her cups, is she no'?"

Jay extemporised quickly. "Her brother was drowned by one o' the wicked Fairgean," he said. "She is cut up pretty bad about it."

"She canna be more than twelve, too young to be drowning her sorrows in a tankard," he said roughly, seizing her hair to look down into her face.

Jay nodded and the soldier let go of Finn's hair so her head fell back against the wooden partition with a thump. He moved away, and Jay moved quickly in front of Finn to hide her from the seeker's eyes. It was too late. His gaze had sharpened at the brief glimpse of the girl's face and now he moved forward, his crimson robes leaving a trail in the straw on the inn's floor. He came right up to the booth and Jay held his ground, despite the terror the man's cold eyes provoked in him.

"Ye know this lass?" the seeker said.

Jay remembered his promise, and shook his head. "No' really. She was cold and greetin', and I felt sorry for her, so I brought her wi' me." He gave an indifferent laugh, wishing he had Finn's talent for deceit. "Wish now I had no'—she drank everything I've earned to-night, and now I'll have to find her somewhere to sleep."

The seeker pulled back the mop of pale curls and stared down into Finn's face. He slipped a hand into her bodice and withdrew the medallion she always wore there. A faint smile curled his thin lips and he tugged at the thong so it snapped, the medallion falling into his hand. "Let me relieve ye o' the trouble, fiddler. I ken this lass, we shall take her with us."

Before he could stop himself Jay shook his head and

saw the seeker's mouth harden. "I promised I'd look after her," he said lamely.

The seeker made a mock pious gesture with his hands. "The Awl has relieved ye o' your responsibility, lad."

He gestured to one of the soldiers, who picked up Finn's limp body and threw it over his shoulder. "Arrest the innkeeper and take him to the dungeons for questioning, along with his servants. I shall interrogate the child myself."

To Jay's dismay, the Red Guards marched out, taking Finn with them. Her fair hair swung as she was carried, her head lolling a few feet above the floor. She looked very small and helpless, and Jay's throat closed with emotion. He would have to rescue her. But how?

Anghus MacRuraich woke out of an uneasy sleep with a jerk. He had spent the evening sampling his host's fine whiskey and listening to the discussions of the rebel leaders. He had been amazed at how well organized the rebels were, and how many of the nobility and merchant class they had attracted to their cause. So fine was his host's whiskey that Anghus had had to be put to bed by his gillie, and he had been asleep only a short time.

It had been a swift and exhausting journey from the mountains to the city, on the trail of Cathmor the Nimble and the rebels. After Tabithas had plunged into the Muileach River, his only hope had been that the rebels would lead him to where Lachlan was, and so his daughter. He was sure now that Fionnghal was with the winged prionnsa, and that the whirling dislocation that had come over him at the sight of her was caused by a reverse spell on her medallion, just as Meghan had surmised.

He had easily found Cathmor and sworn allegiance to the rebellion. "I have come too far now to turn back," he had said. "I hear the MacCuinn is dying. I canna bear the Banrìgh to rule, knowing what she has done, and so I give my support to the Rìgh's brother, young Lachlan. For now there is just my sword and the sword of my men, but I pledge the support o' my people in days to come as well."

As Prionnsa of Rurach and Siantan, Anghus had been eagerly accepted by Cathmor the Nimble, and had been quartered in a safe house in Ban-Bharrach Cliffs, the wealthiest of the city suburbs. The greatest shock had been to walk into the sitting room his first night and find Meghan of the Beasts knitting by the fire. When last he had seen her, Meghan had been shackled and chained, a prisoner of the Awl. He had not heard much news on the road and so had not known of her escape. She had smiled at him and patted the seat beside her. In a flood of joy and relief, he had broken down and wept. His betrayal of their friendship had weighed heavily on him these past few months. She would not tell him how she had escaped, only quirking her seamed mouth and saying, "Lucescere has many secrets."

He had told her of his decision to seek out Fionnghal and what had eventuated, including the disappearance of the wolf. Meghan had been distressed, and hoped Tabithas could survive the rough waters of the Muileach. "If she did, the river will lead her here, Anghus, ye can be sure o' that."

Anghus had begged her for news of his daughter, but Meghan had none. Lucescere was a cesspool of seekers and witch-sniffers, many of whom had their own clairvoyant powers. She had dared not scry when her discovery would smash the rebellion and betray her hosts, who had risked much to hide her.

It was the knowledge that his daughter was nearby that had woken Anghus. He could feel Fionnghal loud as a clarion call, bright as a bonfire. She was so close his skin tingled. He was on his feet in a moment, calling to Donald. Within minutes, he was out in the rain, Casey Hawkeye and the gillie at his heels.

"This way!" Anghus called, feeling his blood pounding quick and heavy in his temples. "She's this way! Hurry!"

Ahead they could see the gates of the palace. A troop

of Red Guards were gathered before them, one carrying a small figure slung over one shoulder, a quantity of fair hair hanging down. He drew his sword, prepared to battle the Red Guards there and then, but Casey pulled him back. Seething with frustration, Anghus watched the gates swing open and the troop march through, a tall, crimson-clad seeker at their head. The gates clanged shut behind them.

Anghus cursed and slammed his fist into the wall. If only they had been quicker! They could have surprised the troop in the streets and wrested Fionnghal from them.

"Ye probably would have been killed and the lassie with ye," Casey said comfortingly.

"We shall have to storm the palace, rescue her!"

"It is too soon—we shall ruin all the rebels' plans," Casey objected. "They are no' ready yet. They all wait for Samhain Night."

"Why?" Anghus raged. "Is there any point to waiting? The men are in place, they have weapons, why do they wait? I canna wait! I want my daughter!"

"If ye can follow her, if ye can find where she is hidden, perhaps stealth is better anyway," Casey said.

Anghus turned to him with a thankful cry. "Aye! We shall sneak in and retrieve her. My poor Fionnghal, in the hands o' the Awl! I canna stand it."

Donald said, "My laird, I do no' think it is a guid idea to be so risking yourself and your daughter. The Awl have had her for five years—wha' does one more night matter?"

"No' one more night, no' one more hour!" Anghus vowed. "Donald! Casey! Are ye with me? Ye can return to the safe house if ye wish, no dishonor. But I find my daughter now or die in the attempt!"

"I'm with ye, my laird, wherever ye go. Ye ken that," Donald said. "But I think we should go and seek help. We do no' ken the layout o' the palace, or wha' sort o' guard they're likely to keep. And it is half past the hour.

Soon everything will be locked up tight for Samhain. We canna risk being locked out on Samhain Eve, my laird."

Some of the glare in Anghus' eyes faded. He nodded. "Very well, but let us be quick about it. I do no' want to lose Fionnghal again."

Dillon crouched in the dark little alley, watching anxiously for his friends. It was well past the hour and there was no sign of them. Jed whined and pressed against him, and he pulled the puppy into his lap, hugging him tightly.

Just then two small figures emerged from the mist and rain, and Dillon recognized Anntoin and Artair with relief. They crouched with him behind the huge barrels, whispering him their news. They had met up with Cathmor the Nimble, who had managed to bring all five hundred of his men into the city, disguising them as refugees. Together with the members of the underground already active in Lucescere, there were several thousand men and women just waiting for the signal to attack the Red Guards.

Their bottoms were getting numb from the stone and Dillon shifted restlessly. "Wha' about Finn and Jay? Where can they be? If they are no' here soon, we shall have to go back without them."

They heard running footsteps, then Jay dashed into the side alley, taking no care at all to make sure he was not observed. Before Dillon could reprimand him, Jay had flung himself on them, his dirty face strained and white. "Finn! The Awl has got Finn! She was right—they do know her, and they took her away with them."

"Flaming dragon balls!" Dillon cried. "Wha' do they want wi' her?"

Jay shrugged, trying to clear his throat. His voice broke as he said, "The seeker knew about her charm—he looked at it and smiled, and said he knew this lass and he would take her wi' him."

"Where did they take her?"

"Into the palace. I followed them until I was sure, then ran here as fast as I could. We have to rescue her."

Dillon clambered to his feet, pushing the puppy off his lap. "Come on then, we'd best be moving. We've got news to tell and Lachlan is going to need to know that one o' us is in the hands o' the Awl. We may have to change our plans."

"Finn will no' betray us," Jay cried.

Dillon looked at him gravely. "No' even if they put her to the Question?"

Jay said nothing, his face white and miserable.

Isabeau was half asleep in her chair by the fire, listening to the rain striking the windows, glad she was inside. After her months traipsing through the countryside, she had lost all idealism about such adventures, knowing there was no protection from the cold and wet on the road.

Isabeau was very tired. She had tended the Rìgh all the long day and fought for his life all evening. Each hour that passed he sank further and further toward death. About ten minutes ago the Banrìgh had sent for the Rìgh's council. It was clear even to her that her husband had only a few hours left to live. She wanted him to declare Bronwen his heir and Maya the Regent, and have the documents properly ratified and signed. Isabeau was not, of course, needed for such official business and she had been kindly but firmly told to go and get some rest.

She had been only too glad to obey. Maya had dressed for the occasion in her crimson velvet, and Isabeau found the sight of it almost unbearable. The Banrìgh looked very beautiful in the tight gown, its rich color highlighting the ivory pallor of her skin, the blue-black sheen of her silky hair. Her beauty meant nothing to Isabeau. To her that color entailed only blood, terror, agonizing pain. The Banrìgh's dress was the original model for the seekers' robes, buttoned to the throat with twenty-five velvet buttons that reminded Isabeau powerfully of Maya's position as the ultimate leader of the Awl. She had been glad to take Bronwen and hide away in the nursery, her severed fingers throbbing in remembered pain.

Something knocked against the window, jerking her awake. She got to her feet and walked over to the window embrasures, concealed behind heavy brocade curtains of silver, blue and gold. Outside it was dark. She could see the trees tossing in the wind, the clouds racing across the moons. Perched on the windowsill was a small dark shape. Bending so that her nose was almost pressed against the glass, she saw two bright eyes and a bedraggled tail.

"Gitâ!" She fumbled to unlatch the window. "Gitâ, what are ye doing here?" Immediately she remembered Meghan saying she would send someone to her and she smiled. She swung open the window, the wind swirling into the room so the curtain billowed up behind her. She gathered the wet, shivering donbeag into her arms and he crept up to snuggle against her neck. Tears stung her eyes. Gitâ said, *Sad?*

She closed the window again and went back to her chair. *No, happy.*

My witch says ye sad and lonely.

I was, but oh, Gitâ, I am so happy to see ye. Where have ye been?

With your mirror-face.

My mirror-face?

Dragon sister.

Dragon sister?

The donbeag sat up on his hind legs and patted her face with his paws. *Dragon sister. Born of the one womb.*

Isabeau was so flabbergasted she did not say a word. For a moment she thought she had misunderstood the little creature, but he put his paws together and bobbed his head, donbeag for "truth speaking."

Ye have been with my twin? I have a twin sister?

He chittered in agreement, and sent Isabeau an image of a sabre leopard.

She's a sabre leopard? Isabeau was more confused than ever.

He hooked his claws in her bodice so he could climb up to her shoulder and pat her earlobe in comfort. *Fierce lass. Fierce as a sabre leopard.*

She felt excitement fill her. A twin sister!

Where? How?

Dragons.

"Dragons!" she cried aloud, and the baby in the cradle whimpered.

Dragons, the donbeag repeated. He slipped down into her lap again and curled up in a ball so he could groom his rain-slicked fur.

Where is she?

Near.

Isabeau gripped her fingers together. A twin sister! No wonder she had always felt so alone, as if half of her was missing. Dreams of sisterly love flowered in her mind. *What is she like?*

Sabre leopard.

Isabeau frowned. Sabre leopards and dragons did not sound altogether promising. *Where is she? Is she with Meghan?* Jealousy stabbed her unexpectedly in the stomach.

No, my witch gone.

Ye did no' come from Meghan?

My beloved tell me you sad and lonely, come look after you. I with mirror-face.

Where is Meghan?

My witch not far.

Canna ye tell me, Gitâ? I've missed her so much, and I do no ken what it is she expects me to do.

Beloved waits for moons to cross.

Isabeau gave up. The fact that Gitâ was here meant that Meghan could not be too far away. "Will ye stay with me, Gitâ?"

Stay till beloved calls me. Watch over you, keep you safe from harm.

Isabeau did not smile. Instead she sighed with gratitude and hugged the donbeag closer. He licked her hand with his warm tongue, and said, *Sleep, I will watch over you.* So she did.

It was a nerve-wracking trip back to the ruined tower. By the time they had made their way through the garden, the rain had stopped. It must be perilously close to midnight.

Dillon ran for the tower door first. By the time Jay had burst in, Iseult and Lachlan had all the news. The prionnsa was pacing the floor, his wings upright and slightly spread, his fists clenched. His eyes were bright with tears. "It canna be true, Jaspar canna be dying!"

"But Lachlan, we've been hearing for months how ill he's been. Ye must have known he was dying! All our plans are based on the fact that he would die!"

"That's no' true!" Lachlan cried. "Always I hoped that we would be able to save him. Meghan would have known what to do. I thought once I had the Lodestar and could prove to him who I am . . . that once I realized how much damage Maya has done . . ." He laid his arms along the fireplace and wept, great, harsh sobs.

Iseult went to him, but he shook her away, struggling to control himself. Duncan spoke quietly to the other Blue Guards in the room, sending them out to patrol the tower. Once they had gone, he stood with his shoulders against the wall, his hands resting on his dagger hilt.

Lachlan took a deep breath and raised his head. "It is too soon! I have no' spoken to him, explained. He does no' ken the truth."

"But Lachlan . . ."

He talked on, not heeding her or the wide-eyed children. "He will die thinking Maya the banrìgh o' his dreams, no' knowing how she has killed and tortured and ensorcelled . . ." His voice broke.

Jorge said quietly, "It does no' matter, Lachlan. He will die happy."

"No! No, do ye no' see?"

"I see that the time has come for Gearradh to have a

hand in this weaving. It is no' for us to say when a man must die, Lachlan. It is for she who cuts the thread.''

"Jorge, canna ye see it is all wrong this way? Meghan said we had to wait for Samhain to retrieve the Lodestar, that its song was dying and we needed to bathe it at the hour o' its birth to save it. So I waited to confront that cursehag and I waited to talk with Jaspar and explain— I waited because Meghan said he would never believe me, that her blaygird ensorcelment was too strong, that I would die as an *uile-bheist* on the fire . . ." A sob tore in his throat, and he stopped, clenching his hands into fists. "I told him! I told him when first he married her. I *knew* she was no' what she seemed. Then when I held her boot, I knew. She's *Fairge!*" He spat the word. "No matter what ye all say, I ken she is Fairge."

"Lachlan, we have no' got the Lodestar," Iseult said, troubled. "Ye canna be storming the palace without it!"

"I have the Bow!"

"And have no' even seen if ye can string it yet! Let alone got used to its balance and thrust, used it until it is as much a part o' ye as your own hand!"

He was silent. Jorge said persuasively, "Lachlan, it is only one more night. Today is the last day o' autumn; tomorrow it is Samhain, and we can penetrate the maze. Meghan told ye that was the time. Join the Key, retrieve the Lodestar, bathe it in the pool when the two moons have crossed and the water is again filled with power. Then, when it is in your hand and potent again, then ye can use it to prove to Jaspar who ye are, and protect yourself from her . . ."

"But it might be too late. They say his heart stopped, his face was blue and the healer was breathing her own breath into his lungs. They say she pounded his chest. Dillon heard it all."

"What was strange is that they called the healer the Red. As we all call ye, Iseult." Dillon thought it was time the conversation grew more constructive.

Iseult and Lachlan shot a look at each other. "Isabeau!"

Jorge said excitedly, "It must be! She will have the rest o' the Key!"

"We canna get into the maze without the Key," Lachlan said swiftly. "If we want to get the Lodestar, we need to join the Key first, ye all ken that! We'll have to go into the palace to get it . . ."

"Do no' be a fool, lad!" Jorge cried.

"I am no' a lad!" Lachlan shouted. "I am Lachlan Owein MacCuinn!" He spun round, his talons scraping against the stone. "The Lodestar will have to wait! Do ye no' see, if I do no' convince Jaspar who I am and what his horrid wife has done, he will name his Fairge daughter heir! That is what she wants! All this time we've been so careful to never strike against Jaspar, only against her! Is it my fault or Enit's fault that there were so many pirates or bandits? They said we were in league with them but we never were. I need to make him understand and name me heir. That was all I ever wanted! She ensorcelled the babe into being. Jorge, ye ken that. It was the comet spell—a Spell o' Begetting. It is no' a true growth o' love, like our babes will be. If they name her Regent and the babe heir, then it will truly be civil war, for I will no' stand that woman—that *uile-bheist*— to rule! She has killed Jaspar, as surely as she killed Donncan and Feargus, as surely as she has tried again and again to kill me!"

Jay, who knew nothing about the Lodestar and did not care, started forward, his voice shrill, "What are ye all blabber-mouthing for! Do ye no' understand Finn is in the hands o' the Awl?"

Finn opened her eyes cautiously. There had been no sound for well over ten minutes. Though every sense warned her of danger, she could not wait any longer.

She was lying on a velvet couch in a dimly lit room. On the table near her foot a chess game was set out, the players engaged. She let her eyes rove over the room and then noticed a thin, white hand lying amongst the crimson velvet thrown over the chair opposite. Her heart hammering, she raised her eyes and saw a high-templed, white face, heavy-lidded, thin-mouthed, smiling. Amongst all the dull crimson, there was only the white of his face and hand and stiff ruff.

"So ye have decided to wake, Fionnghal."

"Why do ye call me that?" She lifted her hand to her throat. "Give me back my charm!"

He smiled and said nothing. She launched herself from the couch, nails raking, but he caught her throat in his thin, white hand and bore her to her knees. He gripped so hard she could barely breathe. Her small hands caught at his, but he did not relent. She knelt, quiescent. "Wild as an elven cat, ye are, Fionnghal." She jerked under his hand and he looked at her, puzzled. "That moves ye, I see. I wonder why." He looked her over, a smile-sneer on his face at her rags and general filth. "The MacRuraich would no' be so proud if he could see ye now, would he?"

She tried to speak, but her throat was paralyzed. He clenched a little closer, then threw her down. She lay still, swallowing air as if it were wine. He sat back, and his hand on his thigh was so still it was like marble.

"Ye slipped Glynelda's leash. A bad time ye gave her, ye and that red-haired wench. And auld Kersey dead, one o' the best bounty-hunters there ever was. Completely ruthless and corruptible. Just the way we like them. Did ye kill him, Fionnghal? I doubt he treated ye well. Did he hurt ye, Fionnghal?"

"Why do ye call me that?" she whispered.

"It is your name. A beautiful name. It means 'fair one,' and indeed ye are fair now, Fionnghal. When last I saw ye, ye were a dark imp, a wee goblin.' Again she startled involuntarily, and his gaze sharpened.

'Ye prick to the most unexpected barbs, Fionnghal. Ye intrigue me. I wonder what ye are doing here. We had tracked ye down to a gang o' filthy beggar bairns, stealing moldy bread from trash heaps and playing at intrigue. Where are they now, your friends? Where is the lad with the healing hands? Ye ken such sorcery is evil, Fionnghal? Ye ken such evil enchantments need to be cleansed by the fire? Ye ken the penalty for treason and witchcraft is death, Fionnghal?"

She lay still, watching him, waiting. He sat back. His hand smoothed his velvet coat, lifted to the tiny button at his throat, the first button of twenty-four. She saw his tightly tailored coat bulged slightly over one hip. He had something in his pocket. Something round. She lifted her eyes to his face.

"Death by fire, Fionnghal."

She gave a little whimper and lifted her hands to her throat. "Ye hurt me," she said piteously.

"Where are your friends, Fionnghal?"

"Please, can I have some wine? To soothe my throat?"

He poured some wine, red as his velvet. As she drank, he talked, startling her with his knowledge. He knew the King of Thieves had helped them escape, that the boy who lead the beggar children had a puppy with a black-patched face.

"Please, I feel faint. I do no' understand what ye mean. My head is spinning. I need something to eat," Finn moaned. At last he rang a bell. His servants brought them bread, white and soft as the cheese, and ripe red bellfruit on a tray, with a curved silver knife and linen napkins. She took her time over it, pretending to fumble in drunken clumsiness.

He laughed sardonically. "Only twelve and a cub unto her father! No wonder the family is weak, with a taste for the demon drink."

"Wha' do ye mean?" Finn mumbled. "All this mysterious . . . mutter!"

He watched her, suspicious. "I hope the supper is to your liking, my lady Fionnghal. Surely better than what ye are accustomed to."

"Indeed 'tis," she slurred and knocked over the pepper pot with her elbow, so pepper poured out. Babbling apologies, she tried to scrape it back into the crystal container. He glanced at her sharply, and she gave him a drunken smile and burped loudly. Finn had spent half of her life with Kersey Witch-Sniffer, a man who was drunk more often than not—she could mimic every expression, belch and stammer. The seeker looked away, disgusted. With a quick fling of her wrist, she threw the pepper straight into his face. He sneezed violently, his eyes streaming. Before he could cry out she had brought the heavy silver tray crashing down on his head. He crumpled and slid to the ground.

She retrieved her medallion and knotted it round her neck again, then dragged down one of the curtains and carefully rolled him up in it. It should muffle his cries and restrict his movements for quite some time. When he was as neatly swaddled as any baby, she smiled and gave a little jig. *Now to get out o' here!*

Meghan and most of the ringleaders were still in the sitting room, finalizing their plans. Anghus burst in, shouting for men, for arms, for directions. It took some time to work out what was wrong. Anghus was keeping his temper on a tight rein, but was unable to stand still in his impatience. At last he shouted, "That's it, I am going! Stay, ye cowards! I care no'."

A thin young man called Culley stood up, yawned and stretched. "I know how to get into the palace unseen, my laird. I will take ye for a price."

"We are to wait for the signal," another said. "Culley, ye ken we were told to lie low until the signal came."

"Stow it, Lunn. The man wants his daughter, I want his bag o' gold. Seems like a fair bargain to me."

Meghan stood up, draping her plaid about her. "I will go with ye too, Anghus. I am uneasy in my heart. Too much has happened to alter my plans and I am no' there to steady my young hotheads. Ye plan to enter through the sewers, Culley?"

"Aye," he said, awed.

"Do ye ken the way or is it just bravado?"

"I have marked many o' the most important turns."

"But no' all o' them? Then I will call Ceit Anna. It

will no' suit my plans to be lost in the sewers under Lucescere, no, indeed."

"I do know the way, my lady. I have used it several times."

"Very well, then, but let's be quick about it."

Within minutes they were in the boulevard, and Culley was pulling up an iron manhole to climb down below street level. With twenty rebels to help guard them, they clambered down into the reeking darkness.

Through endless passages they hurried, illuminated only by the light of their candles, gagging at the foul stench. Culley found his way by checking for scratch marks on the wall. He told them the story of Tòmas the Healer, and how he had helped the King of Thieves and his followers escape the dungeons of Lucescere Palace. They had been led through this maze of ducts and drains by a nyx. Culley had not trusted the black-winged faery and so had scratched his mark here and there on the wall in case the nyx left them somewhere to rot. Realizing the usefulness of the underground system, he had spent time in the following few months exploring the sewers and marking key turnoffs. His foresight had paid off later when he had been arrested again and had managed to escape through the sewers a second time.

They had just begun to climb an upward sloping drainpipe, wading through storm water, when Anghus suddenly cried, "No!"

"What be wrong, my laird?"

"I've lost the connection! Something has happened—I canna feel Fionnghal any more!" They looked at each other in foreboding.

"What could have happened?" Casey whispered.

"Did ye no' say it was a spell on her medallion that prevented ye from sensing her?" Donald said placidly. "Happen she has just put it back on."

Anghus nodded, trying not to think about what else it could mean. He was tense and undecided, the others waiting to see what he thought was the best course of action. After a moment he said, "Let us push on. It will be much harder to find her now, but I canna leave her there another minute. We shall just have to track her down with our mere human senses."

Finn thought swiftly. There would be guards beyond the door. It was a miracle they had not heard her scuffles already. She wrapped the cloak about her and climbed out the palace window, closing it gently after her. It was dark, the rain beating against her back. She moved cautiously along a ridge of decorative stone, came to an open window and crawled inside. It was too dangerous to be hanging out there in that rain, particularly when the hour to midnight was already trickling away.

She tiptoed through the sleeping palace, came at last to the great staircase, and leant over the marble balustrade. Four floors below her was the entrance hall. She could see soldiers, stiff-backed and straight-speared. She ducked back, thinking furiously. There must be a servants' staircase, and at this time of the night it was likely to be empty. All she had to do was find it, slip down it and out through the kitchens into the garden.

Desperately she hoped Goblin had stayed with Jay, that Jay and Dillon and the others had returned safely to the tower, that they would do nothing rash. Surely they knew she could look after herself?

As if her thought of Goblin had summoned her, Finn saw the tiny cat poke her black nose through the front door of the entrance hall. Finn closed her eyes. *No, Goblin*, she prayed. *They will see ye, go back.* Then she opened them again, desperate to see what was happening.

The cat had slinked around the perimeter of the hall, almost invisible in the shadows, and was now bounding silently up the stairs. She was very black against the white marble. Finn could see her clearly, but the soldiers were all staring in front of them and did not notice.

The little black cat pranced up the final flight of steps, her tail raised high. She bounded into Finn's arms, kneaded her neck painfully, then demanded to be put down with one of her high-pitched, almost silent mews.

Clever kitty! Finn said, dropping her on the ground. *Let's get out o' here.*

Ten minutes later she had reached the western wing of the palace, the one closest to the gardens. She had to hide behind some curtains as a group of men passed by, talking in low voices, their heads bent together. They were richly dressed, in doublets and embroidered hose. She wondered what they were doing, wandering the palace in the wee small hours.

She followed the men, unable to help speculating about what they were up to. Their expressions had been so serious, the air of furtive excitement so intriguing, that Finn thought she should take advantage of being in the palace to find out what she could. Besides, they were going in the direction she wanted to, and surely it could not do any harm to see what they were up to.

The corridor was dimly lit, lanterns casting an occasional pool of light. She had wrapped herself well in the cloak, keeping the hood pulled forward. The cloak protected her against the cold, and she felt safer with her face hidden. Conscious of time running away, she began to hurry, turning a corner without first checking to see if the hall beyond was empty. She came to an abrupt halt, terror beating through her. Four soldiers stood only a few feet away, talking in low voices. One was facing her, and as she stared helplessly, he raised his eyes and stared straight at her.

Terror held her motionless. She waited for the inevitable shout. Nothing happened. The soldier's eyes passed over her as if she was not there, even though the light from the nearest lantern must have fallen upon her.

He made a gruff comment and touched his fingers to his helmet. Then he and his companion wheeled away and came down the hall toward her. Finn stood still, unable to believe they did not see her when she could see them so clearly. They passed within a foot of her, saying something about the Rìgh, and disappeared

around the corner. Finn did not move. The other two
soldiers talked a while longer, then marched off, somehow not noticing the cloak-shrouded little girl pressed
against the wall in full view. Trembling with reaction,
she waited a full minute before slowly and carefully
continuing.

She reached the end of the wide corridor and carefully
peered around the corner. Her heart hammering, she
whipped her head back. Two guards stood outside a
grand door, spears at the ready. Another two were
standing at the top of the marble staircase opposite.

Her only thought now was to get back to the tower
but she could hear voices behind her, and the beat of
marching feet. She picked up the elven cat, tucked her
into the cloak's capacious pocket, pulled the hood further over her head and tiptoed across the corridor to
the door opposite.

Within was a bedroom, thankfully empty. She put
back the hood so she could look about her. It was a
lofty room, its ceiling painted with clouds and suns and
the delicate shape of dancing nisses. In the center of the
room was a wide bed with carved and gilded posts. The
satin brocade curtains were blue and silver, fringed
with gold.

In one corner was a gilded mirror on a stand.
Thoughtfully Finn went to stand before it. To her disappointment she could see herself clearly. She was about
to turn away when, on an impulse, she lifted the hood
over her head. A thrill went down her spine, electrifying
her. She was invisible. She had simply disappeared. She
could see the room behind her reflected in the mirror,
but there was no image of her at all. She pulled the
hood away, and there she was, a small, black figure in
the cloak, her face rather white, her eyes glittering
with excitement.

Realizing the mantle she had found in the tower's relic
room was a cloak of invisibility made her escape from
the palace a much easier proposition. Smiling, she
looked about her consideringly. There was a set of dou-

ble doors in the right-hand wall, standing slightly ajar. She slipped through, careful not to move the doors, and found herself in a dressing room. By the richness of the gowns she knew she was in the quarters of one of the aristocracy, and wondered where the lady was. *Probably gone to visit her amour*, Finn thought with a grin. Beyond was a lady's boudoir, daintily furnished and quite empty.

She went quietly through the next set of double doors and found herself in a room lit only by the flickering flames on the hearth. Glancing about she saw someone asleep in the chair by the fire, Gitâ curled on her lap. The firelight played over her copper-red curls. "Iseult!" Finn cried. "Wha' are ye doing here?"

She threw back the hood of her cloak and shook the sleeping girl vigorously. The redhead woke and stared at Finn with bemused blue eyes. "What?" she said sleepily. "What's wrong?" Then her eyes opened wide and she sat up hastily. "The Rìgh! Has he taken a turn for the worse?"

She got to her feet, setting the donbeag back down on the chair. Finn stepped away, feeling scared. As soon as she had heard the girl's voice, she knew it was not Iseult. She saw now the girl was wearing a plain gray gown with a white apron, quite unlike Iseult's white leather jerkin and breeches. As the girl yawned and stretched, she saw one hand was tightly bound up with bandages.

"Well, answer me!" the stranger with Iseult's face cried. "Has the cat got your tongue, lassie? What's wrong?"

"Nothing, I'm sorry, I made a mistake," Finn babbled, staring at her with astonished eyes. Apart from the bandaged hand and the clothes, she was identical to Iseult, down to the red-gold curl that dangled into her eyes and was pushed away with an impatient hand.

The girl cast Finn a shrewd look from her vivid blue eyes. "What do ye mean, ye made a mistake? Ye wake me from the best sleep I've had in weeks to tell me ye've made a mistake? Who are ye? I have no' seen ye before. What are ye doing in the royal suite?"

Finn felt her jaw drop, her eyes widen. The royal suite? She cast a wild look around the gilded and painted room, noting the luxurious furnishings and the grand dimensions. She decided she had to get out of here, fast! Her eyes fell on the donbeag, now sitting up and watching with bright eyes. *Gitâ?* she thought incredulously, and the little donbeag chittered in welcome.

"Ye know Gitâ?" the girl said. "Who are ye?"

"I'm Finn," she said limply. "Who are ye?"

"Isabeau the Red," she answered and suddenly Finn knew she was a fool. She had heard of Iseult's twin sister Isabeau; indeed, she had known Isabeau was in the palace for she had heard Lachlan and Iseult worrying about some key she was meant to have. She sat down and said, "I'm an idiot!"

Isabeau laughed. "Are ye? Why?"

Finn thought there were more differences between the twins than she had thought. Isabeau's face was much more expressive, and she was quick to both laughter and words. Iseult had a quality of coiled stillness about her, like a spring about to be released. She rarely laughed, and when she did, it was involuntary and quickly smothered.

"I should have known who ye were as soon as I saw ye," she answered. "Ye look exactly like Iseult!"

"I do?" Isabeau replied swiftly. "Who is Iseult?"

Again Finn was staggered. "Your sister—I thought."

"Ah, the sabre-leopard girl." She chittered at Gitâ, who chittered back excitedly. She smiled at Finn. "Do no' look so startled. I only found out I had a sister twenty minutes ago. Is she here too? What are ye doing here?"

Finn explained to Isabeau how she came to be sneaking through the palace. Isabeau's interest quickened as Finn told her how she and her companions were hiding out in the ruined witches' tower. Isabeau gave a little laugh. "Half o' Rionnagan is being turned upside for this mysterious rebel leader and ye say he's in the very midst o' the Awl's headquarters!"

She hammered Finn with questions, but the little girl was growing restive. Even with her cloak of invisibility, Finn was dreading the return to the tower and worried about what her companions might do. How dreadful if they tried to rescue her and were caught themselves!

Jay's words cut through the impassioned speech like a knife. There was no need to articulate the danger. Apart from their fears for Finn's safety, they all knew the possibility of their hiding place being tricked or tortured from her. Lachlan seized the bow and bent it. "Iseult, I need to string it!"

Iseult's face was impassive. "I will get ye one o' Cloudshadow's hairs." The Celestine had pulled out a handful of her coarse mane for them, and they were coiled in one of the many compartments of Iseult's satchel.

It was a tall bow, and strongly made. Few men could have bent it and strung it, but Lachlan managed it. All the muscles in his neck and shoulders bulged, and a sheen of perspiration sprung up on his brow, but it was done in moments. Iseult gritted her jaw. It seemed her pupil was outstripping her.

"We must hurry. How are we to get to the palace safely? It is almost midnight, and the rain is blowing over."

"Call back the rain. And mist, a thick mist." Iseult spoke quickly. "We have watched Meghan do it, and she says we are both strong in the Element o' Air. And ye have a Talent with water, Lachlan, ye ken ye do. All ye have to do is use it!"

He nodded, his jaw determined. Iseult held out *The Book of Shadows*. "It will help us, I know it will."

Their eyes locked and he smiled. "Ye must all stay here," he said to the others. "Nay, no arguments. Iseult and I can do this better alone." Lachlan caught up Finn's hunting horn, which lay on the table with Jay's viola. "I will blow on the horn if I am in trouble. One blast, I want ye to come to me. Two blasts, and ye must get out as fast as ye can. Either way, someone must ring the tower bell to alert our friends in the city. Understand?'

Jorge said urgently, "Be careful, my dears. It is Samhain, night o' the dead. I feel death is very near. I am afraid . . ."

"That is why I must go, Jorge. It is Jaspar's death ye feel, and he is the last o' my brothers. Ye do understand?'

The blind seer nodded, though his cheeks were wet with tears.

MIRRORS

Iseult and Lachlan ran up the stairs, taking two or three steps at a time. Out on the balcony they knelt between the delicately fluted columns and set *The Book of Shadows* on the ground before them. They were both afraid.

They did not know how to ask the book for help and so they just stared at it. The cover flung itself open, the pages riffling in a rising wind. They clasped hands. "Come rain, come mist, come darkness, come concealment," they chanted, drawing in their will and focusing their desire as much as they were able. "Come rain, come mist, come darkness, come concealment," Lachlan sang, finding a melody in the chant, "Come rain, come mist, come darkness, come concealment."

The pages fell open, and a small tornado rose out of the book. It spun, gaining height and force, and they gripped hands, rain spitting over their faces. Leaves began to twist into its heart; lightning speared out, needle-thin but quick and deadly. Thunder shook the pillars, and the tornado veered out and into the night, gathering momentum. Their hair blew away from their faces, and in another flash of lightning much greater than the first, they saw each other's terrified faces.

"How did we do that?"

"It was no' us, it was the book," Iseult cried. She closed it, goodwishing it fervently, and thrust it back into the pouch at her belt. They scrambled to their feet and ran to the stairs. An eerie sound was rising. Suddenly ghosts were all about them, frail, white, shredded into cobwebs.

"It is midnight," Lachlan cried, and cowered down. He knew ghosts were only psychic emanations of what had gone before, but the grief and horror of their passing quivered the air like the aftermath of lightning. Iseult caught his hand. She was used to ghosts, for the Towers of Roses and Thorns was thick with them and they did not wait till Samhain to cry. She dragged him forward, and the ghosts passed over them like a shiver. Down the stairs they raced, flinging open the door and running across the garth, not looking to see if anyone was watching. There would be no patrol on the ramparts now.

Snow swirled about them. A wolf howled, close behind them. They could feel coldness at their necks and they quickened their pace. Never before had Lachlan been so nimble and quick on his claws, the beat of his wings propelling them forward over the flagstones. The wind battered them with leaves and twigs, swept away, then returned with a spurt of sleet. The lanterns along the palace were blurred globes of yellow. Lights burnt in only one wing, and Lachlan panted, "There."

"How do we get up?"

"We fly, *leannan*. What else? If we can conjure a storm, can we no' fly?"

He spread his wings and leapt toward the lights, and she leapt with him, not thinking, just following where he led. In one graceful arc, they reached the windows and caught at the shutters, which banged once again the wall. They hung there, shaking, triumphant and amazed.

Curtains inside were dragged back, and they flinched back against the wall. Iseult transferred her grip to the stone fretwork, and took her dagger from her belt. The window was flung open. "Just the shutter banging in the wind, Your Highness," a man's voice said. Lachlan nimbly swung over Iseult so he was hanging from the fretwork beside her. The shutter was banged closed, and they heard the window slammed down again.

They hung there in the snow-whirling darkness. It was bitterly cold. Lachlan smiled with stiff lips and whispered, "Let's find a way in, *leannan*."

Step by slow step they made their way along the wall. They passed two sets of shutters, but they were both locked tightly. They inched their way along to the next set of windows. The shutter was ajar, and they hung outside, arms aching, and looked inside.

They saw a fire burning low, its light shining copper and gold on the heads of two girls, close together, talking. Just as they recognized the faces, the red-haired girl looked up and saw them.

Her pupils flared in instant recognition. She rose and walked toward them, her intense blue gaze never faltering. She raised her hand, and outside in the snow Iseult raised hers. Their fingers touched through the frosty glass.

Jorge sat still for a time, the children staring at him. The raven hopped restlessly from foot to foot and gave a caw that sounded like mocking laughter. He lifted his blind face and said huskily, "Dillon, call in the soldiers. They canna guard us against banshees. Anntoin, my lad. Extinguish the fire."

"But, master . . ."

"Do it, lad. Johanna, do no' weep. Come close, all o' ye."

They gathered around him, and he showed them the Samhain cakes he had baked that afternoon and the Samhain cider he had concocted with apples, honey, whisky and spices. "Do no' be afraid, my bairns. Most o' the spirits that fly at Samhain are no' evil. We will light a bonfire and have a feast, and leave the night for the ghosts."

The Blue Guards came in, followed by a restless and

worried Duncan. Jorge tore a page from the end of a book, grimacing a little as he did so, and gave them all scraps of paper. "Tonight is the time we cast away our weaknesses and seek to make ourselves strong and vital. Write down all your failings and we shall cast them into the festival bonfire."

"But we canna write," Johanna cried. "None o' us know how. Only Finn knew." She burst into tears again.

"I can write a few words," Duncan volunteered. With a quill plucked from the raven, he wrote down their failings one by one, in their own blood. That macabre suggestion was Dillon's, and only done because they had no other ink. By the time they had argued over each other's weaknesses—which ranged from Johanna being a scaredy-cat to Dillon liking to get his own way too much—it was midnight.

Jorge had cleared the gate of ashes and laid a bonfire there with the sacred woods—ash, hazel, oak, blackthorn, fir, hawthorn and yew. He drew the ceremonial circle with ashes, water and salt, making it large enough to contain all of them. The children sat cross-legged around the fireplace, with the soldiers pressing close behind them. Most of the soldiers were very superstitious and would rather have been spending Samhain Eve at any other place but the ruined witches' tower.

"Midnight on the eve o' Samhain is the time when the veil between worlds is thinnest," Jorge said. "I shall do a sighting, and so ye must all have a care for me."

Carefully he added herbs and powders to the kindling, lighting the fire with a thought. As flames began to flicker up, he swayed back and forth, chanting, "In the name o' Eà, thee who is Spinner and Weaver and Cutter o' the Thread, thee who sows the seed, nurtures the life, and reaps the harvest, feel in me the tides o' seas and blood . . ."

He was whirled away in a vortex of visions. A rainbow-striped viper writhed out of the sea—Lachlan struck it again and again with his claymore but each time the snake gave birth to smaller, more vicious serpents that twisted and squirmed all over the land. He saw Lachlan raise a bow of fire and shoot arrows like comets. One of the fiery stars turned into a child, winged and haloed with light. The child fell, and Jorge saw he had a shadow of ice.

Dreams he had had many times came to him, more vivid and sinister than ever. He saw a white hind being hunted through a dark forest, blood on its breast. He saw a black wolf leaping. He saw a girl-child with one foot on the land and one on the oceans, the Lodestar blazing white in her hand. He saw mirrors, some breaking in tinkles of silvery glass, some dissolving into water. He saw the moons embrace and devour each other, and heard a strange song swell and deepen into an orchestra of sound.

The dreams changed. He dreamt of snow whirling and fire leaping; he saw an owl flying over a snowy, shadowed landscape, a white lion racing beneath, a star falling overhead. The land was torn apart by war, blood soaking into the cornfields. A tidal wave rose, taller than any tower and seething with glinting scales and fins. It broke upon the land and swept away town and village, faces sucked down despairingly. The visions swirled faster—he saw Tòmas with incandescent hands in a whirlwind, he saw him dead on a field of war. He saw Dillon with a bloodied sword in his fist, howling with grief; he saw Finn wrapped in darkness, wandering lost, he saw her flying with wings of night, stars on her brow; he saw Jay playing a blind viola as the hand of a storm clenched around him. Then Jorge saw his own death and understood both the time and place of its coming.

Isabeau and Iseult sat and stared at each other. Neither had said a word since Isabeau had hauled Iseult in through the window, their hands gripping each other's wrist. Finn had filled their silence with words, dancing about excitedly as she told Lachlan all about her adventures. The winged prionnsa was drying the string of his bow by the fire, melting snow dripping from his cloak.

It had been a strange, uncanny feeling, that first sight
of her twin. As Isabeau had walked toward the night-
black window, her reflected image had merged with
Iseult's, so that she had stared into her own eyes and
touched her own fingers as well as those of Iseult. It had
been like looking into a mirror and seeing your counter-
part move with its own vivid, independent life.

Now her sister sat opposite, staring at her with the
same troubled fascination. She had a thin scar on either
cheek, but otherwise she looked exactly how Isabeau
had looked a year earlier—a faded tam o'shanter
crammed over bright curls, a torn shirt and shabby
breeches, two long-fingered, capable-looking hands.

It was not that Isabeau could think of nothing to say
to her twin. Since Gitâ had mentioned her mirror-face,
Isabeau's brain had been whirling with questions. At this
moment, though, she was content just to stare at her
familiar yet strange face, to feel the connection between them.

Lachlan cut short Finn's explanations with a chopping
gesture. "Glad as I am to see ye, Finn, we canna be
wasting any more time. I need to see Jaspar—now!"

Isabeau tore her eyes away from Iseult's face and
looked at Lachlan. She had barely noticed him before,
all her attention absorbed by her twin. She recognized
him at once, even in the uncertain light of the fire.

"Bacaiche?" she whispered. Color swept into her
cheeks. She remembered how she had rescued him from
the Awl, and had been hunted and tortured as a result.
Worse, he was the lover of her dreams, the one who
came most often.

Lachlan colored also. A sullen expression settled over
his face. He said haltingly, "I be sorry, Isabeau, I did
no' ken who ye were . . . We heard about your hand
and everything . . ."

Isabeau looked down at her linen-swathed hand. Bitter tears stung her eyes. She glanced up at him. "Ye
could have trusted me. If I had known . . . things might
have been different."

Lachlan scowled. "I thought I was doing ye a favor, all right? As far as I knew ye were just some country lass who'd made the mistake o' getting mixed up in the Awl's business. I dinna ken they were going to track ye down . . . Besides, I never asked ye to rescue me."

Isabeau flushed red with indignation. She opened her mouth to argue, but Iseult said sarcastically, "Lachlan, we do no' have time to chat now, ye know we do no'. Can ye save the pleasantries for later?"

Isabeau's eyes had widened at Iseult's accent, which was none she recognized. Her twin looked at her, color rising also, and said, "Isabeau."

". . . Iseult?"

Iseult nodded. She took a deep breath and said, "We have so much to talk about. I ken ye have been away for months and do no' know anything about me or how Meghan found me . . ."

"Why did she no' tell me?" Resentment welled up in Isabeau.

"I do no' know," Iseult replied.

Lachlan laughed harshly. "Ye lived with my aunt all those years and ye can ask such a question?"

Isabeau flashed him a look. "She does like to keep secrets," she admitted. "But surely this was no' her secret to keep? She knows how I have always longed for kin o' my own . . ." Her voice broke slightly.

"She trusts no one," Iseult said. "No' even Lachlan or me."

Now Isabeau looked at her twin with jealousy and resentment. "Or me, her ward and apprentice?" she asked harshly. "She only raised me as her own."

"She trusts no one," Iseult replied, coloring up again. "I suppose she has been betrayed before—and no' all betrayals are on purpose. I know she trusted ye as much as she trusted anyone."

"Even ye and . . . Lachlan?" Isabeau frowned, knowing the name Lachlan should mean something to her.

Lachlan and Iseult exchanged glances. "This is no' the way we were meant to meet," Iseult said. "There is so much we all do no' understand about each other yet. We do no' have time, though, to talk and tell each other all the things we want to know. Firstly, does the Rìgh still live?"

"If he lasts the night, it will be a miracle," Isabeau answered. "Twice now I have kept him breathing when he could not breathe for himself. Meghan begged me to keep him alive until after Samhain and I have done my best."

"Meghan! Ye've seen Meghan!"

"No' seen, spoken to." She told them quickly about her accidental scrying to her guardian.

"I am Jaspar's brother," Lachlan said. "I was ensorcelled by the Banrìgh and have no' seen him for thirteen years. I must see him before he dies! Ye must help us."

They heard the scrape of a door and the sound of heavy footsteps. Lachlan stepped back into the gloom of the corner, beckoning to the others, his hand drawing the cloak up to muffle his face. Quick as a thought Iseult was beside him, her dagger drawn, but Finn had only time to draw her hood over her head.

An immensely fat woman bustled in, keys clinking at her waist, her eyes almost lost in red and swollen eyelids. "Isabeau, I'm afraid . . . the Rìgh is sinking. His pulse seems so faint, and we can barely rouse him to confirm the settlements. Have ye any more *mithuan*?"

"It may make his heart flutter too fast . . ."

"Isabeau, he's dying! Nothing can save him now! We must make sure everything is in order. Just a little *mithuan*—just so he can say what he needs to, and sign the papers and make sure all is well for the babe. For the babe, Isabeau!"

"I'll need to mix some up, Latifa, I had no' planned on giving him any more. I will no' be more than a moment."

The cook nodded and sighed hugely. "Be quick, lassie, we are afraid he will slip away before we have everything settled."

She turned and went out the door, not noticing Lachlan and Iseult backed against the wall. To Isabeau, they were as clear as if it were daylight, but she remembered that her eyesight had always been abnormally sharp.

Lachlan came out of his corner like an arrow from a bow. "He is declaring the baby heir? I knew it! I knew it!"

"We only have a few minutes, tell me what ye can," Isabeau said. "I seem to know nothing whatsoever." Her voice was harsh. Lachlan objected, and she said calmly, "There are a half dozen guards within calling distance, Bacaiche. If ye want my help, I suggest ye tell me all ye know for I will no' help ye otherwise. I remember ye only as the man who stole my witch knife."

Hurriedly he told her about their plan to retrieve the Lodestar and how its song had grown so faint Meghan said the only way to revive it was to wash it in the Pool of Two Moons at the hour of its birth.

"Aedan Whitelock wrought the Lodestar during a full eclipse o' the moons," he said. "Meghan is convinced there will be another eclipse tomorrow night."

"The time o' the two moons crossing," Isabeau murmured.

He nodded and told her he had only just heard the news of the baby's birth and Jaspar's declining health. Meghan had forbidden him to confront the Rìgh and Banrìgh until the Lodestar was safe and restored, but none of them had expected Jaspar to die so soon. "He's only ten years older than me," Lachlan said with tears in his eyes. "He's no' even thirty-five yet."

"Ye want to see the Rìgh?" Isabeau said, making her decision. "He lies in the room just beyond, with the Banrìgh at his side and the chancellor and councillors, and probably the Grand Seeker too. The only way he'll be able to speak with him is if they do no' ken ye are there—unless, o' course, ye want to have the Red Guards swarming all round! Ye'll have to wrap yourself in Finn's cloak o' invisibility. Do ye see? The bed is against one wall—I'll take ye in ..."

"What about me? How will ye conceal me?" Iseult said.

"Ye'll have to wait out here with Finn . . ."

"No!" Iseult cried, then added more reasonably. "I canna risk Lachlan so, I must be there to guard him and make sure he is safe."

Isabeau looked at her in some amazement. "I am a Scarred Warrior," Iseult explained. "And Lachlan is my husband . . ." Unconsciously her hand dropped to her abdomen, pulling the loose shirt against the bulge.

Isabeau looked from her to Lachlan, her color fluctuating. Then she bit her lip and began stripping off her apron, saying to Lachlan, "Can ye turn away? I will no' get undressed with ye watching, brother-in-law though ye may." She was conscious of a cold knot in her stomach, but that could have been fear. "Quick, Iseult, ye'll have to give me your clothes else I'll freeze."

"But . . . why?"

"Iseult, ye will have to pretend to be me. They have no idea there are two o' us so no one should suspect a thing." They swapped clothes and dressed again hurriedly, because even by the fire it was cold. "Tell them all to leave ye with the Rìgh while ye tend him. Try no' to speak with such a strong accent, else ye'll give the game away. Give him some o' the *mithuan*, a mouthful or two, no more else ye'll kill him. Pull the curtains around the bed to shield him from their eyes, then keep watch while Lachlan talks to him. The *mithuan* will rouse him and he should be clear-headed enough." She hesitated, then slowly unwound the bandages from her left hand. "Here. Bind up your hand."

Isabeau's hand was horribly scarred and maimed. Her smallest two fingers were missing, great red pits where they had been. The other fingers were stiff and bent at odd angles, her thumb hanging uselessly. They all drew in breath at the sight of it, and she closed her other hand about it protectively. "Go. Be careful," she said and turned away from them into the shadows.

Iseult knelt by the side of the great bed and helped the Rìgh sit up. He swallowed a mouthful of the *mithuan*, coughing a little as the bitter potion burnt his throat. Under her fingers his pulse leapt erratically.

Iseult made sure the Rìgh was screened from the group clustered around the fire, then gave a small nod. Lachlan's figure emerged from the shadows as he unclasped the cloak and let it fall. He shook out his wings and bent over the wasted figure of his brother. "Jaspar," he whispered.

The Rìgh turned his head and smiled faintly. "Lachlan."

There was silence for a moment, then Lachlan knelt beside the bed, his face pressed against his brother's arm. His voice was incoherent, but at last he managed to say, "Ye know it is me?"

"Lachlan," the Rìgh said again. His voice was so weak they could hardly hear it, even bending so close over the bed. "O' course I know it is ye. Ye've troubled my dreams for years, ye and Donncan and Feargus. My nights seethe now with the faces o' those I have loved. And lost. Soon I shall be with ye."

"Nay, Jaspar, I'm alive. I'm with ye now. Feel my hand." He grasped the Rìgh's thin, cold hand in his big, warm one. The frail fingers stirred. "Your hand is warm," the Rìgh said with an inflection of surprise. "Am I so close to the world o' the dead that ye should feel so alive?"

"Nay, Jaspar, ye are alive too, we are both alive. Look at me, Jaspar. Canna ye see that I live? Feel my breath on your face, the pulse in my wrist."

"Lachlan," the Rìgh said dreamily. "Where did ye go? Ye've been gone so many years."

Lachlan's whole body stiffened. "I was ensorcelled, Jaspar. Look at me. See my wings, see my talons. All this was the result o' a spell."

"A spell? There are no spells any more, Lachlan." He sighed. "No magic. No witchcraft. All gone."

"So they say," Lachlan said bitterly. "But there are witches still, Jaspar. Your wife is one!" Despite his attempt at self-control, he spat the words out.

"My wife is one," Jaspar repeated. "My wife . . ." He

seemed to dream. Then he said, in such a clear voice
that Iseult cast a glance over her shoulder, "No, Lachlan,
ye canna be thinking! Maya is no witch. Maya is the
only one . . ."

"Jaspar, it was Maya that cast the spell on me, Maya
that turned me into this hideous half man, half bird. She
tried to kill me, Jaspar, and she did kill our brothers. I
saw her do it! Ye must believe me!" His voice was rising
and Iseult made discreet shushing motions. He lowered
his voice. "Jaspar, ye know it is me, do ye no'? Hold
my hand. Ye ken it is I, Lachlan, your brother?"

"Yes. Lachlan. So good to see ye, my brother. I
thought ye were dead."

"I almost died, Jaspar, if she had had her way I'd be
dead. Maya is no' who ye think. She is no human
woman, I swear to ye. She does no' love ye . . ."

"My Maya," Jaspar said, smiling. "She is the only one
to love me, the only one to stand by me."

"No, Jaspar, she has ensorcelled ye! Ye lie here dying
because she has ensorcelled ye. Canna ye see she is a
murderess?"

"Murderess? Who?"

"Maya, o' course,' Lachlan said with barely controlled
impatience. "Your wife. She has done nothing but evil
since she came to our country, Jaspar. Do ye no'
understand?"

"No, Lachlan. It is ye who do no' understand. Maya
is the only one to love me and no' betray me. Ye all
left me . . ."

"*She* made us leave ye! *She's* the one who kept us
apart. She turned me into a bird, Jaspar, a bird! And set
her hawk on us. *She* murdered Donncan and Feargus."

Iseult glanced over her shoulder again and saw the
eyes of the beautiful woman in red were fixed upon the
bed. She was frowning slightly.

"Please believe him," she whispered hurriedly to the
Rìgh. "He really is your brother and he is speaking
the truth."

The Rìgh's dark, unfocused eyes moved her way. "Is

that ye, Red? What are ye doing in my dreams? Or are ye real?"

"I am real, Your Highness, and so is Lachlan."

"I can hear voices in my head. I canna tell what is real and what is no'."

"I am real, Your Highness, and so is Lachlan. We are both here and both alive. Trust us."

"Lachlan . . ."

"Yes, Jaspar?"

"Let me feel your hand again."

The two brothers clasped hands. Lachlan's cheeks were wet. "Do no' die, Jaspar," he whispered. "Live! We can fight the Fairgean together. We'll rescue the Lodestar and renew it, we'll . . ."

"The Lodestar is gone," Jaspar said so loudly that several of the people around the fire looked up, and the Banrìgh rose to her feet.

"Quickly!" Iseult hissed.

"No, Jaspar, it's all lies, all lies that she's told ye. Please listen to me . . ."

"Red, what do ye do?" the Banrìgh called. "Ye take so long, is all well?"

"Aye, Your Highness," Iseult said, mimicking Isabeau's voice as best she could. "Just a few more minutes."

"It is late . . ."

"I will no' be long. Your Highness." She saw Latifa look up, puzzled, and bent her head over the Rìgh so the old cook would not wonder what was wrong.

Lachlan was whispering, "Can ye no' see my wings? See how my body has been ruined? She turned me into a blackbird and set her hawk upon me. They are Fairgean, Jaspar, and it is all a trick, a scheme to destroy our power and win back the coastlands for themselves."

Jaspar said hazily, "Your face is swimming. I feel strange."

In desperation Iseult gave him another mouthful of *mithuan*. It was two hours past midnight, and they had not much time.

"She is an evil sorceress, Jaspar, who cast such a spell on ye that ye turned against your friends and family! Ye must see she is evil!"

Jaspar was distressed. "No, Lachlan, how can ye say such things? Nay, ye've taken a notion into your head and let it take root there, growing bizarre fruit. Maya is good and kind; she looks after me and does her best to care for the people."

"Then why is the country in revolt? Why do people disappear from their beds at night, never to be seen again? Why is there so much murder and torture?"

Jaspar was shaking his head, his lips so white they were invisible. "Evil people . . . ."

"It is Maya who is evil!" Lachlan's voice rang out. Iseult heard the waiting courtiers murmur and shuffle, and slipped her hand into the pocket of the apron, where she had hidden her *reil*. "Her and that babe o' hers! She ensorcelled the babe into being, Jaspar. She used the comet to cast a spell o' such strength . . . How could ye no' know it? How can ye still think she is good and kind when she is a foul, scheming, murdering . . . ."

"Maya is my wife," Jaspar said with tremulous dignity. "I think ye forget yourself, Lachlan."

There was a step behind Iseult, and she flashed a warning glance at Lachlan who hurriedly draped the cloak about him, dragging the hood over his head. As he disappeared from view, Jaspar sighed and moved his head restlessly. Then there was a cool hand on Iseult's shoulder and the Banrìgh stepped past her to lean over and kiss the Rìgh on his forehead. "What is wrong, my darling? I heard ye cry out?"

Jaspar gripped her hand, tears leaking from his eyes. "Maya, Lachlan was here, *he was here*! I saw him. Did I no', Red? Ye saw him too."

Iseult bowed her head and said nothing, conscious of those dark-lashed silvery-blue eyes looking her over. Maya said, "It was only a dream, my darling, only a dream. Come, we have the papers all ready, we have done as ye instructed." She gave a light laugh. "We have even named your cousin Dughall as the next in line, as ye requested, though he says he will no' renounce his father's name . . ."

"Maya, he was here. I saw him. He had wings and claws . . ."

The Banrìgh stiffened all over, her pupils dilating. "I fear the Rìgh wanders in nightmare," she said loudly. "Red, canna ye help him?"

"I dare no' give him more *mithuan*," Iseult said, moving around the other side of the bed, her hand upon her *reil*.

"Ye must. He must sign the papers. Give it to him now." There was steel behind the silken voice, and the Banrìgh gestured imperiously to the councillors to bring the scrolls and royal seal.

"Aye, Your Highness," Iseult said and lifted the Rìgh's head to trickle a few more drops of the potion in. His eyelids flickered and he swallowed.

They clustered around the bed. A few wept—the man in black velvet and jewels, a tiny old man with bags under his eyes. He was the one to spread the papers out before the Rìgh and to place the quill into his trembling hand. "Your will and dispositions. Your Highness. Drawn up as ye requested. The Banprionnsa Bronwen Mathilde MacCuinn will inherit, but her mother will act as Regent until she comes o' age at twenty-four. Sign here, my laird, and here."

As the frail fingers tightened around the quill and the Rìgh lifted himself in the bed, Lachlan seized the papers and threw them across the room. At least, Iseult assumed it was Lachlan for all she could see were the flying papers. Everyone gasped and looked around nervously, fully aware it was Samhain, night o' the dead, when ghosts flew and banshees wept.

The Banrìgh alone showed no fear. She gathered the papers up and placed them before the Rìgh, guarding them with her arm. Gently she set the quill in his hand and said softly, "Sign, my darling."

"No!" Lachlan shouted and tugged off the cloak so

all could see him. There were gasps and cries, and most
of the councillors shrank back in fear. The man in black
velvet started forward, saying tentatively, "Lachlan?"

The winged prionnsa knelt by his brother, clasping his
arm. "Please believe me, please, Jaspar! Name me your
heir! I am a true MacCuinn. I would no' lie to ye, please
believe what I have told ye ..."

The Banrìgh stood still, white as her husband, waiting
to see what he would say. Latifa gasped and pressed the
baby to her shoulder.

Jaspar put up a hand and touched Lachlan's burly
shoulder, the soft feathers of his wings, the skin of his
face. "Ye are back again," he whispered. "Ye feel real,
but ye step in and out o' shadows like a ghost. Am I
dreaming? Am I dead?"

"No, brother,' Lachlan wept. "I live, I swear it. Name
me heir! Why should Maya the Unknown rule? Who is
she to steal the throne? I am Lachlan Owein MacCuinn,
youngest son o' Parteta the Brave. Ye should name me!"

'"It is my daughter I name heir," Jaspar said slowly,
his voice strengthening. They could see a pulse beating
rapidly in his temple. "My daughter."

"She is a halfbreed!" Lachlan screamed. "Ensorcelled
into being! Ye canna allow a Fairge halfbreed to inherit!
She is the seed o' evil!"

"No," the Rìgh moaned. "Get ye gone, fiend!"

"Jaspar, it is the truth!"

"Maya is my wife, my beloved wife."

"She's a sorceress!" Lachlan cried desperately. "It is
she who made me this . . . this *uile-bheist*!" He indicated
his wings and claws with one sweep of his hand.

"Maya could never do such a thing. Never."

"I saw her!"

"Ye're naught but a nightmare, an evil ghost come to
confuse me and frighten me. Shame on ye, shame!" With
the last of his strength he seized the papers and scrawled
his signature along the bottom of first one, then the
other. Lachlan tried desperately to seize the papers,
reaching across the wide bed but Jaspar held them out

of his reach, passing them to the chancellor. "Seal them for me, Cameron." Trapped in his corner, Lachlan could only watch helplessly as the chancellor shakily pressed Jaspar's seal into the warm wax and stamped the papers.

"It is done," the Rìgh said, slumping back against his pillows. "Bronwen shall rule when she is grown. The land is safe."

"Thank ye, Jaspar!" Maya cried and fell to her knees beside the bed. She was weeping. She kissed his hand and it was flaccid in hers. With a soft cry, she called to him and pressed his hand to her mouth. He lay still. She turned and waved to one of the councillors and he brought the candelabra closer. As the light spilled over the pillow, they saw the Rìgh's face, slack and gray, his eyes between the half-closed lids glassy.

She screamed, a strange, high, echoing sound that bounced off the walls and shattered the mirror. They all ducked, hands to their ears. She screamed again and fell over the bed. Latifa began to sob, her whole body quivering. The baby began to wail. Lachlan cried, "No! Jaspar!" and seized his wrist, shook his arm. He pushed Maya violently, so she fell to the floor, and flung himself onto the bed, clutching Jaspar's shoulders and trying to rouse him.

"Seize him!" Maya cried. "Guards! Guards! Treason!"

"Lachlan, quick! We must go!" Iseult cried.

As the door swung open, the chancellor said thickly, "The MacCuinn is dead! Long live the NicCuinn!"

"Long live the Banrìgh, Bronwen NicCuinn!" the councillors all echoed.

"No!" Lachlan shouted and would have dived over the bed if Iseult had not tripped him with her foot. He fell on to his brother's body and began to weep, and Iseult caught his arm and dragged him away. With her free hand, she flung her *reil* and it sliced neatly through the throat of the soldier running through the door. Blood spurted across the cloud-blue walls and Latifa screamed.

Iseult got them through the door and managed to get

Lachlan composed enough to heave a cream and gilt wardrobe against the doors. It was a flimsy piece of furniture and she did not think it would hold long, so she dragged him into the nursery as quickly as she could, where Finn and Isabeau were waiting anxiously.

"The Rìgh is dead," Iseult said as soon as they had secured the door behind them. They could hear hammering on the other door and shouting.

"We guessed. Meghan is on her way. Gitâ has gone to her so she must be near enough to call him."

"Lachlan!" Iseult cried. "Blow on the horn! We must summon help, we canna withstand the palace guard by ourselves!"

Lachlan had stumbled to a chair, his head in his hands. Finn seized the horn, ran to the window, leant out into the wintry night and blew on it with all her might. Long and hauntingly beautiful, the peal rang out into the dark, lingering and lingering.

At the first note of the horn's call, Duncan was on his feet and shouting at the guards to seize arms. Dillon jumped to his feet in excitement, and the other children milled around him, waiting for his orders. Jorge sat up, his hands trembling.

"We need someone to ring the bell!" Dillon said. "To warn the rebels. Johanna, ye should do it."

She shrank back. "I . . . canna."

"Ye have to, canna ye see that? Jorge must no' go, he is too sick, and we must keep Tòmas safe."

"I will be needed," the little boy said solemnly. "I can feel death."

"Jaspar MacCuinn is dead." Jorge's face was haggard. "But there will be more deaths. Many more deaths."

"Tòmas will be needed *after* the fight, no' during. He'd be no use during. Neither would ye, Johanna! Ye must stay and look after Jorge and Tòmas and the other children."

"I do no' want to go," the girl said, shaking with tears.

"But someone has to ring the bell. If ye canna fight,

surely ye could do that—so all o' us who can fight are where they are most needed."

Although he spoke with brutal frankness, there was such the air of seriousness and clear thinking about the boy that both Duncan and Jorge murmured, "He's right."

Outside the tower a wolf howled. They all flinched back, even Jorge, and the raven croaked loudly. Johanna was trembling. But she remembered the delicate gray ashes of her Samhain wish, floating up the chimney with the words, magical loops of writing, that said, "I do no' want to be afraid any more." To all their surprise, she squared her shoulders and said, "All right then, I will."

The wolf howled again.

Anghus lifted his head in amazement. He had never heard the MacRuraich war horn before but he recognized its sound straightaway. He stopped mid-stride and Casey, following close behind, collided with him in the enveloping mist.

"The MacRuraich horn!" Meghan cried and grasped his arm. Gitâ was clinging to her shoulder, chittering with excitement. "They must have removed it from the relics room. But why? I never mentioned the horn!"

From somewhere in the mist the howl of a wolf rose, taking up the sound of the dying horn. "Tabithas!" Anghus and Meghan cried together. More howls arose, chilling and drawn out. The men following them all shuddered and drew closer together, but on Anghus and Meghan's faces there was only joy.

Out of the darkness drifted a battalion of ghost warriors, wielding swords of ice. They were dressed in the fashions of many different centuries, but all wore the ghostly remnants of the black MacRuraich kilt, the wolf rampant engraved on every sword and shield. The rebels shouted in fear and stumbled back, but Meghan and Anghus watched with fearless and fascinated eyes. Floating silently through the storm and mist, the ghost warriors converged on the palace. Shouts of alarm rang out, and red-clad soldiers ran to engage. Soon there was fighting in the big square and on the rampart, and the palace began to blaze with lights.

"Only Fionnghal could have called up the MacRuraich ghosts," Anghus said in exultation. "How could she have known that blowing the war horn at Samhain would call up the warriors o' ages past? How did she know what the horn was?"

"Luck? Instinct? Who knows? The ghost warriors have come and the Red Guards canna stand against them. Let's hurry!" And Meghan did not wait for them to follow her, but picked up her skirts and ran toward the palace, the donbeag clinging desperately to her plait.

Anghus followed her, shouting the MacRuraich war cry. Those behind him took up the cry, shouting, "The wolf! The wolf!" There were close on a hundred following them now, Meghan having unlocked the doors to all the cells in the dungeons below the palace.

A Red Guard struck at Anghus from the shadows, and he retaliated with quick, hard strokes. Somewhere inside was his daughter—nothing would stand in his way now! A large, black shape leapt out of the shadows and tore out the throat of a guard who would have spitted the prionnsa on his spear. "Tabithas!" Anghus cried, and the wolf turned and grinned at him, her jaws dripping with gore.

Meghan hurried ahead. Somehow all who stood against here were unable to land a blow on her. Anghus ran after her, the wolf at his heels, and dived into the confusion of the fighting. Red Guards grappled with blue-kilted soldiers, ghost warriors swarmed in the shadows, wolves leapt and snapped.

Anghus took intense pleasure in the thrust and strike of his sword. Too long he had had to bend his neck meekly! At last he could avenge the insults to his pride, the injuries to his family. Donald was at his back, shooting at those who fought to catch them from the rear. Casey was at his side, sword darting. The black wolf

streaked ahead. "Tabithas!" Anghus called. "Find Fionn-
nghal! Find my daughter!"

Iseult thrust the bow and quiver into Lachlan's reluctant
hands. "Lachlan, the Red Guards come! We have to
go!"

"No!" he snarled. "Where is that cursehag? She has
stolen my birthright! Where is she?"

"She's with the soldiers, Lachlan. They will kill ye!
This place is swarming with them, *leannan*, we canna
fight them all. Let us go!"

He threw her away, got to his claws and prowled the
room, gripping his bow, his golden-brown eyes so savage
the others kept silent. "I will kill her and that Fairge
baby. I will strangle her! Let us see if her death breaks
the spell and restores me, since nothing else has. Call
her the NicCuinn! That squalling brat, that halfbreed
uile-bheist . . ."

"If Cloudshadow is right, then both Iseult and I are
half faery and thus *uile-bheistean*," Isabeau said, facing
him, her whole body poised for movement. They were
all surprised, and Iseult glanced at her twin with grudging admiration for her courage. She would not easily
have crossed Lachlan in this mood.

"And ye have promised to stand for the faeries,"
Iseult said, "and ye should no' judge the babe for its
parentage. She is your niece."

At that, Isabeau gave her sister back the same look
and the twins felt their strange connection grow.

They heard wolves howling outside, and then the clash
of arms. "The Blue Guards come!" Lachlan cried, and
bent the longbow, testing it.

There was a loud crash, and they knew the wardrobe
had given way. They looked at each other and ran
through into Maya's boudoir, securing the door behind
them. Suddenly bells began to peal out, loud and insis-
tent. Iseult and Lachlan shared a quick, exultant look.

"The League has done it again!" Lachlan said, grinning. "Now we shall see how long the Ensorcellor rules!"

"Lachlan, we have to get out o' here," Iseult said urgently. "I canna fight them all—we canna! We have to join the Key and save the Lodestar if we wish to prevail. Ye ken that! Ye have precipitated the rebellion before we have the Lodestar and ye ken Meghan says—"

"I do no' give a damn what Meghan says," Lachlan snapped. "If I had gone to Jaspar earlier, I might have convinced him!"

"And ye might have burnt on the fire," Iseult retorted.

There was hammering on both the inner doors and the grand entrance to the Banrìgh's suite from the hallway. "We need to retreat and find our friends," Iseult said. "Please, Lachlan, let us go!"

"Where?" Isabeau asked. "They are at both doors—I bolted them while ye were with the Rìgh, but they will no' last long."

"Out the window!" Lachlan cried, and threw it open.

"What about Isabeau and Finn?" Iseult cried. "They canna fly!"

Isabeau felt a peculiar sensation, like a hand closing over her heart. She had not had time to wonder how Lachlan and Iseult had reached the royal suite's windows, five storeys from the ground.

"We shall have to carry them," Lachlan said. "Are ye strong enough to hold Finn? She's only a skinny wee thing."

The sound of one of the inner doors breaking stilled Finn's protests. She clambered onto the windowsill as Lachlan commanded, Isabeau following, her heart slamming in long, hard beats.

"Put your arms about my neck," he commanded, not looking at her. Isabeau obeyed stiffly, keeping a distance between them. With an irritated snort, he grasped her, gripping her so tight she lost all her breath and was not able to take another. He launched off into the air, Iseult following a few seconds later. Behind them soldiers reached the window just as Iseult's foot left the sill. One grasped at her skirt but she kicked him in the face and he fell, nose smashed.

Behind the palace the darkness was lifting, the stars beginning to fade. They fell swiftly into mist, Lachlan struggling to slow their descent. Gradually the powerful beat of his wings steadied and they dropped more slowly, surrounded by gloom. Isabeau could only see his face dimly.

"How does Iseult fly without wings?" she asked.

"Her mother is Ishbel the Winged," he replied and felt the electric shock that ran through her.

Through the mist came the dull clash of swords, the screams and cries of dying men. All over the western square, Red Guards were in desperate hand-to-hand combat with warriors that seemed strangely insubstantial in the swirling mist. Here and there the dark, lean shapes of wolves leapt, dragging down the red-clad soldiers.

Then they saw the flowing, changing shapes of ghosts all about them in the mist. As the ghosts flowed through them they both felt a quiver run down their spine, a sudden shock of cold. Isabeau clung to Lachlan, unable to stifle a scream. He landed heavily, stumbling and falling, knocking all the breath out of her. She lay still, her face pressed against his neck, then he hauled his heavy body away from her, scratching her legs with his claws. Red Guards materialized out of the mist, but the ghost warriors swarmed to meet them, so Lachlan had time to unsheathe the claymore. Isabeau knelt behind him, trying to catch her breath, as he moved to engage with the closest Red Guards.

Iseult fought her way towards them, Finn keeping close behind. "Where did all these ghosts come from?" Iseult asked, showing no fear, her dagger dark with blood.

"Who kens? All I know is that they fight for us and no' against us," Lachlan responded. She and Lachlan fought side by side, anticipating each other's every move, fighting as one. Slowly they moved across the square, seeking to reach the garden, but as the light grew the

ghost warriors began to fade, and they had difficulty in
keeping the Red Guards from overwhelming them. From
the garden came the hesitant melody of the first bird.

There was a roar, and a huge man in a faded blue kilt
came charging through the mist, swinging his claymore.
With him were thirty or more soldiers, and soon it was
the Red Guards retreating toward the palace walls.

"Duncan!" Lachlan cried. "Thank Eà ye are here.
Come, I have unfinished business in the palace!"

Duncan nodded and directed his men to pursue the
soldiers. Lachlan leant on his claymore, breathing heavily. He flashed a look at Isabeau and said roughly, "Do
ye have the other two parts o' the Key?"

Isabeau looked at him warily. "Latifa has them."

He swore and cast a look of intense dislike at her.
"The auld fat one. I remember her. Ye were meant to
have it! Why do ye no' have it?"

"Latifa guarded it."

"Ye fool! It is dawn now. Are ye no' meant to join it
at the turn o' power? Is that no' what Meghan said?"

"We joined it at sunset, moonrise on Midsummer's
Eve, but I think any turn in the tides would do it."

"Iseult, *leaman*," he said, the harshness gone from his
voice, "ye must get the Key. It was your task, yours and
Isabeau's, to join the Key if Meghan was no' with us."

"Meghan is near," Isabeau cried. "She will be here!"

"I have to go and put my sword to that black-hearted
witch's throat," Lachlan said. "Then we shall see if she
restores me! Then we shall see if her blood flows red or
black like the blood o' fish."

"No, Lachlan! Ye must come with us. I fear for your
safety. We must stick together, please, Lachlan!"

"Go! Join the Key. I will meet ye at the Pool o' Two
Moons. If ye need me, blow the horn and I will come.
Do no' fear for me—the rebels will have heard those
bells, they will be at the palace gates already. Ye ken
this is our plan, we have just done it backwards. Please,
leannan, let me go. Did Isabeau no' say Meghan was
near? And I have the Bow!" He flourished it.

"Lachlan, it's too dangerous! Wait . . ."

"No, *leannan*. I must confront the cursehag. She will turn her foul sorceries against us. Ye do no' understand her power!"

"No, Lachlan . . ."

"She killed my brothers!" he snarled and ran to join the fighting.

From all sides they could hear the clash of arms, screams, and the howling of wolves, closer than ever. As they watched Lachlan swipe and thrust his way through the fighting, Isabeau held her twin's arm comfortingly. For the first time emotion was written clearly on Iseult's face—both longing and terror mingled.

Latifa hurried through the corridors, the babe pressed to her heart. *The puir wee babe, the bonny Bronwen*, she thought and felt the babe stir in response. She was not crying now, her silvery-pale eyes wide open, her hand clenched into a tiny fist.

The old cook reached her room and locked the door behind her. Her heart was hammering, her breath wheezing. *Too auld and too fat for this*. She laid the baby tenderly on her bed and turned to rummage through her drawers. Her fingers closed upon a thick braid of red hair, as long as she was tall. She pulled it out and held it to her. Indeed, she had thought it may come in useful, this plait of hair that she had cut from Isabeau's head. Already she had used it several times—to call Isabeau to the kitchen that first dawn, to get her to gather the groundsel that had wrought the sickness in Gwilym the Ugly's guards, to call her when she needed her.

She felt a little guilty, but the lass had been feverish and incoherent and would have died if Latifa did not bring her temperature down. Latifa had some knowledge of herbs, but her skills were in cookery, not healing. The only way she knew to break the fever was to cut away the great length of curly hair. Admiring its fiery vigor, she hid it away and told Isabeau that she had burnt it.

Latifa had been sorely troubled by the scene in the

Rìgh's bedroom. Apart from her grief at the death of Jaspar, who had always been her favorite of the prionn-sachan; apart from the sudden appearance of the winged apparition, the ghost that had said such dreadful things and appeared so disturbingly familiar; apart from all her misgivings and confusion, there had been the peculiarity of Isabeau. She had sounded all wrong; worse, she had smelt all wrong. She had smelt of someone who had eaten meat—and Latifa knew Isabeau had never tasted the flesh of any living thing. And she had killed a guard as easily as she would swat a fly. Latifa could not imagine Isabeau, who wept to see a lamb taken to the slaughter, so nonchalantly cutting the throat of a man. It puzzled her greatly, and she could only think that someone had been impersonating her apprentice.

Either that, or Isabeau was not what she had seemed.

Within a moment the naked emotion on Iseult's face was gone. She said impatiently, "Well, we'd better get the other parts o' the Key then. Do ye know where they are?" With a nonchalant kick of one foot, she knocked out a Red Guard trying to attack them from the rear.

Isabeau closed her eyes, trying to locate Latifa amongst the confusion of minds. "I think she's in her room. I hope she's got Bronwen away safely!"

"Who's Bronwen?"

Isabeau looked her warily. "The babe."

"The Ensorcellor's babe?"

"Maya and Jaspar's babe," Isabeau said, a little shakily. Lachlan had said he would kill them both! Isabeau had cared for the little Banrìgh since her birth a month earlier, and she could not bear the thought of her death. "We have to find Meghan!" she cried. As Iseult protested, she said, "Meghan will guard Lachlan—she will stop him doing anything stupid."

Her twin nodded eagerly. "That's true. She will protect him."

Isabeau now sent out her senses in search of her guardian, and with a glad hammering of her heart, cried,

"She's close, she's very close. Let us find her and tell her what's happening, then we can run and find Latifa. Come on!"

They ran along the side of the square, Finn clutching the elven cat to her breast, and came around the corner. There the fighting was thick, red-cloaked soldiers hand to hand with rough-clad rebels. Wolves were fighting with them, led by a black she-wolf with a thick, upstanding ruff. She was at the head of the rebels, fighting by the side of a tall red-bearded man in a black kilt. The mist was melting away in the pale sunshine, the sky above a wash of blue.

As Finn pushed her fair head between Isabeau's and Iseult's to see, the black wolf raised her muzzle and sniffed the air. Suddenly she howled in triumph and leapt into a ground-eating lope across the square. The three girls drew back. It looked exactly as if the wolf was heading for them.

The wolf tore out the throat of a guard who tried to stop her, fixed her terrible golden eyes on the girls, and leapt toward them. Iseult pushed the other two behind her and drew her dagger.

"No!" They heard Meghan's voice and saw her standing across the square. With her was the man in the black kilt, an agonized expression on his face, his hand thrown up. "No, Iseult!" Meghan cried. "The wolf is a friend. Do no' harm her."

It was too late—the dagger had already left Iseult's hand and was spinning through the air, straight for the black wolf's breast. Isabeau threw up her hand and the dagger spun away, clattering to the ground. The wolf flung herself on Finn. The little girl fell with a scream, only to have her face licked enthusiastically, the wolf's paws on her chest.

Meghan and her companion hurried toward them, the man staggering, his hand to his head. He was supported by an old man with a long beard thrust through his belt, while a spearhead of rebels slashed through the ranks of palace soldiers. Finn tentatively stroked the wolf's thick ruff, trying to wipe her face dry with her other hand.

The red-bearded man fell on his knees before her, and with one hand wrenched the medallion away, the much-knotted string snapping. Finn wriggling and protesting in his arms, he clasped her to his chest and wept. "My Fionnghal, my Fionnghal," he muttered, rocking back and forth. "I have ye at last, my Fionnghal."

"What's wi' this name all the time?" Finn sighed, pushing herself away from him. "Who are ye? Stop squeezing me!"

"I'm your father," he cried. "Do ye no' recognize me at all? I'm your father!"

Her hazel-green eyes widened, and she tugged herself free. She stared at him and said, "I have no father."

"Ye were stolen from me," he cried. "The Awl took ye, to make me do what they said! Five years ye've been kept apart from me. Do ye remember nothing?"

She shook her head, suddenly frightened.

"I gave you this medallion when ye were born. See, here is mine." And he pulled out the medallion he too wore around his neck and showed her the crest on his sword and brooch. The wolf, lying beside them, thrust her black muzzle into the man's hand. "We are MacRuraichs, clan o' the black wolf," he said. "This is your aunt, Tabithas."

Finn said with a quaver in her voice, "This is no' a joke, is it?"

"No, no! I have been searching for ye five long years. Ye think I would joke about such a thing? And see! Tabithas knows who ye are. She tracked ye here from the mountains. And did ye no' call the horn? Ye must have, no one else could have called up the ghost warriors."

"I do no' understand," she said.

Meghan panted up beside them and said, "Anghus, this is she? Ye have her?"

"I have her," he wept and held her so close that Finn could hardly breathe.

"I am glad," she said and dropped her hand on his shoulder. Then she turned and stared at the twins, ignoring the fighting surging around them. "Well, well, Iseult in Isabeau's clothes and Isabeau in Iseult's clothes. Did ye seek to trick me?"

Isabeau shook her head, tears thick in her throat. Meghan smiled at her and embraced her fiercely, her head only coming up to Isabeau's shoulder. "Good it is indeed to see ye, my bairn. Ye are well?"

She nodded.

"Nothing to say? Things have changed indeed if my Isabeau is speechless." She smiled at Iseult and grasped her hand, but did not let go of Isabeau, who had begun to cry. "Obh obh! No time for tears, dearling. Where is Lachlan? What are ye doing here in the palace?"

"The Rìgh is dead," Isabeau said, unable to stop her sobs. "He died about half an hour ago. And Bacaiche says he is going to kill the baby! Ye have to stop him, Meghan! She's only a babe, no' more than a month auld, and the dearest wee thing!"

Meghan looked at her closely. "I see. Where is Latifa?"

"She has the two parts o' the Key still, Meghan. I did no' ken I was meant to get it, no one told me I was meant to have the Key now."

A troop of Red Guards charged them, shouting, their claymores raised. Meghan lifted her hand and they tripped and went down in a red seething mass. "Anghus!" she said sharply. "Ye must get your daughter out o' here. It is no place for a bairn. Take her to the tower. Jorge is in the tower?"

"Aye," Iseult replied.

"Take her there—she will know the way. If the fighting spreads and it looks as if we shall lose the day, flee out the secret gate into the forest behind. Tell Jorge to take the children to the summer palace. He will remember the way."

Anghus nodded and picked Finn up. She put her arms

about his neck and said shyly, "I think I remember the beard."

He smiled and pressed his cheek against hers. "Come, my Fionnghal, let us get ye to safety. Come, Tabithas!"

"Bye bye, Iseult, Isabeau! Will we see ye at the tower?"

"Perhaps," Meghan replied, and the twins both kissed Finn and said they would see her there for sure.

The soldiers had picked themselves up and were again charging toward them. Meghan waved her hand, and their legs tangled and down they went again. Anghus stepped around them, the wolf growling so menacingly the soldiers pressed themselves closer to the floor. Then the prionnsa was running across the flagstones, the old man in the tam o'shanter at his heels. The wolf ran with them, tail wagging.

"Isabeau, Iseult, we must penetrate the palace. I will go in search o' Lachlan if ye can find Latifa. Tell her I am here and that we must join the Key! Dawn has passed, so we have until noon to do it. I charge ye with the task—whatever else happens, ye must join the Key!"

"Latifa has Bronwen," Isabeau said.

"Bronwen?"

"The baby."

"Tell her to keep the babe safe. No matter what Lachlan says, she is a NicCuinn and there are far too few o' the clan left to be quibbling about her parentage. I will seek out Lahclan and keep him safe, I assure ye. Now let us go!"

Maya lay across the foot of the bed, weeping. Great sobs shuddered through her. Pain like she had never experienced before penetrated her like a spear. Jaspar was dead.

She had never thought of how she would feel when he died. His death had been part of their plans from the very beginning. If she had conceived an heir when they first married, he would have been dead years ago. But it had taken her sixteen years and an ancient, powerful spell to plant the seed in her womb, and by that time she had drained all the life force from him. She and Sani had known his death was coming since the night she conceived—it had been Jaspar's powers she had used as well as her own that night, and he had had little left to give.

Yet she wept for his passing as if she had truly loved him, as if he had wound about her heart and in the uprooting taken great chunks of her flesh with him. Sixteen years she had played the role of loving wife, and now found it was not such a charade.

At last she lay silent, composing herself with a great effort of will. Dimly she had been aware of the soldiers trying to break down the doors; dimly she had felt anger at Red's betrayal, and fear at the sudden appearance of the winged man when she had been sure they had hounded him far away. Now she was aware of light seeping in around the curtains, and the singing of birds.

"My lady?" A guard bent over her, voice worried. She ground her teeth at the change in her title—her husband not twenty minutes dead, and already she was merely "my lady."

"What is it?"

"We could no' catch the *uile-bheist*—he and his conspirators escaped from a window."

"Escaped from a window? We're five stories from the ground, man. What did they do, fly?"

"Aye, my lady." His voice and face were wooden.

Fear and chagrin flashed through her. It had been a shock to see her husband's little brother, caught halfway between blackbird and man. Ever since they had first heard the rumors of a winged man, she and Sani had feared that somehow one of the lost prionnsachan had survived. It had seemed impossible, however, and equally impossible that he could evade their grasp for several years. He obviously had powerful magic at his command.

Suddenly she thought of her daughter, the newly declared Banrìgh of Eileanan. Her hands gripped into fists.

Bronwen was in danger. She sat up, wiping her cheeks surreptitiously.

The Rìgh was laid out on the bed, candles burning all about. Guards stood against the wall, backs straight, cloaks as red as blood. The door into the dressing room lay in splinters, a broken wardrobe half blocking the way. There was blood on the floor and the walls, but they had taken the dead soldier away.

"Guard!" she said peremptorily. "Where have they taken Her Highness?"

"Latifa the Cook took her, my lady, for the babe was much distressed."

"Tell Latifa to bring the babe to me at once."

She stood up and went to the mirror to straighten her dress and hair. There was only the empty frame, the mirror lying in glittering shards on the floor. A shudder ran over her, and she had to stand still, hand on the table, before she could collect herself again. There was a jug of water by the Rìgh's bed. Ignoring the soldiers, she washed her face and hands and drank a mouthful of wine.

As she paced the floor, she heard the sound of fighting grow ever fiercer. It was coming from within the palace now as well as outside and, despite herself, her agitation grew.

The chancellor came in, flanked by guards. "My lady, there is bad news."

"Worse news than that my husband is dead?" Even roughened by grief and fear, her husky voice was melodious.

"The city has risen, my lady. There is a mutinous crowd at the palace gates, and the guards are having trouble keeping them back. They were all taken by surprise, no' expecting the witch-lovers to take action on Samhain Day."

"Surely there are soldiers enough to put down the city rabble?" she said scornfully.

He hesitated. "The palace guards are already engaged in repelling an attack from the rear, my lady. Somehow the grounds themselves have been infiltrated with a battalion o' rebels, and they now close in on the palace."

"This is incredible!" she said. "Ye tell me the rebels attack in the very hour o' the Rìgh's death? What conspiracy is this?"

He said nothing, and then lifted his grief-reddened eyes to her face. "The winged *uile-bheist* said he was Lachlan MacCuinn, my lady? The Rìgh's brother?"

"It is all a foul plot o' the rebels to discredit me!" she cried. "Jaspar knew it was no' true."

He did not believe her, she could see. Rage engulfed her. She had to fight as hard to control her anger as she had her grief, for she needed the chancellor and could not afford to strike him or screech at him, as she so wanted to do. It would be twenty-four years before Bronwen would be able to rule in her own name. By that time Maya would be an old woman and ready to step aside. Until then, though, she needed the support of those around her.

She hid her emotions under the guise of a grief-stricken woman who needed help and advice. The chancellor was an old and kindly man. He could not maintain his stiffness. She clung to his hands and wept, "Ye must secure the palace. Ye must keep the wee Banrìgh safe! Where is she? I sent for her half an hour ago, and yet they have no' brought her. Find me my Bronwen!"

He went to give orders to the seanalairs, and the Dowager Banrìgh went slowly through the wreckage of the doors and into her chamber, ordering the guards to leave her alone. She needed to have her clàrsach and the magic looking-glass to hand. It seemed she was beset on all sides.

For the first time she wished she had not decided to trap Sani in the shape of a hawk. The priestess would be useful now—Maya could use her far-seeing and clear-seeing skills, and the benefit of her advice. She wondered if the hawk would come if she called it to her hand. It was probably too late now. Sani would never forgive her for not changing her back after Bronwen's birth on the road. At first Maya had been too unwell, and she was never left alone, surrounded by servants and guards until they arrived at the palace. Later, Maya had procrastinated, enjoying the freedom from Sani's cutting tongue, her constant reminder that Maya was a mere halfbreed, begotten on a mute slave.

Maya opened the cabinet and took out the Mirror of Lela wrapped in its silk. She carried it carefully, knowing any mischance would deprive her of much of her power. It was the mirror which helped create Maya's illusion of youthful, human beauty. It was the mirror that facilitated her ability to transform others.

She brushed her hair and massaged cream into her cheeks. In the mirror her face looked hollow-cheeked and haunted. She stared at herself and imagined herself in the first flush of youth and beauty. Slowly the marks of grief faded, and subtly the strangeness of her features modified until she looked more human than ever.

She stood at the window, wondering why no one had brought her the baby, and saw how the fighting washed around the palace like a wild sea-storm. Her throat constricted with fear. Surely the palace would not fall? The battle was loud in the corridors now, so loud she could hear it, and she wondered if she should go in search of her daughter herself. If Latifa did not keep her safe, everything was lost.

She heard a door open behind her, and turned, eyebrow raised. There was no one there. She looked around uneasily, her skin prickling. There was a scrape on the floor. She remembered how the winged prionnsa had sprung from the shadows, a dark cloak falling from him. Her heart quickened. She sat at the table and pulled her clàrsach to her. With the mirror concealed in her lap, every sense aware of danger, she caressed the strings so sweet, lilting cadences filled the room. "Be at peace," she sang. "Rest and be at peace."

As long as Maya could remember, her singing and playing had charmed those who listened to her will. She had spun the spell of love with her music and tied Jaspar to her for sixteen years. She had soothed angry crowds, beguiled recalcitrant prionnsachan and won enemies to her cause.

"Ye think I do no' know what ye do?" A man's voice said scornfully. "Ye sing the song o' sorcery." And to her chagrin, he began to sing, his baritone skillfully blending with her contralto. She felt the silken strands wrap around her, soothing her, sapping her will. With an effort, she quickened the tempo, saying, "What coward is this that hides behind evil enchantments and sneaks into a widow's room, mocking her grief?"

"Grief! That's a joke! Ye think I do no' see through your play-acting?"

"How do ye know what I feel? Ye think I have a heart o' stone? Jaspar was my husband, and the father o' my babe, and I loved him well!"

She heard his claws click on the marble floor and turned her head, trying to conceal her fear.

"Loved him well enough to drive him to an early grave, steal his throne and murder his family?" The voice was thick with grief.

She strummed the clàrsach, lightly, delicately, and said, "Why do ye no' show yourself? Are ye afraid?"

"I am no' afraid!"

"Yet ye skulk behind some enchantment so I canna see ye. Who is it who speaks?"

He threw back the cloak and stepped forward proudly, his wings erect. He was dressed in the MacCuinn tartan and carried a bow as tall as himself. She ground her teeth with anger to see him wear the crest at his breast, as if he were the head of the clan and not his baby niece. "As if ye do no' remember me," he said. "Did ye no' wake us so we could see ye and understand what it was ye did to us? Did ye no' smile as we watched our own faces being swallowed by feathers and beak?"

Her fingers wandered into a lullaby, and she said thoughtfully, "How did ye escape the enchantment? I thought it would be impossible."

"Meghan o'the Beasts brought me back with the help

o' some friends," he answered, pacing closer. "Yet ye can see they were unable to restore me fully."

She looked him over, flinching a little at the sight of his talons, which were bloodstained. "No," she said softly. "No, I can see they could no'."

He cried, "Why would ye do this to us, Maya? Why?"

The lullaby wrapped the room in soft rhythms of sound. "I was cursed, Lachlan, born o' a Yedda and the King o' the Fairgean, trapped between sea and land, trapped between cultures and races. Ye call me the Unknown, but if I am a stranger here I was no less a stranger among my father's people."

"Ye are Fairge! I knew it, I always knew it." Lachlan sat and clasped his head in his hands, propping the bow against his knee. His shoulders heaved.

"I am sorry ye were so trapped, Lachlan. I was young and jealous o' Jaspar's love for ye. Ye would never have let me be. It was *peace* that I wanted, it was to be left alone, it was *peace* that I wanted. Indeed I loved your brother, and I grieve much at his passing, but now he is at *rest*, he is at *peace*, be at peace with me, brother, be at *peace*."

She saw him cover a yawn. His face was gray with tiredness. She let one hand drop from the clàrsach into her lap, and she talked on in a gentle sing-song as she unwrapped the mirror. Lachlan had thought she had forced them to watch their own ensorcelment out of cruelty, but it was imaginatively changing their reflection in the mirror that effected the actual shape-shift.

Lachlan shook his head and wiped his eyes angrily. "Be at peace with ye? I think no'," he said, glancing up. She had just lifted the mirror, and his eyes dilated at the sight of it. With a cry he brought the bow up and shot the mirror from her hand. There was a tinkle of falling glass and she screamed in pain, bringing up her hands to cover her face. She fell from the chair and writhed on the floor as changes rippled over her. Gray sprang from her brow, crinkling through the blue-black sheen. Her face altered, grew wider and more strongly sculpted, her nostrils flaring, her nose flattening. The webs between her fingers grew, and her skin grew paler and moister, a fine iridescent sheen to it almost like scales. Blood seeped up through a fine web of cuts on one cheek, patterned like the broken mirror that lay at her feet.

Lachlan shuddered in horror. She gasped, "Ye fool! Ye just lost any chance ye had o' being transformed back into a man. The mirror was magical—ye are trapped forever now!"

SONG OF THE KEY

Isabeau and Iseult fought their way down the hall, heading away from the battle. It was only the surge of fresh rebels from the city that gave them the momentum to enter the main wing of the building. Dillon and the League of the Healing Hand had somehow managed to raise the portcullis, so the city rabble had surged into the palace grounds.

The twins reached the cook's rooms, and Isabeau whispered to Iseult, "Perhaps I had better speak to her alone. Why do ye no' keep guard for me?"

Iseult reluctantly nodded, and Isabeau knocked on the door. "Latifa," she called. "It is I, Isabeau."

The door opened and a suspicious round face peered out. The old cook's face was swollen and red with tears, her eyelids so puffy her tiny raisin-black eyes could hardly be seen.

"Isabeau?"

"Let me in, Latifa, we need to talk."

The cook pushed the door open and Isabeau went in. She saw the baby lying on the bed. At the sound of Isabeau's step the baby opened her silvery-blue eyes and gave a little dreamy smile. "Bronwen!" Isabeau picked the baby up and swung her to her shoulder. "Ye are safe! I was so worried."

Latifa sat heavily, looking down at her plump, work-chapped hands.

"Latifa, it is time to join the Key," Isabeau said gently, laying the baby down again. "Ye must give it to me now."

Latifa clutched the keyring at her waist. "No," she said.

Isabeau sat down, facing her, taking her hands in hers. She could see the cook was dazed with grief and shock. "Latifa, what is wrong? Why no'?"

"Ye heard the Rìgh," Latifa said stubbornly. "He wanted his wee babe to inherit. If ye support that *uilebheist* she will be disinherited. Puir Jaspar—all he wanted was to make sure Bronwen would be protected. He made me promise I would watch over her, keep her safe. Ye canna tell me she will be safe if the rebels win the day? I heard how that winged man spoke about my wee Bronwen. He called her evil."

"We will keep Bronwen safe," Isabeau said. "Ye and I will look after her. Meghan will make sure nothing happens."

"Meghan is gone," Latifa said harshly, and a sob shook her.

"Nay, Meghan is here. I just saw her."

"Ye try and trick me," Latifa said suspiciously, staring at Isabeau. "Ye sound like Isabeau . . ."

"I am Isabeau," she said, puzzled. "I speak the truth. Meghan is here. She needs the Key. She is the Key-bearer and she needs it back."

"Meghan is dead," Latifa said. "This is all trickery and deceit. Before they said it was ye, and I knew it was no'. Now ye say it is ye again, but I canna tell. Ye smell all wrong, o' smoke and blood."

Isabeau persisted gently. "Latifa, ye ken Meghan needs the Key, ye've guarded it for her all these years. Why will ye no' give it to her when she needs it?"

"Meghan is no' here, she's disappeared. Ye've been tricked, Isabeau."

Sunlight was striking in through the cook's window, and with a shock Isabeau realized how much time had passed. The last few hours had been a blur. "I have no' got time for this, Latifa, ye need to give me the Key!"

A cunning expression crossed the old cook's face. Her hands slipped under her apron and her lips moved silently.

A strange lethargy crept over Isabeau. Her bones felt soft as butter.

"Ye are mistaken, Isabeau."

"I am mistaken?" she said with a questioning inflection.

"Ye are mistaken."

"I am mistaken."

"Ye do no' want the Key."

"I do no' want the Key."

"Latifa will keep it safe."

"Latifa will keep it safe."

"Ye must leave now. This will soon be all over, and we will all be safe. Go, Isabeau."

"I must go now," Isabeau repeated and felt herself standing. Her legs were stiff, and her head muzzy. She shook it. The cook's face swam before her and she tried to concentrate. Suddenly an image flashed before her—an old skeelie's face, murmuring words, her gnarled fingers playing in her lap.

Her eyes flashed to Latifa's lap; she held something there, under the cover of her apron. Isabeau reached forward and seized it. Despite Latifa's shriek, Isabeau was able to wrest it from the old cook's hands. To her bemusement, it was a long snake of ruddy hair.

At once she realized what had happened. Latifa had not burnt her hair but kept it. Meghan had often warned her to have a care for her discarded nails and hairs and flakes of skin—indeed, Isabeau had been trapped before by a single strand of hair. The Grand-Seeker Glynelda had used it to hunt her through the highlands. What could Latifa do with several feet of braid?

Isabeau remembered gathering great armfuls of groundsel in the forest, mindlessly, like a puppet. She remembered many occasions when she had felt compelled to go to the kitchen or storeroom and had found Latifa there waiting for her. She remembered not eating the day before Midsummer Eve, despite her hunger, and how she had later thought how lucky it was she had fasted before they held the rites. Color flamed over her face.

"Ye were compelling me!" she cried. "Why, Latifa, why? Compulsion is forbidden!"

"An auld witch has to have a care for herself," Latifa muttered, rocking back and forth in her seat, tears streaming down her face. "Sixteen years I spied for Meghan in the very heart o' the Righ's household—ye think that was easy? No, no, an auld witch has to look out for herself."

"Give me the Key!"

Latifa shrank back, clutching the keyring with both hands. "No!"

Isabeau tried to wrest it from her but the old cook was strong and clung to the keyring desperately. Isabeau had the use of only one hand and could not pry her fingers free. They struggled, panting, then Isabeau was thrown back onto the bed. She clenched her fingers and concentrated. Her will was much stronger than her body and had been forged in the fires of the Awl's torture room. The Key wrenched itself free of Latifa's belt and flew to Isabeau's hand, jangling loudly with the many keys that hung from it.

"Latifa, I swear to ye I am doing the right thing," Isabeau said. "Meghan is here; if ye would just open your mind, ye would sense her . . ."

The cook rocked back and forth, weeping. "I'm sorry," Isabeau said. "I have to go. Look after Bronwen, keep her safe." She kissed the baby then she was gone.

As soon as Isabeau emerged from the cook's room,

her face flushed, her short curls in disarray, Iseult caught her hand and they ran. They could smell smoke and knew the city rabble must have fired part of the palace. Now they had all three parts of the Key, they could not risk being separated or injured.

"Where?" Iseult cried.

"This way!" Isabeau skidded as she tried to round a corner. They brushed past the milling servants, found the door into the kitchen garden, and ran through to the great paved square beyond.

A group of Red Guards saw them and recognized them from an earlier confrontation. With a shout they ran to engage, but the twins fled into the garden.

The snow crunched underfoot, and they saw they were leaving a trail of footprints. The sun was high in the sky, and there was nowhere to hide. All they could do was try and outrun the guards.

For almost an hour the twins played a breathless game of chase-and-hide with the soldiers. At last they took shelter in the trees, baffling the soldiers by swinging from tree to tree so that no footprints were left behind. Even with only one hand, Isabeau was as nimble in the branches as any donbeag, and she told Iseult about the tree-house in the secret valley and how Meghan had made her do this every time she came or went.

The twins had their first chance to talk as they crouched in the sweet-scented cave at the heart of the evergreen oak. Since their first meeting they had been in constant motion, running, fighting, climbing out of windows. Now they had the leisure to examine each other's faces and have some of their most pressing questions answered.

Isabeau had the most questions to ask; since she had been isolated from Meghan for so long, she knew nothing about the discoveries the old witch had made at the palace of the dragons or the Towers of Roses and Thorns. By the time the soldiers had given up their search, she knew almost everything. She knew she was a banprionnsa, descendant of Faodhagan the Red and a Khan'cohban. She understood how she came to be abandoned on the slopes of Dragonclaw and the significance of the dragoneye ring. She knew that her mother really was Ishbel the Winged, the fabled witch who could fly as easily as any bird, and that she had taught Iseult the secrets of flight. She was thrilled, frightened, bewildered and jealous, all at once.

It was a strange sensation, to see her face upon another's, to feel a bond between them as strong as steel. In some peculiar way Isabeau felt as if the missing parts of her jigsaw self had at last been found, and she was whole at last.

At the sound of Maya's scream, the guards outside came running into the boudoir. Lachlan shot two down before they had taken more than a few strides, but had to throw the bow down and reach for the claymore as the two behind charged him. Claymores clashing, they beat him back toward the wall as the Banrìgh moaned.

From down the corridor came a shout, and then the sounds of fighting. Lachlan held the two guards off, but he had been in violent action most of the long night and morning and was exhausted. One slashed his thigh, and he stumbled.

Duncan burst through the door, roaring with rage. Behind him ran Meghan, her face ashen, her hand to her chest. The big man killed the other soldiers with a single, sweeping stroke. Lachlan swung around unsteadily, advancing on Maya with his bloody claymore. She had her hands to her face, blood seeping through her fingers from the spider's web of gashes that covered most of one side of her face.

Meghan leant against the table and drank a few mouthfuls from a little bottle. Gitâ screeched from her shoulder, all his fur on end, his eyes huge and black. "No, Lachlan," she said tiredly. "Ye canna kill her now. There is too much we do no' know."

"She says she canna change me back now the mirror

is broken," he said in soft, silky tones. "We shall see if her death effects the miracle."

"No, Lachlan. Surely ye can see it would be better to put her on trial, to show the country the evil she has done? We still have much to do to win the people to our cause and help us drive out the Bright Soldiers. If she is murdered, the common folk will make o' her a martyr. Canna ye see that?"

"No," he said. "All I can see is that at last I have her at my feet. I shall show her the same mercy that she showed my brothers and me." He raised the claymore.

Meghan wearily raised a hand and he found he could not move. Maya crawled away from him, her silvery-blue eyes retaining their old beauty amidst the wreckage of her face. In her hand she clutched the remnants of the mirror.

"Meghan, what do ye do?" he cried. "Do ye turn against me now?"

"Do no' be a fool," she said and sat down heavily. She was ashen in the morning light, her face heavily lined. She sighed. "Lachlan, the rebels have won the palace. There is fighting still all through the city and grounds, and the countryside belongs to the Bright Soldiers, but we have won the first battle. We can join the Key, enter the labyrinth and save the Lodestar. Tonight is the time o' the two moons crossing. We will wash the Lodestar and it will sing again for us. We can use it to free the countryside and drive the Fairgean back into the sea. The land will be ours, and ye will be Rìgh as ye wanted. It is time to think like a Rìgh. If ye kill Maya, who will ever know the truth o' what happened? Ye will say she was a sorceress and murdered your brothers. Her supporters will say she was the rightful Regent and ye murdered her to win the throne. Think, Lachlan, think!"

She released her hold on him, and he staggered and went down on one knee. "Jaspar is dead!" he wept. She rose and went to him, soothing him with one hand on his sweat-tangled curls.

Maya managed to get to her feet, and looked at her bloodstained hands in disbelief. The unscarred side of her face showed faint lines at the corners of her mouth and eyes that had not been there before. She said, "Kill me now and be done with it! Indeed ye are a cruel, unforgiving woman, Meghan NicCuinn! Ye would rather shame and mortify me, parade me in public, play out a farce o' a trial and then watch me die a traitor's death. Ye have no mercy."

For the first time Meghan looked at Maya, and there was no pity on her face. "Nay, Maya, I will show ye greater mercy than ye showed the witches. Ye will no' die on the fire, the cruelest o' all deaths. Ye will be tried and judged by the people, and the people shall choose your punishment."

She turned to Duncan, standing on guard nearby. "Duncan, glad I am indeed to see ye. How are ye yourself?"

"Glad to be here, my lady," he replied, bowing to her deeply. "Though I never thought it would take sixteen years for the Blue Guards to overcome the Ensorcellor."

Maya laughed, a bitter sound. "The Ensorcellor! Well, at least it is better than the Unknown." She stood straight as an arrow in her crimson gown, her ruined face proud and unrepentant.

"We need to make a circle and star," Isabeau said. With a stick she drew as perfect a circle as she could, the ground under the snow hard. She left it open, stepping inside and carefully drawing a hexagram within—it seemed appropriate to have the star the same shape as the one in the Key, and there were only two of them so she thought they should try and balance the power. Hurriedly she built a fire in the center, gathering kindling from under the yew trees and breaking dead branches from an oak tree, a hazel tree and a hawthorn bush, the only sacred woods to hand.

These actions were familiar to Iseult. She sat on the ground and began unpacking the bottomless bag. *The*

Book of Shadows was followed by a pouch of essential minerals, including salt, which she passed to her twin. She found her *sheyeta*, which Meghan had carried for so many months, and ran her fingers over it lovingly. As soon as she pulled it free of the pouch, it began to hum, it strange melody rising through the air, and Isabeau gestured to her to keep it hidden.

Iseult took the salt and scattered it with a handful of snow and earth around the circle, chanting, "I consecrate and conjure thee, O circle o' magic, ring o' power, symbol o' perfection and constant renewal. Keep us safe from harm, keep us safe from evil, guard us against treachery, keep us safe in your eyes, Eà o' the moons."

"Meghan obviously managed to teach ye something." Isabeau said.

"No' much," Iseult admitted. "She often compared me unfavorably to ye."

"Ye must be bad, then," Isabeau said with a laugh, tossing handfuls of rosemary, roseships and thyme that she had cut from the garden into the fire.

Iseult scattered salt, earth and melting snow along the lines of the six-sided star, chanting the rites. They sat opposite each other, Isabeau at the southern point, Iseult at the northern, and closed the circle about them. Isabeau lit the fire with a thought and rejoiced to have her powers returned to her.

Fingers shaking, Isabeau removed the reverse spell from the thrice-crossed hoop, a green signal of fire flaring up. They both felt the power of the Key thrumming around them. Holding her breath, Iseult suspended her triangular talisman above the hoop. It hung there, singing. Hovering a few inches away from each other, the song swelled. They waited for the sun, and as it reached the zenith of the sky, Isabeau and Iseult chanted the rites.

With a little jerk, the circle and triangle clicked together as if they had never been dismembered, and the song burst into triumphant orchestra. The key spun and hovered, pulsating with power. Kneeling together in the snow, Isabeau and Iseult struck their hands together in jubilation. It was done!

Margrit of Arran raised the twelve-thonged whip again, preparing to lash the torn and bleeding back of her chamberlain one more time. Khan'tirell hung before her, his wrists manacled to the wall, his horned head hanging. The steel-tipped whip was whistling down when suddenly the banprionnsa staggered and the stroke fell awry.

She clutched her head in her hands. "No! It canna be! They've united the Key!" Her face distorted with rage. The Khan'cohban glanced at her sideways, one side of his pain-twisted mouth lifting. She caught his thought and grasped the whip again in a fury, savagely thrashing his sinewy back.

"If they recover the Lodestar, I swear someone will suffer for it," she hissed. "As ye shall suffer, Khan'tirell, for allowing my son to escape. As my son shall suffer, and his mealy-mouthed bride. As the MacCuinns shall suffer. One does no' thwart the Thistle without pain!"

Deep in the forests of Rionnagan, Iain and Douglas stopped mid-stride, looking at each other in amazement. The air seemed to resonate as if somewhere a giant gong had been struck, and they could feel the ground thrumming under their feet. All around them the cold wind sang.

"Wha' is that music?" Dide cried.

Enit's face was alight with triumph. "The Key! Thank Eà, they have joined the Key! We must be near a line o' power to hear its song so clearly. Och, this is grand indeed—soon the Lodestar will be renewed, and then the land shall be free. We shall all be free!"

Dide grasped Lilanthe by the waist and waltzed her round, shouting with excitement. A smile of satisfaction and relief spread over Gwilym's pock-marked face, transforming it. The children jumped up and down, laughing and clapping their hands, even though they did not understand the adults' animation.

"What force and strength canna get through,

With a mere touch, I can undo," the cluricaun chanted, dancing a jig.

"If only we could travel faster," Dide cried. "I want to be there! The master is storming the palace, and I am no' there to fight at his side. They've joined the Key, the rescuing o' the Lodestar canna be far away."

Excited chatter burst out, and the cluricaun did a forward roll in his excitement. Suddenly Enit cried out, and her blue-veined, twisted hands clutched her breast. "No!" she moaned. "Meghan!"

From the garden there came a sound as if of trumpets, and a wave of power washed over them all. Meghan turned, her face lighting up. "They've done it! Lachlan, they've done it! The Key is joined!"

They clustered together, laughing with delight. Suddenly Gitâ gave a shriek of warning. Meghan turned and saw Maya darting towards her with a shard of mirror held in her hand like a dagger. Before the witch had time to do more than stumble back, Maya brought the dagger of glass down, plunging it into Meghan's breast. The old witch fell into Lachlan's arms, blood beginning to well up around the silver glass. Maya laughed with bitter triumph, catching up the cloak of invisibility from where Lachlan had discarded it on the floor. As Duncan lunged forward, his claymore whizzing down, she disappeared and the sword clanged fruitlessly on the floor.

Both Isbeau and Iseult were clinging to each other with joy and the glow of accomplishment when suddenly Isabeau staggered, her hand to her breast. Iseult felt the shock of the blow as well, though without the intensity of Isbeau's pain. "Meghan!" her twin whispered through white lips.

They looked at each other in horror, their thoughts flying to the palace. Isabeau would have set off for the palace at a run if Iseult had not caught her and kept her still. "Ye must never step outside the magic circle—there is a cone o' protection about us! Wait! We must finish the rite."

White-faced and trembling, they opened the magic circle and scattered it and the fire's ashes into the muddy snow. Isabeau put the Key in her pocket, ignoring Iseult's imperious hand. Then they set off in a staggering run toward the palace, the fastest pace they could muster after twelve hours of constant action. Tapping his way along the walkway was the blind seer, led by a small boy with fair hair. Isabeau and Iseult ran to meet them.

"Jorge, something has happened to Meghan!" Isabeau cried.

"I felt it. We are on our way to see if we can help. She lives still, and while there is life there is hope."

The warlock's pace was too slow to satisfy the twins, and they ran on ahead. They reached the palace and, holding their sides to ease the stitch there, bounded up the stairs toward the royal suite.

Breathing harshly, they raced into Maya's room and saw Meghan lying back in Lachlan's arms. She was gray to her lips, blood splashing crimson down her dress. Gitâ was keening in distress, clinging to her neck, his fur wet with her blood.

Lachlan was distraught. Iseult had to fling her arms about him to make him release Meghan so Isabeau could examine her wound. Kneeling by her side, Isabeau cut Meghan's dress away so she could probe around the wedge of glass. Red blood was pulsing up around it.

"It's arterial blood," Isabeau said. "I do no' think I can save her." She caught her breath, tears making tracks through the soot and grime on her face.

"Isabeau, listen to me," Meghan whispered. "If it is time for my thread to be cut, then nothing ye can do can stop Gearradh. Ye must save the Lodestar. Look after this for me, Isabeau, and look after Lachlan and Iseult. They are Eileanan's only hope. Ye must go to the labyrinth near sunset. It is designed to trick those

that enter without the secret—I could have shown ye
the way through, but I canna now. Read *The Book of
Shadows*, Isabeau. Ye are the only one who can do it. I
am trusting ye, Isabeau, do no' let me down."

The old witch fell back in a faint. Isabeau dared not
pull out the shard of glass and, without her herbs and
potions, could do little but press with her hand to try to
slow the pump of blood. Jorge came in, tears on his face,
the little boy trotting ahead. As soon as Tòmas saw the
sorceress, her eyes sealed shut, the breath barely whistling through her lips, he stripped off the black gauntlets
he wore. Immediately Isabeau felt the power concentrated in his hands and cried out. She had heard rumors
of the lad with the healing hands, but had certainly not
expected him to be this cherubic-looking boy, no more
than eight years old.

Tòmas knelt and laid his hands on the wound. He was
frowning. "She slips away," he whispered. "The glass
has pierced her heart's wall. I will try . . ."

They saw the shard of glass slowly rise out of the
wound as the flesh and muscles beneath began to knit
together. The pulsating blood began to slow and then it
clotted, black and sticky. Meghan moaned. Tòmas was
ashen now, panting with the effort. He pulled the shard
free and fresh blood leaked through, but at the touch of
his fingers it dried. He fell back. "I can do no more
now," he said, his voice thin. "She was at the very gates
o' death. I have used her own strength as well as mine to
save her. She may still slip away, but I can do no more."

Duncan lifted him away and set him at the table, giving him wine to sip. Tòmas was shaking with exhaustion
and said piteously, "There are so many hurt, I can feel
them crying to me."

"They will have to wait," Duncan said firmly. "Ye will
do no guid killing yourself to save them."

Isabeau was kneeling beside Meghan, weeping. The
sorceress lay still, gray-faced, her breathing only margin-
ally stronger. On her breast was a great scar, as large as
Duncan's fist and black with clotted blood. "Help me

lift her to the bed," she said. "Get me some o' that *mithuan* and the poppy syrup from beside the Rìgh's bed—she will be in great pain when she wakes."

They set Meghan in the great bed, Gitâ curled by her side, and closed the curtains against the afternoon sun. Isabeau would have sat beside her, but she was so white and trembly that Jorge himself tucked her up in her cot in the nursery. He sent one of the rebels standing guard outside to fetch food and tea for the three of them, and insisted on Lachlan and Iseult sleeping as well.

"Meghan said ye must enter the labyrinth near sunset. Ye have no' slept all night and it has been a long and hard one. Sleep, my bairns, and I shall watch over ye."

TWO MOONS CROSSING

orge woke them in the late afternoon and made them
eat and drink some wine. All were white and tired
still, but the overcharged tenseness had left their faces
and bodies and he no longer feared one would collapse.

Duncan Ironfist had searched the palace and grounds
for the Dowager Banrìgh but there had been no sign
of her. The old cook had also disappeared from her
room, and there was no sign of the baby, declared
Banrìgh only that morning and now already dispossessed. They all hoped Latifa's disappearance was not
related to Maya's, for if the Dowager Banrìgh escaped
with her daughter, they could be a rallying point for any
future insurrection.

Isabeau slowly led the way through the garden. Even
if they had felt the urgency of the morning they were
simply too tired to move any faster. "So where in the
name o' the White Gods is this blaygird maze?" Iseult
asked wearily.

"Good question. I was hoping Meghan had told ye."

"Nay, all she ever said was something about *The Book
o' Shadows* having the answers."

"Ye have the Book safe?"

Iseult nodded. Isabeau smiled wanly. "We should no' have any problems then."

Her twin groaned. "Ye think so? We've only managed to make *The Book o' Shadows* work for us once and we have no idea what we did."

"Ye never do, with *The Book o' Shadows*," Isabeau said. They reached a long, high hedge, wild with brambles.

"Do ye have any idea where we are going?" Lachlan asked in a surly voice. He was blaming himself for Meghan's injury and had hardly said a word to either of them.

"No' really," Isabeau admitted. "I tried to work the maze out the other day but just got lost and frustrated. We have the Key now, though, and the Book, so we should manage."

They came to the parterre garden and sat on the stone bench. The yew trees and hedges were black, the sky a pure blue-green, only the dome of the observatory still burnished with light. A wind ruffled the leaves, making them jump.

"I was here the other day," Isabeau said, "and could no' help thinking how much this garden looked like it was built around something. Do ye see what I mean? There is the pathway up the center, quite wide, the clipped lavender bushes and cypress trees, the archway— and then just a hedge. Why would they design it that way?"

Iseult shrugged. She knew nothing about gardening and did not want to. Isabeau had always loved plants and flowers, though, and had spent a lot of time with Riordan Bowlegs in the palace gardens at Rhyssmadill.

"I think this garden is enchanted, too. The other day I stumbled across it twice, in different parts of the garden. I've never yet heard o' a garden that could move itself at will, so it stands to reason it's enchanted. That's why I headed here. Do ye have the Book?"

Iseult got it out of the pouch at her belt, and Isabeau received it with a pleased cry. It filled her arms, bound with embossed red leather and iron. She laid it on the bench between them and rested her hands on the cover. She was still for a moment, breathing deeply, relaxing her muscles. Then she held the book between her hands and let it fall open.

On the open pages were a carefully sketched design and many lines of writing. Isabeau pored over the tiny, crabbed words. "It is a description o' the planting o' the gardens and maze by Martha the Wise. She designed it while the Tower of Two Moons was under construction. It says here her father, Lachlan the Stargazer, had built an observatory at the sacred pool o' the Celestines. Once the pool had been protected by forest, but the Coven had torn down the forest to build the city and palace. Martha the Wise decided to protect the pool and observatory with a maze, for she had discovered the pool had great magical powers that could be used by the dishonorable for their own ends . . ." Her voice trailed away.

"Well, that's about as useful as anything else I've ever got out o' *The Book of Shadows*," Iseult snorted in disgust.

Isabeau stared at the page, then said softly, "No, do ye no' see? Look at the drawing. It is a sketch o' Martha MacCuinn's plan for the maze—see?"

Iseult looked carefully, but all she could see were circles, triangles and squares set in harmonious patterns on the page. Isabeau's finger traced out a square at one end. "See, this is the parterre garden. We are sitting on this bench, and that long oblong is the hedge. But look! From where we sit the hedge is solid, but in the drawing the path runs straight ahead, lined with hedges on either side. Come on!"

She jumped to her feet, closing the book before Iseult could warn her not to, and walked down the flagstones. Her twin followed closely, her dagger drawn, with Lachlan by her side. Together they came to the hedge. Iseult and Lachlan stopped before their faces were scratched but Isabeau kept on walking and the hedge disappeared as if it had never been. Instead it formed into an arch over their heads.

They were standing at one end of a long path, lined on either side with ancient cypress trees and enclosed with tall hedges. At the far end of the path was a tall, thin gate, made of wrought iron. Beyond the gate they could see more hedges, with the dome just visible above.

"Are we in the maze?" Iseult said. "That was easy."

"Too easy," Isabeau agreed. "But let us go on."

They walked down the path, cool in the shadows of the cypress trees, and came to the gate. It was locked with a chain. Isabeau carefully examined it and smiled. "Look, we need to fit the Key into the lock to open it." She showed Iseult the shape of the circle and hexagram set into a padlock about the size of their hand. The Key fitted easily into the depression, and the chain fell open at a single turn.

"That was easy too," Iseult said.

"At the risk o' repeating myself, I have to say too easy again," Isabeau replied, and let Iseult push ahead through the gate. They closed it behind them but could not lock it again. This troubled her all, with the maze now open to the garden and the Ensorcellor still at large.

Directly ahead was a hedge, with the path now running south to north so they had to choose between turning left and right. Isabeau recalled the shape of the maze and said, rather hesitantly, "Left."

"Ye should no' have closed the Book," Iseult said. "It had the design o' the maze in it and now we'll never find the page again."

"We had to close the Book," Isabeau said. "It will only ever give ye an answer once. I memorized the layout o' the maze from the tower, and then checked it against the design when I had the page open. They were the same."

Iseult looked at her in grudging admiration. "Ye can do that?"

"Did Meghan no' teach ye visualization and memory skills?"

Iseult laughed. "She tried to."

After wandering the maze for close on an hour, they were all tired, hot and bad-tempered. The dome mocked them, swinging so close they thought they were almost there, then swinging away again. By now it was just a black curve against the sunset sky, and it was dark between the hedges, so that Isabeau had to summon a light.

Lachlan would not believe that Isabeau knew the way, and he kept insisting on exploring different paths. They were all jumpy, and at last they sat in the shade of the hedge and Iseult made tea for them all, heating it with her finger. That made Isabeau give a weary smile, for that had always been her trick.

"I canna understand it," Isabeau said. "I swear I memorized the path. We should have been there by now."

"Ask *The Book of Shadows*," Iseult suggested.

Isabeau reluctantly agreed, and they got out the massive tome again. The wind rustled the hedge near them so they looked around warily, but they could sense nothing near them but mice and hedgehogs. Out in the night a hawk shrieked, and they heard the death squeal of a dormouse. Isabeau looked up, startled and worried, and waited long moments before turning back to the Book.

The clue to using *The Book of Shadows* was not to ask it or order it or even beg it for its secret knowledge. Instead, one just had to trust to its wisdom and open it, knowing the answer would be revealed. Isabeau had read through the pages of *The Book of Shadows* since she was a child, but still she had to focus her thoughts and let go of her doubts to make it work. She did so now, but when the pages fell open on the reverse spell— a page she had read a hundred times—she swore and slapped it with her hand and said, "I do no' understand what is wrong with it!"

Iseult looked gratified, and Lachlan said impatiently, "By the Centaur, Isabeau, Meghan said ye knew how to use this thing."

She cast him a seething look and bent her head over the page again, the light from her finger casting strange shadows over the words. Suddenly she smiled. "O' course!" She scrambled to her feet, slammed the book shut and set off back the way they had come.

"Where are ye going?" he demanded.

"I've been a fool!" she cried. "I should have worked it out the first time I realized we had something gone astray. The maze works backward. Instead of trying to reach the dome, we should be trying to go away from it!"

By the time they reached the end of the maze it was dark. They stepped with relief from the claustrophobic closeness of the hedges and saw a great, stone temple, ringed by wide steps leading up to arched cloisters. They climbed the steps and found themselves by a wide pool, edged with stone and open to the sky. All round the pool were thick pillars made of a stone so ancient the many symbols carved all over them were worn almost to obscurity.

Both Iseult and Lachlan immediately saw the resemblance to the pool on Tulachna Celeste, except that the great menhirs were here topped with decorated arches, and at one end was a raised platform with great bronze doors into the domed observatory. All the stone was beautifully fretted and carved, and stone faces looked down at them from the curve of each arch.

The water was very low in the pool, and murky green-brown. At one end of the pool was a stone channel where water once ran. At the other end was carved the crest of the witches' tower—two crescent moons and a star.

They wandered around the pool, exclaiming over its beauty and wondering where Meghan would have hidden the Lodestar. She had given them no clue, but now they were sure the answer would be somewhere in *The Book of Shadows*. Then Isabeau gave a startled cry.

She was staring up at one of the arches. Perched on

its apex was a white bhanais bird with a magnificent white sparkling tail. It looked as if it was studded with diamonds, but as the bird spread his tail for their admiration they could see it was silver iridescent feathers that caused it to sparkle so.

Who is it that disturbs the rest of the Keeper?

They all jumped. _I am Lachlan Owein MacCuinn_, Lachlan answered politely, bowing to the bird.

And these two, alike as if one is a reflection in the pool?

My wife, Iseult NicFaghan, and her sister, Isabeau NicFaghan.

It has been a long time since we have had a MacCuinn visit the stargazer. Indeed, it has been a long time since anyone has visited.

The Pool o' Two Moons has been locked away and only now have we managed to unlock it again.

I am pleased. It has been lonely here for my wife and I. We have had nothing to eat except worms and bugs since the last MacCuinn was here—gone are the days when we supped on cake and wine.

He spread his wings and drifted down slowly, his magnificent tail shimmering. _Ye wish to see the observatory, I suppose?_

Lachlan looked at the other two and Isabeau shrugged and nodded. The Keeper promenaded before them, his tail spread so they could admire its curled and plumed feathers. The doors opened as he approached them, and he led them into the interior of the observatory. They examined the instruments and charts with great interest, Lachlan becoming so absorbed Isabeau had to remind him why they were here. She could not help a certain tartness to her tone, for Lachlan had been consistently rude and quick-tempered with her since their meeting last night.

Reluctantly he put down the chart and followed them back outside. Gladrielle had risen, looking blue and delicate, and Magnysson was close behind her, swollen and red on the horizon.

"Ask *The Book of Shadows* where the Lodestar is hidden," he ordered.

Isabeau bridled at his tone but nonetheless lay down on the ground, setting the ancient book before her. She gathered her will, emptied her mind and thought of what she needed to know. Then she opened the book.

Although it was windless in the shelter of the hedges, a breeze sprang up and riffled the pages of the book. Isabeau tried to save her place with her finger but the pages fluttered over and she could not see where the book had first opened.

"That's what always happened to me!" Iseult said with a certain satisfaction.

"That is what happens if ye go to the Book without a clear question, or if there are many pages in the book that the subject is mentioned," Isabeau said, despair on her face. "Ye must always make your question as defined as possible."

"So what did ye do wrong?" Lachlan's voice was angry.

"I did nothing wrong!" Isabeau glanced down at the book and saw it had at last settled on a page. She read what it said, and a little smile sprung up.

"What does it say?" Lachlan said and snatched the book away so he could read. She let him, sitting up on her heels. She watched his expression fall, and he said, "Eà damn it, this is useless! It's just a faery story!"

"Eideann and the Nightingale," Isabeau said. "It was always one o' my favorites."

He slammed the book shut and got to his claws in a rage. "This is useless! Why did Meghan no' just tell us where she hid it?"

"She did," Isabeau replied and clambered to her feet, the Book cradled in her arms. Refusing to say another word, she went back up the steps to where the white bhanais bird was perched.

Keeper, may I ask ye a question? she asked.

He gave her a hoarse chortle. *Ye may ask three, my dear. Not counting that one.*

*Were ye here when the last MacCuinn came through
the maze?*

*No, but my father's father was then Keeper of the Pool
of Two Moons. I was told all I needed to know before
my father died.*

*Do ye know if the last MacCuinn was a little old
woman with black eyes and a white streak through her
hair?*

Indeed she was, my dear.

*She carried something and hid it. Can ye tell us where
it was hidden?*

I may only tell the one that carries the MacCuinn crest.

Lachlan started and came forward to show the Keeper
the brooch he wore to pin his plaid together.

The orb she carried was hidden at the pool, the bird
said promptly. *Behind the crest of two moons.*

Almost before his harsh cries had died away, Isabeau,
Iseult and Lachlan were running up the stairs. They
hung over the pool, pushing and pounding the crest, trying to make it open. Then Isabeau's fingers pressed the
star, and immediately the stone carving swung forward
and they saw a dark space behind. With a cry, Lachlan
reached in his hand and pulled out the Lodestar.

It was a dull white stone, about the size of an apple,
only perfectly round. Mist drifted within its glass walls.
Lachlan cupped it in his hands and a frail silvery light
sprung up in its heart. For a moment they could hear a
trace of music, like sleigh bells. Then the light flickered away.

"It is dead!" Lachlan cried in horror. "Look at it! We
are too late, it is dead."

"We have to bathe it in the pool," Iseult reminded
him. "Meghan said it would fade as its birthday approached. It should be washed in the pool at the time
o' the two moons crossing. Then it will be renewed."

They all looked at the sky, where the two moons were
so close. Gladrielle had a strange murky color. They all
sat to wait, Lachlan cradling the Lodestar in his hands

and crooning to it. The fragile wisp of light occasionally twisted within but otherwise there was no response.

Lachlan rose to get the far-seeing glass from the observatory, and they took turns to stare at the sky through it, amazed at what they could see. Planets with rings of fire, drifts of violet and green cloud, stars bright and dim, great stretches of impenetrable blackness. The moons grew closer and closer as they rose, Magnysson seeming to swell as Gladrielle grew frailer. Then he leant toward her, and they saw a crescent-shaped bite in her side.

"That is the shadow o' the larger moon," Lachlan said. "It looks as if they are merging, but in fact they are a long way away from each other, it is just the angle that we see it from."

"Two moons that reach out to each other, sometimes to kiss, sometimes to bite," Isabeau murmured. She felt tears prick her eyes, for the words reminded her poignantly of her first meeting with Jorge, when she had been an eager acolyte, dreaming of magic and adventure.

Slowly Magnysson ate into Gladrielle, and then they saw an even larger shadow move across his red-hued flank. "That is the shadow o' the earth," Lachlan said. "Soon the earth will be between the sun and the moons and we will have a total eclipse."

"How do ye know all this?" Iseult asked him in irritation. He smirked at her, and said, "Did ye read none o' the books Meghan gave us?"

Gladrielle was swallowed, and only a curve of Magnysson remained. A hush had fallen over the garden and all the yews rustled mysteriously. Then the last thin curve of red was blotted out and immediately all the stars sprang out, brilliant against the velvety blackness. Where the two moons had been was a round dark hole in the sky, a great whirlpool of darkness.

Gradually the larger of the moons moved aside, and light began to spill out from one side. The water in the pool began to slowly rise, bubbling up from the center. Lachlan stood and sang the winterbourne, and a sparkling fountain gushed into life. Silver light shone through the archways into the pool, and all the water was lit up mysteriously.

Lachlan walked down the steps, the shimmering light blazing on the white lock at his brow and sculpting the planes of his face. His face was triumphant. The steps led straight into the water and he walked into it, and bent and dipped the Lodestar in the bubbling, light-filled water. There was a flash of bright light and music sounded. He held up the Lodestar triumphantly, streaming with glittering water like the bhanais bird's tail. "It is done!" he cried. "The Lodestar is renewed!"

At that moment a hawk dropped out of the sky and snatched the Lodestar from his hands. He shouted in dismay, but the hawk beat its powerful wings and rose in the air. In two quick strides Lachlan caught up Owein's Bow and shot an arrow into the sky. It curved in a perfect trajectory and pierced the hawk's breast. The bird gave a dreadful cry and fell, the Lodestar dropping from its claws. Lachlan flung up his hand but he was too late. Across the dark garden a tall shape sprang free of the shadows. With their night vision Isabeau and Iseult could both clearly see Maya, with the baby Bronwen in her arms. The baby laughed and held out its hands for the Lodestar and it flew to her.

As soon as the baby's tiny fingers touched the orb it swelled with music. Isabeau and Iseult could hear words among the melody, words of welcome and connection. "No!" Lachlan screamed. "No!"

Maya walked across the garden toward them, while the baby balanced and spun the great orb on her fingertips as if she were a jongleur and it a juggling ball. "They say the Lodestar responds to the hand o' any MacCuinn," Maya said in a gloating voice. "We have it now, and as they say, *whoever holds the Lodestar shall hold the land* . . ."

"So they say," Lachlan agreed grimly. Maya climbed the stairs and stood, the ruin of her face twisted into a smile. To Isabeau's grief, she saw Latifa's round form huddling in the shadows of the garden and she knew the old cook had shown Maya the way through the labyrinth.

"So at the end ye have lost, Lachlan MacCuinn, and I win. My daughter is very powerful, ye ken. She was conceived at the height o' the comet with a Spell o' Begetting, and it was made sure it would be born at the most potent hour . . ."

"Except Lasair made ye give birth prematurely," Isabeau pointed out, "so Bronwen was born at the autumn equinox, not at Samhain."

They ignored her, Lachlan and Maya facing each other over the length of the pool. He said savagely, "No matter how powerful she is, Maya, she is but a babe." He held out his hand and called to the Lodestar with all his will and all his desire. The Lodestar lifted from the baby's hand and soared towards him over the pool. The baby whimpered in disappointment and held up her little hand again. The Lodestar faltered, as if unsure whom to respond to. Isabeau was irresistibly reminded of her trial in Caeryla, when the young laird had made Lasair choose between her and his rightful owner, the Grand-Seeker Glynelda.

The orb hesitated only a moment, then flew to Lachlan's hand. His fist closed about it in triumph. "See, I am more powerful and the Lodestar chooses me. Prepare yourself for death, Ensorcellor!"

Unable to use his bow with the Lodestar gripped tight in his hand, he drew his claymore and started towards them.

Maya glanced around in fear, then looked at the pool before her. The water was still bubbling with light, but it had begun to twist away at the center, like water running out of a sink. She flung Bronwen into the pool and dived cleanly into the swirling heart.

"No!" Isabeau cried and dived after them.

The water boiled with silver light. She saw Maya's feet disappear into a swirl of bubbles. Bronwen swam nimbly as a tadpole after her, reaching out one hand to grasp Maya's hair.

Deeper and deeper into the sparkling, fizzing water Isabeau dived. Her eyes were wide open, but all she could see was luminosity, as if a great light shone from the depths of the pool. She kicked strongly, and saw Maya's feet ahead of her, both braceleted with flowing fins, as she dived straight into the heart of the spring. *Bronwen*, Isabeau called and the child looked back at her, her eyes shining strangely, her body glinting with scales, frills floating all about her hands and feet, a long, serrated fin curving out of her baby spine. Then she wriggled ahead, following her mother.

Desperately Isabeau caught her tiny foot, then the baby was squirming in her arms. She turned and struck for the surface, her lungs burning. It seemed a long, long swim to the surface, all the light beginning to die. At last she floundered to the surface, gasping and choking, the baby in her arms.

Lachlan strode into the pool, the water swirling up to his knees. He grasped Isabeau and helped haul her out. "What did ye do that for?" he grumbled.

"Save . . . Bronwen . . . from drowning," Isabeau gasped, turning her body so the baby was out of his reach.

He gave a harsh laugh. "By the look o' those scales and fins, she would no' have to worry about death by drowning."

Isabeau, dripping wet and shaking with cold, realized with a jolt that he was absolutely right. Bronwen had swam as easily as any fish and had seemed quite happy in the water. Maya was gone, lost somewhere in the waterways below the garden. With two great rivers on either side, Isabeau had no doubt she would find a way free. Bronwen could have escaped with her and probably would have been safer with her than with a vengeful uncle who would see her as a potential threat to his throne and that of his heirs. With tears welling up in her eyes she realized her impetuosity had again led her to act before she thought.

Lachlan suddenly gave an almighty shout. "Look at me!" he cried. "Look at my feet!"

They stared in stupefaction, for where Lachlan's black, scaly talons had been were two very white, shapely human feet. He lifted one, then the other, his swarthy face breaking into a delighted grin, then he threw back his head and sang, a clarion call of joy and triumph that rang through the garden. The Lodestar shone bright as a tiny moon in his hand, and birds rose from their roosts in hedge and tree with a clatter of wings, caroling with startled delight.

"When Magnysson shall at last hold Gladrielle in his arms, all will be healed or broken, saved or surrendered . . ." Isabeau cried and looked desperately at her hand. A sharp and bitter disappointment pierced her, for in the bright moonlight she could clearly see her hand was still missing the last two fingers. It took her a moment to realize her remaining fingers were straight and smooth as they had ever been. Even then, clenching her two fingers and thumb open and shut, grievous tears burnt her throat and dampened her cheeks, and she bent her head to Bronwen's so her tears were hidden from the others. Through the baby's dark hair she saw a silver lock glinting in the moonlight.

"It is done!" Lachlan said with immense satisfaction. "I have saved the Inheritance. Now I hold the Lodestar, I shall hold the land!"

A NEW THREAD IS STRUNG

To Rear a Child

Isabeau sat by the dying embers of the fire, rocking the child in her cradle with one foot. It was cold in her little room but she made no move to blow the ashes into flame. She was tired, chilled and dispirited. It was nine months since she had set out on her adventures with such high hopes. So much had happened. So much had changed. If she had not left Meghan on the slopes of Dragonclaw, how different would her destiny have been? She might have her body and her soul intact, her loyalties undivided, her future clear before her. She might have won the MacCuinn to love herself, and now be Banrìgh of all Eileanan. She might have been the one to whom Ishbel the Winged taught her secrets.

Instead, she had no place, no future, of her own. Meghan had called Lachlan and her twin the only hope of the country, yet what was she, apart from Iseult's maid-in-waiting and the baby's nursemaid? Tears trickled down her cheeks and she lifted the sleeping baby to her shoulder.

The door creaked open, and Meghan came in slowly. She had aged terribly since her wounding—her face was heavily lined, and her snowy lock was lost among many other white streaks. Gitâ rode on her shoulder; he was rarely to be seen more than a few paces from his witch any more, and he clucked over her until she grew exasperated. At Meghan's waist hung the Key, polished to brilliance.

Meghan saw the tears on Isabeau's face and sat beside her, taking her hand. "I think this is the first time I have seen ye alone since we first parted ways."

Isabeau nodded, rocking the baby gently. Meghan said, "I have no' got very much time, they are all so foolishly fussed about my health and insist I stay most o' the time in my bed. I thought ye would like to talk though." Isabeau nodded again, and the old witch said, "I wish ye were no' so silent now, Isabeau, I miss my chatterbox."

"I do no' feel much like chattering," Isabeau said, and her voice sounded childish even to her own ears. She made an effort, and said, "I am sorry, Meghan, it is just ye all seem to have a place here and I do no'. I have been a servant to these courtiers and they treat me so still, despite my mirror image sitting on the throne."

The old sorceress sighed, and said, "If I had only known what would come o' my climbing Dragonclaw, I would have taken ye with me, Beau, but I saw only danger and death before me. I thought ye would be safe, but ye had to stop and rescue Lachlan! It is ironic, because if ye had no', he would have been the one in the Awl's hands."

"Baron Yutta would have enjoyed that," Isabeau answered bitterly.

Meghan hesitated, then said, "There are few witches who could have escaped their grasp, Isabeau. Your powers are great indeed, for they are married to imagination and quick thinking. I want ye to ken how proud I am o' ye."

At that Isabeau wept again, though this time there was a little sweetness in the mix. Gitâ flew from Meghan's shoulder to hers so he could comfort her, patting her earlobe with his little paw. She wept some more.

"Have ye noticed many changes in yourself since your

dive into the pool?" Meghan asked, fixing Isabeau's face
with her piercing black eyes.

"Apart from being able to use my hand a little? No,
no' at all."

"What about in Bronwen?"

"I have seen her bring a toy to her hand when it has
fallen to the floor," Isabeau said, "but who is to say if
that is as a result o' the water. She called the Lodestar
to her hand before she swam."

Meghan was silent for a while. "Let me hold the
babe," she said unexpectedly, and Isabeau handed her
over gladly. The old sorceress held the baby gently, examining her closely. Bronwen returned her scrutiny with
her unusual silvery eyes. She was a solemn baby, but she
laughed now and reached for Meghan's face. She placed
one fat starfish hand on the white lock and laughed
again. Then she moved her hand to touch Meghan once,
lightly, between the eyes.

"An unusual babe," Meghan said in a shaken voice.

"Yes," Isabeau agreed.

"I am going to tell ye something I've told no one else.
Do no' ask me why. I have always guarded my secrets
closely, for I am very auld now, Isabeau, and find it hard
to burden others whom I still see as children. Even poor
Latifa. I knew her when she was the fattest and most
adorable baby you've ever seen." She sighed.

"Ye must have heard many things about me, Isabeau,
which ye can no' know are true or no'. I canna help ye
sort rumor from truth now, for I grow tired and need
my bed. This I will tell ye, though. I am four hundred
and twenty-eight years auld. Samhain was my birthday,
and one o' the strangest I've known in all my long life.
I was only eight at the time o' the last eclipse. That day
I had my First Test and saw the moons eaten and the
Lodestar created, and found my first familiar. A big
day indeed."

She paused, gray-faced, and Isabeau rose to pour her
some goldensloe wine. "Now, I have often wondered if
I have lived these many years because I drank o' the

shining water when I was but a bairn. My father had forged the Lodestar in the pool, and I was curious and drank a mouthful—it seared through me like fire. I have often wondered if this long and heavy life is a consequence o' swallowing that water. Ye must be prepared to accept profound changes o' one sort or another."

"Healed or broken, saved or surrendered . . ." Isabeau answered, and Meghan nodded.

The old sorceress rose stiffly and handed back the baby, who tried to catch at the Key on her waist. She hesitated, then said wearily, "Isabeau, I know your path was thorny, but indeed things may have turned out very differently if ye had no' trodden it. I hope the price ye paid was no' too high, for things have turned out happier than I hoped. The Lodestar is safe and in our hands, Maya is dispossessed and, although the land is riven with war, Lachlan sits the throne, with two heirs already on the way."

Isabeau nodded, knowing the witch meant the words as comfort. Meghan paused and said hesitantly, "Beau, look after the babe. I am troubled indeed by Lachlan's black looks at her, and fear he may wish to do her harm. Jorge tells me he dreams o' her, and she has a role yet to play in this weaving. I do no' ken what the future holds for us, but I want ye to have a care for her . . ."

Isabeau nodded, kissed the old witch and bid her good night. She suddenly remembered what Jorge the Seer had once said to her: "I see ye with many faces and many disguises; ye will be one who can hide in a crowd. Though ye shall have no home and no rest, all valleys and pinnacles will be your home; though ye shall never give birth, ye shall rear a child who shall one day rule the land."

She caught her breath and looked down at the dreamy face of Maya's child. Bronwen smiled and reached for Isabeau's bright ringlets, and a pang of sweetness pierced her heart, sharp as any grief. She rocked the babe against her heart, and wondered if Meghan had been right, that only the lame could love, only the maimed could mourn.

"Surprisingly original." —*Locus*

The Witches of Eileanan
BY KATE FORSYTH

In the Celtic land of Eileanan, witches and magic have been outlawed, and those caught for practicing witchcraft are put to death. It is a land ruled by an evil Queen, where sea-dwelling Fairgean stir, and children vanish in the night...But as two young flamehaired twins grow to womanhood, their apprenticeships, as Warrior and Witch, will help them challenge this oppressive ban.

The Witches of Eileanan: Book One
A marvelous quest to save a vanishing world of magic and wonder.

The Pool of Two Moons: Book Two
In the darkness of a land besieged, the light of sorcery will shine.

The Cursed Towers: Book Three
Peace rests in the hands of twin sisters—one a warrior, one a witch.

The Forbidden Land: Book Four
A young girl comes of age—and discovers her abilities when she is called to aid her kingdom.

The Skull of the World: Book Five
In Eileanan, the sea-dwelling Fairgean have refused to sign the Pact of Peace.

The Fathomless Caves: Book Six
In the land of Eileanan, the Pact of Peace has not meant the end of unrest.

Available wherever books are sold or at penguin.com

DENNIS L. MCKIERNAN

HÈL'S CRUCIBLE Duology:

In Dennis L. McKiernan's world of Mithgar, other stories are often spoken of, but none as renowned as the War of the Ban. Here, in one of his finest achievements, he brings that epic to life in all its magic and excitement.

PRAISE FOR THE
HÈL'S CRUCIBLE DUOLOGY:

"PROVOCATIVE...APPEALS TO LOVERS OF CLASSIC FANTASY—THE AUDIENCE FOR DAVID EDDINGS AND TERRY BROOKS."
—*BOOKLIST*

"ONCE MCKIERNAN'S GOT YOU, HE NEVER LETS YOU GO."
—*JENNIFER ROBERSON*

"SOME OF THE FINEST IMAGINATIVE ACTION...THERE ARE NO LULLS IN MCKIERNAN'S STORY."
—*COLUMBUS DISPATCH*

Book One of the *Hèl's Crucible* Duology
INTO THE FORGE
Book Two of the *Hèl's Crucible* Duology
INTO THE FIRE

AND DON'T MISS McKiernan's epic which takes you back to Mithgar in a time of great peril—as an Elf and an Impossible Child try to save the land from a doom long ago prophesied.

SILVER WOLF, BLACK FALCON

Available wherever books are sold or at penguin.com